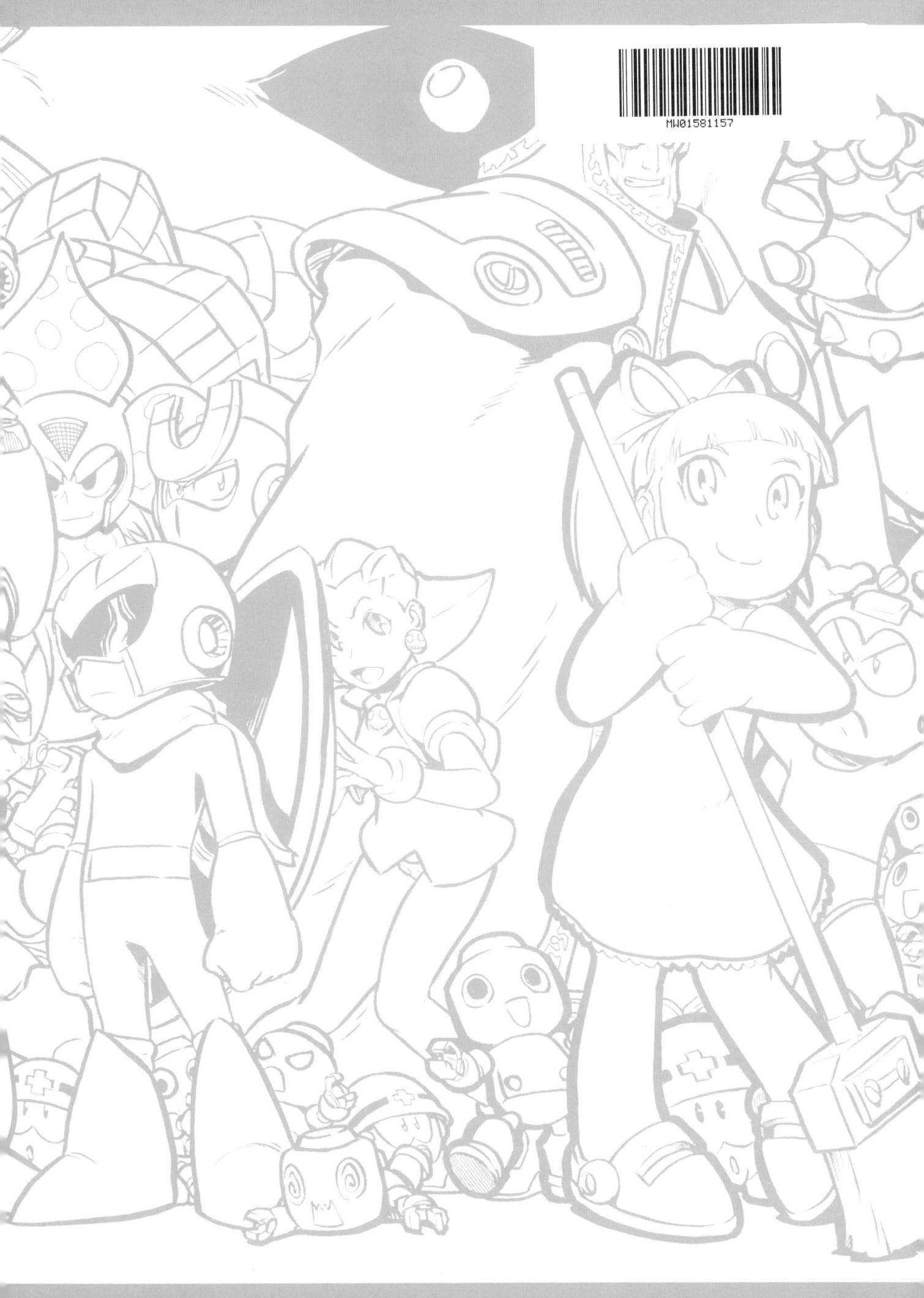

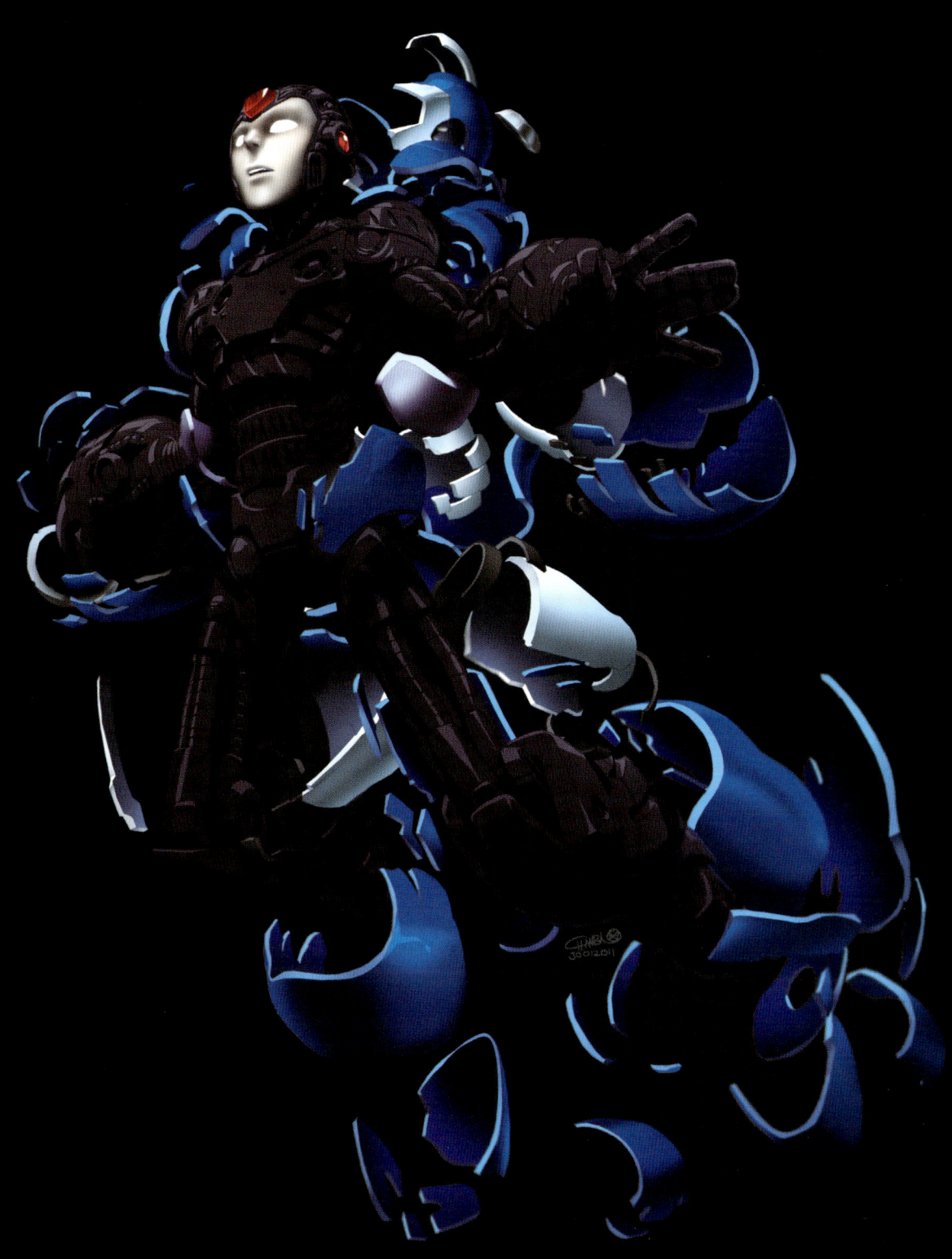

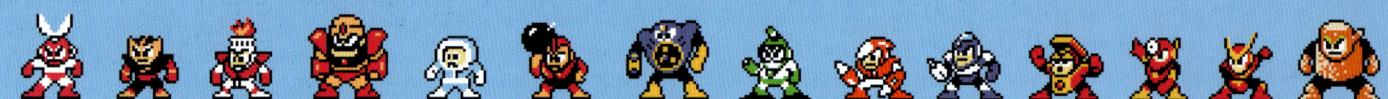

MEGA MAN HAS ENDED
THE EVIL DOMINATION
OF DR. WILY
AND RESTORED
THE WORLD TO PEACE.

HOWEVER, THE NEVER ENDING
BATTLE CONTINUES
UNTIL ALL DESTRUCTIVE FORCES
ARE DEFEATED.

FIGHT, MEGA MAN!
FOR EVERLASTING PEACE!

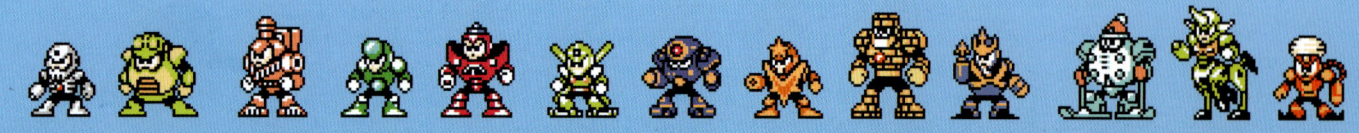

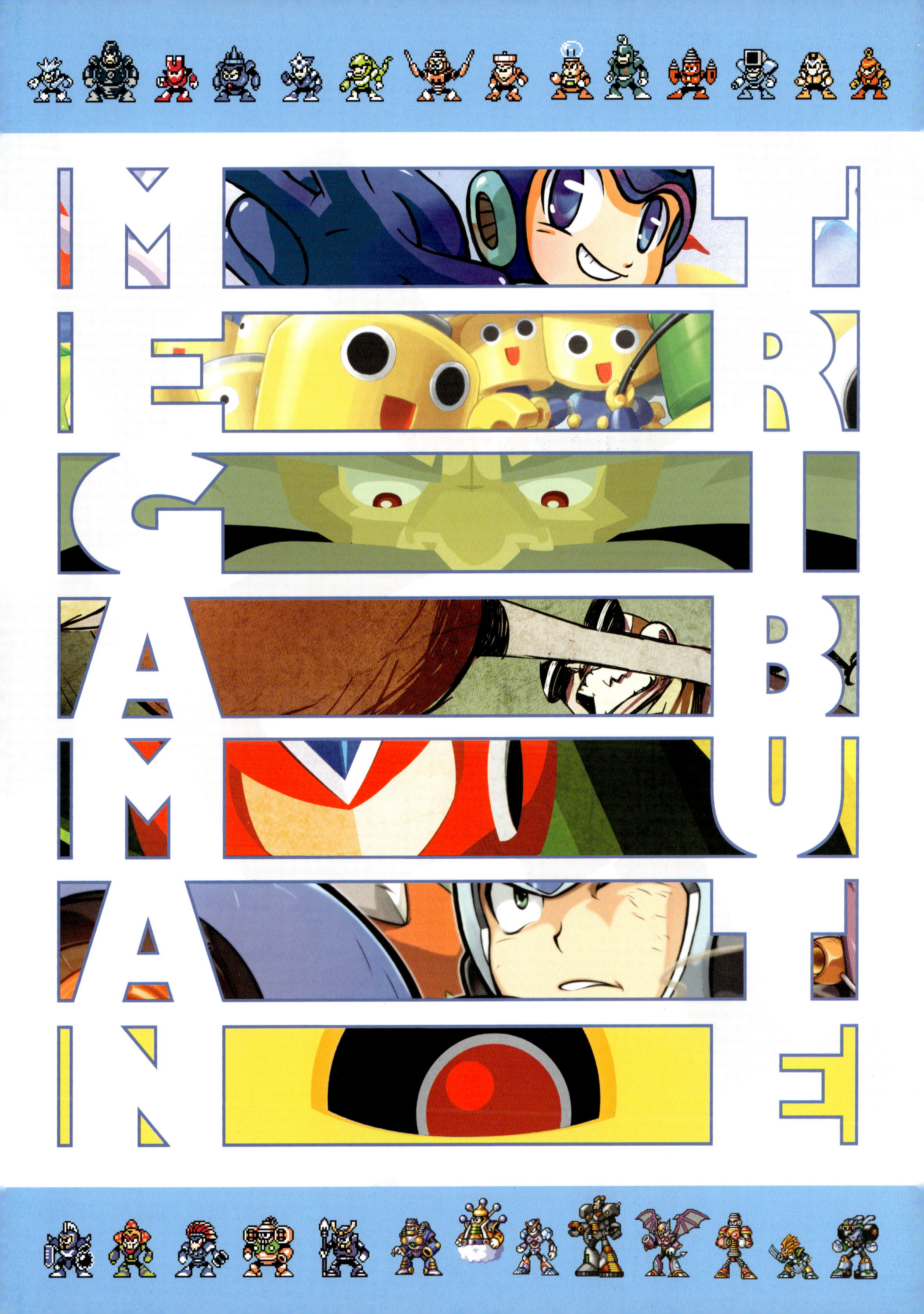

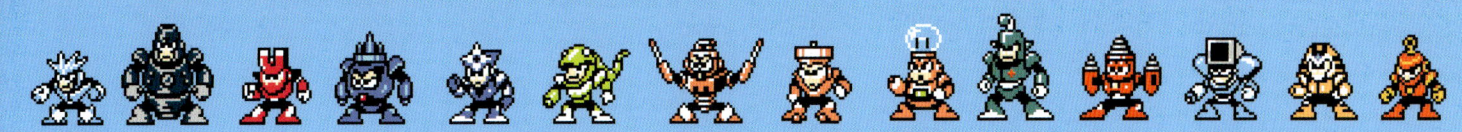

MEGAMAN TRIBUTE

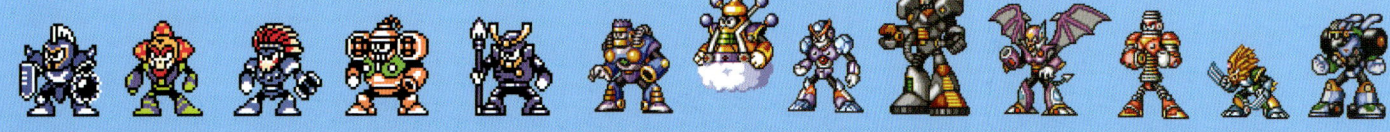

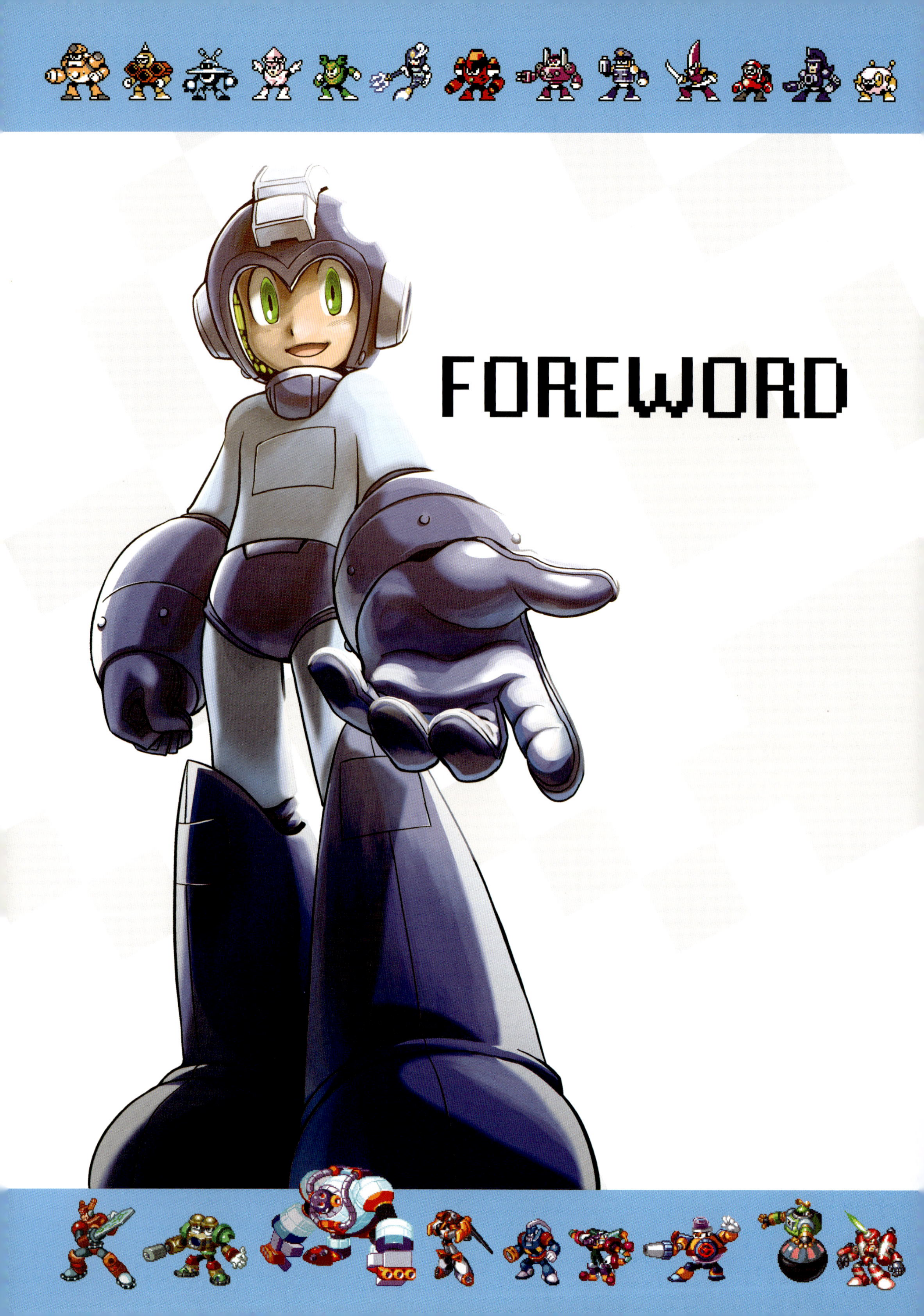

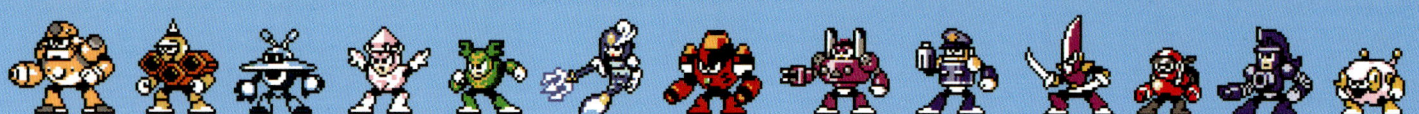

FOREWORD

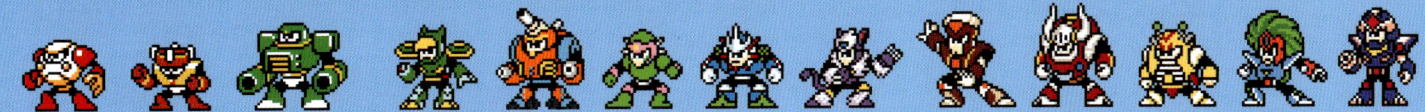

DO YOU REMEMBER YOUR FIRST ENCOUNTER WITH MEGA MAN?

I do. As far as I was concerned, Mega Man was just another character from just another game, among the countless games that populate our world. Back when I first played a Mega Man game, people were really getting into this thing called Role Play Games. I played my share of RPGs, but I always felt like there was something lacking in them. I'd always end up with an action game, and one of them happened to be about Mega Man.

Every Mega Man game I played was tough, but fun. I spent so many hours being beat down by enemies, caught by traps, and failing boss fights. But every time I played, I'd make just a little more progress, and get just a little further ahead. It was pretty difficult, but I would eventually clear the game and move on to the next new game hitting the market. To be completely honest with you, that's all Mega Man was to me. He was just a face on a cartridge in my big pile of game cartridges.

As time went on, they came out with more and more Mega Man games. I had always enjoyed my experiences with Mega Man games, so I was quick to pick up every new game as they came out. I was never disappointed. After more than two decades of new releases, it became clear that Mega Man wasn't "just another game". By that point, I had to admit, he was a permanent part of my life... but the truth is, he had always been there for me, with me... I just hadn't realized it. I think that's pretty amazing. This is how Mega Man became a presence unlike any other in my life.

Games (especially action games) are fun. The player becomes the main character, and becomes immersed in the game's world. Though the world may be a place that was pre-defined by the game's creators, the experiences the player has while inside that world are theirs and theirs alone. All of the defeats, the frustration, and the inspirations leading to victory... are unique to each player. In this way, each player creates "My Mega Man" within their heart. This book is overflowing with the "My Mega Man" of countless people from all across the world. Will you find a "My Mega Man" within these pages that is similar to the "My Mega Man" that you carry with you? Or perhaps you will find a "My Mega Man" that is utterly different from yours, that manages to catch your interest anyway.

A great big thanks to the many creators who brought the Mega Man games to life! And fully-charged enthusiastic thanks to the awesome artists who submitted their art for this book! Finally, one very special thanks to UDON Entertainment for coming up with the amazing idea that is "Mega Man Tribute"!

有賀ヒトシ
HITOSHI ARIGA
Manga Artist - Mega Man Megamix

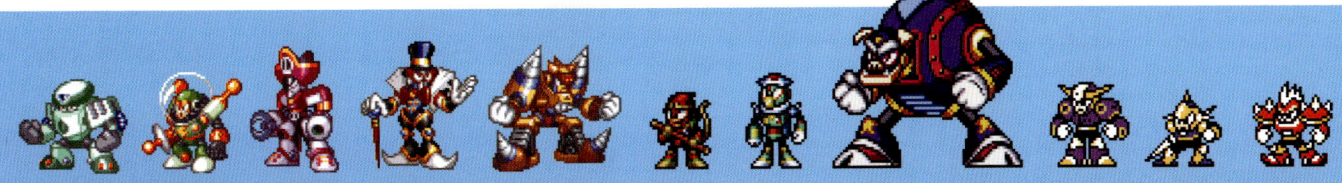

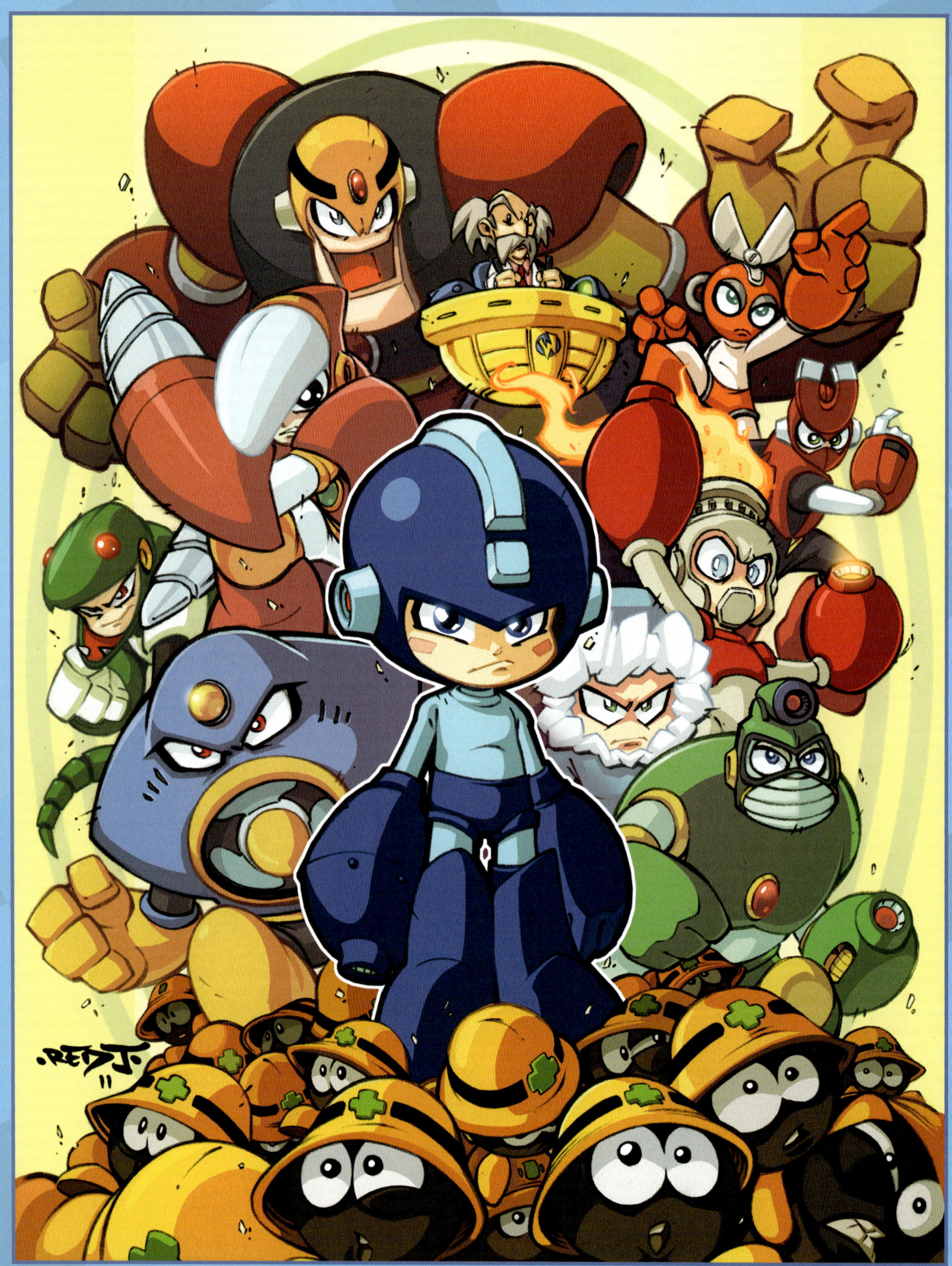

JON SOMMARIVA (RED J)
Sydney, Australia
red-j.deviantart.com
Freelance Artist
(Gemini - Image comics, FreeRealms - WS/DC comics)

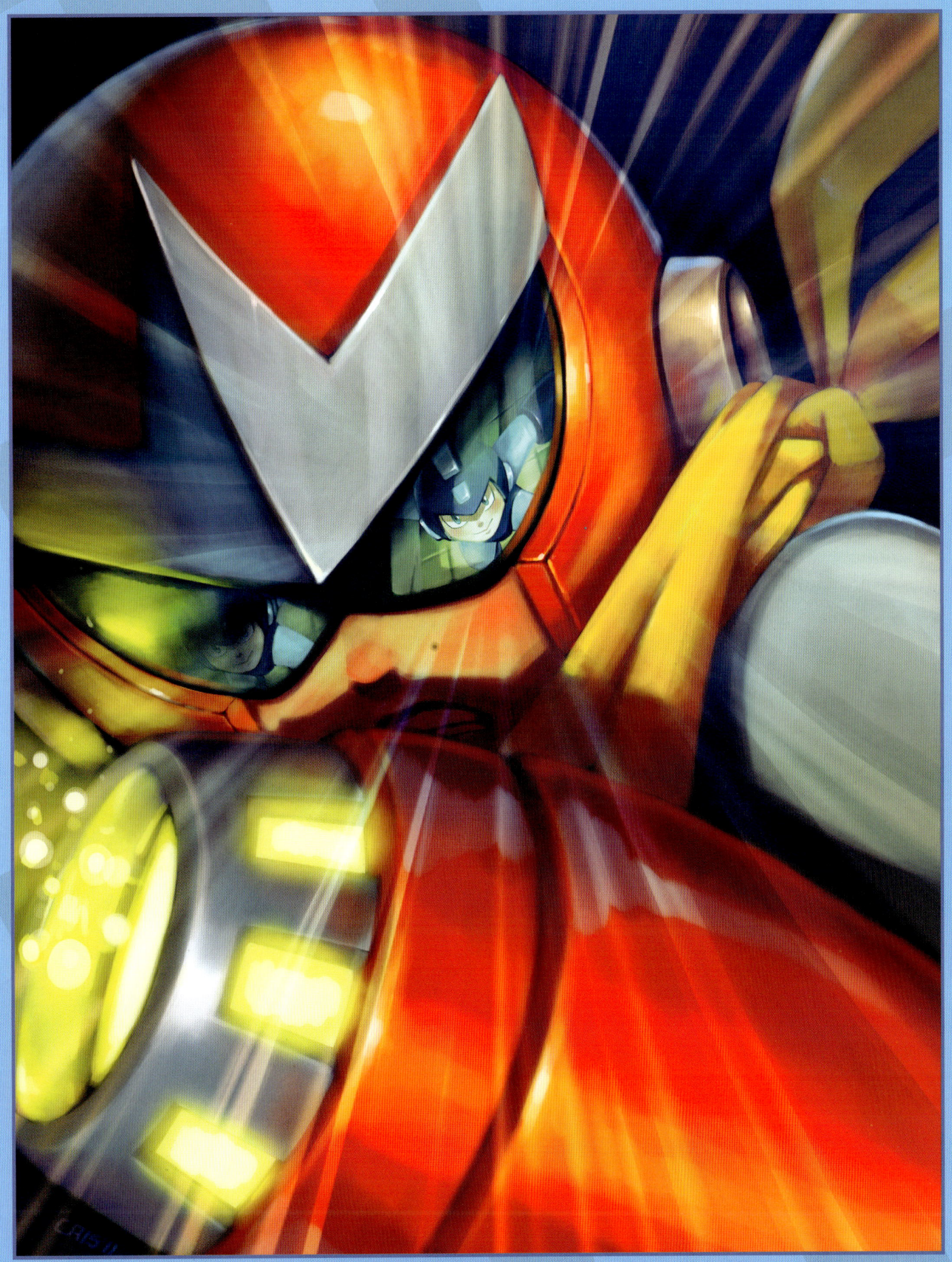

CRISTINA DÍAZ
Santiago, Chile
Illustrator
(AtakamaLabs)

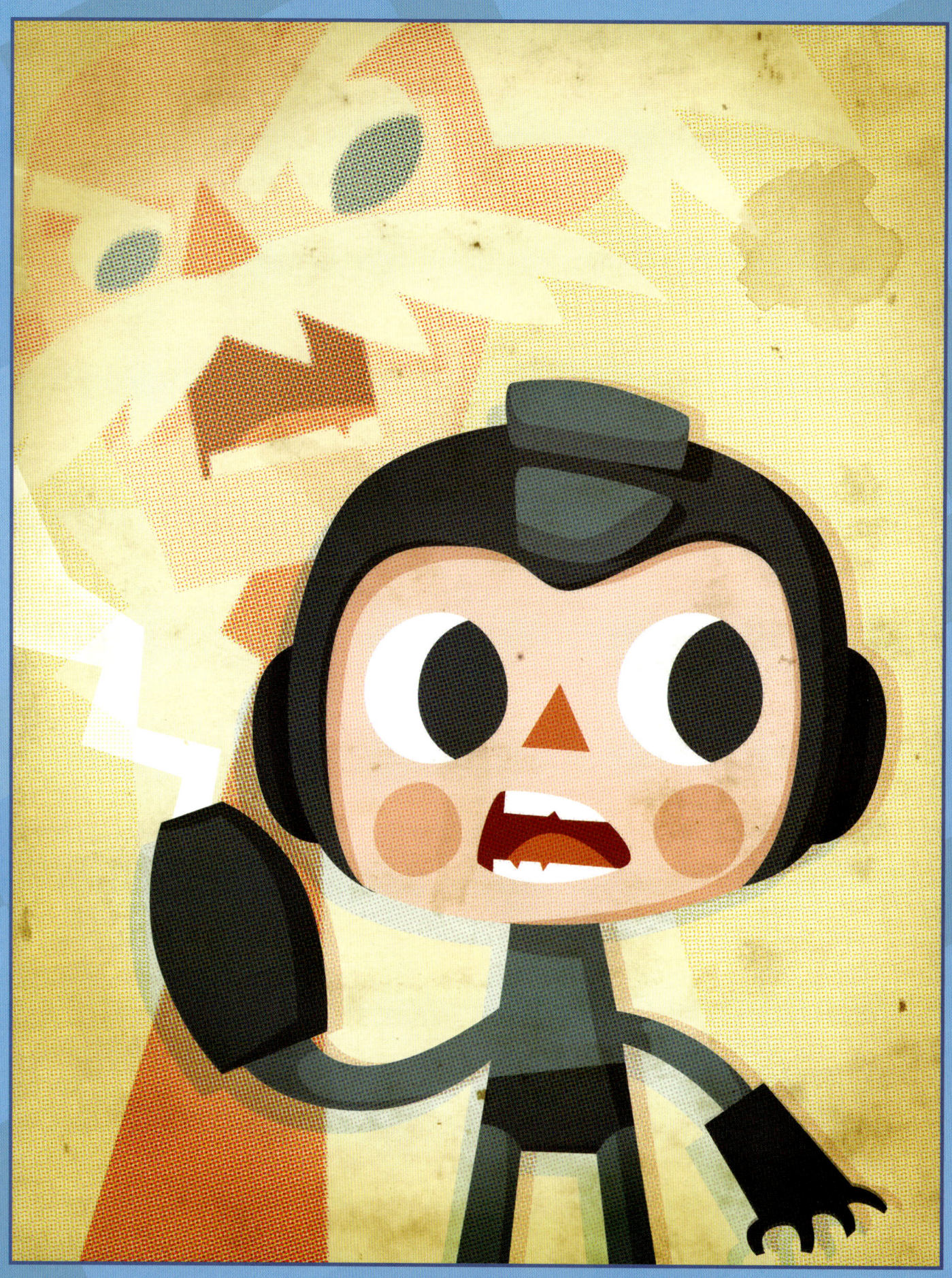

SERGIO LANTADILLA (PEERO)
Santiago, Chile
www.peerro.cl - peerro.deviantart.com
Illustrator / Graphic Designer

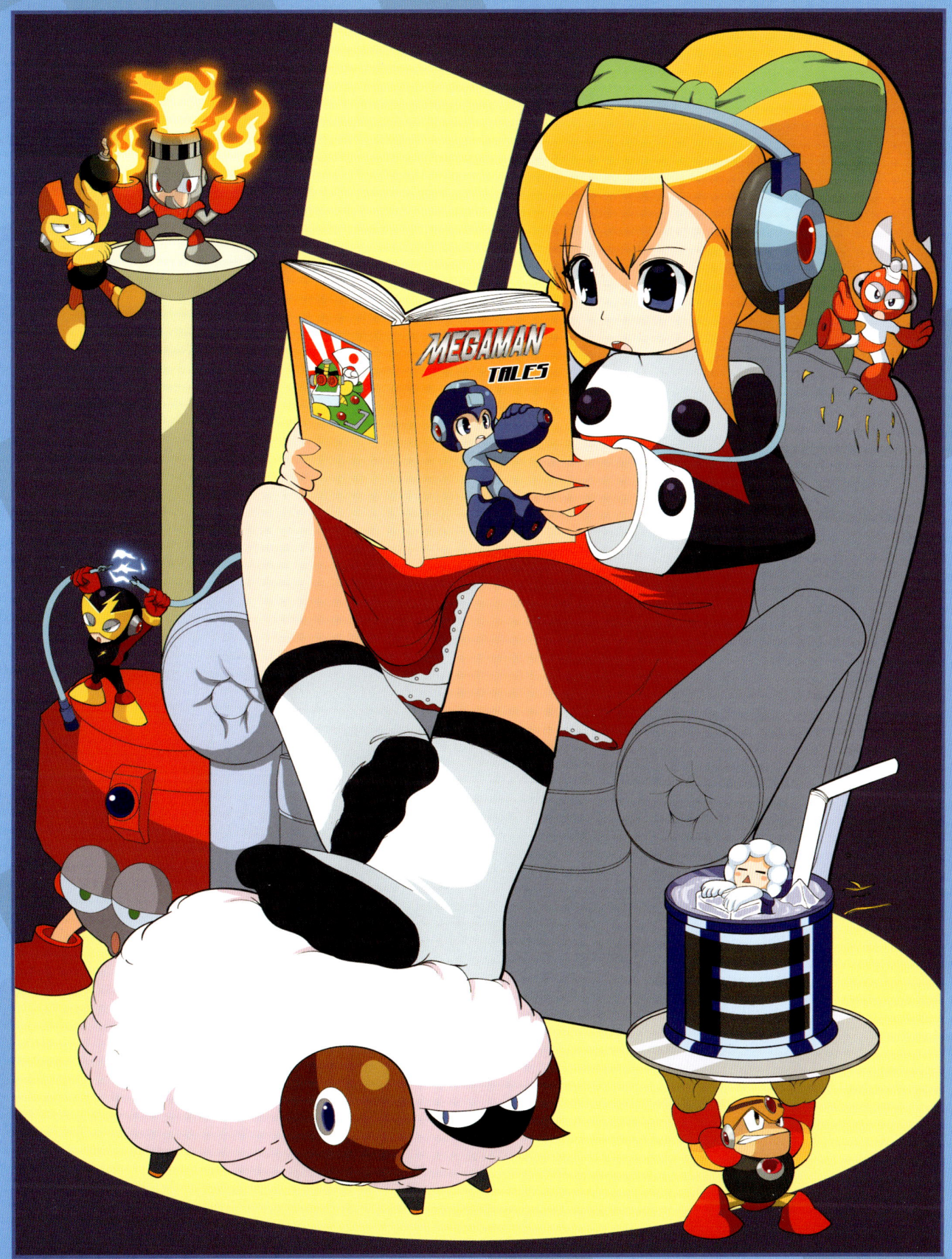

SAMUEL THOMAS
Vernon, CT, United States
Graphic Designer

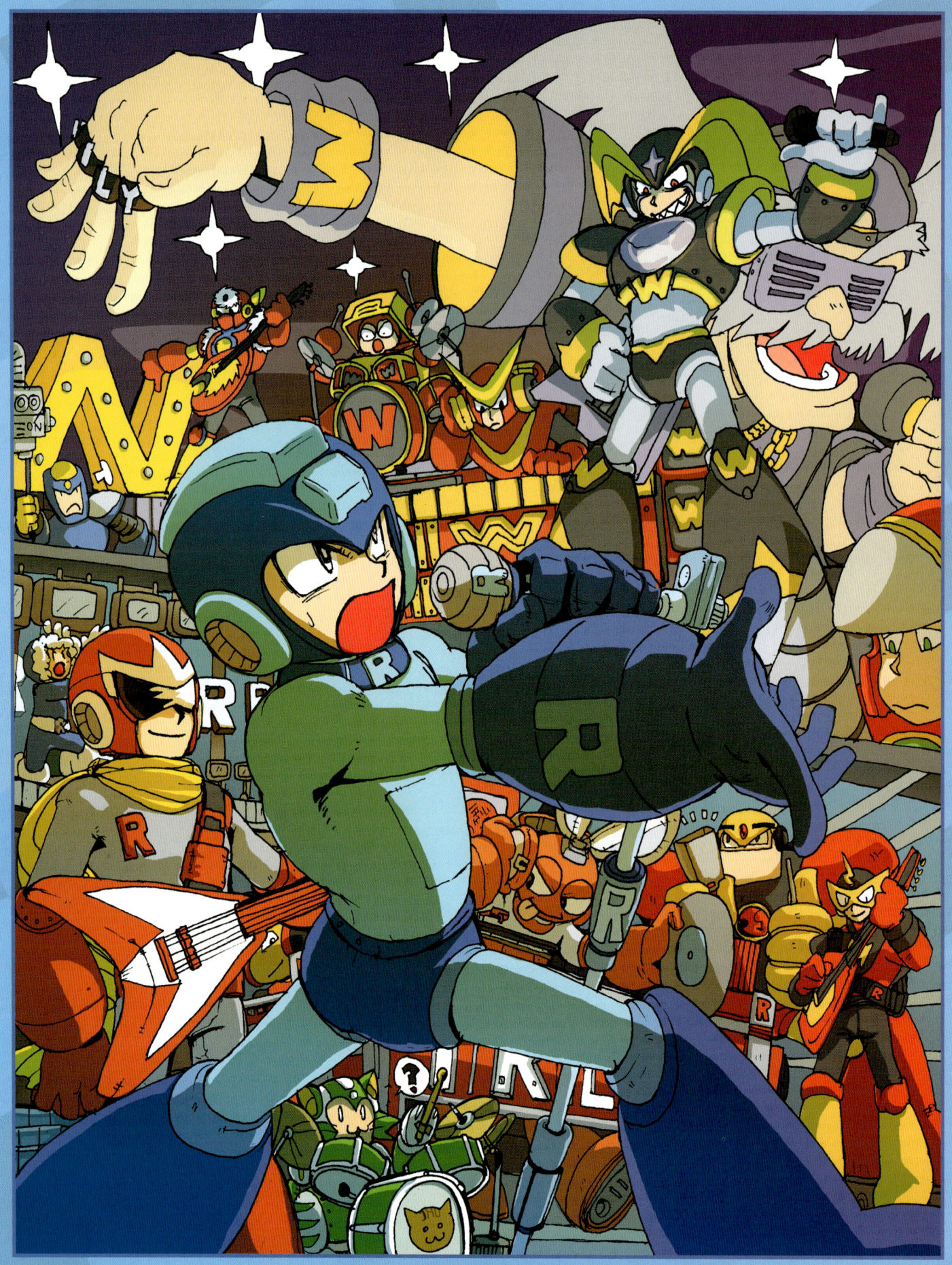

JHOSEPHINE TANUWIDJAYA
Oakville, ON, Canada
www.jho-tan.com
Graphic Artist

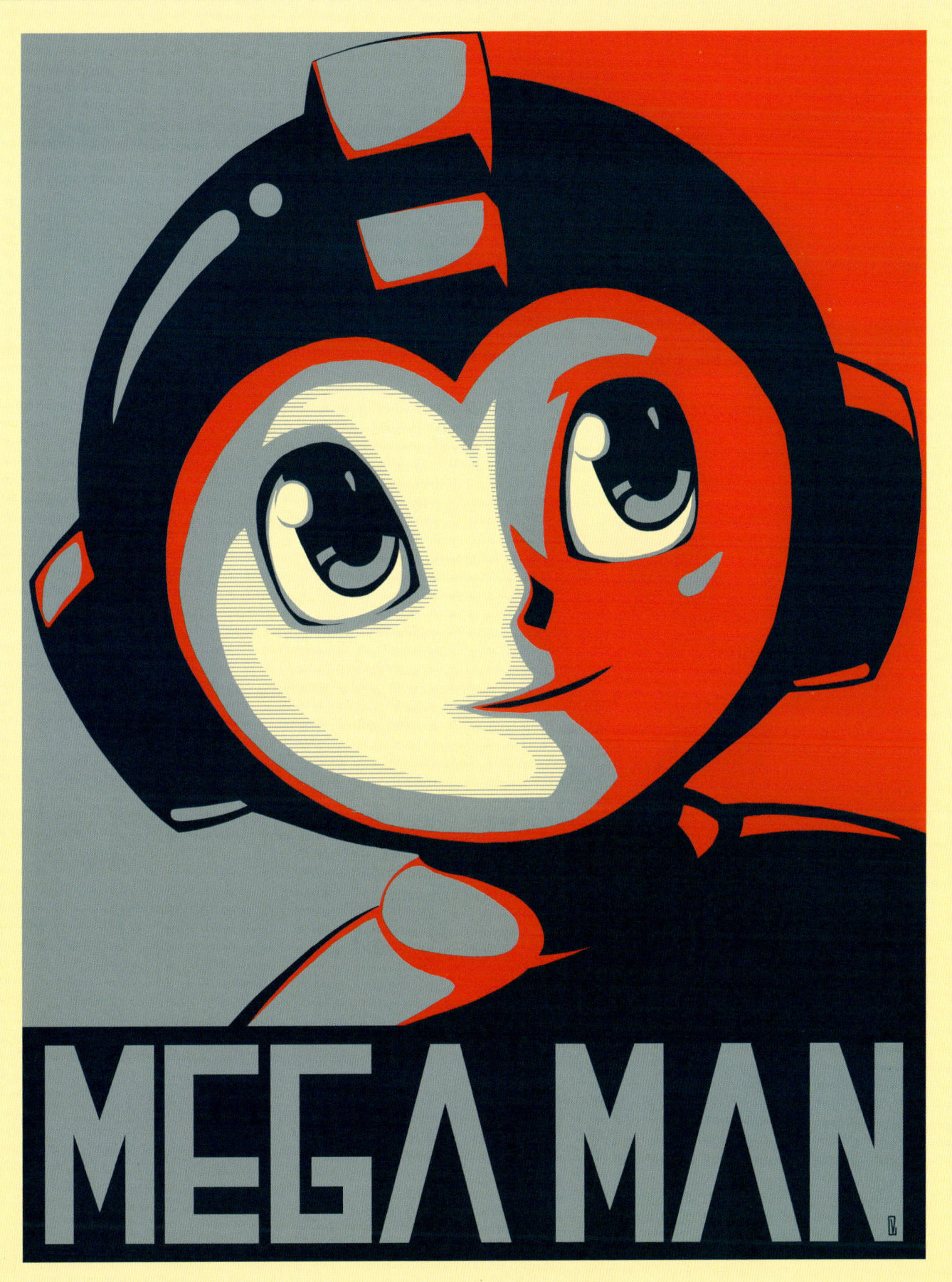

ERIC VEDDER
St. Catherines, ON, Canada
www.ericvedder.com, aardehn.txcomics.com
Illustrator
(Darkstalkers / Aardehn / Too Human / Shade / N+)

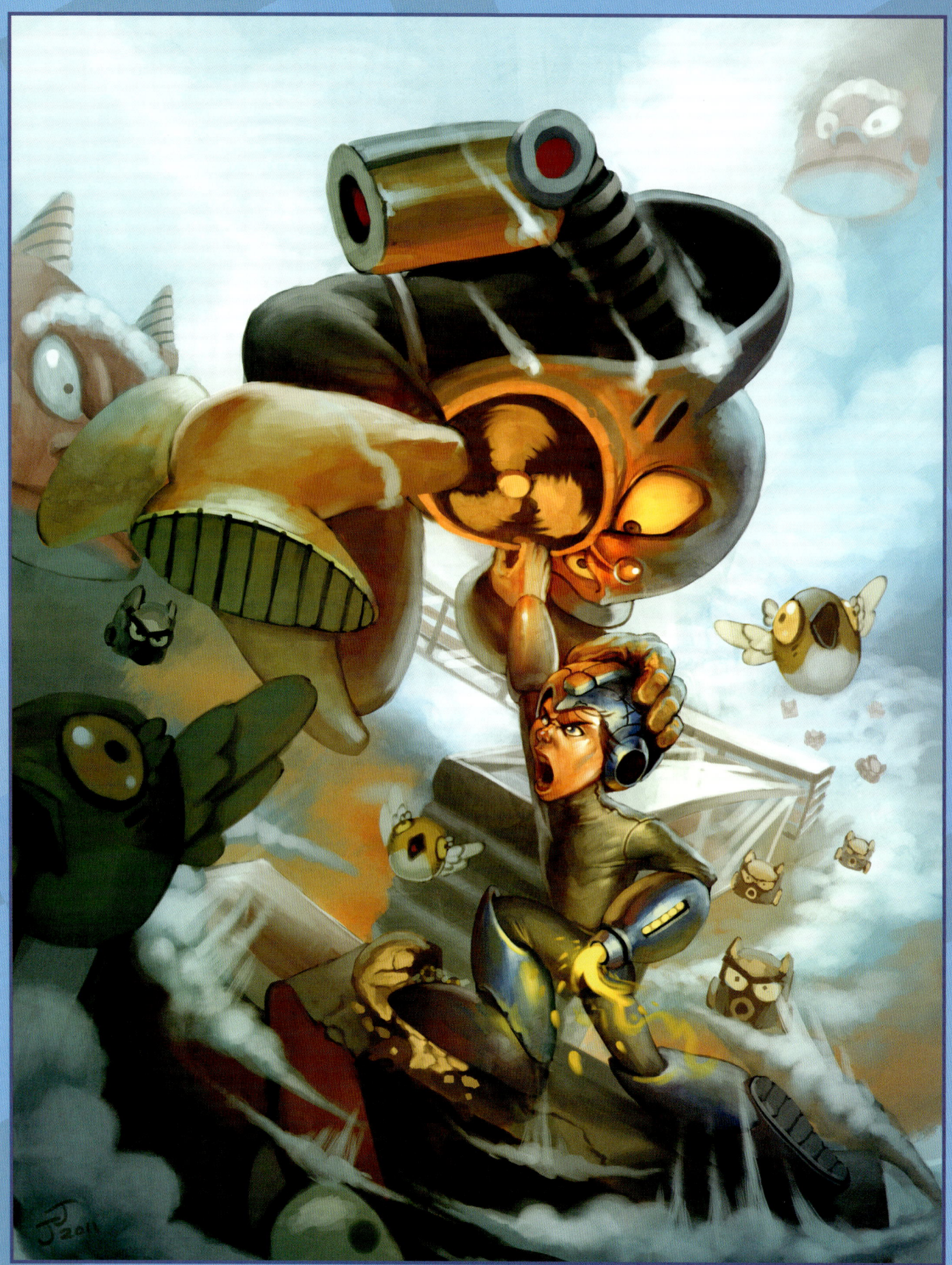

JEROME PATRICK JACINTO
Quezon City, Philippines
chichapie.deviantart.com
Freelance Artist
(UST - College of Fine Arts and Design)

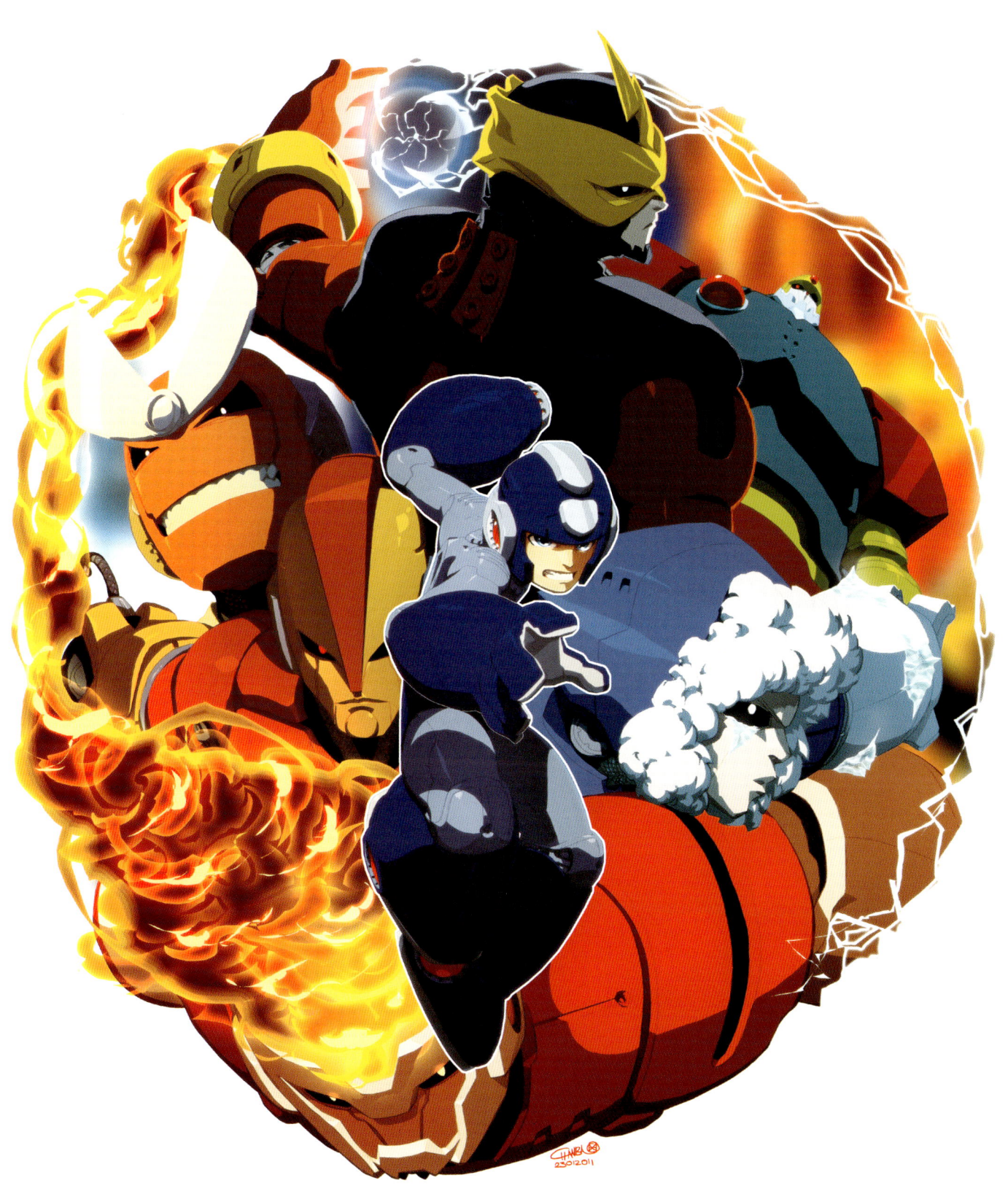

JEFFREY CRUZ (CHAMBA)
MELBOURNE, AUSTRALIA
LASTSCIONZ.DEVIANTART.COM - WWW.RANDOMVEUS.COM
ILLUSTRATOR
(Randomveus / Street Fighter II Turbo)

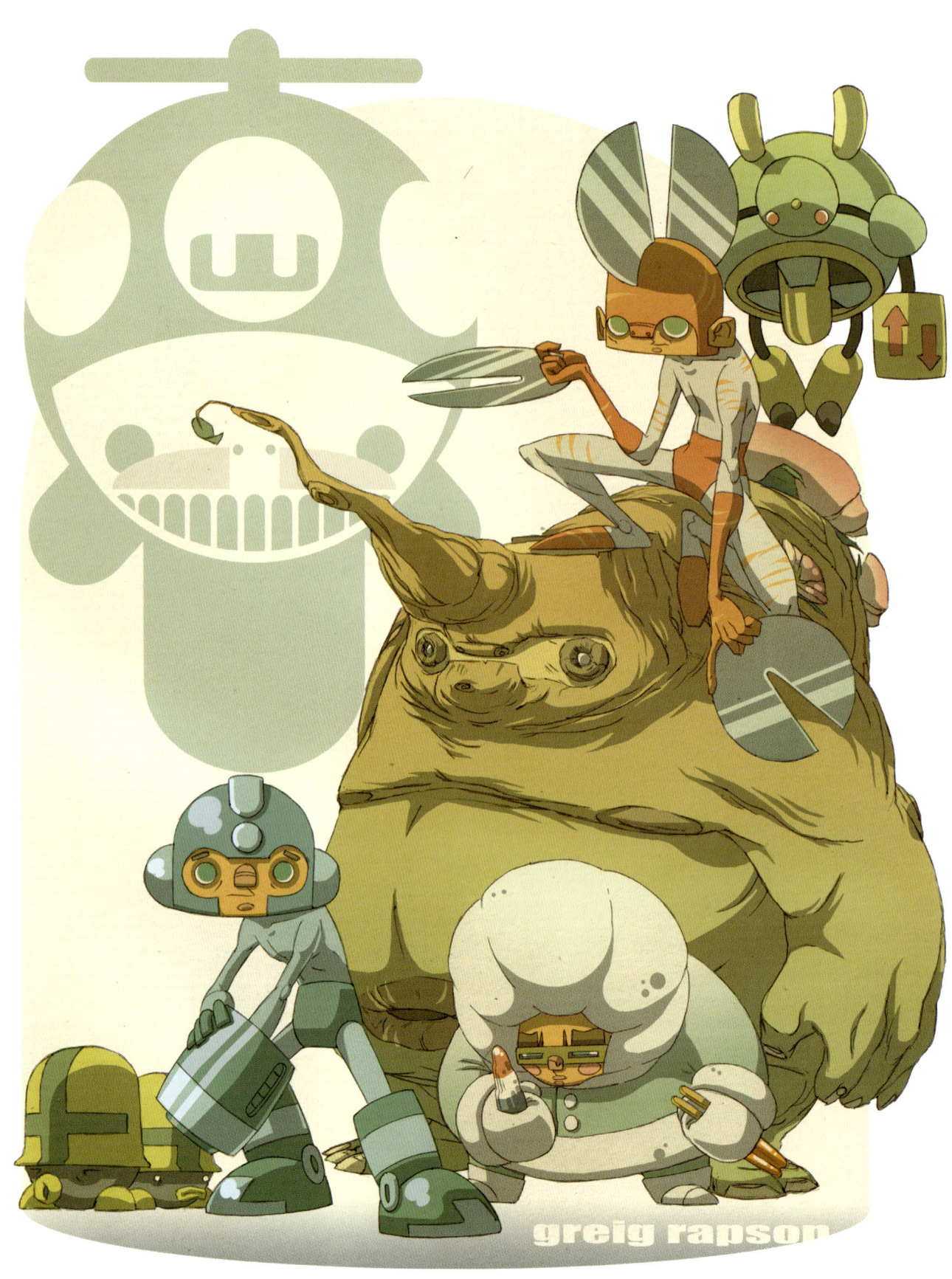

GREIG RAPSON
Pickering, ON, Canada
greigrapson.blogspot.com
Illustrator

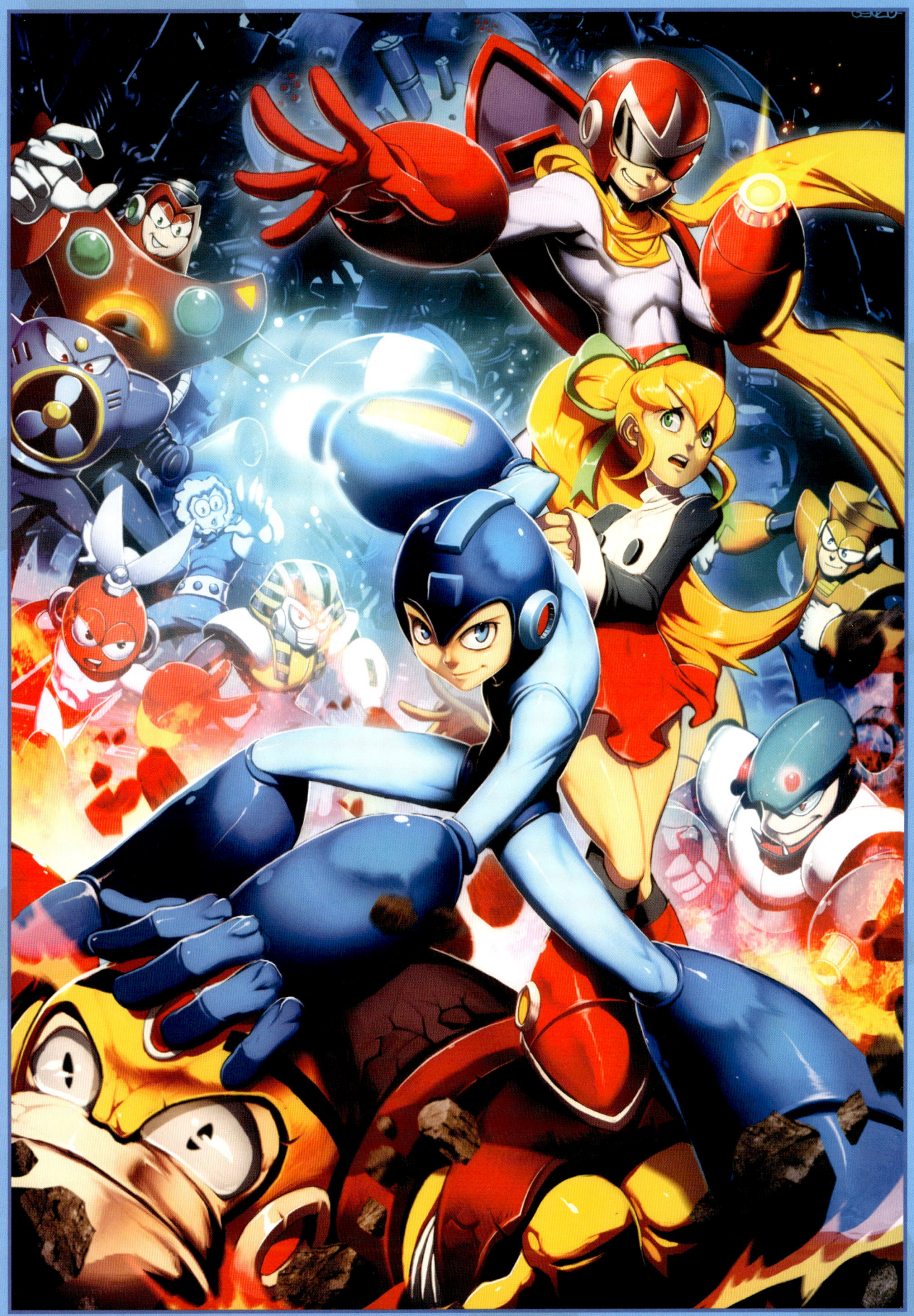

GONZALO ORDÓÑEZ ARIAS
Arica, Chile
genzoman.deviantart.com
Illustrator
(Myths & Legends / The Wanderer / UFS / Clash of the Titans)

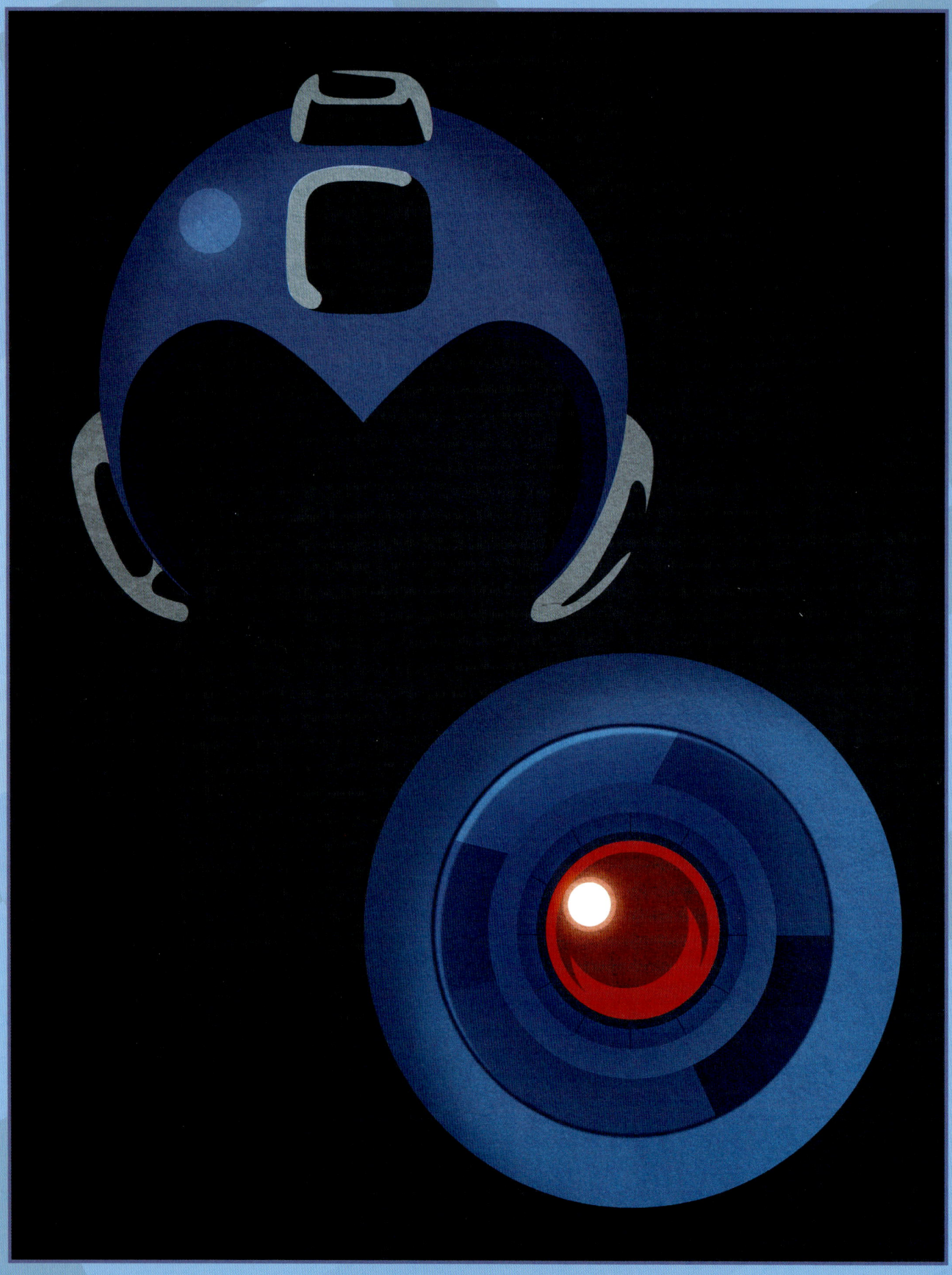

CHRISTIAN RAMIREZ (CREEPSTIAN)
Allende, Mexico
Designer
(Incubo visual branding studio)

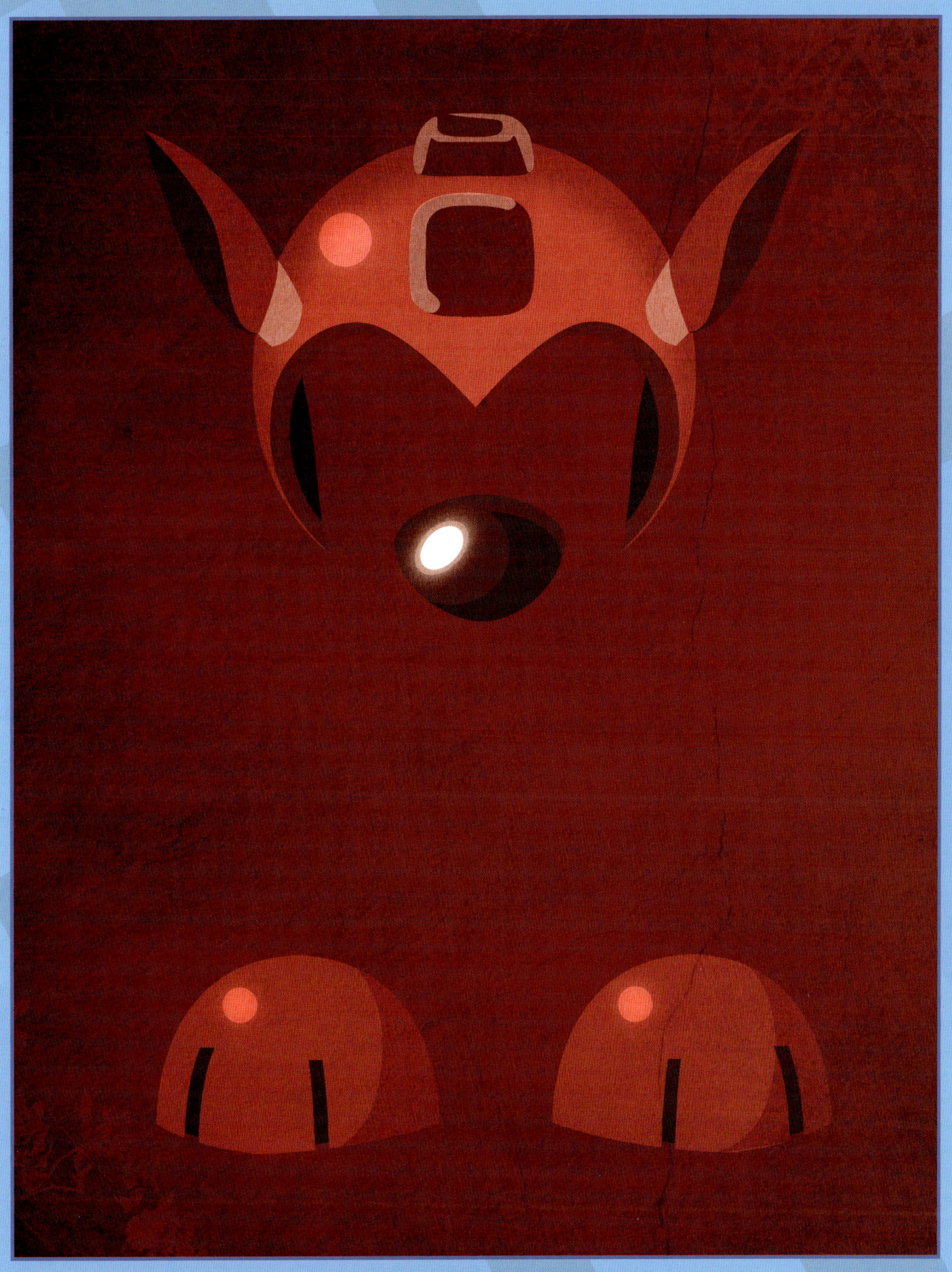

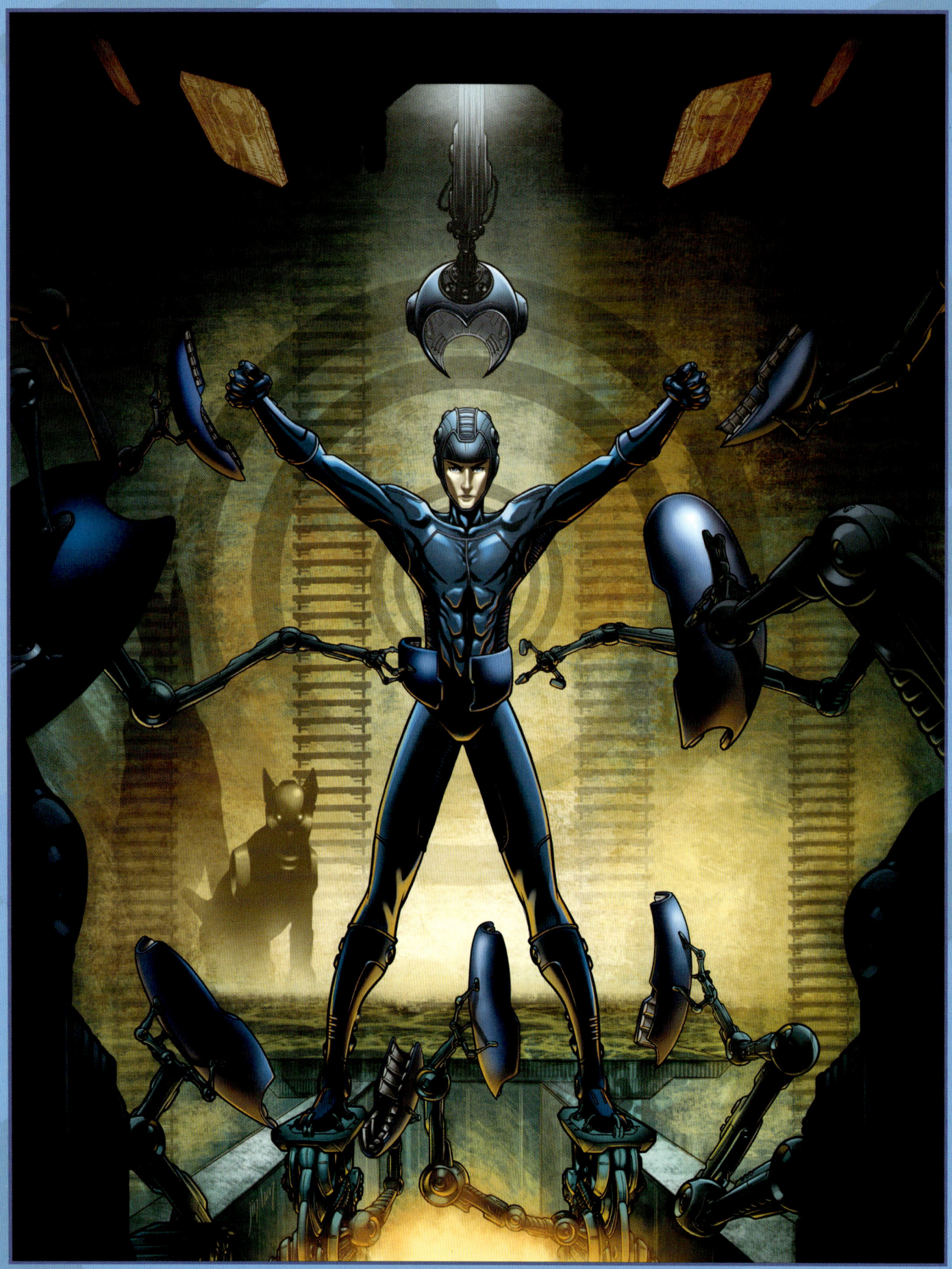

JIN HAN
Hacienda Heights, CA, United States
www.drawjindraw.com
Design Director
(Yellow Tracksuit Entertainment)

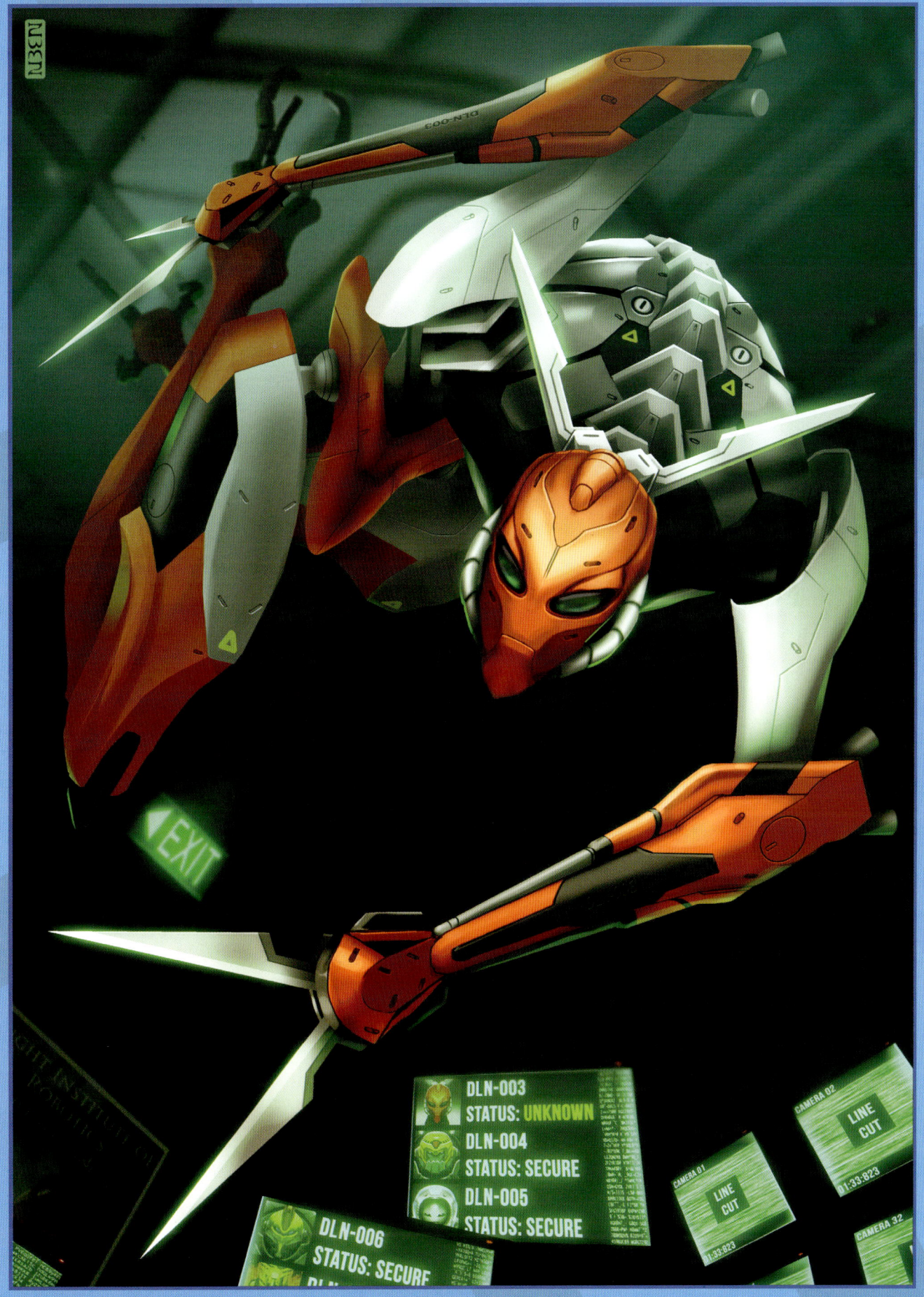

RUBEN DE VELA
Paranaque, Philippines
Illustrator
(Tokyopop/ Blizzard - Starcraft Frontline)

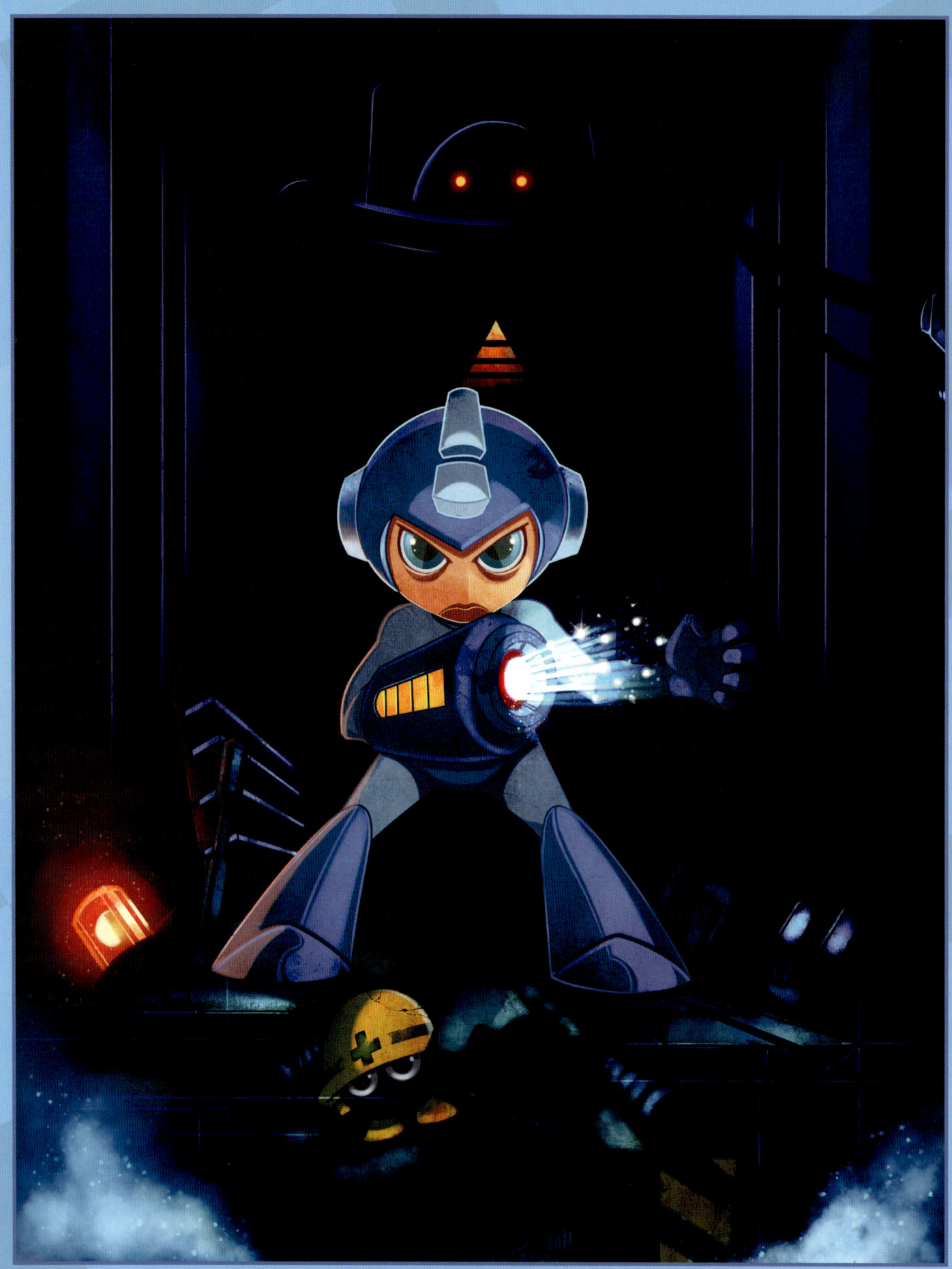

ILIAS PATLIS
Stockholm, Sweden
www.iliaspatlis.com
Illustrator / Stuntman

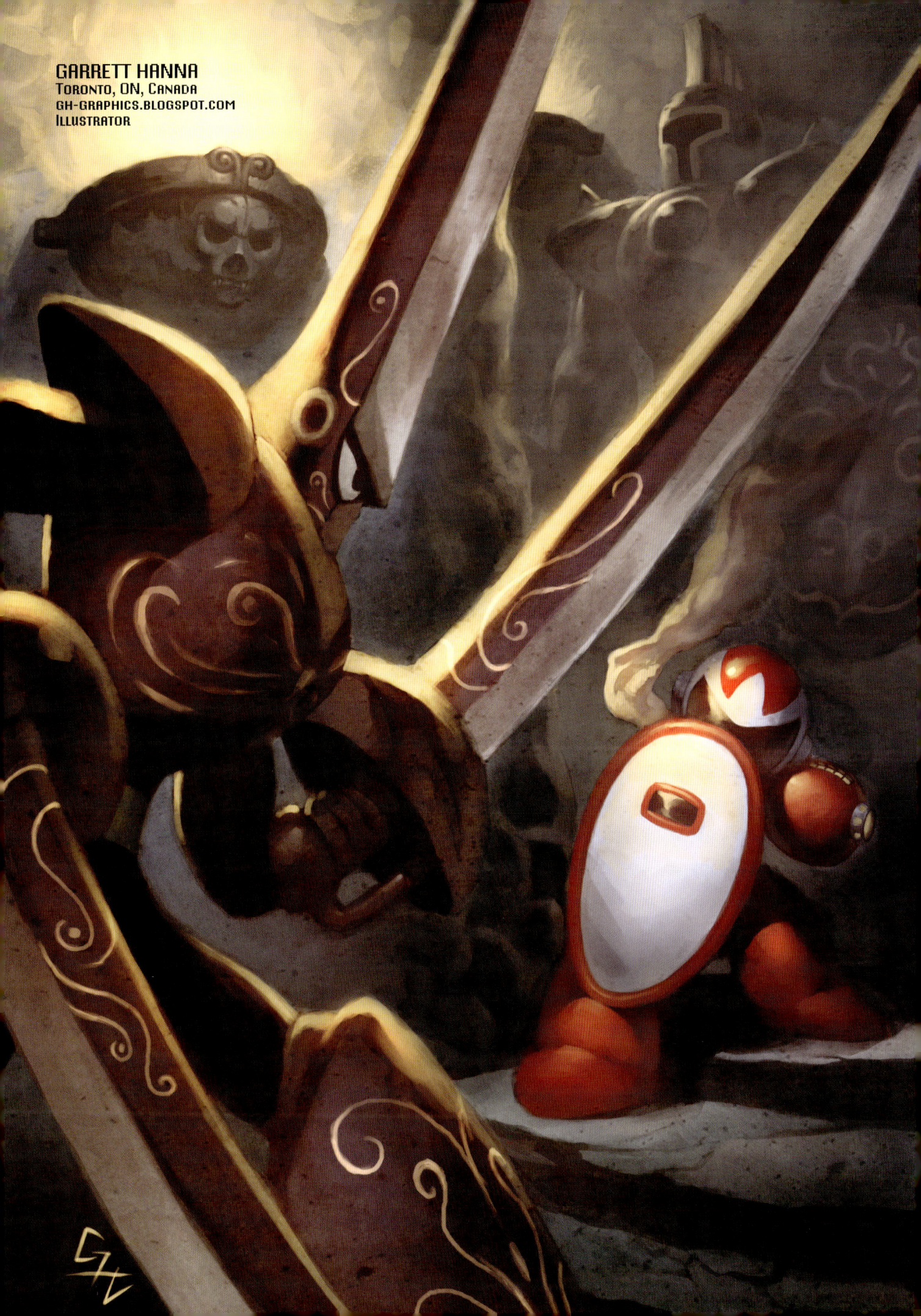

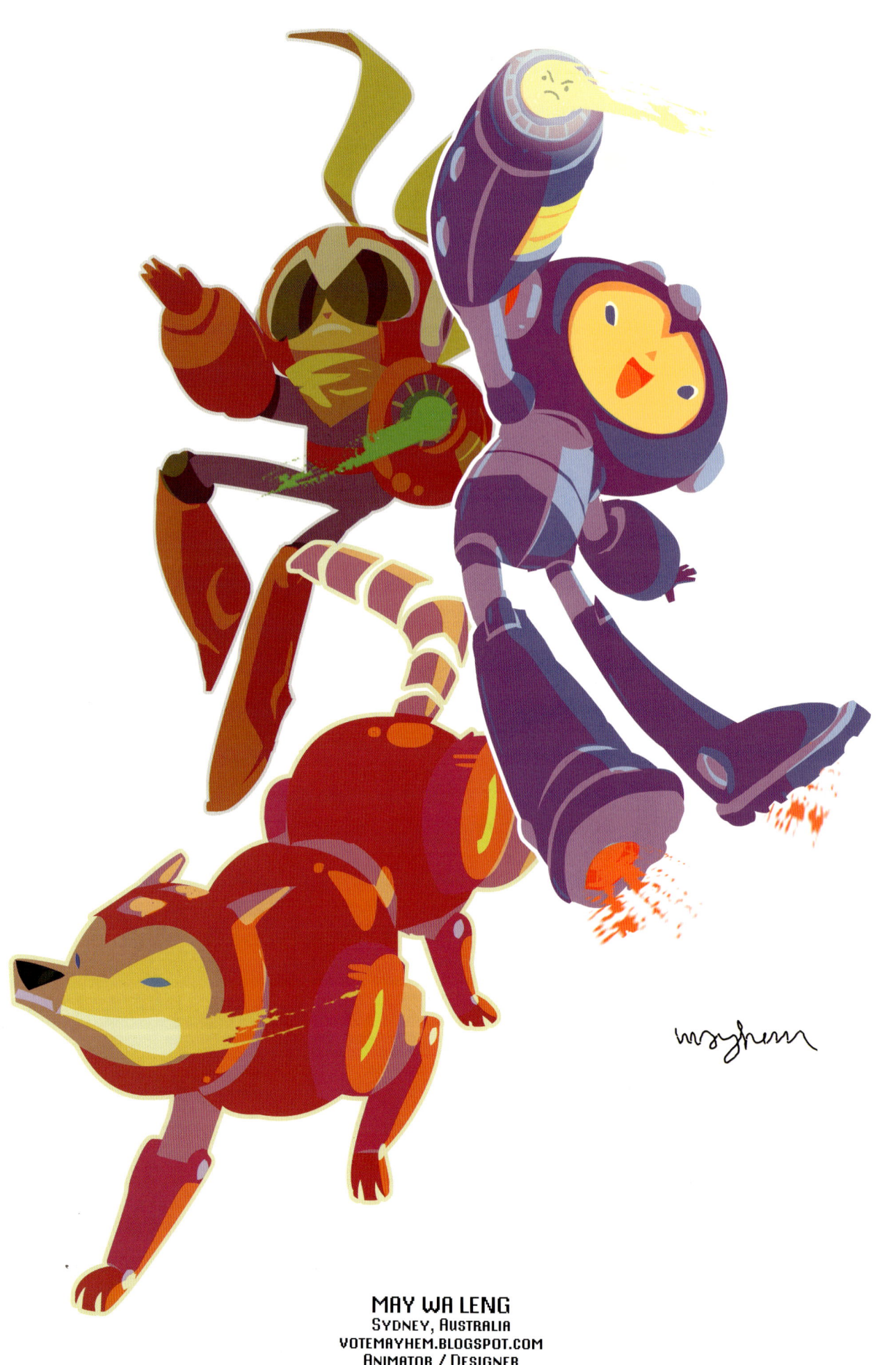

MAY WA LENG
Sydney, Australia
votemayhem.blogspot.com
Animator / Designer
(Disneytoon / StudioB / Bardel)

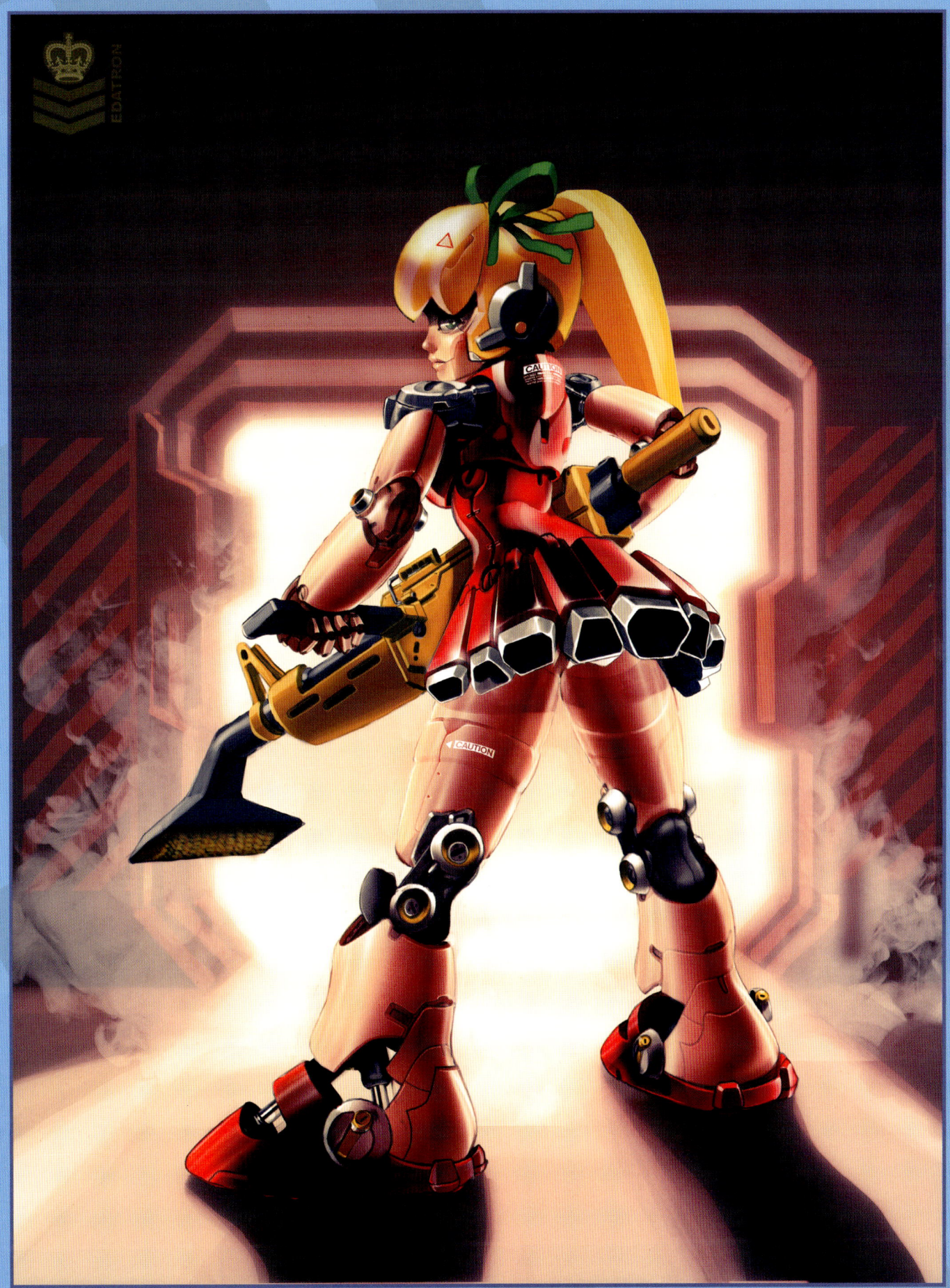

EDWARD CHOW (EDATRON)
New York, NY, United States
motomechanica.deviantart.com
Concept Artist

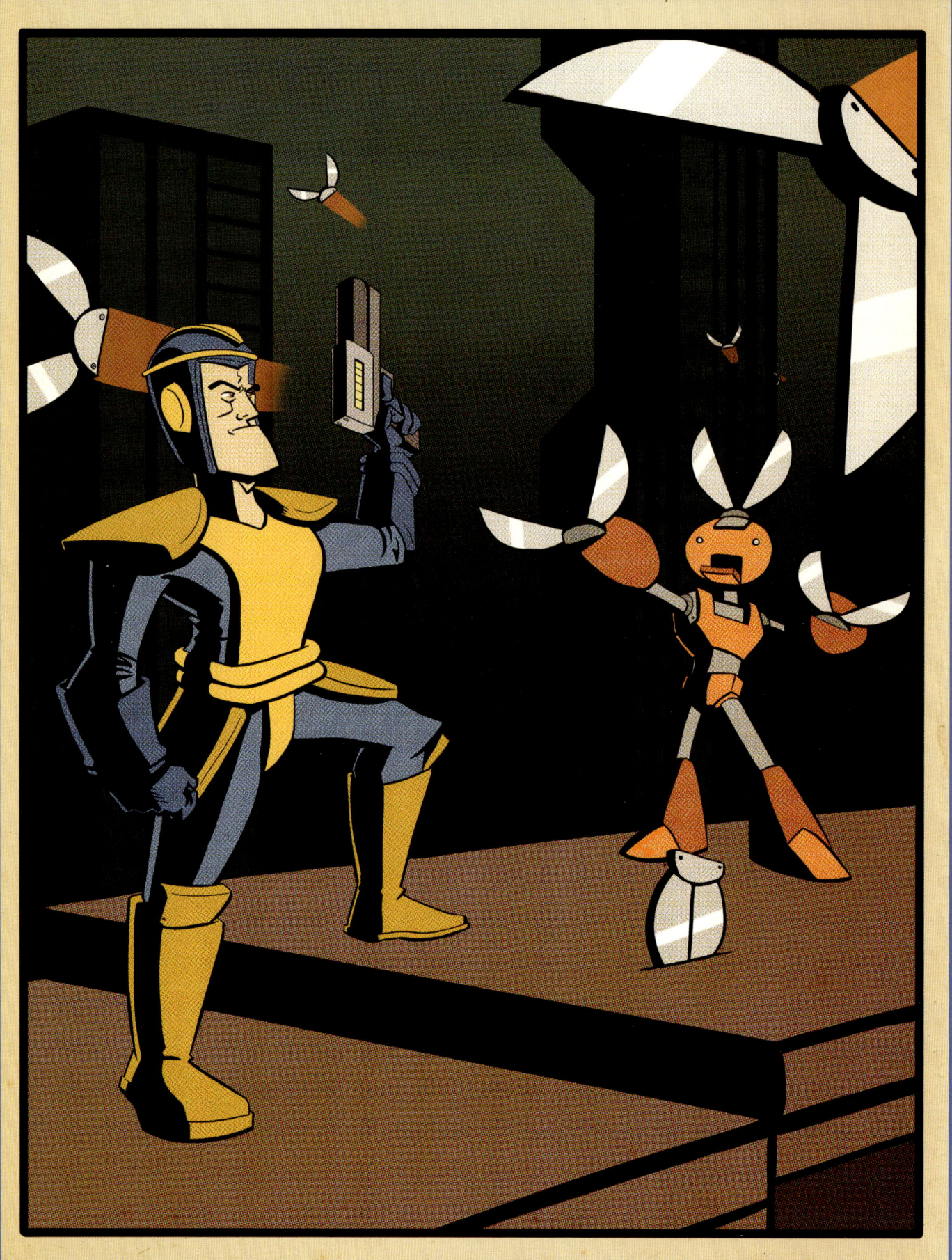

ADAM HINES
Toronto, ON, Canada
Animator

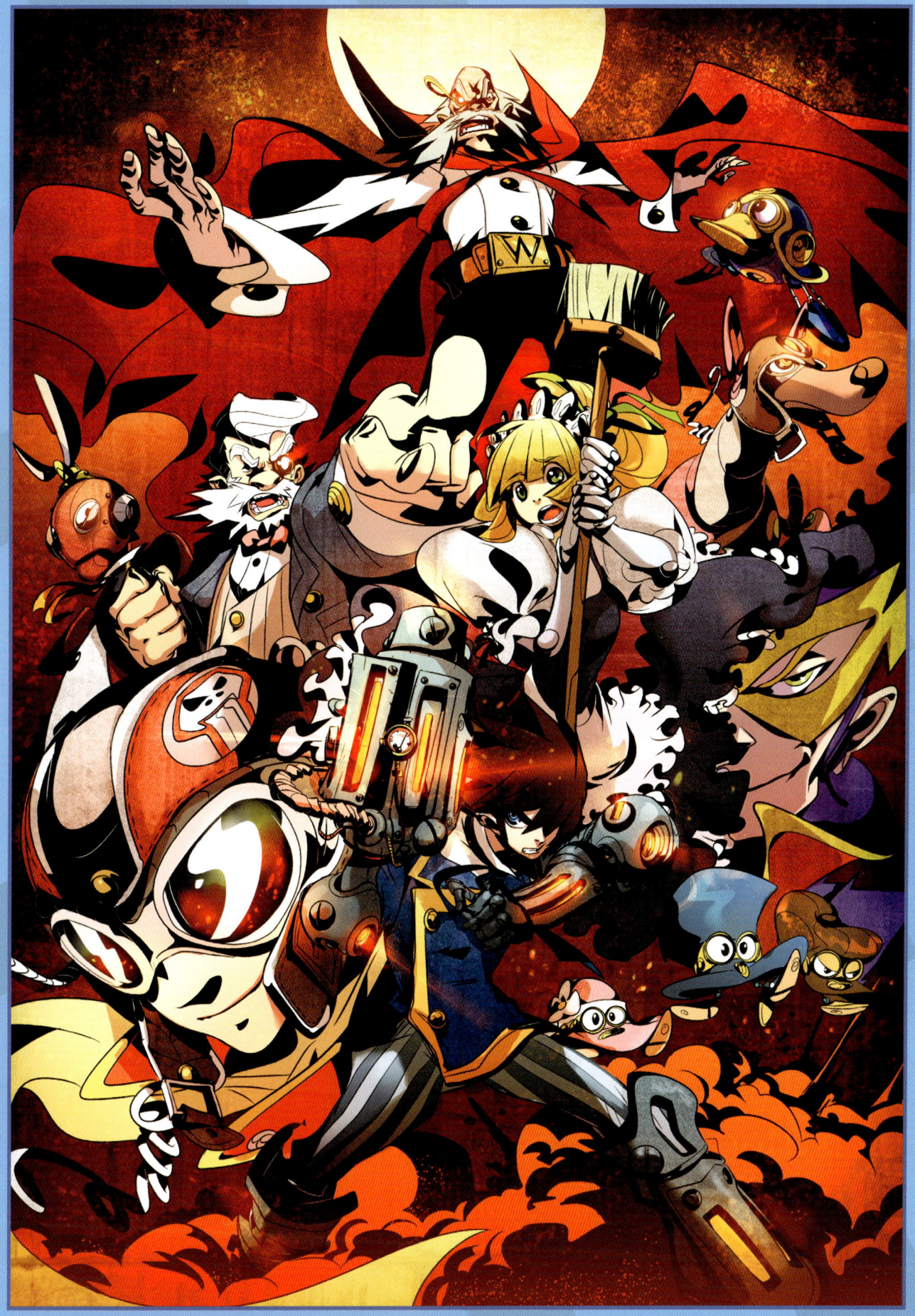

Andres S. Blanco
Santiago, Chile
yin-sakamoto.deviantart.com - ninjamaids.blogspot.com
Illustrator / Concept Artist
(IDW Publishing / Fantasy Flight Games / Jasco Games)

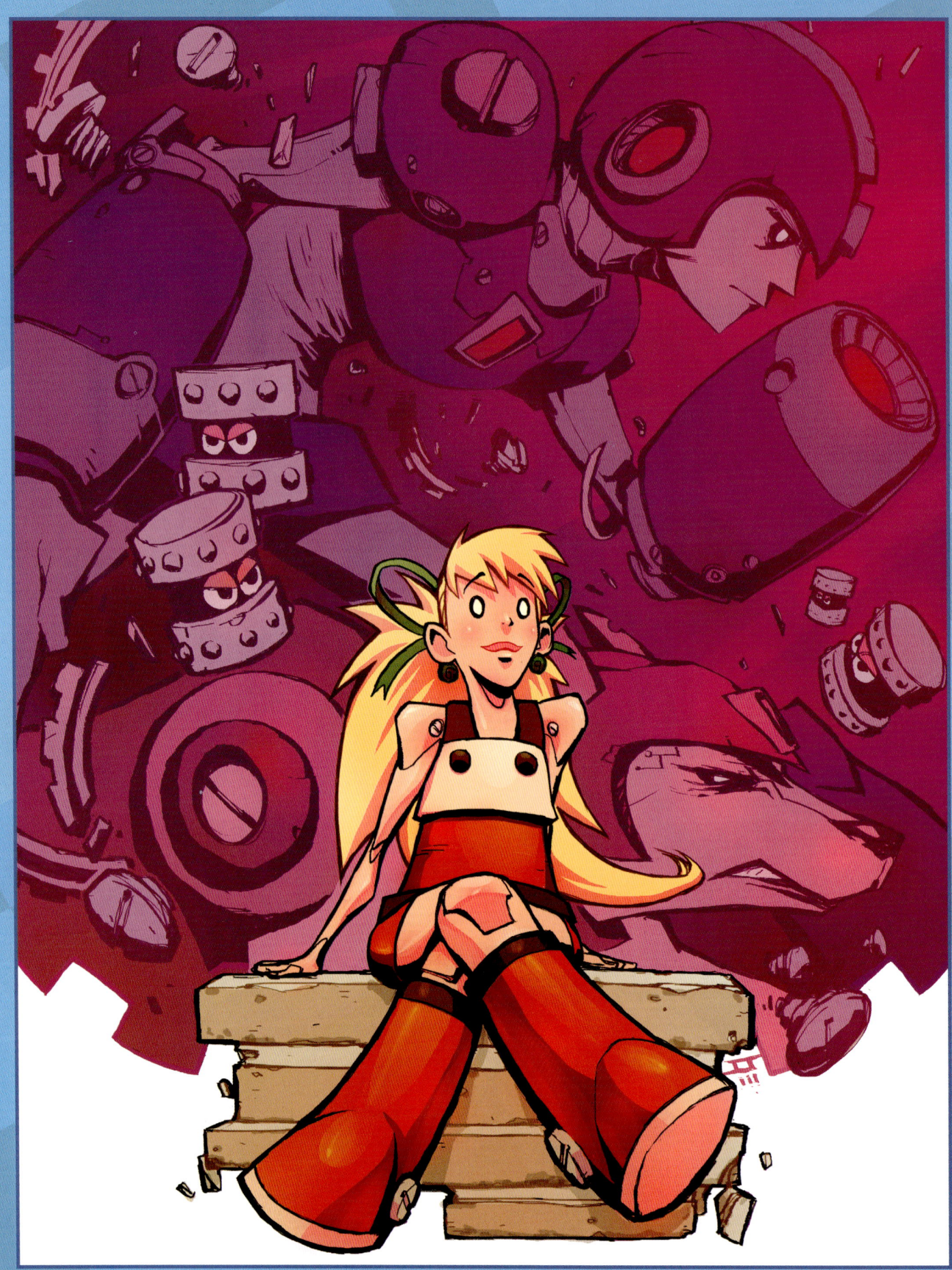

JEFF STOKELY
Manhattan Beach, CA, United States
www.jeffstokely.com
Illustrator
(Fraggle Rock issue 1, vol.1 - Archaia / Masters of the Universe contract artwork - Mattel /
Return to Labyrinth pin-up - Tokyopop)

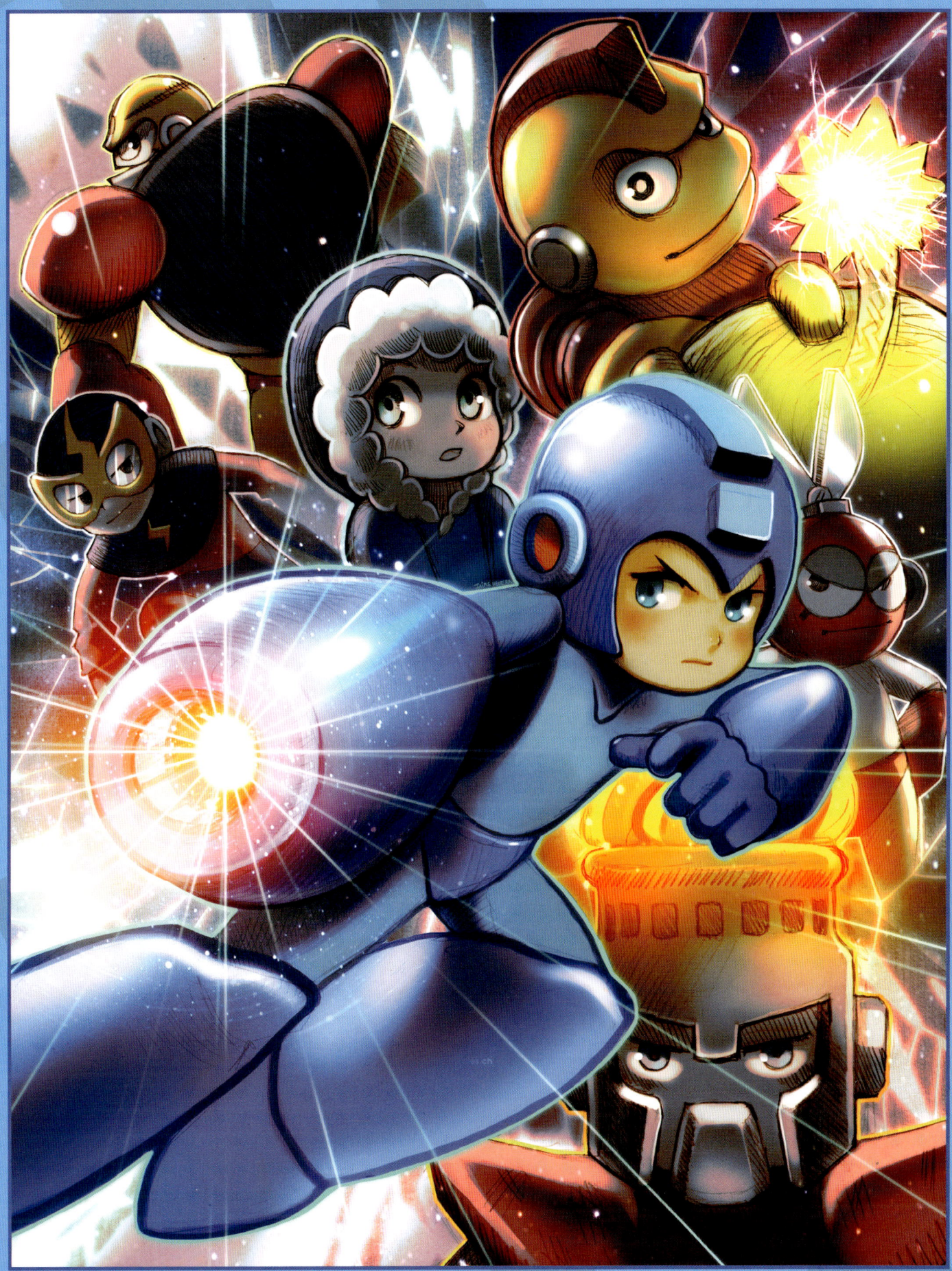

JAIME HERRERA RIVERA
Palma de Mallorca, Spain
jaimito.deviantart.com
Illustrator

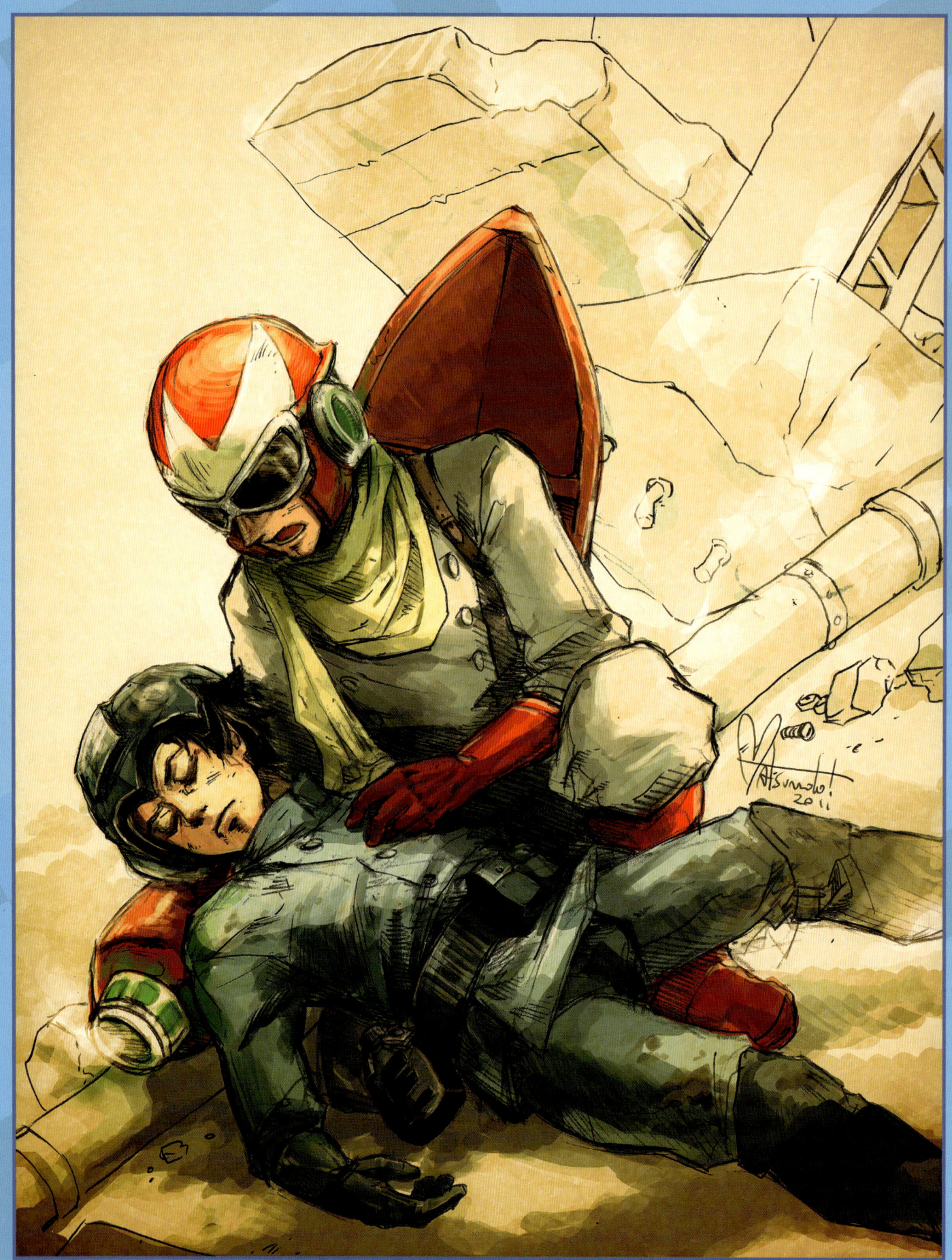

NINA MATSUMOTO
Coquitlam, BC, Canada
www.spacecoyote.com
Comic Book Artist
(Bongo Comics (penciler) / Yokaiden (artist/writer) / The Last Airbender: Zuko's Story (artist))

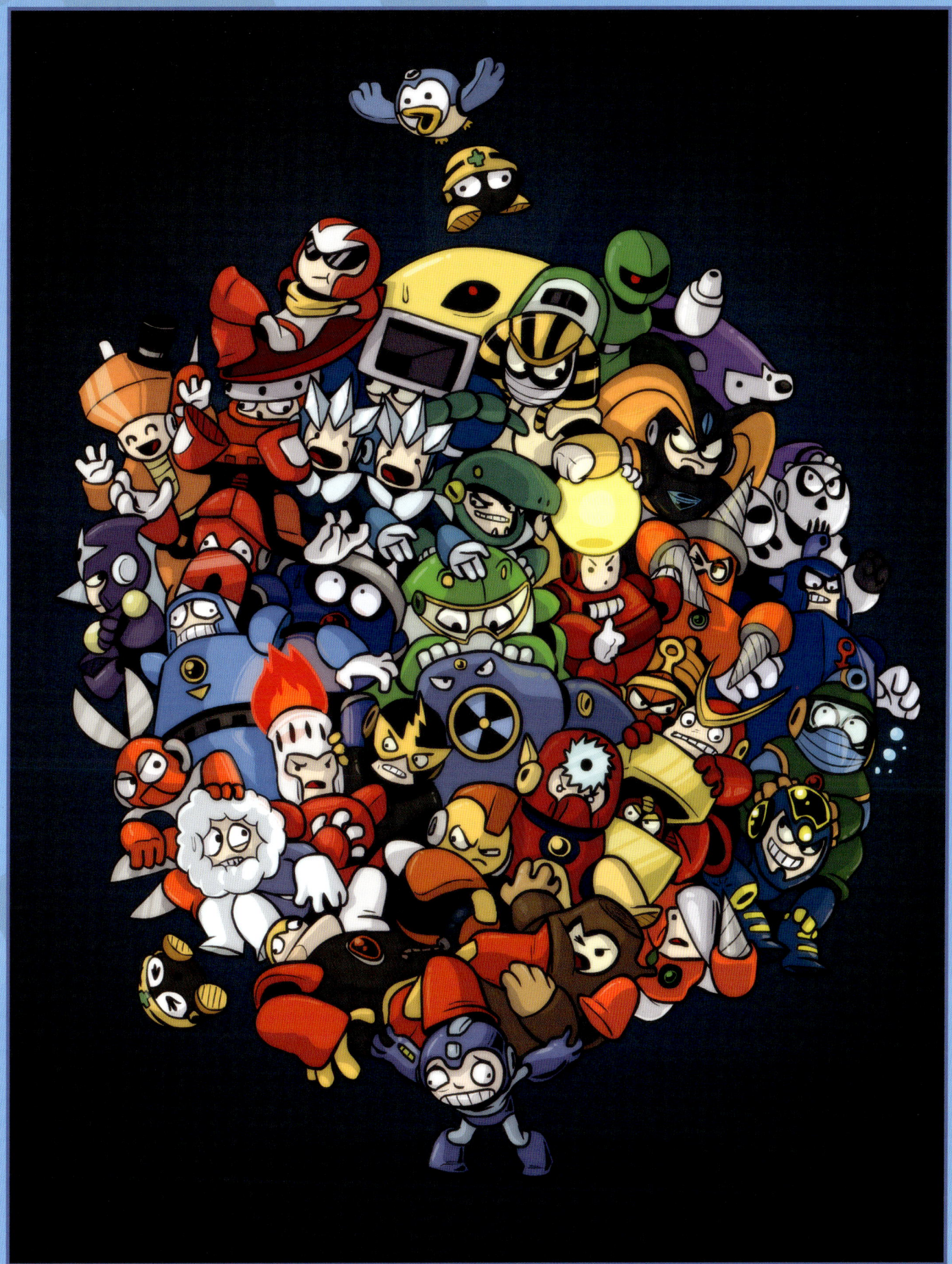

GENE GOLDSTEIN
Schaumburg, IL, United States
www.hyperboystudios.com
Animator Extraordinaire
(Animator on Squidbillies / Animator on Aqua Teen Hunger Force / Animator for Chicago Bulls)

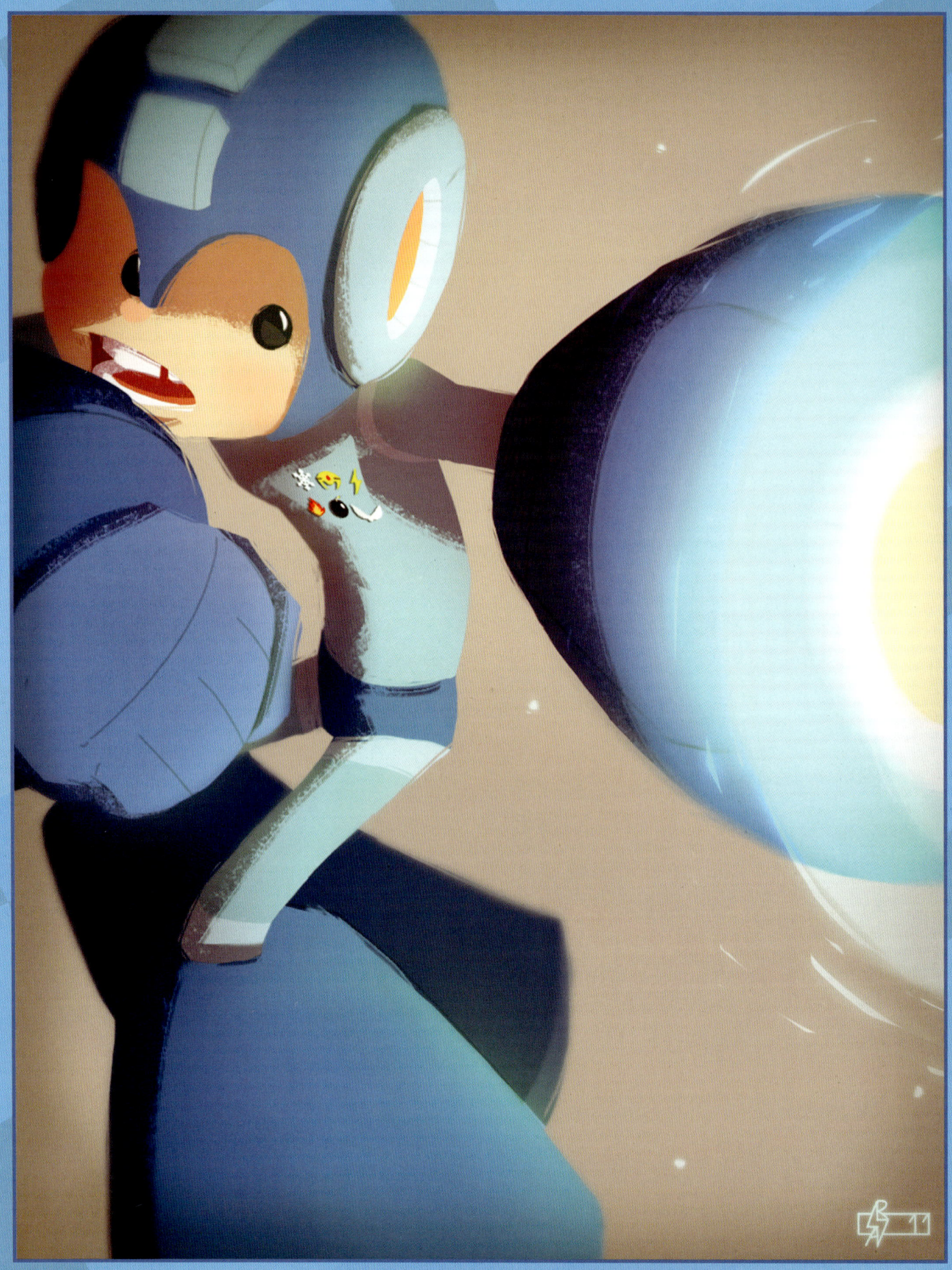

ANDRY RAJOELINA (SHANGO)
Paris, France
andry-shango.deviantart.com
Designer for Animation

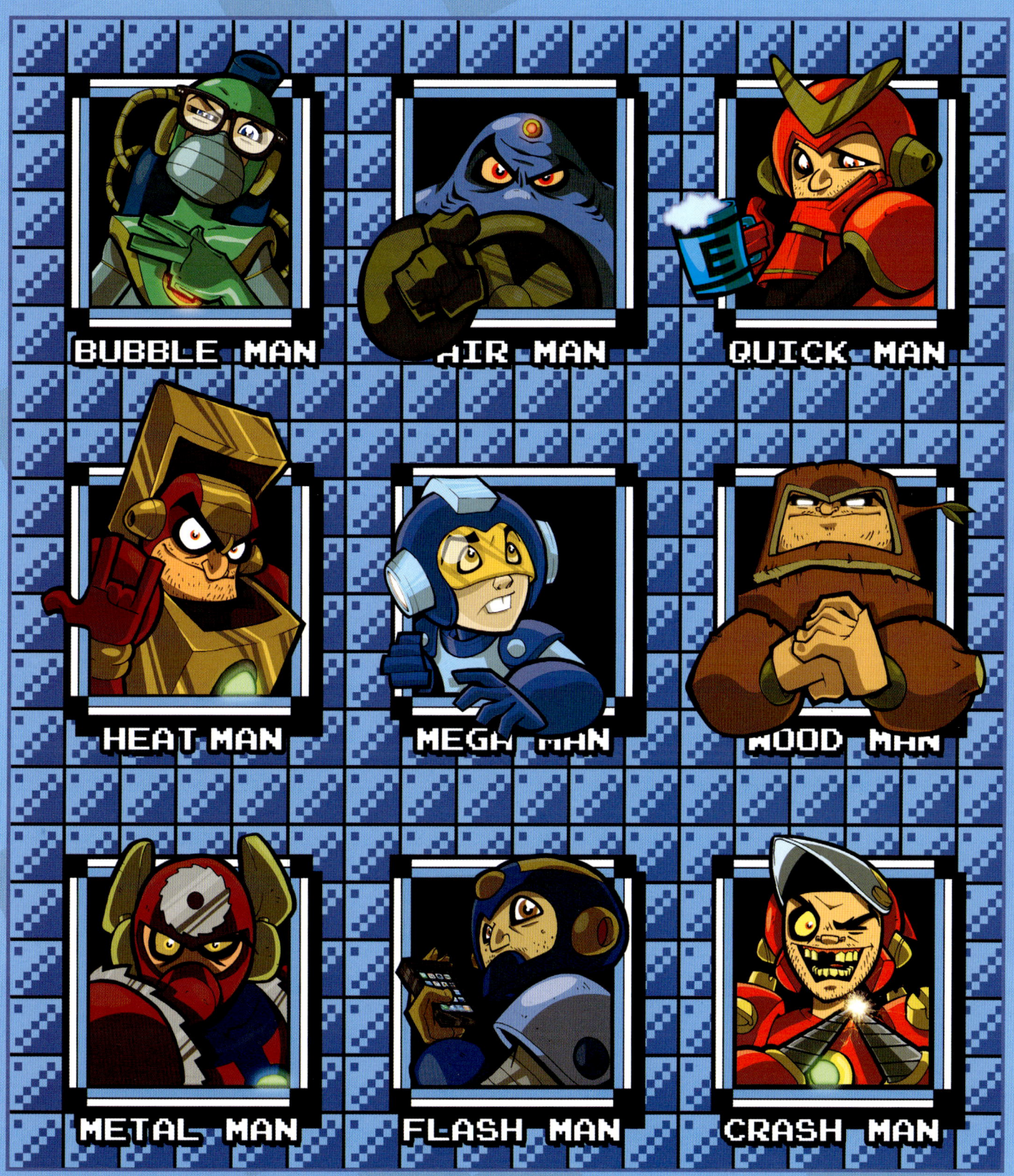

KEITH MORRIS
Toronto, ON, Canada
Designer
(Babar / Beyblade / Bakugan / Franklin / Ruby Gloom / Mike The Knight)

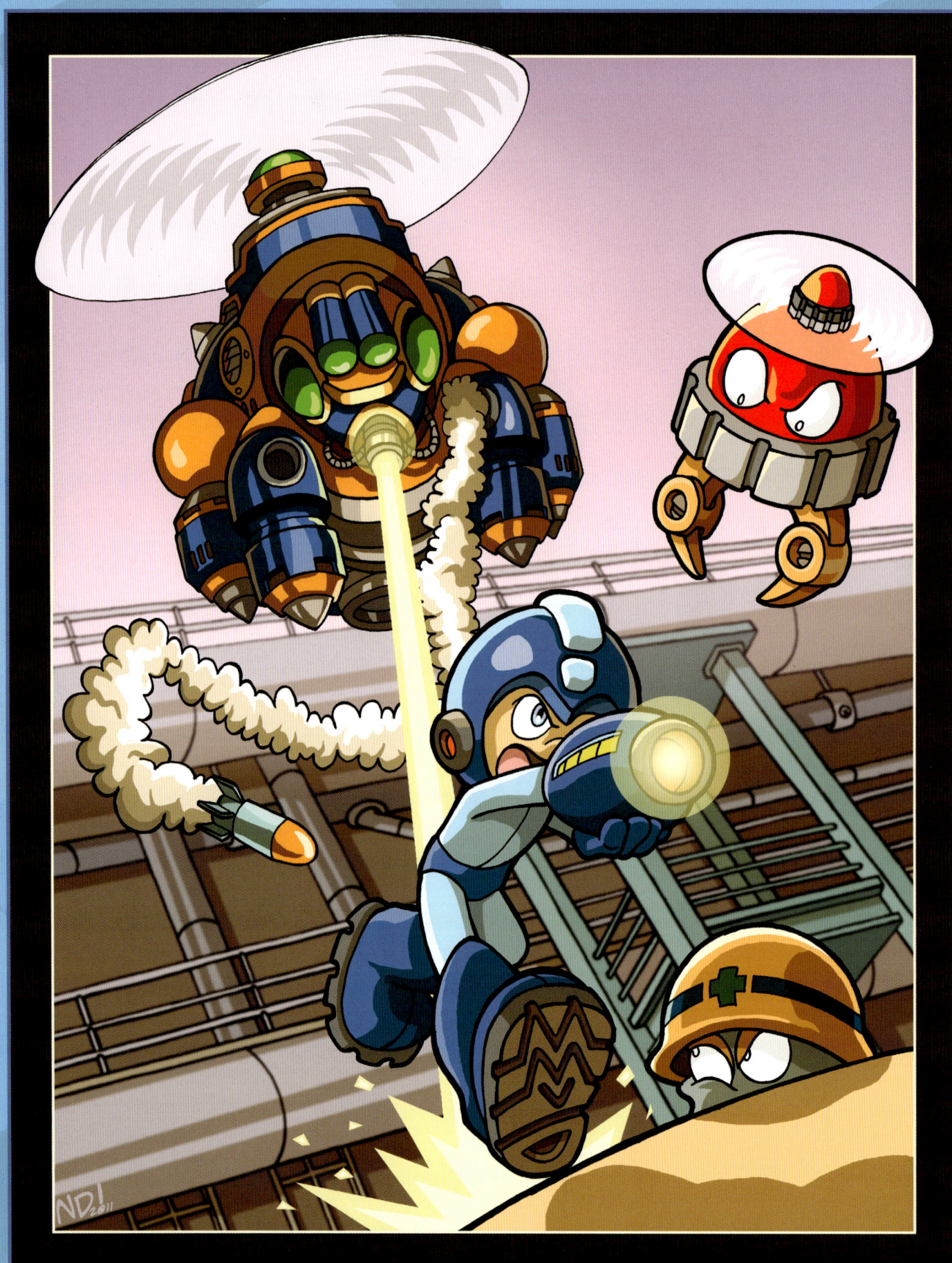

ANDY GENEN (-ND!-)
Aubange, Belgium
scoundreldaze.deviantart.com
Illustrator
(Dream Catcher / De leschte Ritter / Josh Howard presents: Sasquatch)

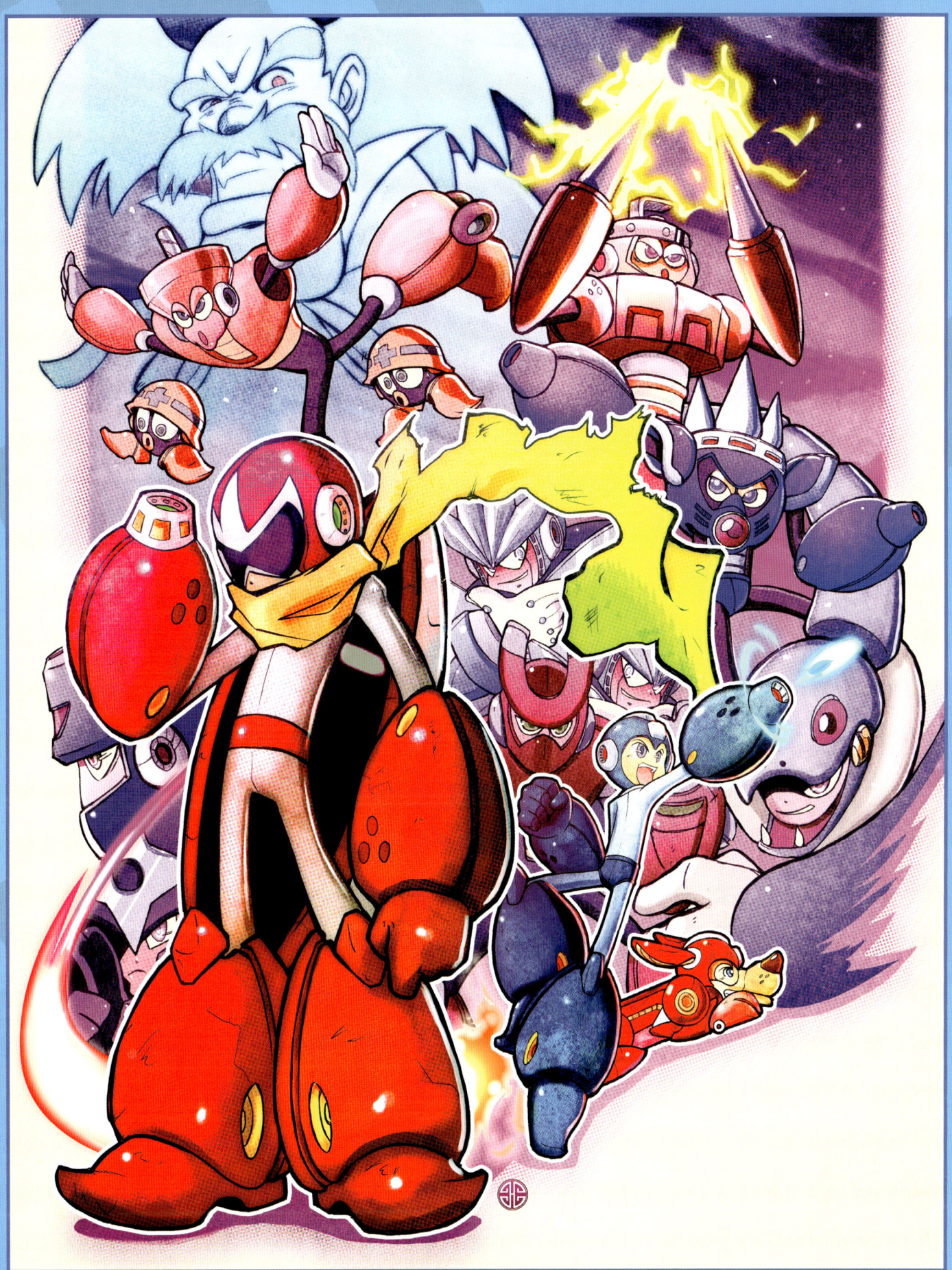

CHRIS HOUSE (RIKYO)
St. Louis, MO, United States
rikyo.deviantart.com
Graphic Designer

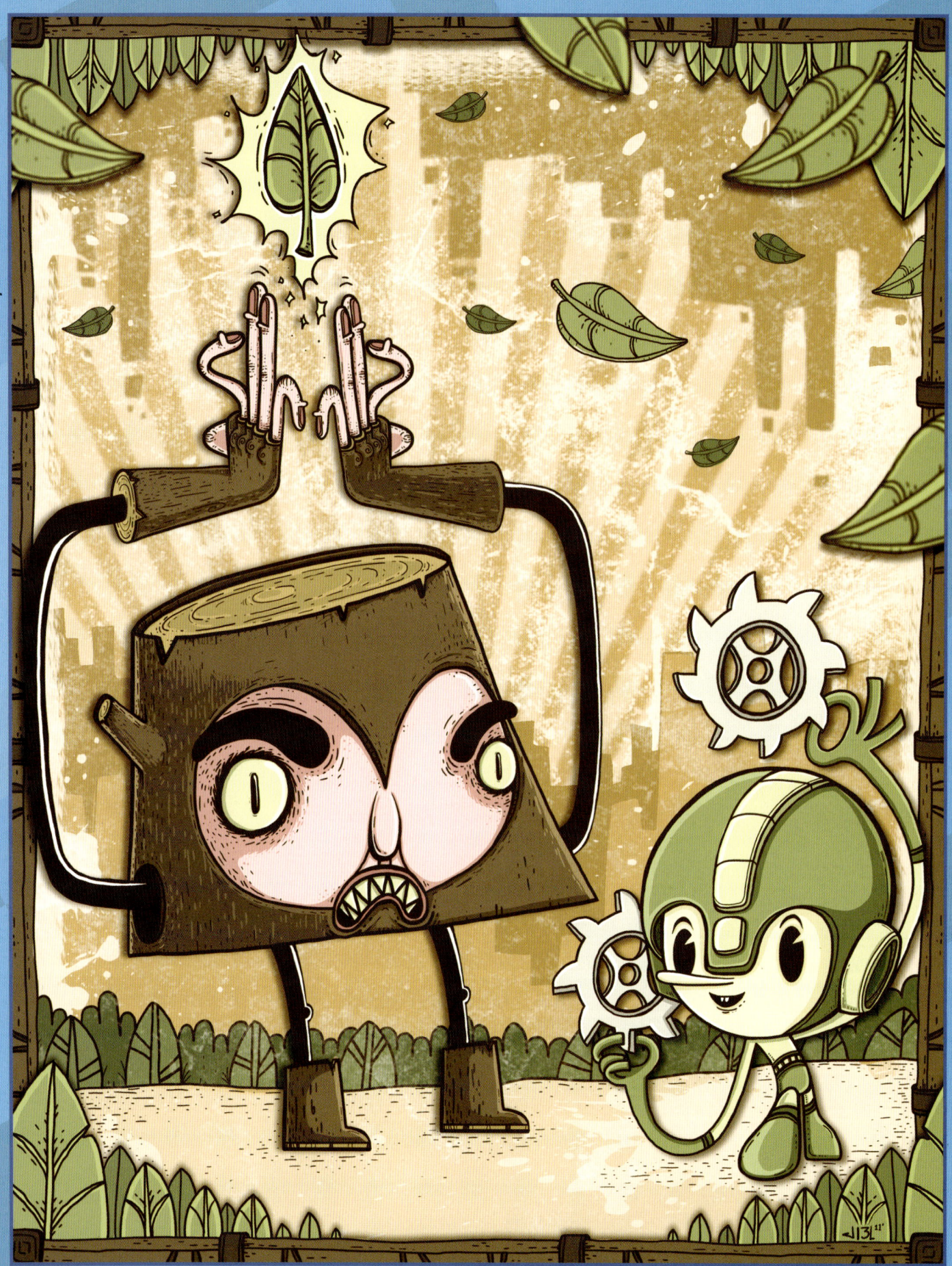

JOEL MACKENZIE
Halifax, NS, Canada
www.flickr.com/photos/joelmackenzie
Animator / Film Maker

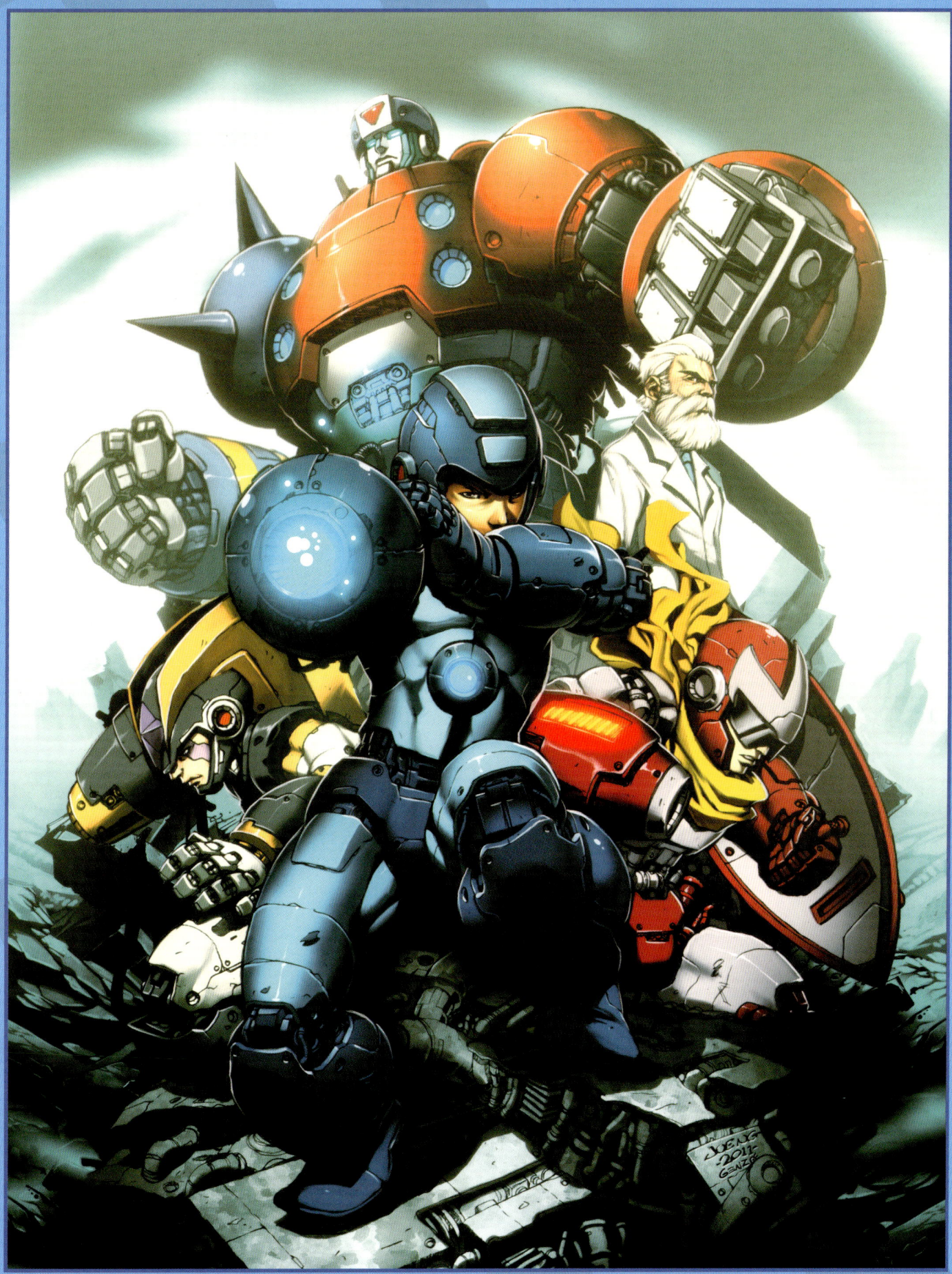

JOE NG
Burlington, ON, Canada
ngboy.deviantart.com
Comic Artist
(Street Fighter IV, Inception: The Cobol Job, Soul Calibur IV, Transformers)

GONZALO ORDÓÑEZ ARIAS
Arica, Chile
Colorist

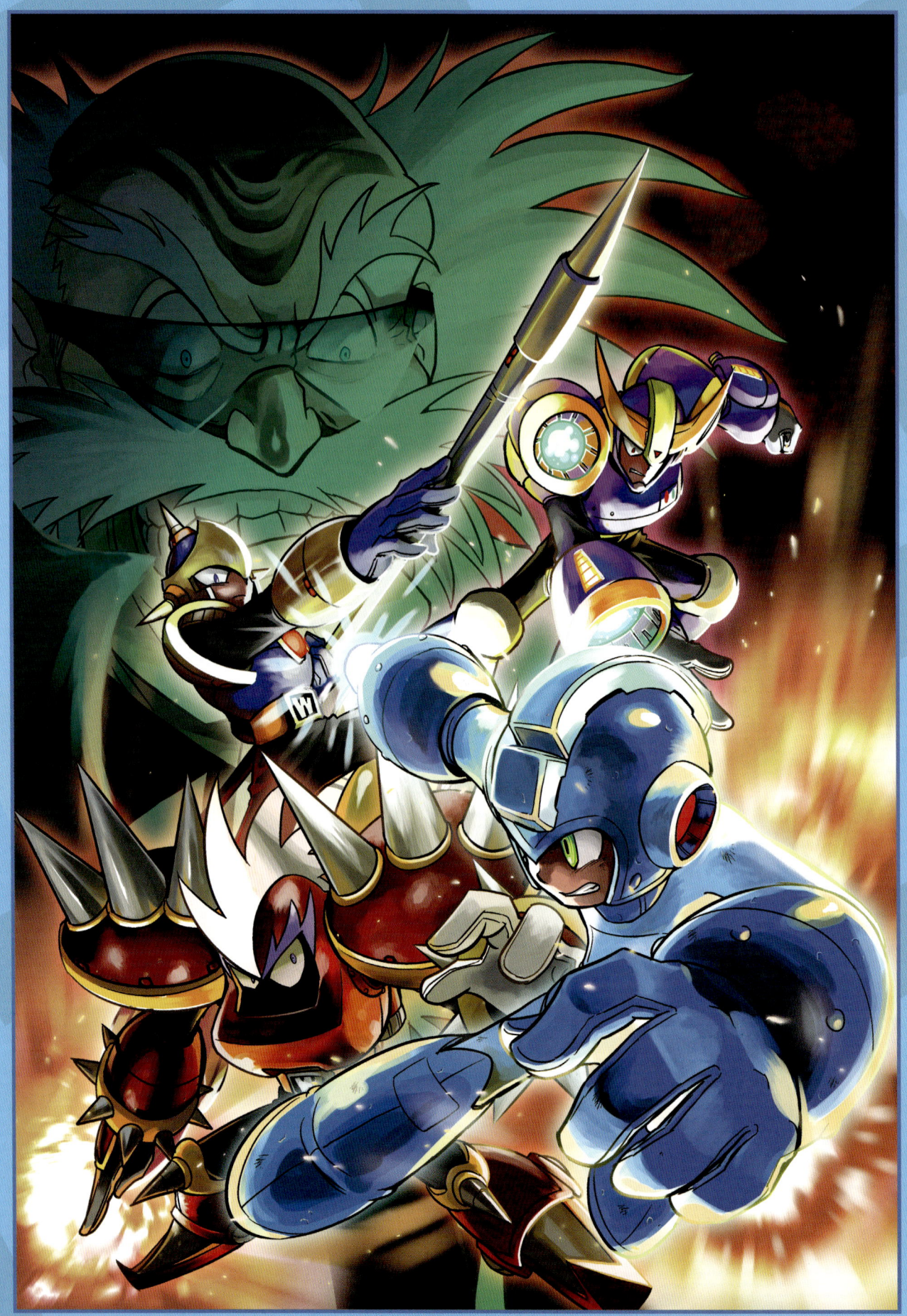

HITOSHI ARIGA
Japan
www.ancient.co.jp/~ariga
Manga Artist
(Mega Man Megamix, MEga Man gigamix, The Big O)

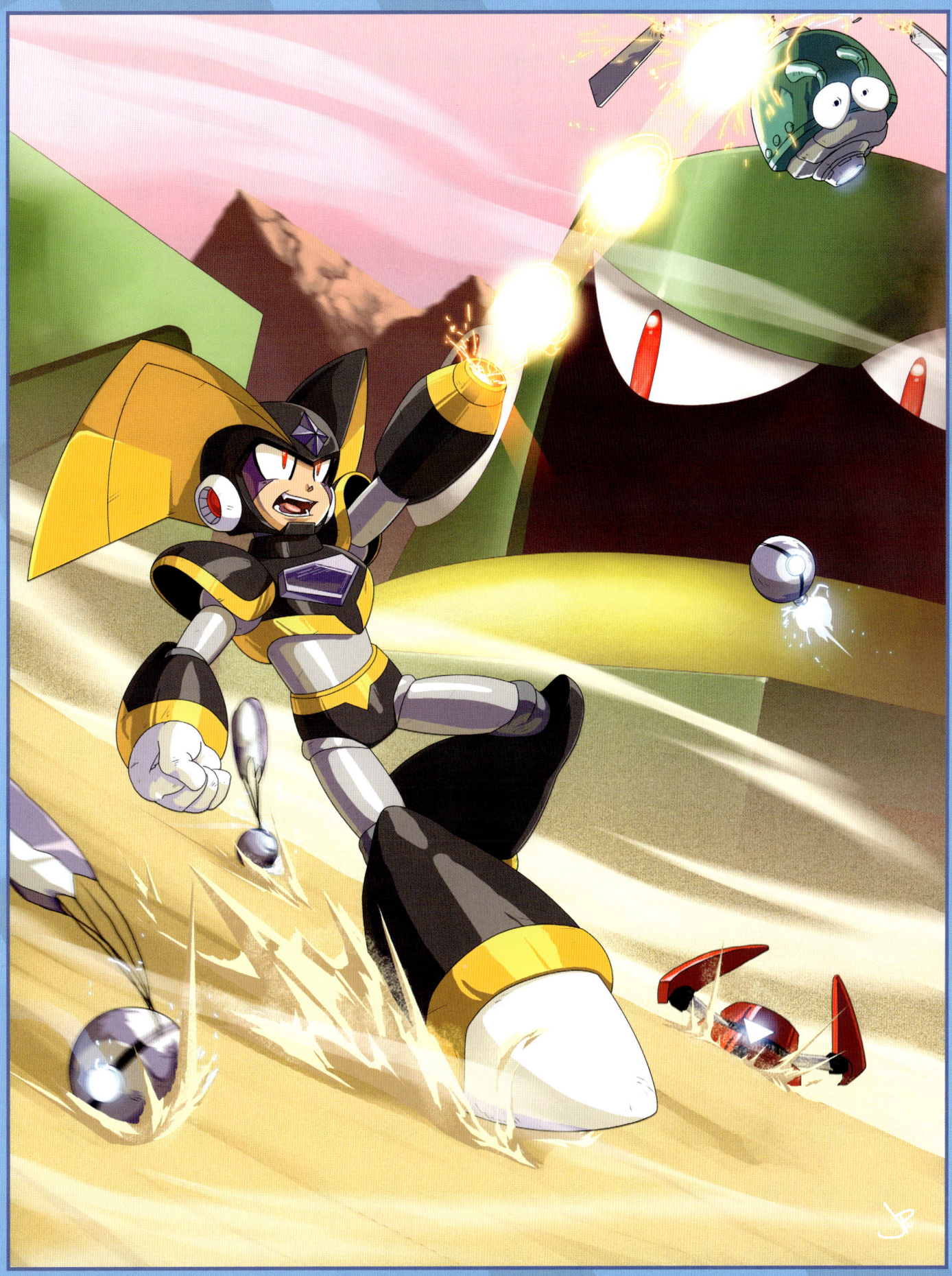

JOSHUA PEREZ (DYEMOOCH)
Killeen, TX, United States
dyemooch.deviantart.com
Freelance Artist/Colorist
(Drift, A-Team War Stories, Jennifer Love Hewitt's Music Box)

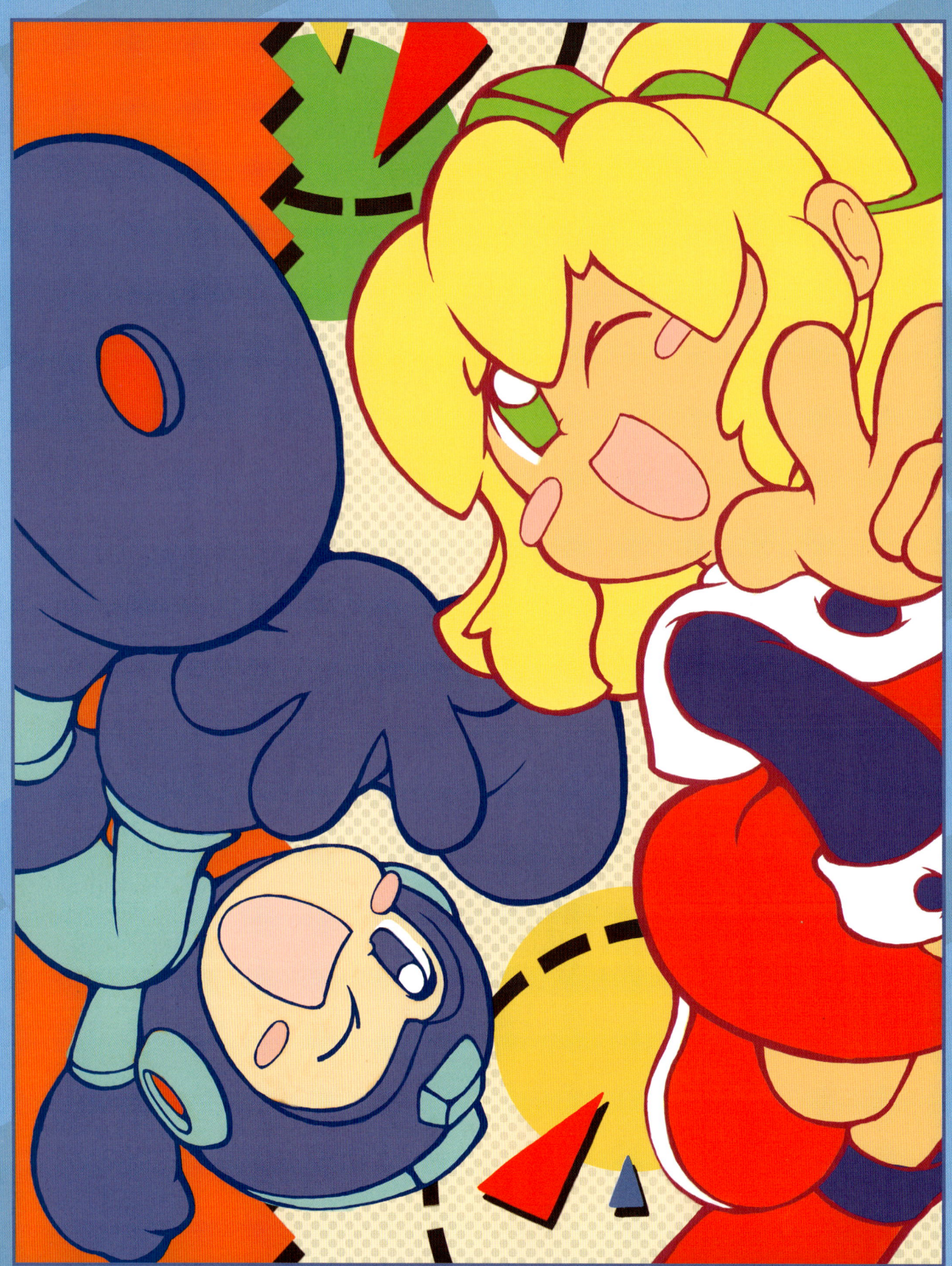

CHRIS AYER (AIR-CITY)
Temple, TX, United States
air-city.deviantart.com
Animator

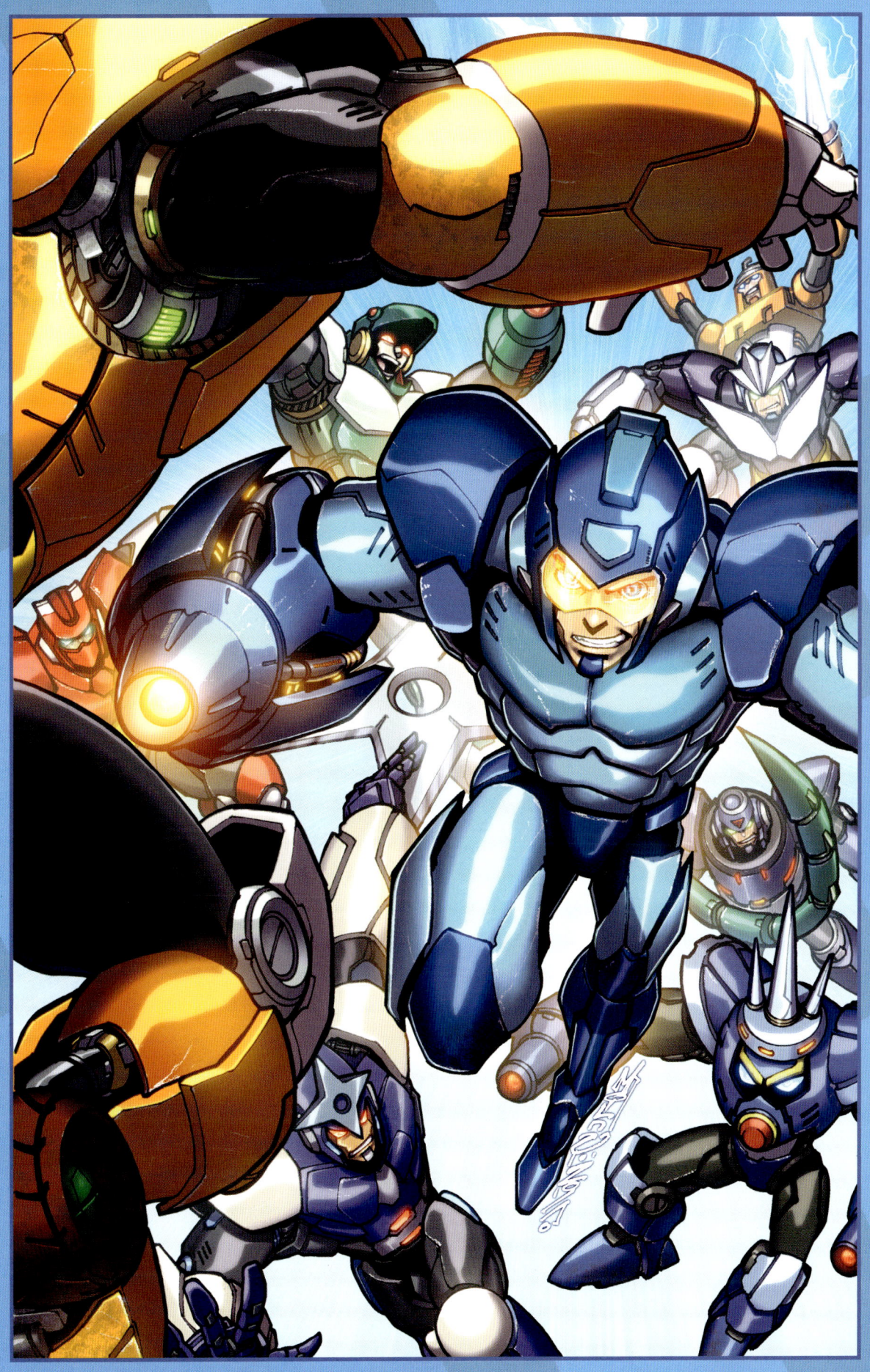

ALEX MILNE
Mississauga, ON, Canada
markerguru.deviantart.com
Comic Artist
(Transformers Ongoing, Drift, Reign of Starscream)

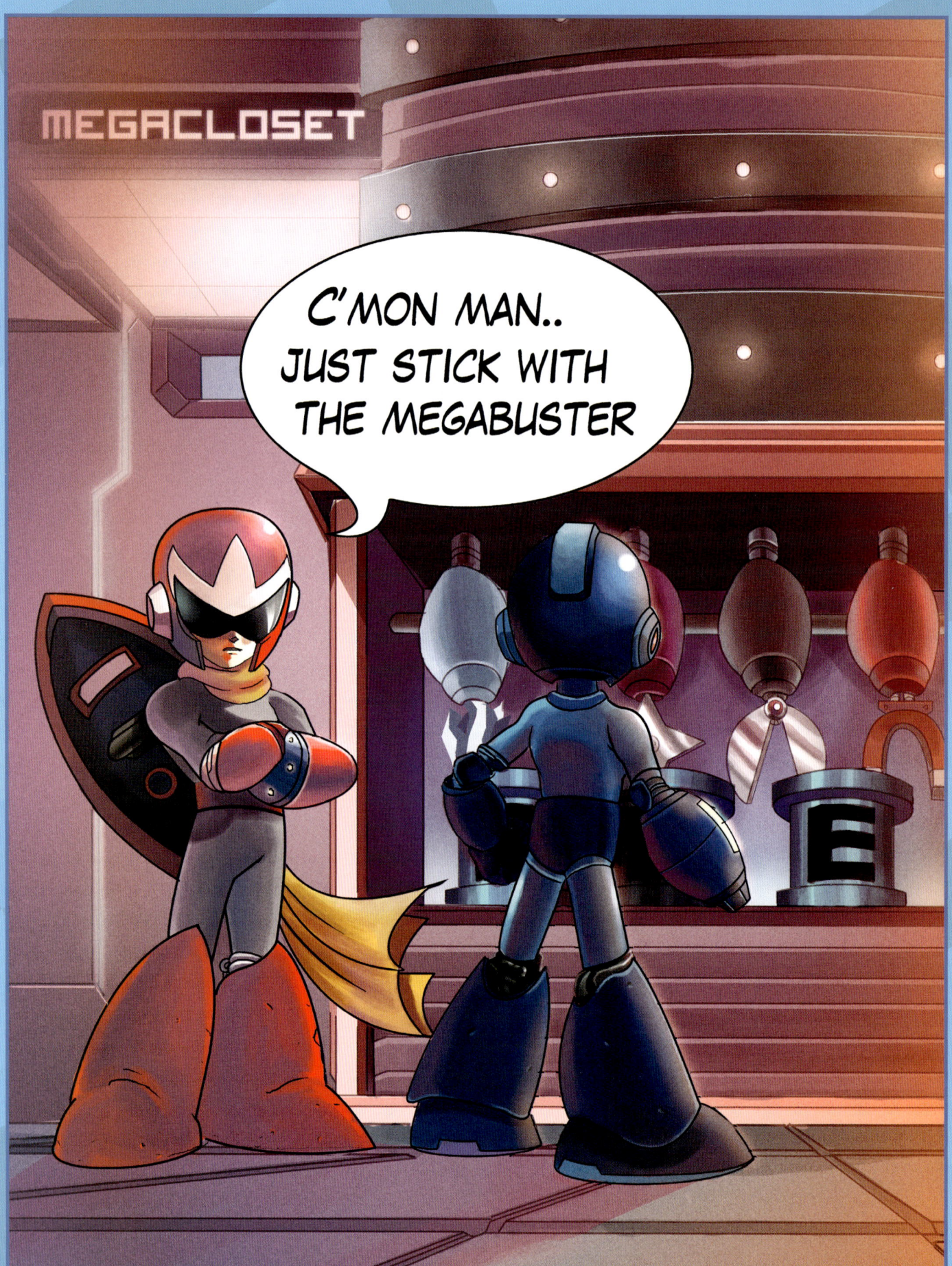

DANIEL ROSINI DIMAS MACHADO (DAMROSSI)
Sao Paulo, Brazil
daniel-shagrath.deviantart.com
Ilustrator/ Concept artist

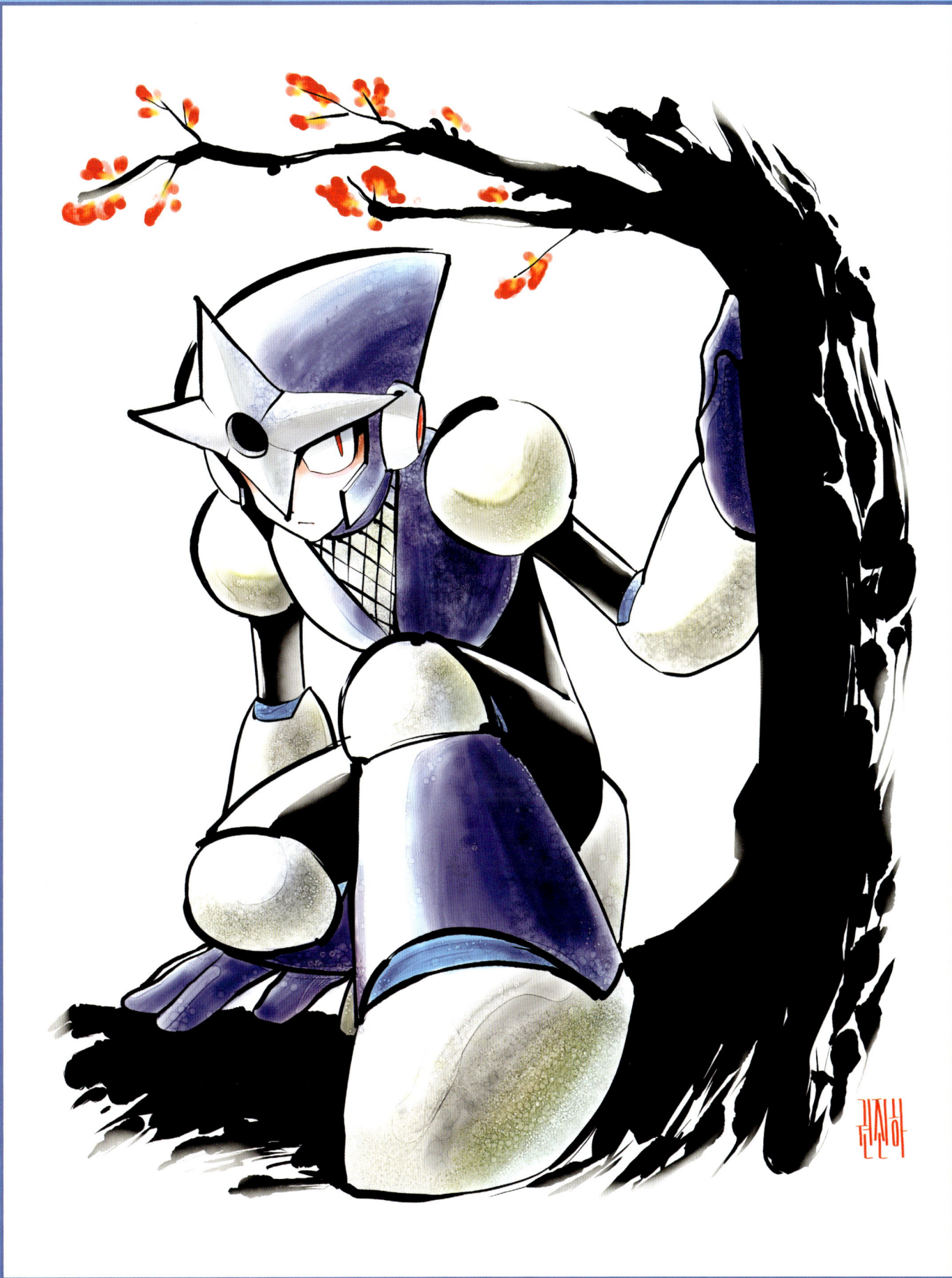

JIN-HA KWON
Korea
Illustrator

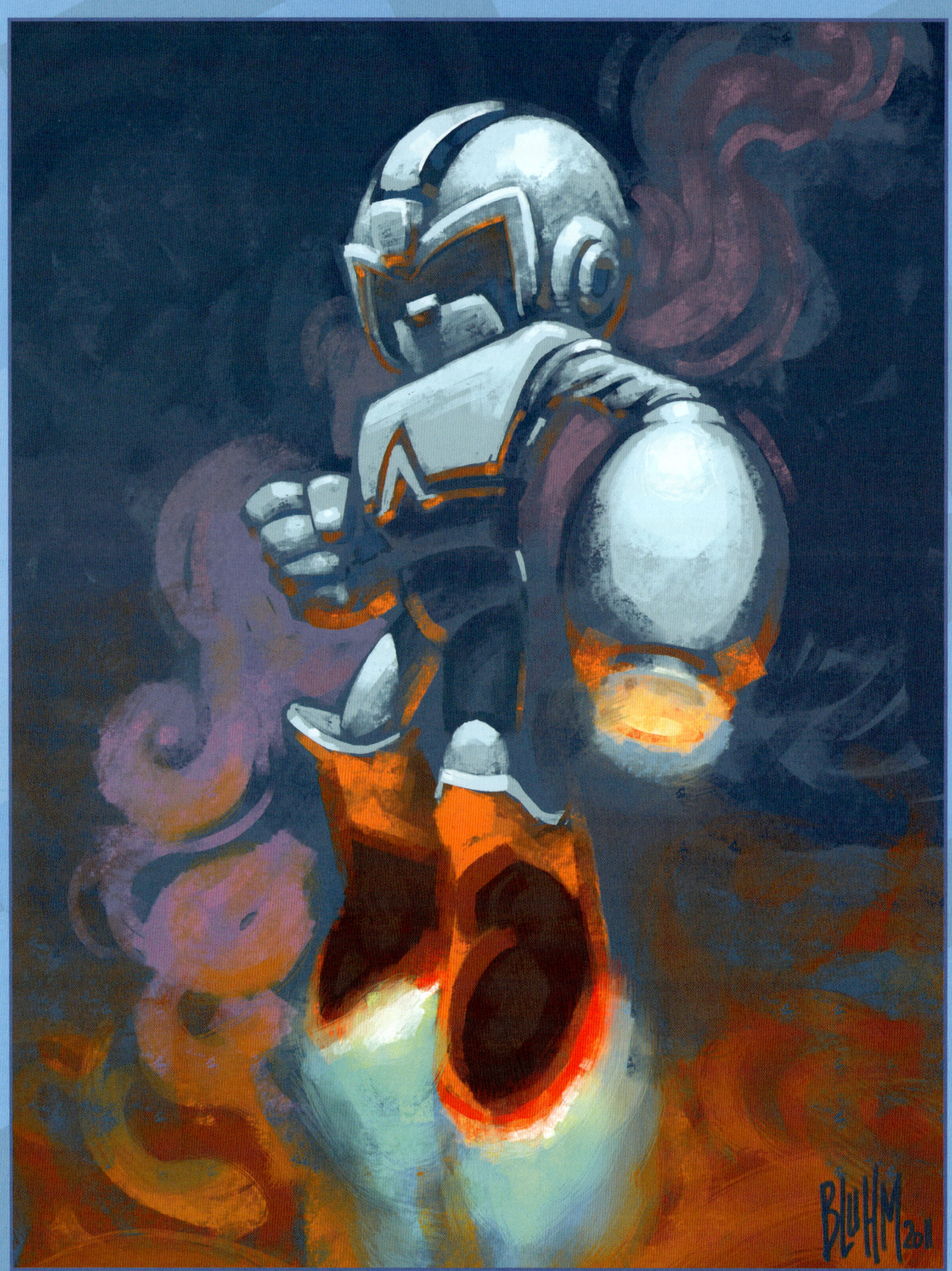

JOE BLUHM
Shreveport, LA, United States
http://www.joebluhm.com/
concept & story artist / illustrator
(Story Artist at Moonbot Studios / Caricaturist and Publisher)

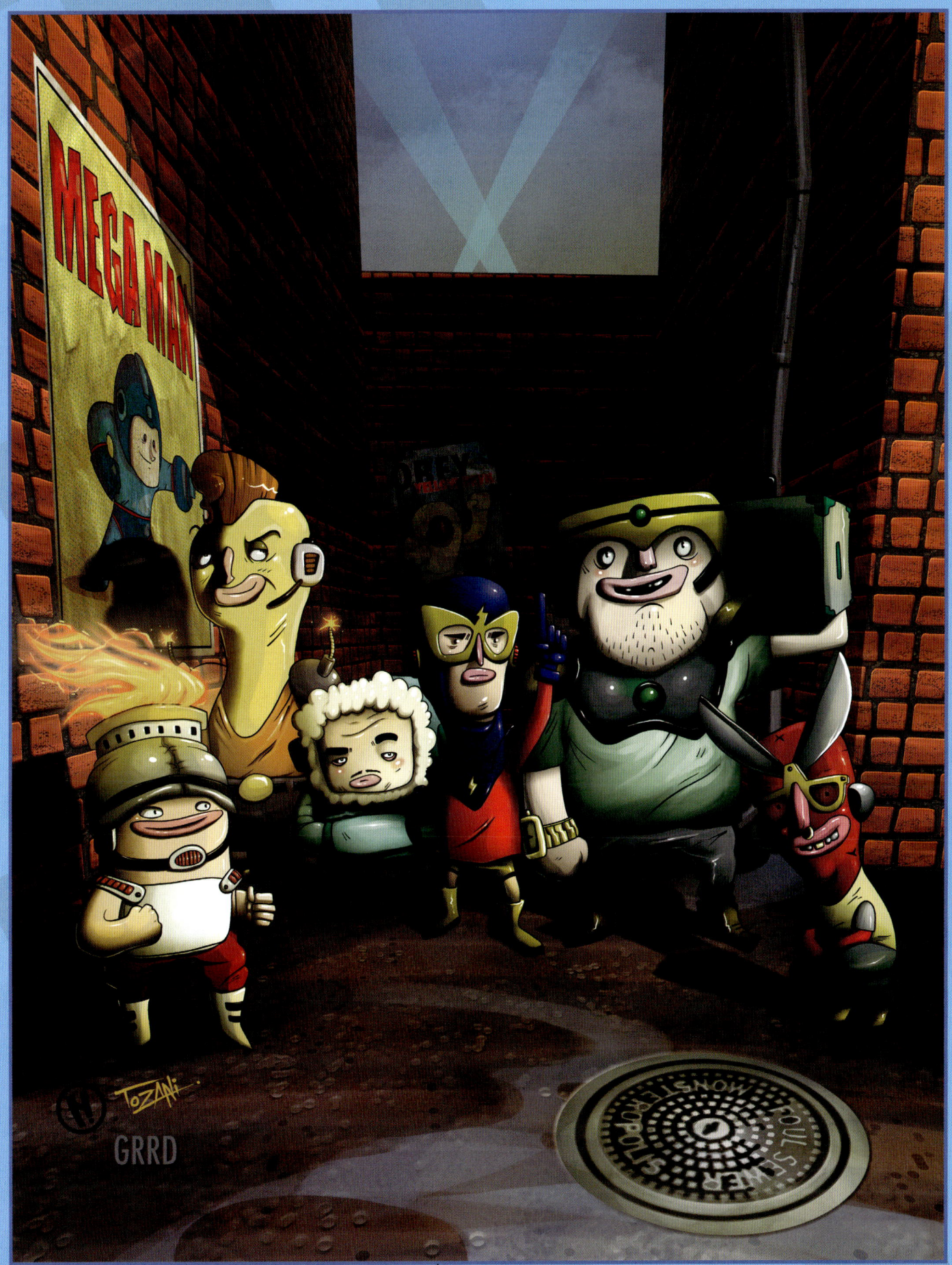

GERARDO ALBA
Naucalpan de Juarez, Mexico
Illustrator

HINO & TOZANI
Mexico
Colourists

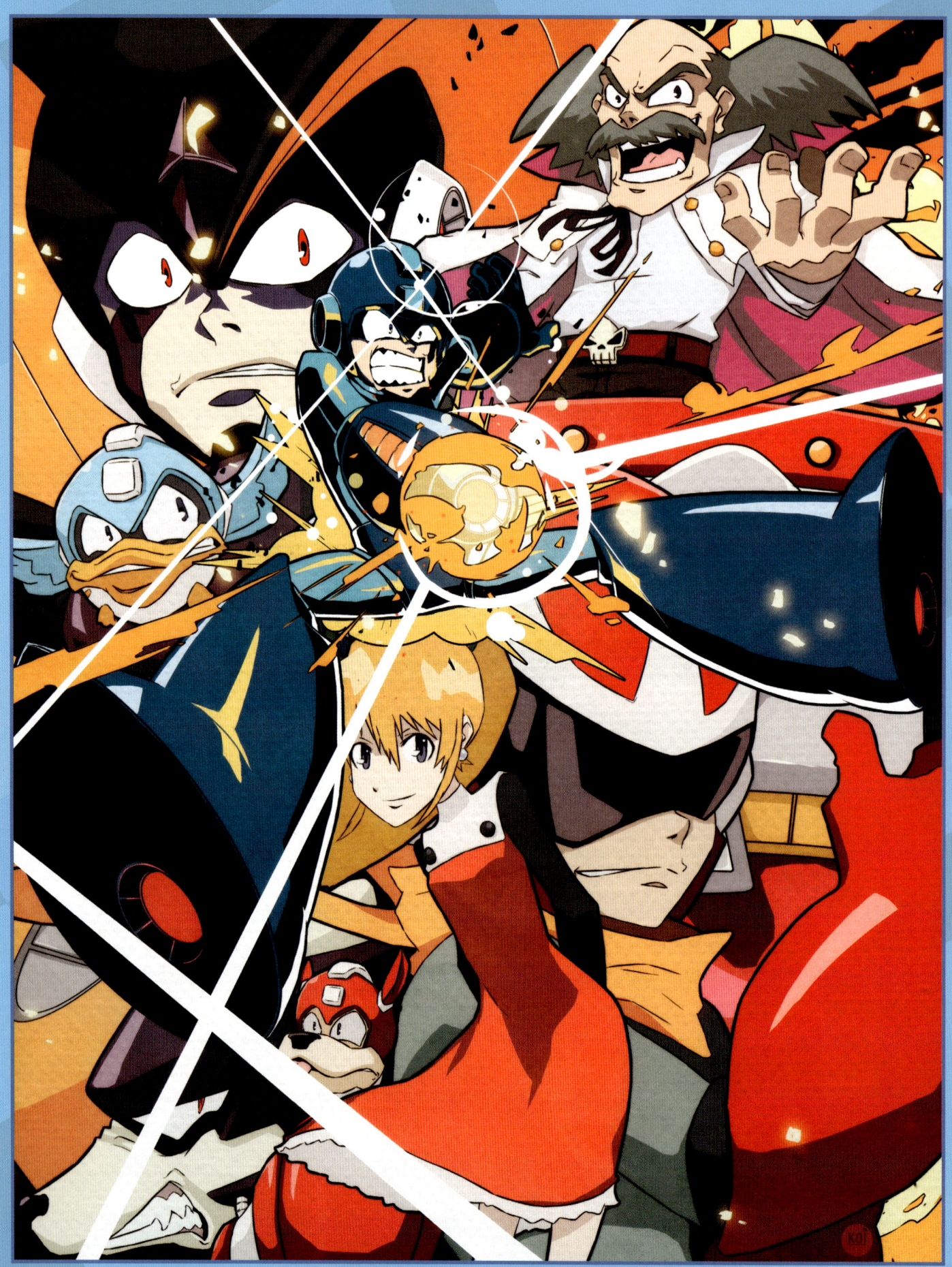

JOHN MICHAEL CARREON (KOI)
Quezon City, Philippines
eclectic-lights.blogspot.com
Graphic Artist

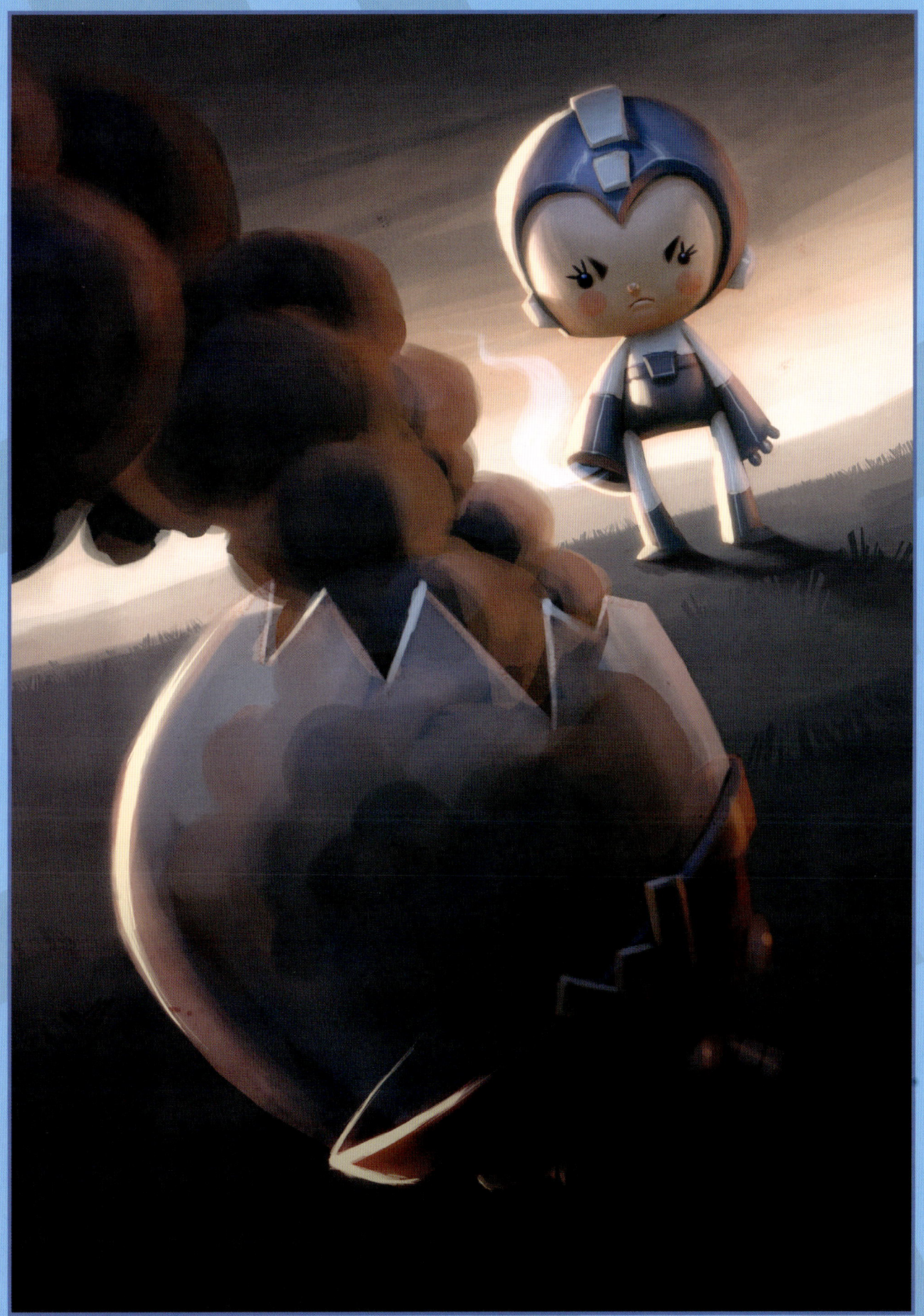

ADAM FORD
Eagle Mountain, UT, United States
adamscreation.blogspot.com
Art Director
(Capoeira Fighter3 / Infinity Blade / Guardians of Altarris)

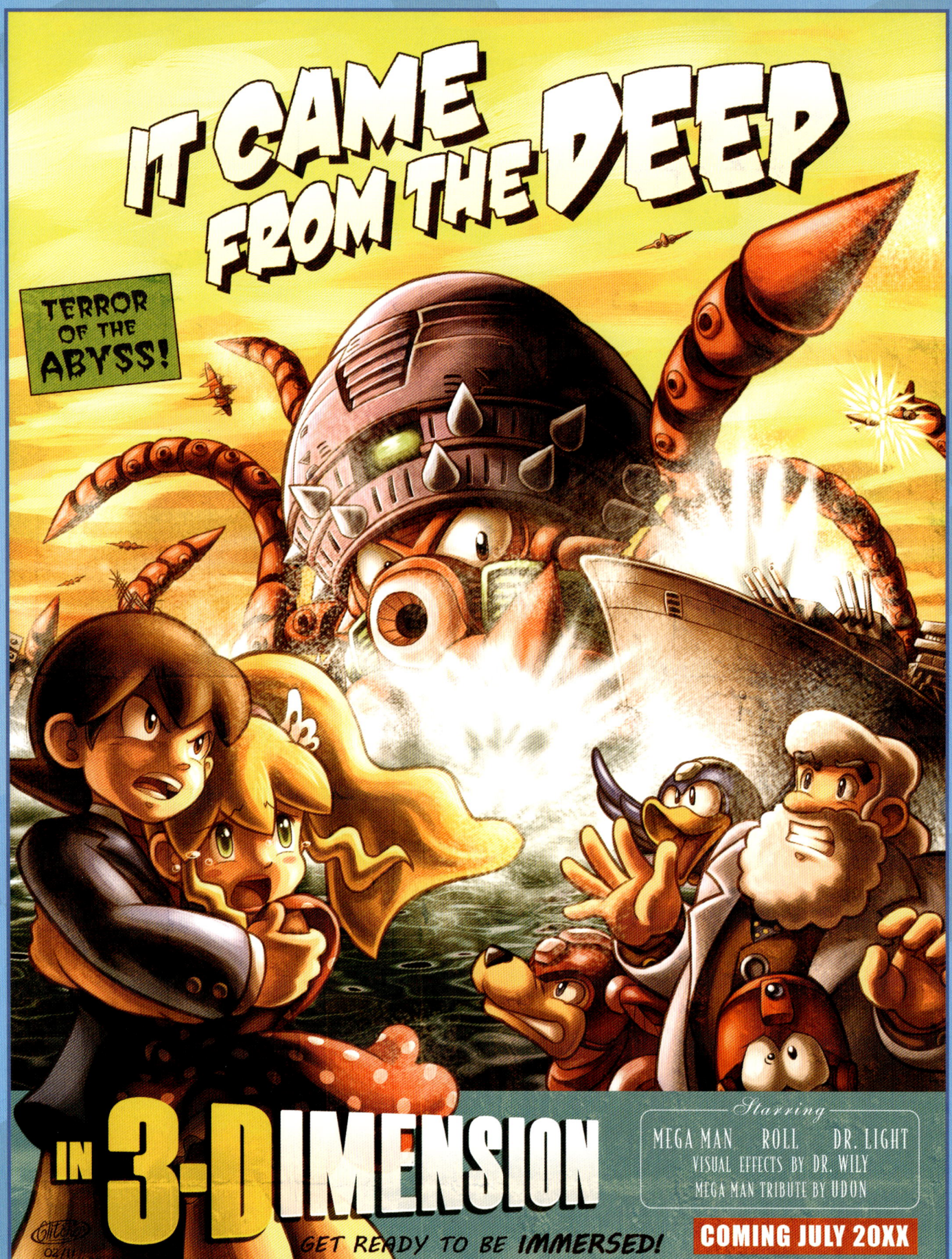

CHRISTOPHER REAVEY (GLITCHER)
London, United Kingdom
glitcher.carbonmade.com
Comic Artist
(Royal Adademy of Fine Arts / School of Arts and Crafts)

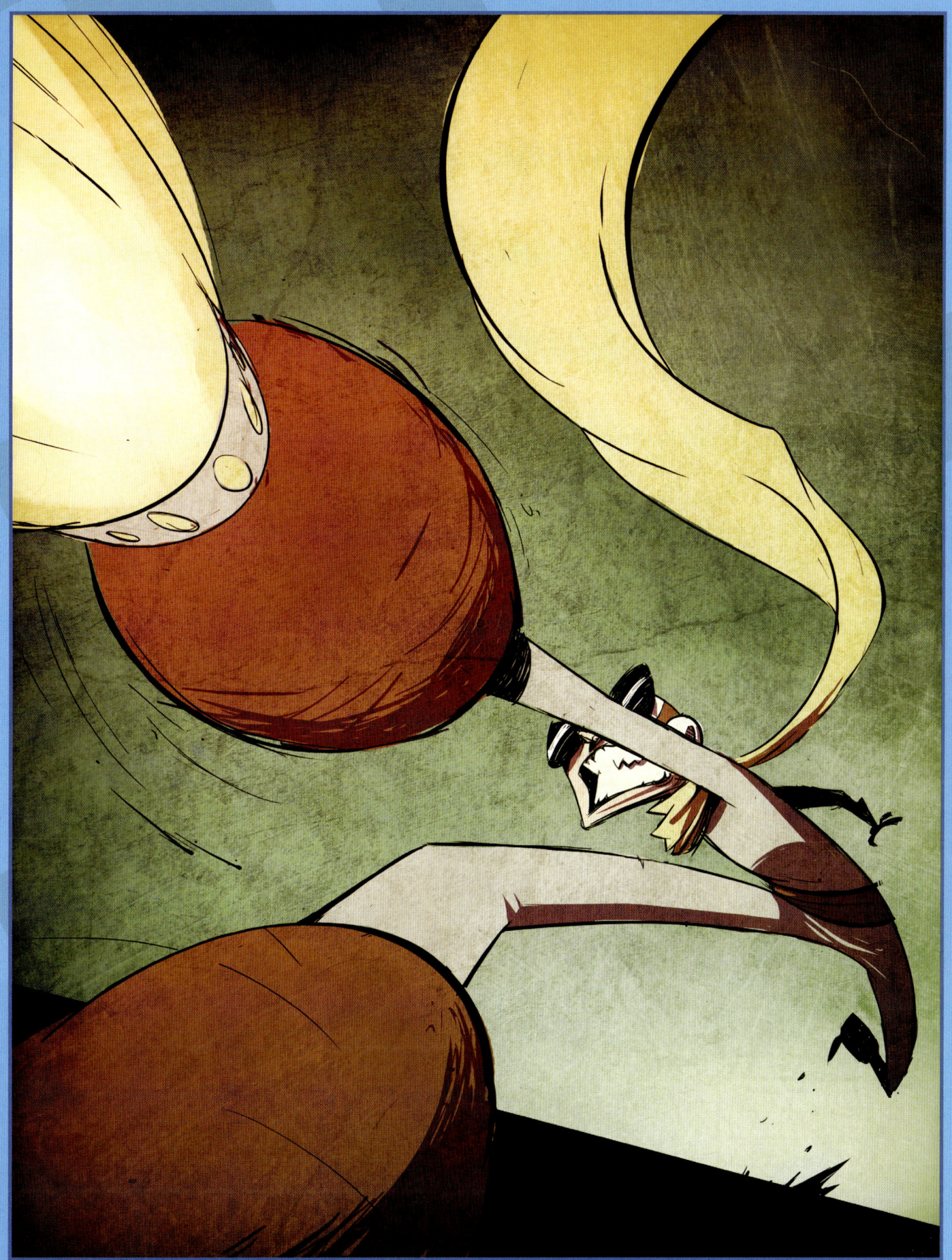

FREDDY CARRASCO
Toronto, ON, Canada
skriblz.deviantart.com
Character Designer & Animator

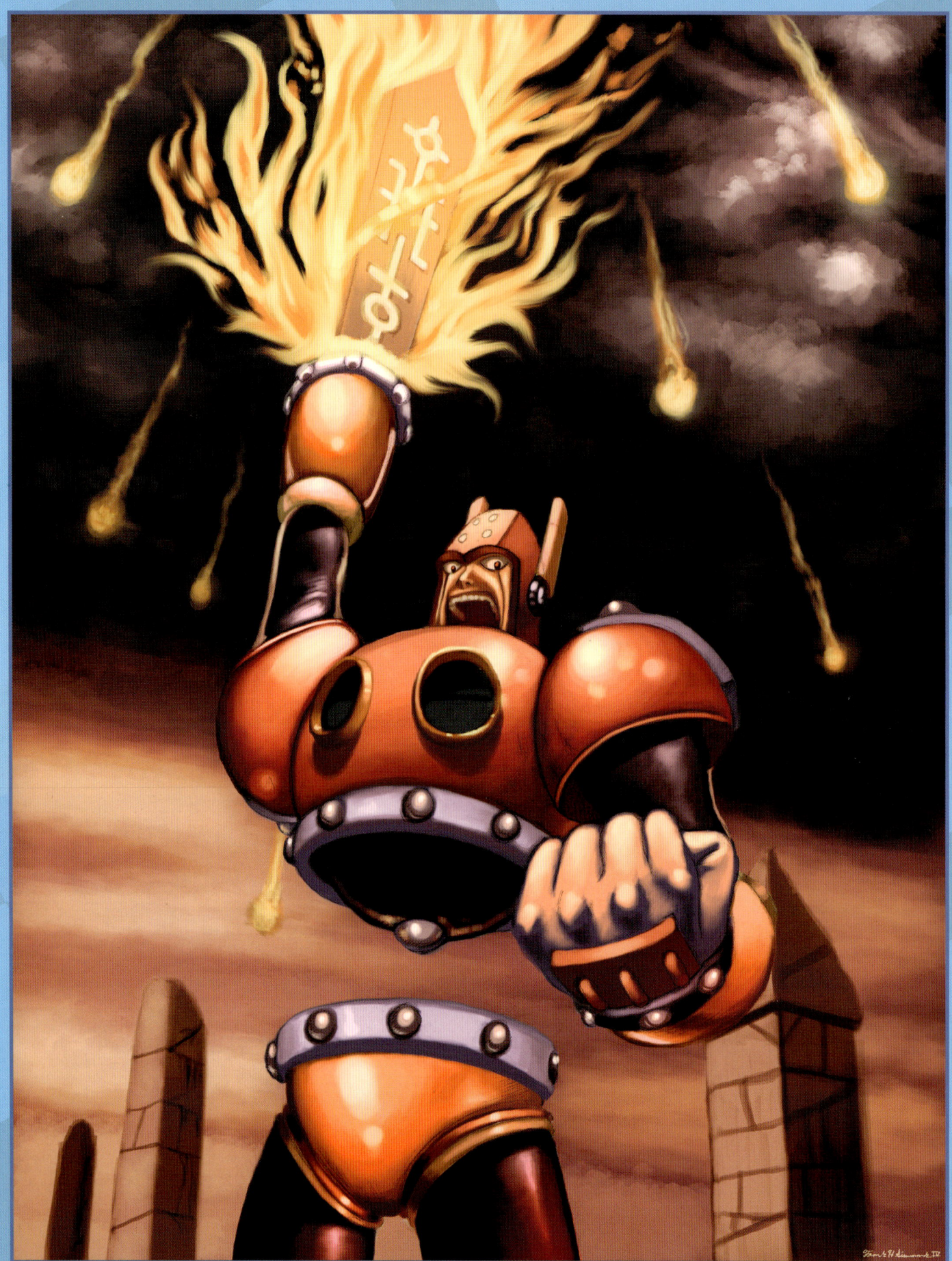

FRANK SIMMONDS
Baltimore, MD, United States
www.fsimmondsart.com
Illustrator

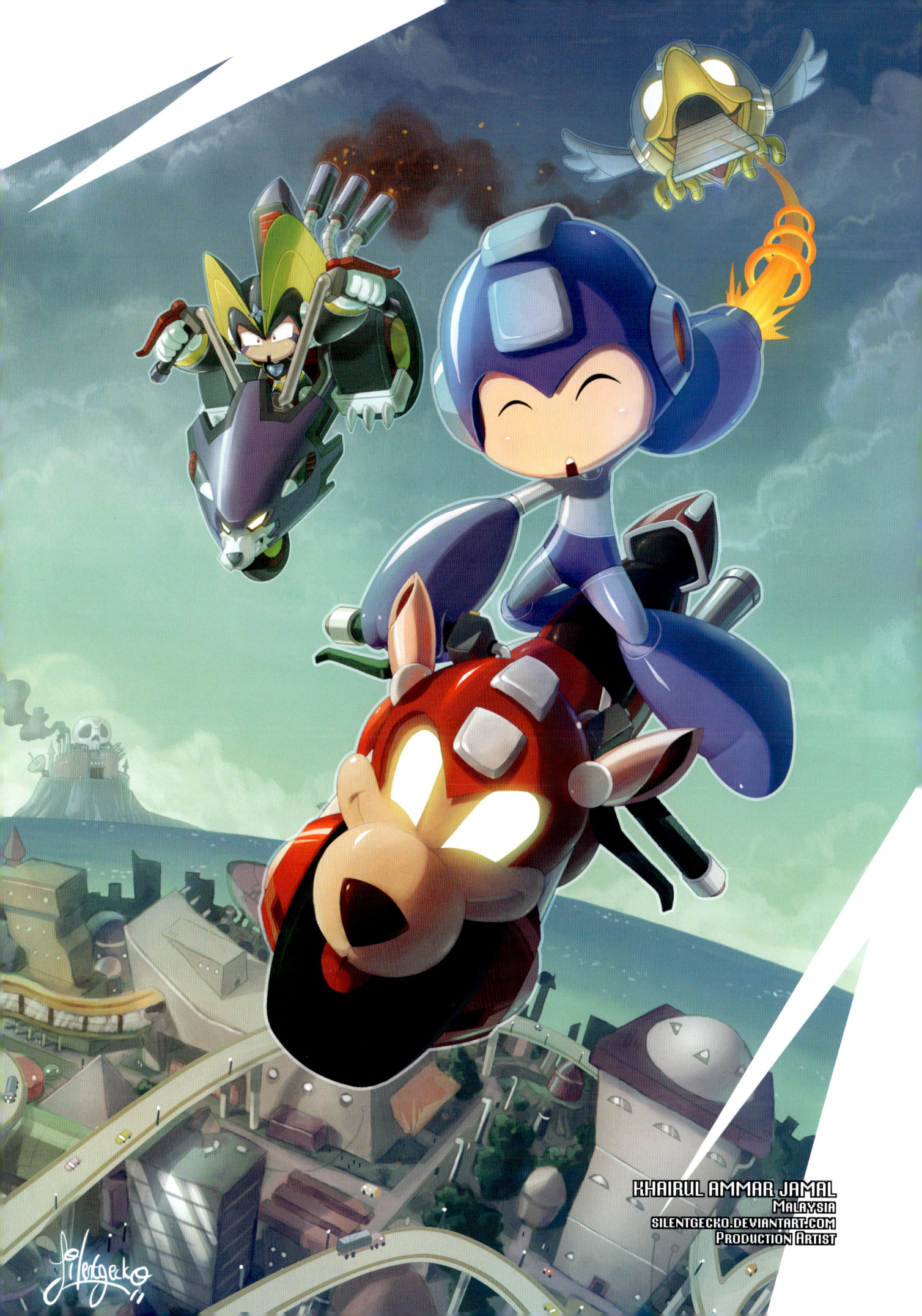

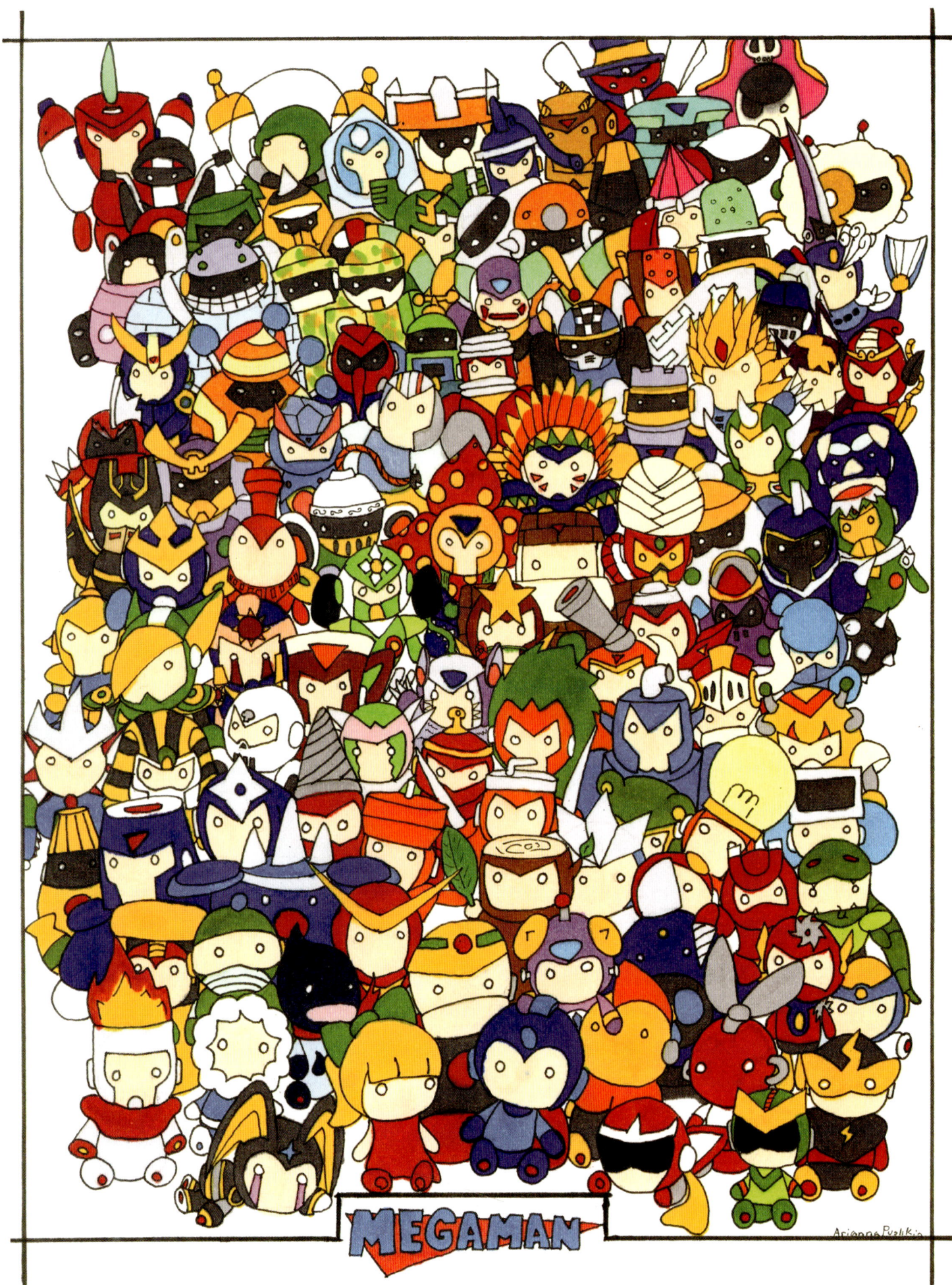

ARIANNA PUSHKIN (AIPE)
Baltimore, MD, United States
Illustrator

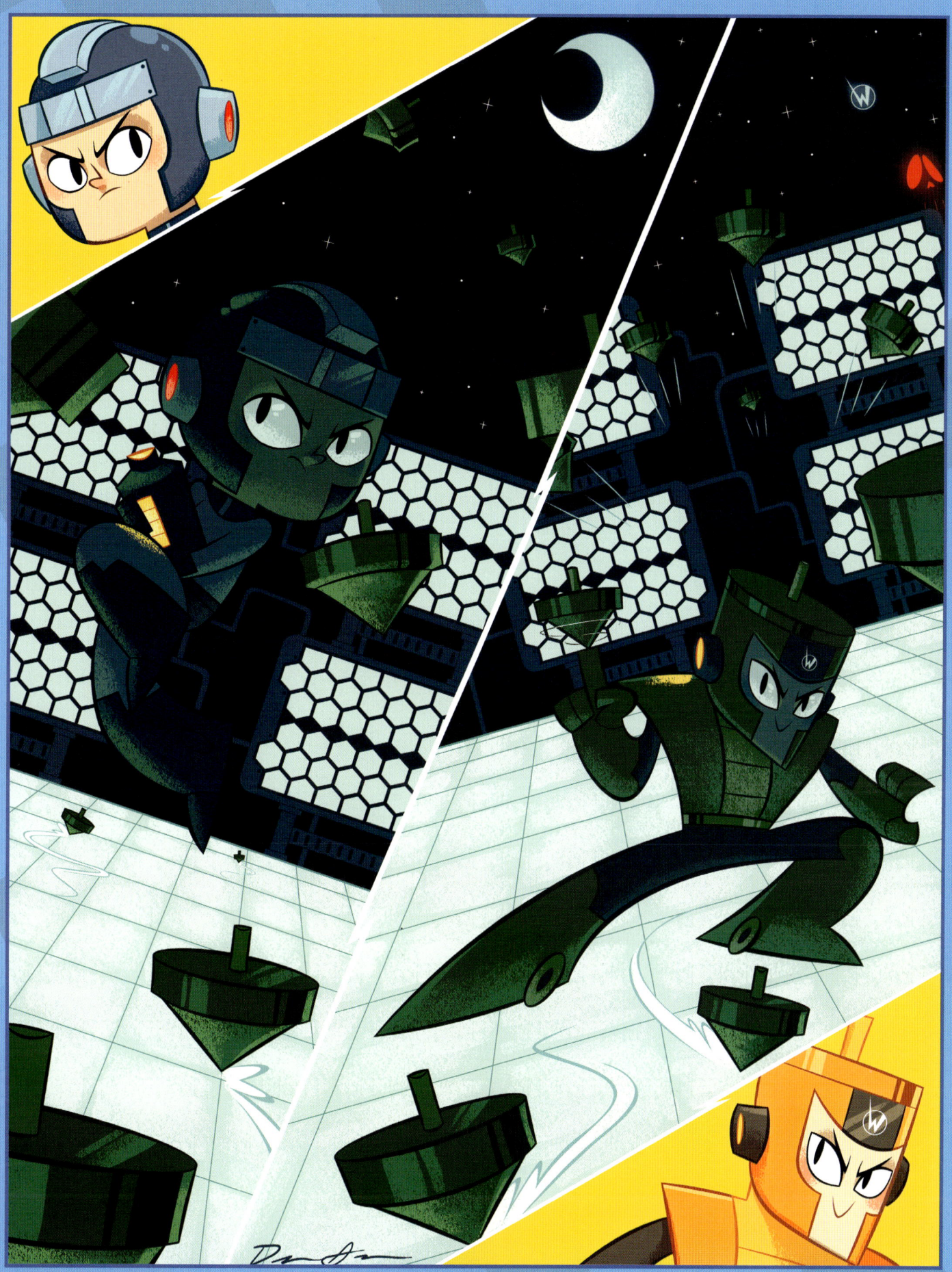

DREW GREEN
Dunwoody, GA, United States
drew-green.blogspot.com
Cartoonist

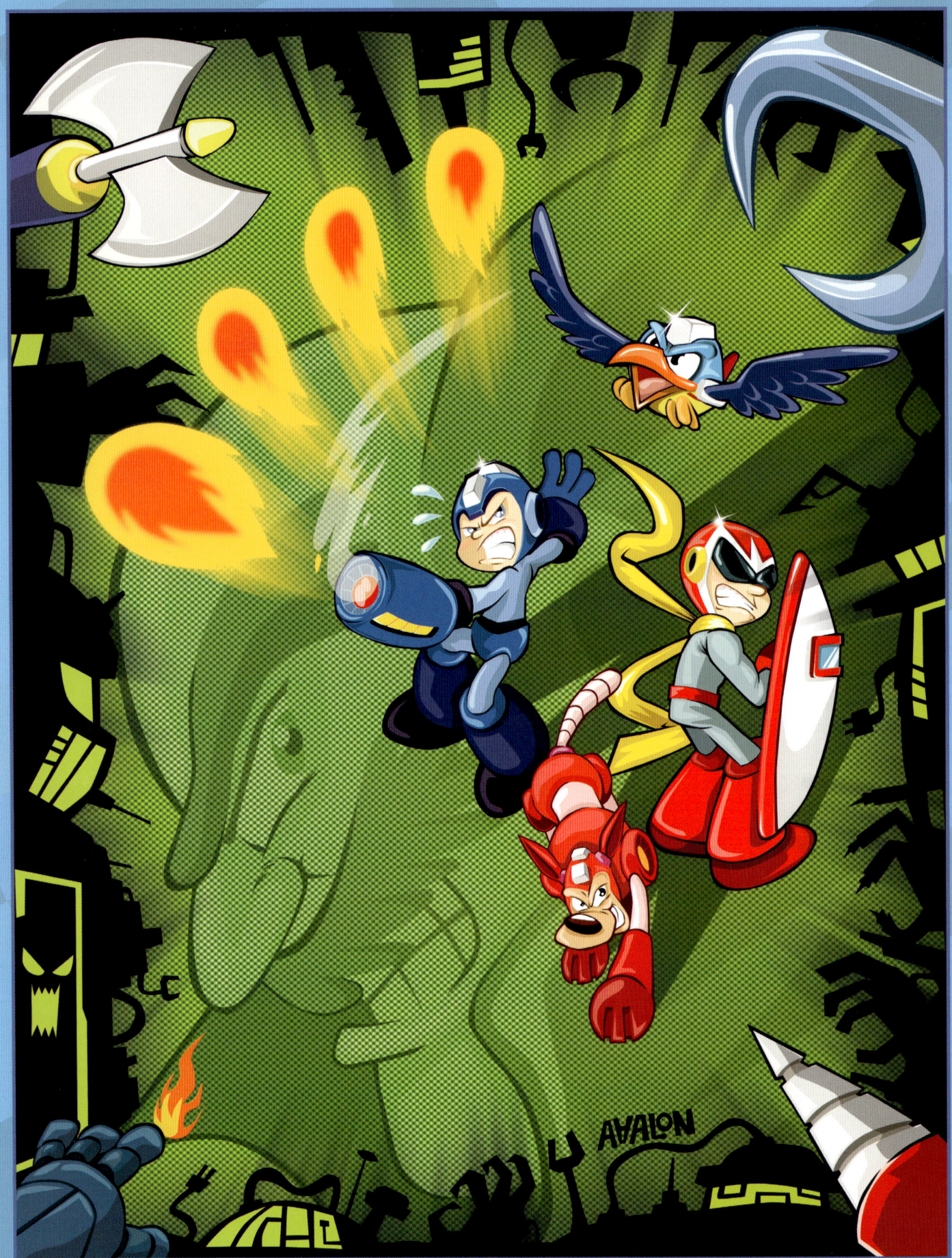

ALVARO AMAYA (AVALON)
Bogota, Colombia
andres-iles.deviantart.com
Illustrator

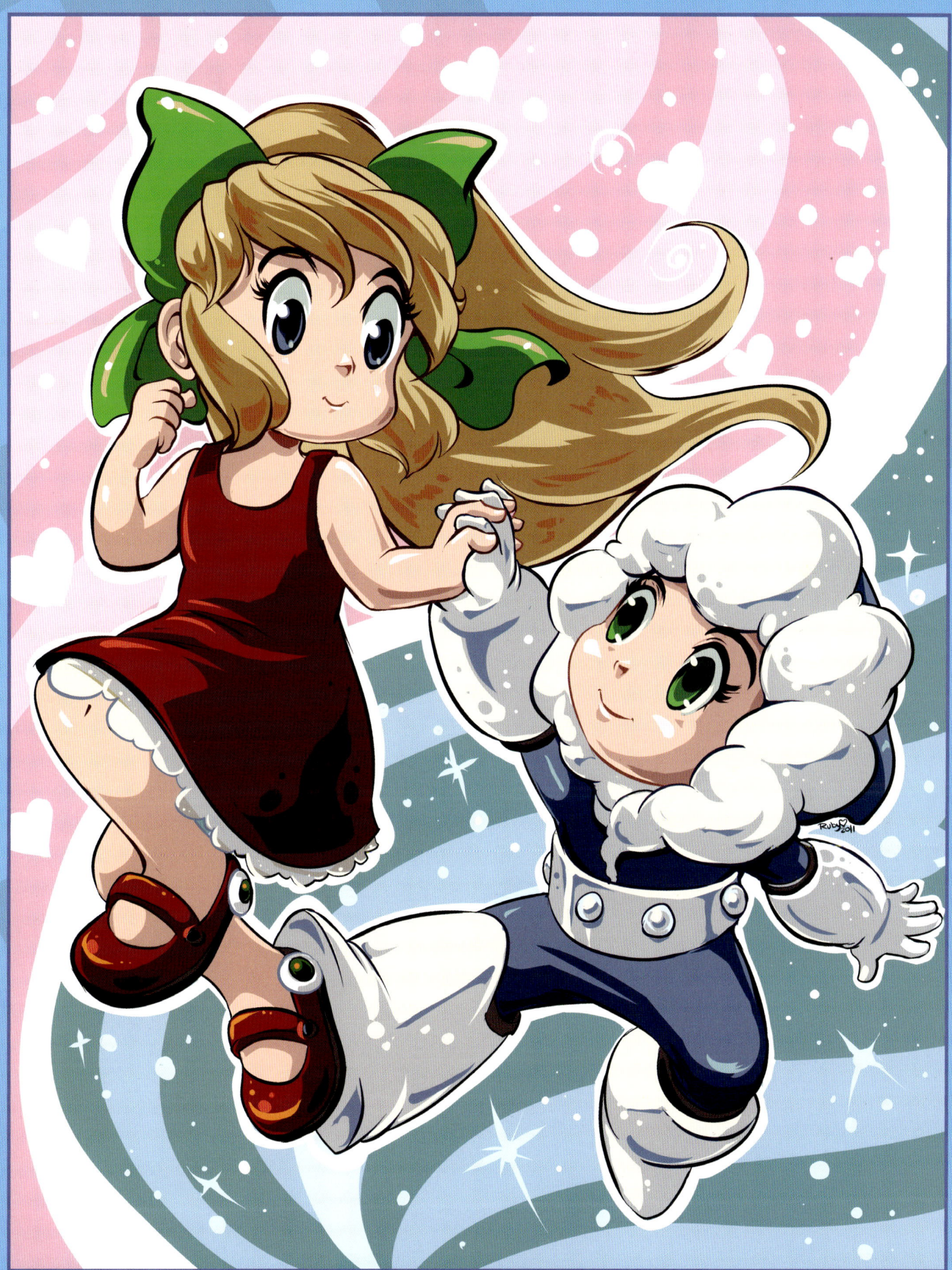

DEANNA BELLE (LADYRUBY)
Baltimore, MD, United States
www.deannabelle.com
Graphic & Web Designer

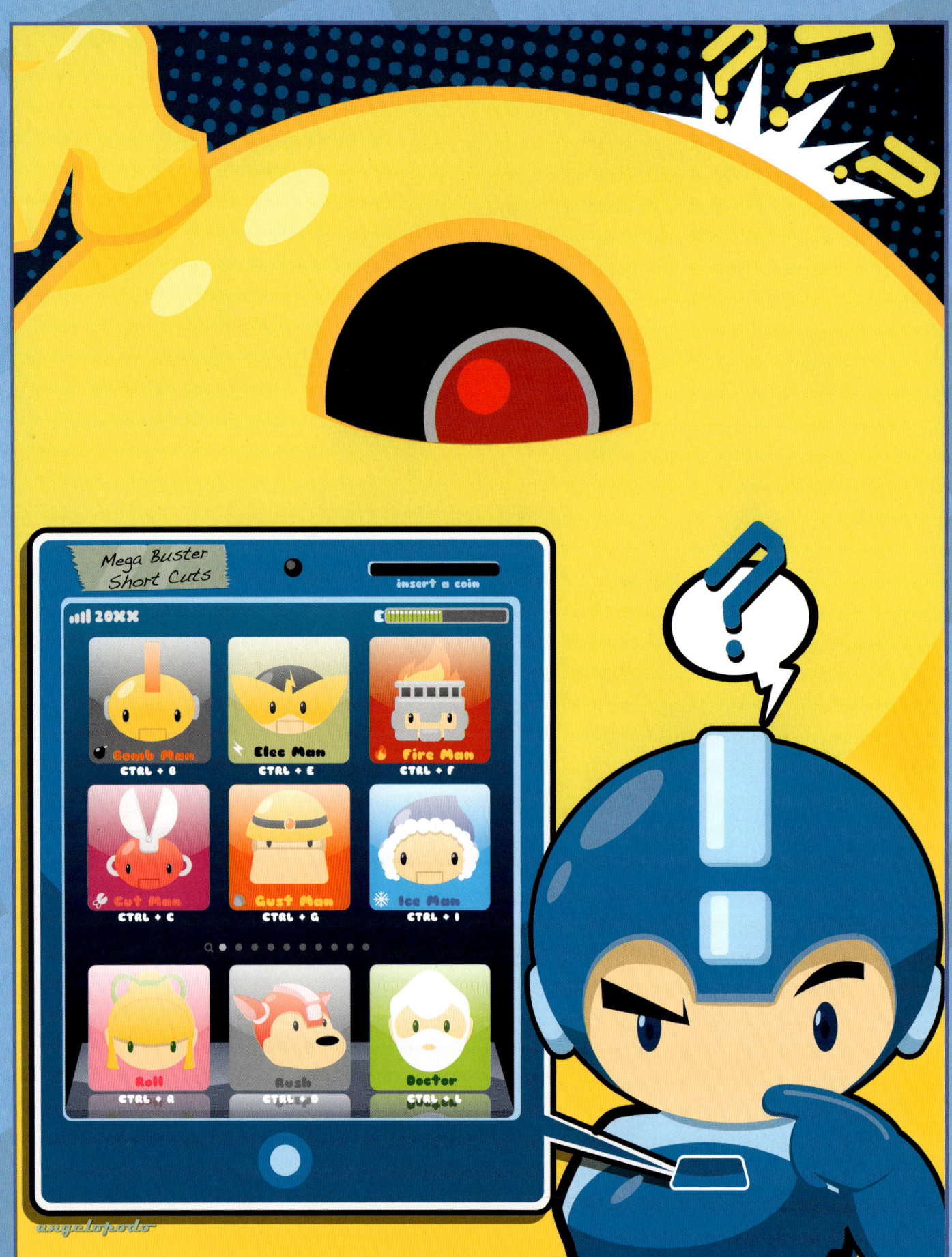

ANGEL BARBA BARRERA
Zapopan, Mexico
www.mostro.com.mx
Designer

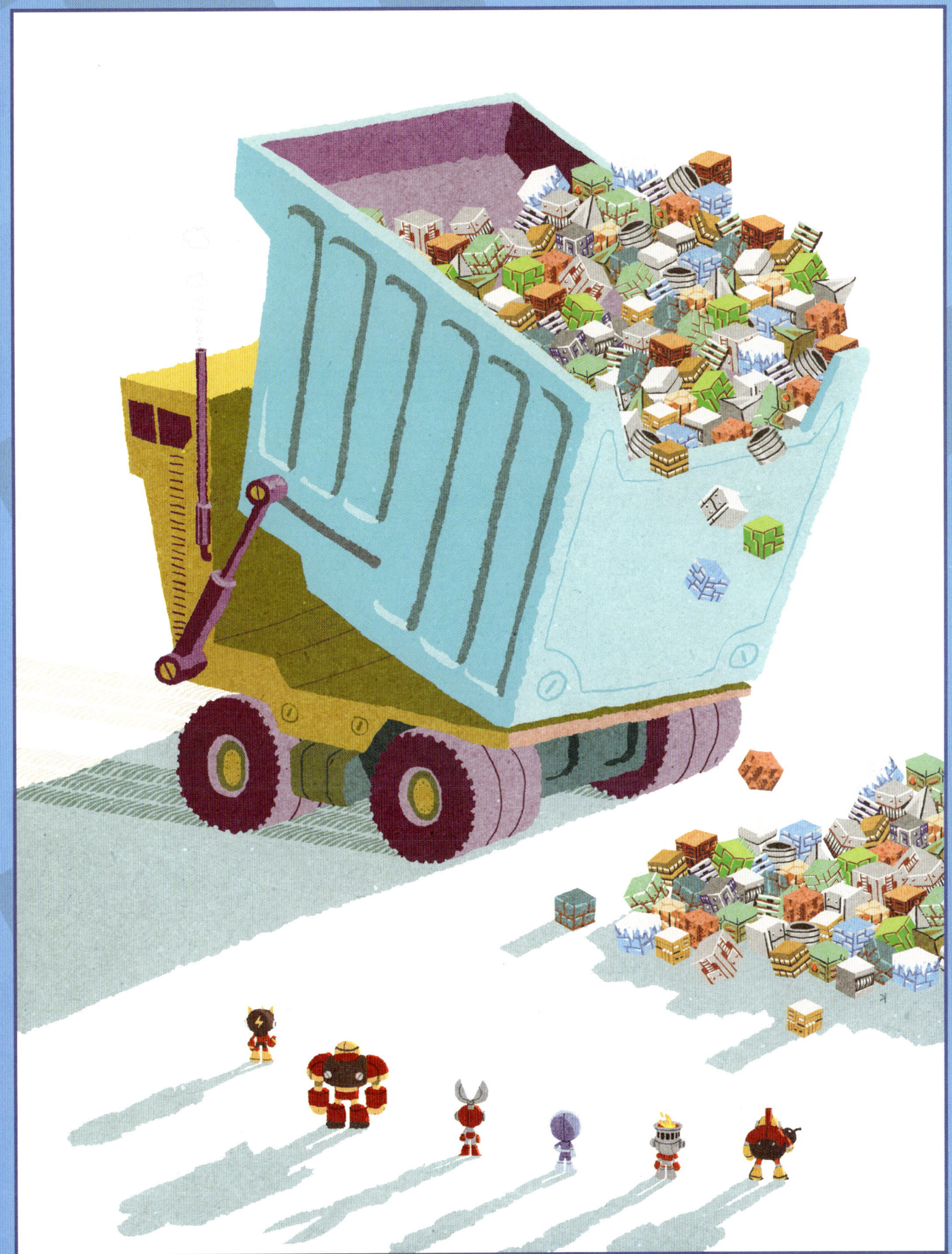

KEN WONG
Adelaide, Australia
www.kenart.net
Art Director
(American McGee's Grimm / Alice 2: Madness Returns)

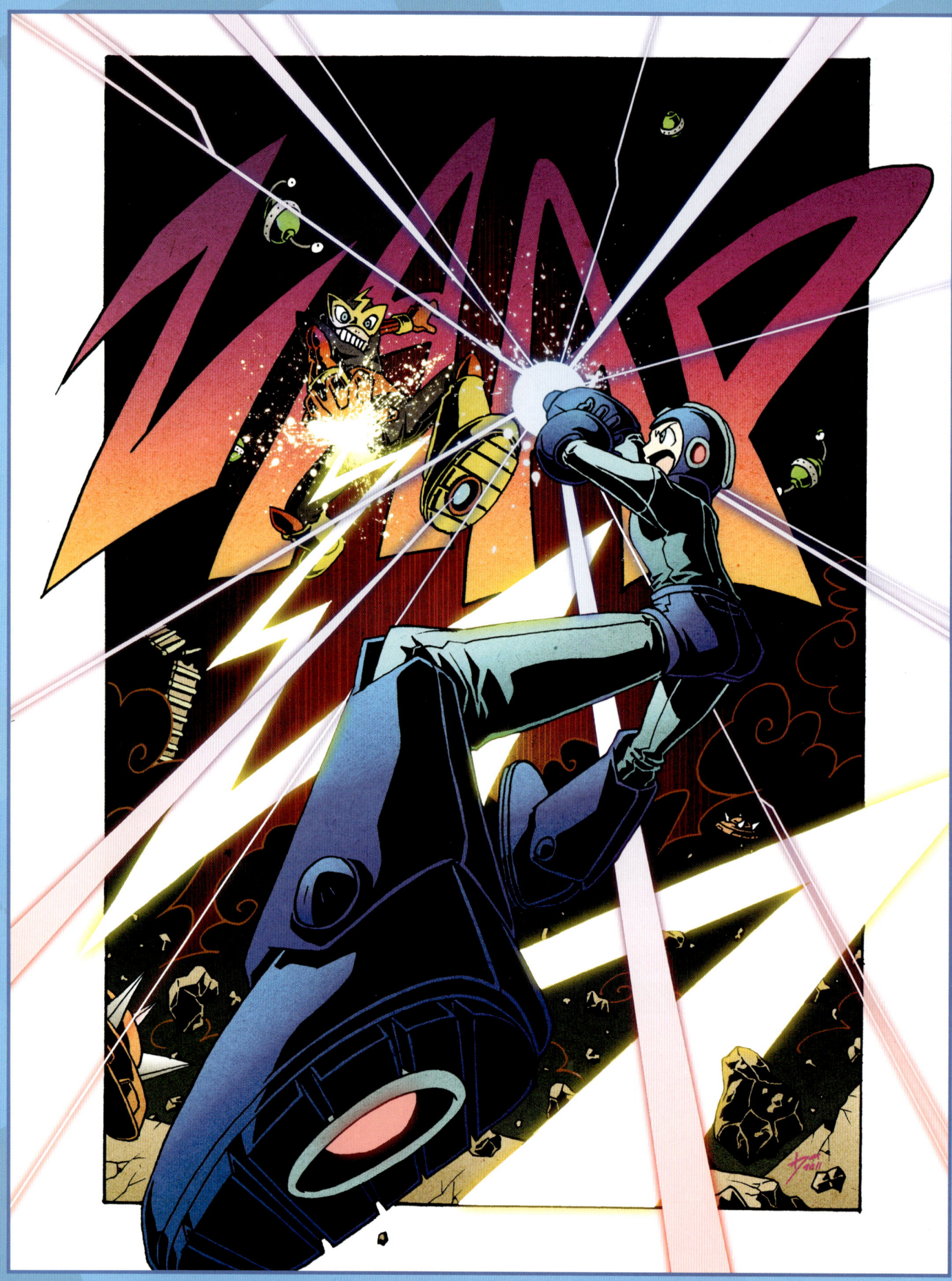

KWOK-HEI MAK (KEI)
Stockholm, Sweden
www.kingdompleased.com
Freelance Illustrator/Comic Artist
(Hofors Comics School (Sweden) / Shonen Jump (Swedish Edition) /
"How to draw manga" book)

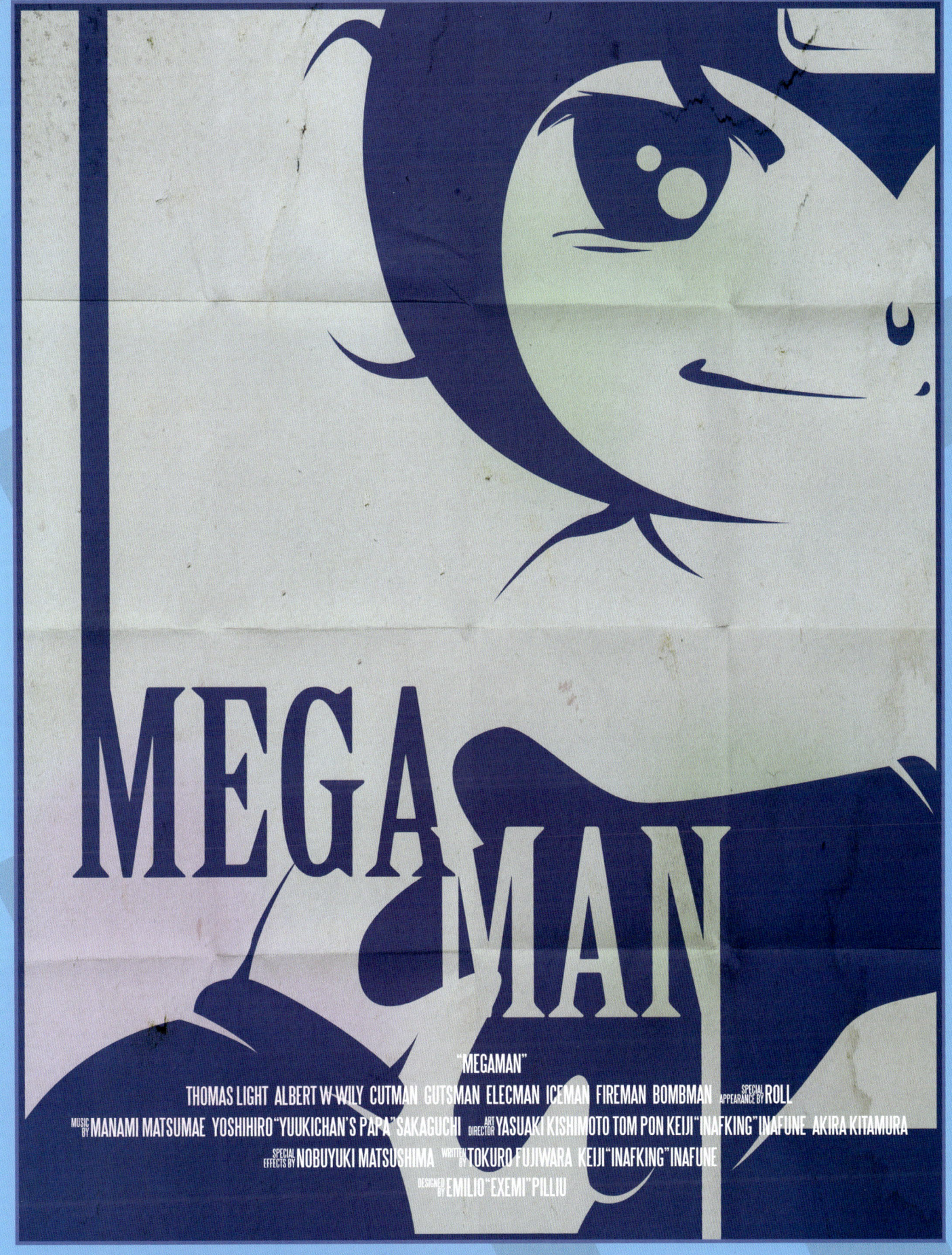

EMILIO PILLIU (EXEMI)
Domusnovas, Italy
exemi.deviantart.com
Illustrator

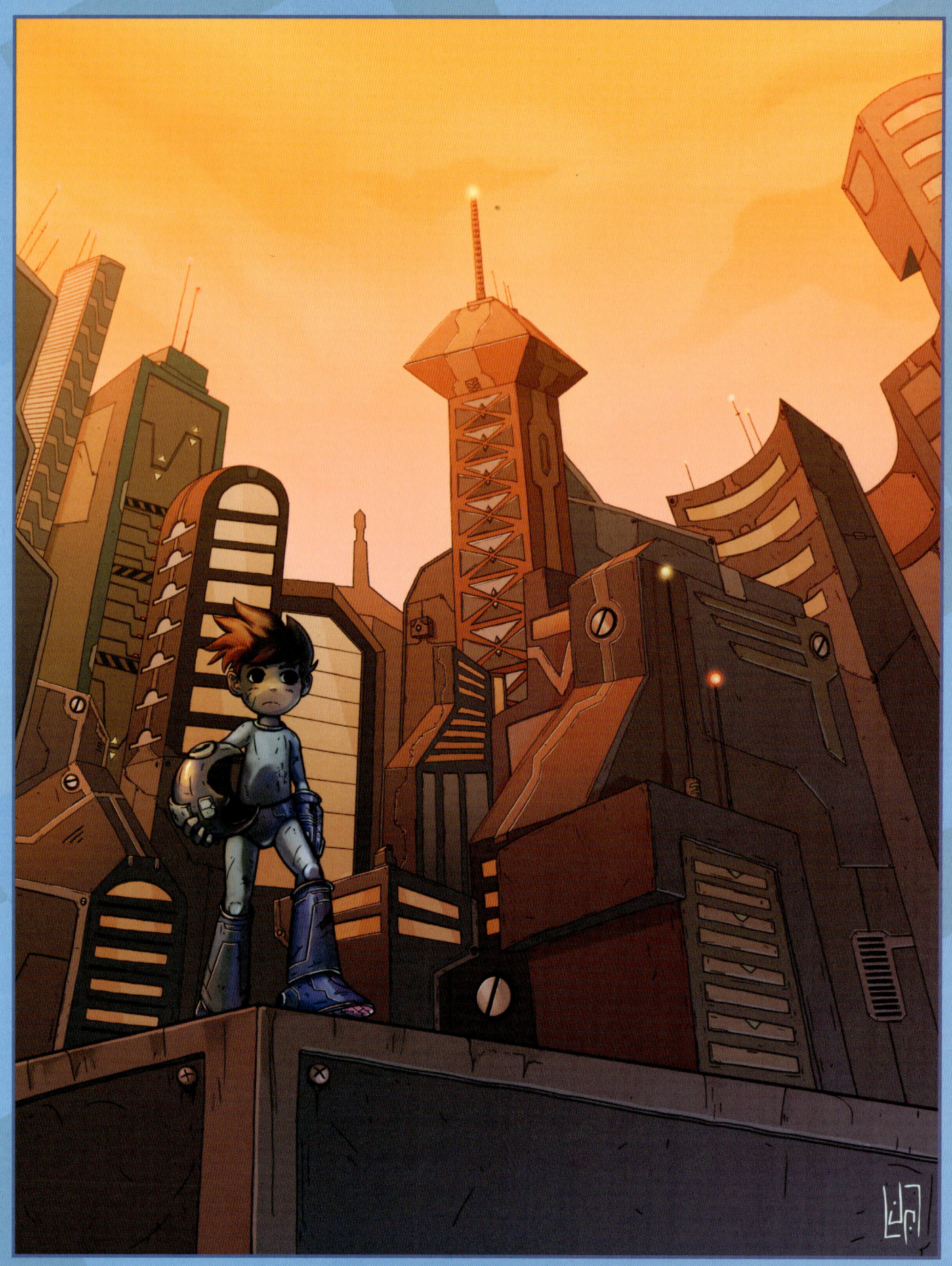

JUAN PABLO RIEBELING (JOVEN PAUL)
Mexico City, Mexico
jovenpaul.blogspot.com
Illustrator

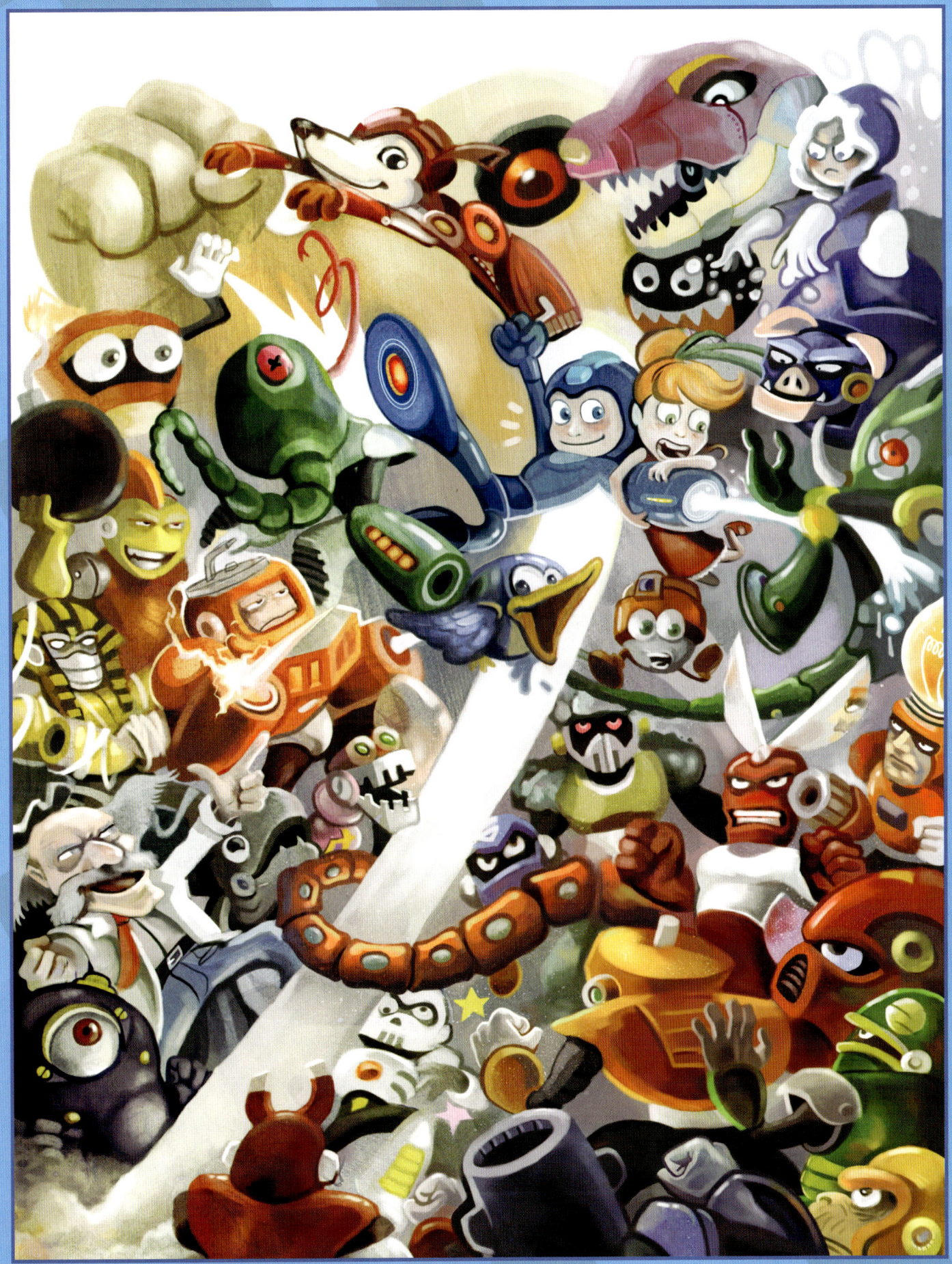

MIGUEL DELICADO
Valencia, Spain
cosasveces.blogspot.com
Illustrator

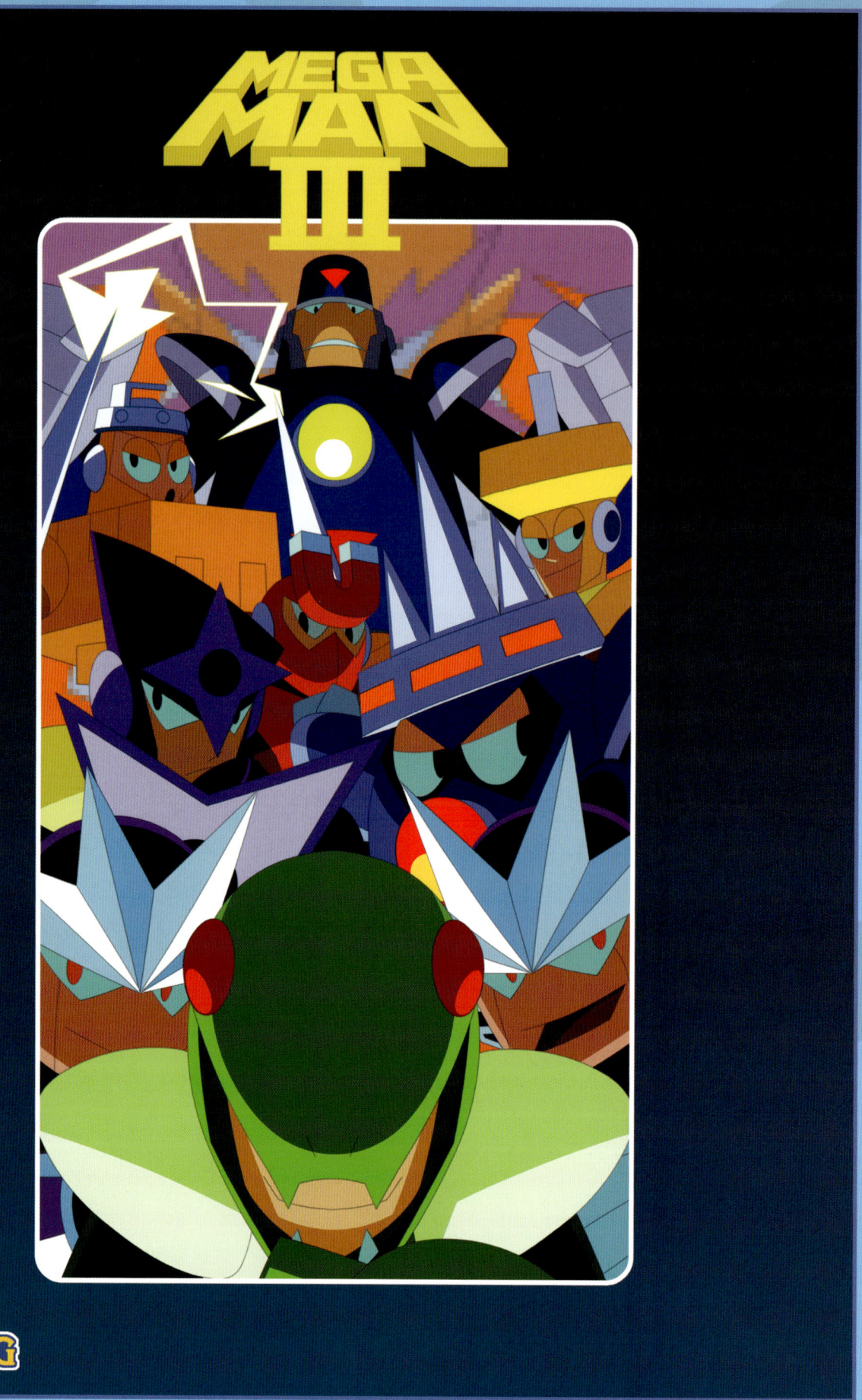

Bob Strang
Somerset PN, United States
vontoten.deviantart.com
Illustrator
(the Creeps, Street Fighter, Booyah)

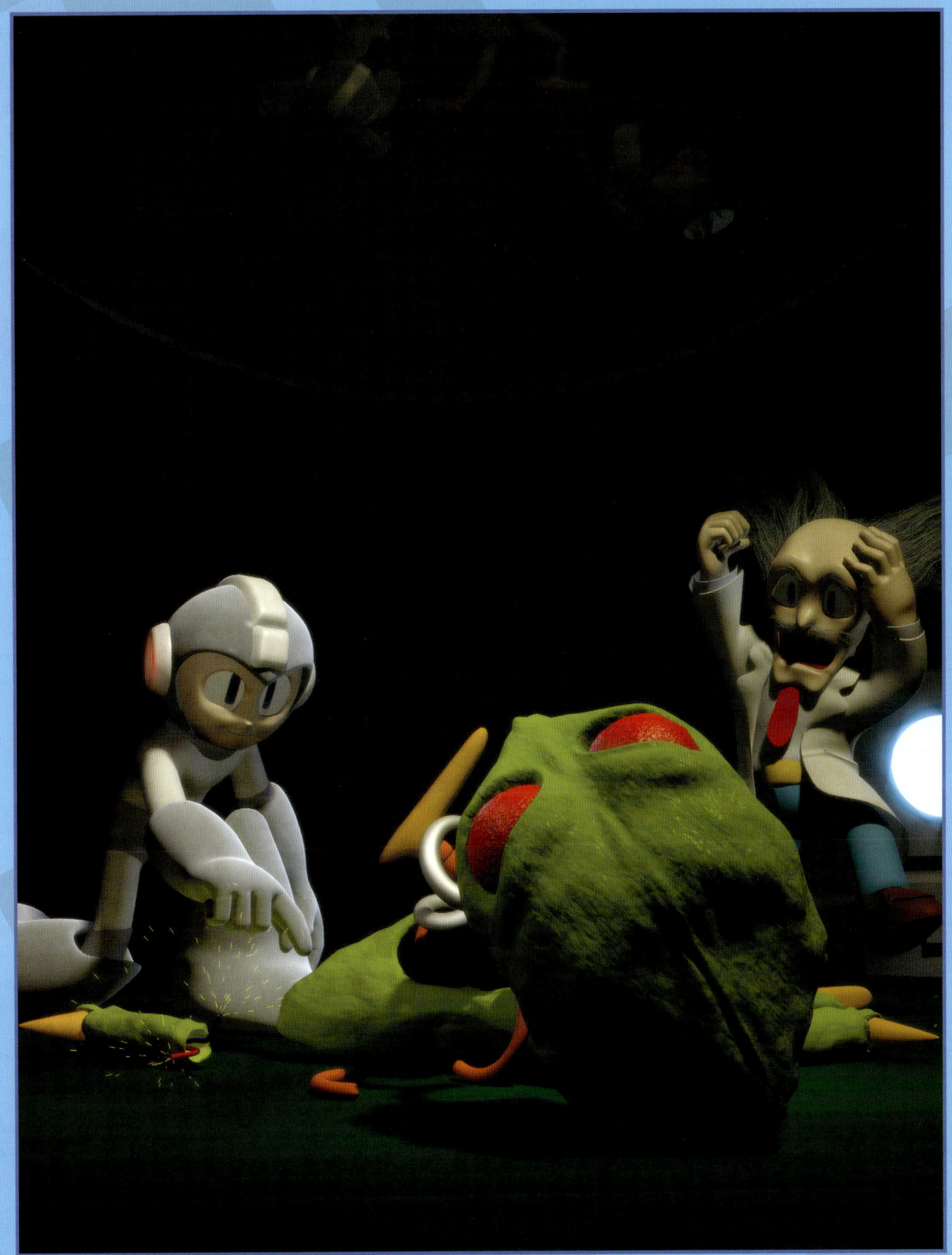

KARITH DENSMORE
Ajax, Ontario
3D Artist

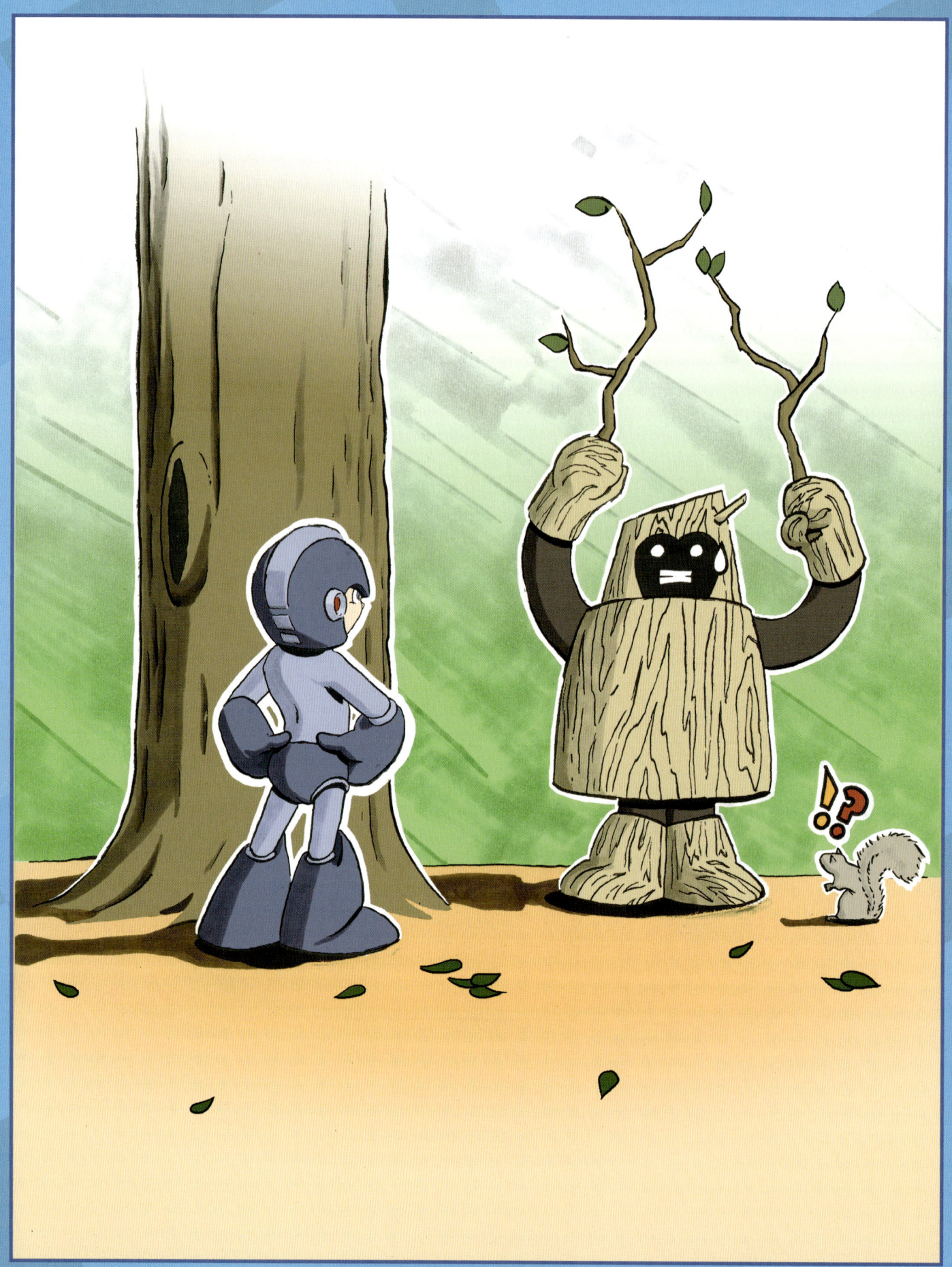

DANIEL HOOKER
Tallahassee, FL, United States
danno84a.deviantart.com
Graphic Designer / Web Designer

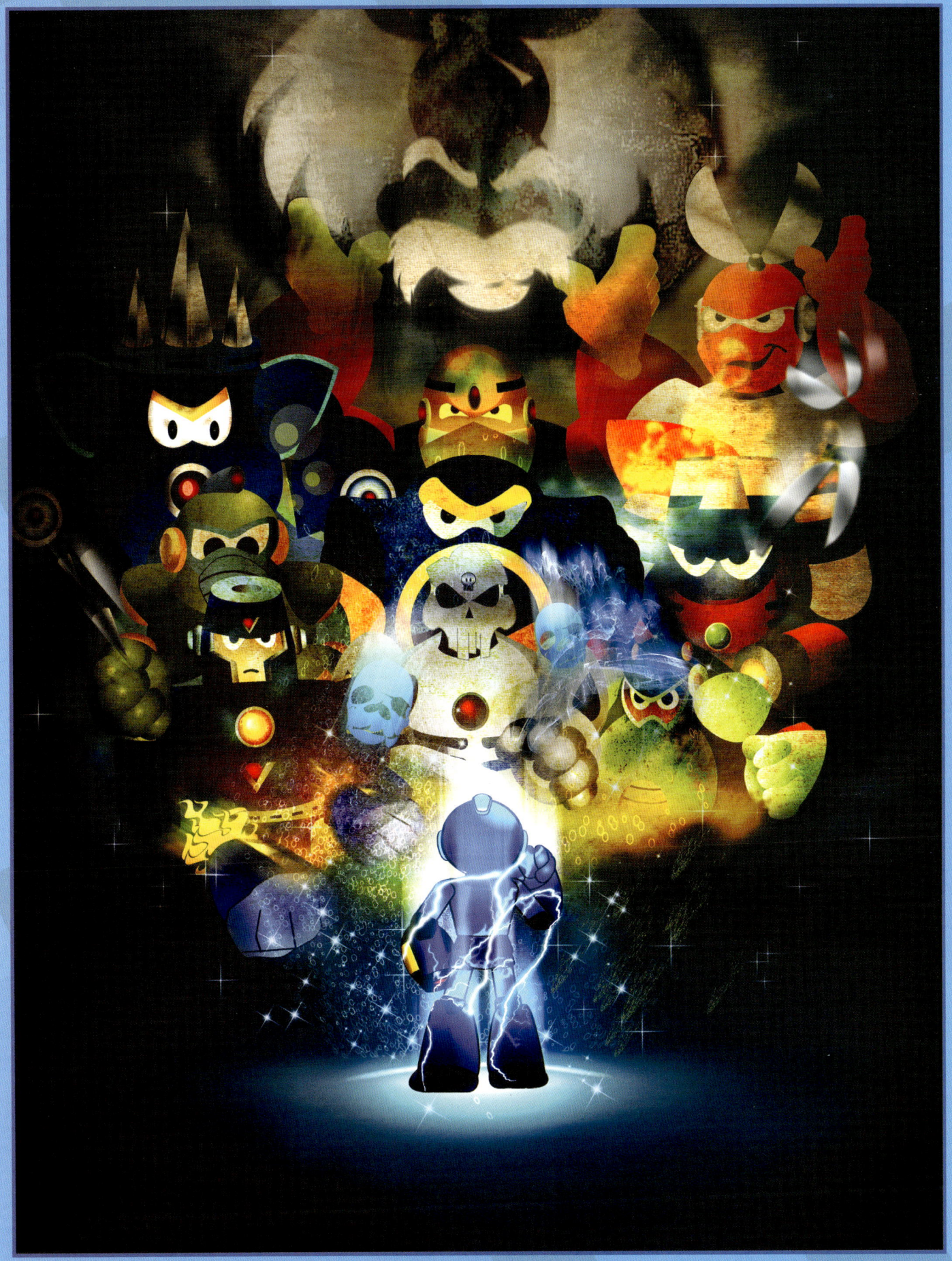

CAMERON AHMADI
San Rafael, CA, United States
Designer

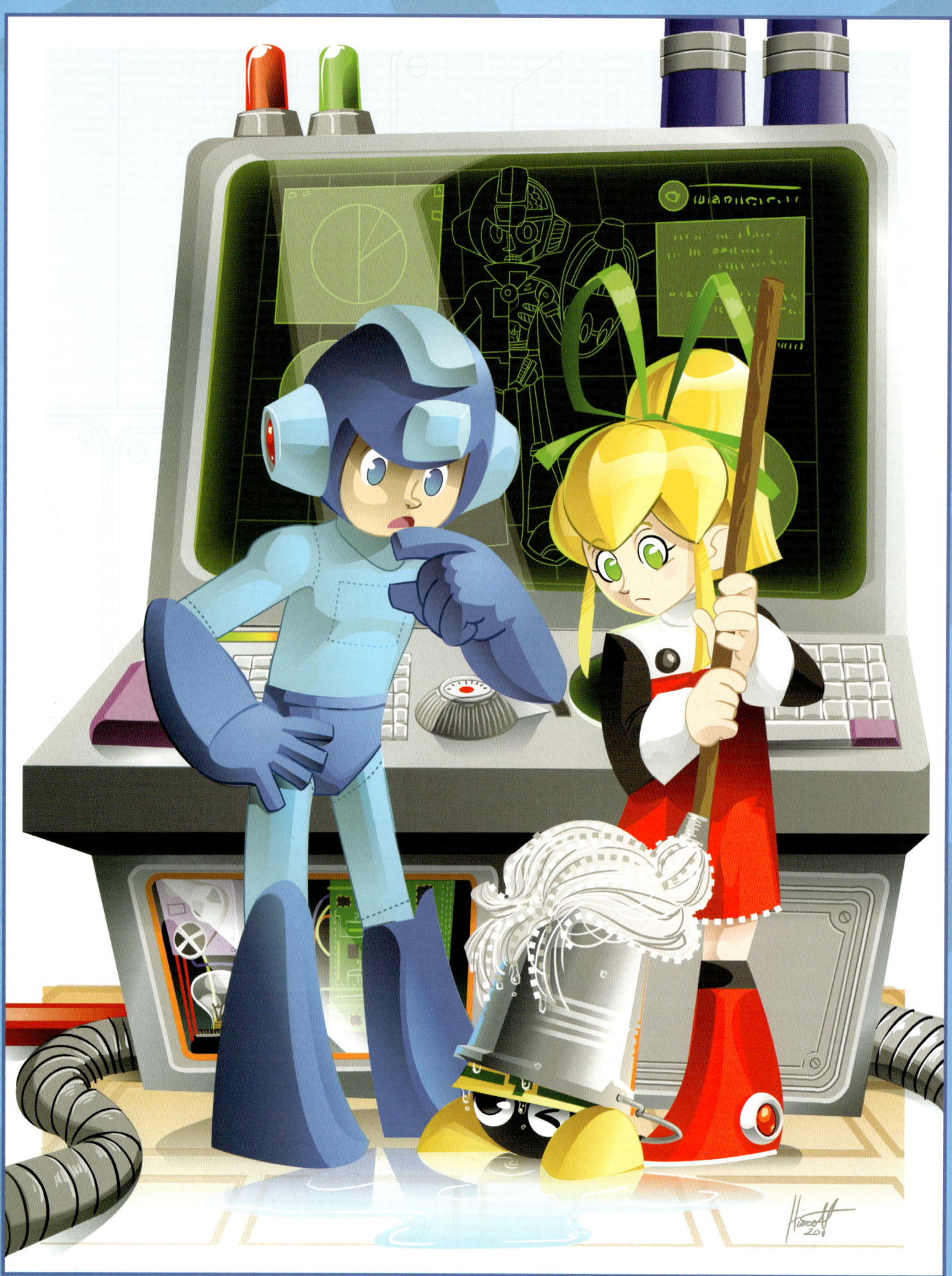

MIKE HISCOTT
Oakville, ON, Canada
crumbelievable.deviantart.com / mike-hiscott.blogspot.com
Illustrator

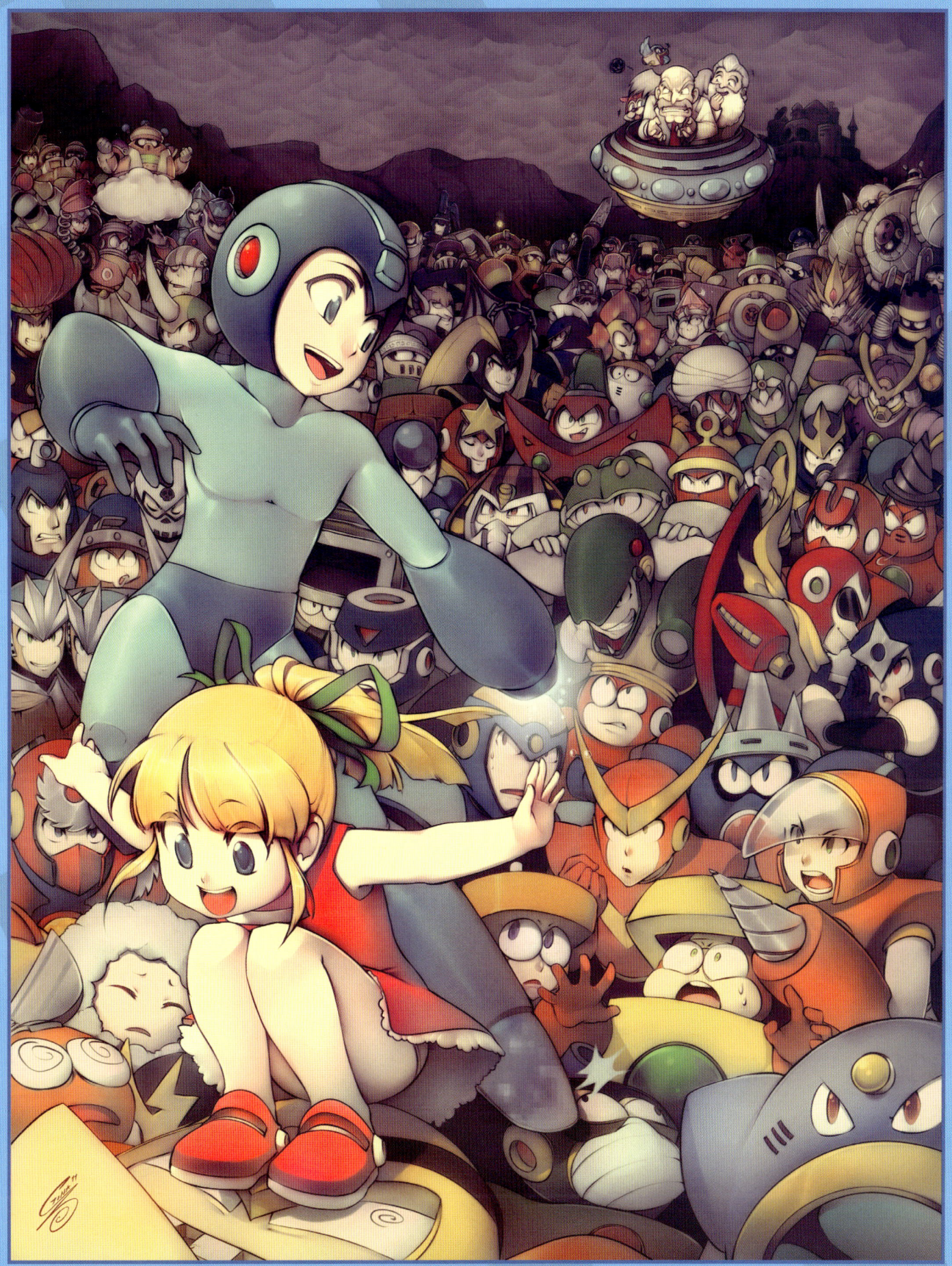

GEORGINA CHACÓN
Chihuahua, Mexico
saiyagina.deviantart.com
Visual Artist

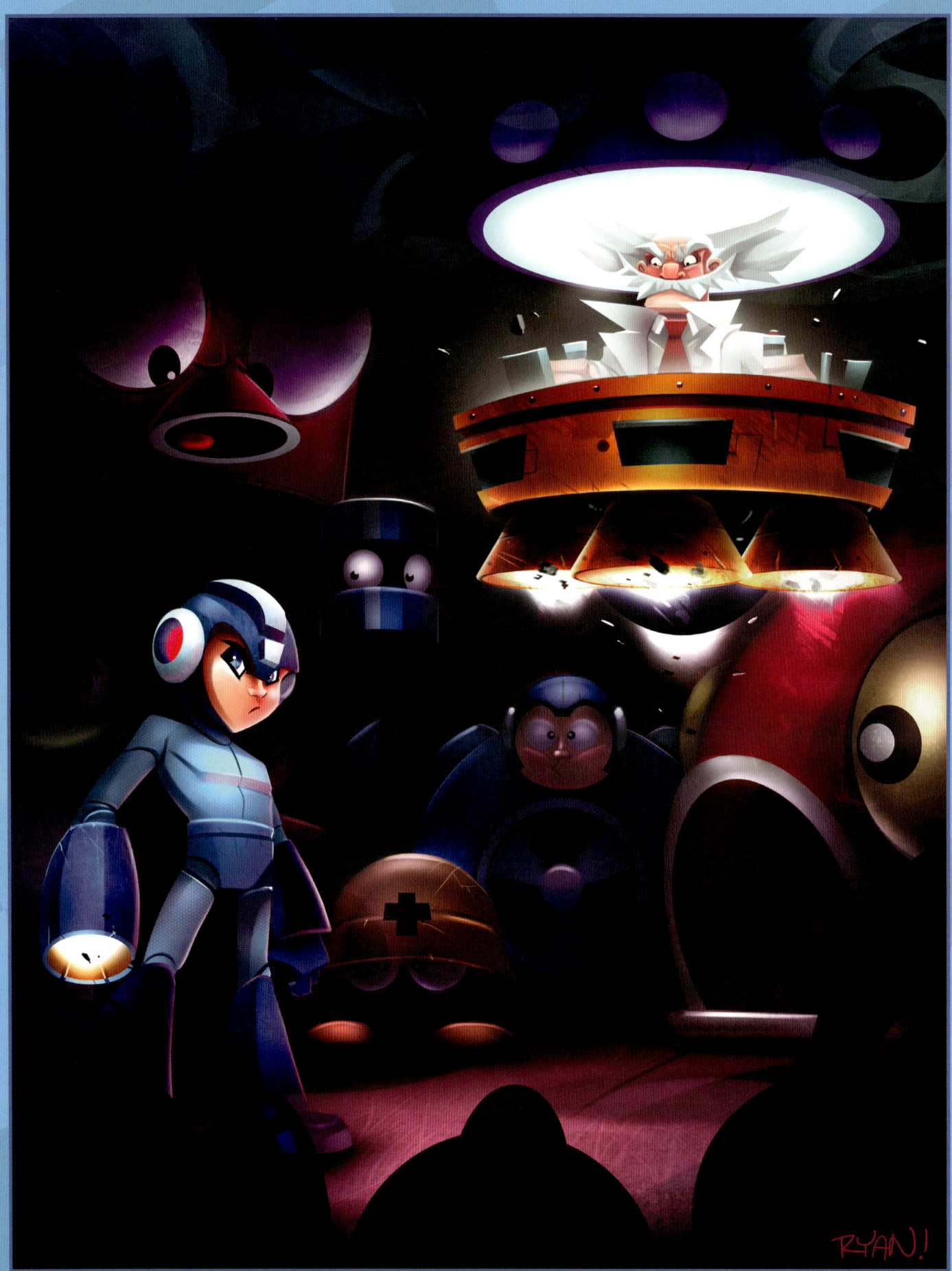

RYAN HALL
San Francisco, CA, United States
frogbillgo.deviantart.com
Concept Artist
(Big Menace Industries Co-Founder)

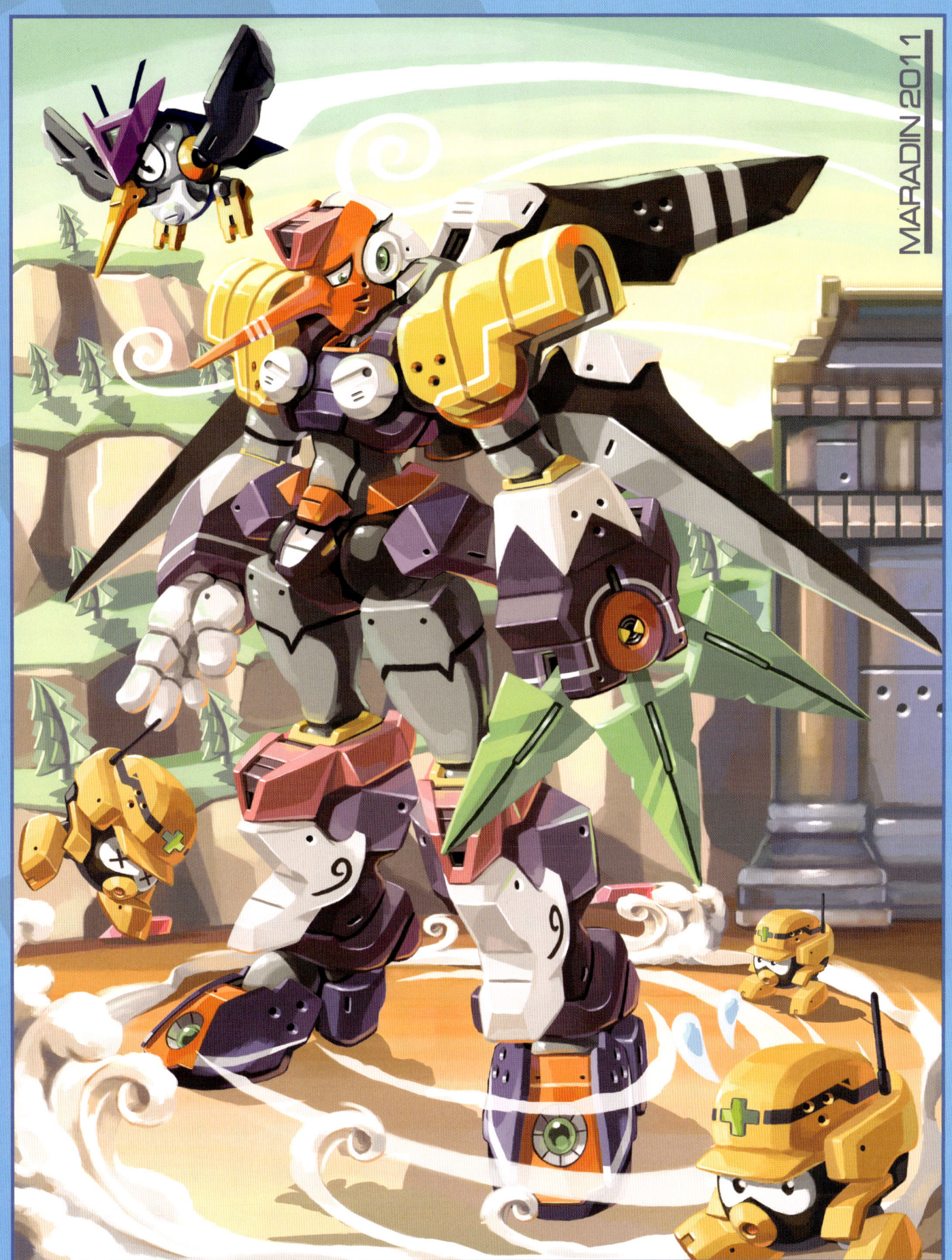

NICHOLAS MARADIN
Coraopolis, PA, United States
nidaram.deviantart.com
Artist/Illustrator

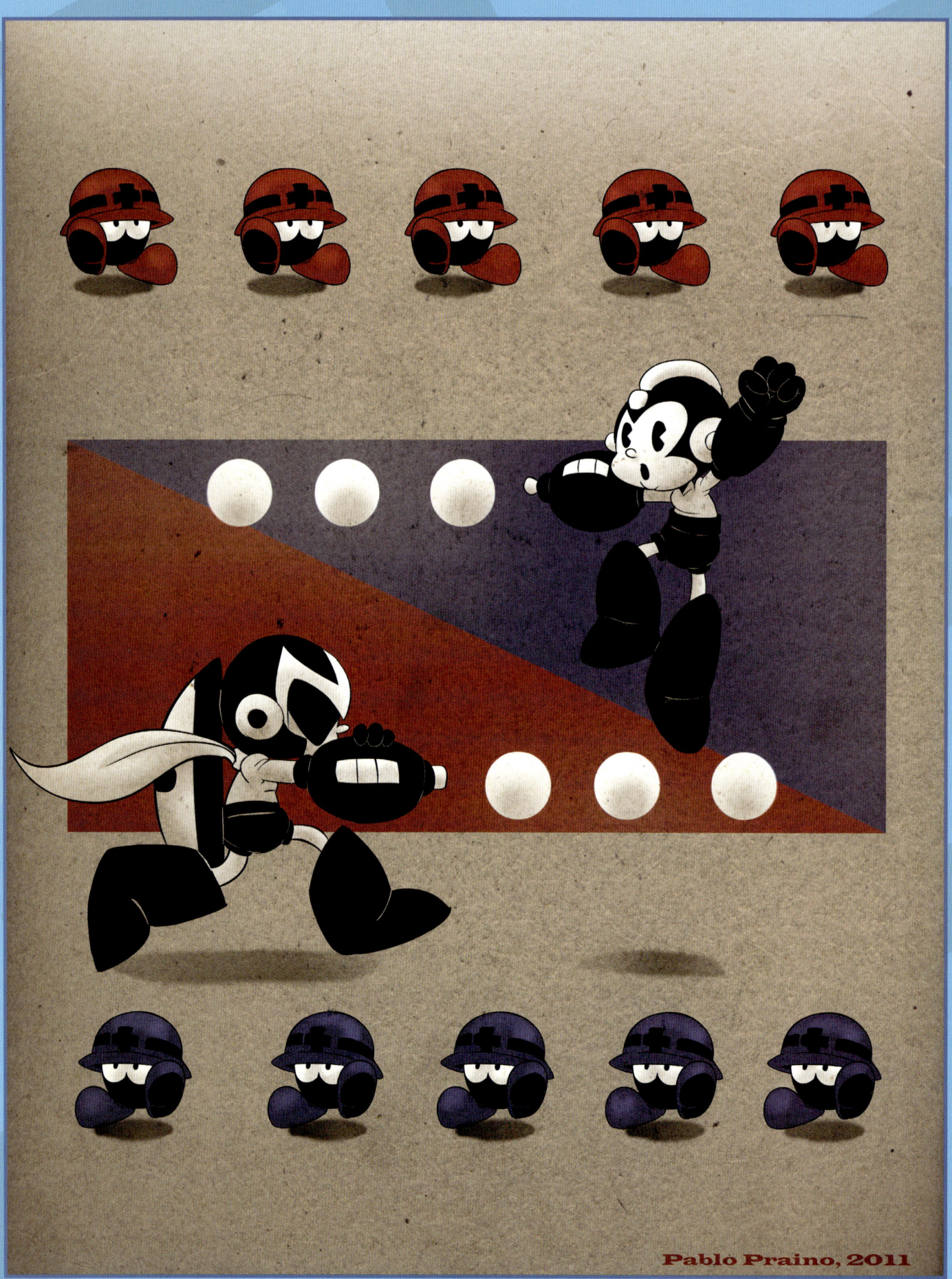

PABLO PRAINO
Montevideo, Uruguay
optimuspraino.deviantart.com
Animator / Artist
(Animator and Co-Director on Forlan Animated Short / Artist & Writer on Gold Digger Special Issues / Hero Academy Webcomic / Marvel Masterpieces Sketch Cards)

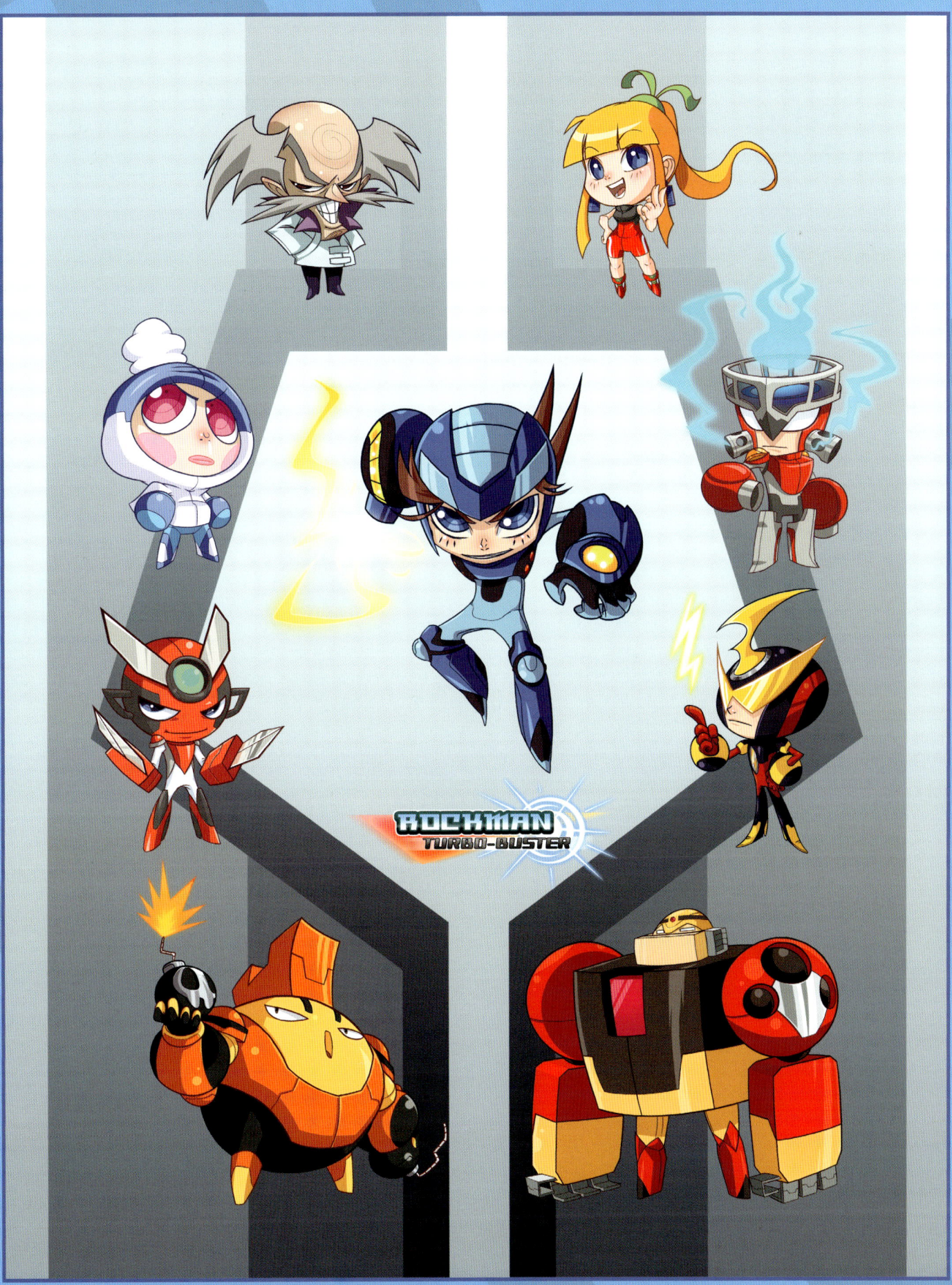

RAUL VELASQUEZ (ZEO)
Caracas, Venezuela
zeoarts.deviantart.com
Character Design / Pixel Artist

HENRIQUE GUIMARÃES BRASIL SILVA
Três Corações, Brazil
http://gmao.deviantart.com/
Colorist

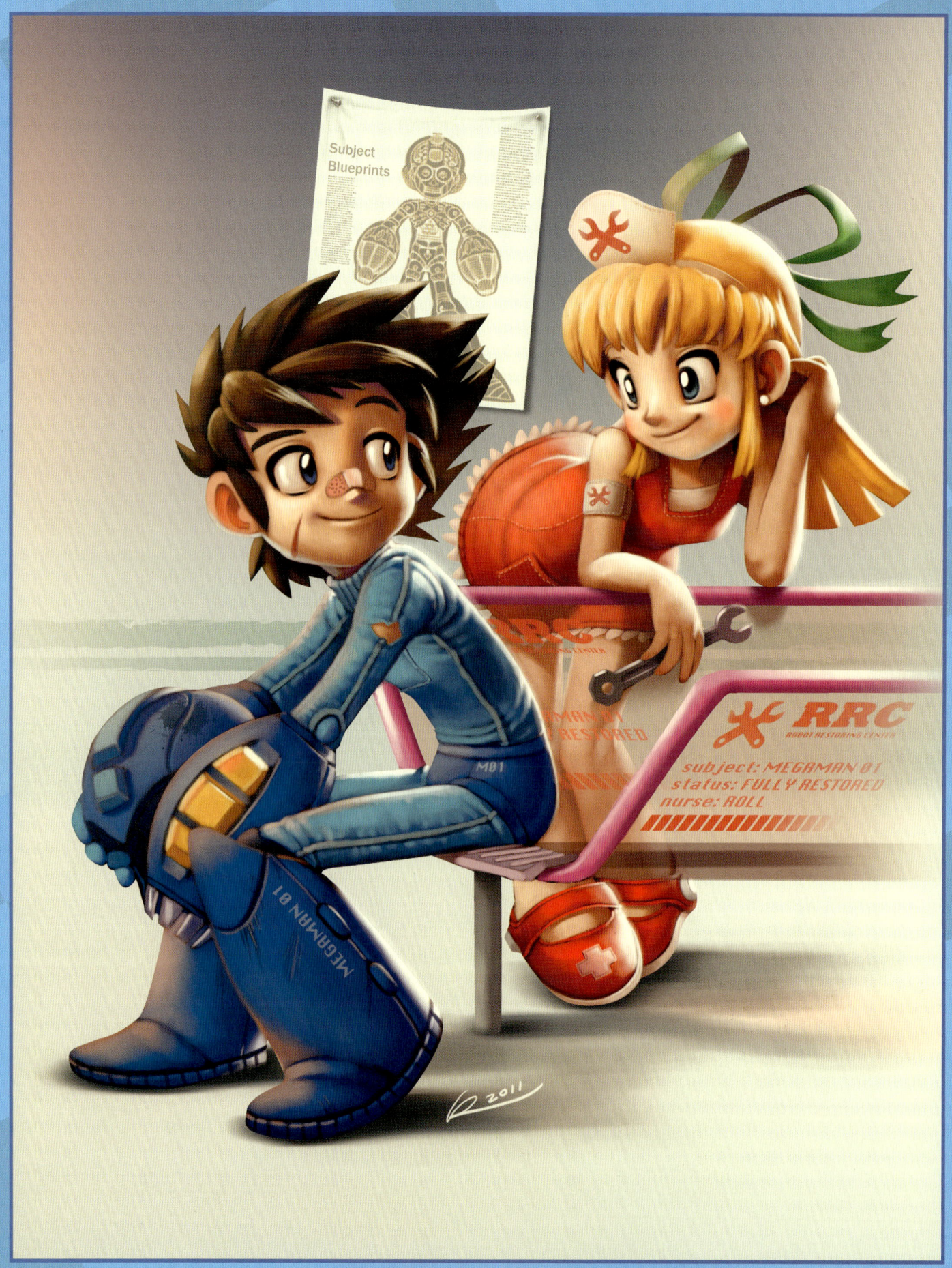

SALVADOR RAMIREZ MADRIZ
Guadalajara, Mexico
reevolver.deviantart.com
Illustrator

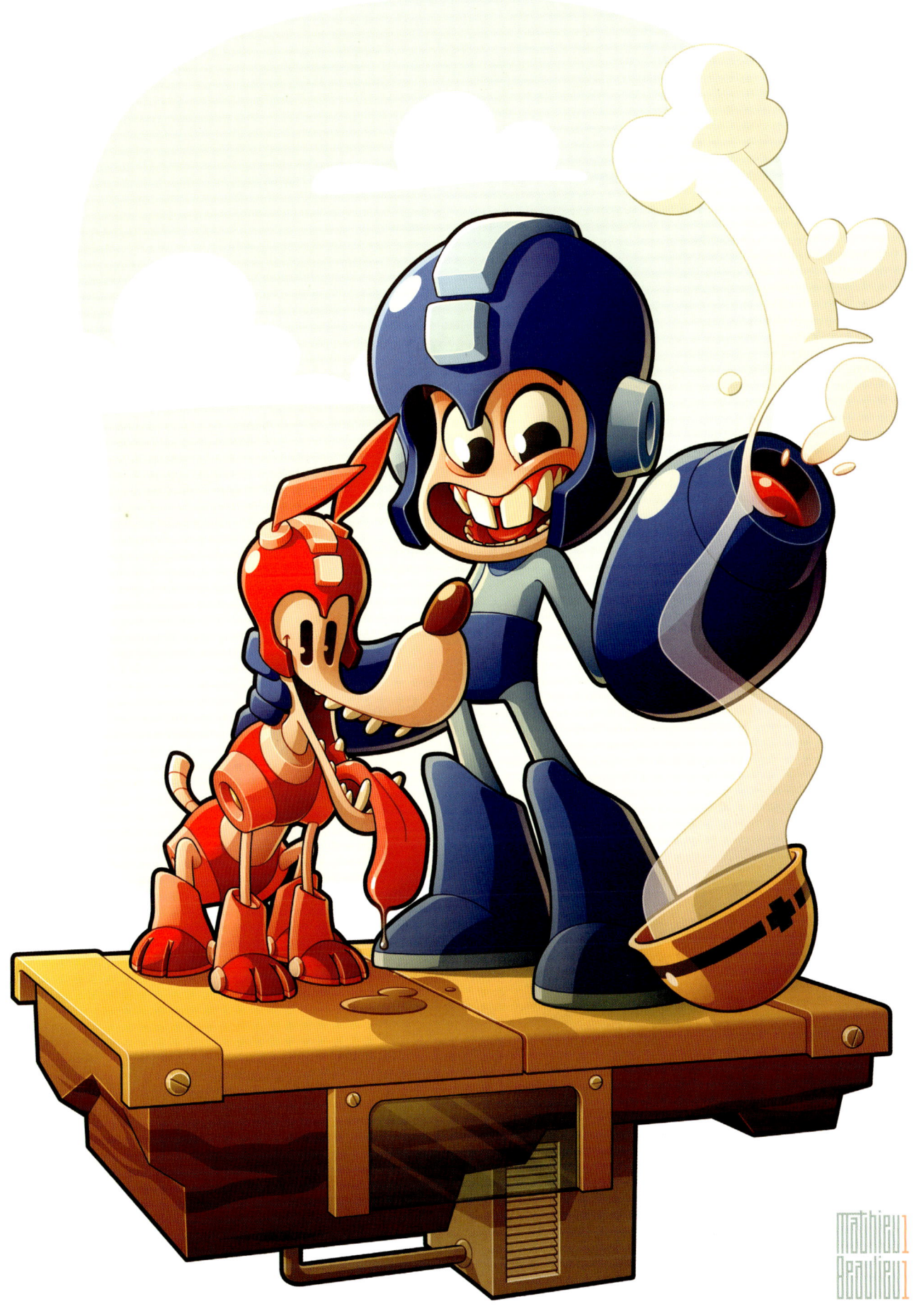

MATHIEU BEAULIEU
Montréal, QC, Canada
www.mathieubeaulieu.com
Illustrator

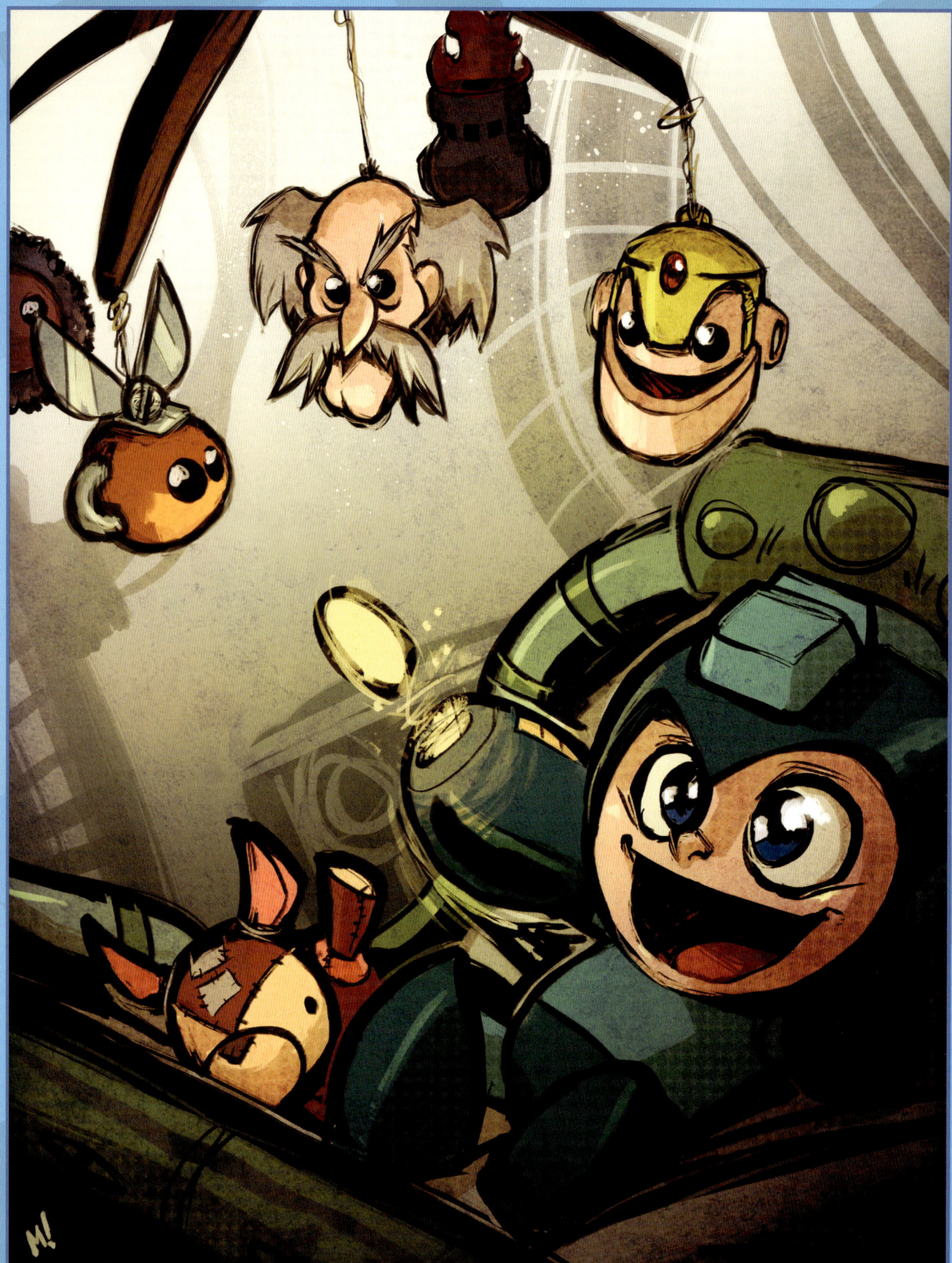

MIKE HENRY
San Francisco, CA, United States
zatransis.deviantart.com
www.bigmenaceindustries.com
Concept Artist

HAINANU SAULQUE
Sacramento, OH, United States
hainanuisance.deviantart.com
Art Assists

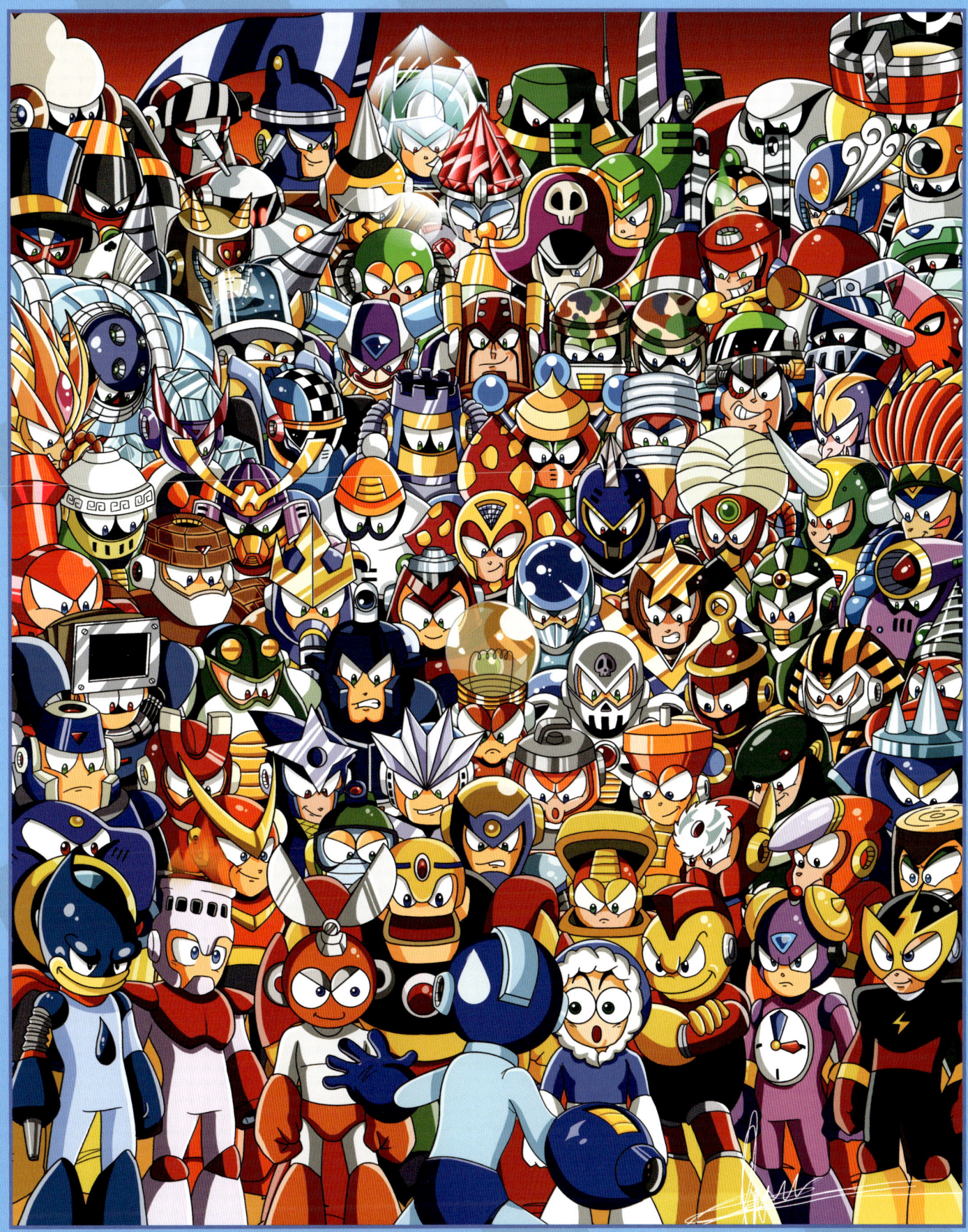

LEONARDO MARTINEZ MANFREDO MORALES
(XAMOEL)
Santiago, Chile
xamoel.deviantart.com
Illustrator

MAXIMILIANO MARTINEZ
Santiago, Chile
Colorist

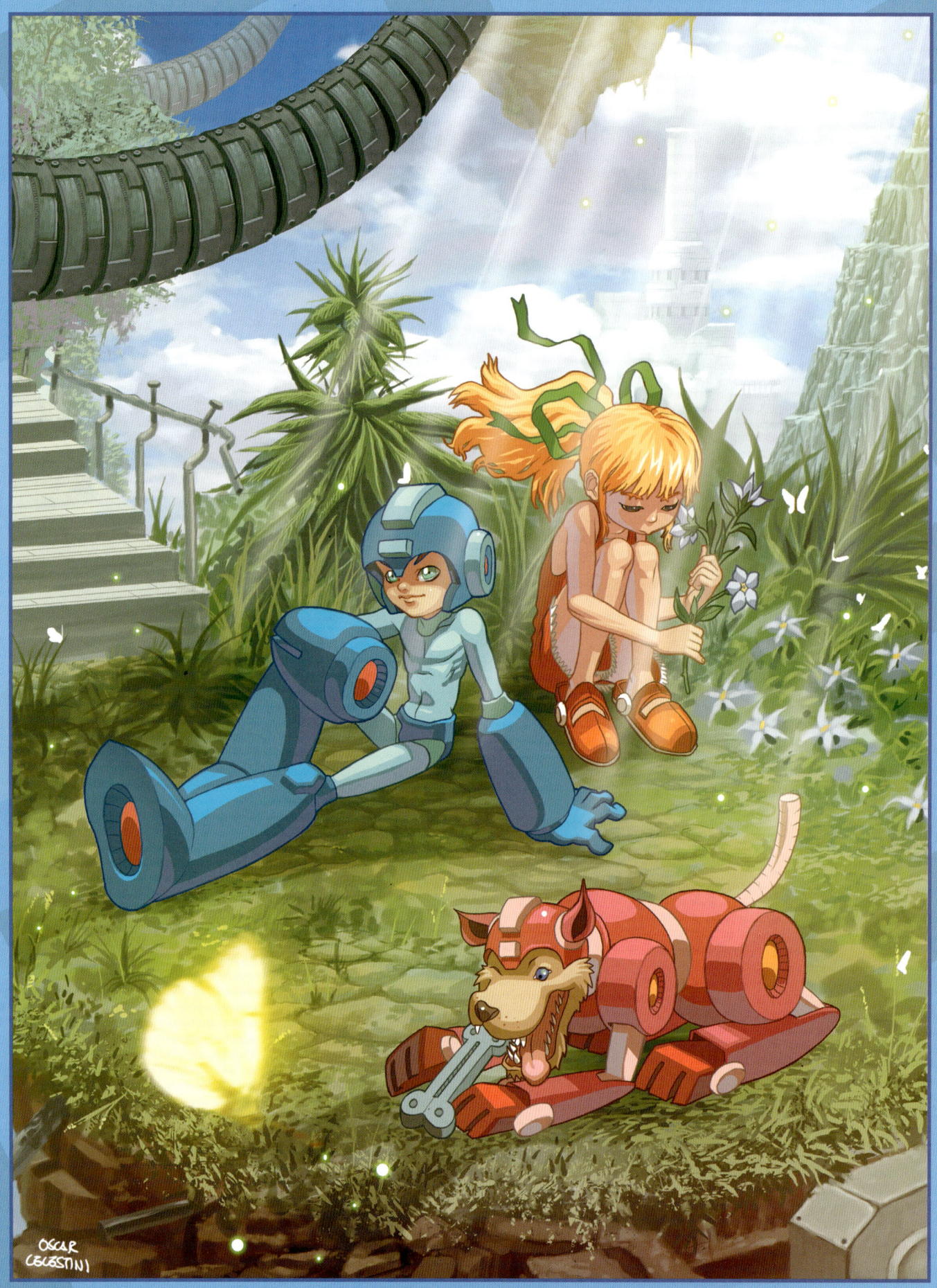

OSCAR CELESTINI
Viterbo, Italy
osk-studio.deviantart.com
Illustrator / Colorist

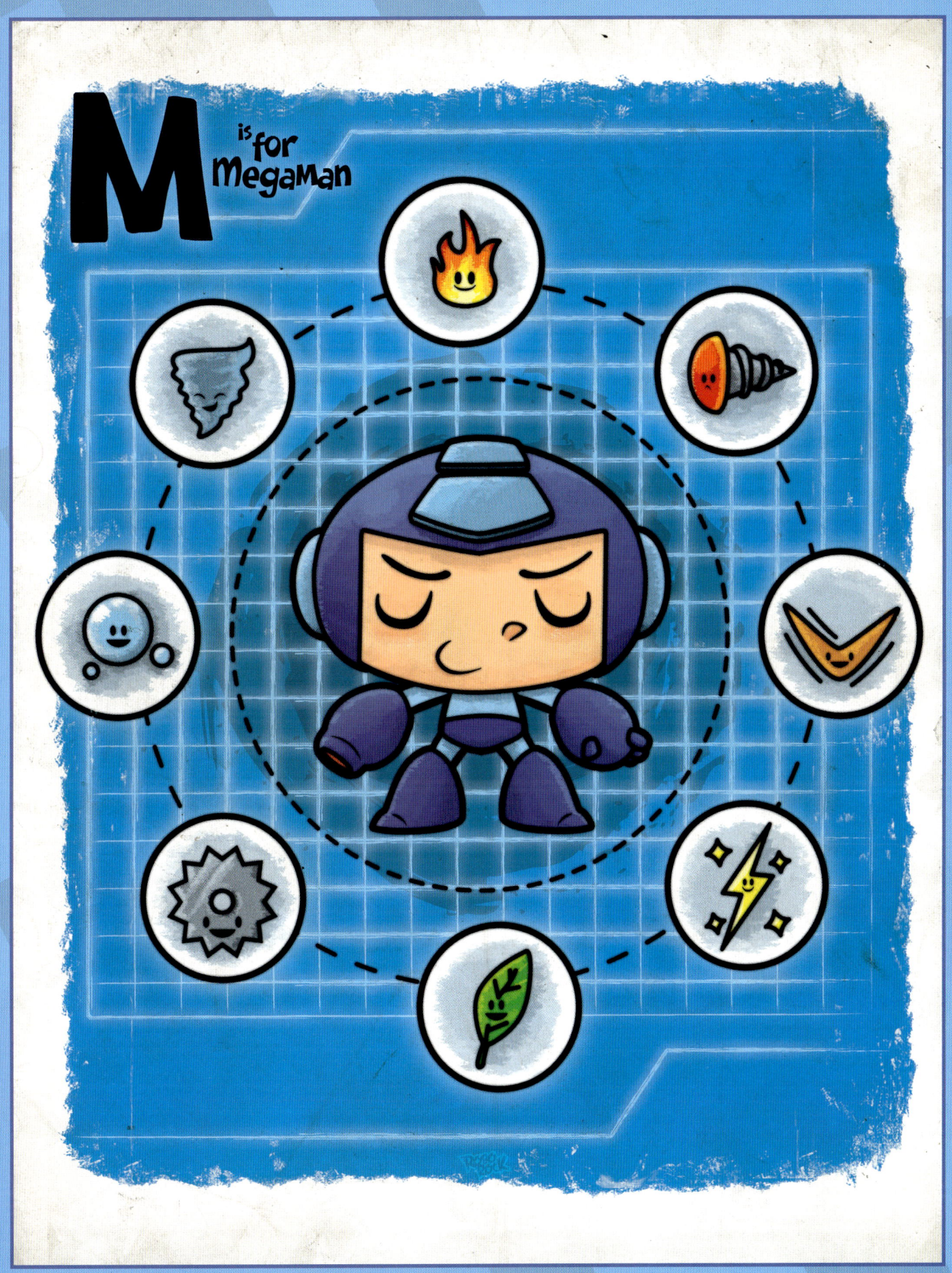

ROBOROCK (ALBERT COVARRUBIAS)
Guadalajara, Mexico
roborock.carbonmade.com / roborockk.blogspot.com
Illustrator

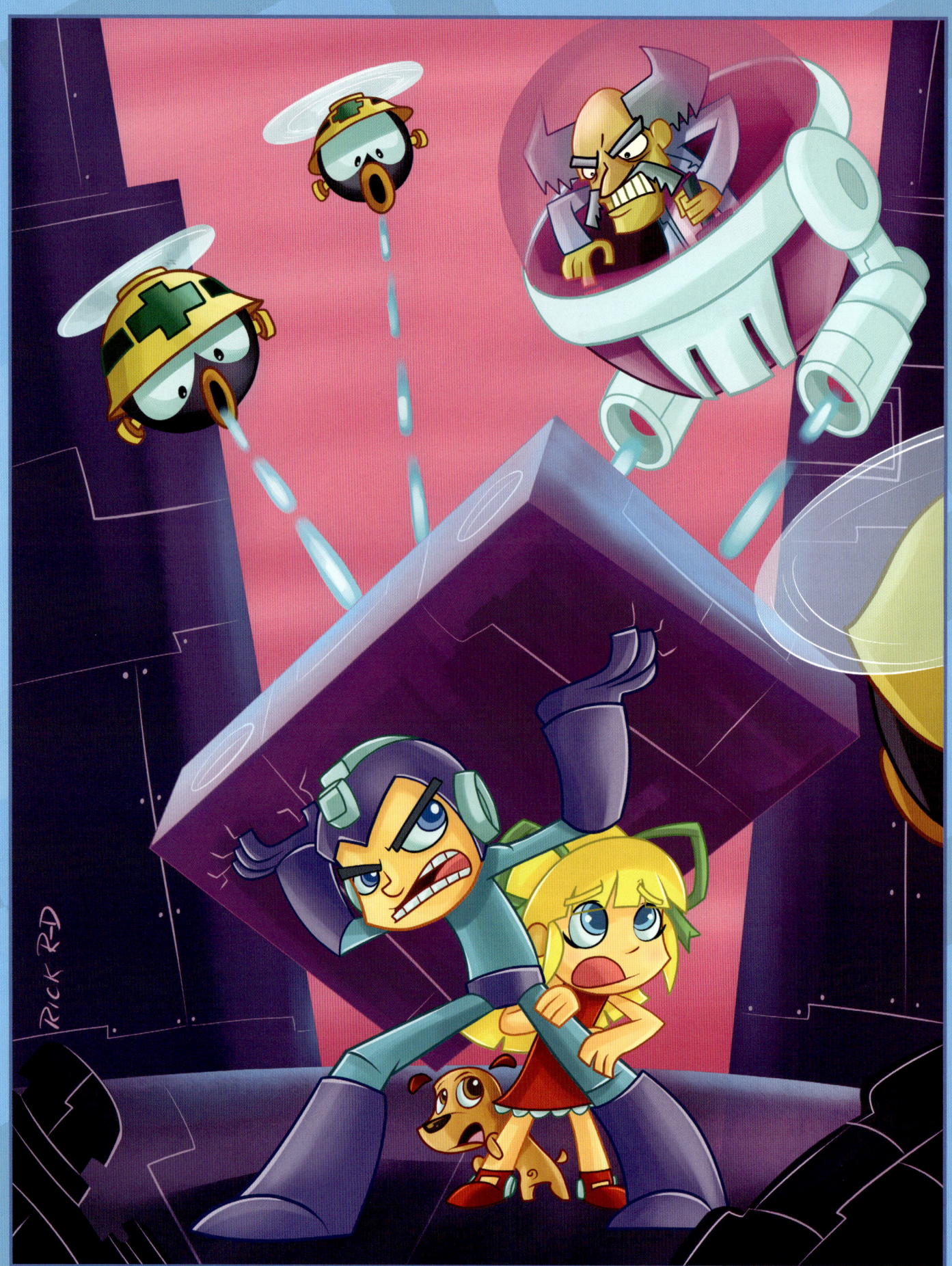

RICARDO RUIZ-DANA (RICK R-D)
Zapopan, Mexico
www.rickr-d.com
Character designer

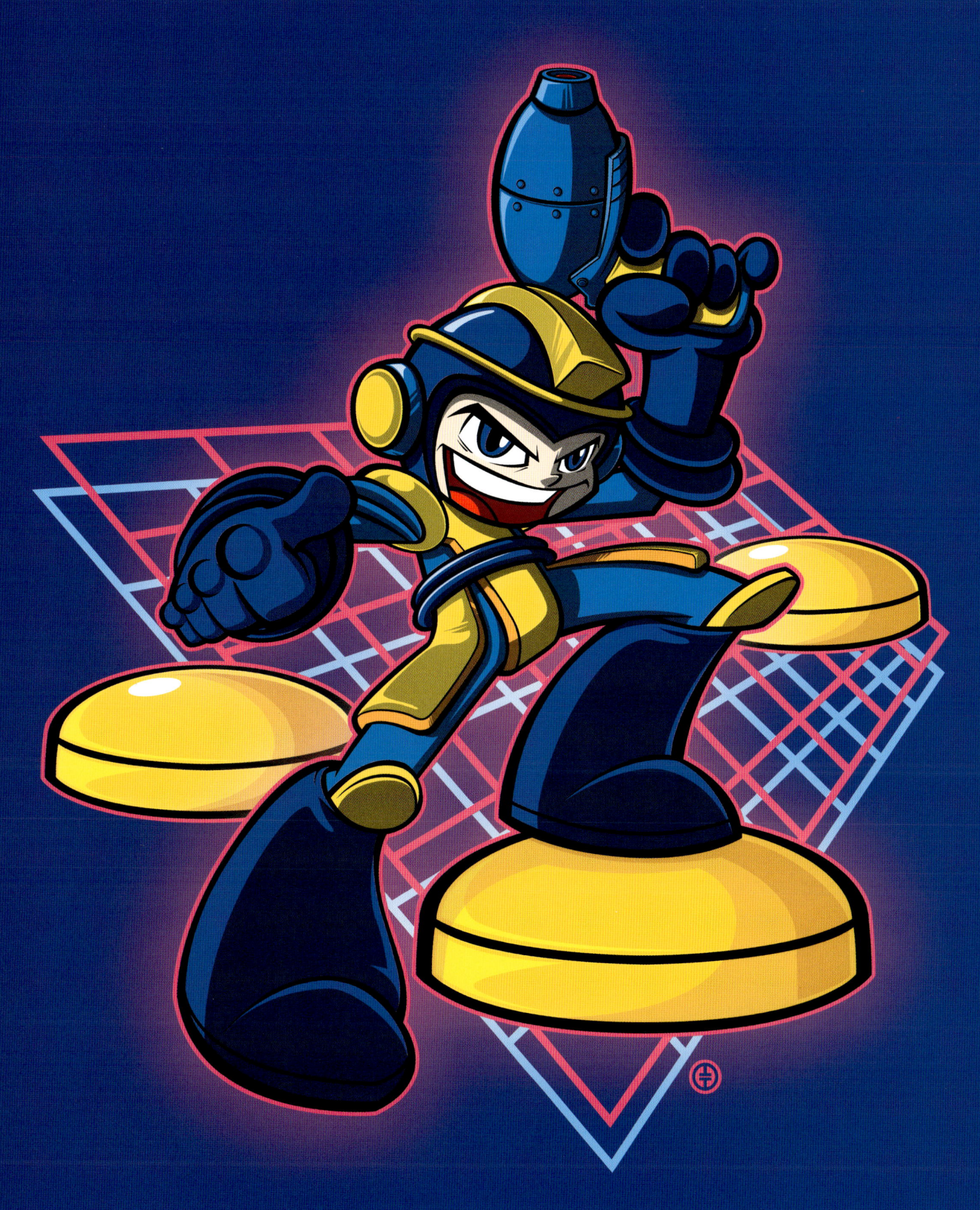

TRACY TUBERA
Pasadena, CA, United States
www.wildgrinders.com
Creative/Art Director
(Rob Dyrdek's Wild Grinders)

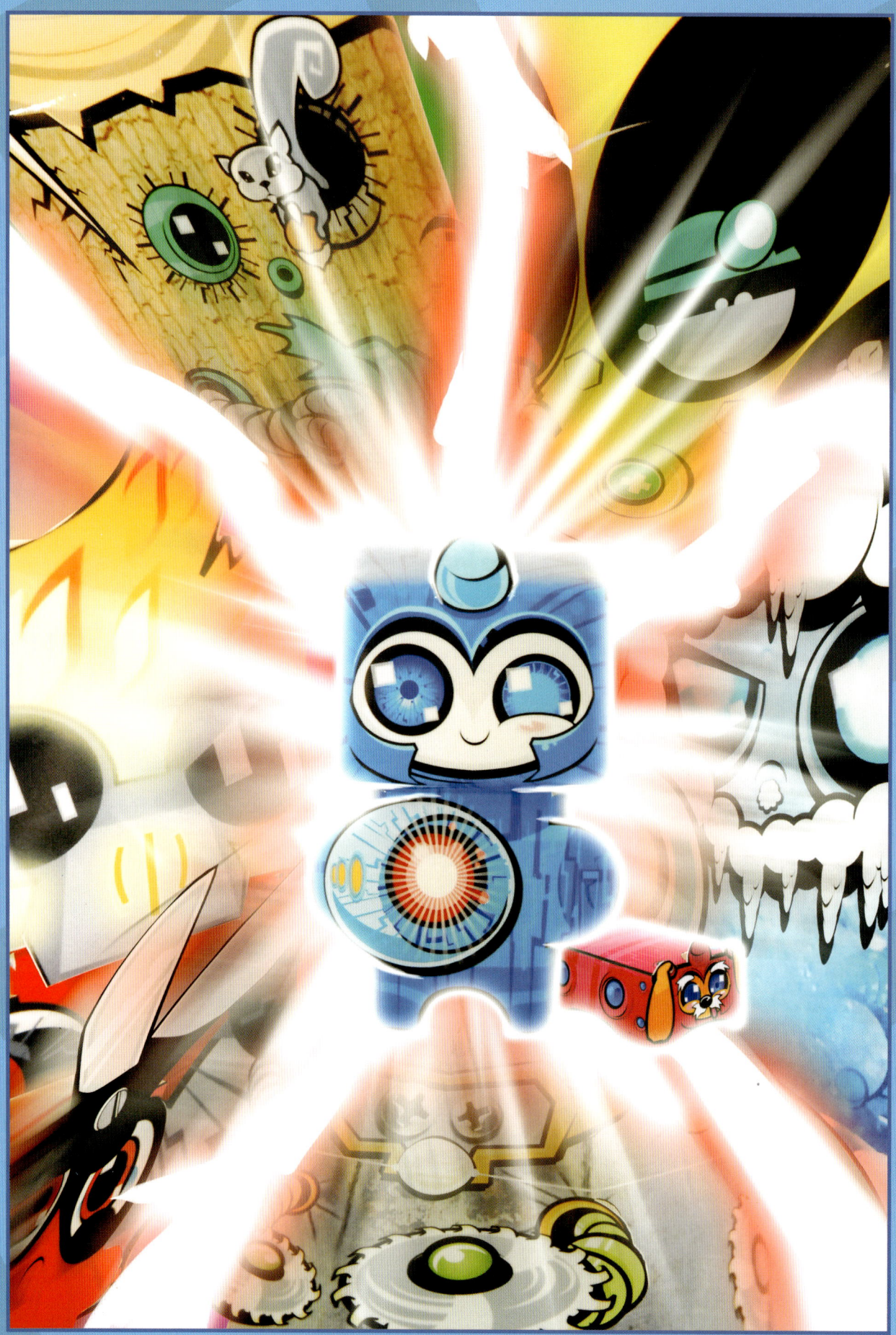

ANTHONY BRENNAN
Mississauga, ON, Canada
www.anthonybrennan.net
Illustrator
(ChickaDee cover artist / Kayak editorial artist /
Tales of the Tundra (book))

JASON BLAKELY (JABONE)
Kingston, ON, Canada
www.flickr.com/photos/jabone
Photographer

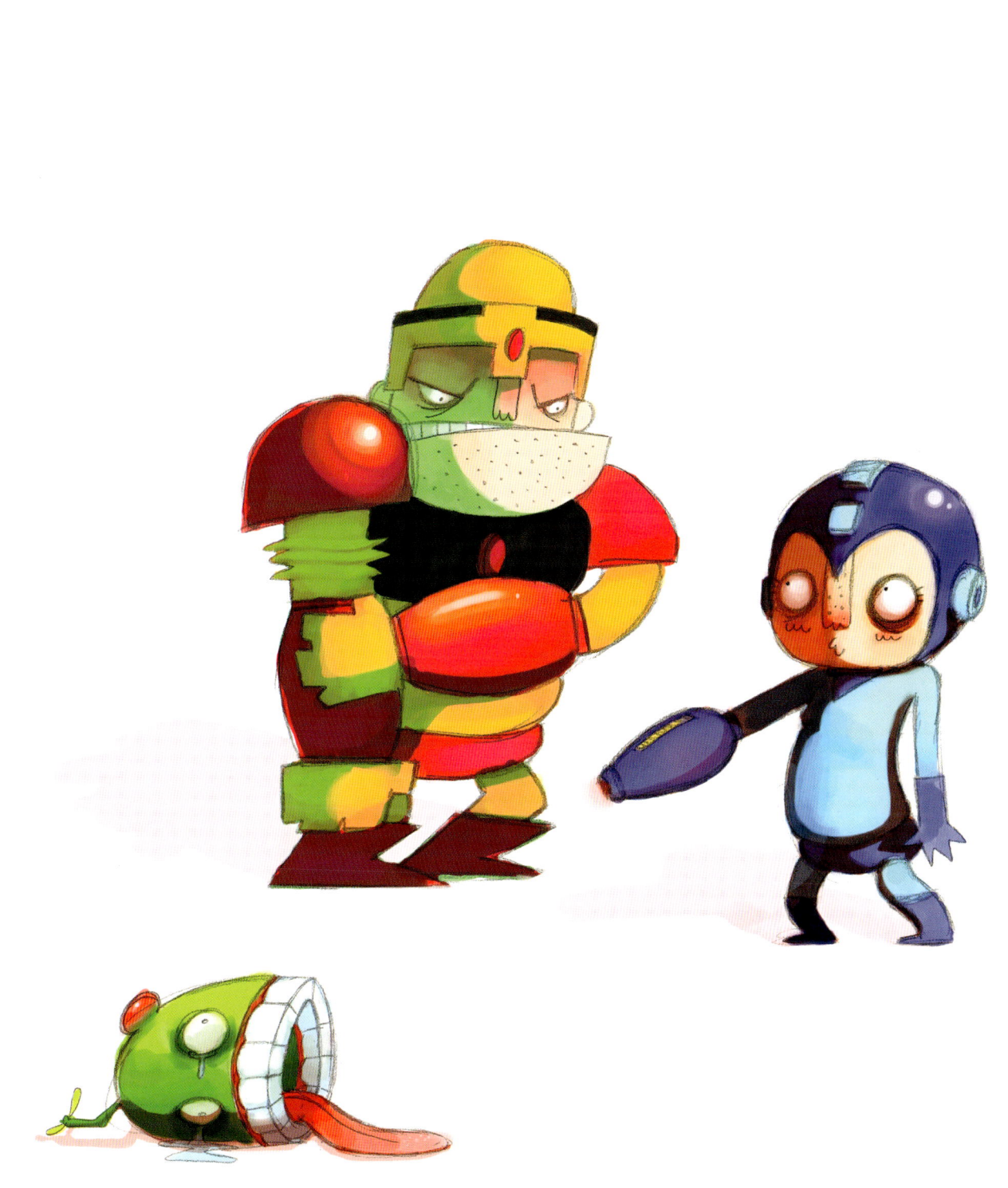

YASMIN SHEIKH
Breda, Netherlands
www.nerderella.com
Illustrator
(Fairytale Fights / Concept artist - Eye Pet / The Bunny Project)

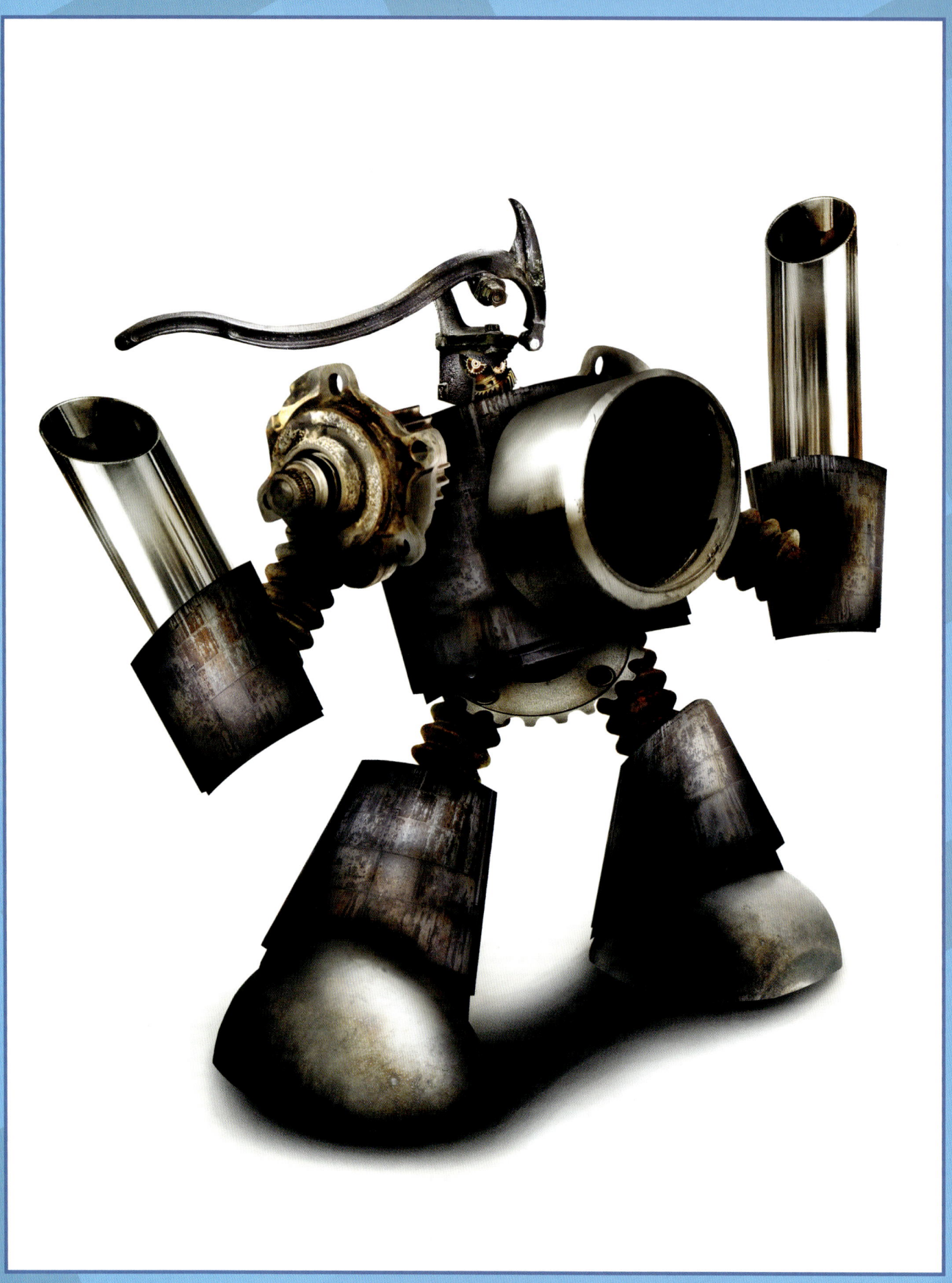

BOB CASSELLA
Atco, NJ, United States
www.bobcassella.com
Graphic Designer

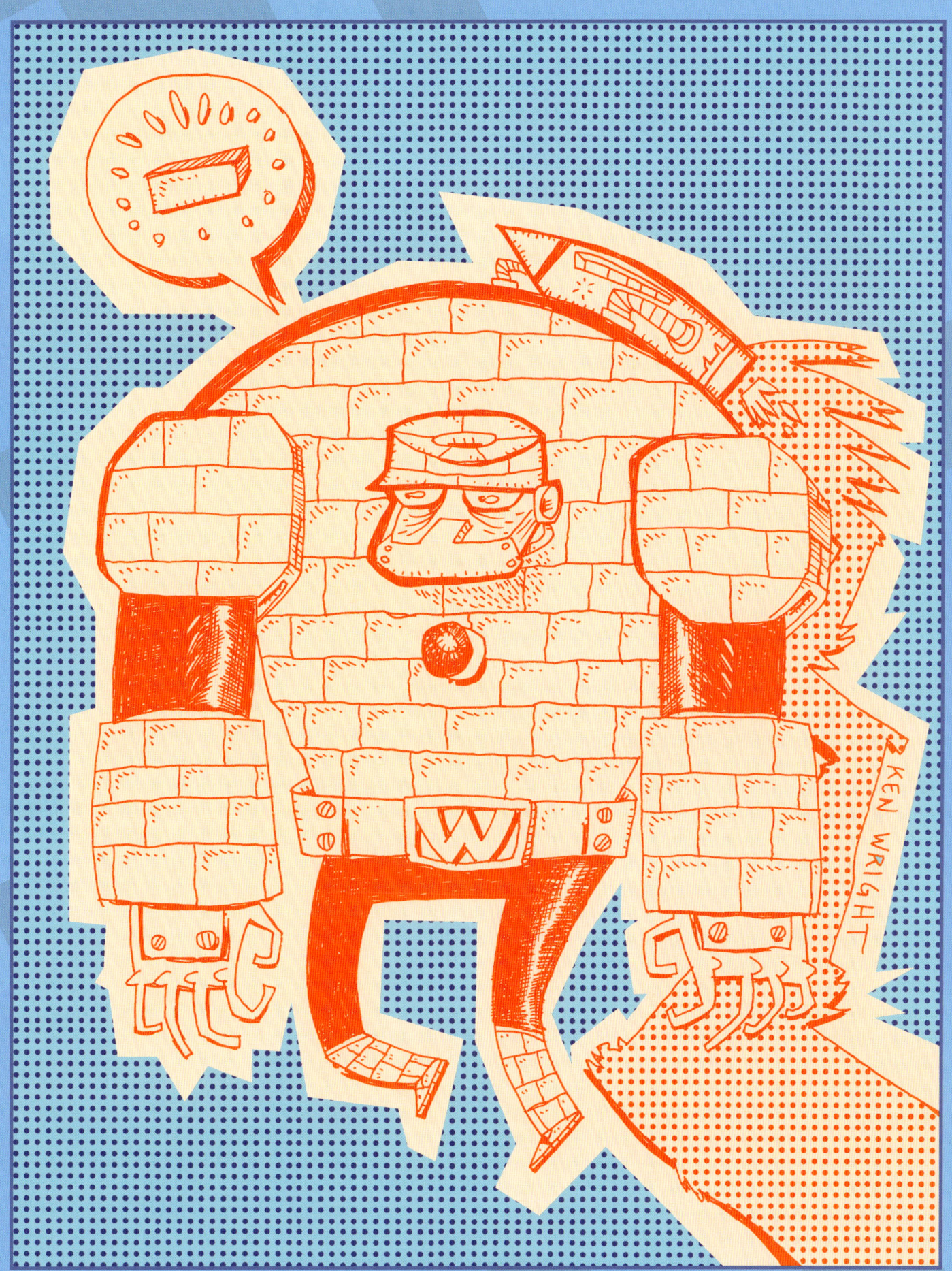

KEN WRIGHT
Tucson, AZ, United States
www.kenwrightonline.com
Illustrator
(The University of Arizona)

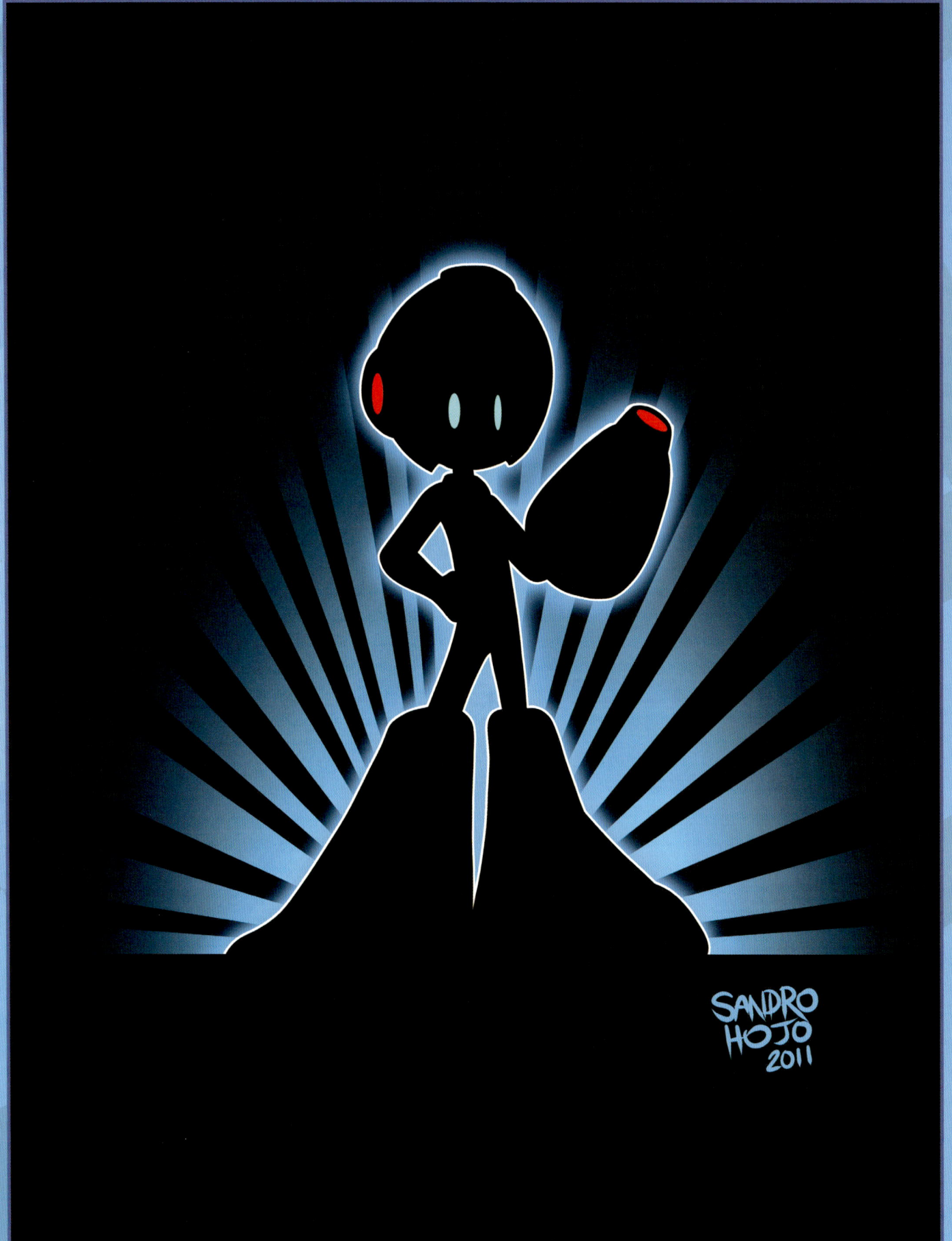

SANDRO HOJO
Guarulhos, Brazil
hojossaurus.deviantart.com
Character Designer

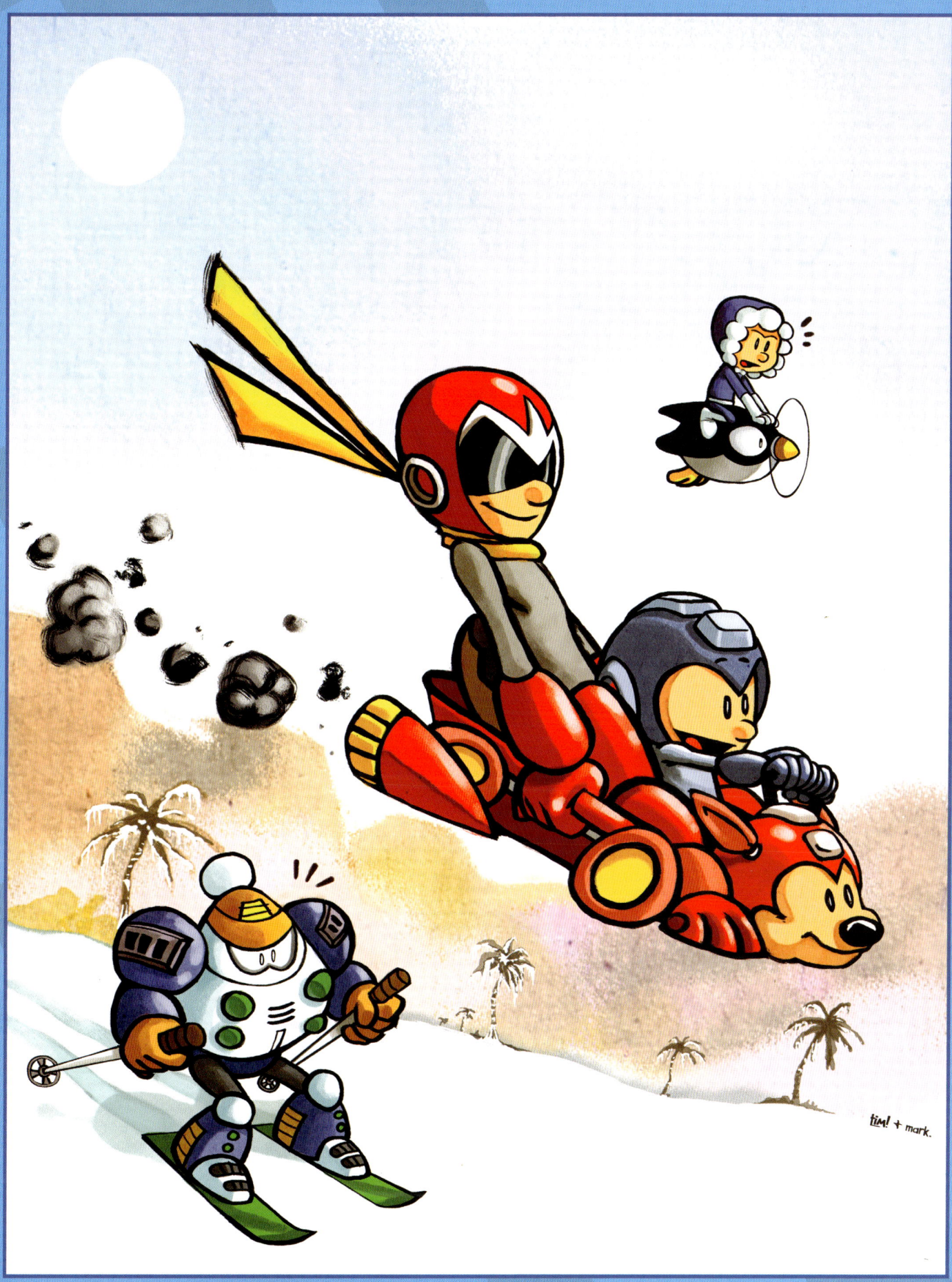

TIMOTHY LIM
Little Rock, AR, United States
ninjaink.deviantart.com
Student

MARK PELLEGRINI
Layout

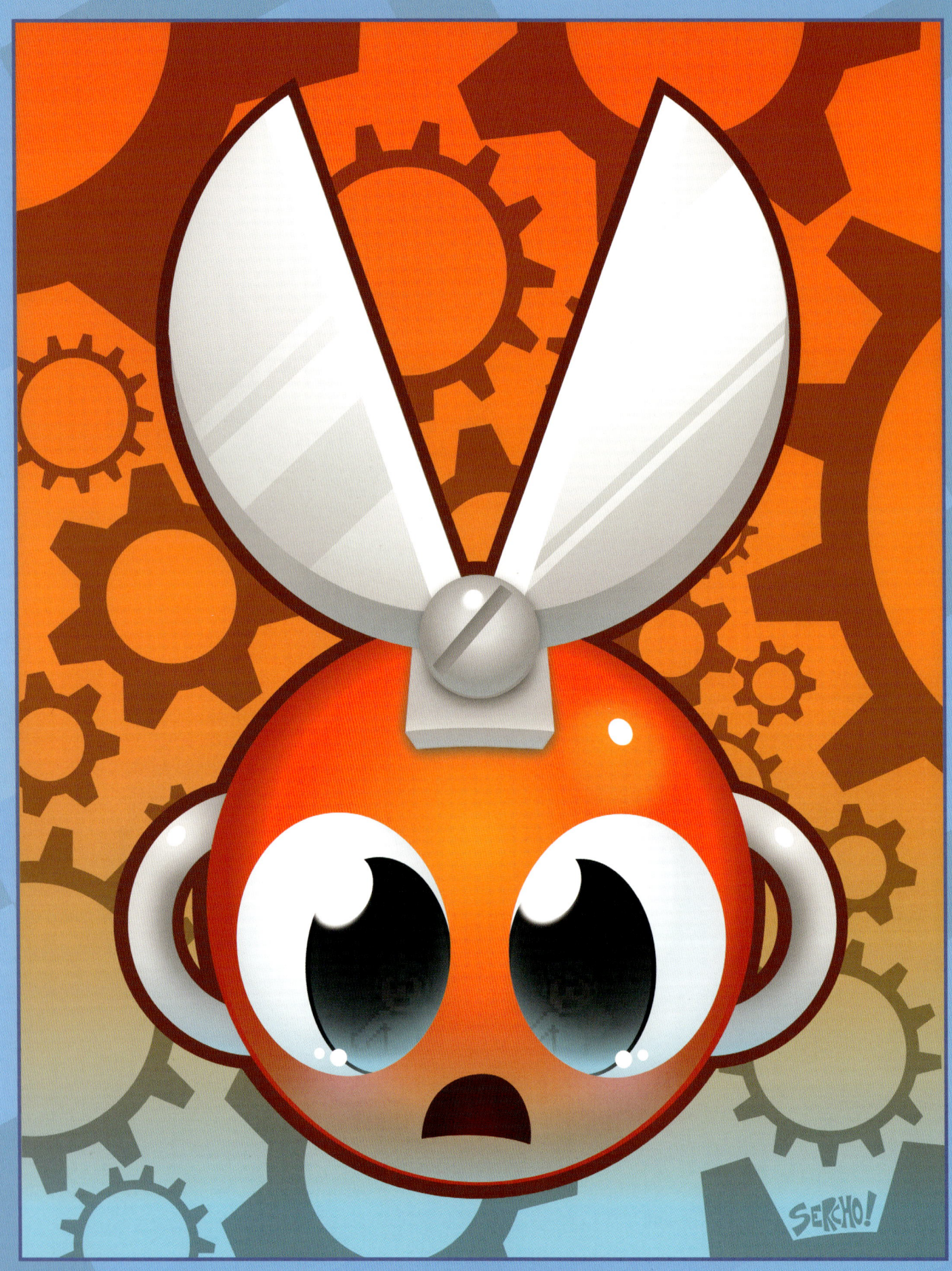

SERGIO OLIVARES (SERCHO!)
Tijuana, Mexico
sercho05.deviantart.com
Graphic Designer

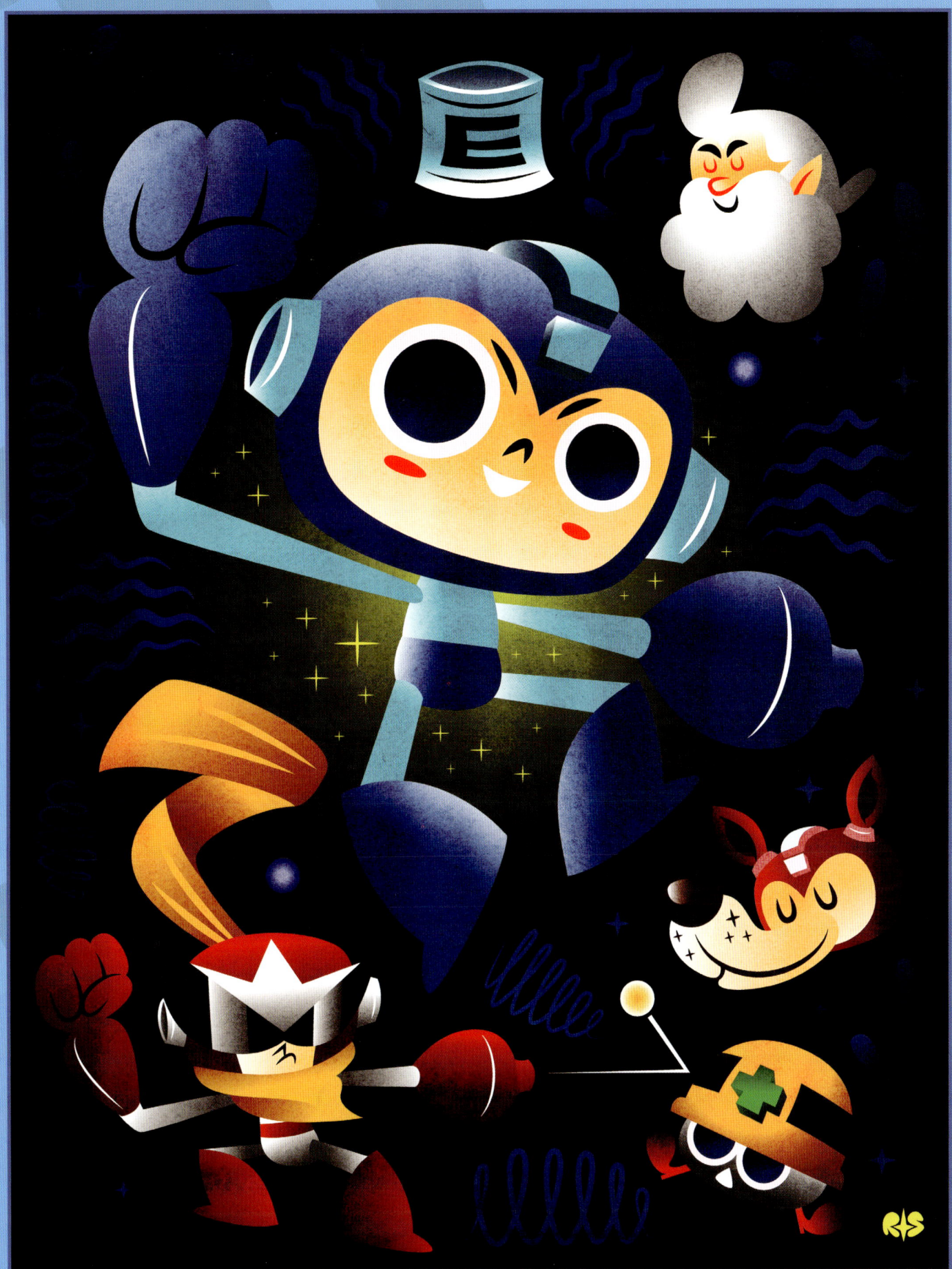

ROBOT SODA
Ensenada, Mexico
www.robotsoda.com
Illustrator

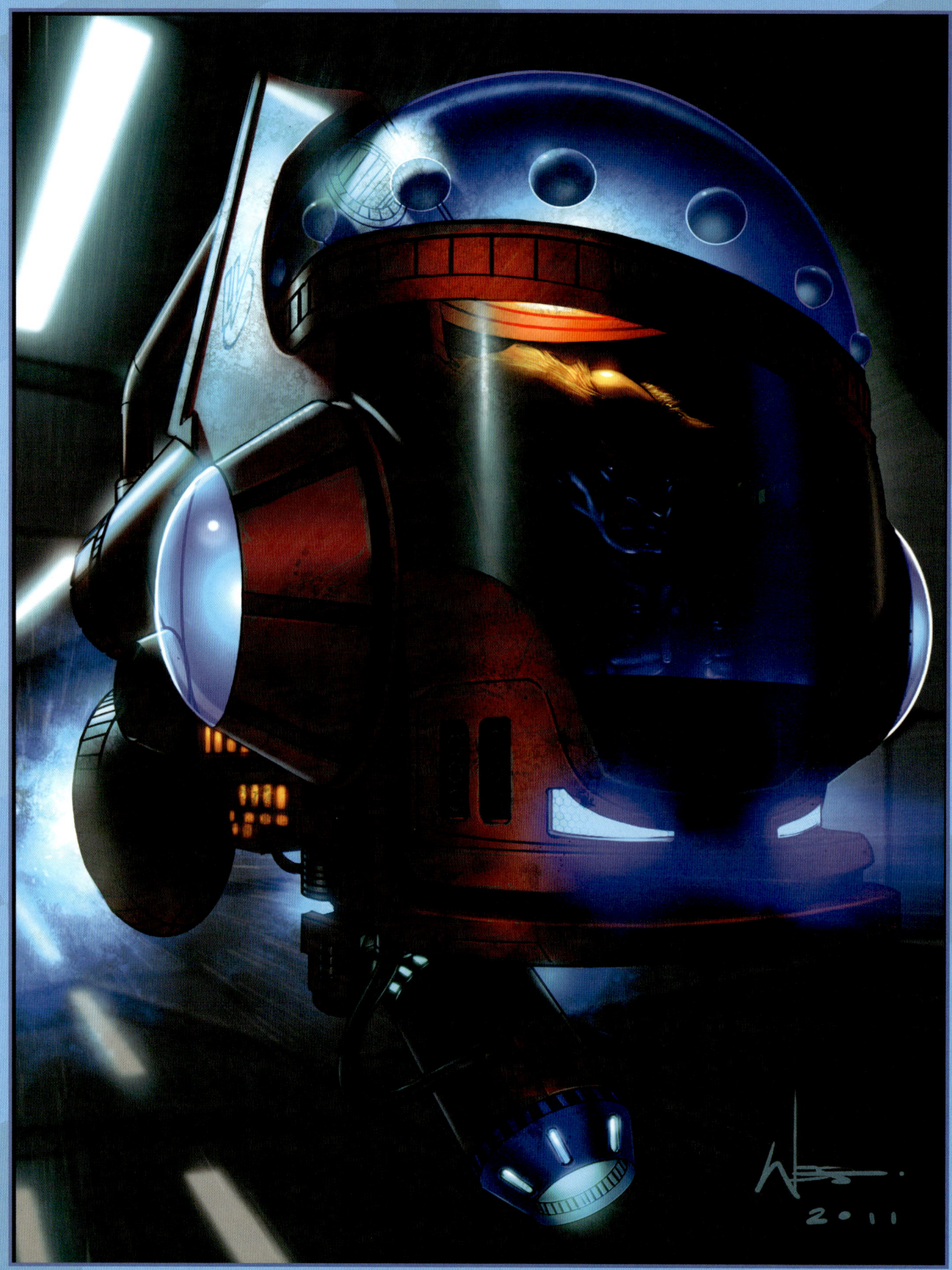

WES LOUIE
Glendale, CA, United States
www.weslouie.com
Concept Designer
(Thor / Epic Mickey / Resistance: Fall of Man)

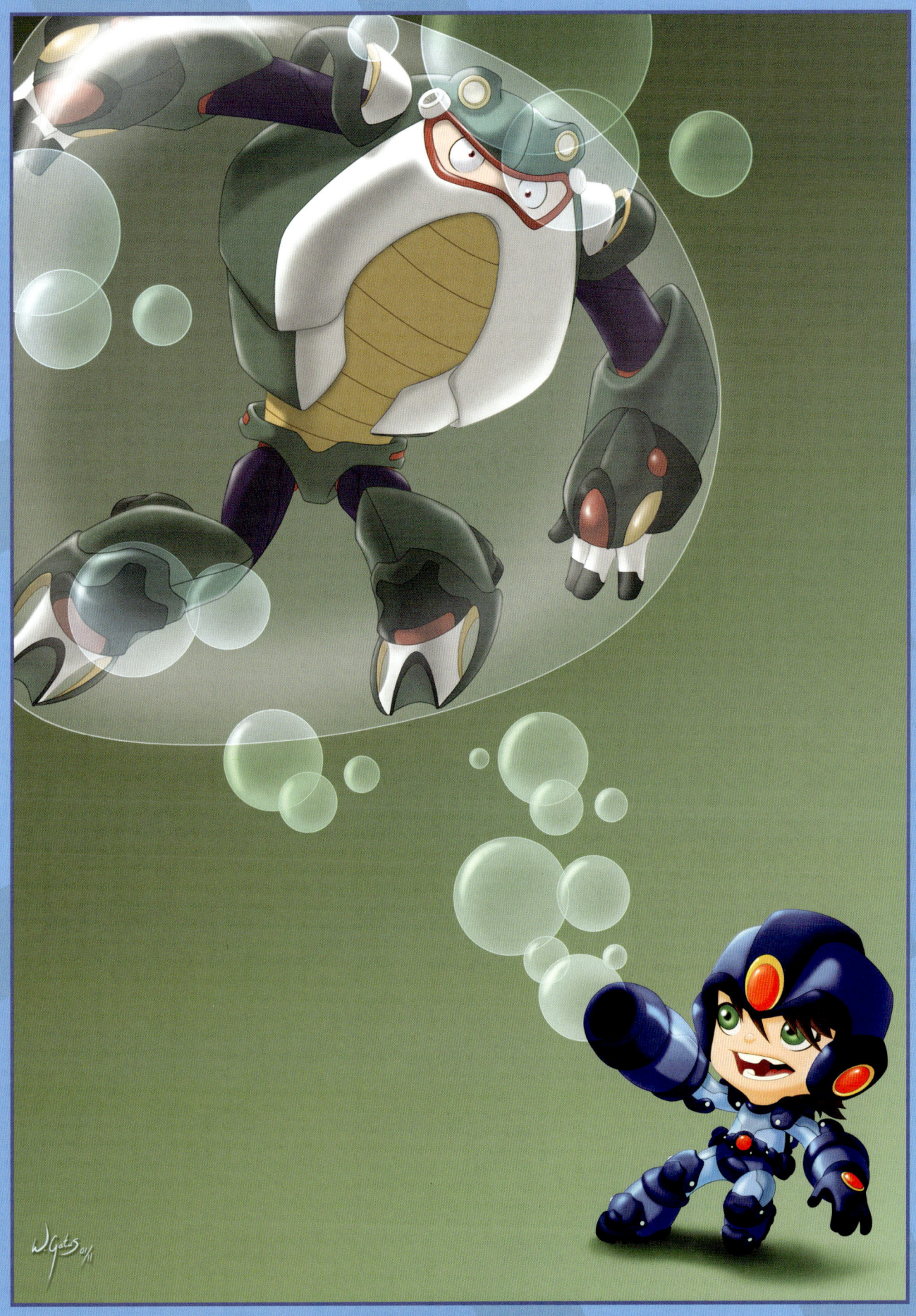

WALTER GATUS (WALTDOG)
Winnetka, CA, United States
waltergatus.blogspot.com
Character Designer
(Transformers: Prime / Avengers: Earth's Mightiest Heroes / Generator Rex)

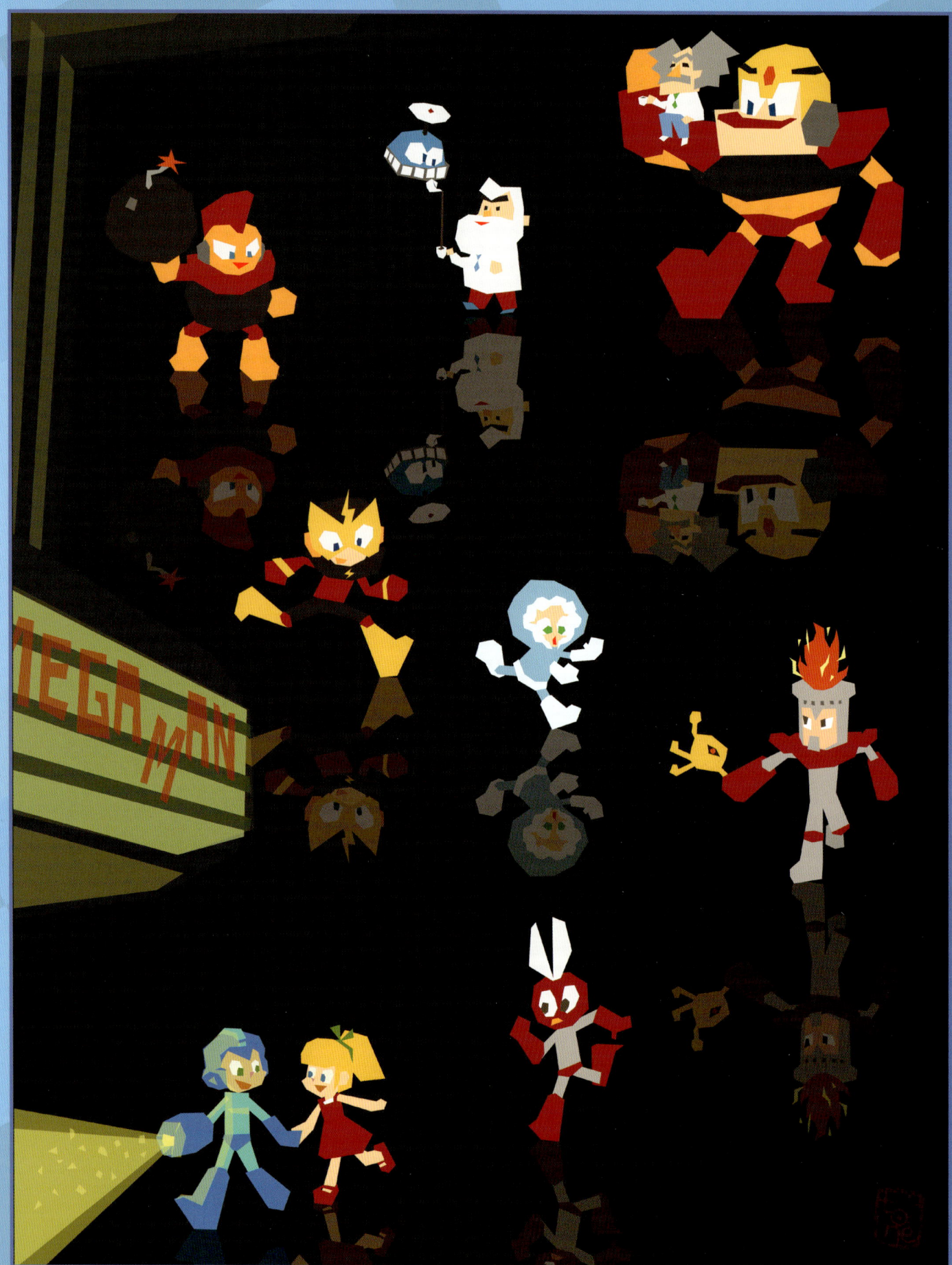

TEERAWAT PALANITISENA
San Francisco, CA, United States
www.teerawat.com
Illustrator

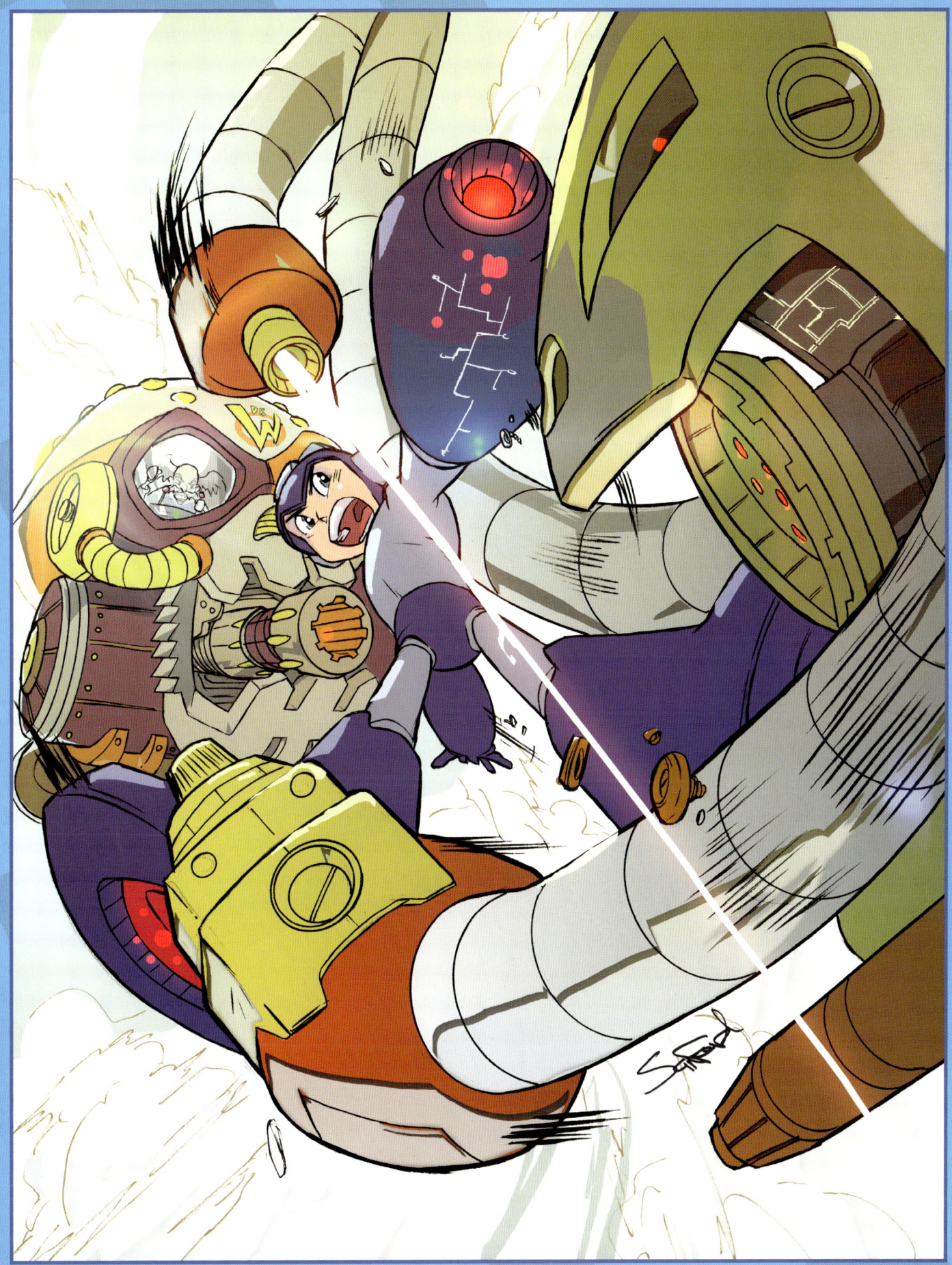

SANFORD GREENE
Columbia, SC, United States
codegreene.blogspot.com / greenestreet.deviantart.com
Comic Artist / Illustrator
(Method Man, Marvel Comics, DC Comics, Disney, Hasbro)

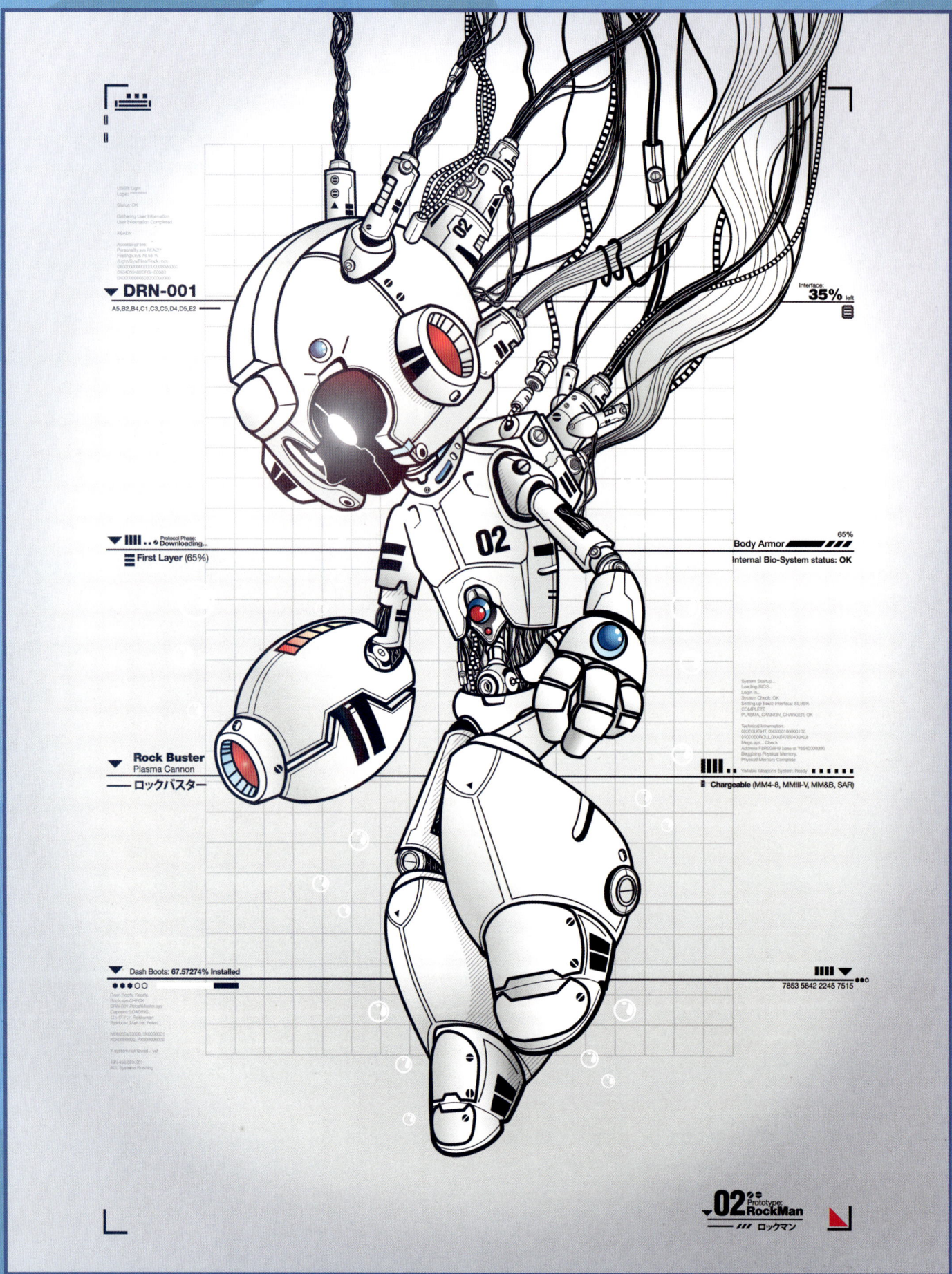

Tonny Jiménez (Anton Van Draco)
South Gate, CA, United States
www.tonnyjimenez.com
Illustrator & Motion Graphics Designer
(Universidad del Valle de Atemajac (UNIVA))

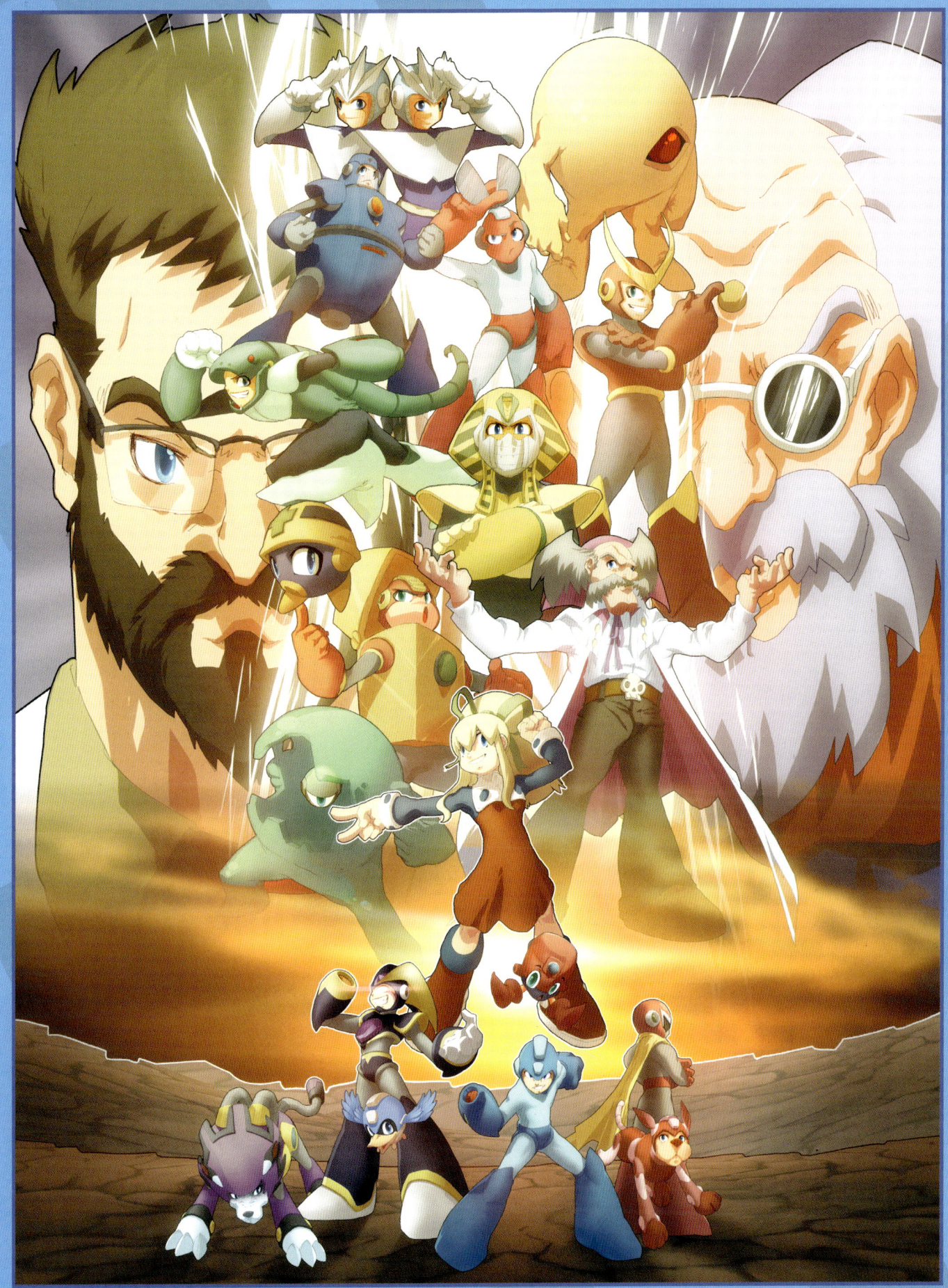

SANTIAGO CALLERIZA
Montevideo, Uruguay
moonfx.deviantart.com
Illustrator

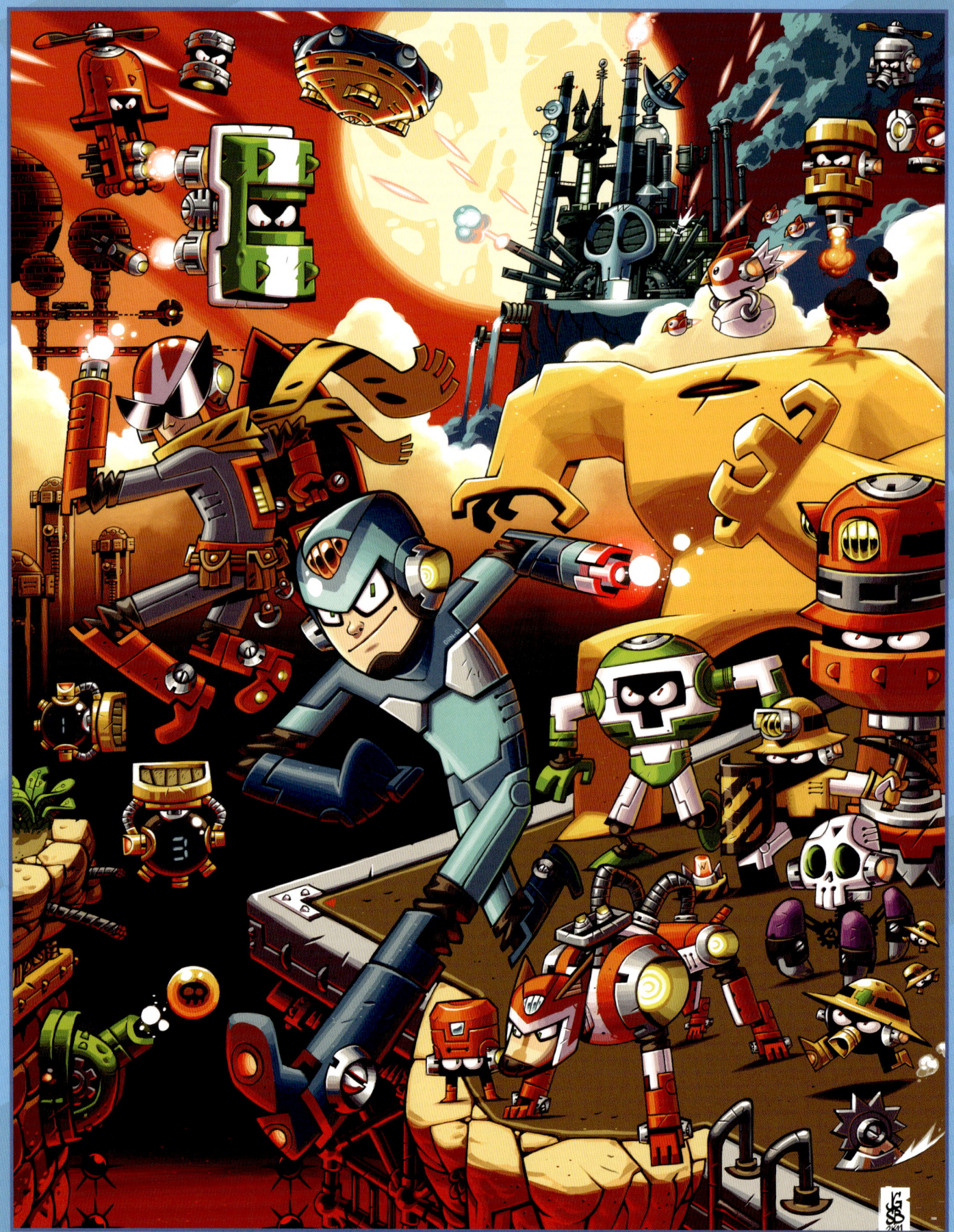

STÉPHANE BOUTIN (JGSB)
Montreal, QC, Canada
boutain.blogspot.com / boutain.deviantart.com
Illustrator
(Scott Pilgrim VS the world: the game)

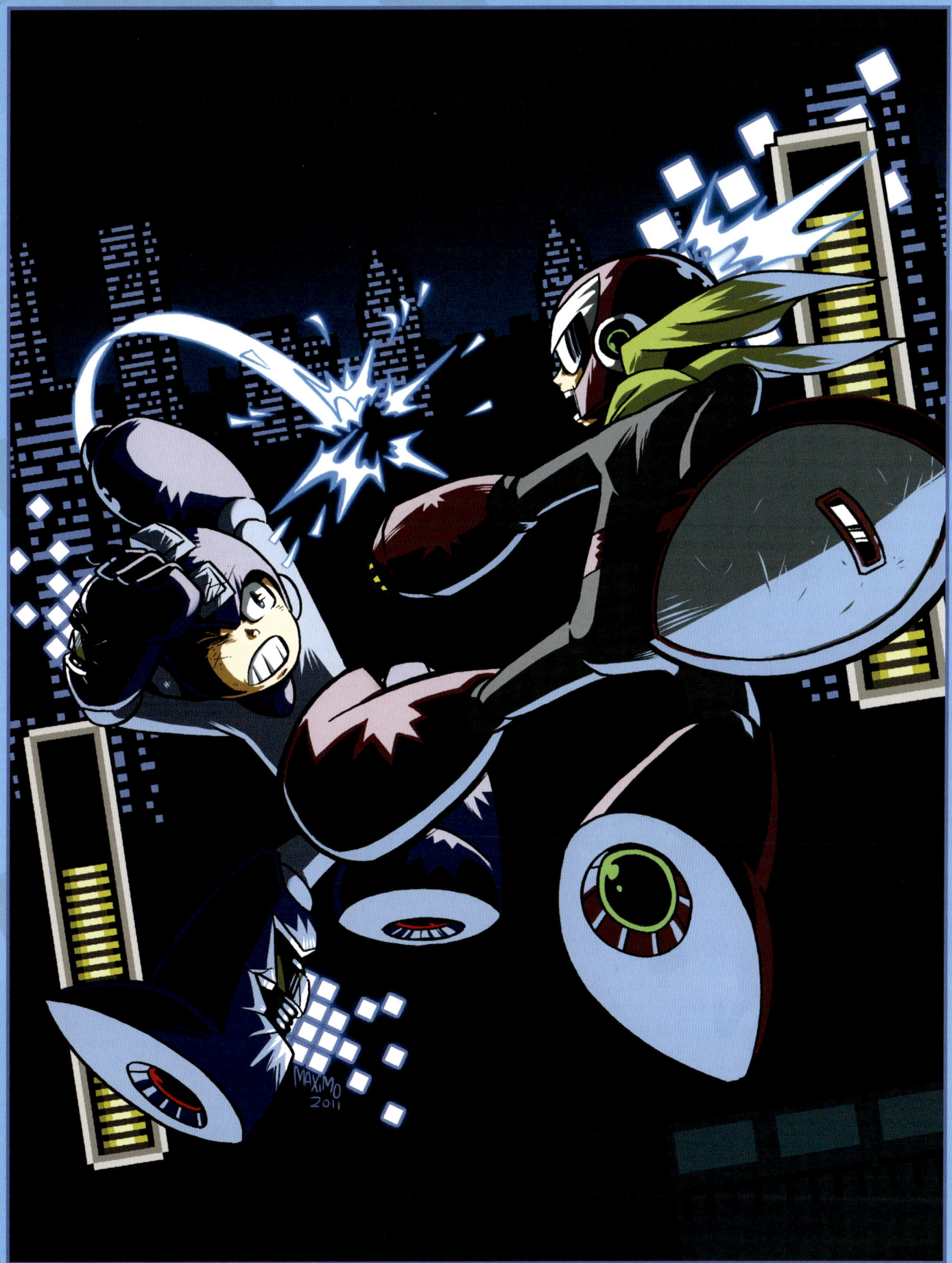

MAXIMO V. LORENZO
Newtown, CT, United States
8bitmaximo.com / speedking.deviantart.com
Comic artist
(Tokyopop Ghostbusters / Popgun 3 / OneHitKnockOut ZUDA)

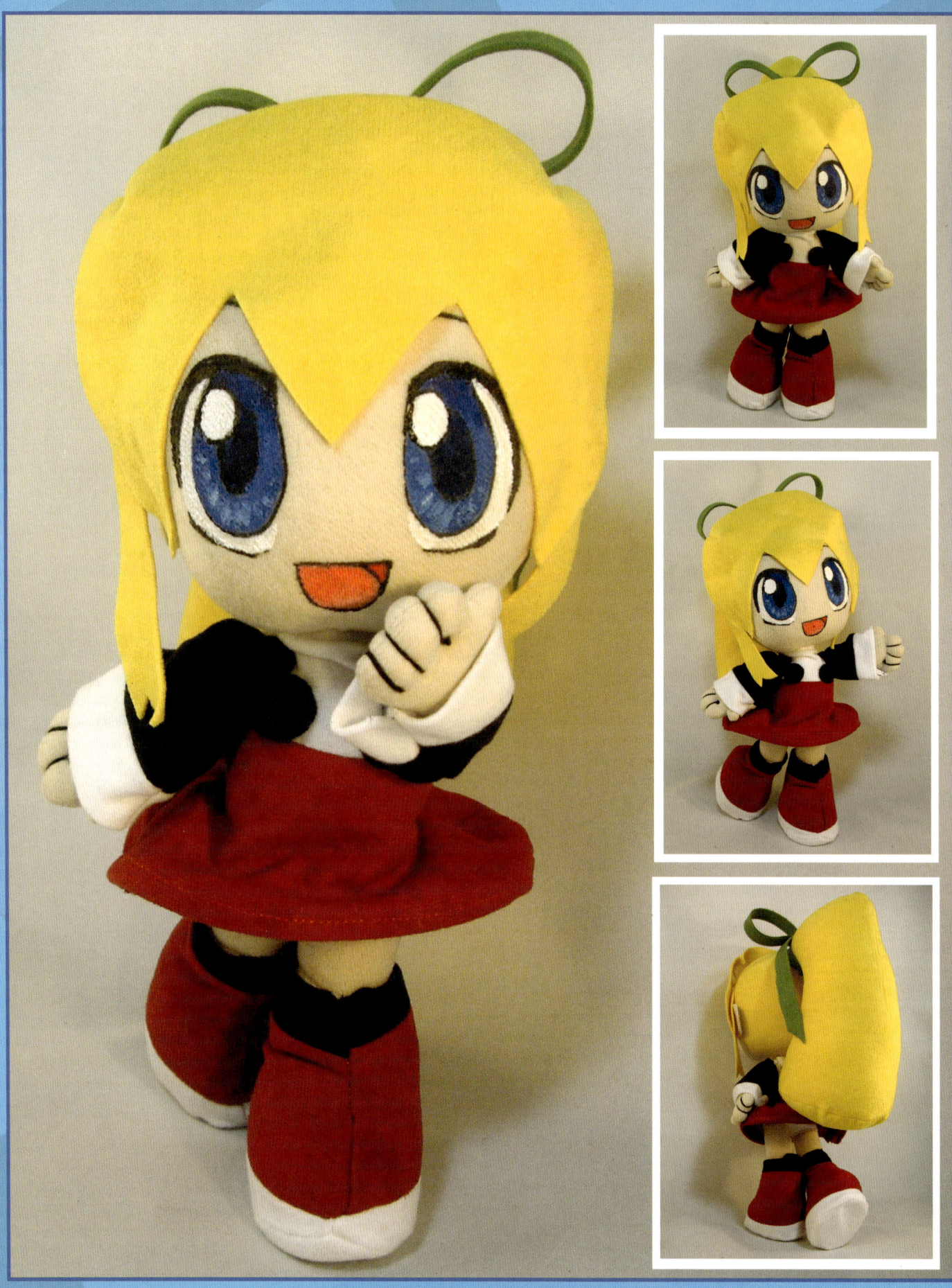

HOLLY SEGARRA
Newtown, CT, United States
www.professionallycute.com / usako-chan.deviantart.com
Illustrator and Toy Designer
(Joe Kubert School of Cartoon and Graphic Arts)

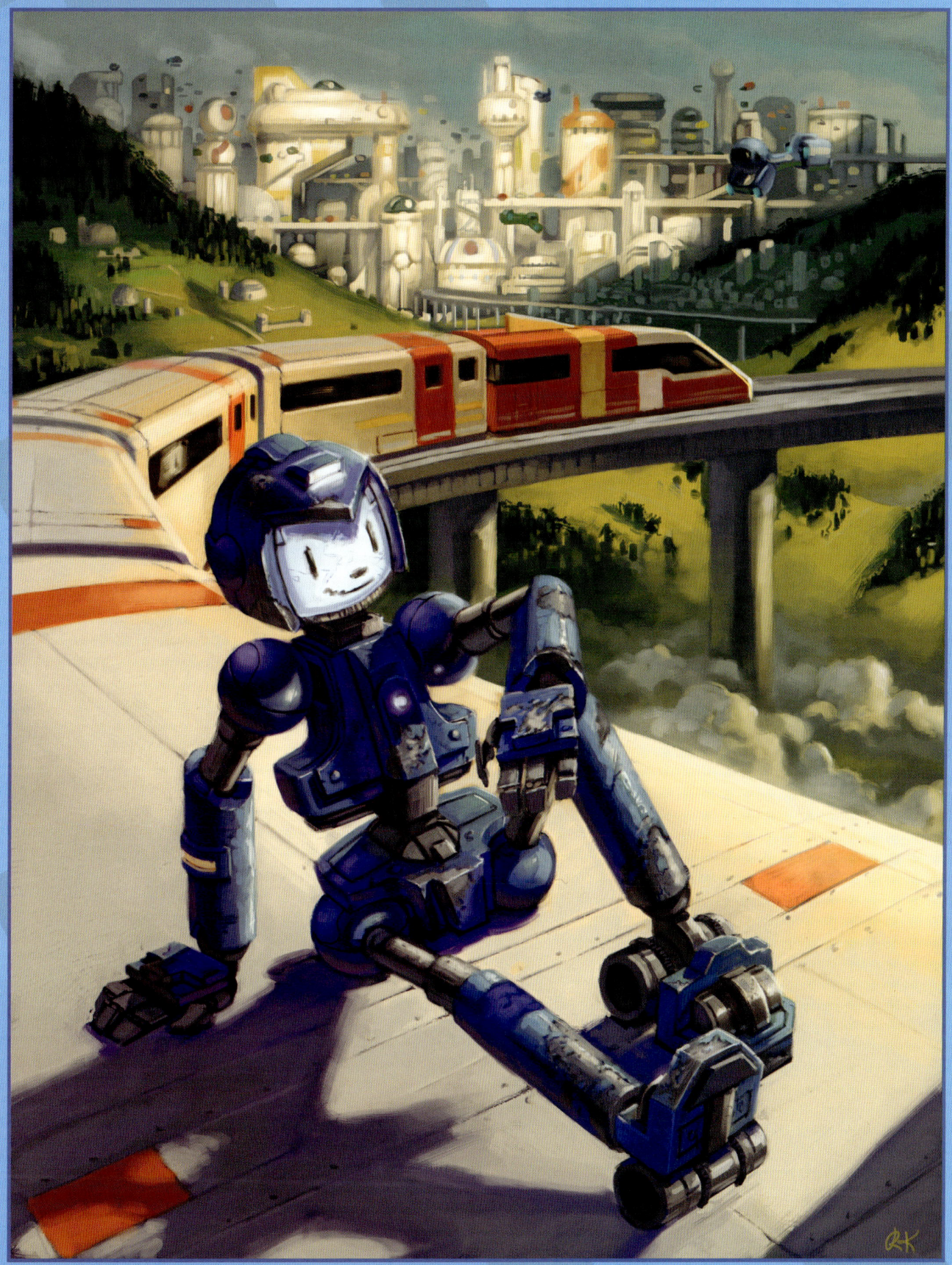

RORY KELLER
Oceanside, NY, United States
rorydraws.tumblr.com
Illustrator

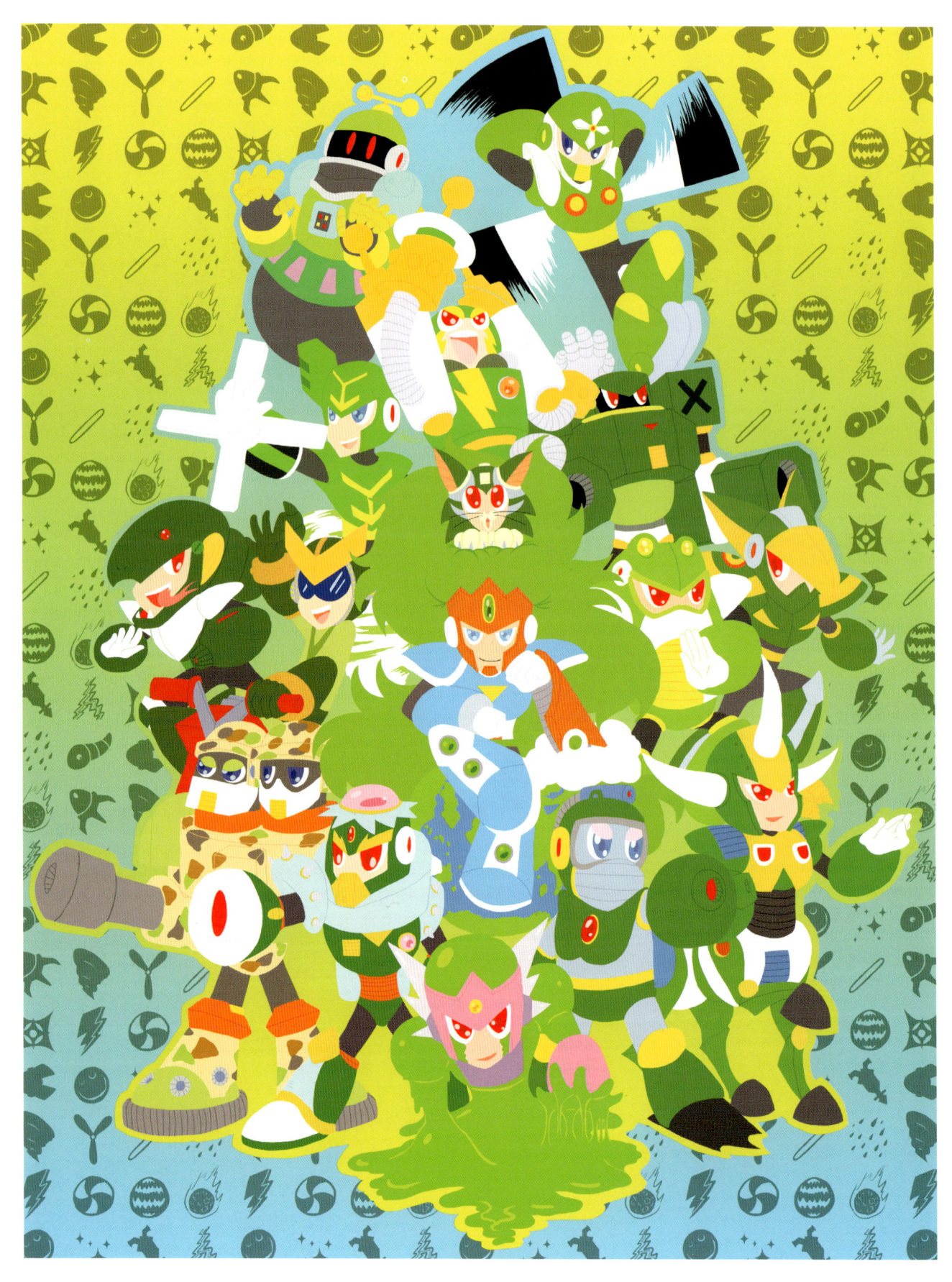

SAWPEA KEO
Milwaukie, OR, United States
Illustrator

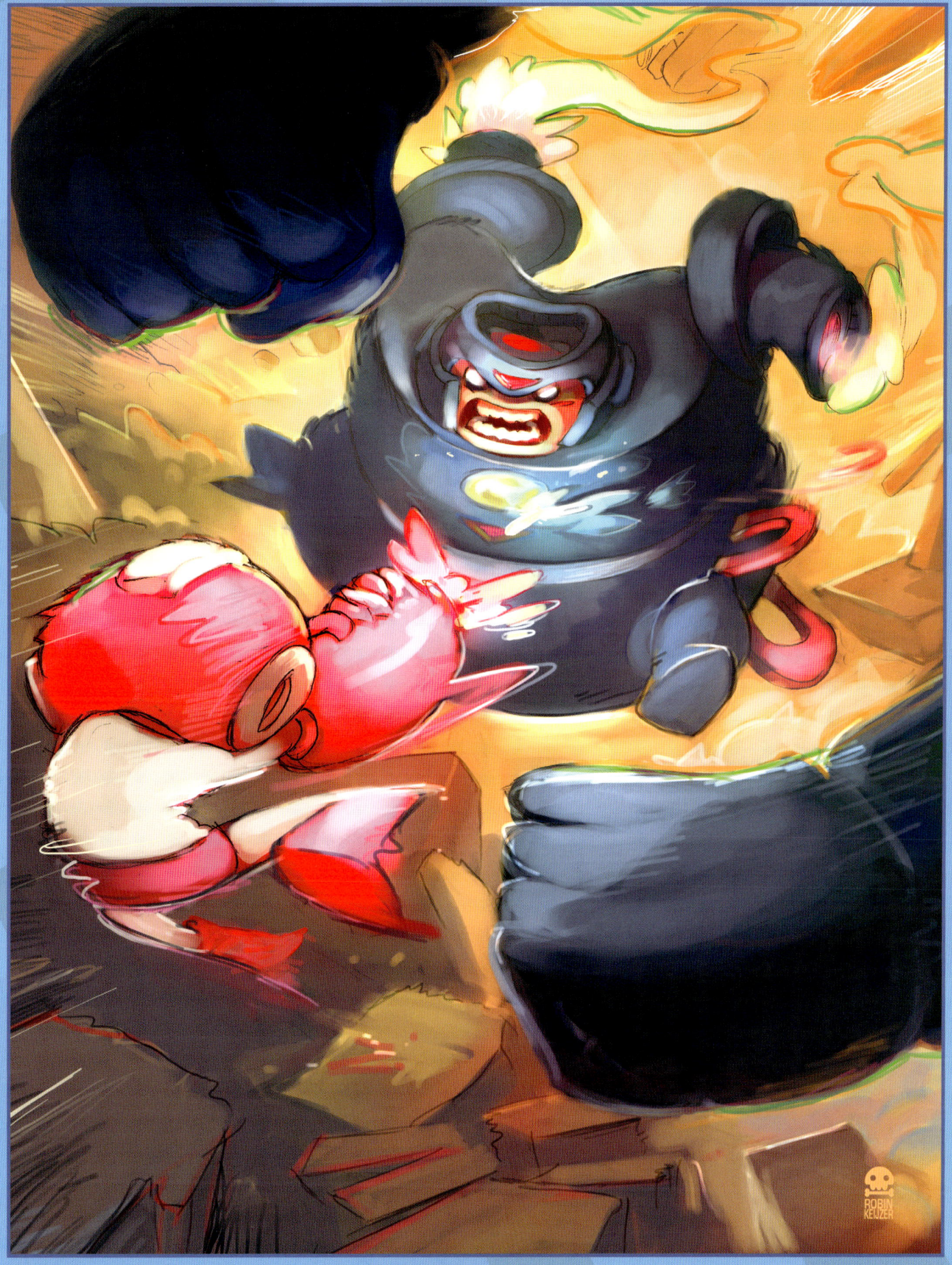

ROBIN KEIJZER
Breda, Netherlands
www.robinkeijzer.com
Art Director / Comic Artist / Illustrator
(Art Director of 'Fairytale Fights' (game) / Creator of 'Splash VERSUS Clean' (comic))

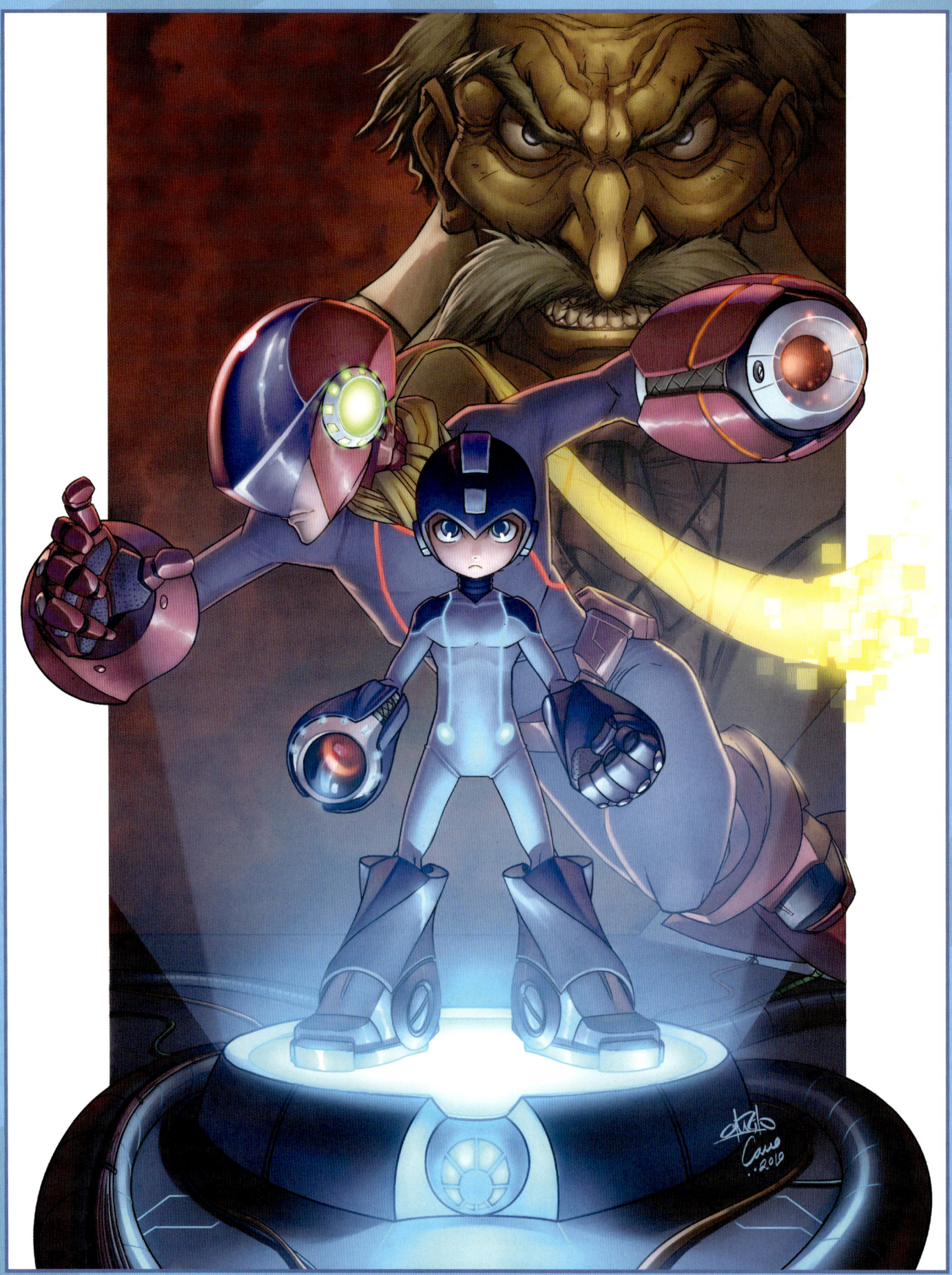

OMAR LOZANO
Nuevo León, Mexico
www.graphikslava.com
Illustrator
(Vanarts Character Animation Summer Intensive 2010 /
Skullgirls / IDW - Colors For Dungeons & Dragons)

FERNANDO CANO
Mexico
graphikslava.deviantart.com
Colorist
(Pathfinder Tabletop Rpg /
Stonearch-Sports Illustrated Kids /
IDW - Colors For Dungeons & Dragons)

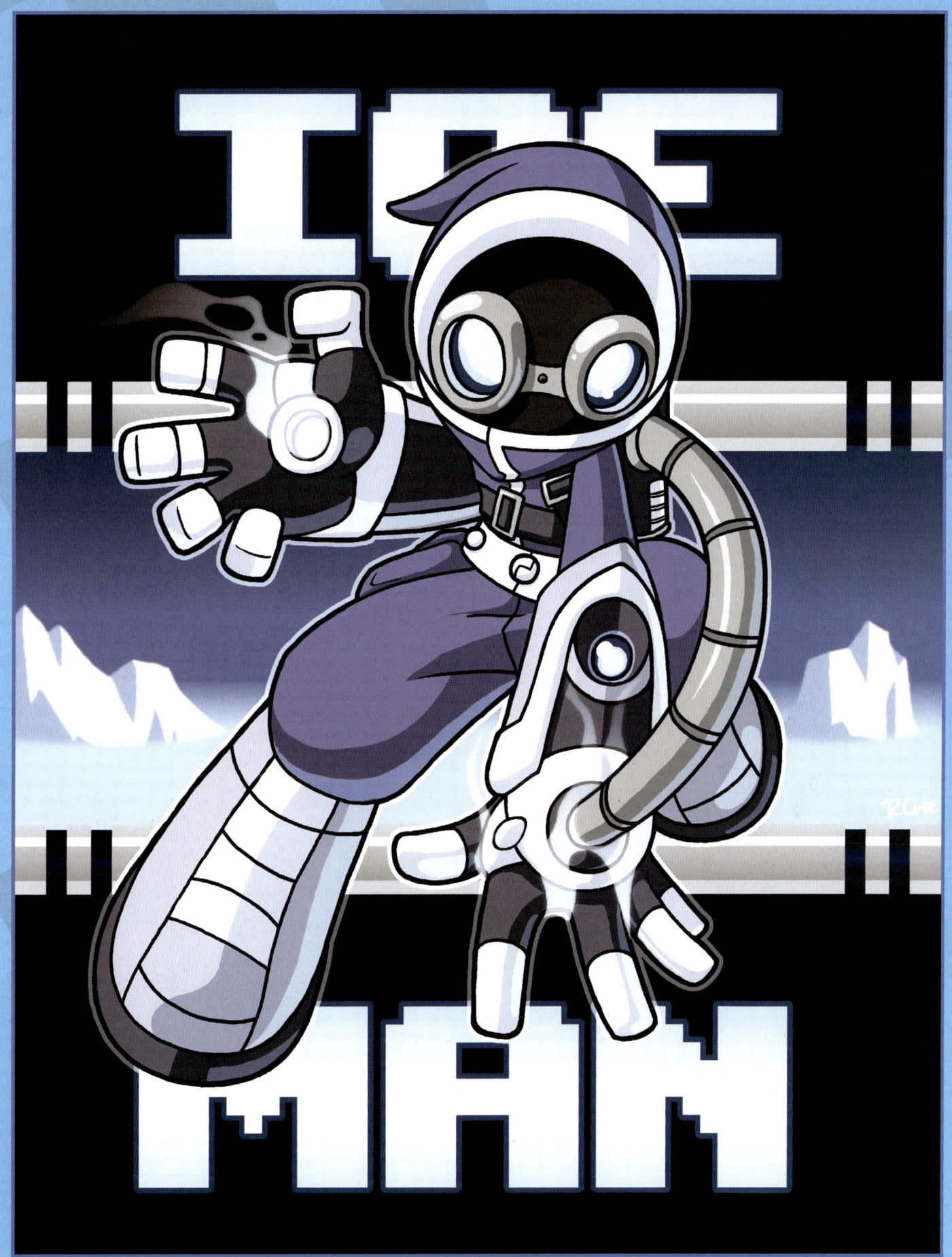

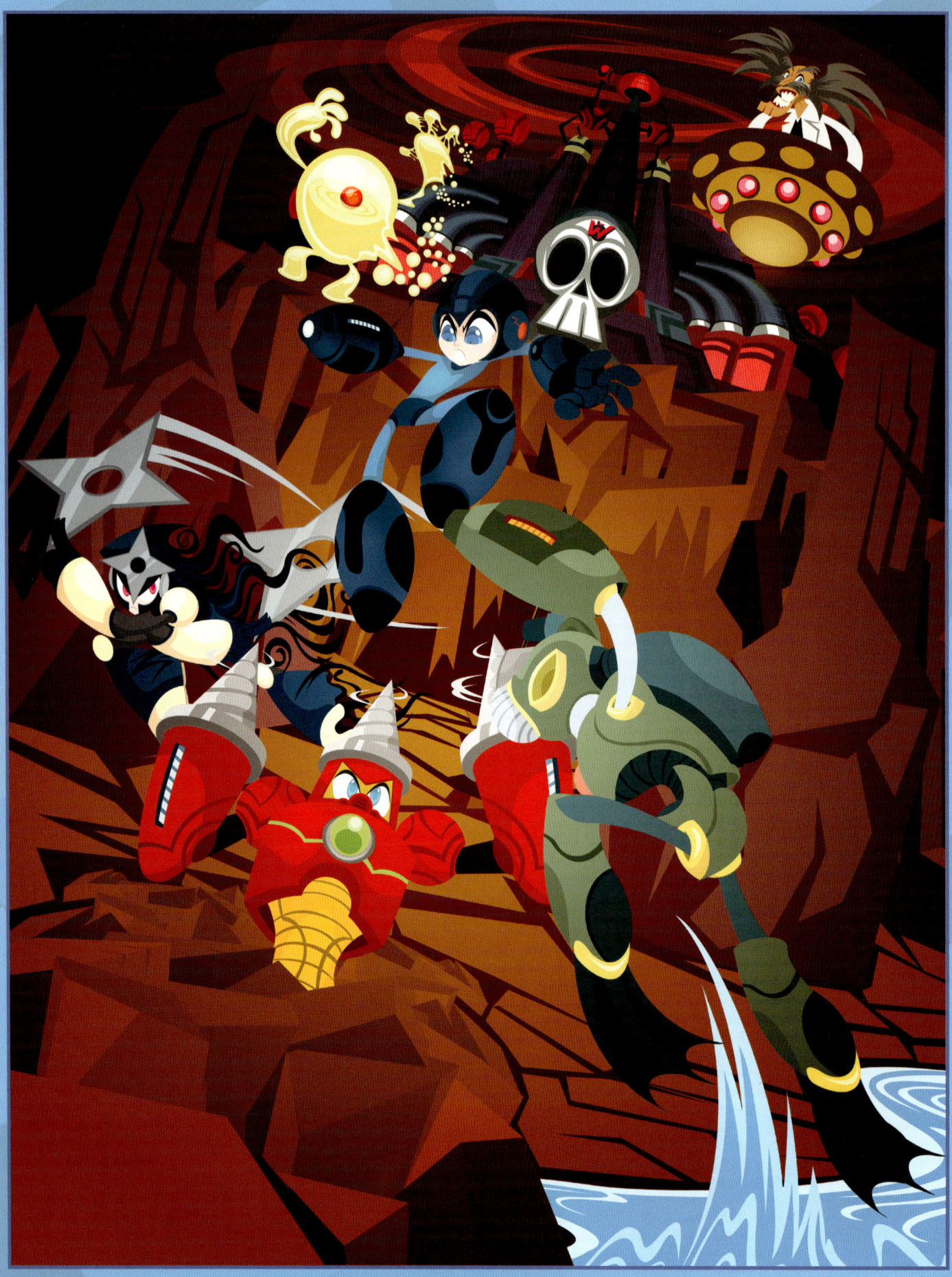

MANUEL MOLOHUA (SAMOLO)
Xalapa, Mexico
samolo.deviantart.com
Illustrator

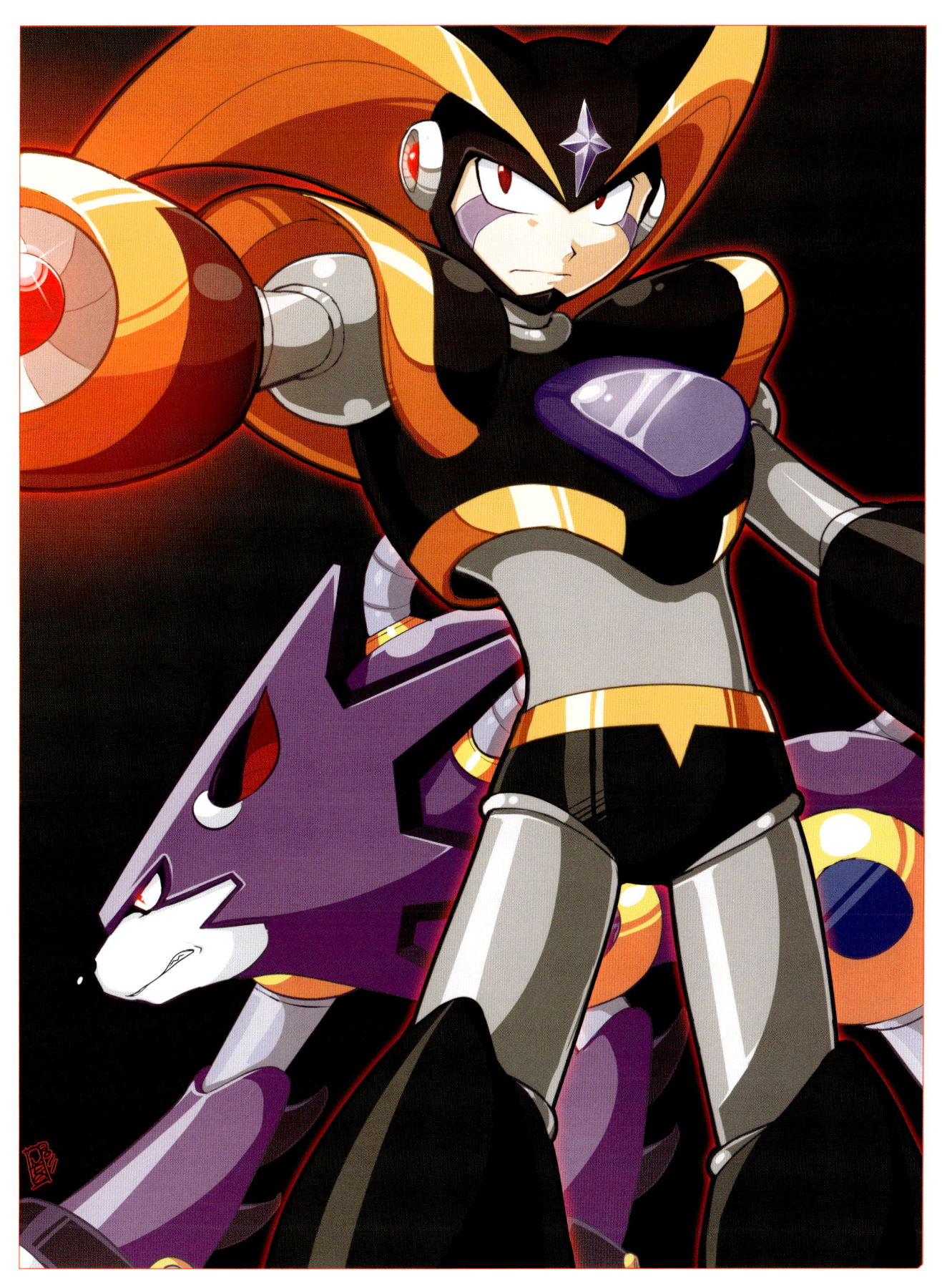

NICOLE DUBOIS (NEOLUCKY)
Poulsbo, WA, United States
neolucky.deviantart.com
Illustrator

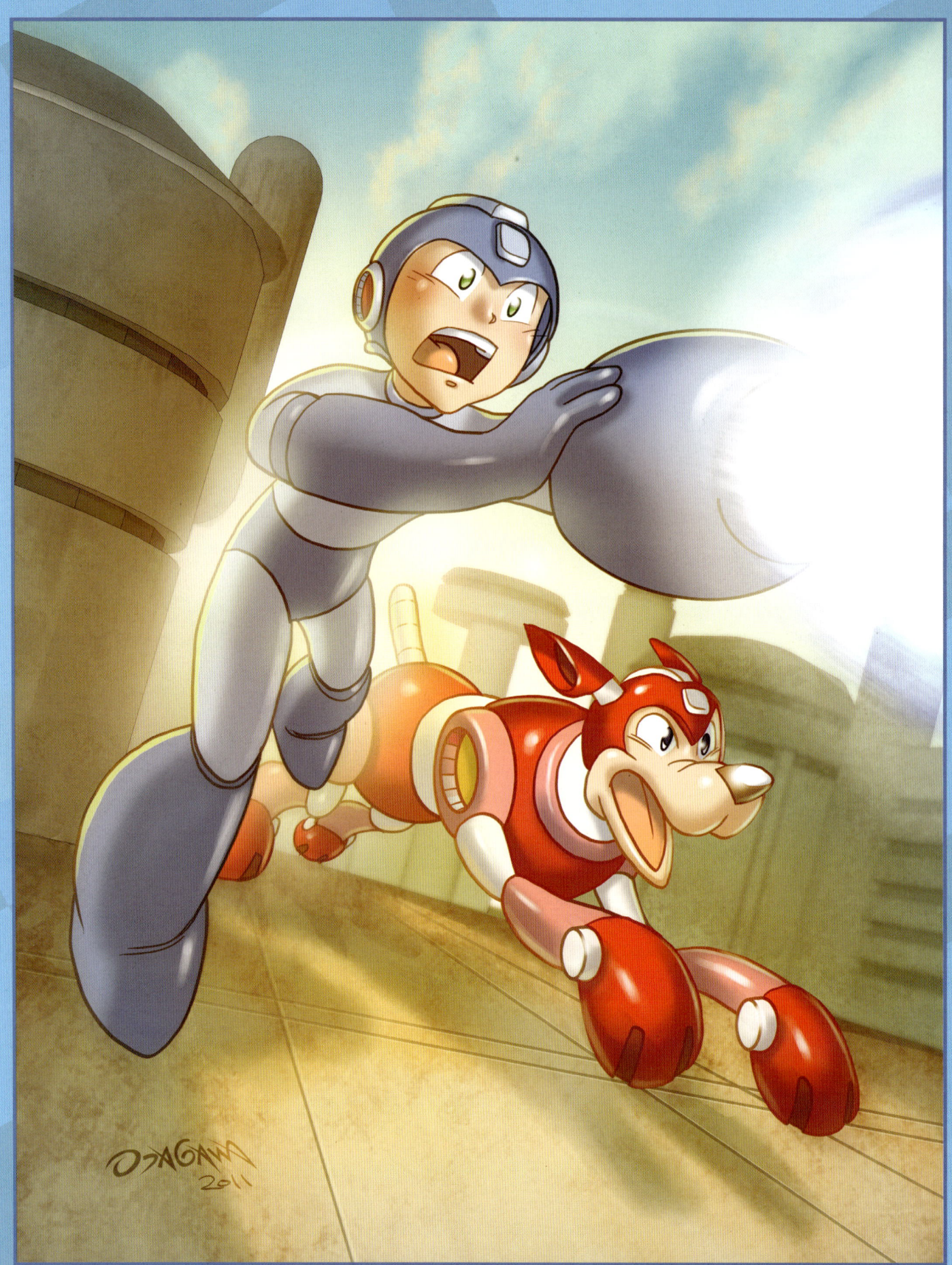

RYAN ODAGAWA
Rosemead, CA, United States
rmo120.deviantart.com
Illustrator
(Heroes Online Comic / Iron Man / Resident Evil)

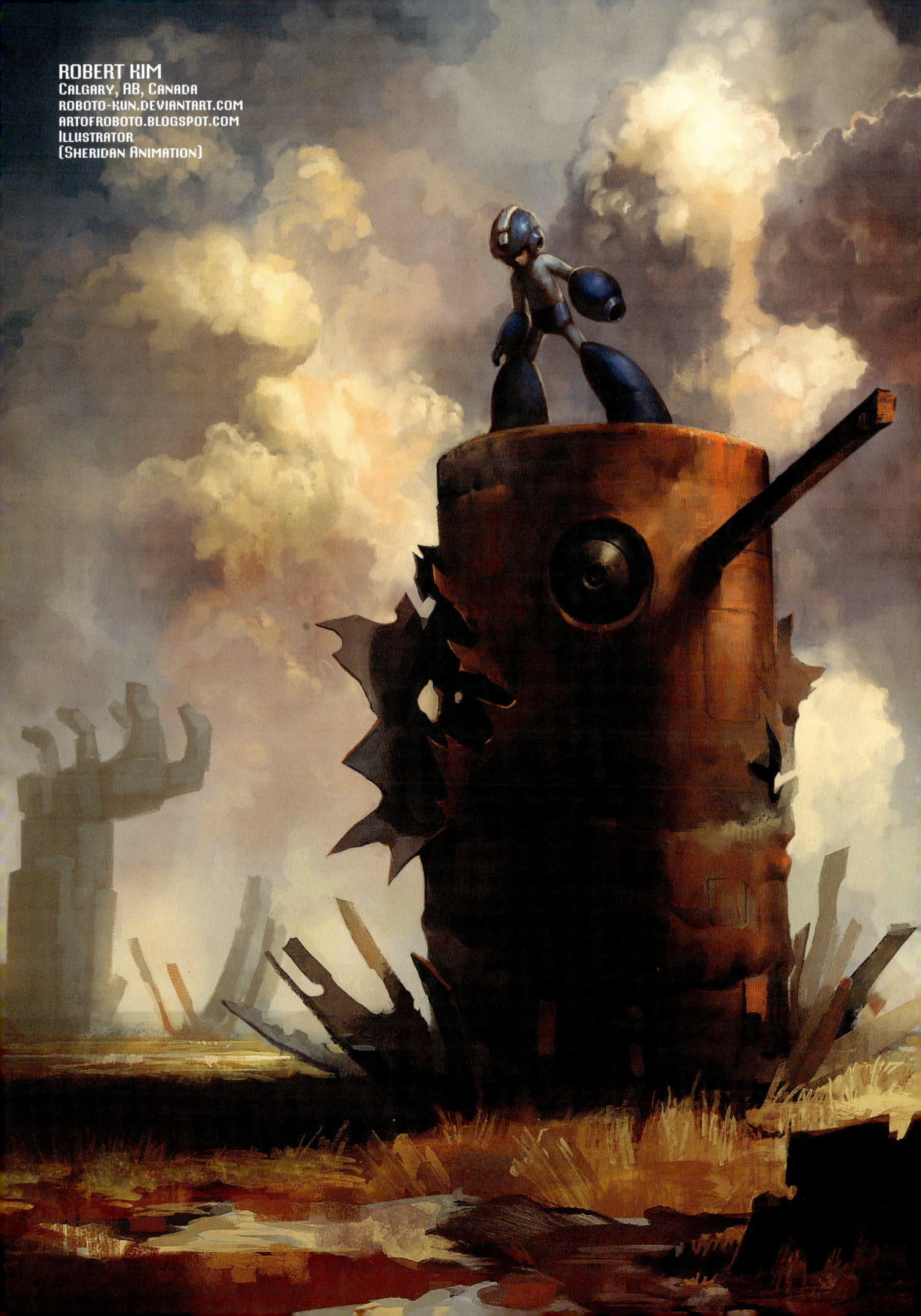

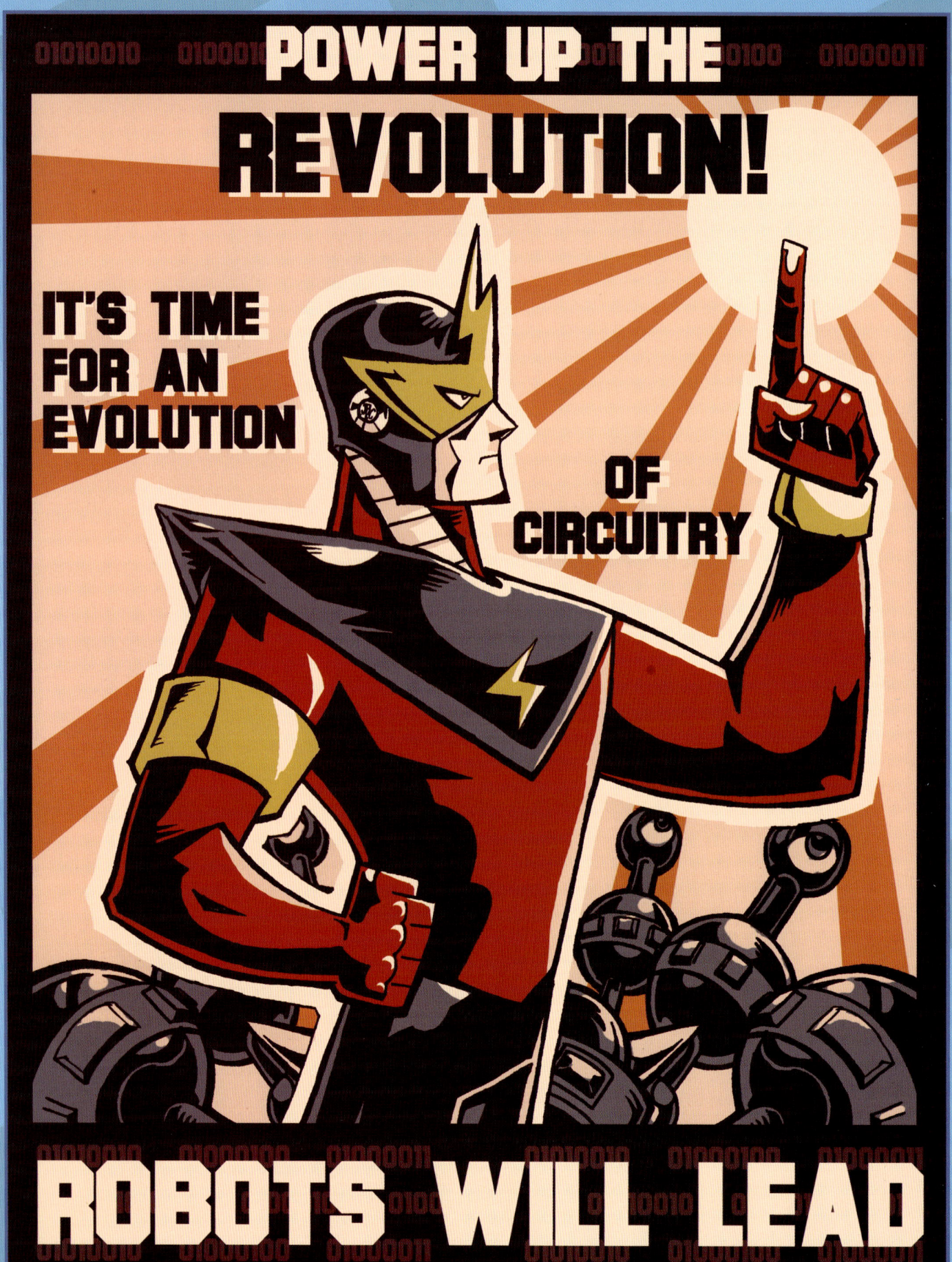

ROCCO COMMISSO
Guelph, ON, Canada
http://www.tippedchair.com/
Illustrator/ Animator
(Darkstalkers Tribute / The MEGAS band artist / Ninja Buger illustrator)

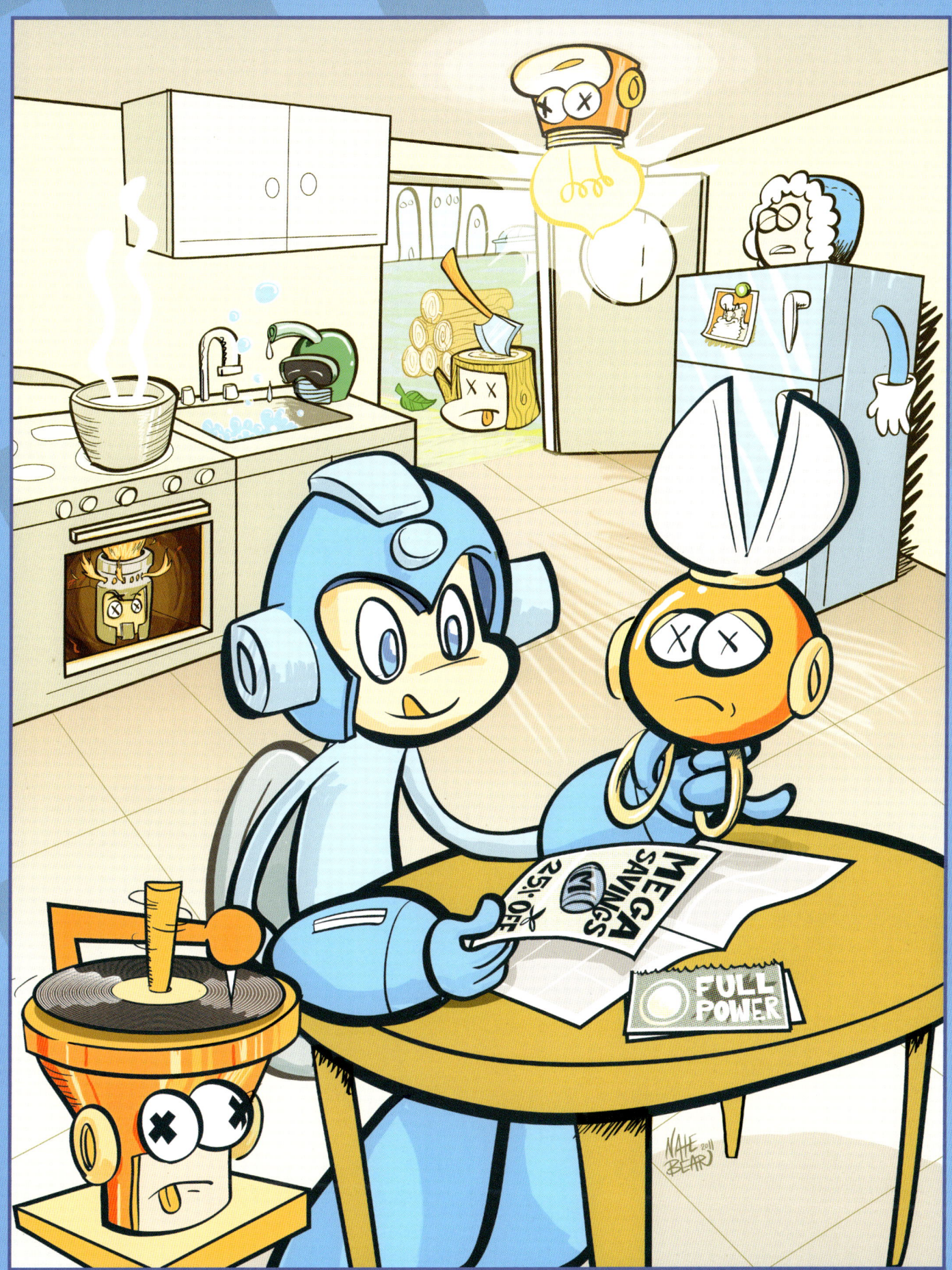

NATE BEAR
Brooklyn, NY, United States
www.natebearart.com
Illustrator
(Bear Brains Comics)

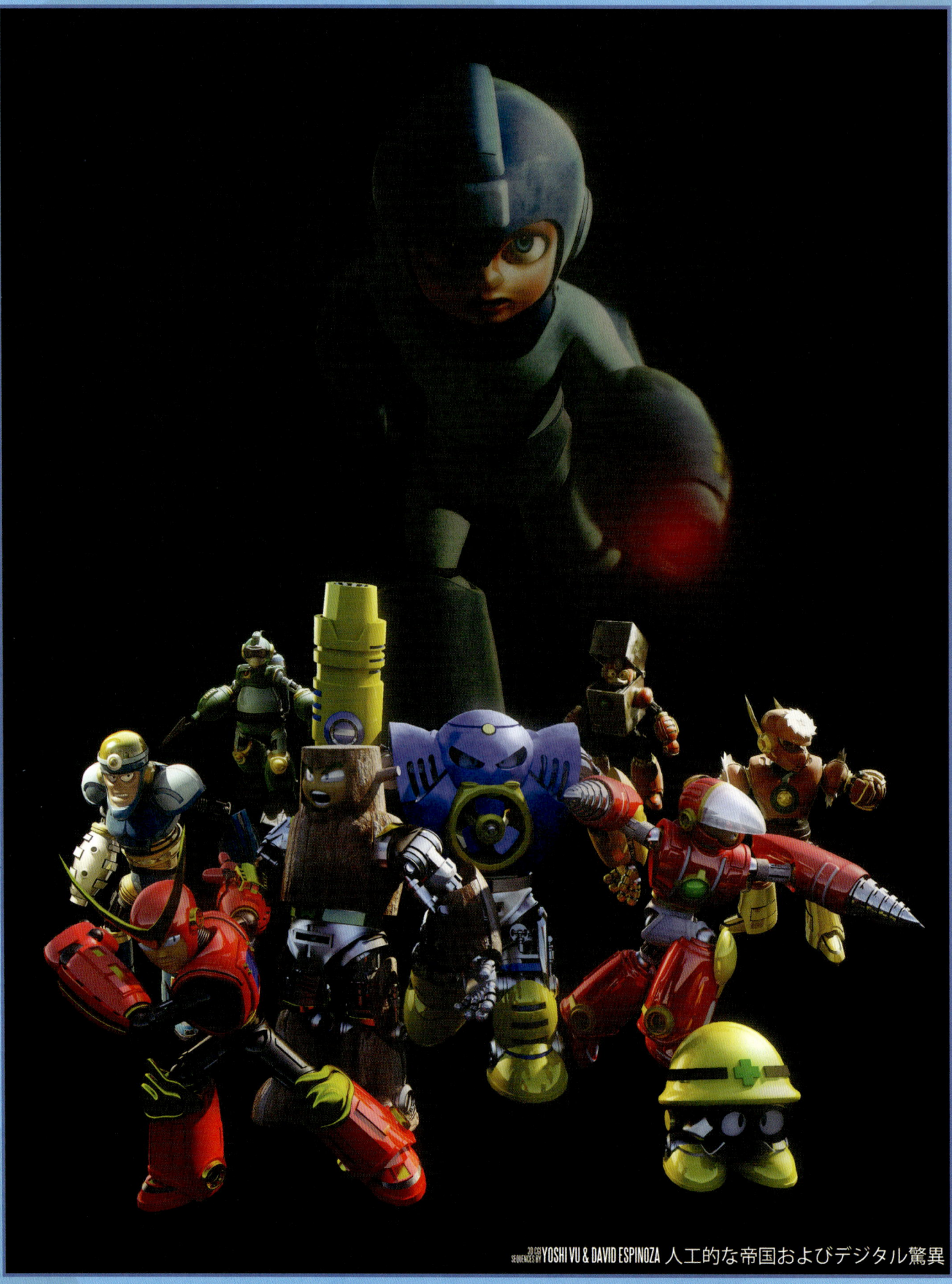

3D CGI SEQUENCES BY YOSHI VU & DAVID ESPINOZA 人工的な帝国およびデジタル驚異

YOSHI VU
Anaheim, CA, United States
3D Artist

DAVID ESPINOZA
Anaheim, CA, United States
www.digitolwonder.com
Digital Artist
(Live Free or Die Hard / Neverwinter Ngiths 2 /
Star Wars: Knights of the Old Republic 2)

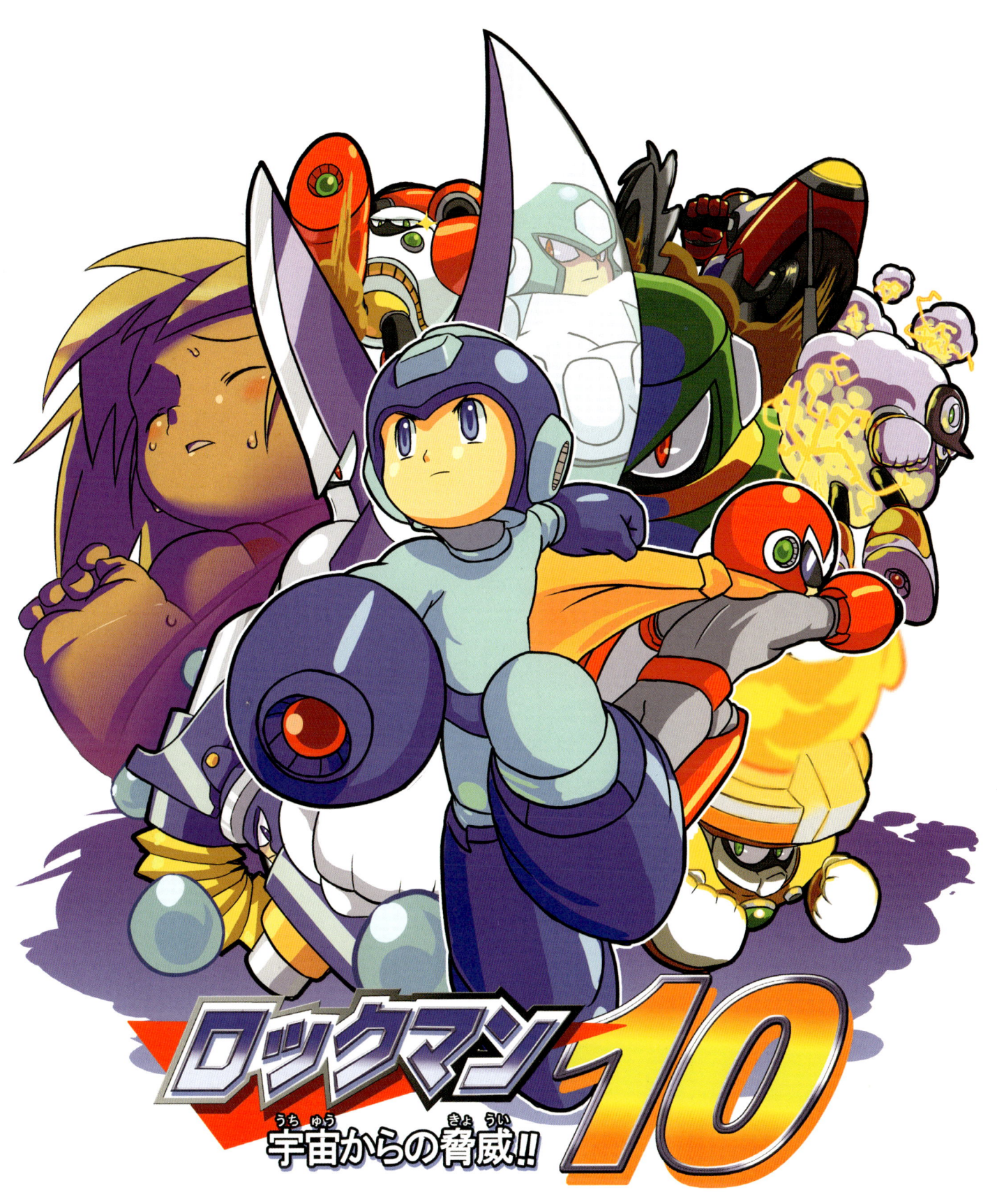

YADZA LAFALIKA (CESSA)
Bogor, Indonesia
Illustrator and Designer

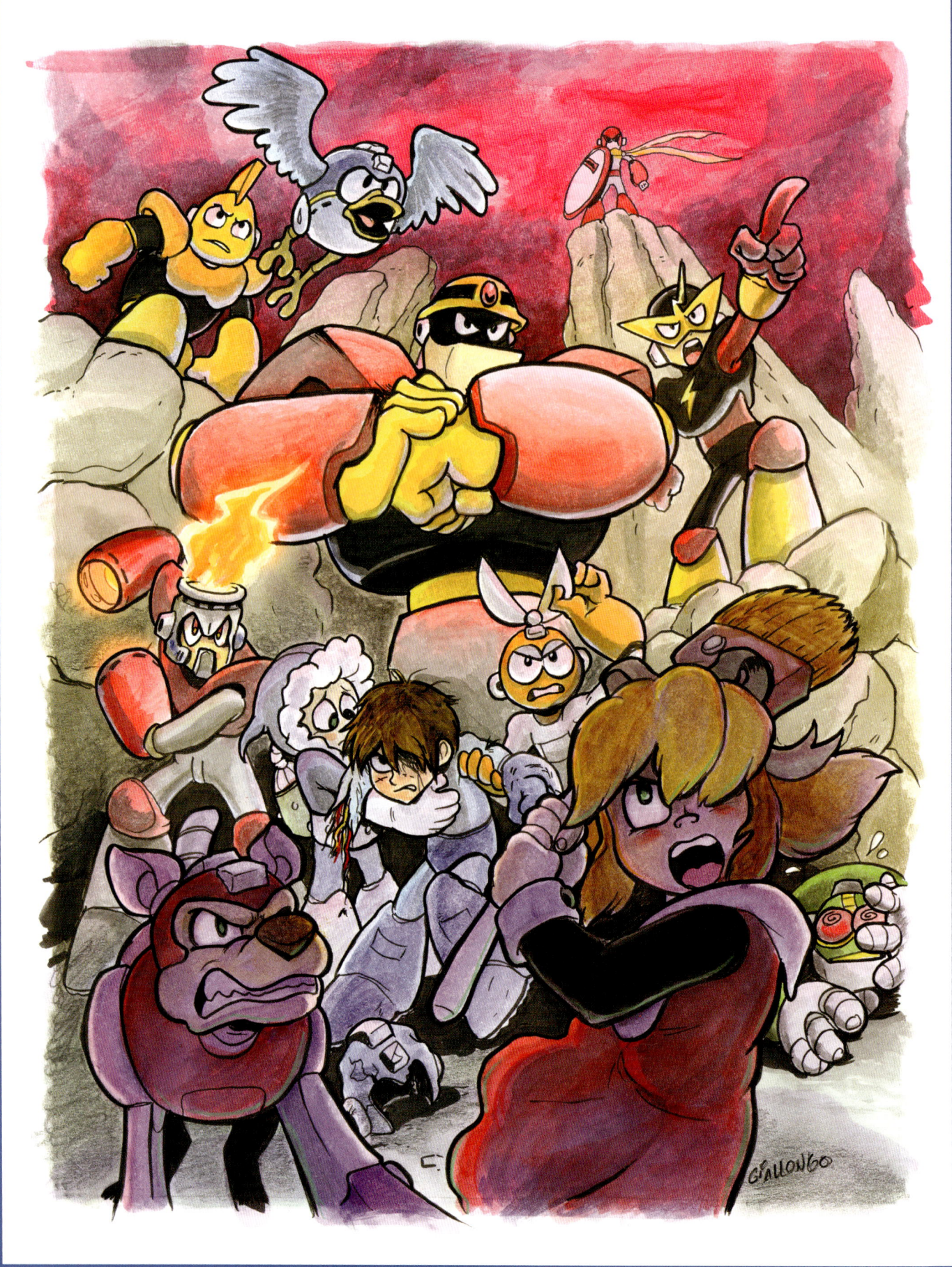

ZACK GIALLONGO
New York, NY, United States
www.zackgiallongo.com
Illustrator

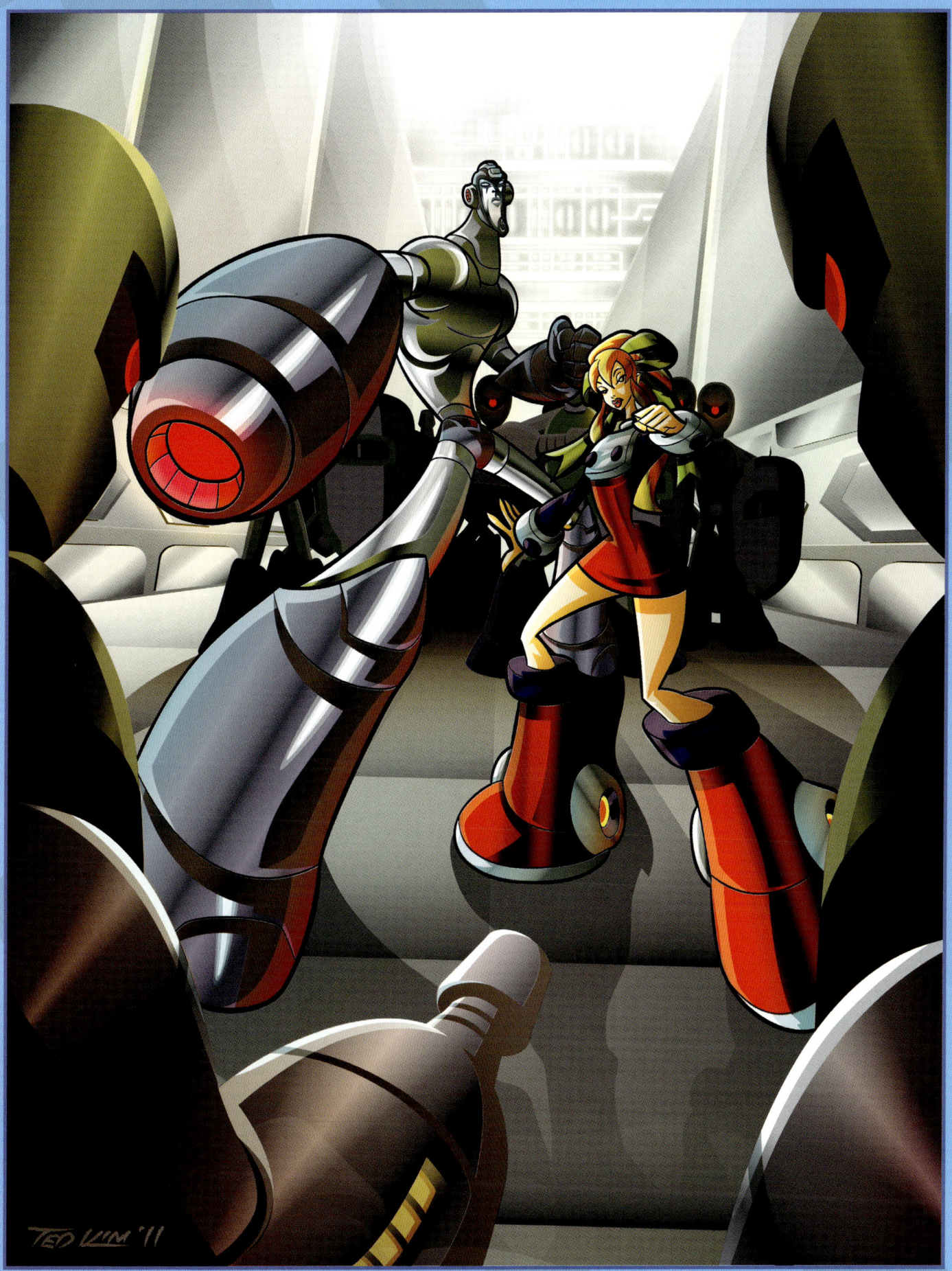

TED KIM
Richmond Hill, ON, Canada
www.tedkimchee.com
Illustrator / Concept Artist
(Full Auto series / Cel Damage / Champions Universe)

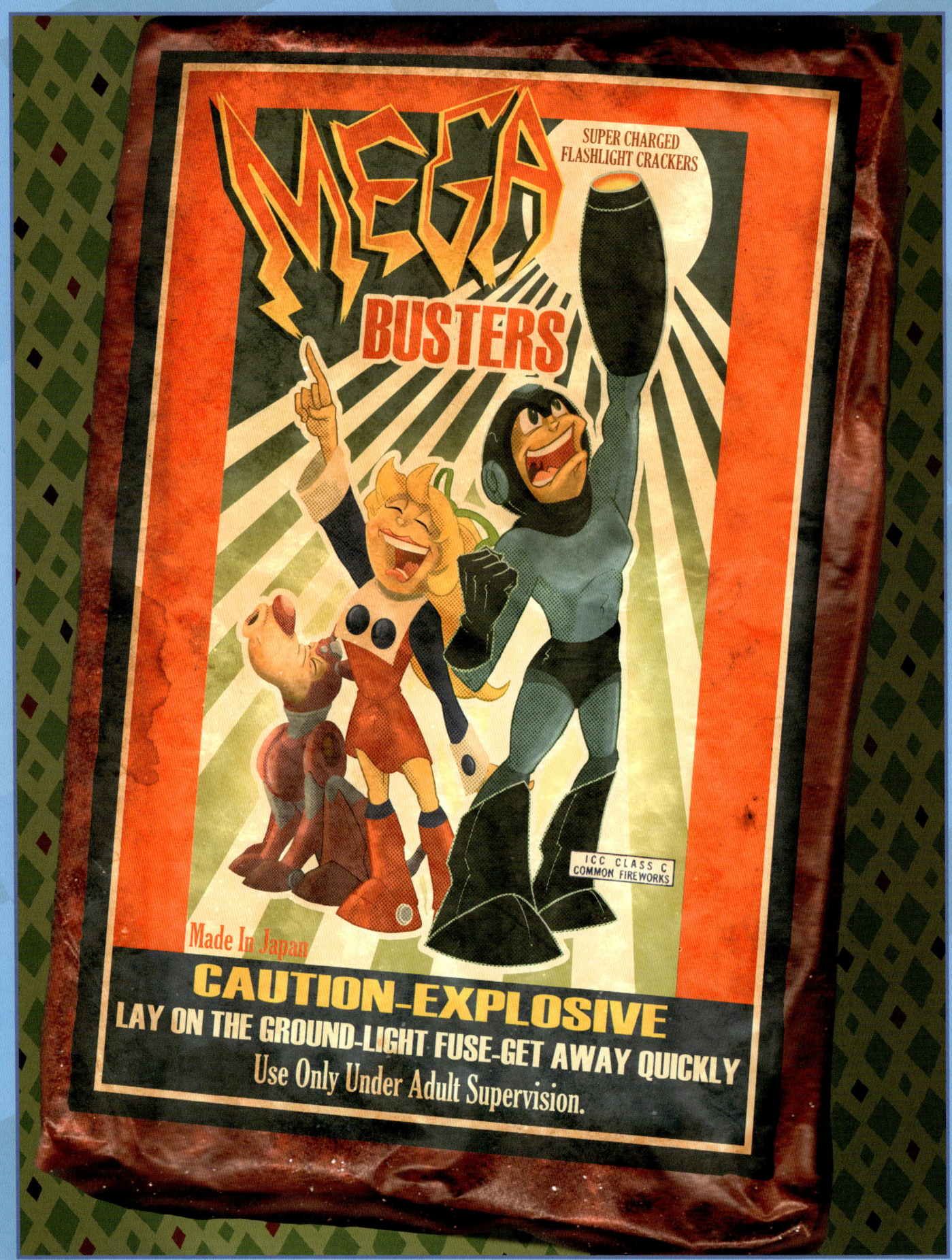

JUSTIN ORR
Parkland, CA, United States
www.jusscope.com
Artist
(Jusscope 2 In One / Jusscope Contents Under Pressure)

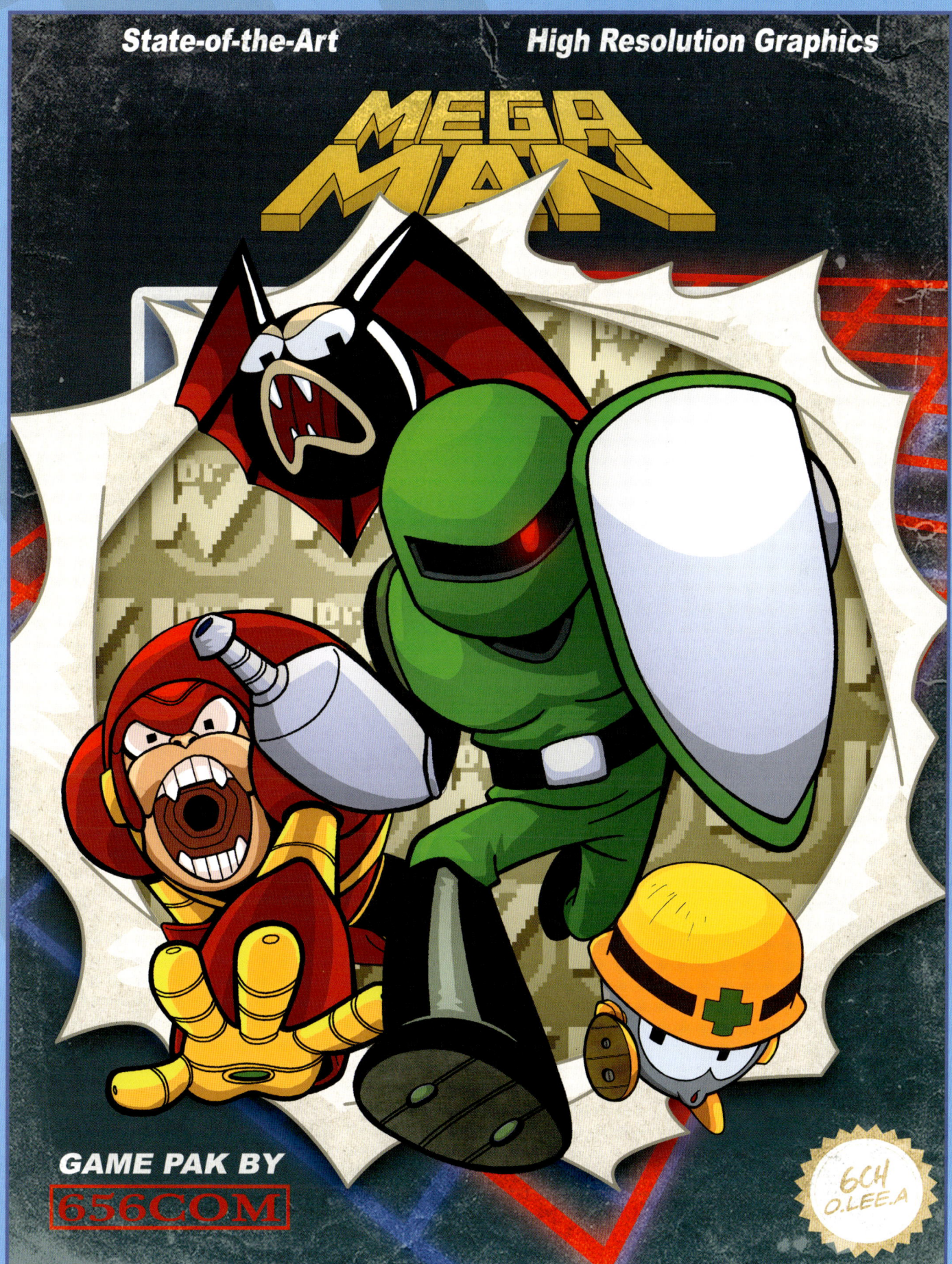

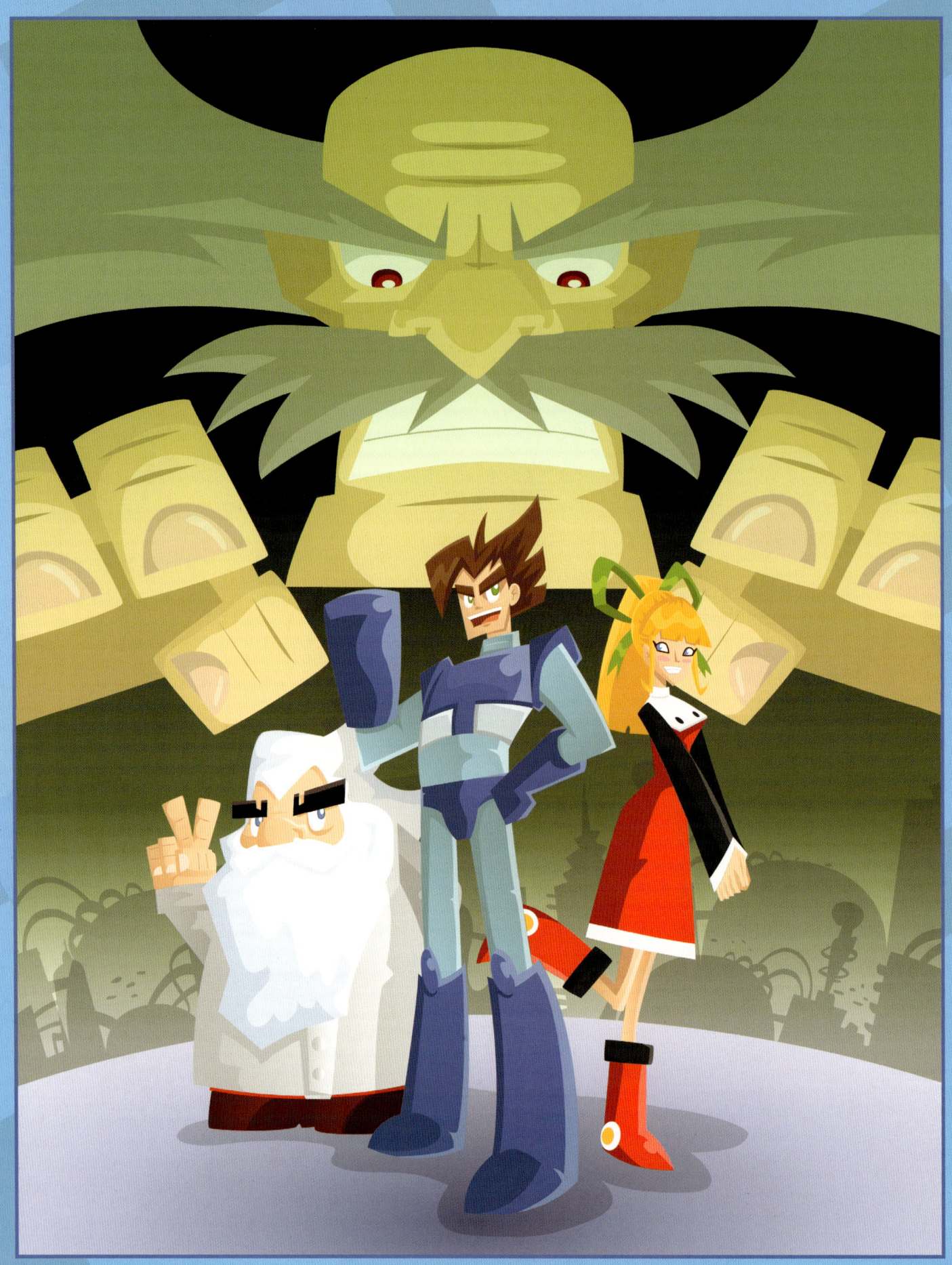

RUBEN LARA (PINGOLITO)
Saltillo, Mexico
pingolito.deviantart.com
Digital Animator

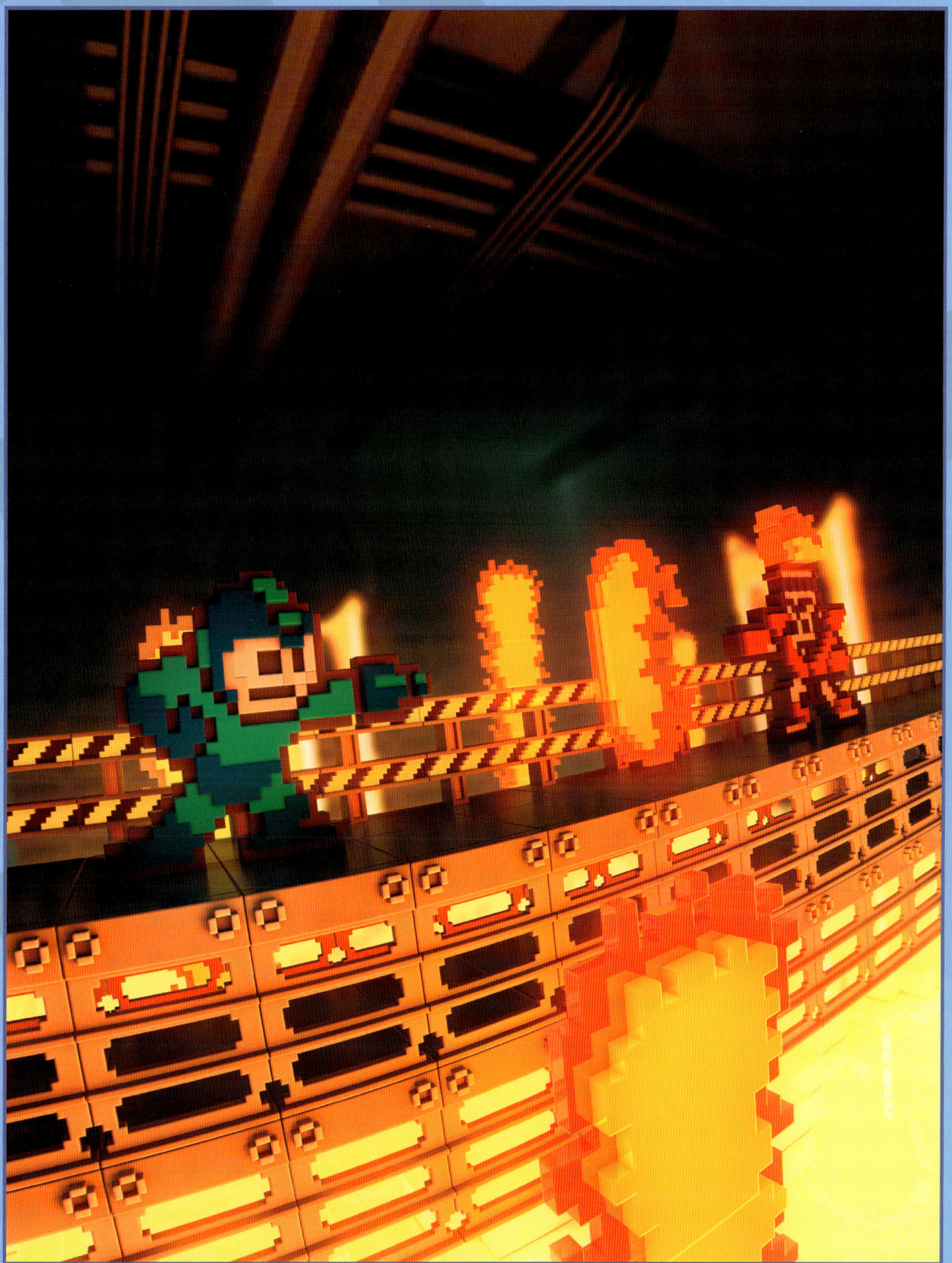

MARCUS PENNA
São Paulo, Brazil
3D and pixel artist
(Colorist on Mesmo Delivery)

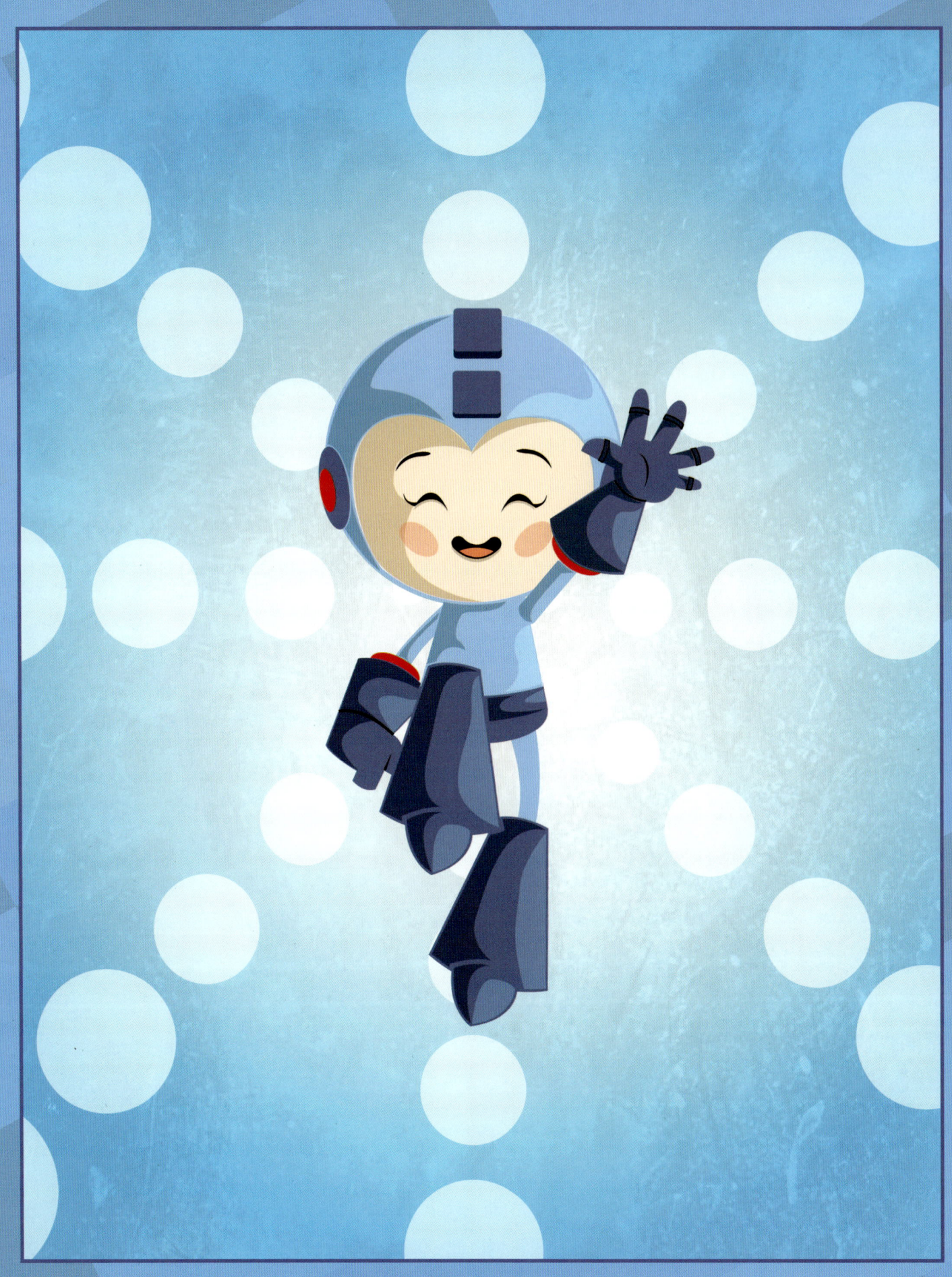

ROSA RAMIREZ (ROSA FRESINA)
Tijuana, Mexico
rosinafresina.blogspot.com
Illustrator

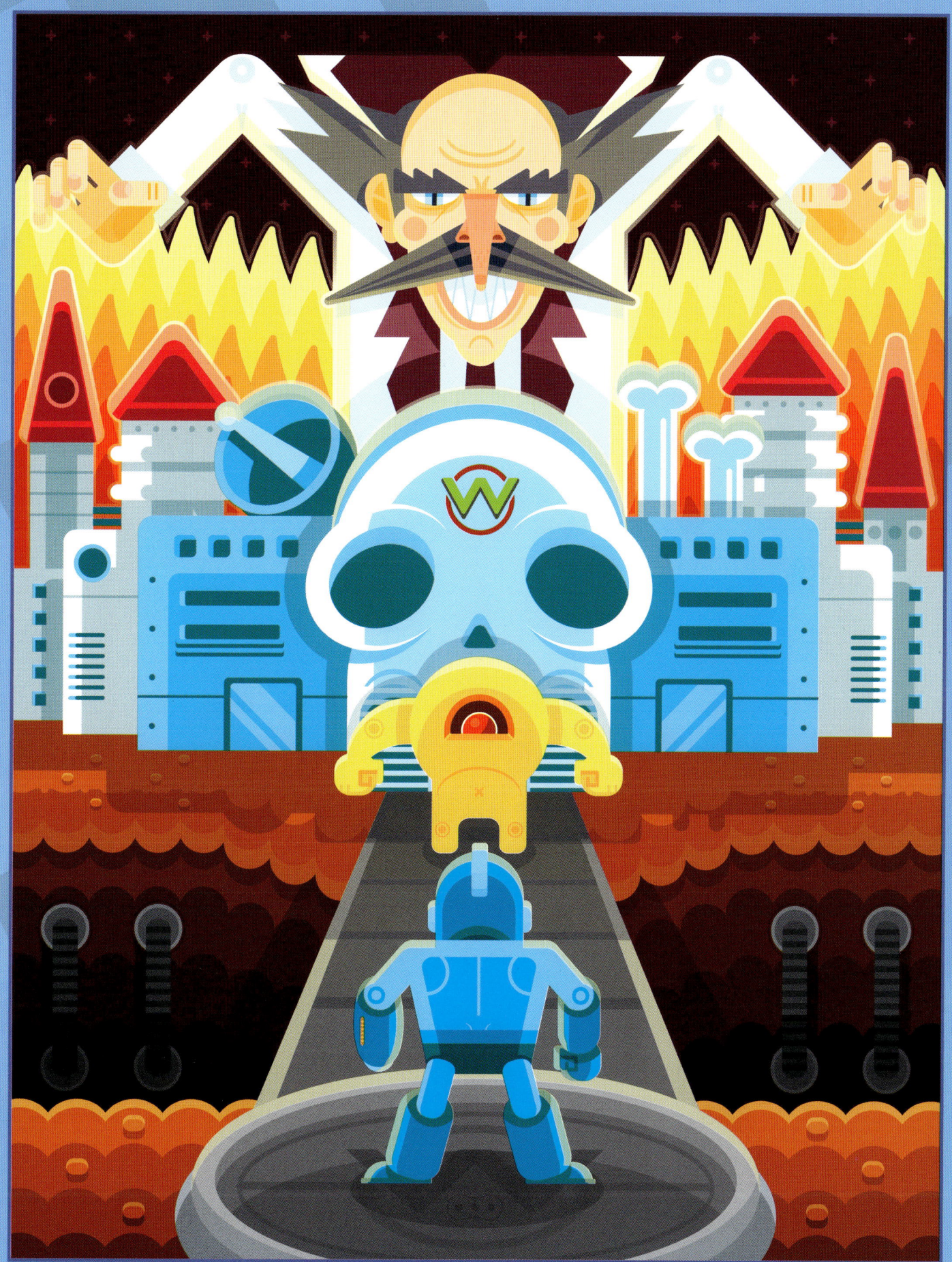

BETO GARZA (HELBETICO)
Monterrey, Mexico
helbetico.deviantart.com
Illustrator

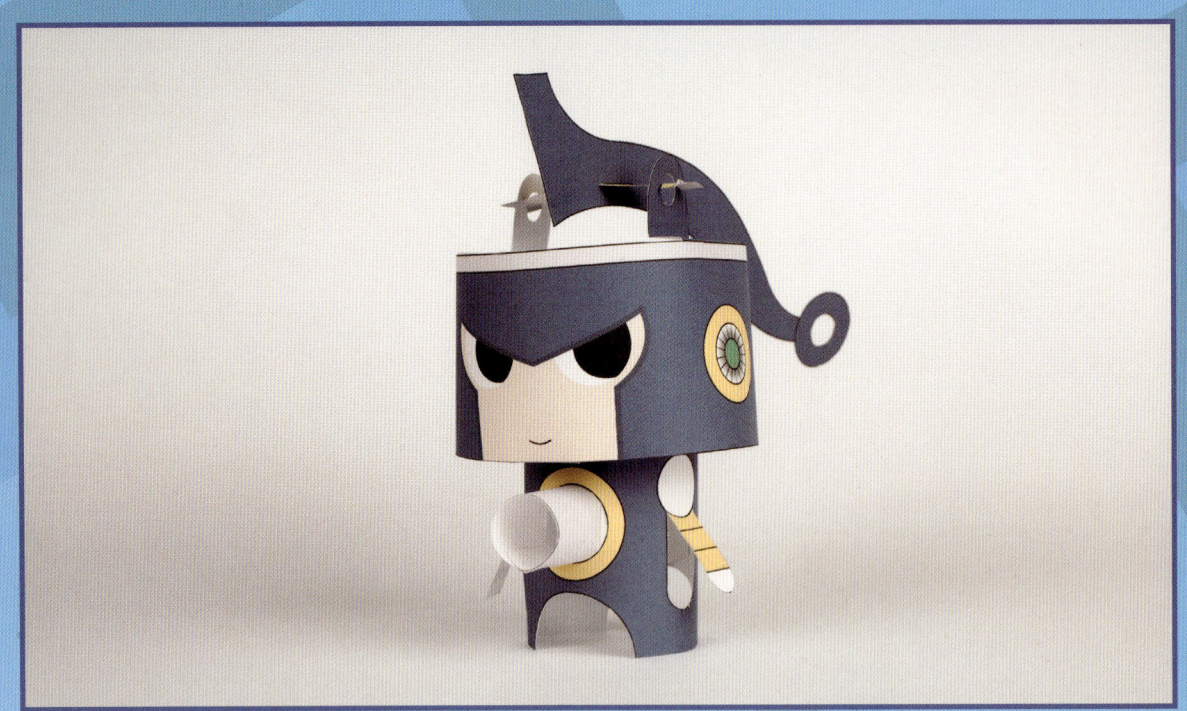

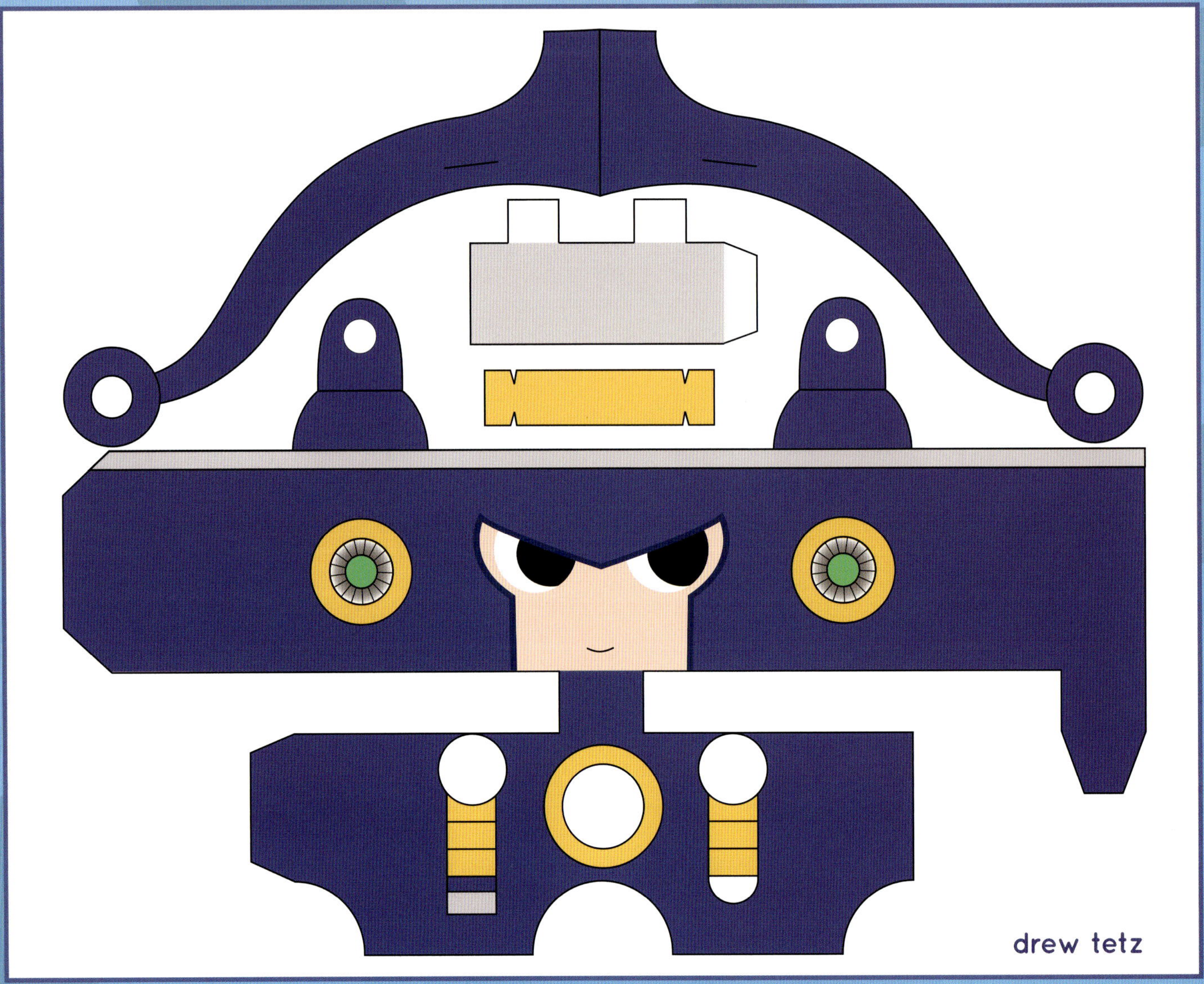

DREW TETZ
Silver Spring, MD, United States
www.drewtetz.com
Graphic Designer

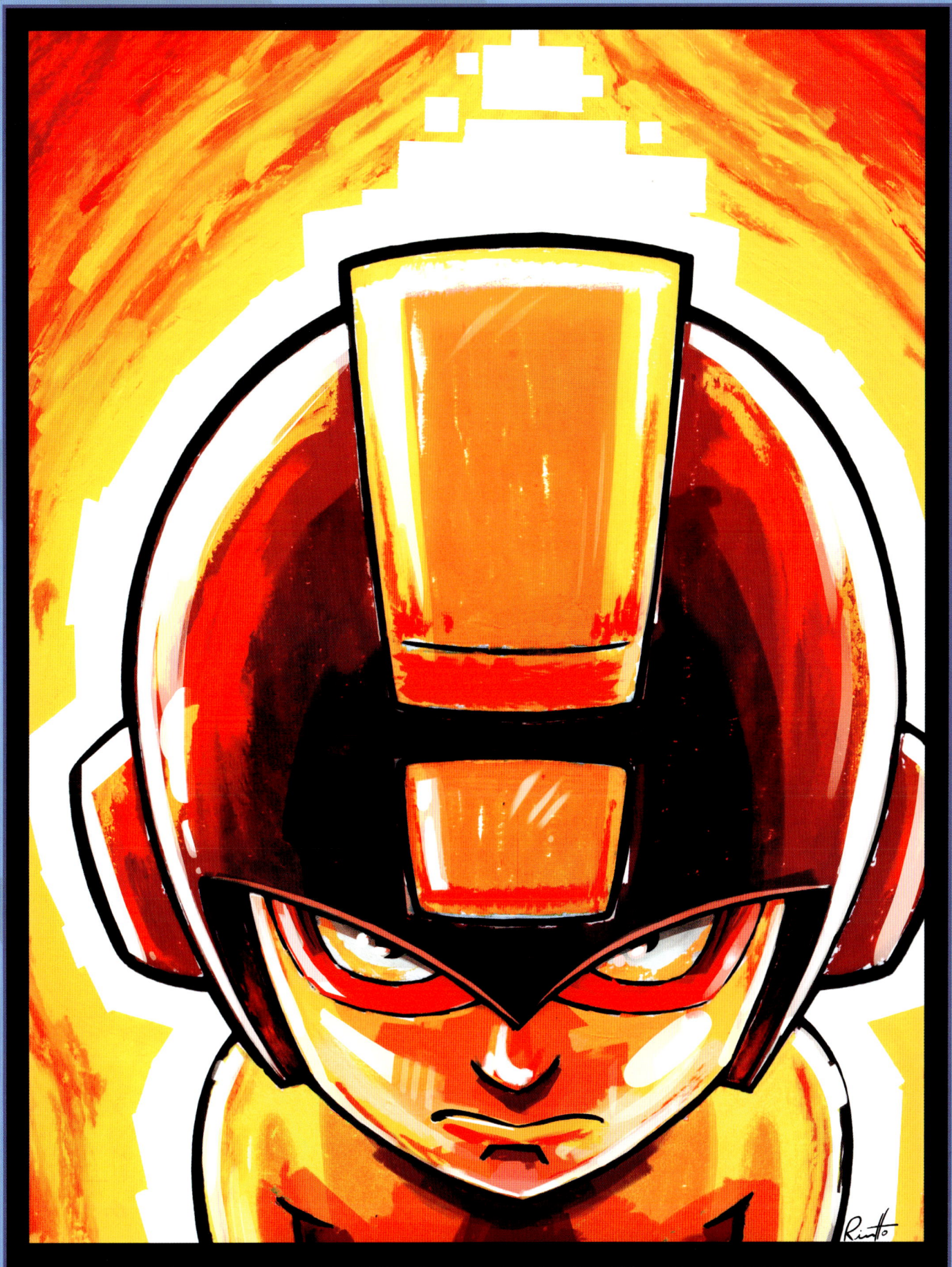

BOB RISSETTO
Elk Grove Village, IL, United States
bobrissetto.blogspot.com
Artist and Animator

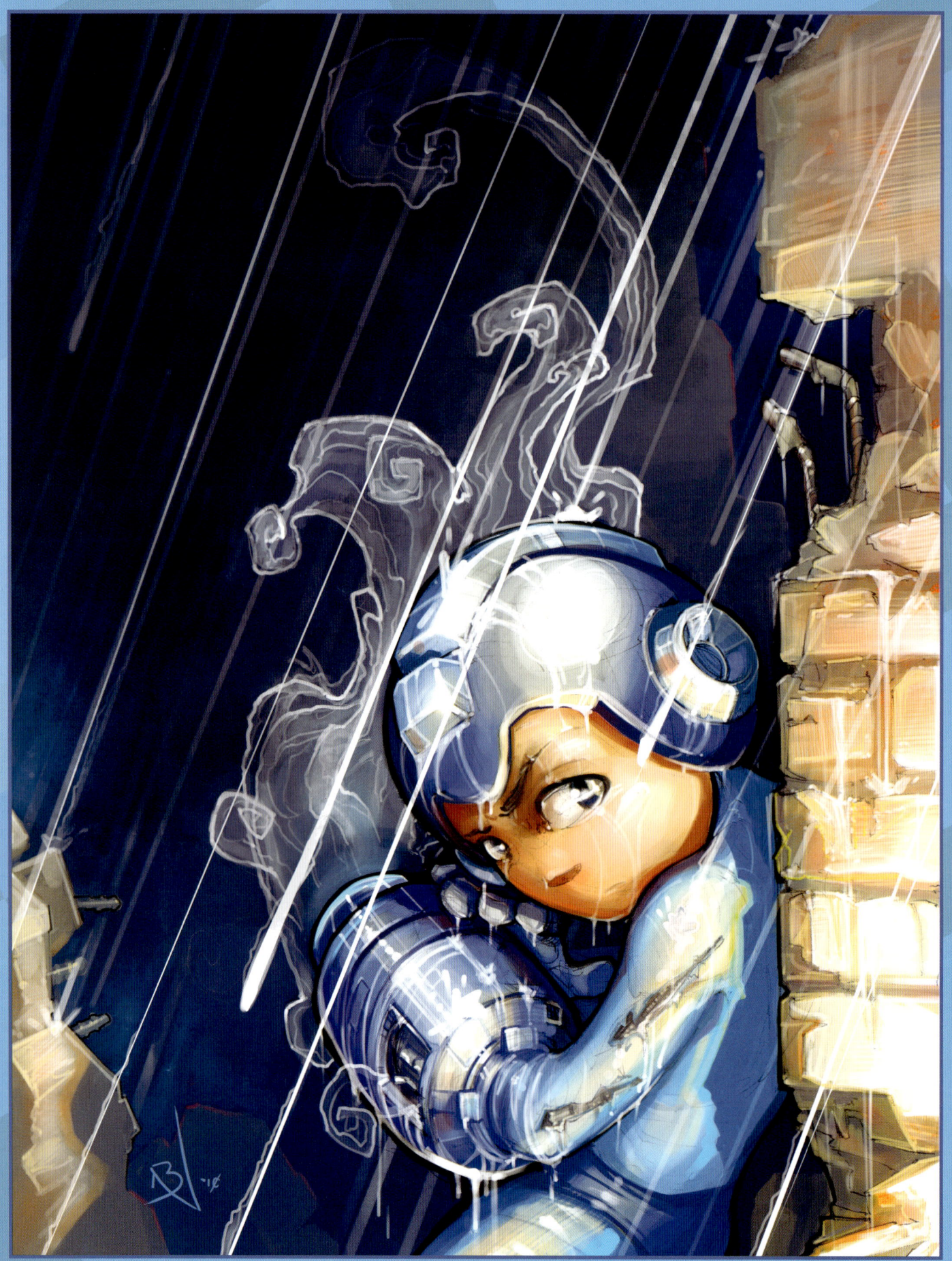

BRETT NIENBURG
Denver, CO, United States
www.brettnienburg.com
Lead Character Artist/Concept Artist

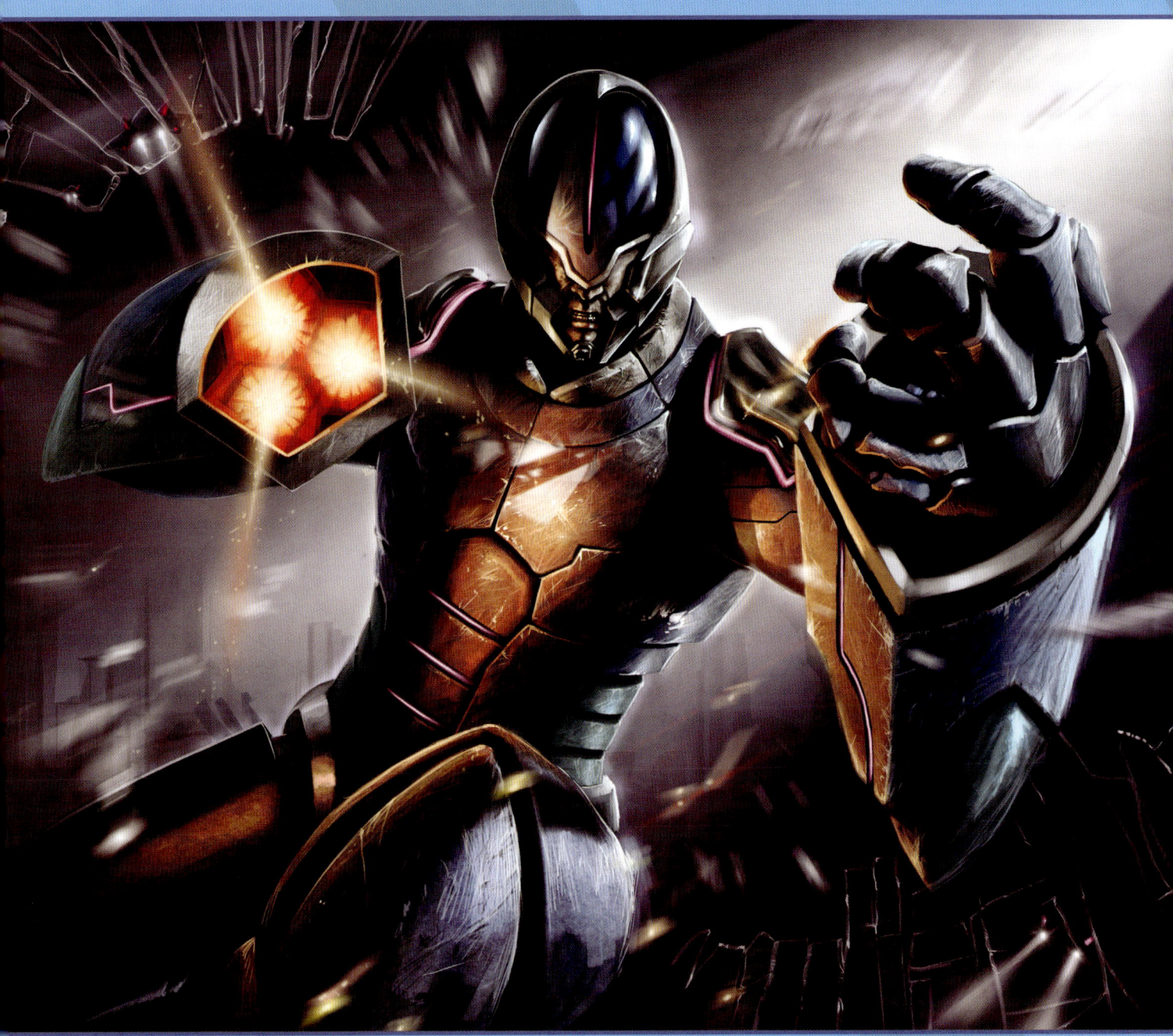

CRISTIAN MELIÁN
Las Palmas, Spain
www.cmcillustration.com
Illustrator

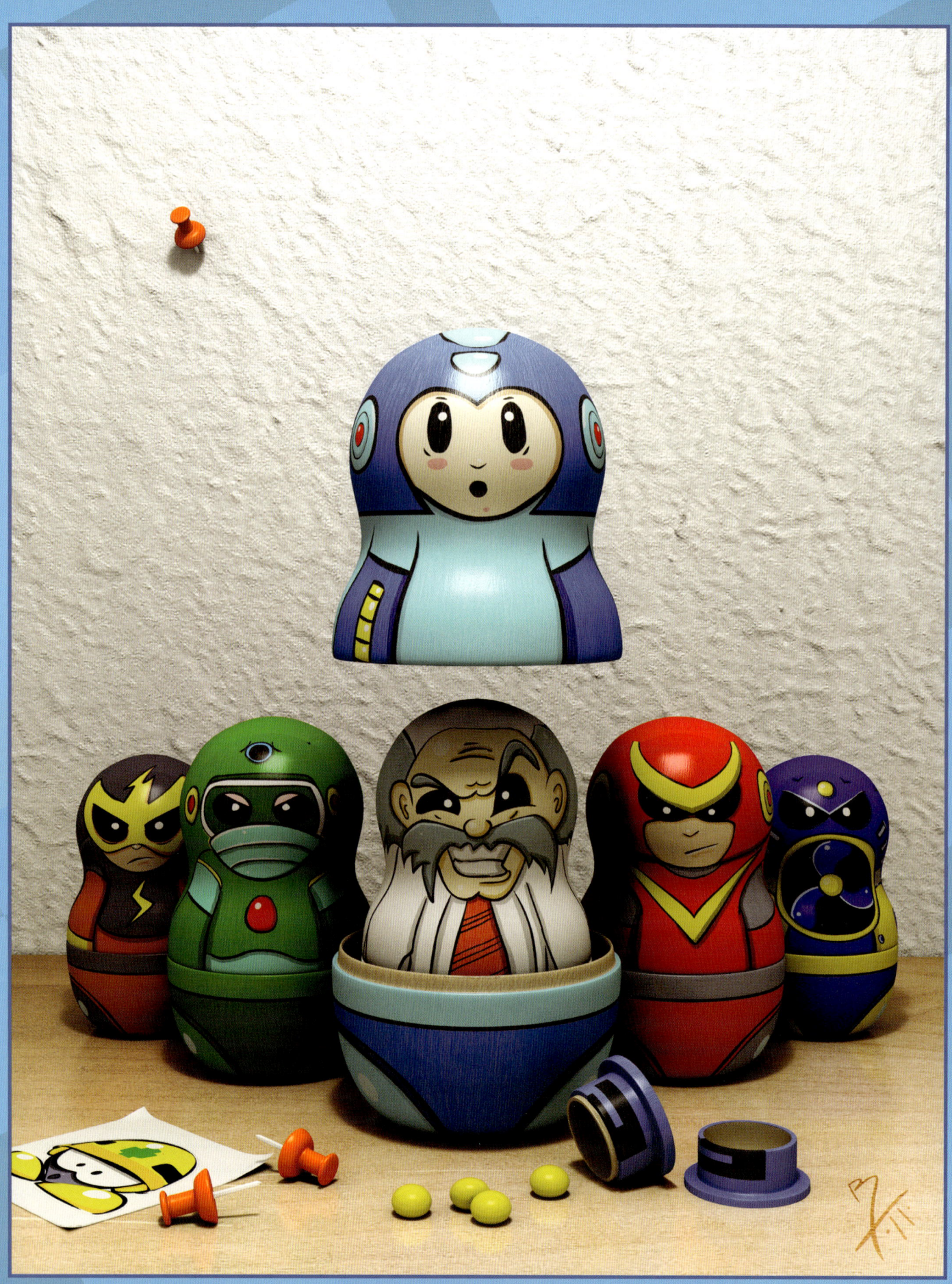

RICHARD BOUDEN
Portland, OR, United States
Texture Artist / Illustrator

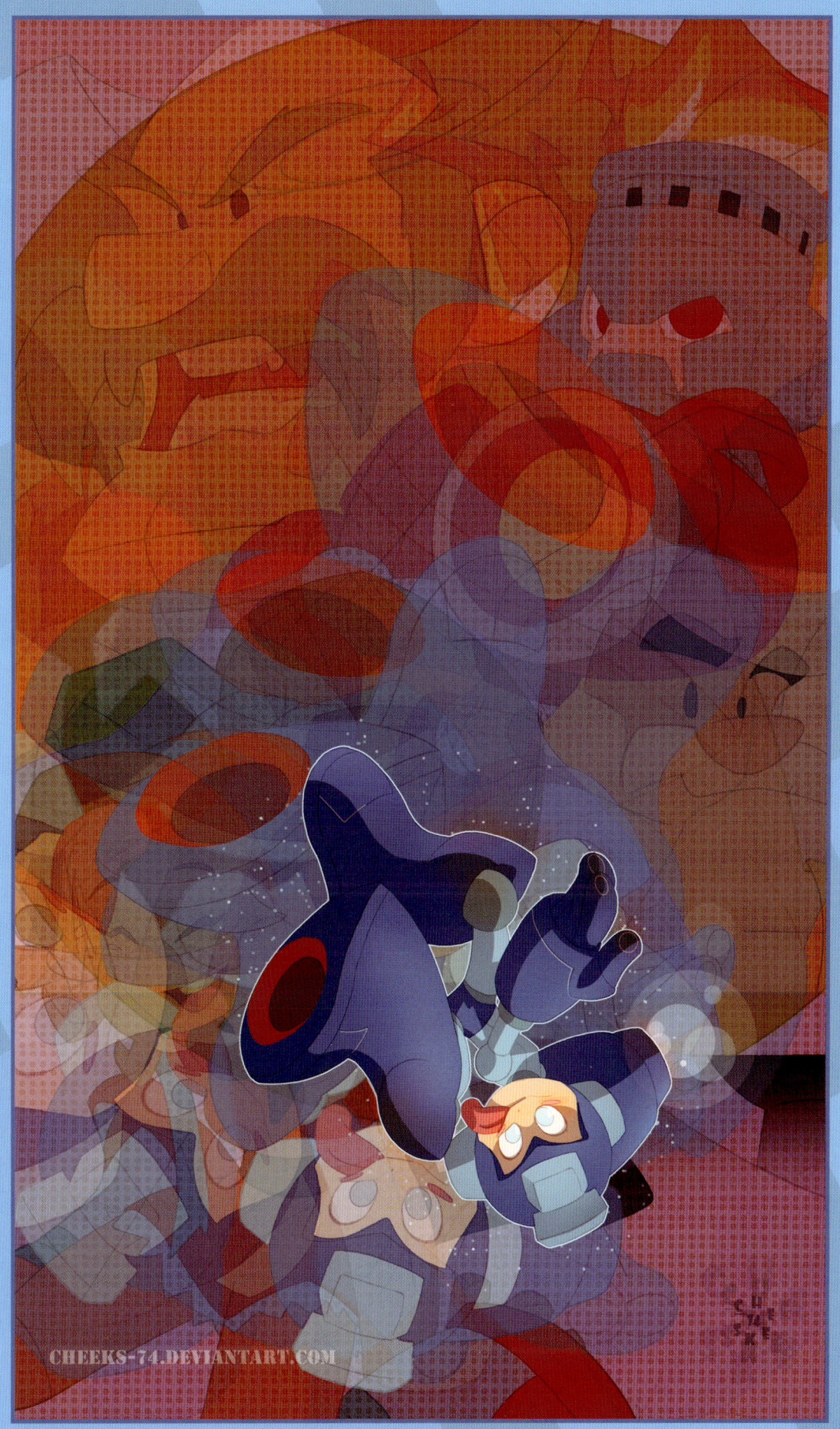

SEAN GALLOWAY (CHEEKS)
Los Angeles, CA, United States
gotcheeks.blogspot.com
Character designer / Comic Cover Artist
(spectacular spider-man, hellboy animated, Transformers Animated)

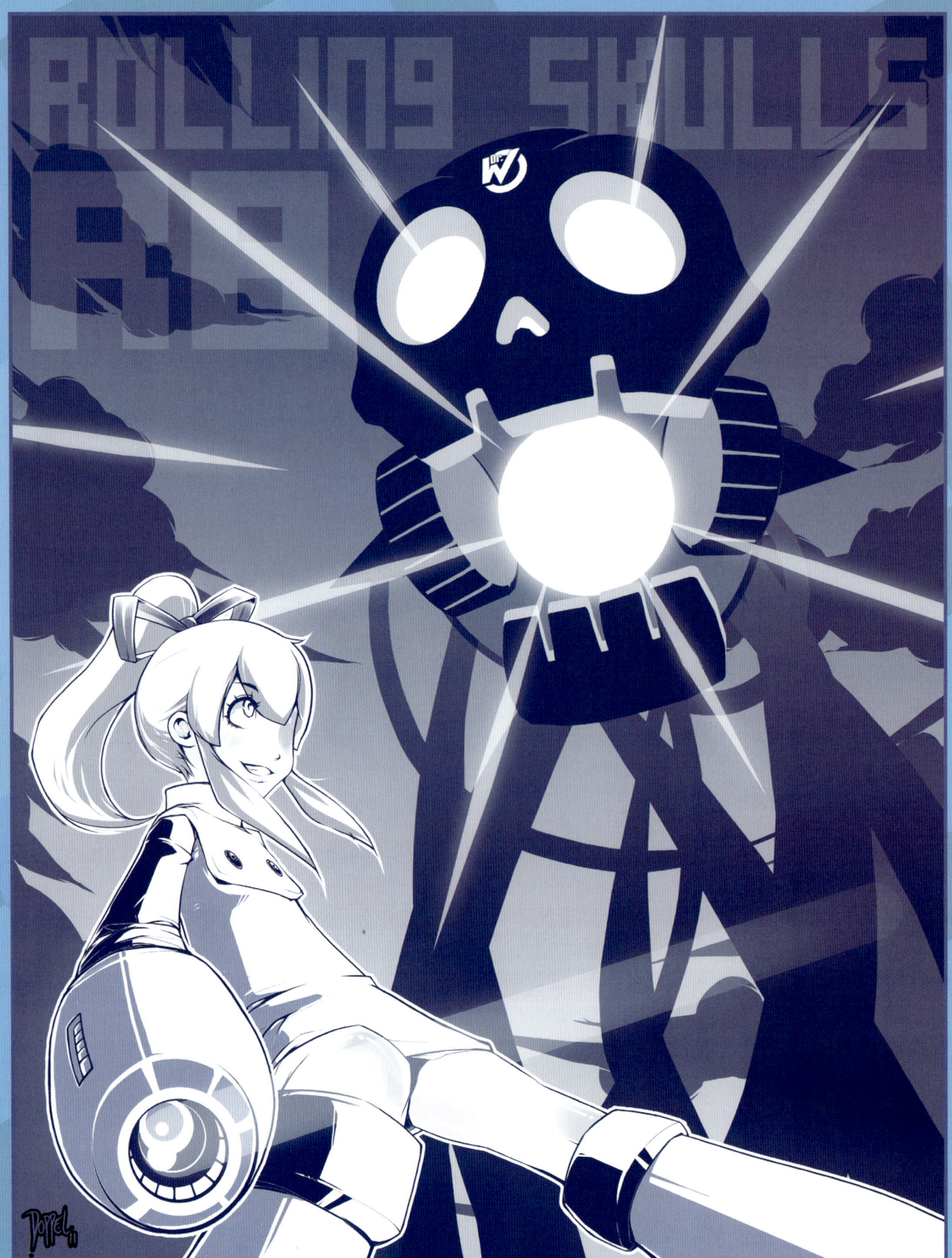

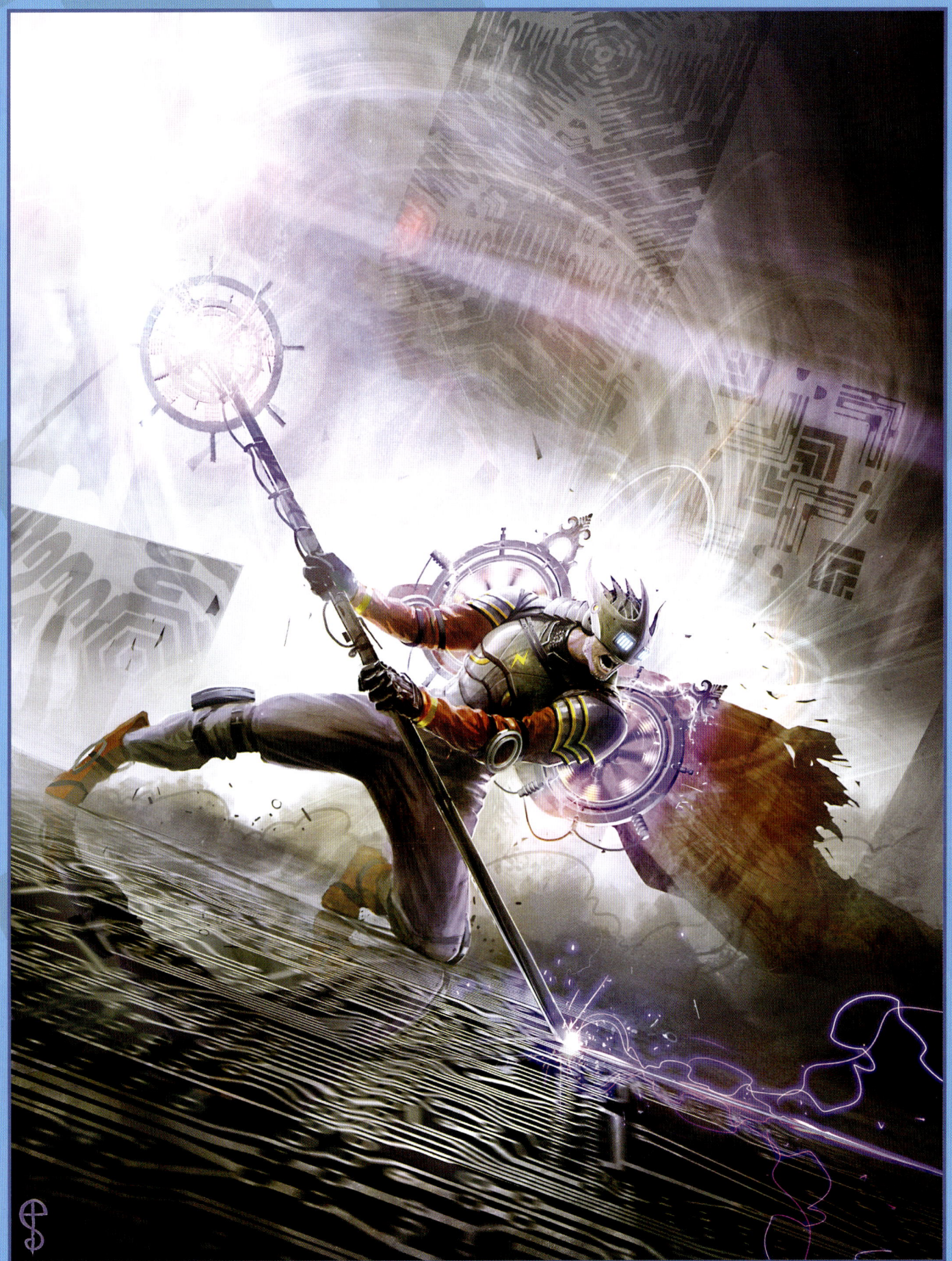

SPIKYTIGER
Montclair, NJ, United States
www.spikytiger.com
Illustrator
(Homefront / Henry Hatsworth / The Pier)

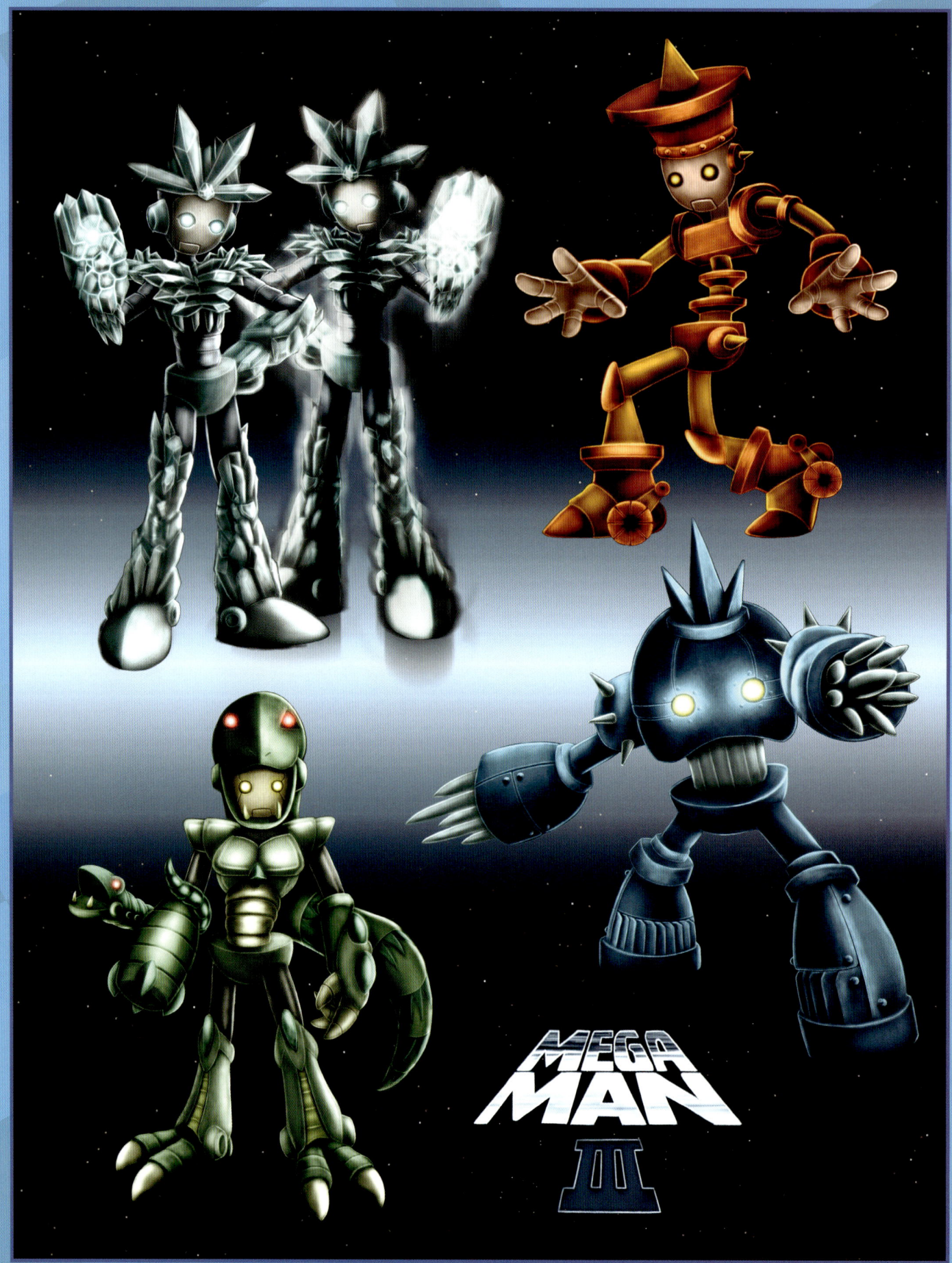

TONY CHRISTOU (PTHALLO)
Athens, Greece
www.TonyChristou.com
Illustrator

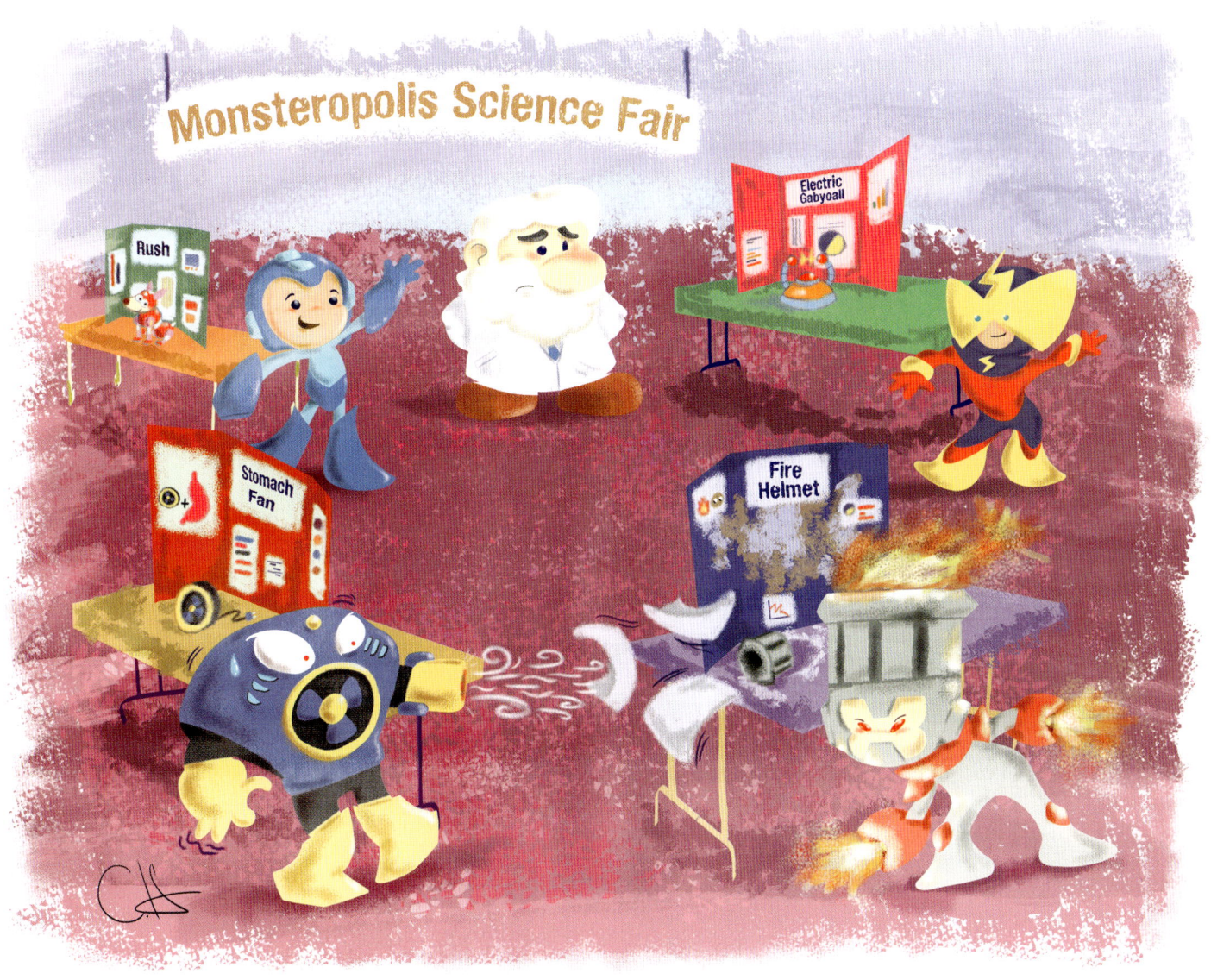

CHARLES HAMWEY
Encino, CA, United States
www.charleshamwey.com
Artist / Animator
(Animation Mentor / Cal State University Northridge)

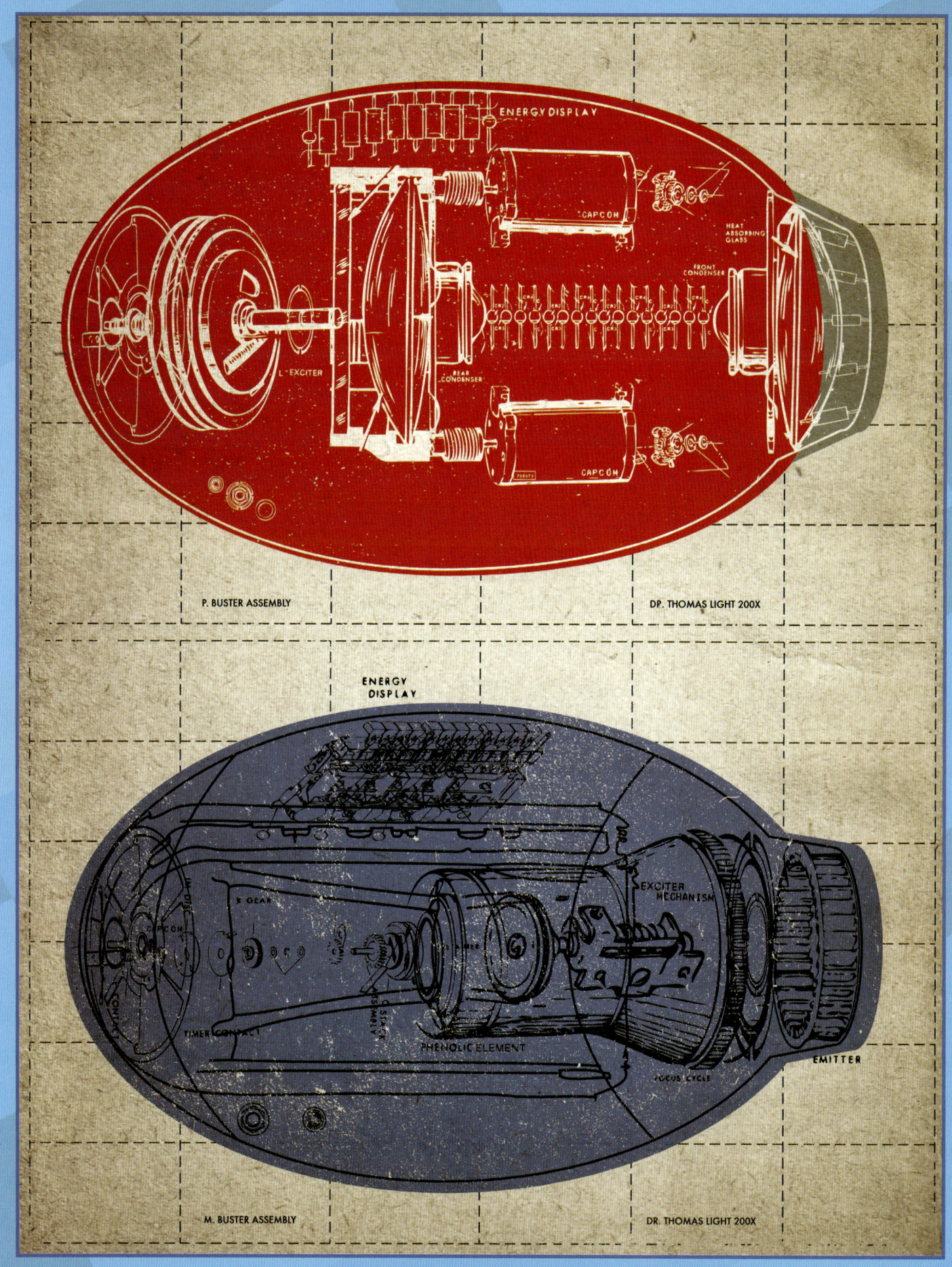

MILES DONOVAN
Somerville, MA, United States
www.thedailyrobot.com
Illustrator

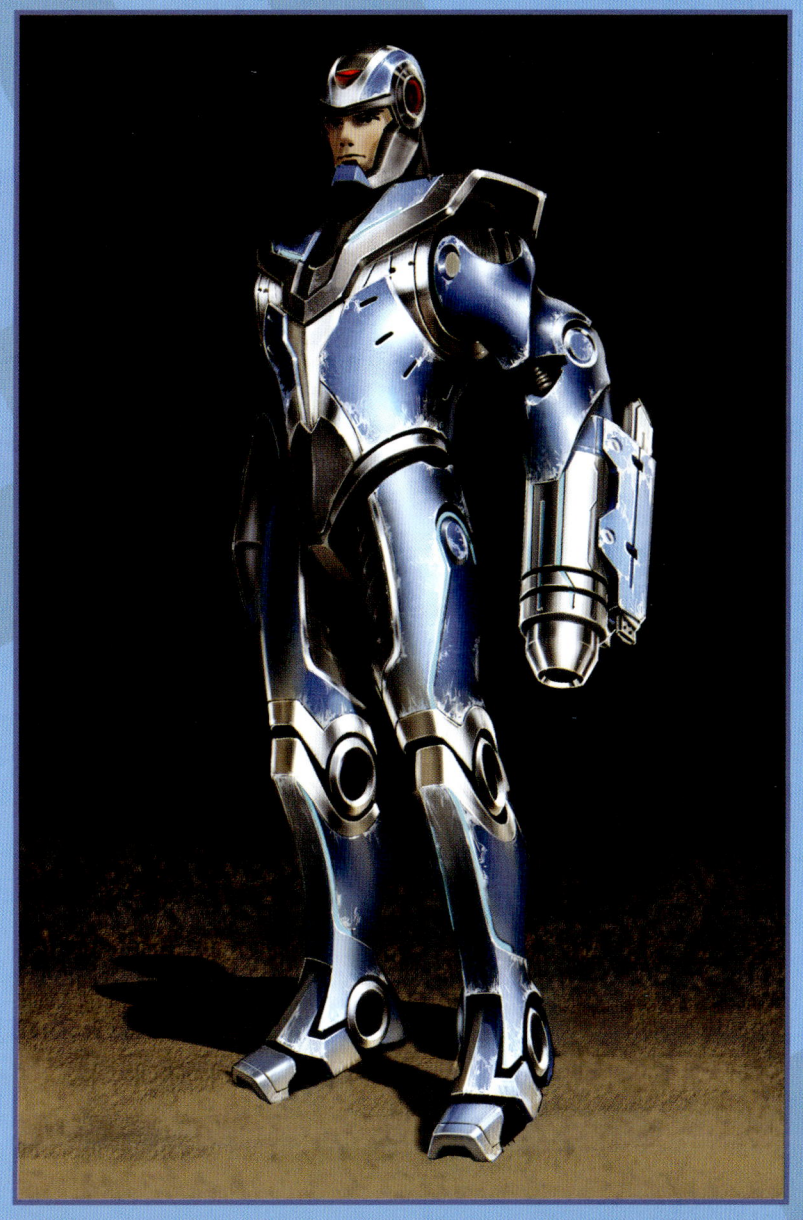

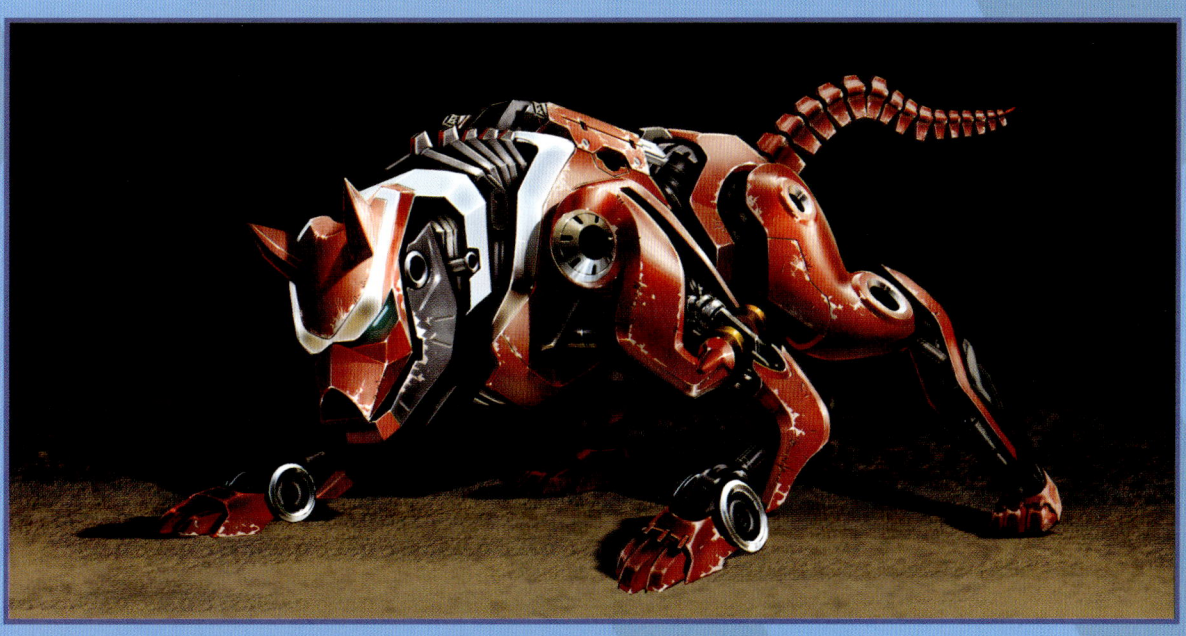

JASON HAZELROTH
Los Angeles, CA, United States
jasianinvasion.blogspot.com
Concept Artist
(Rock of the Dead - Character Designer)

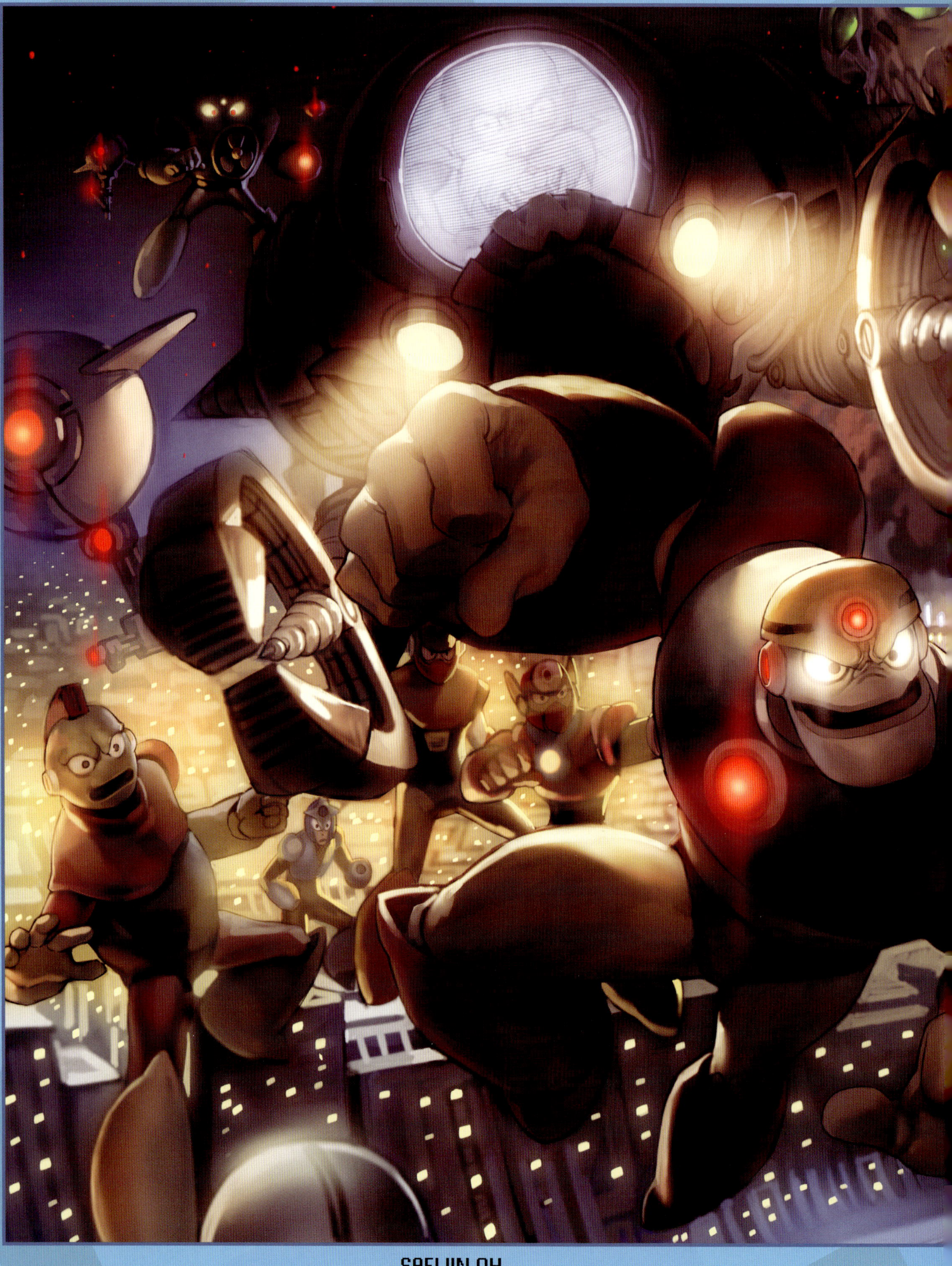

SAEIJIN OH
Korea
saejinoh.blogspot.com
Illustrator (ImagineFX, Dungeons & Dragons, Warcraft/Starcraft Manga covers)

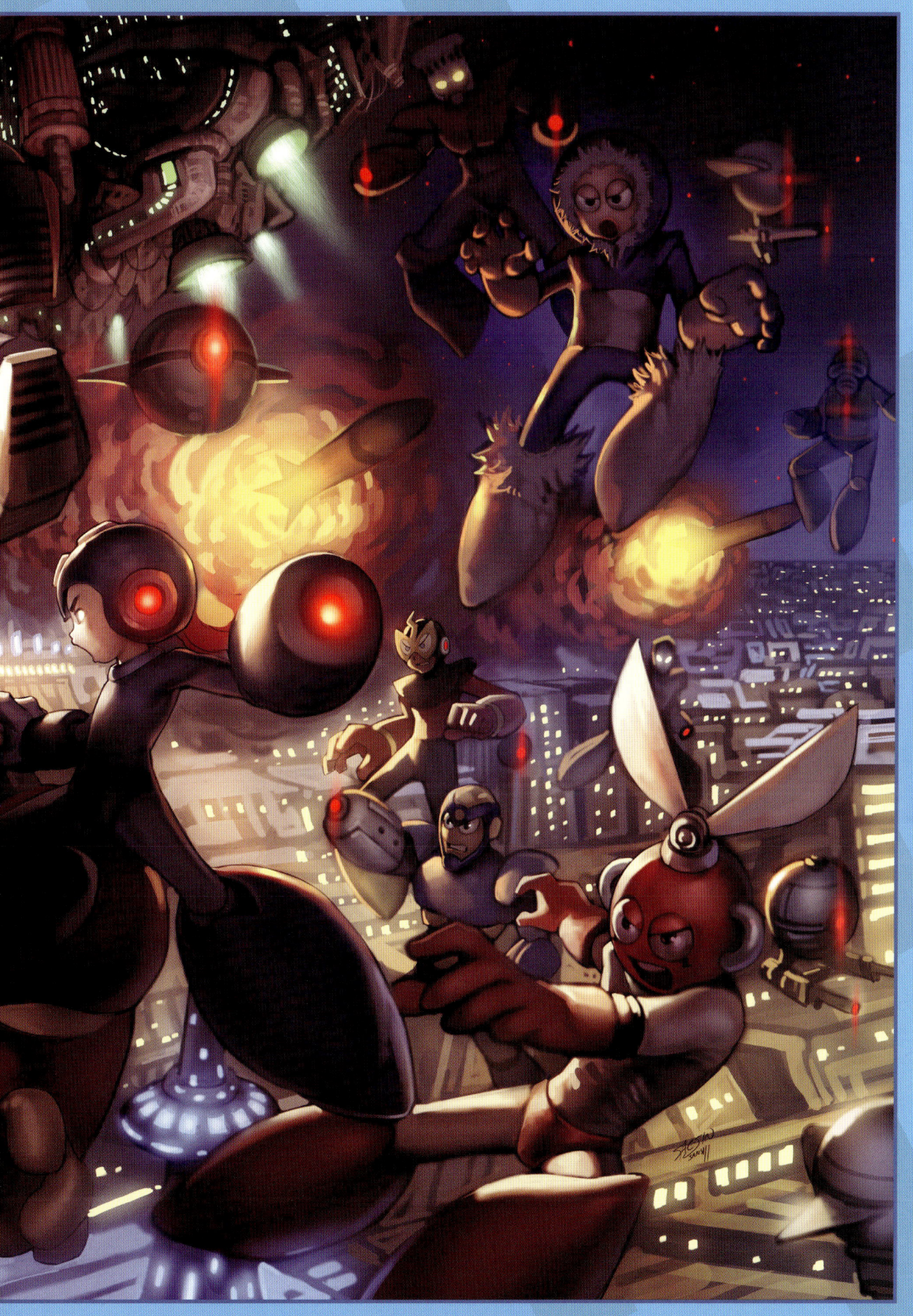

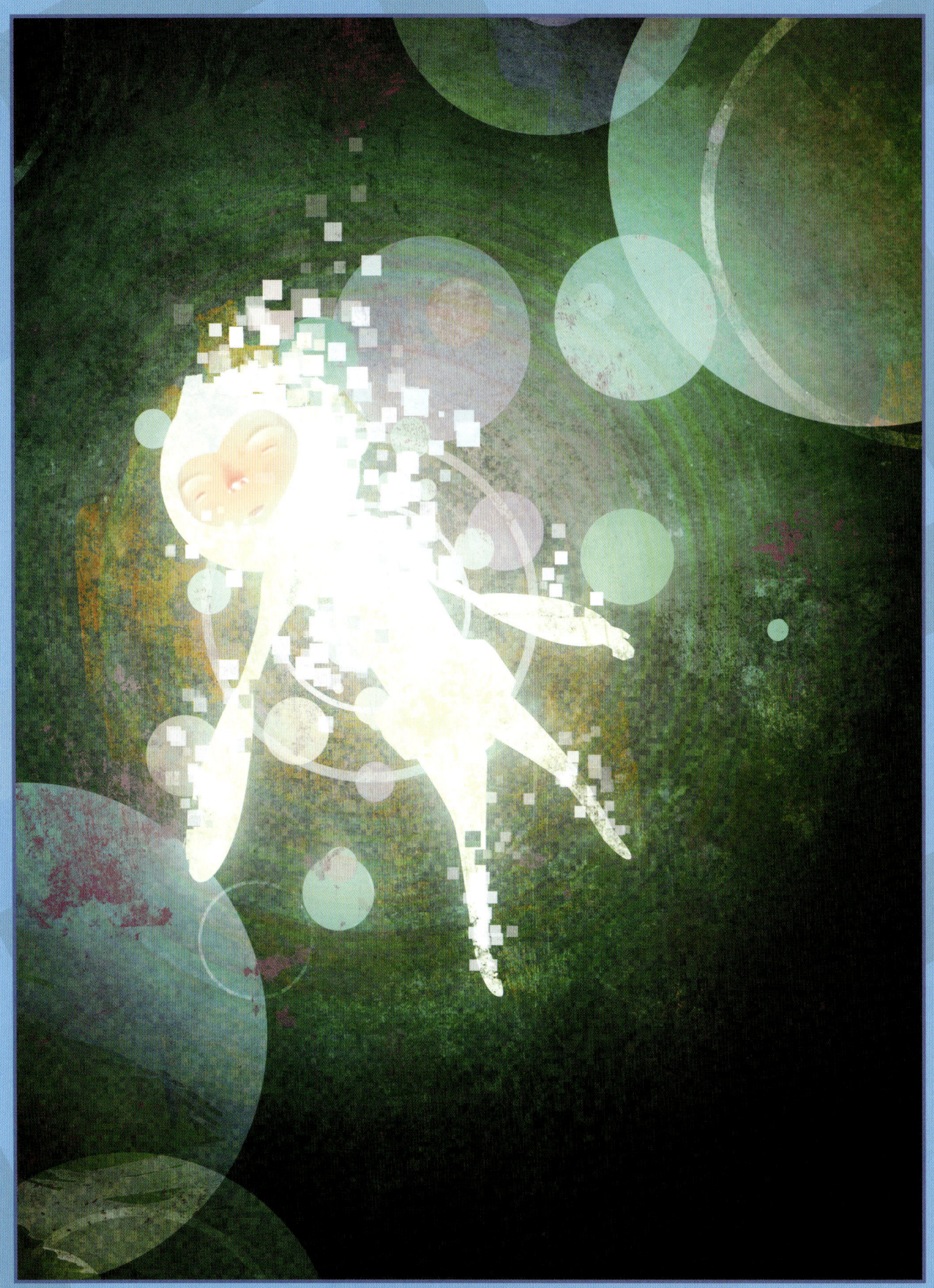

STEVEN TRAN
San Gabriel, CA, United States
stevenmtran.carbonmade.com
Illustrator

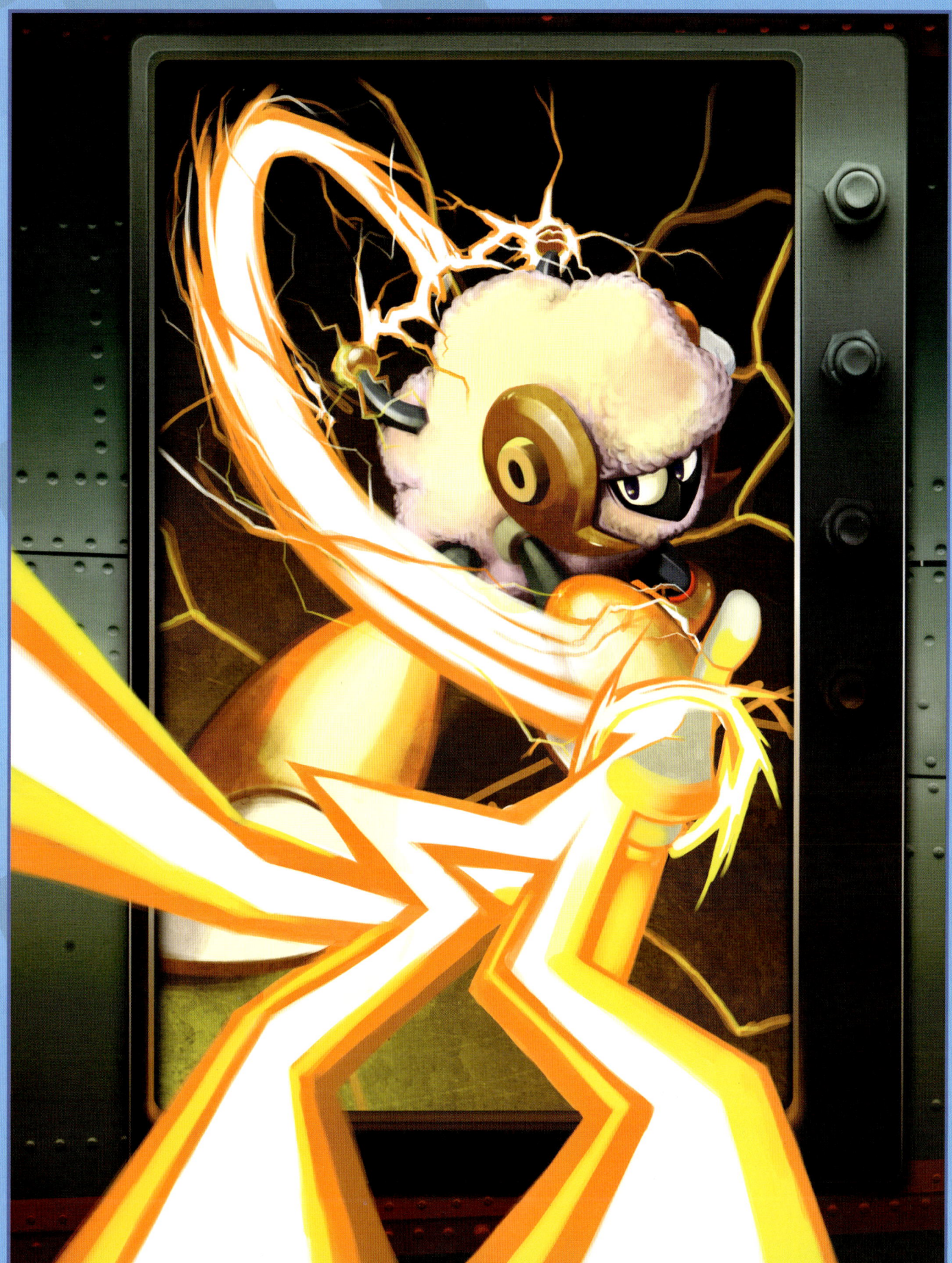

PEDRO REYES (BUG!)
México City, Mexico
bug-productions.deviantart.com
Senior Graphic Designer

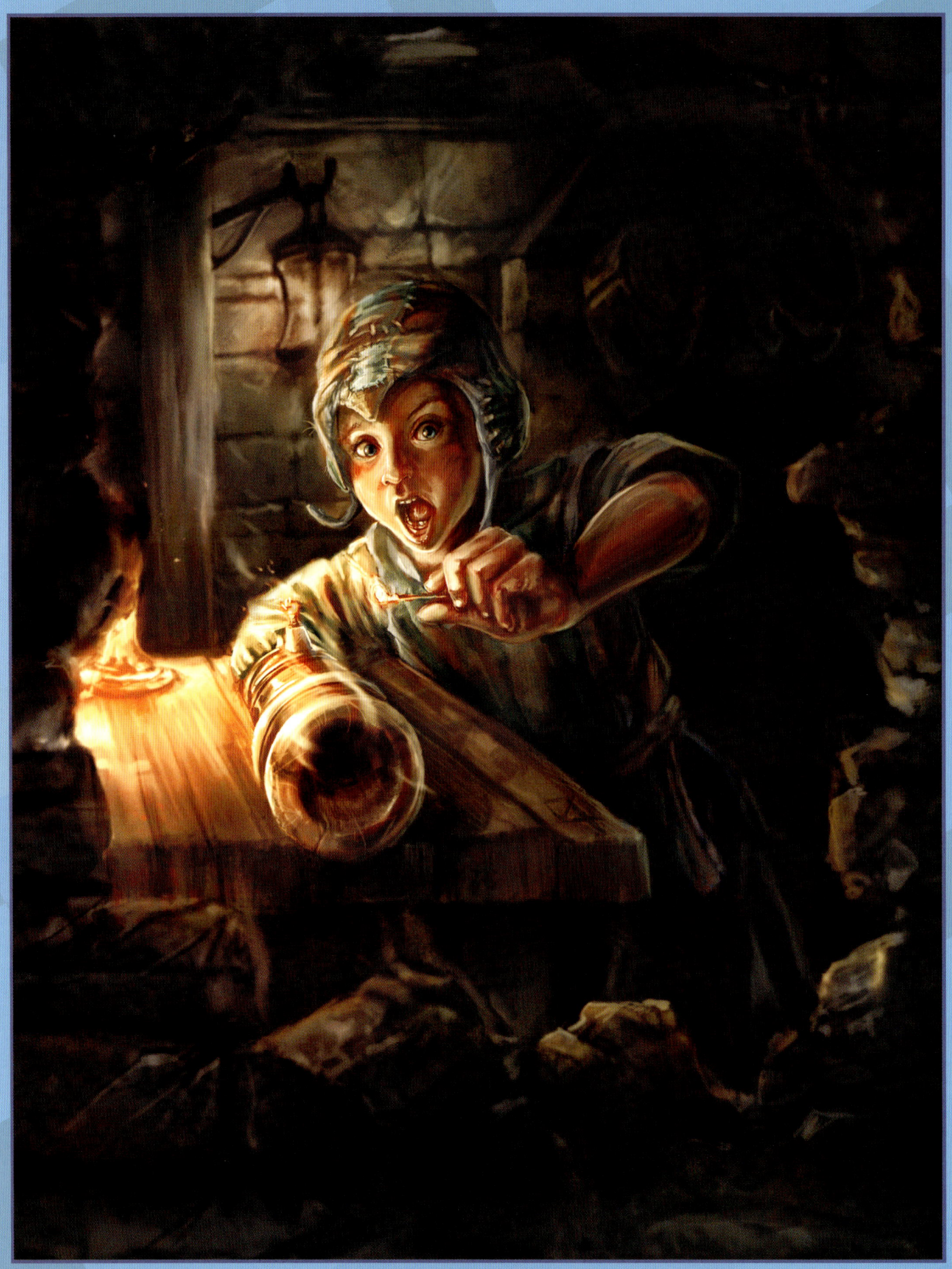

DAMIAN BUZUGBE
Hove, United Kingdom
www.dpbcreative.com/d4
Artist

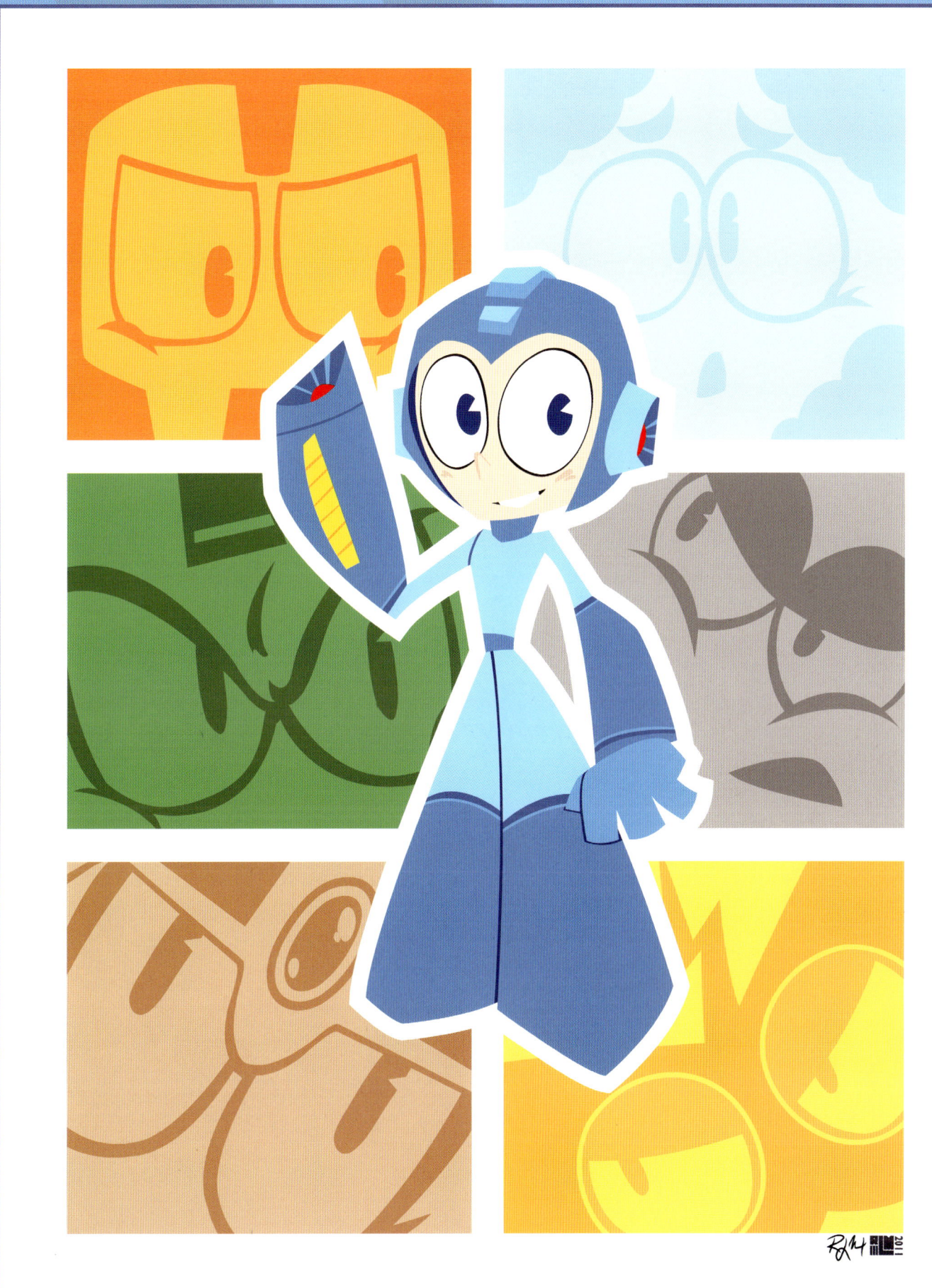

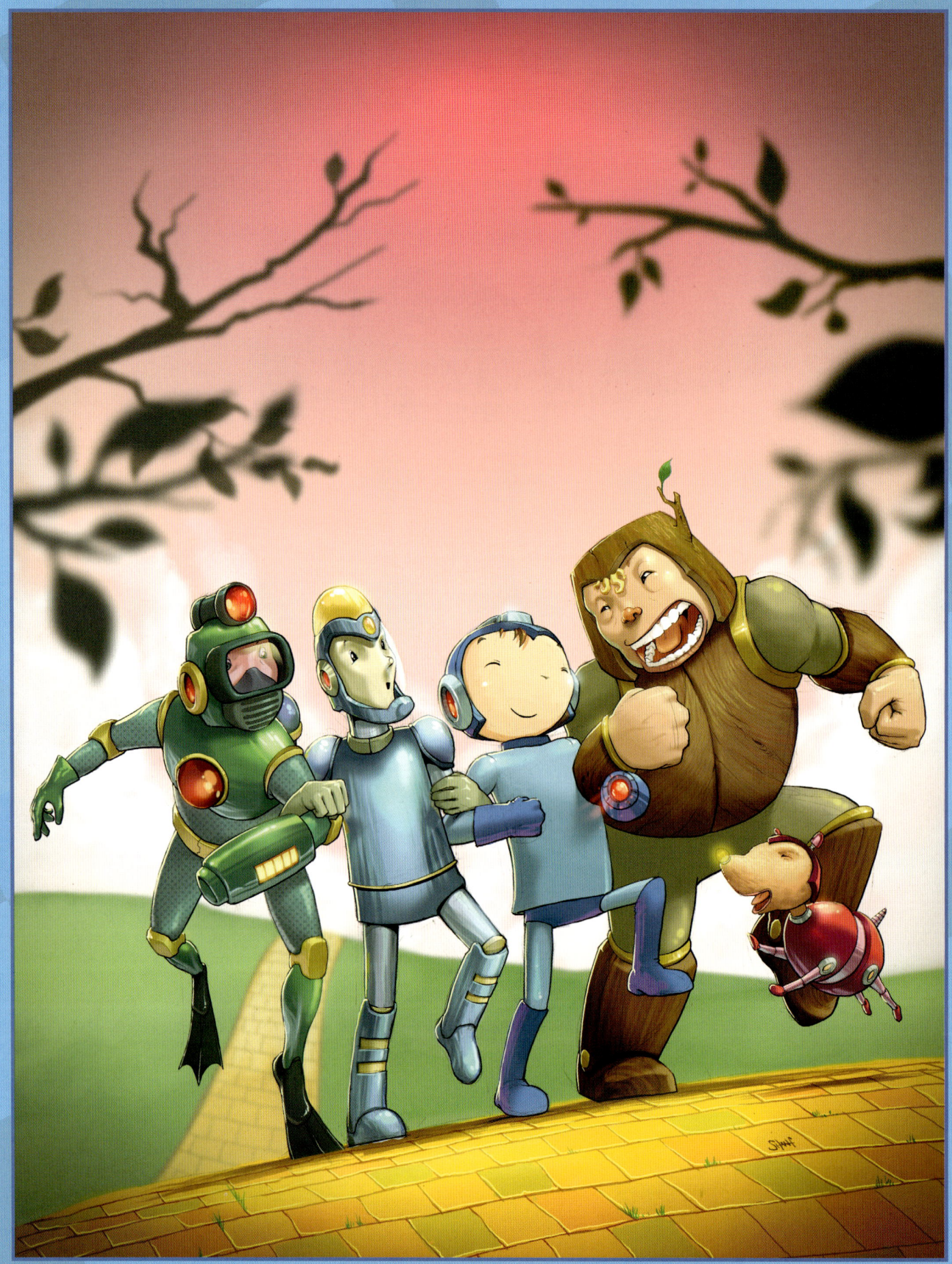

SHANE LAW
Toronto, ON, Canada
UDON Co-Founder / Animator
(Nelvana - Handy Mandy)

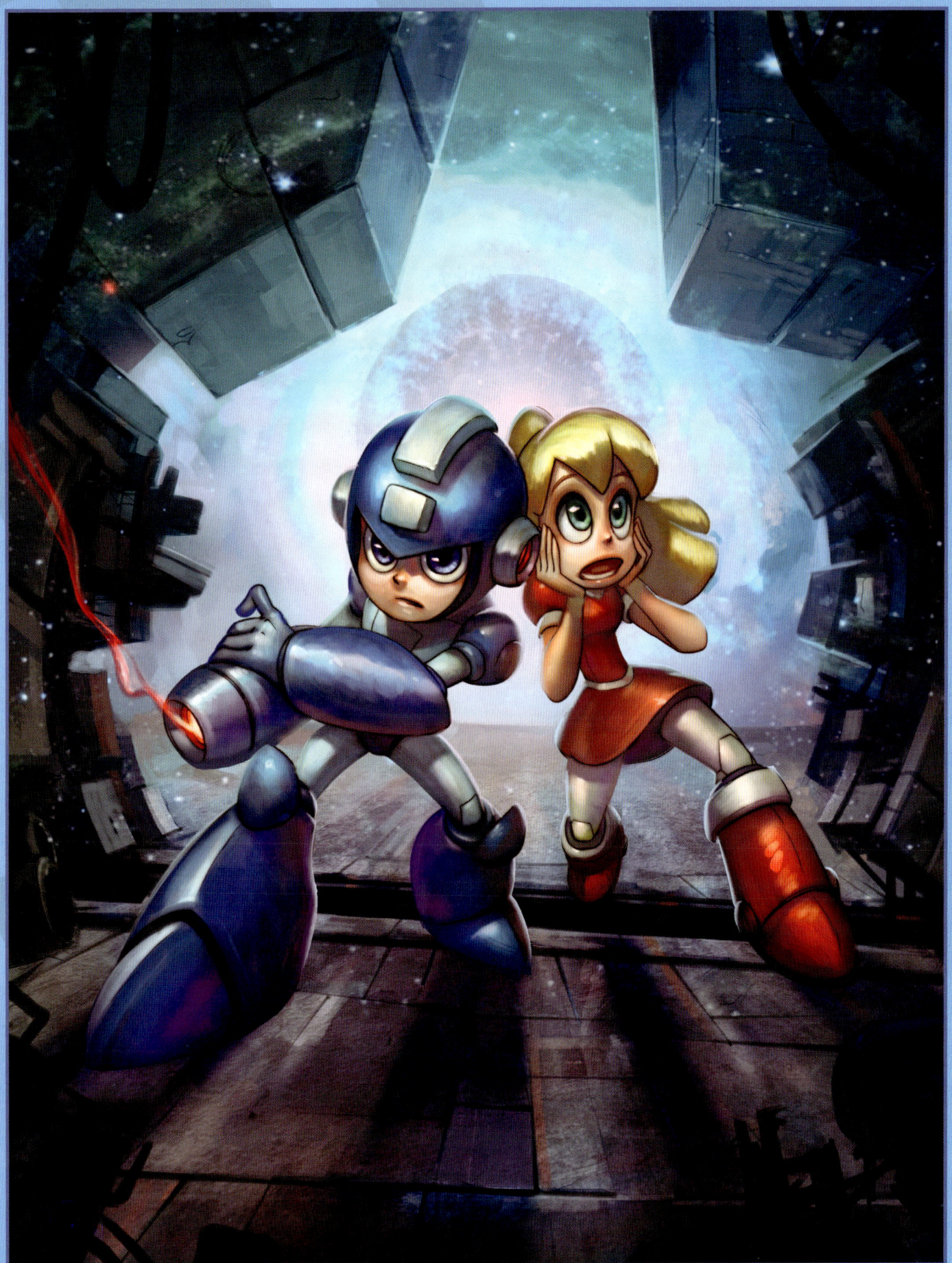

MATTHEW ARMSTRONG
Salt Lake City, UT, United States
www.matthewart.com
Concept Artist / Writer
(Jane and Mizmow)

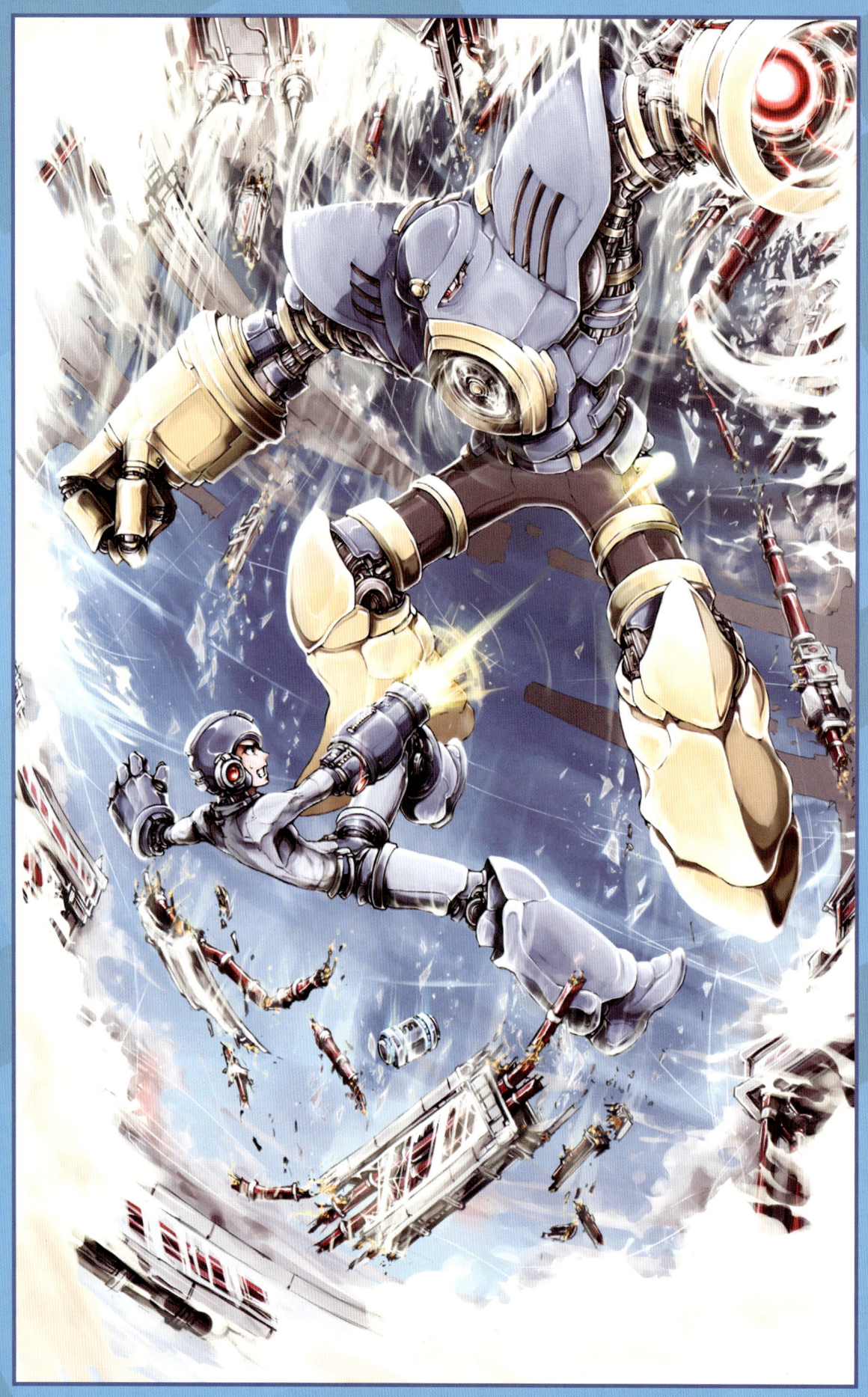

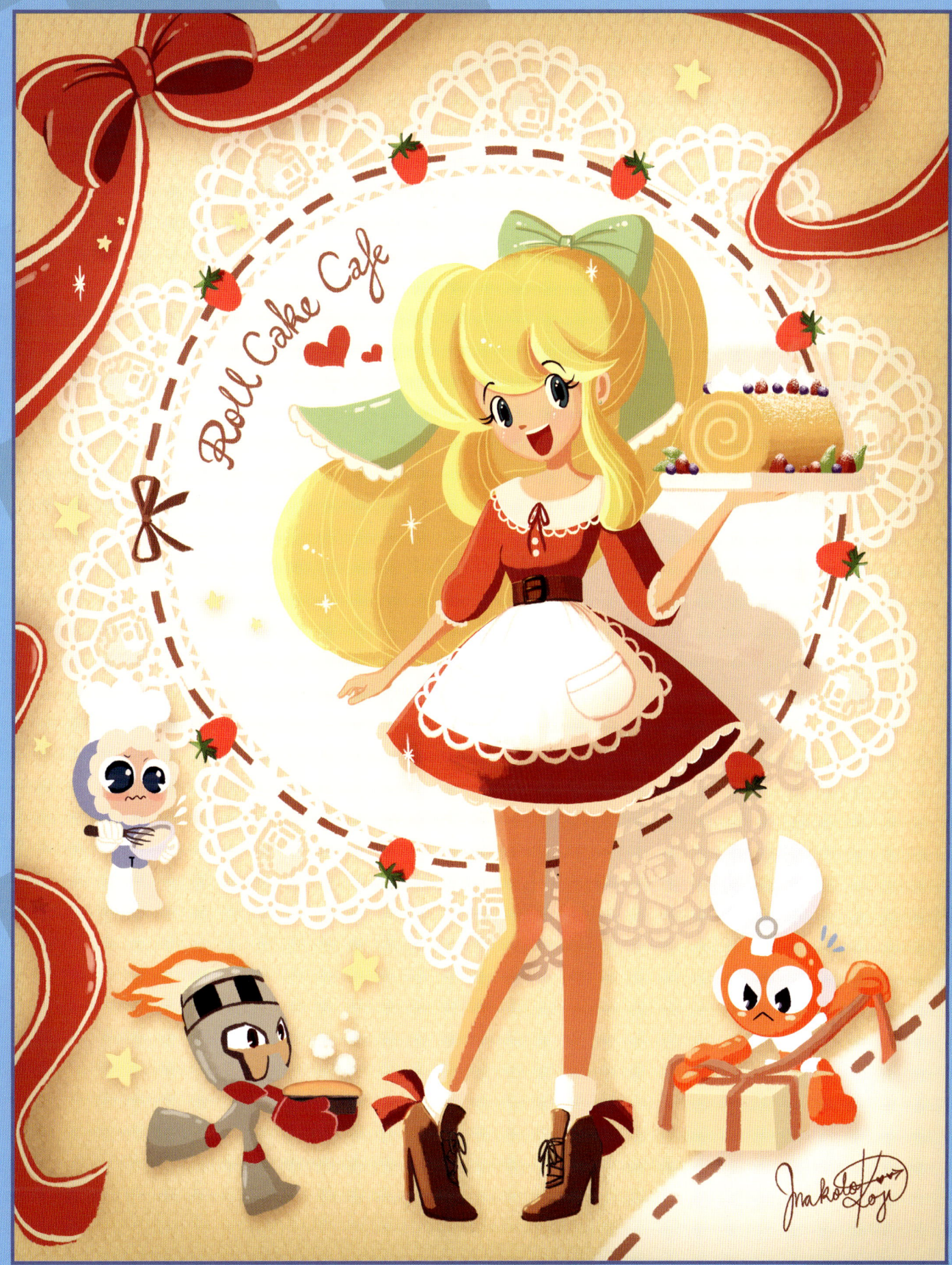

MAKOTO KOJI
Norwood, Australia
makocchi-desu.blogspot.com
Illustrator / Animator

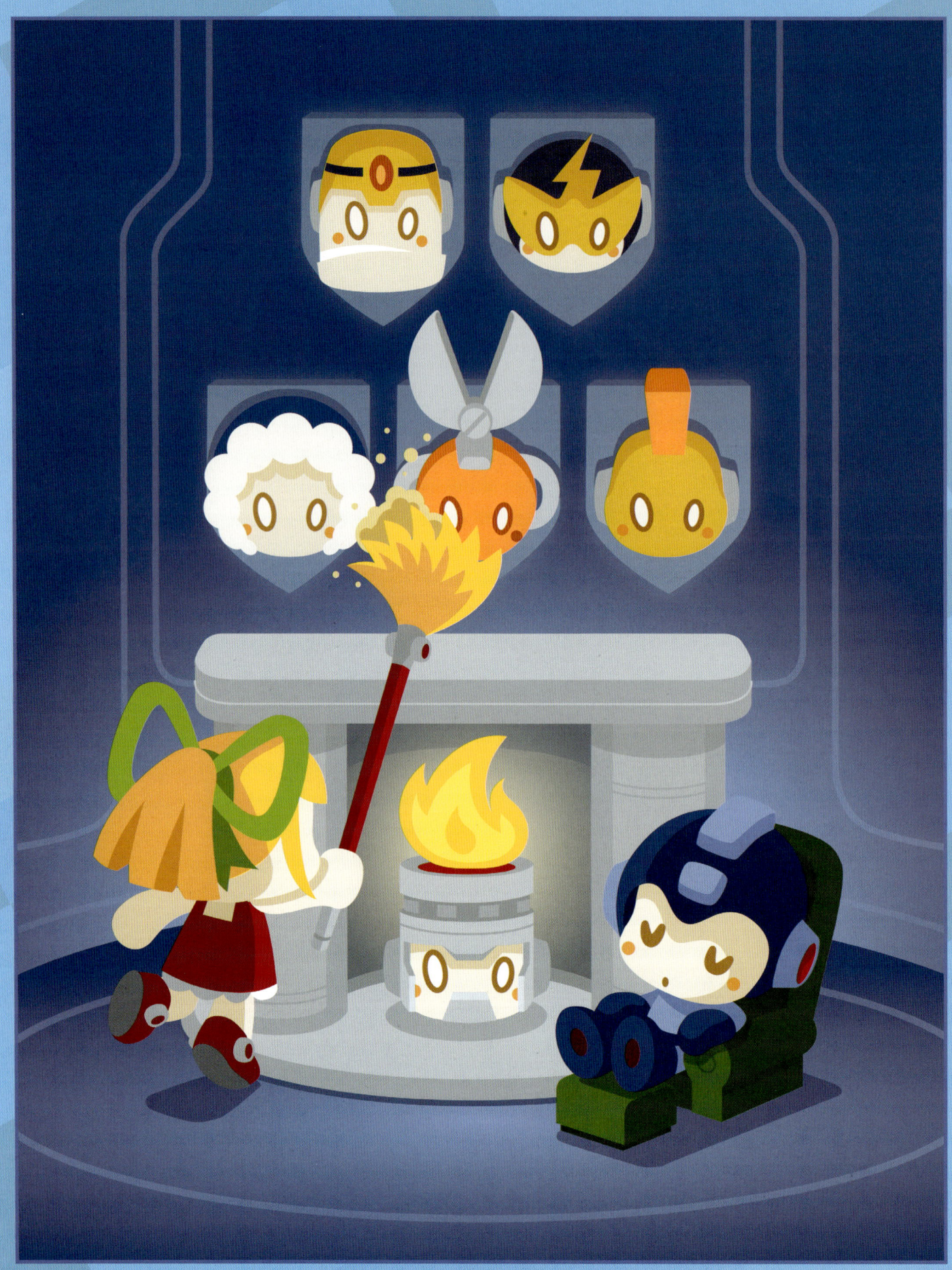

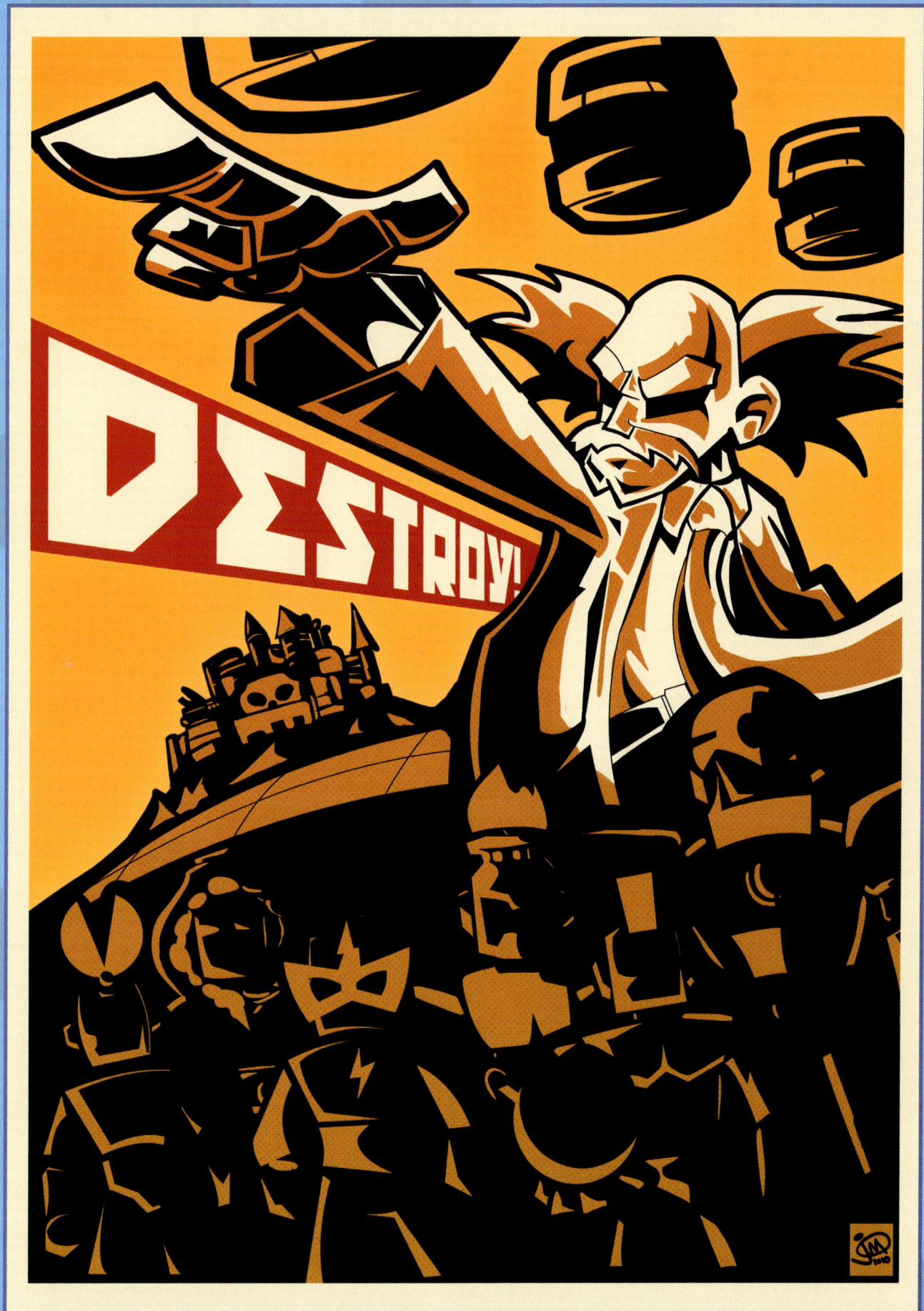

JOE MARTIN (JOEROCKS1981)
Sebring, FL, United States
joerocksart.blogspot.com / joefreakinrocks.deviantart.com
Artist

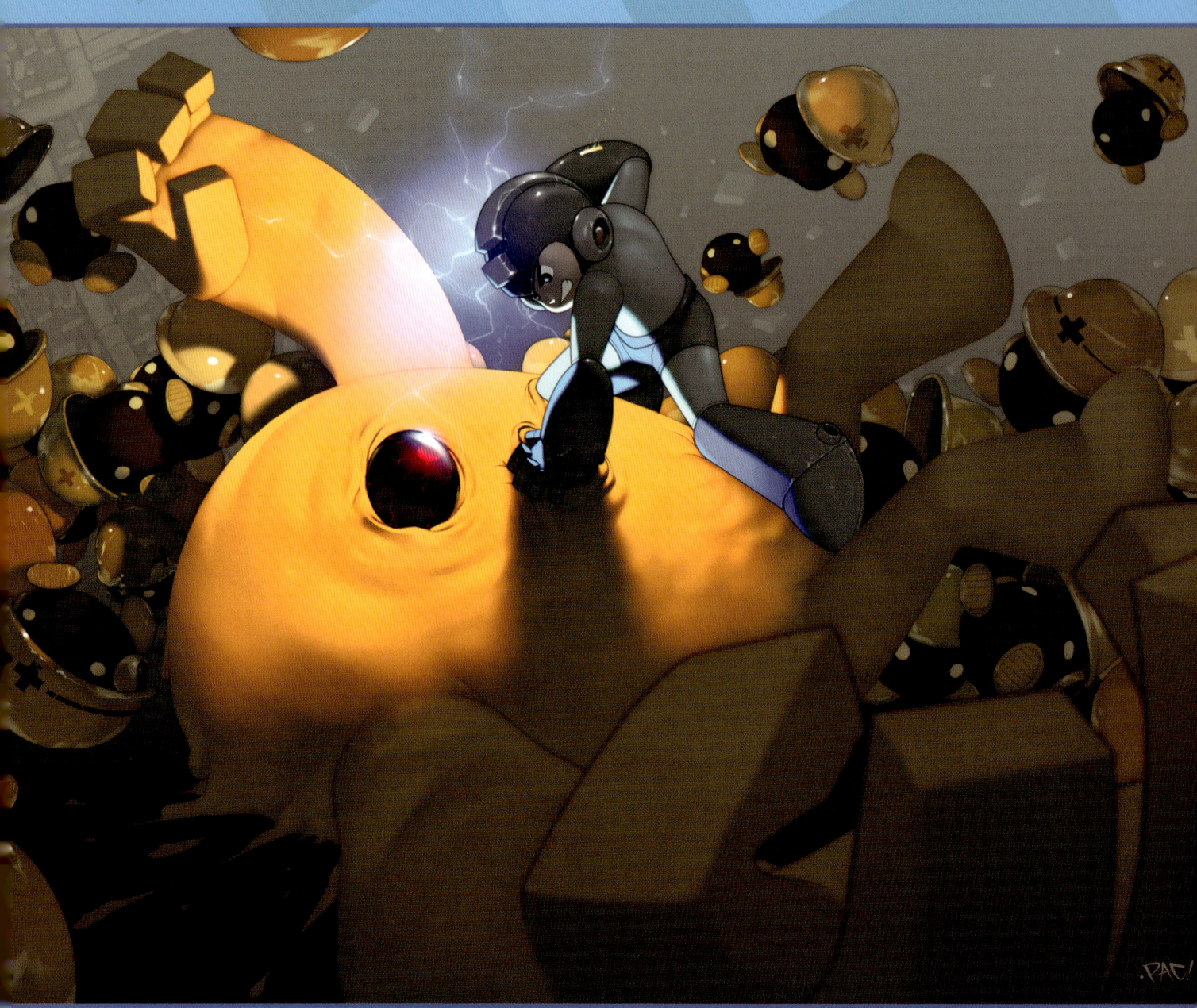

FRANCISCO PEREZ (PAC23)
Coral Gables, FL, United States
pacman23.deviantart.com / www.pac23.com
Illustrator
(ESPN / Popular Mechanics / Leviticus Cross)

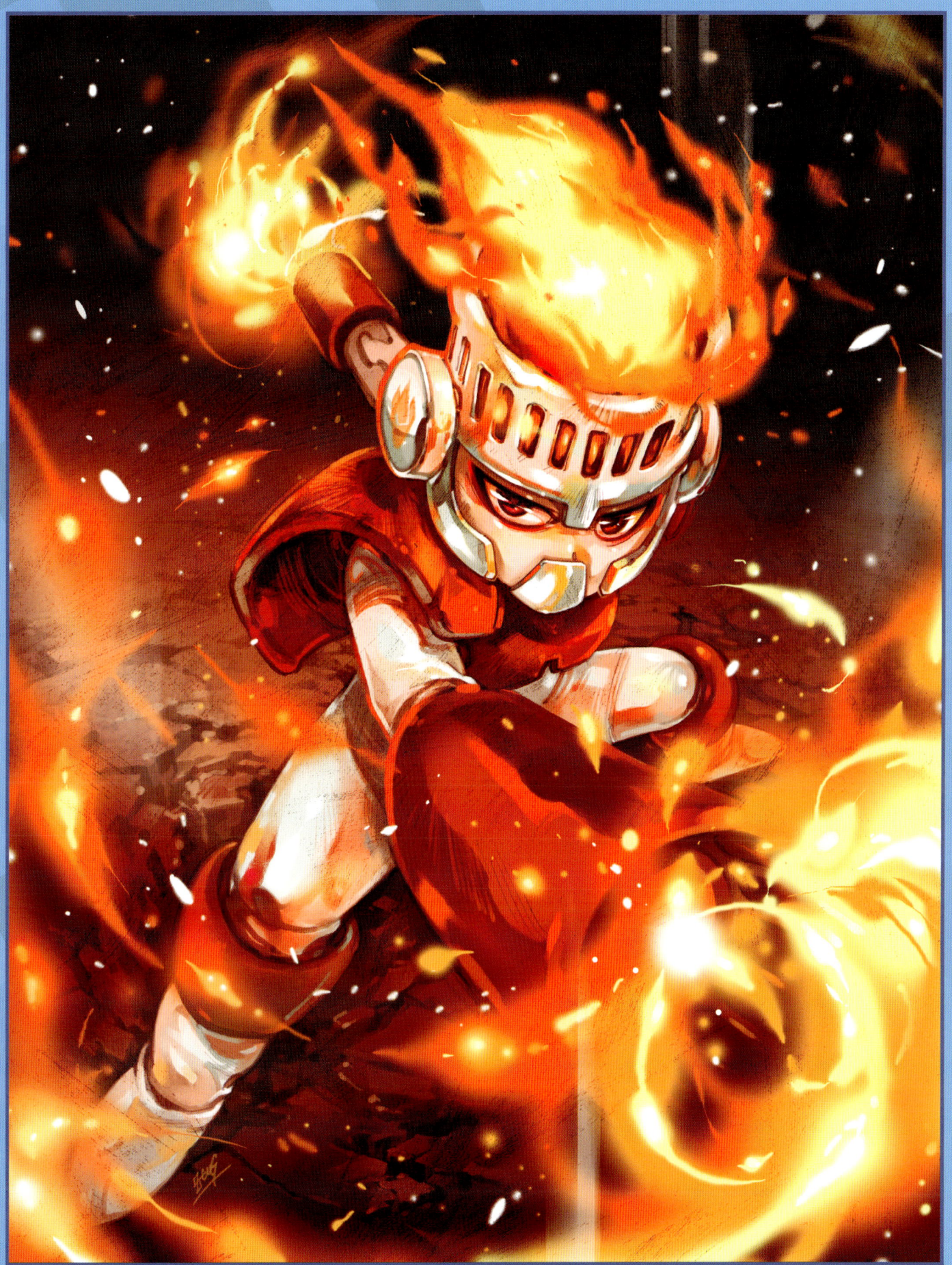

ANDREA JEN
Buenos Aires, Argentina
zengsportfolio.blogspot.com / handrewx.deviantart.com
Comic Artist
(El Delirio de Ani / Las Horas Perdidas)

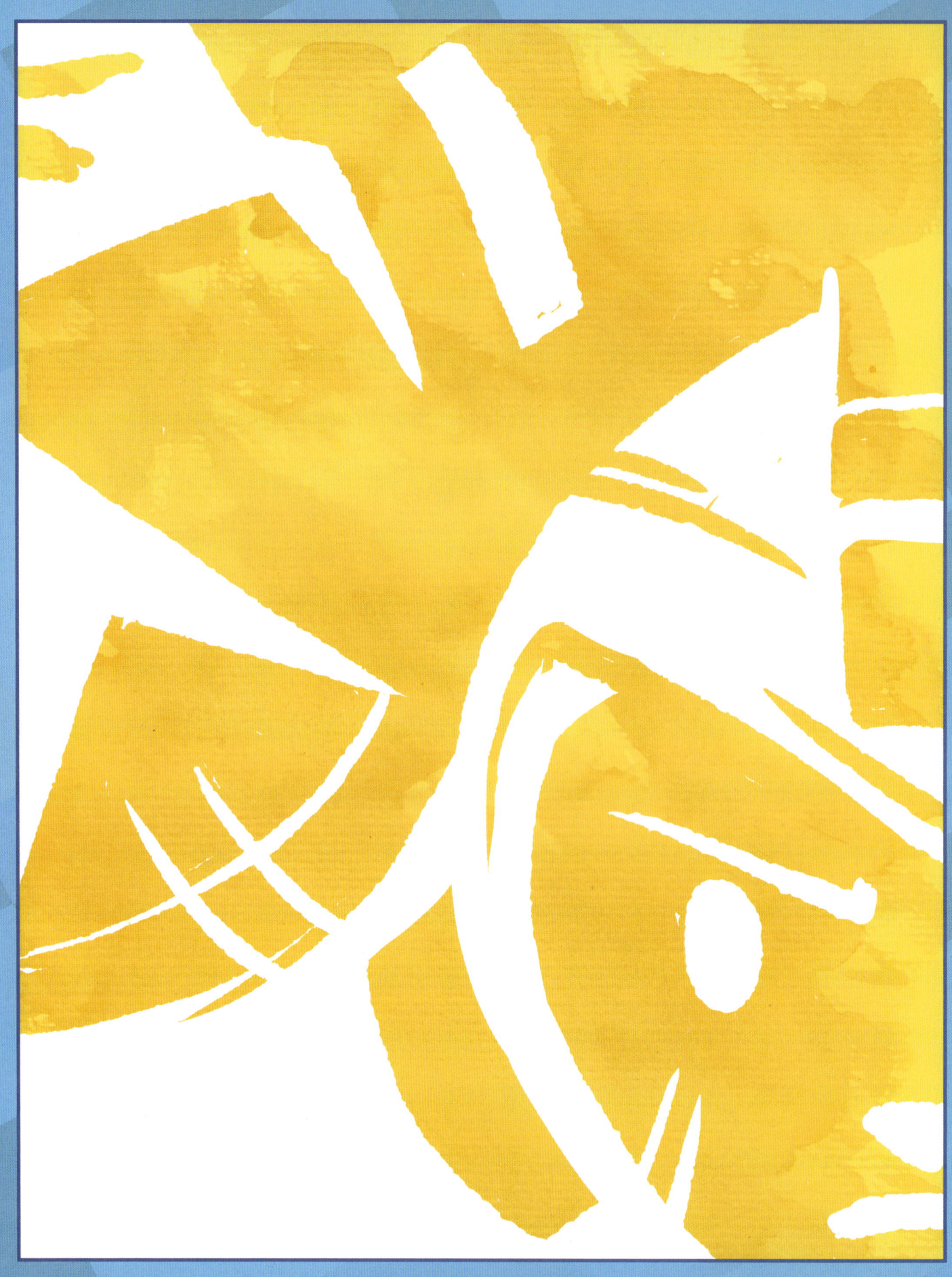

ALEXANDER DIOCHON
Oakville, ON, Canada
stplmstr.deviantart.com
Illustrator
(Storyboarding- Ugly Americans /
Tatoo Design - Eastern Promises End Credits / Deep Down- Comic)

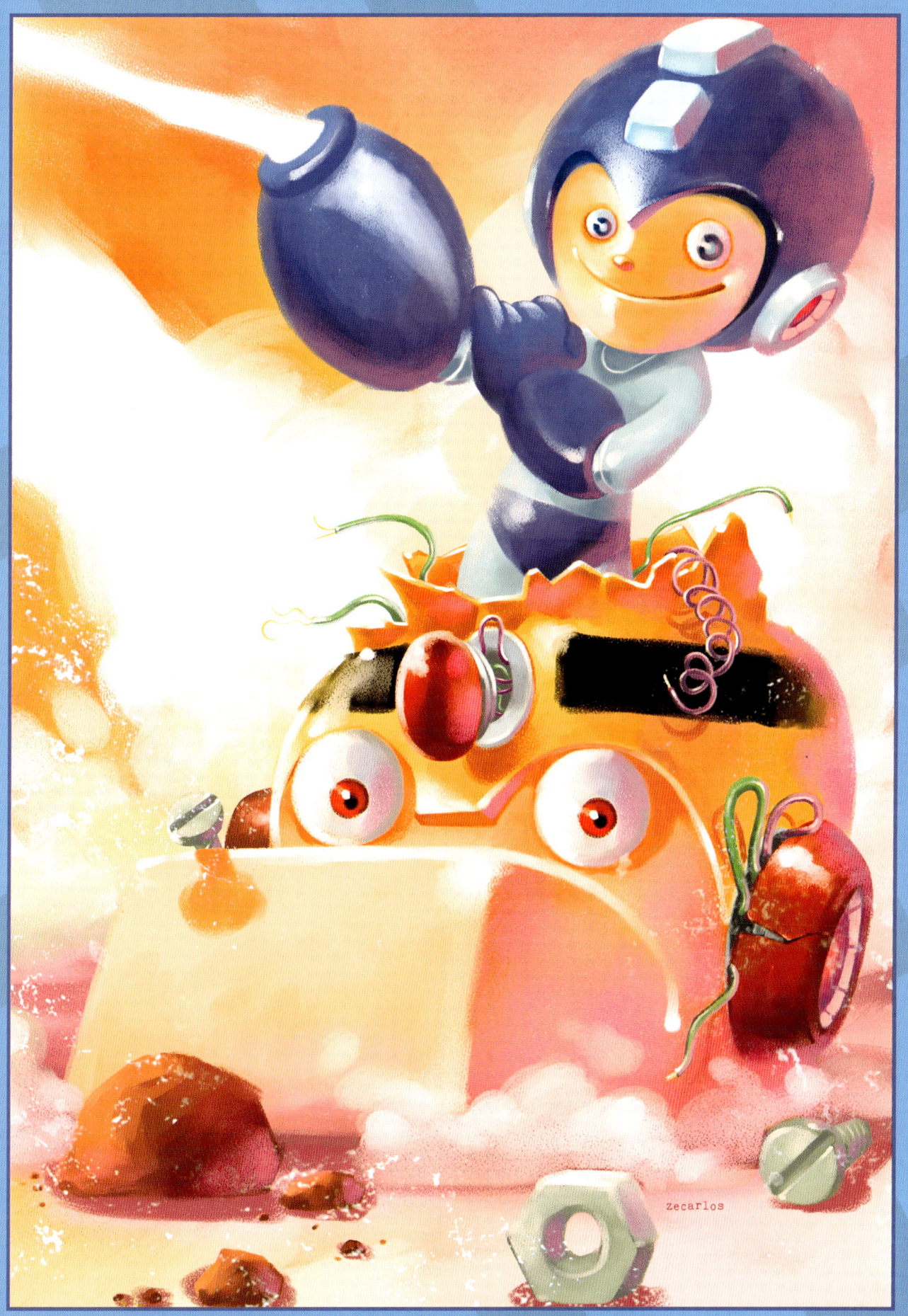

JOSE CARLOS SALVIO PEREIRA JR
Sao Paulo, Brazil
zecarlos.deviantart.com
Illustrator

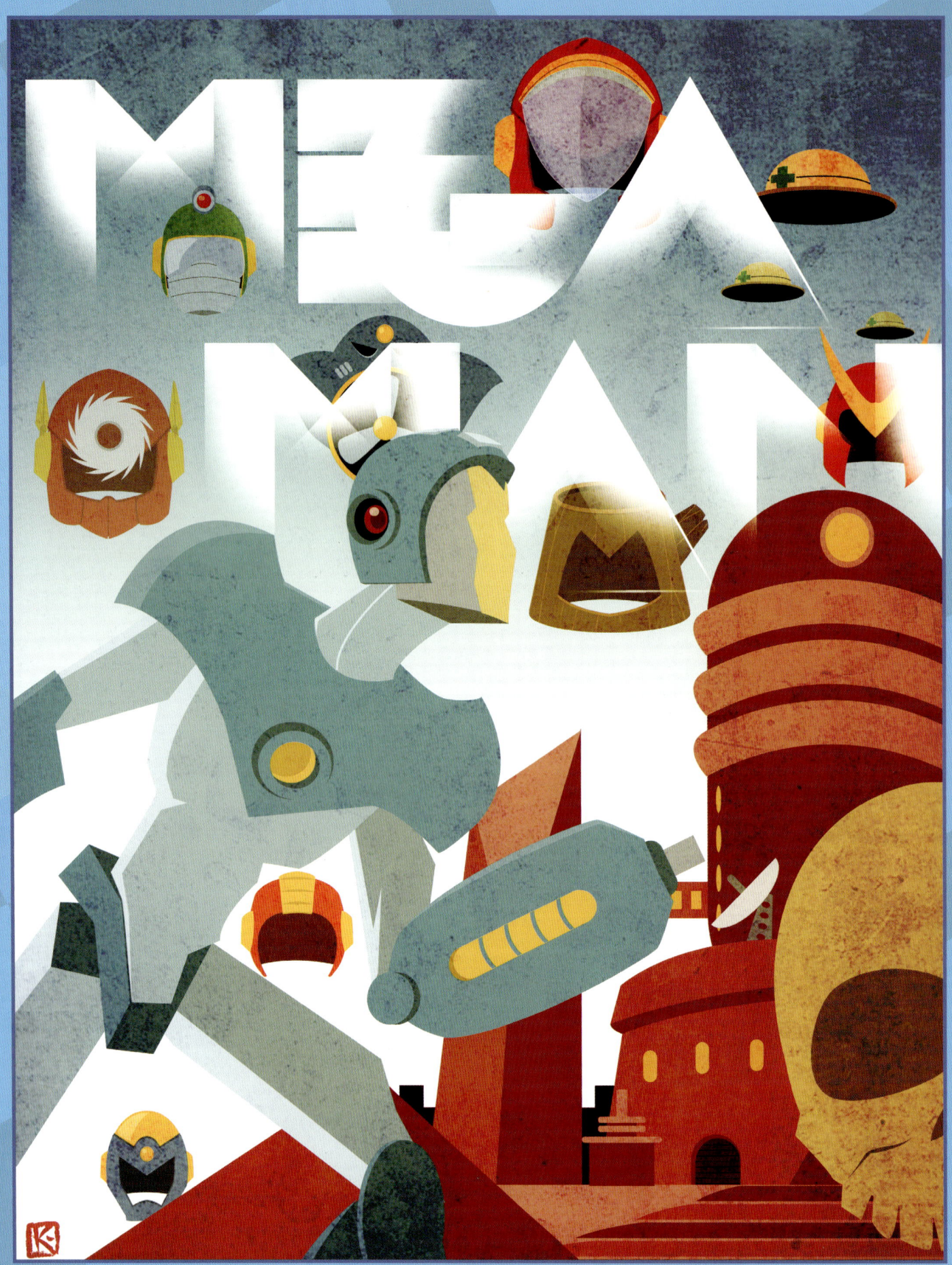

CESAR AUGUSTO SANCHEZ SANDOVAL (AUGUSTO SASA)
Monterrey, Mexico
www.augustosasa.com / augustosasa.deviantart.com
Illustrator

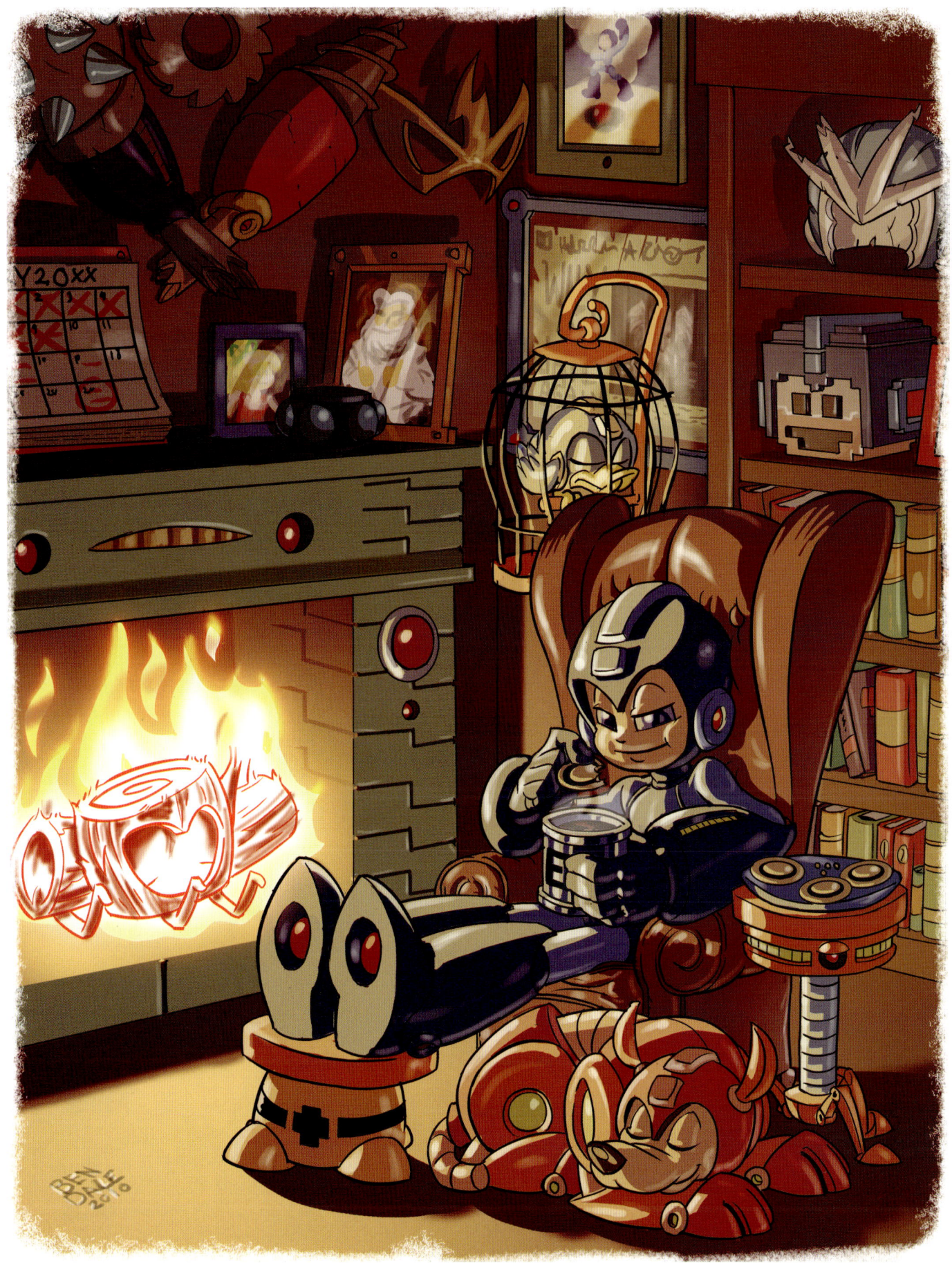

BEN DALE
Brooklyn, NY, United States
bendaledonethat.blogspot.com / crazyskull.deviantart.com
Illustrator
(Joe Kubert School of Cartooning / Creator of "Little Knight")

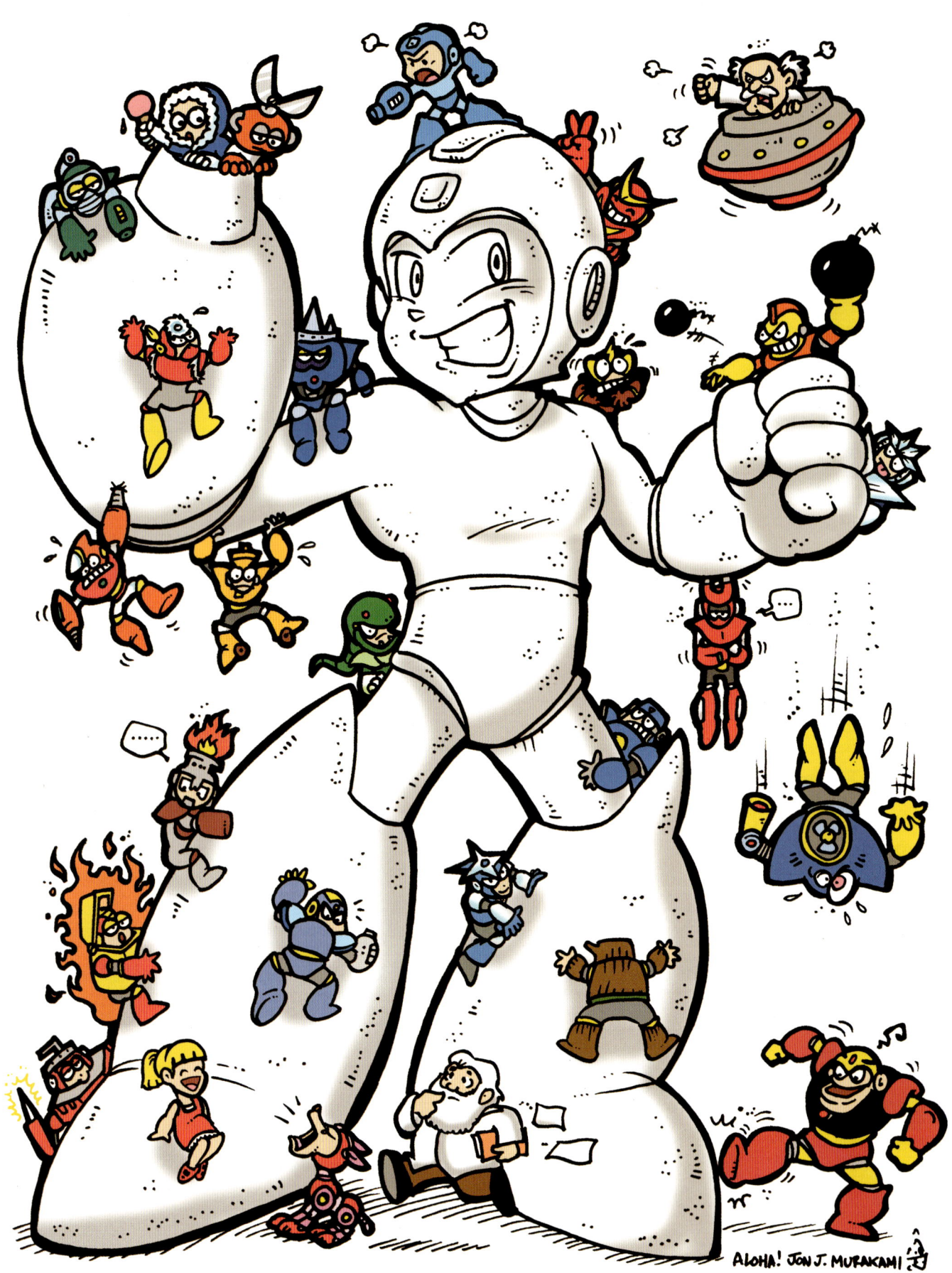

JON MURAKAMI
Honolulu, HI, United States
www.gordonrider.com
Cartoonist

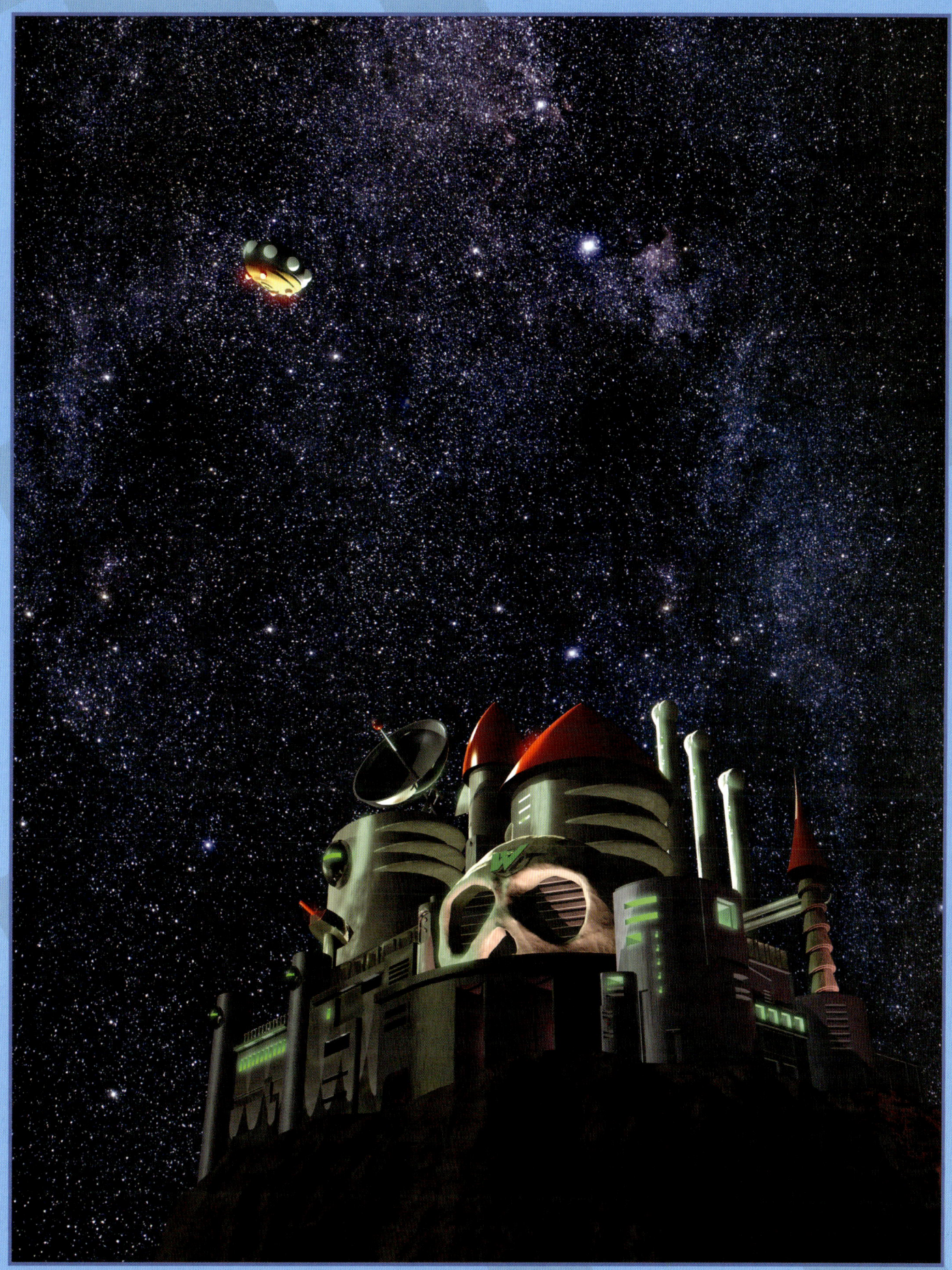

LARRY GILBERT
Marlton, NJ, United States
kiwi-rgb.deviantart.com
Designer

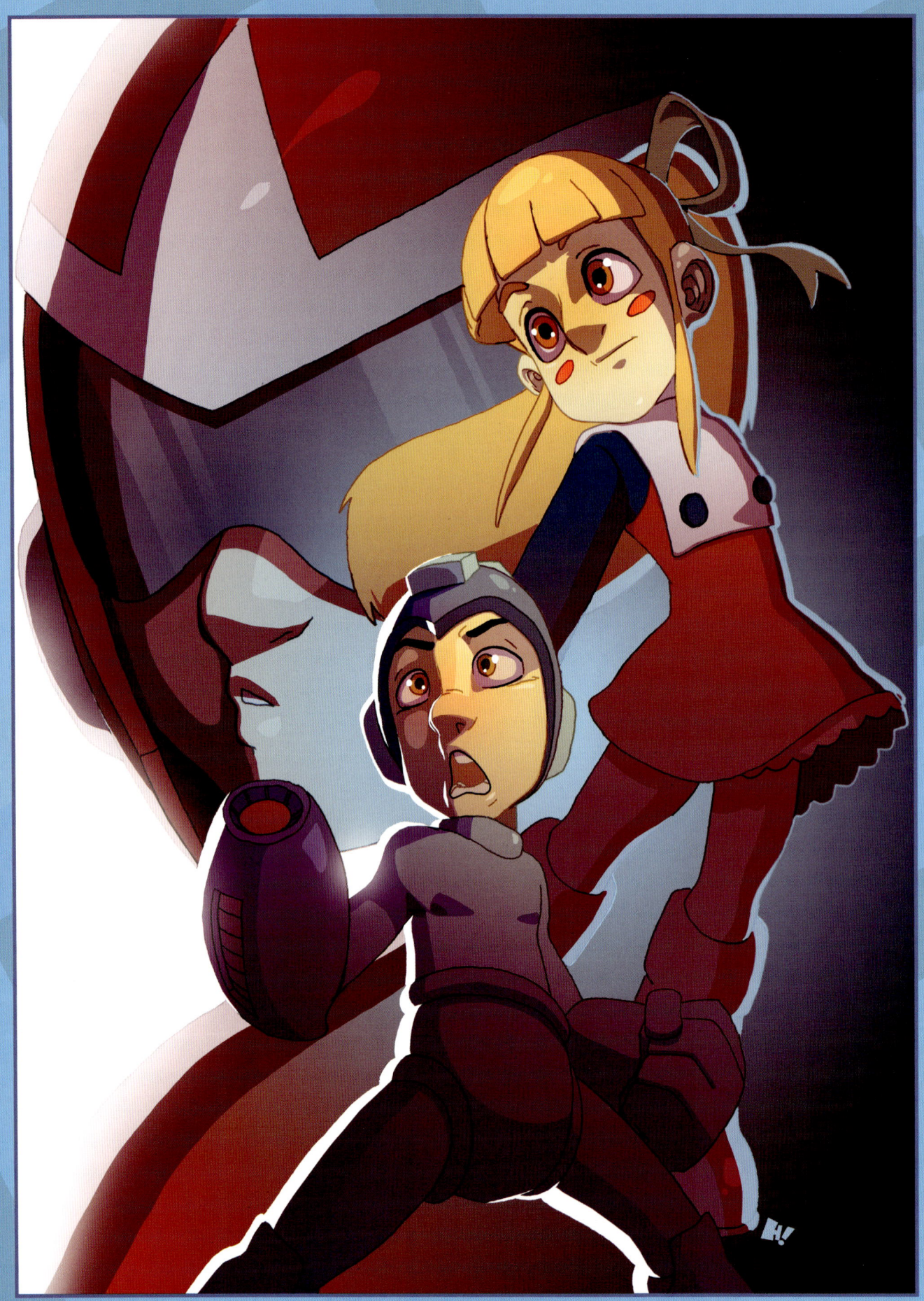

HUGH FREEMAN
Melbourne, Australia
deathbysodacan.deviantart.com
Illustrator
(RMIT University - Animation & Interactive Media)

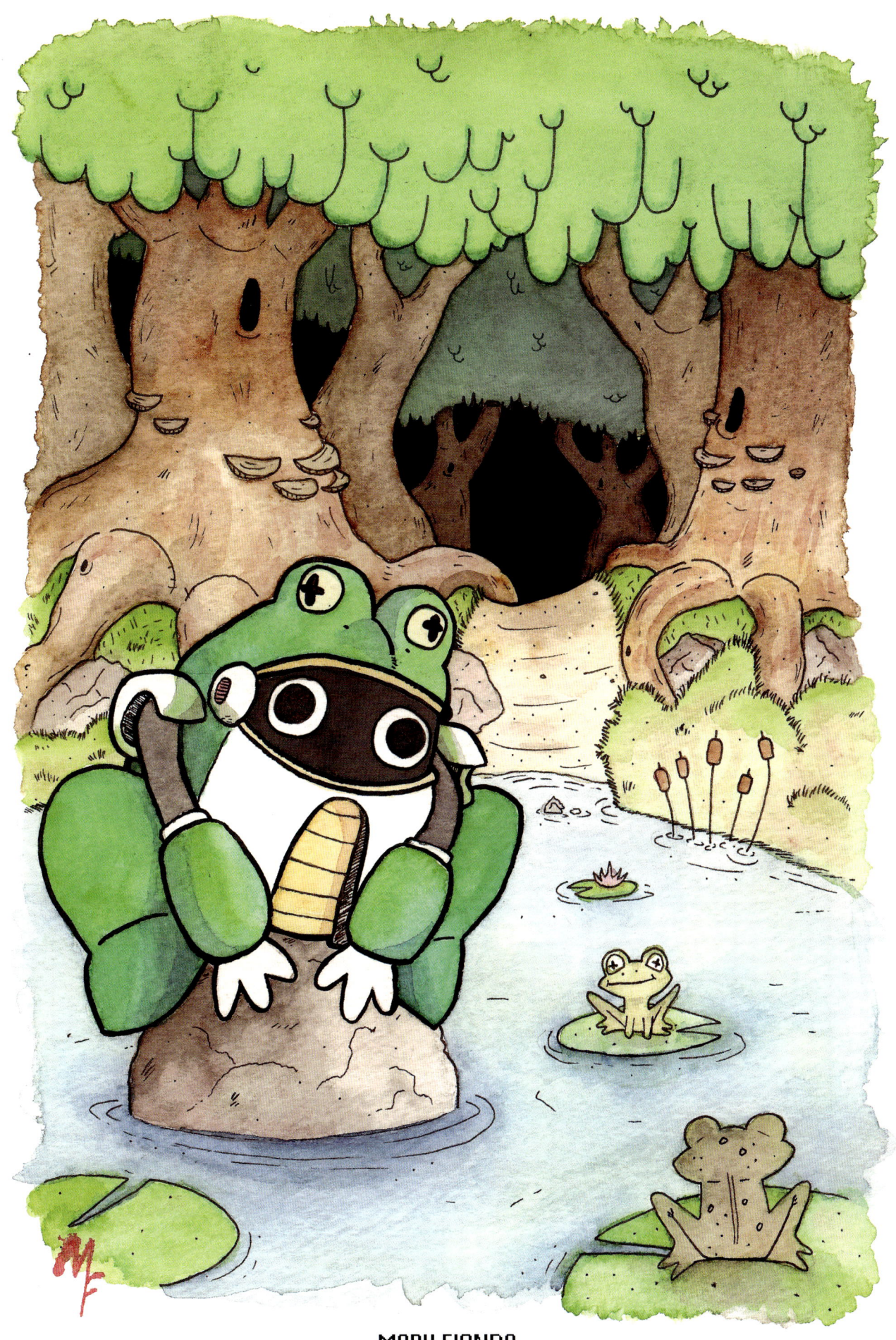

MARK FIONDA
Ridgewood, NJ, United States
www.markfiondajr.com
Illustrator
(University of the Arts / Carnivale de Robotique / Autumn Society)

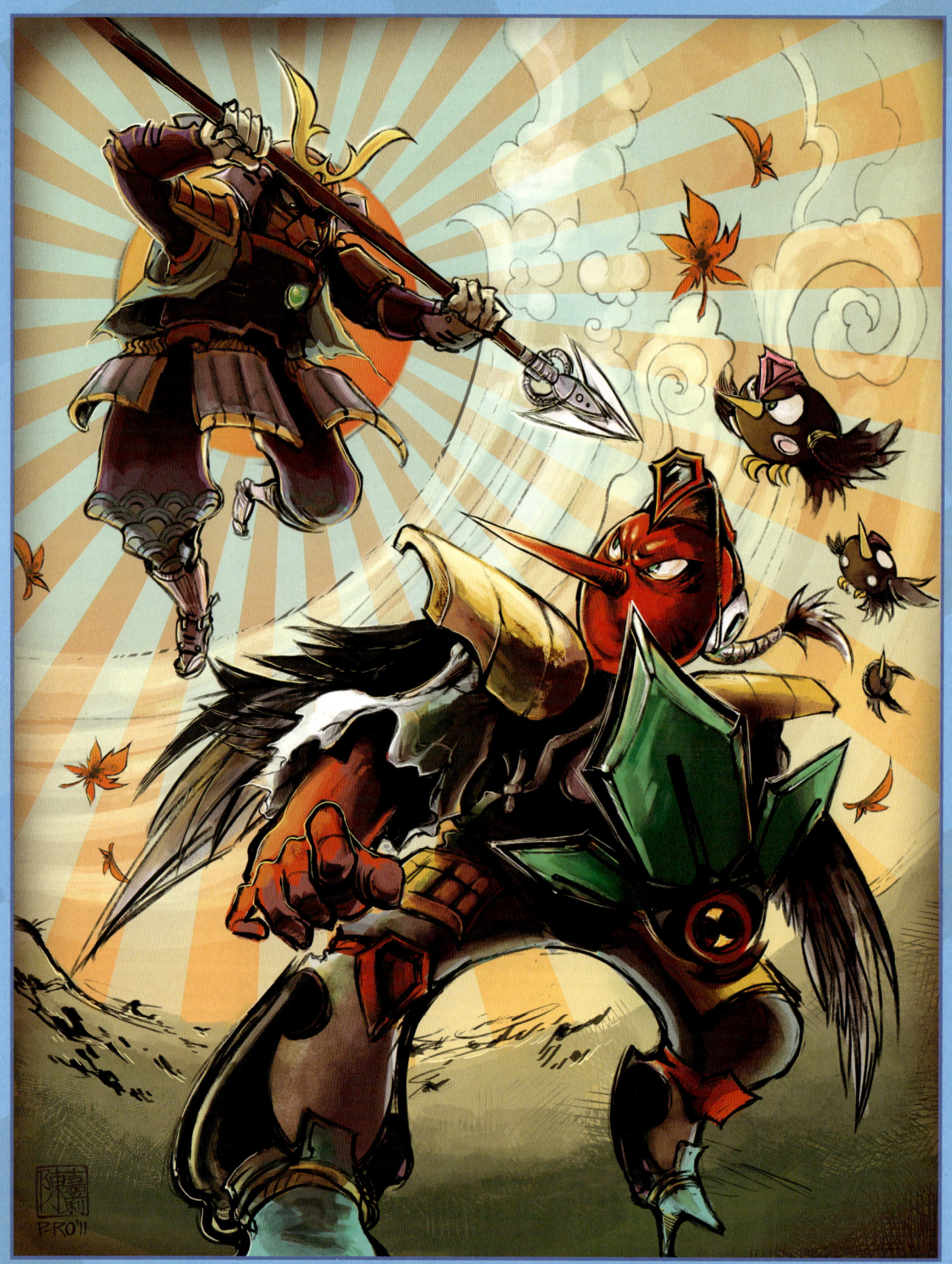

CAREY CHAN (P-RO)
Montréal, QC, Canada
p-ro.deviantart.com
Tattooist / Illustrator
(Cégep Ahuntsic)

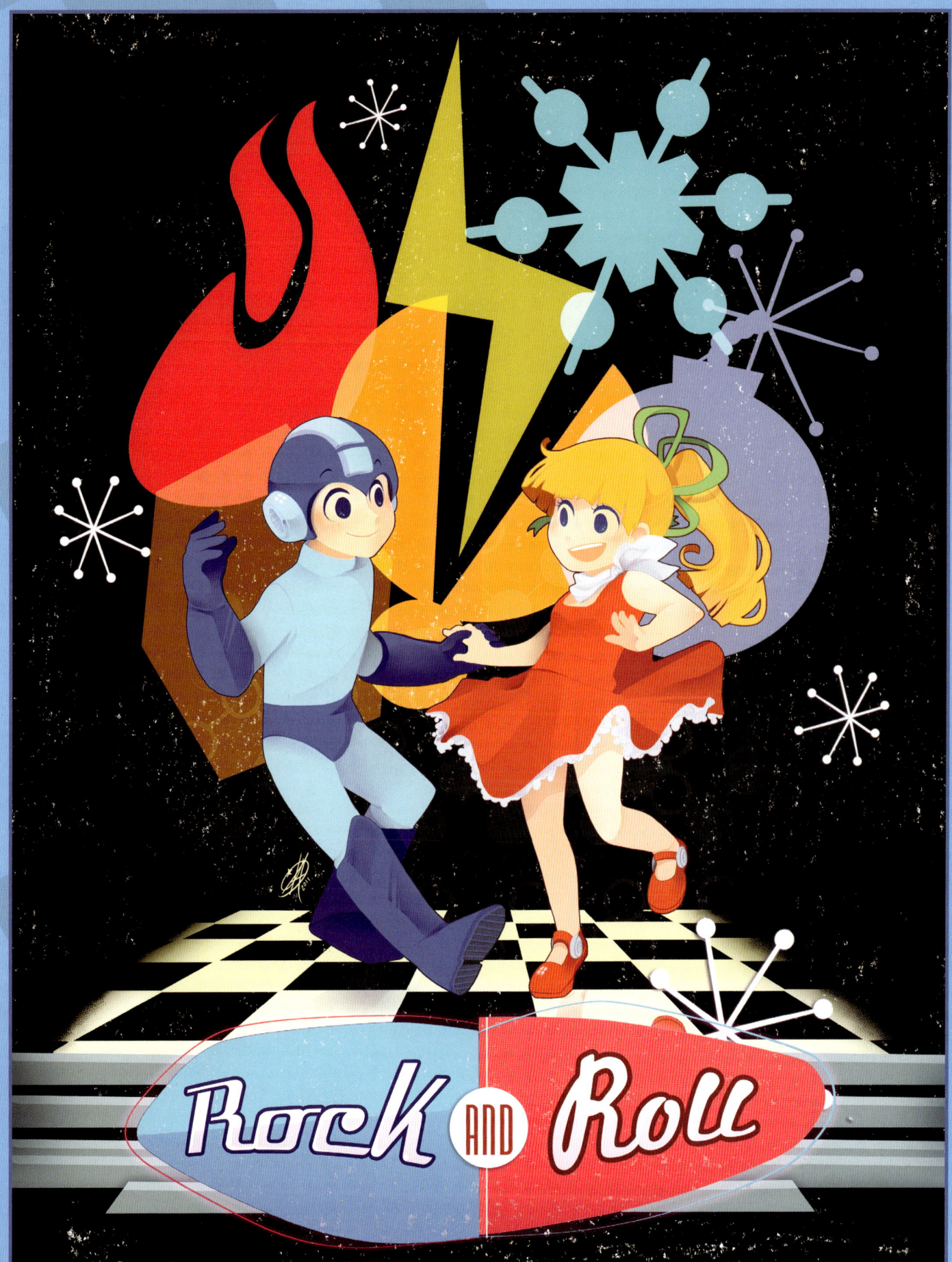

ADRIANA DE LA TORRE (AKIMARO)
Chihuahua, Mexico
akimaro.deviantart.com
Design Student
(Studio XIII, Epsilon Magazine)

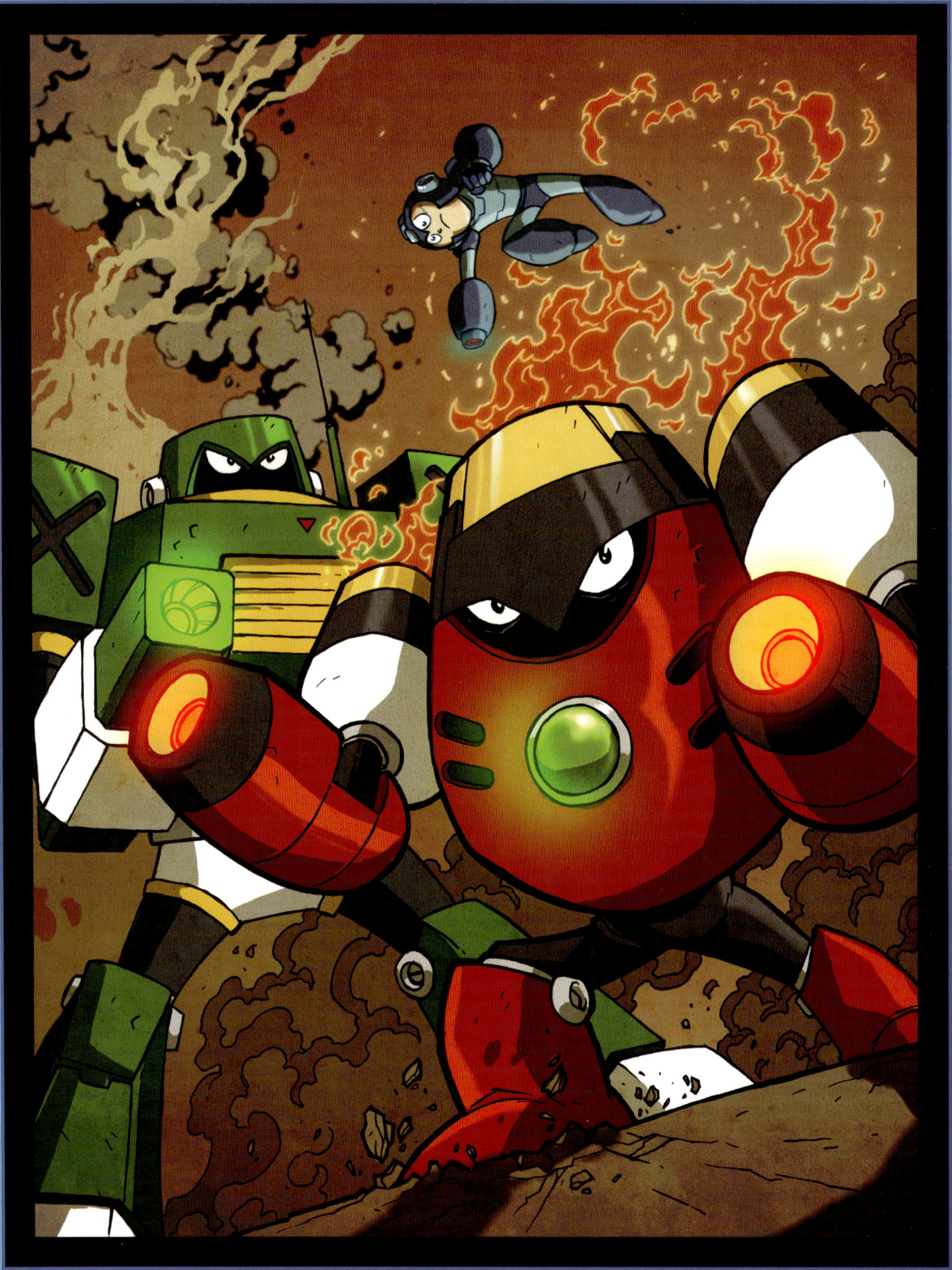

DARREN RAWLINGS (RAWLS)
Brampton, ON, Canada
www.rawls.ca / rawlsy.deviantart.com
Animator/Illustrator
(Popgun v04 - Image comics / The Anthology Project - volume 1&2 /
Agent Orange - Graphic novel series)

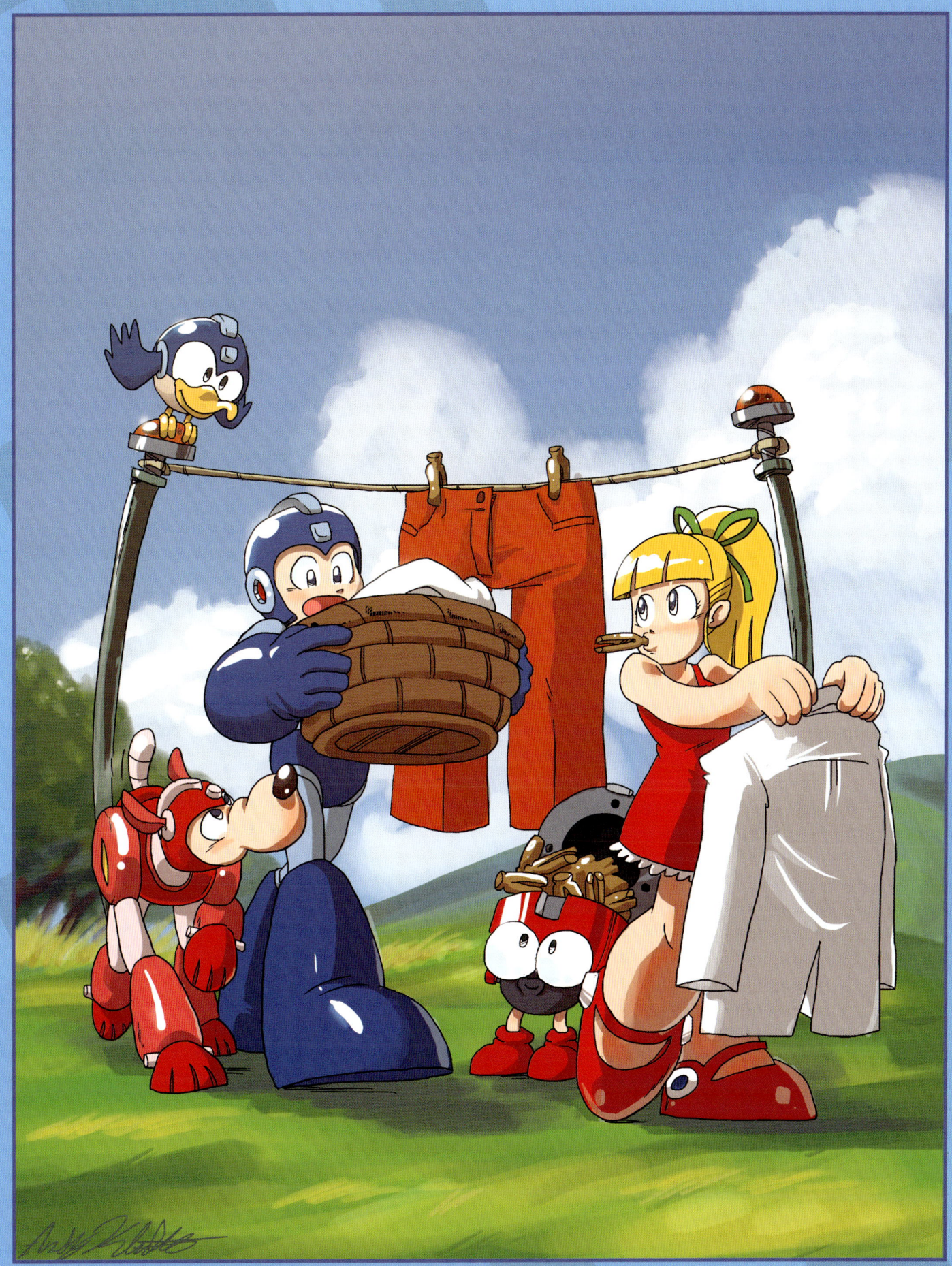

ANDY KLUTHE
Collinsville, IL, United States
www.andykluthe.com
Illustrator

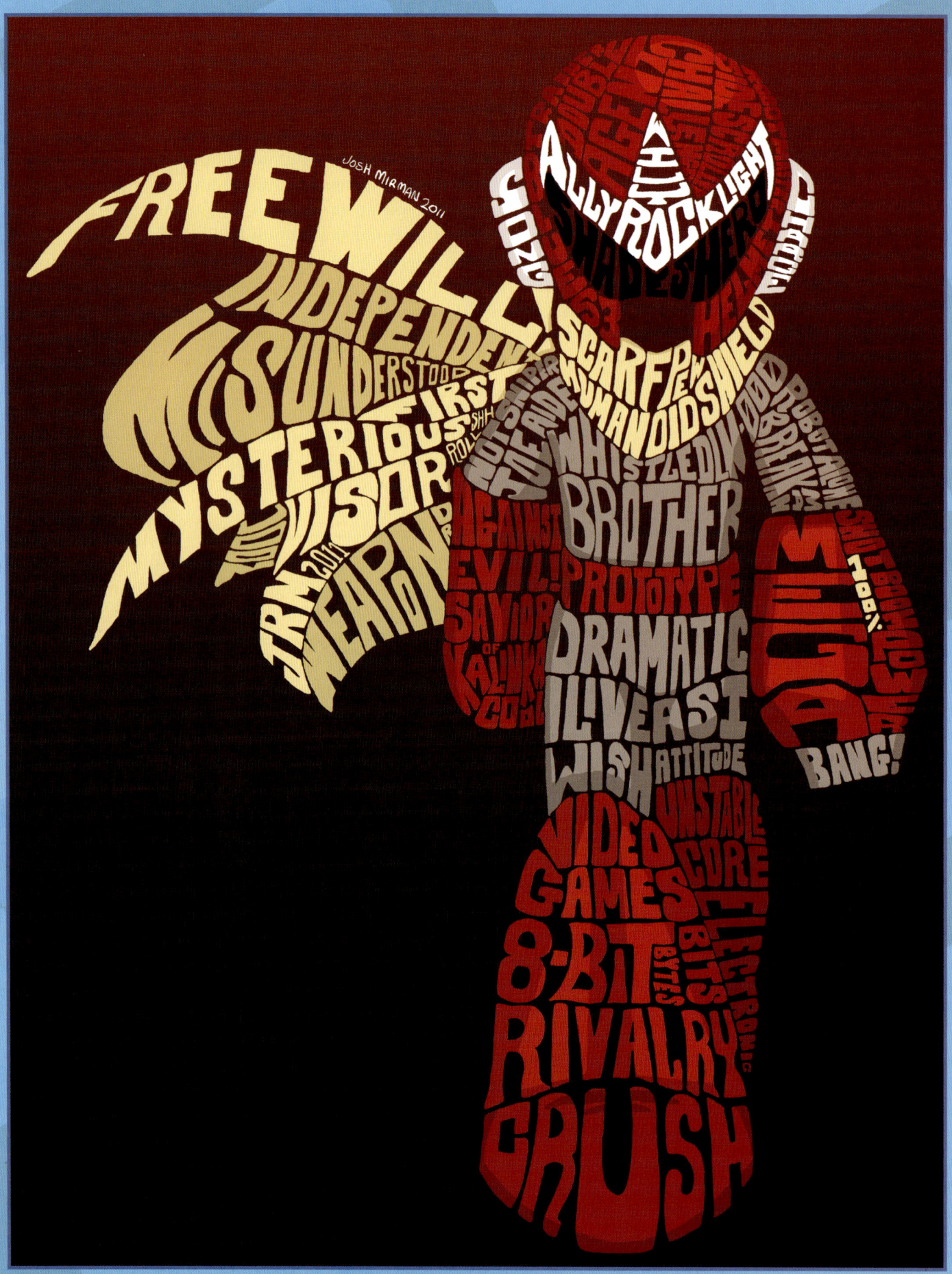

JOSH MIRMAN
Brooklyn, NY, United States
www.mirmanism.com
Artist / Writer
(The Awakening Of A Superhero / Stubble's 10th Anniversary / Punks and Nerds: Quarterlife)

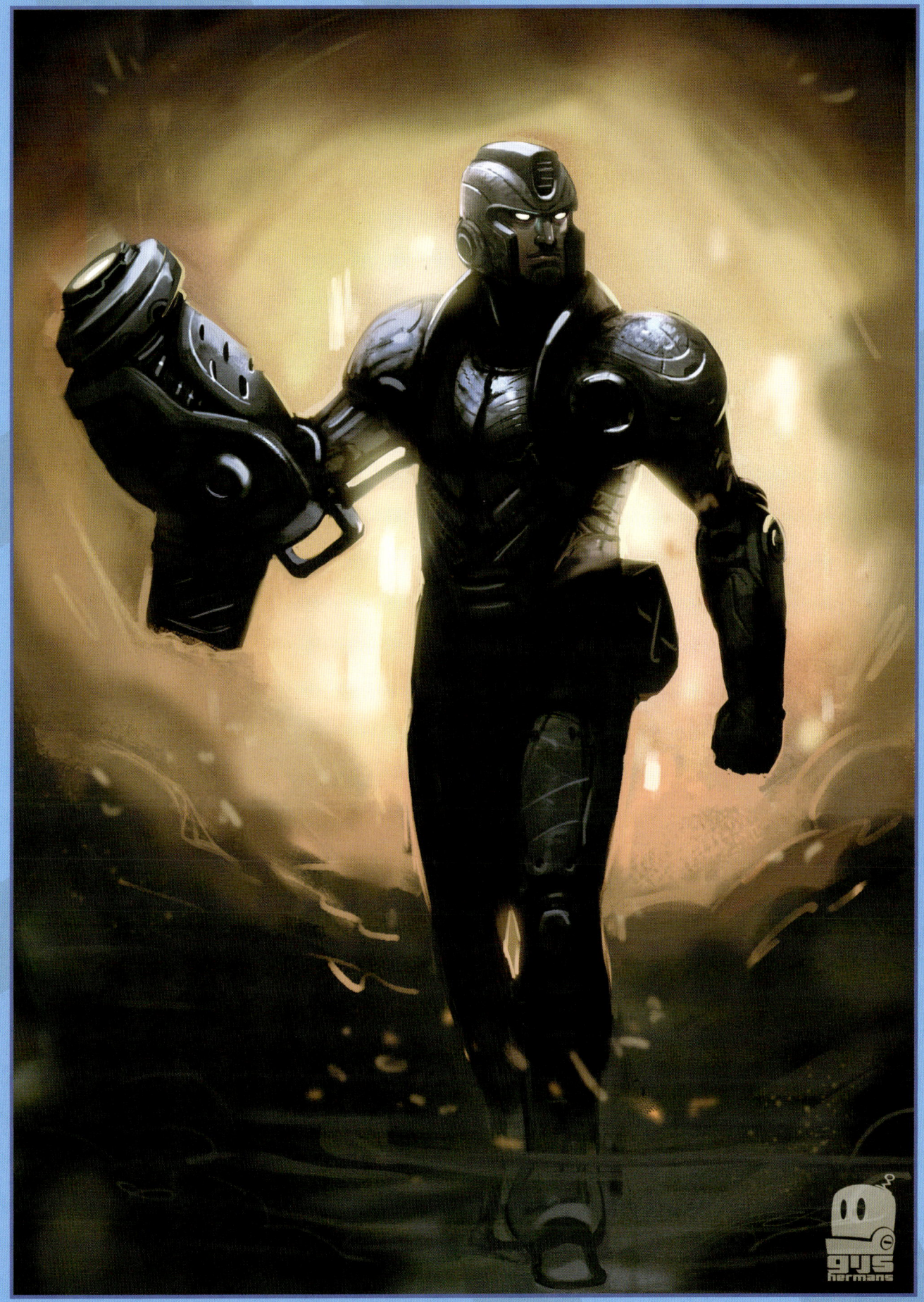

GIJS HERMANS
Reusel, Netherlands
Lead Artist - Ronimo-Games
(Lead Artist Swords and Soldiers / Lead Artist De Blob (the student project)
/ Master in Game Design & Development (HKU))

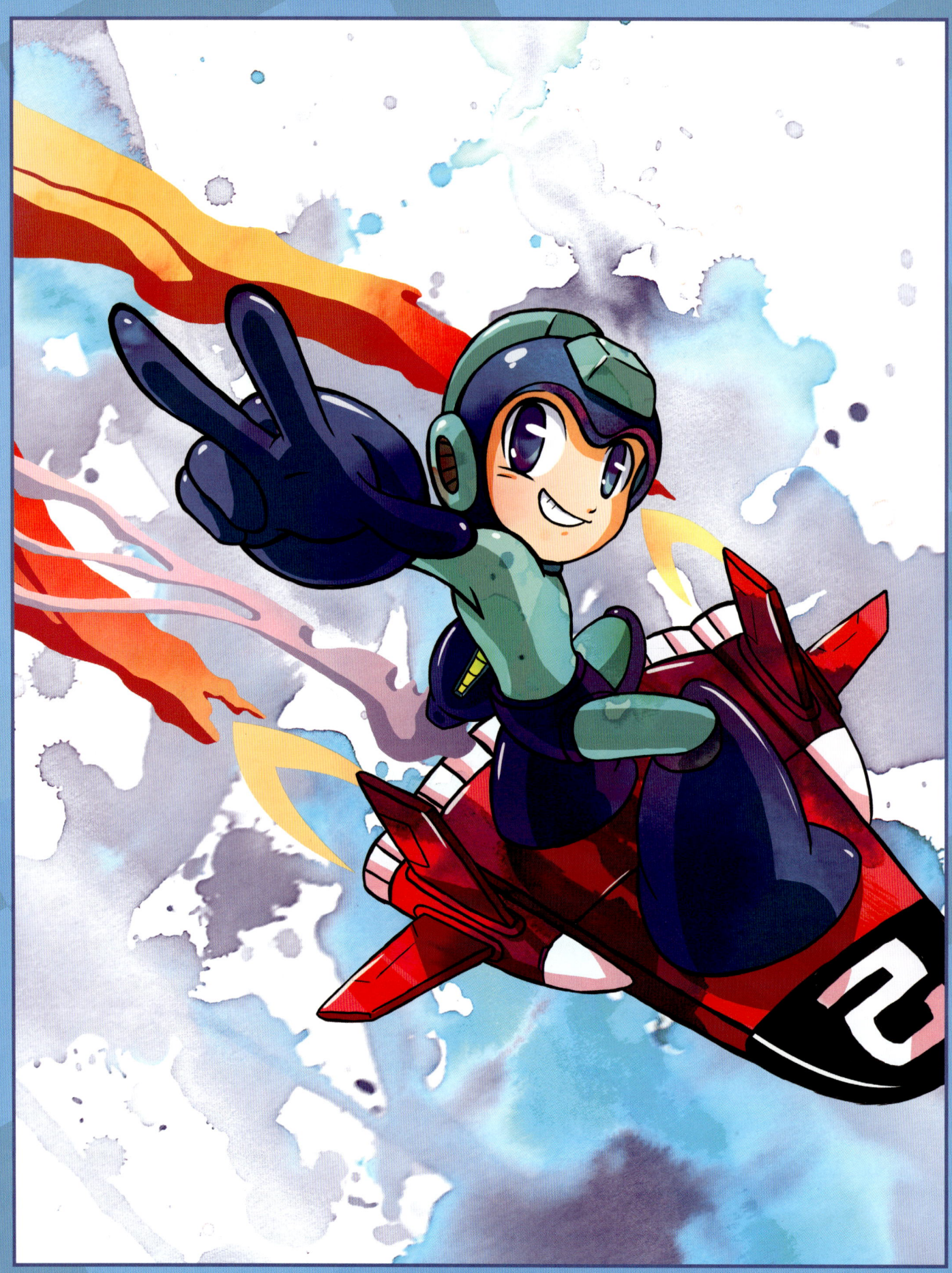

CLAIRE SCHUMACHER
Rotterdam, Netherlands
www.kurea.nl
Artist

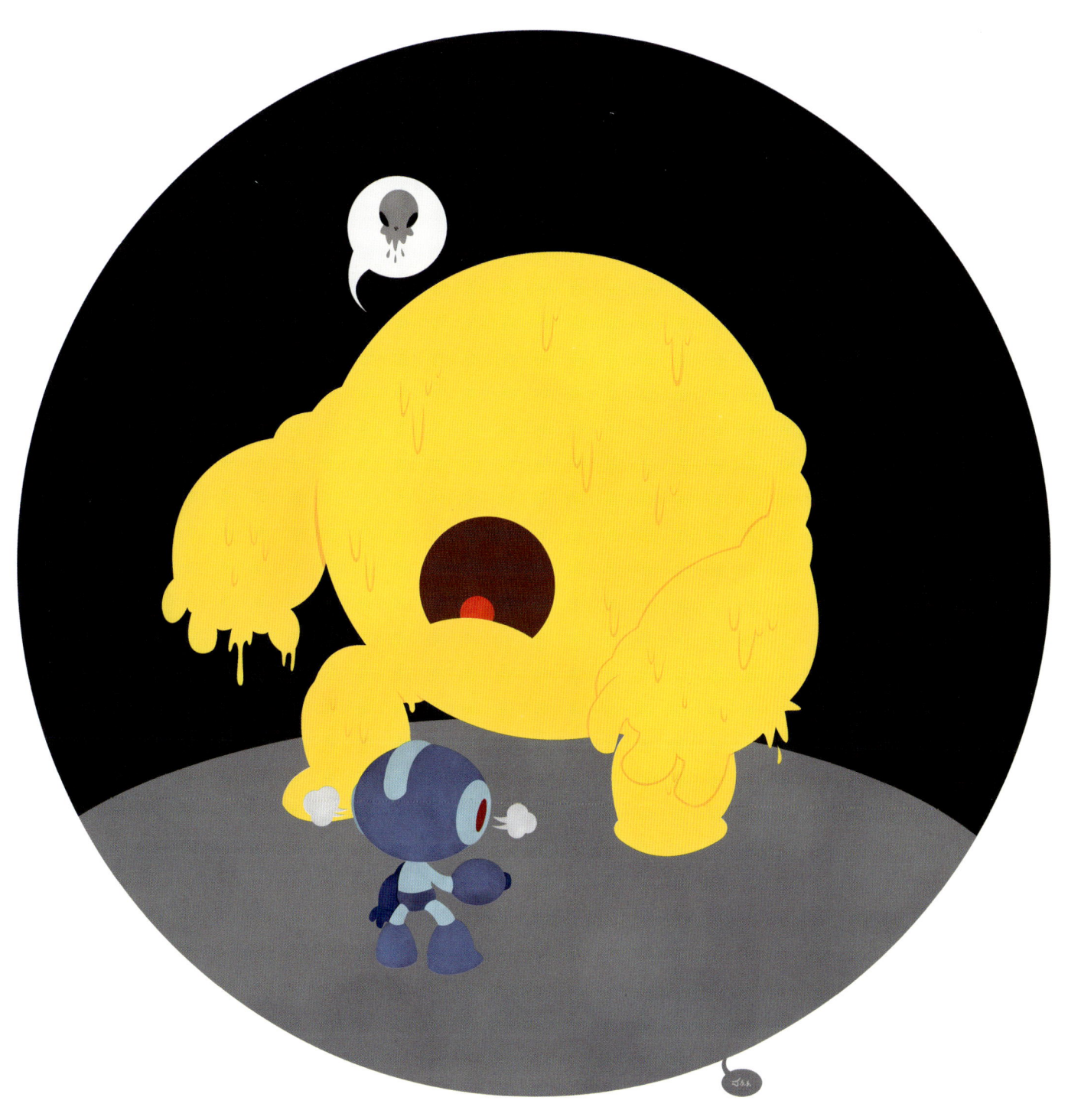

JOSHUA SHEPHERD
Sheffield, United Kingdom
sketchxj.deviantart.com
Illustrator

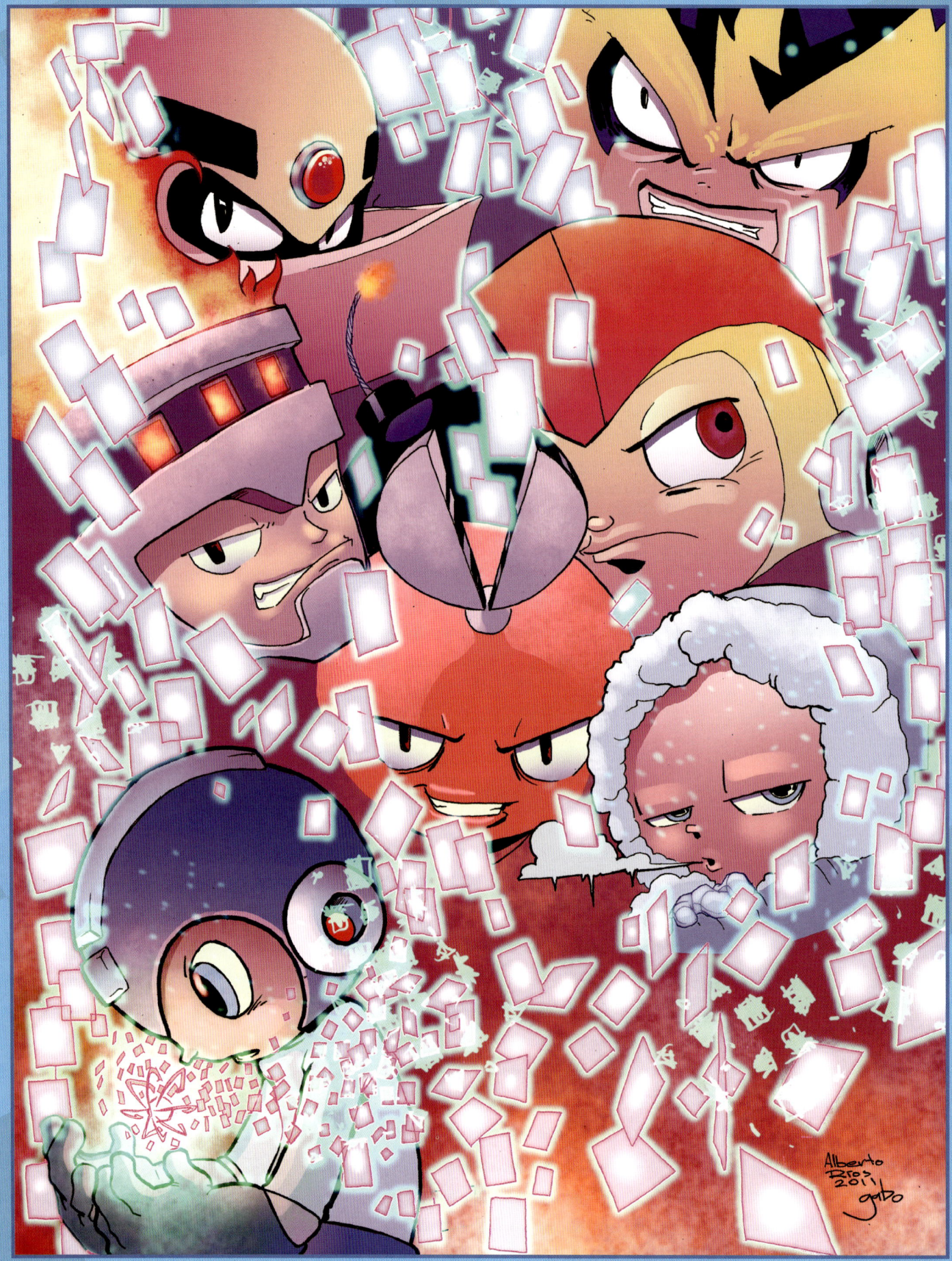

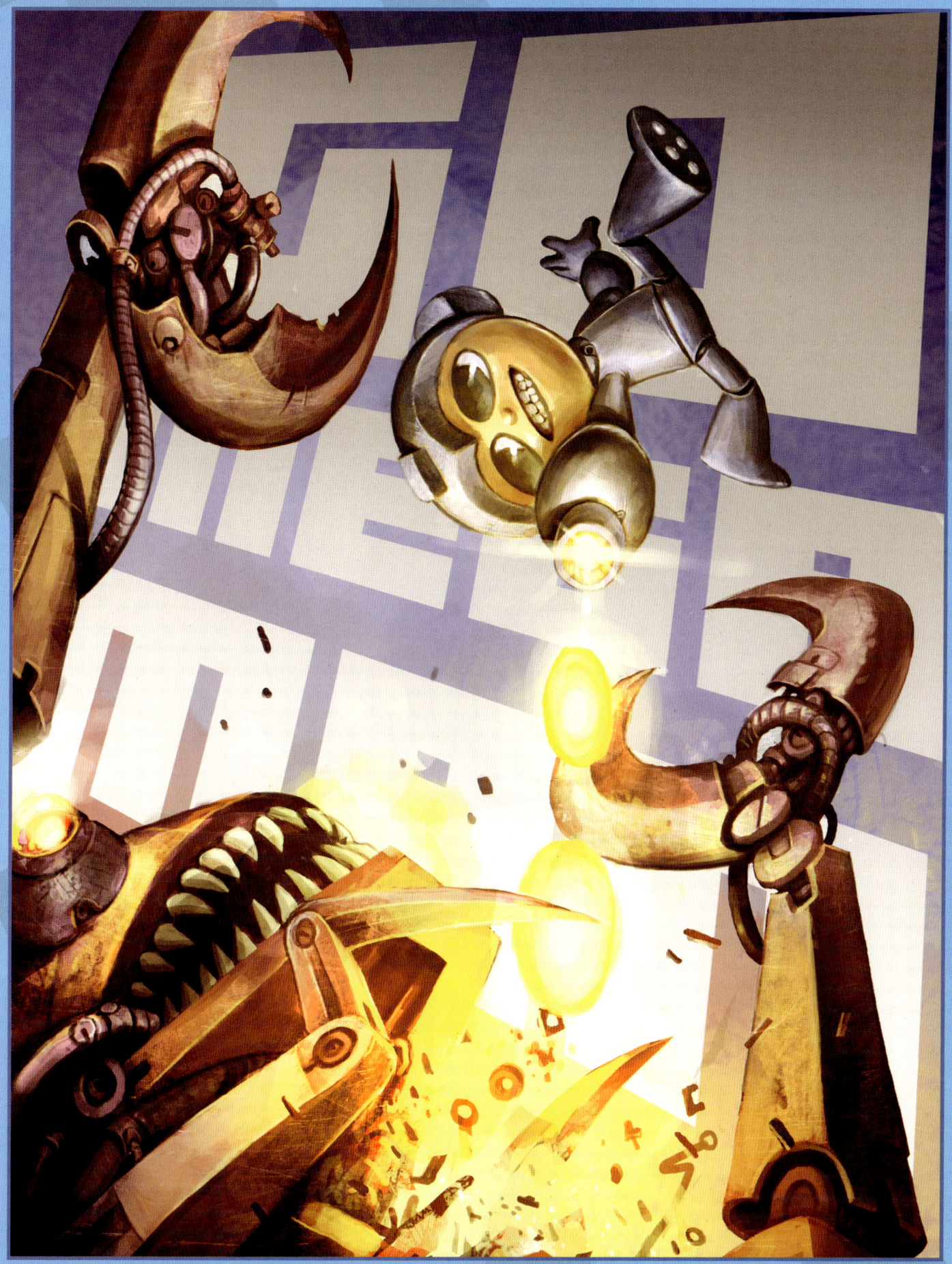

ANCOR GIL HERNÁNDEZ
Santa Cruz, Spain
great-oharu.deviantart.com
Illustrator
(POPGUN Comic Antology Nº2 / Legend of the 5 Rings card game)

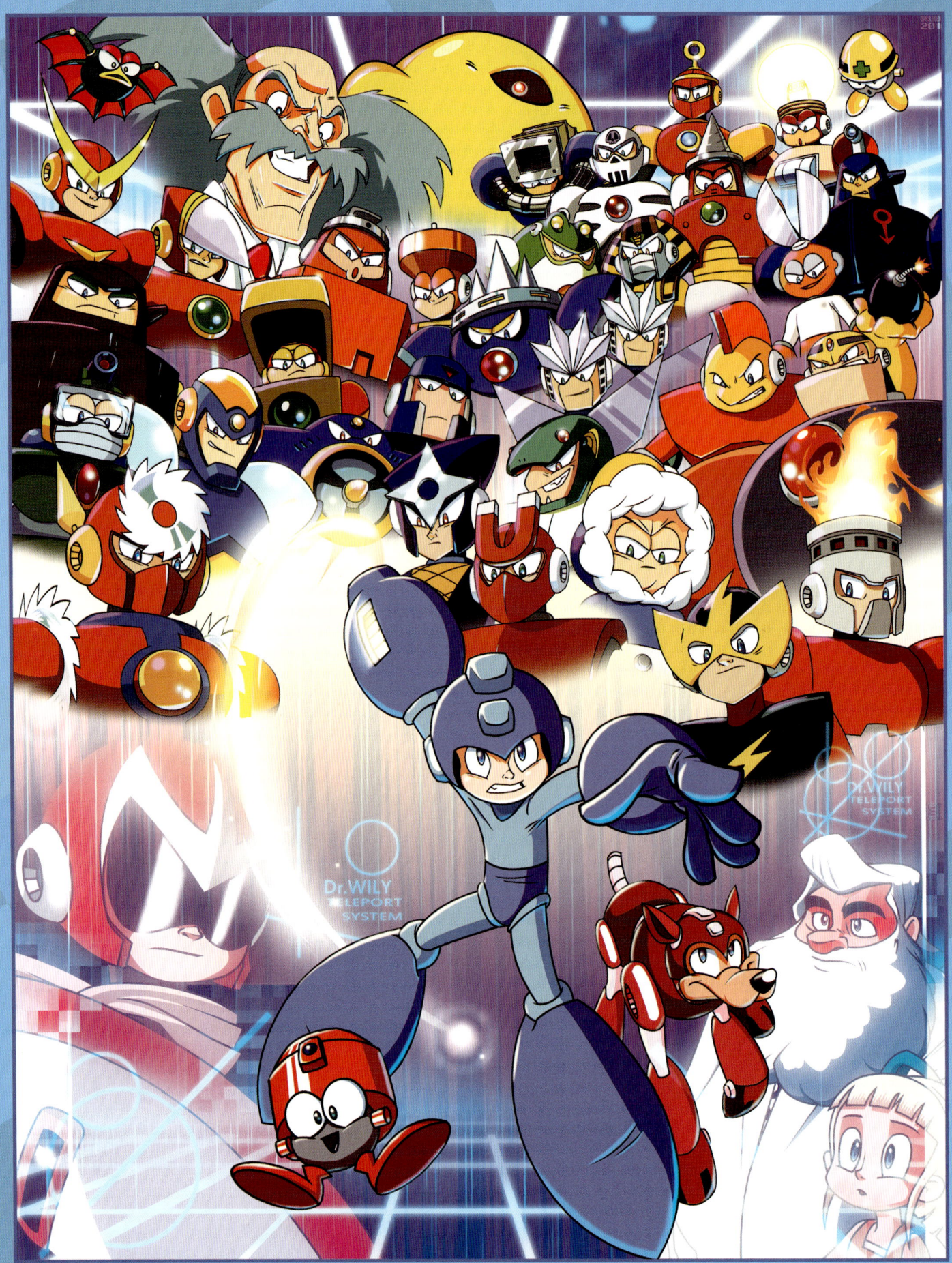

DAN SCHOENING (DAPPER DAN)
Victoria, BC, Canada
www.danschoening.com / traditionaldanimatio.deviantart.com
Animator / Illustrator

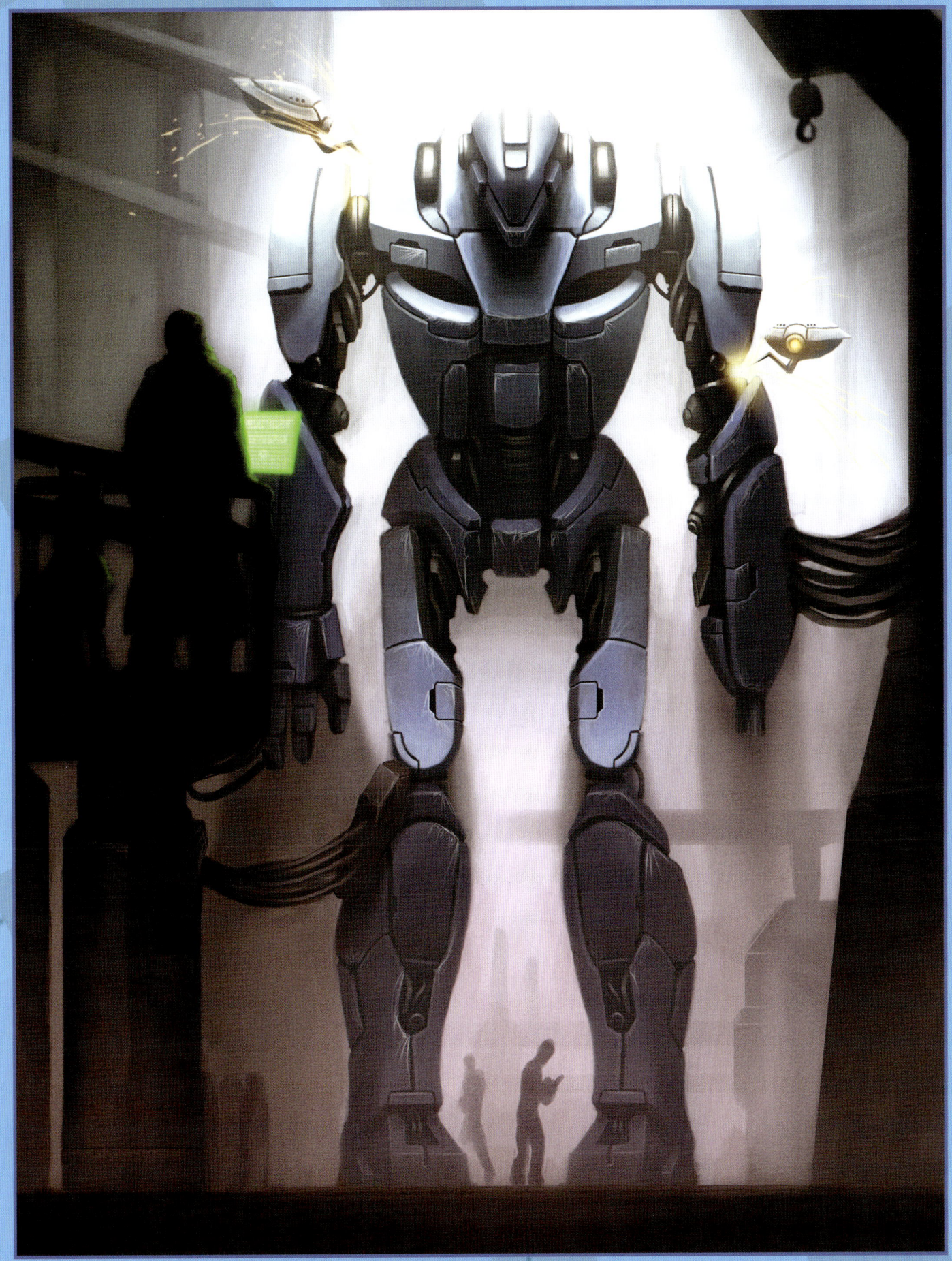

JONATHAN GONZÁLEZ GÓMEZ
Santa Cruz, Spain
brotherostavia.deviantart.com
Graphic Designer

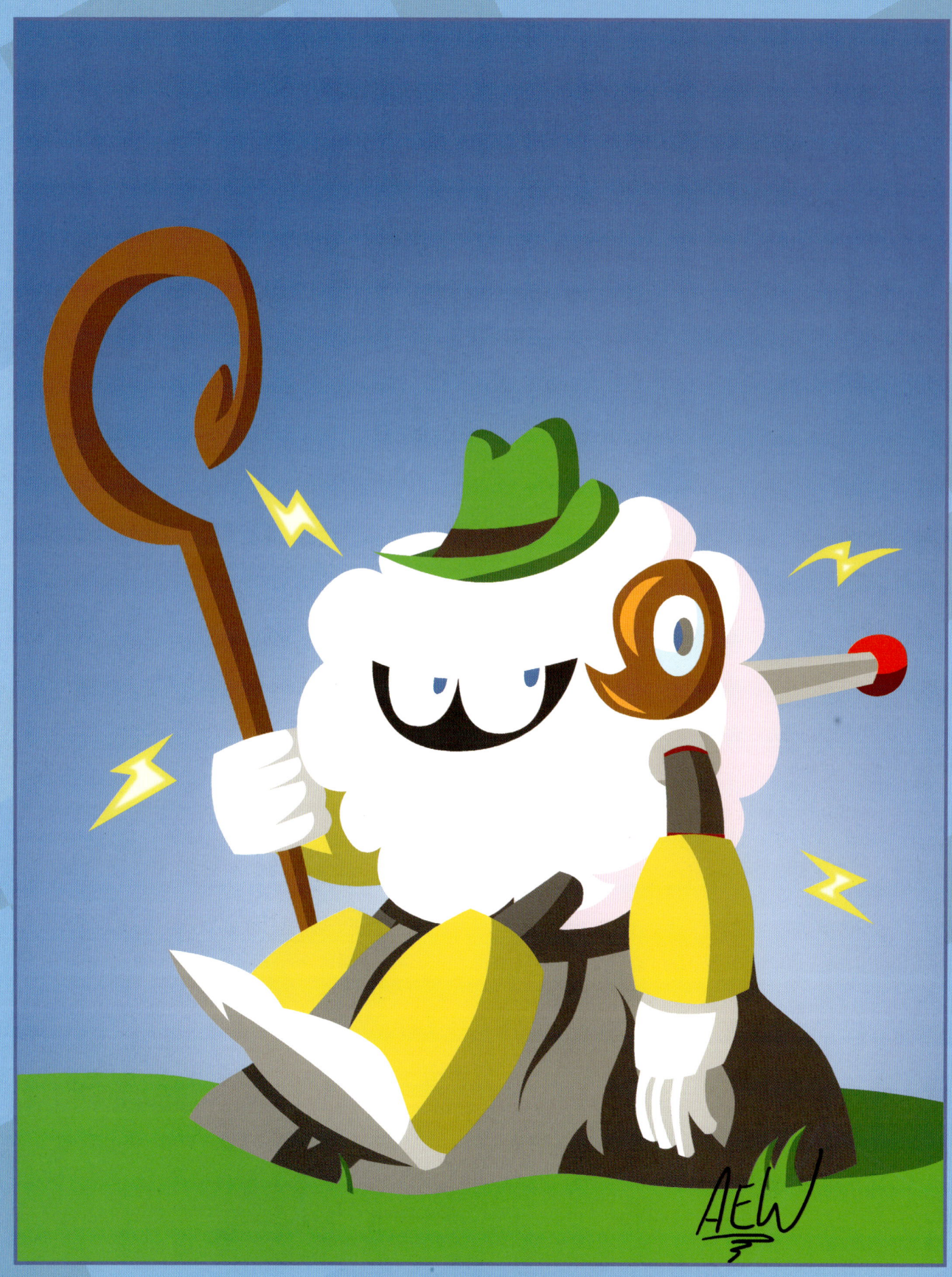

AMR EL-WAKEEL (FROBMAN)
Bath, United Kingdom
frobman.deviantart.com
Illustrator
(BA (Hons) Animation course)

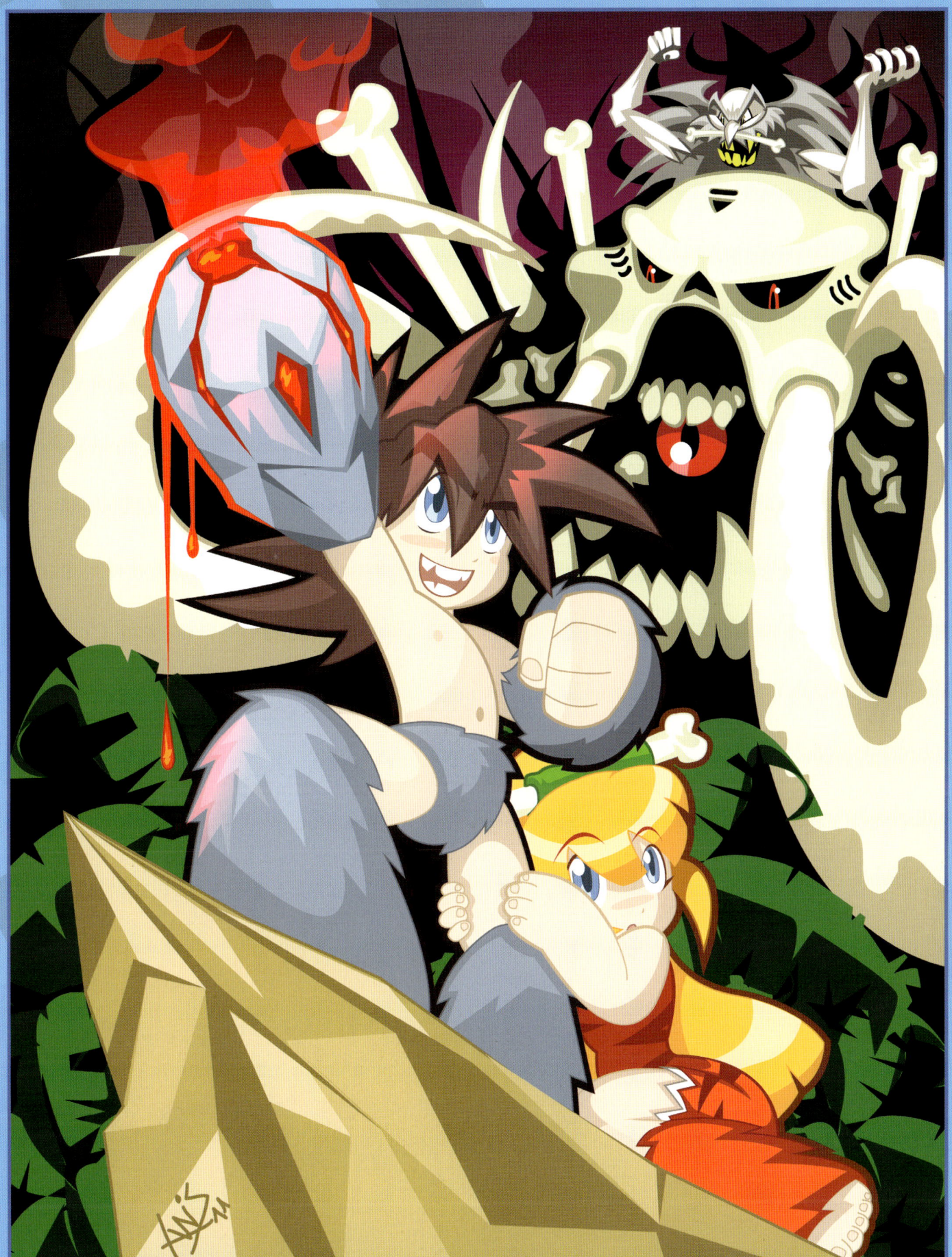

JOSÉ LUÍS JIMÉNEZ DÍAZ (ELDOCTORGOREDEALER)
Bogota, Colombia
http://eldoctorgoredealer.deviantart.com/
Illustrator
(SHARPBALL / AIRE COMO PLOMO / MENTEZ)

CAMILO SUAREZ
Bogota, Colombia
www.camilosuarez.com
Graphic Designer

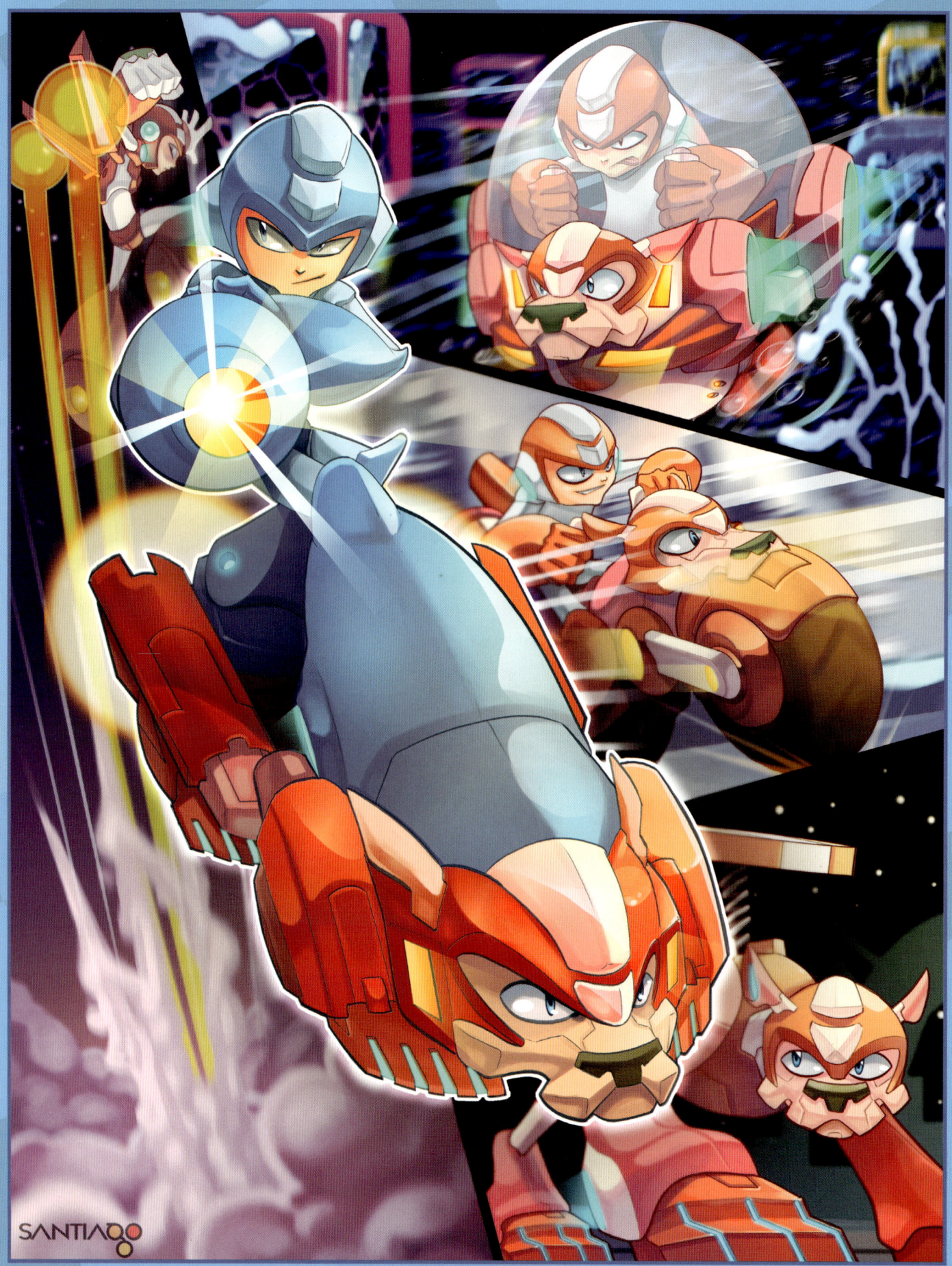

LUIS SANTIAGO
Bayamon, Puerto Rico
pertheseus.deviantart.com
Graphic Designer

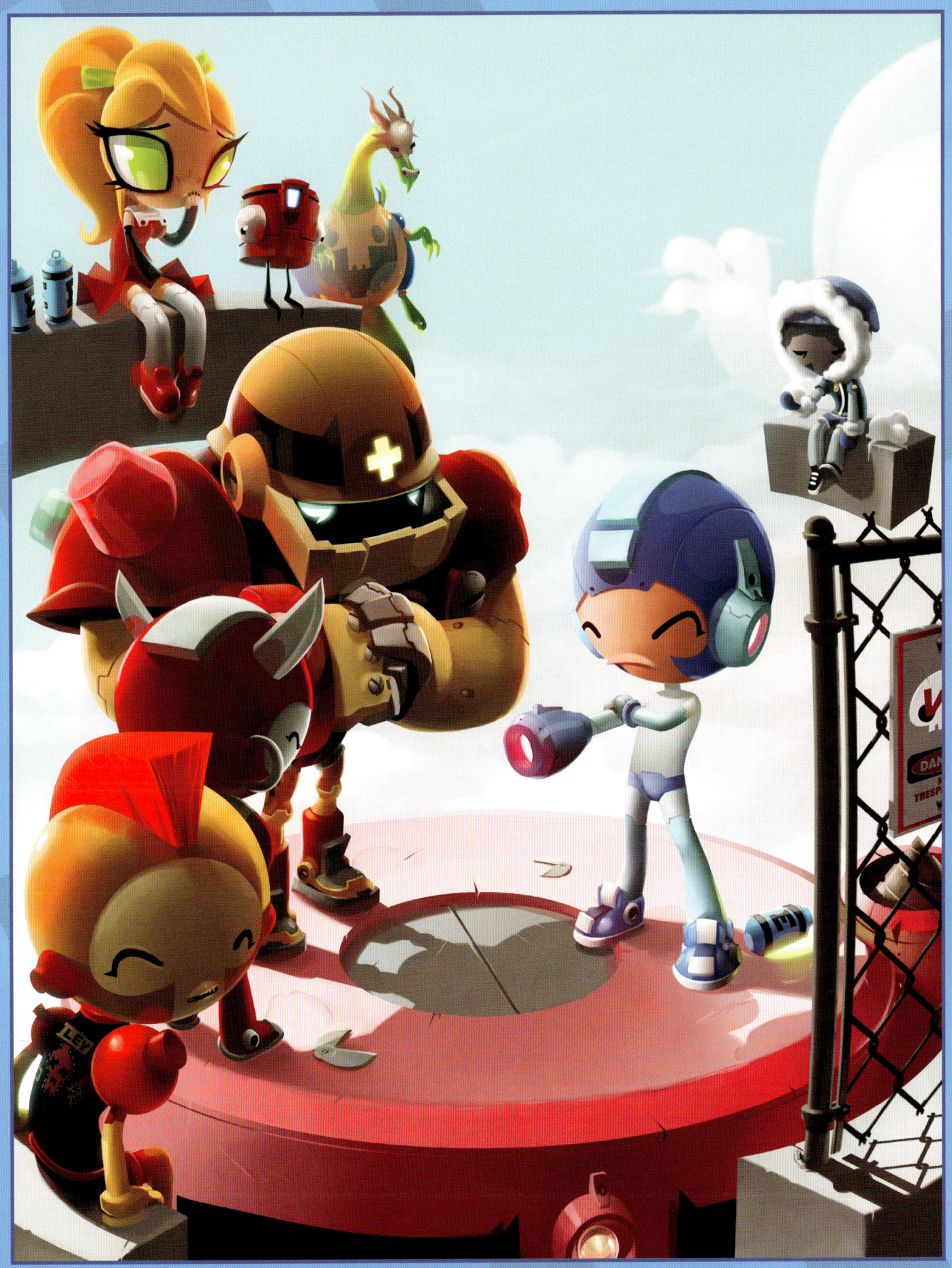

ANDREW WILSON (FOURTHWISH)
ENCINITAS, CA, UNITED STATES
www.theforgottenkingdoms.com
ART FIEND
(FORGOTTEN KINGDOM OF IMAGINARY FRIENDS /
SO NOW WHAT DO WE DO? / RED DEAD REDEMPTION)

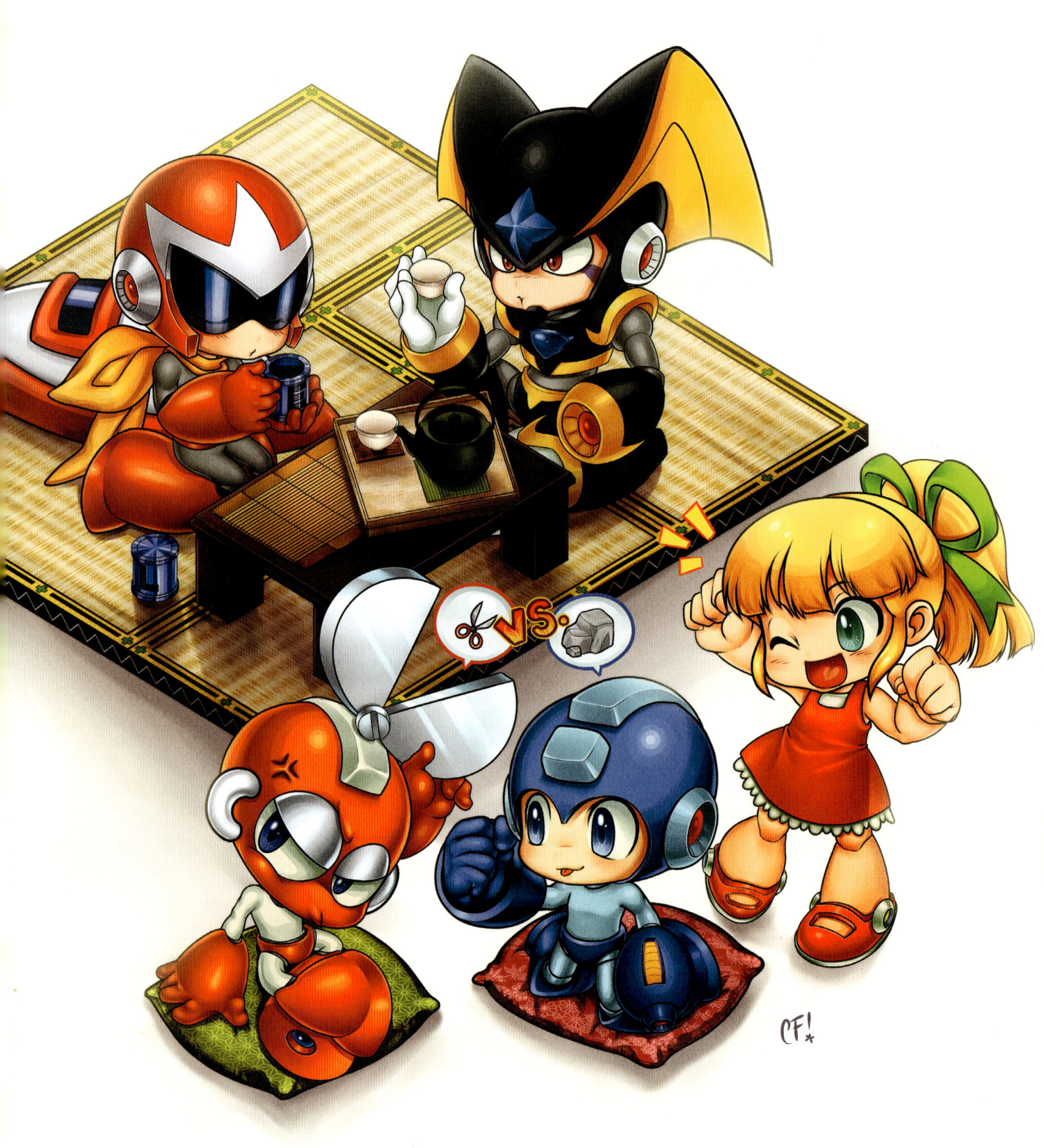

CAMILA FORTUNA
Montevideo, Uruguay
sakura-studio.deviantart.com
Game Artist

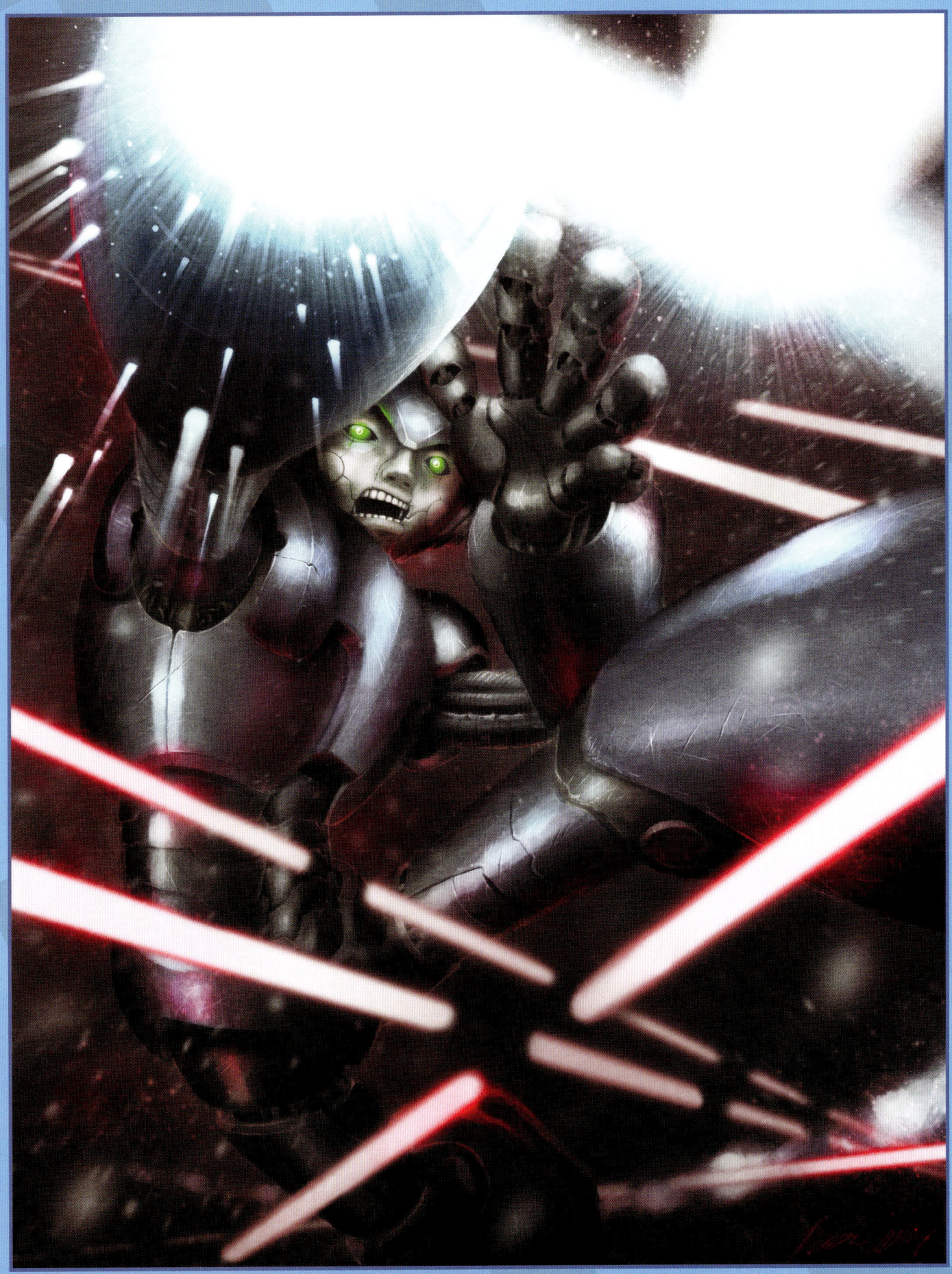

BRIAN LUONG
Simi Valley, CA, United States
artofbrianluong.carbonmade.com / artofbrianluong.blogspot.com
Illustrator

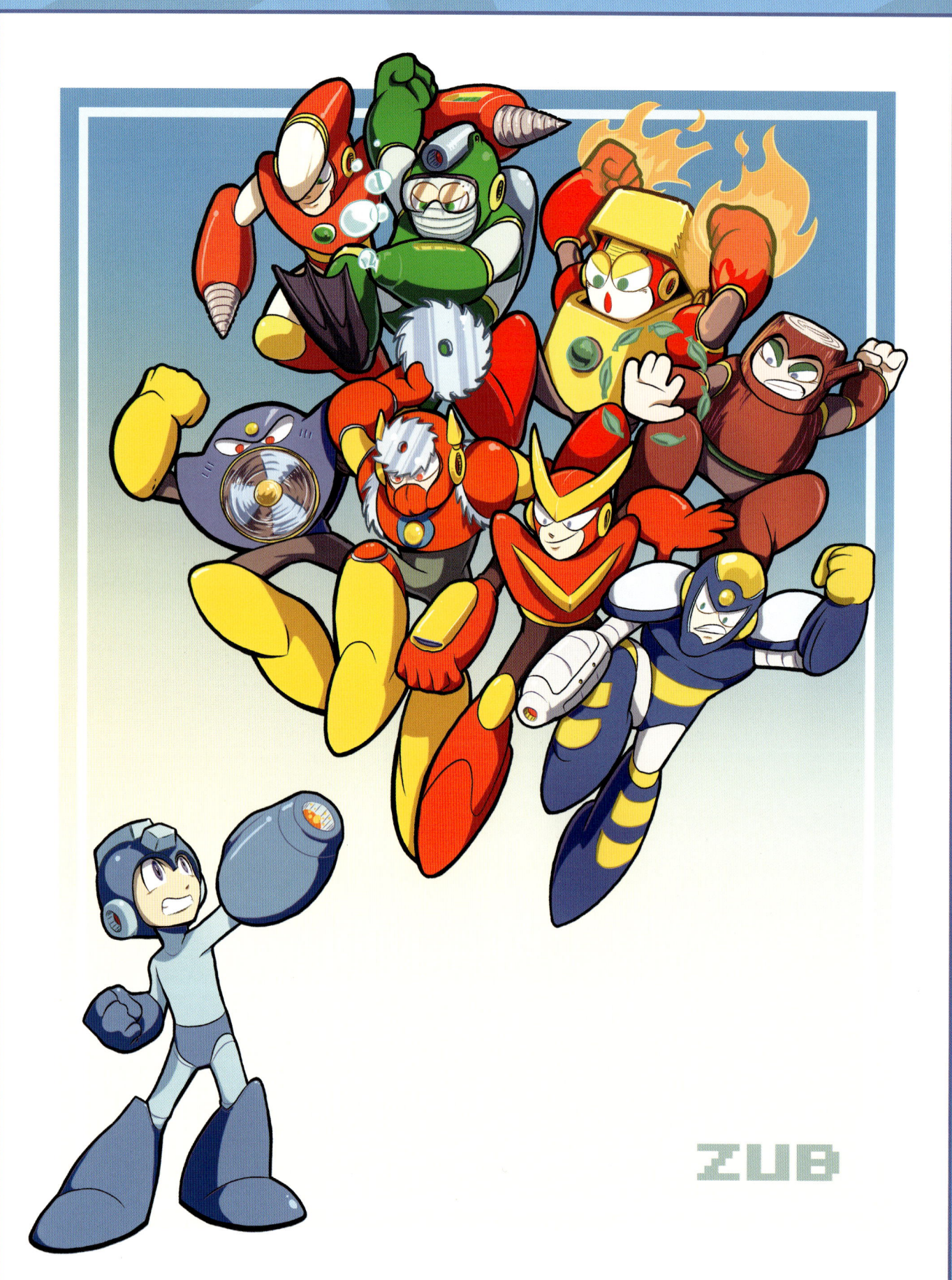

JIM ZUBKAVICH
Toronto, ON, Canada
www.skullkcikers.com,
Writer, Artist, UDON Project Manager
(Skullkcikers / Street Fighter Legends: Ibuki / Makeshift Miracle)

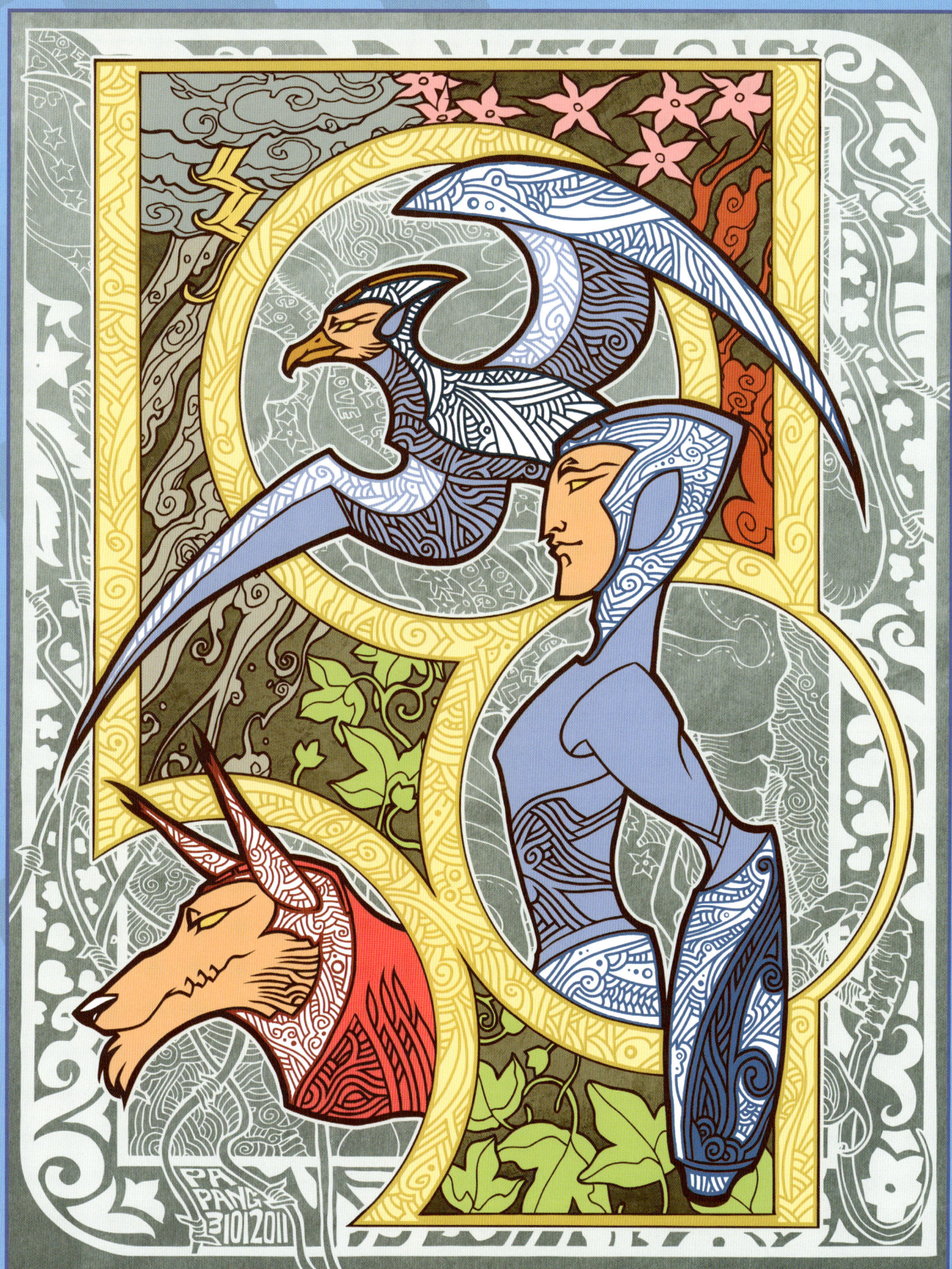

PAPANG PANGKETEPANG
Malang, Indonesia
pangketepang.deviantart.com
Illustrator

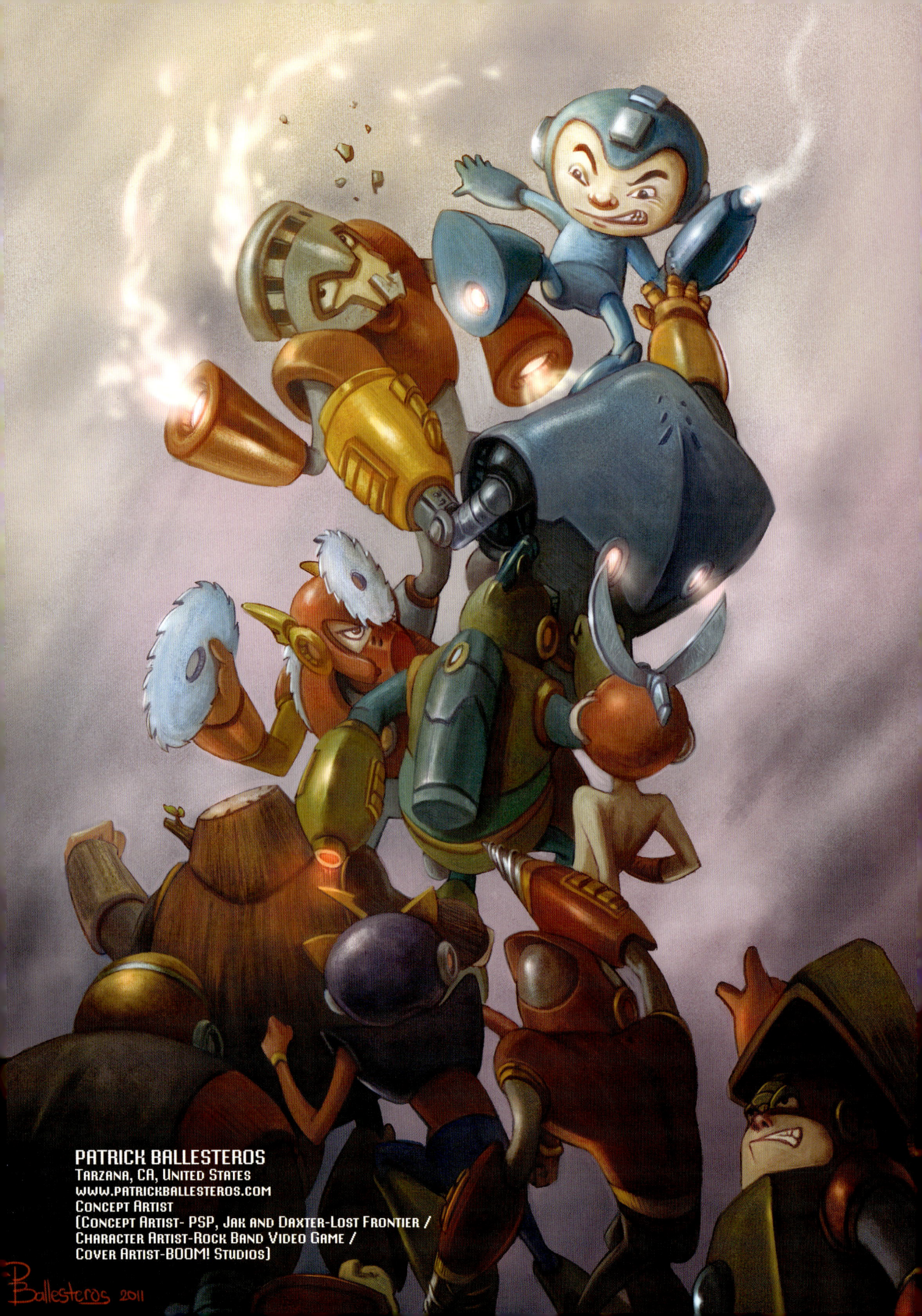

PATRICK BALLESTEROS
Tarzana, CA, United States
www.patrickballesteros.com
Concept Artist
(Concept Artist- PSP, Jak and Daxter-Lost Frontier /
Character Artist-Rock Band Video Game /
Cover Artist-BOOM! Studios)

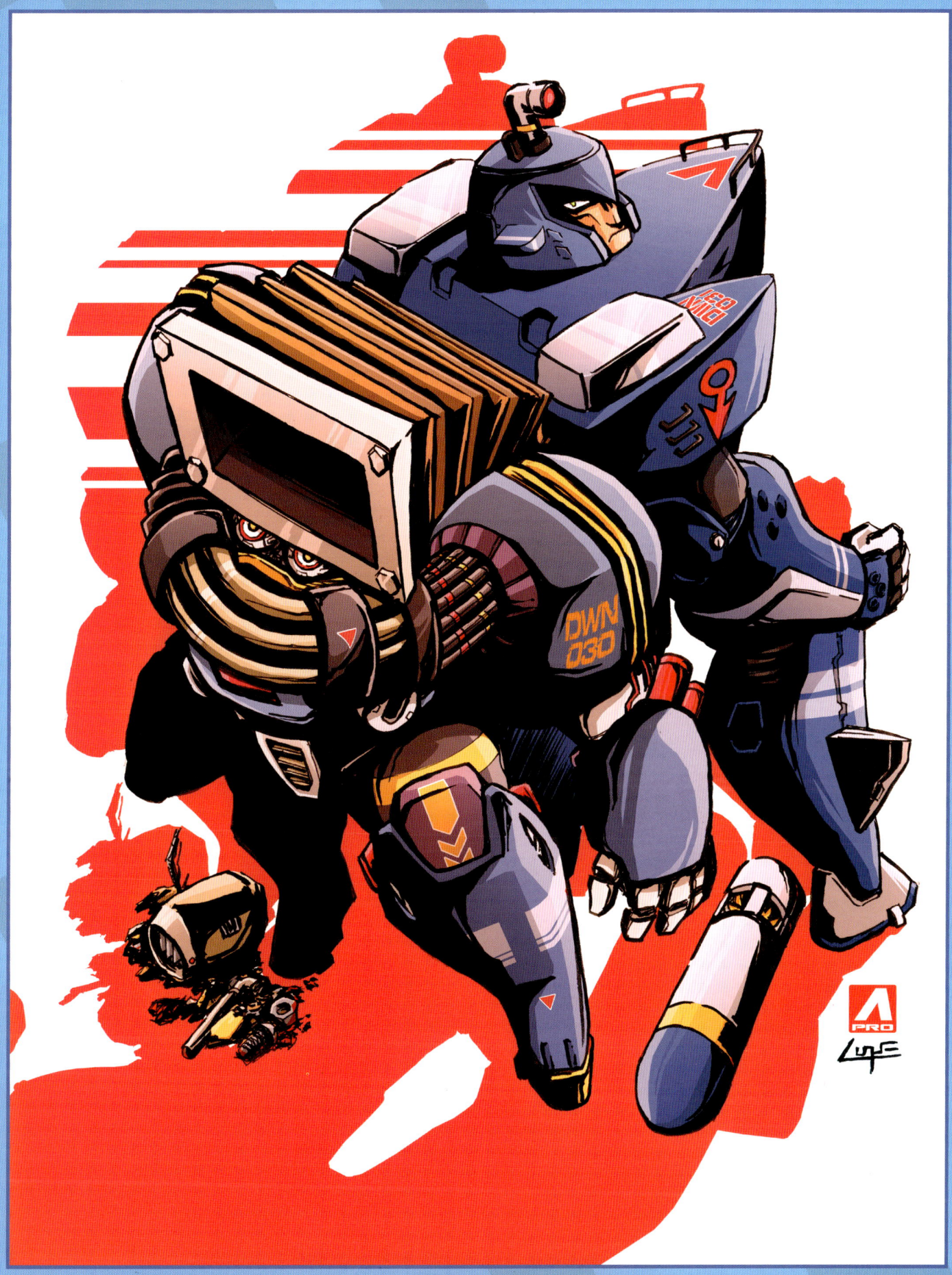

GABRIEL LUQUE
Gonzalez Catan, Argentina
aprostudio.blogspot.com
Illustrator

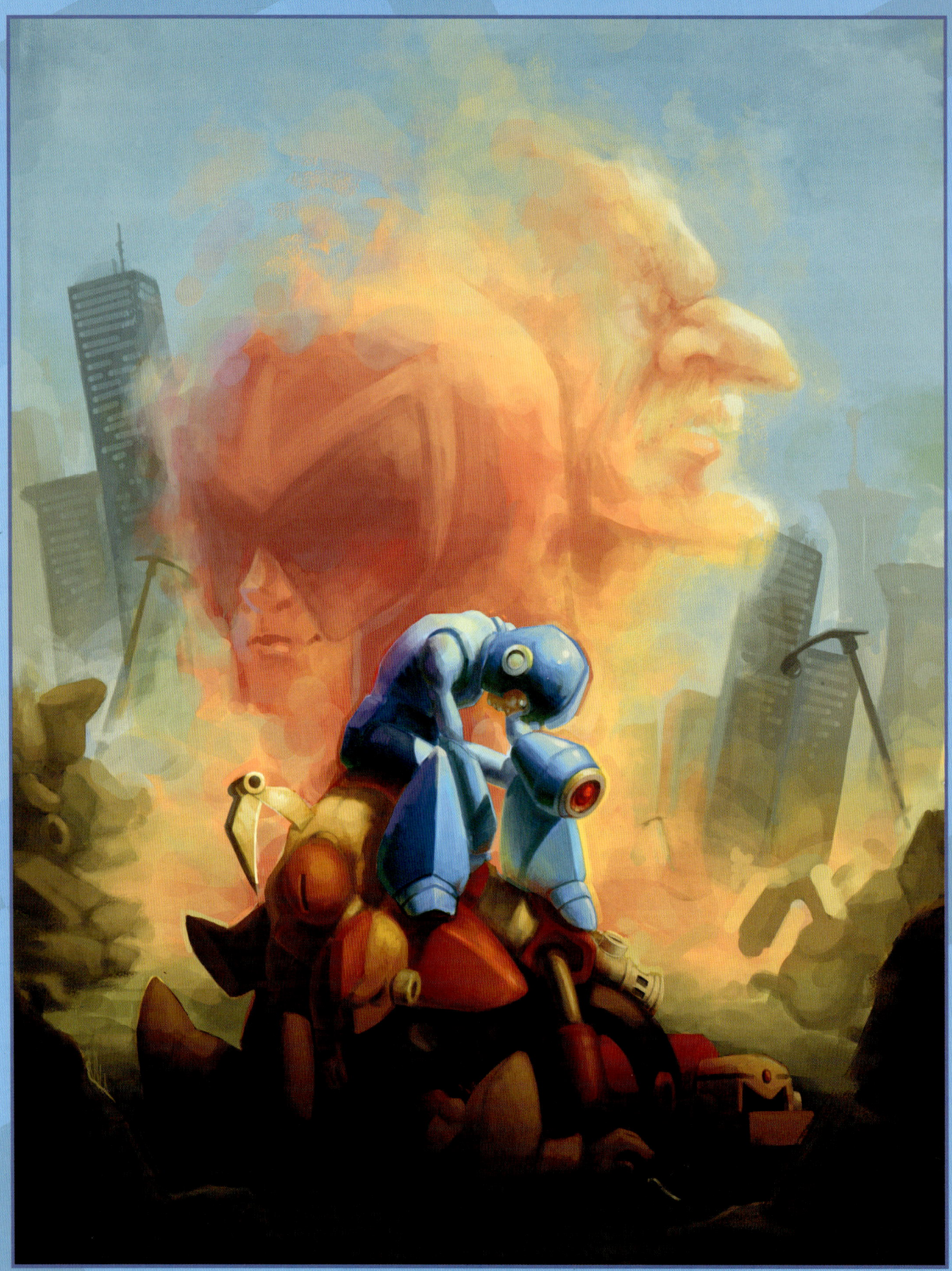

JAKE KALBHENN
Toronto, ON, Canada
j-niff.deviantart.com
Illustrator
(Max the Mutt Animation School)

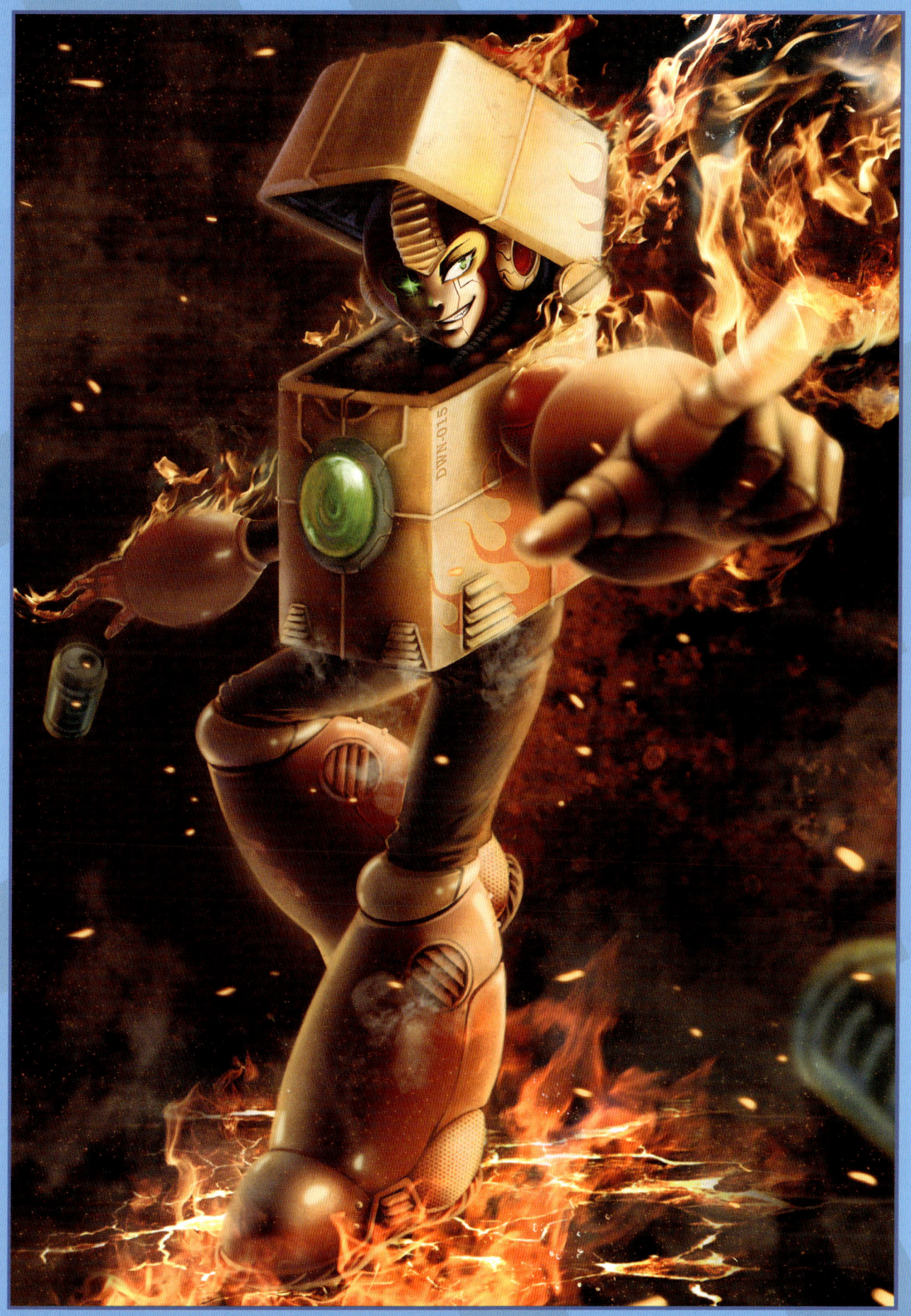

ALISE GLUŠKOVA (ALEXASHARLOT)
Riga, Latvia
alexasharlot.deviantart.com
Illustrator

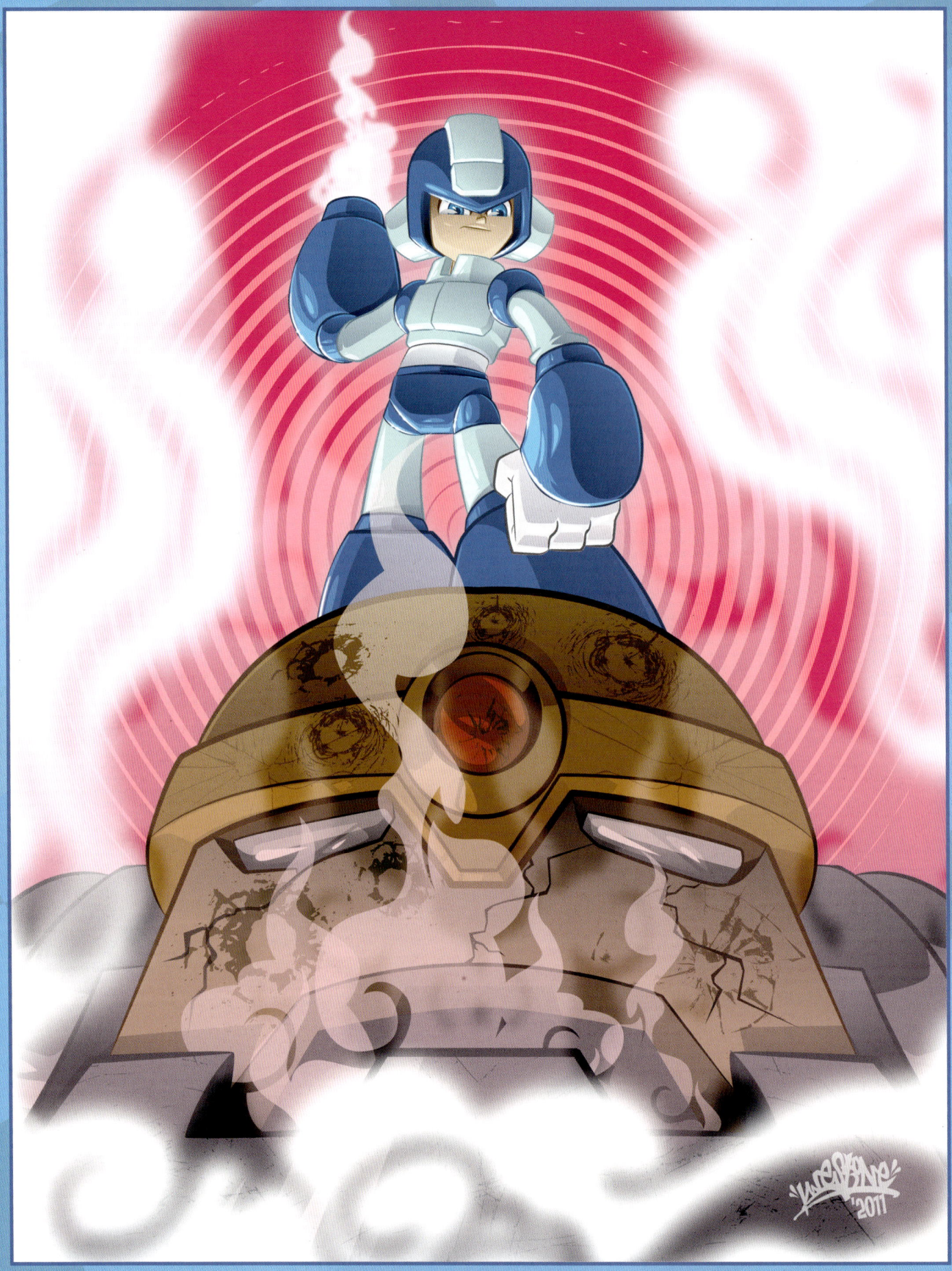

CHITO ARELLANO (KWESTONE)
Long Beach, CA, United States
kwestone.deviantart.com
Content Development / Sr. Artist at Spin Master LTD
(Lead Toy Designer (Tech Deck Dudes))

ERIC PHAN
Art Manager
(Tsunami Tactical)

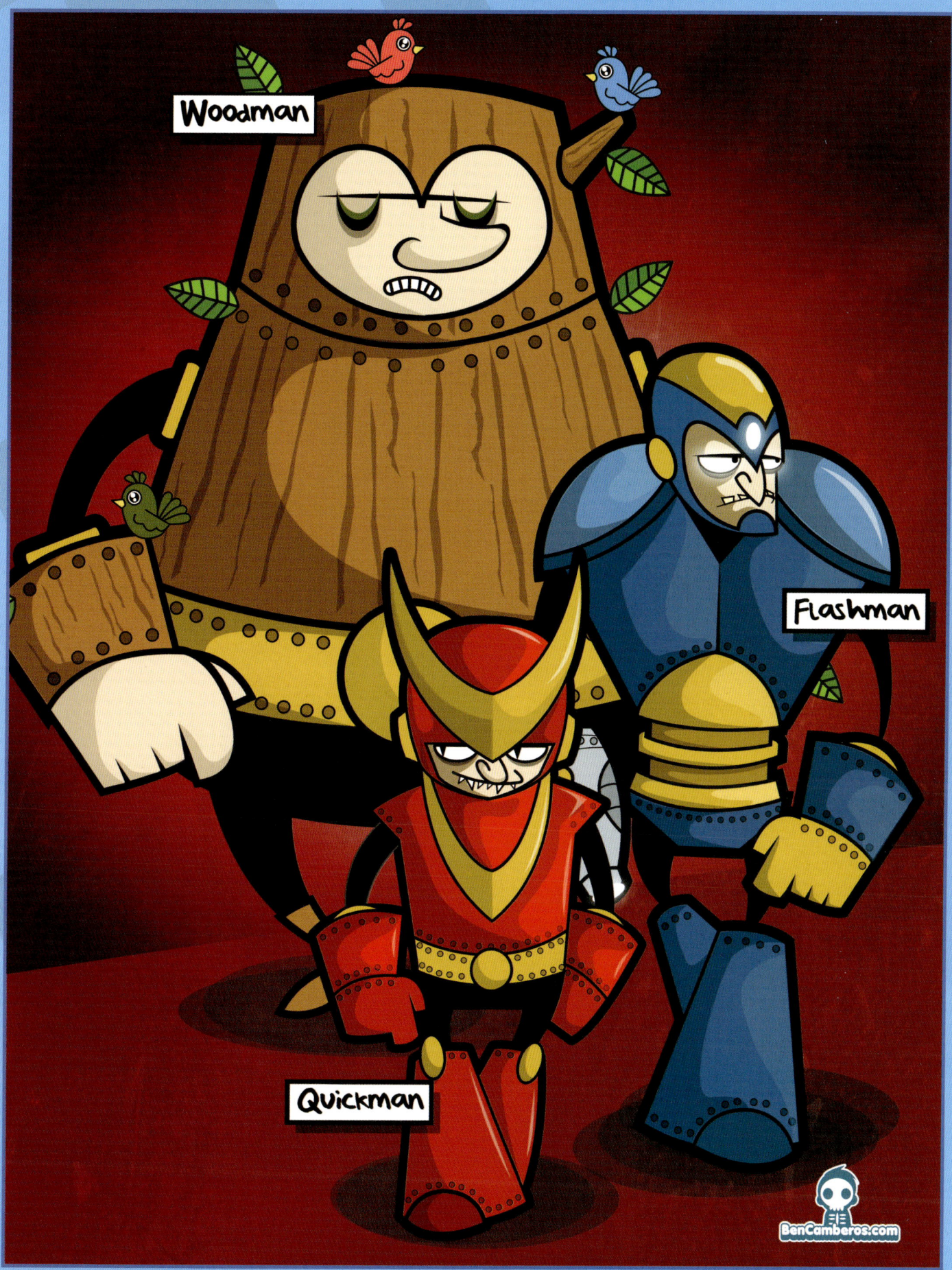

BEN CAMBEROS
Tijuana, Mexico
www.bencamberos.com
Art Director

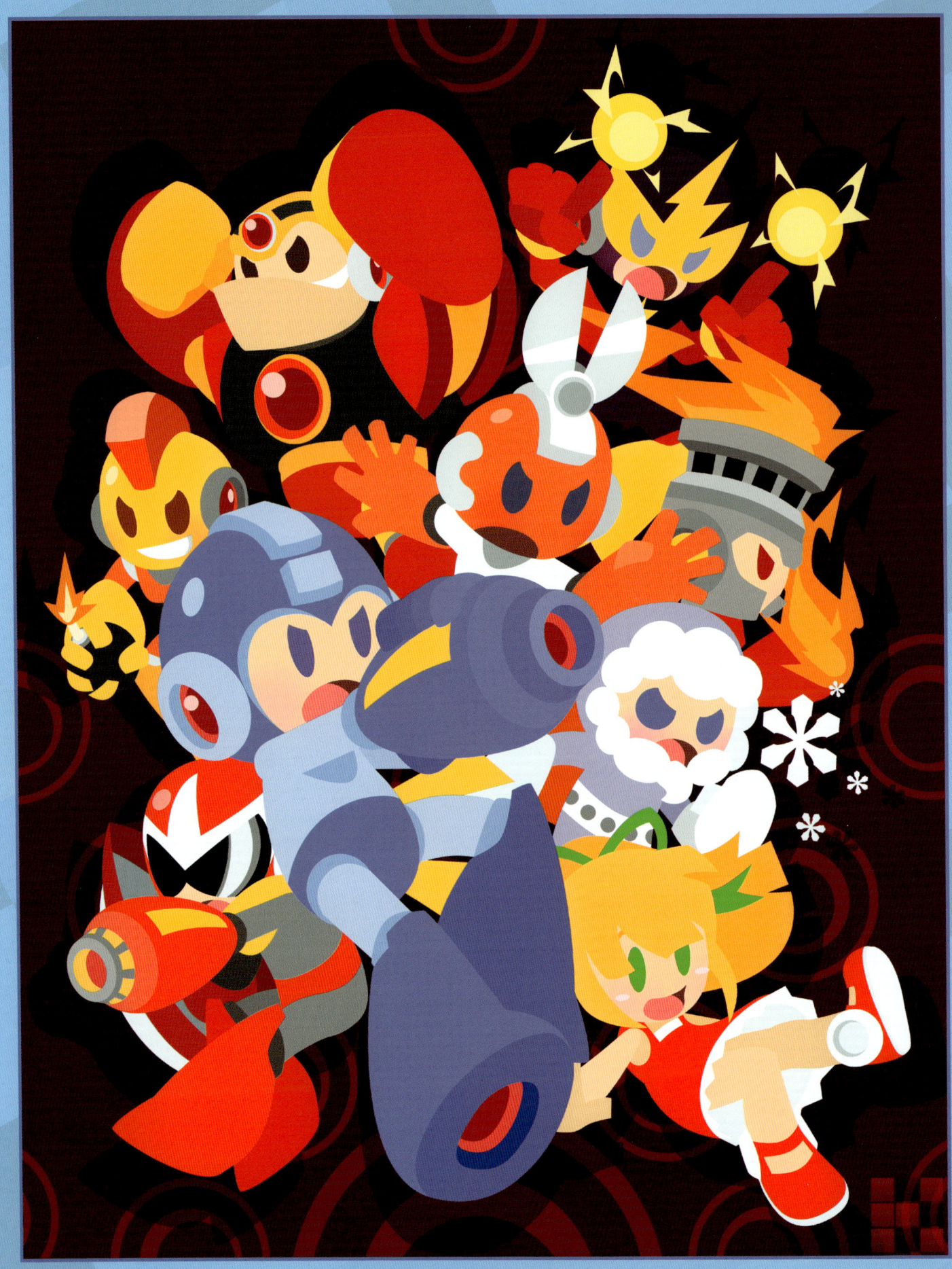

KINSON YUNG (PYAUKI)
Vancouver, BC, Canada
www.kinsonyung.com
Artist

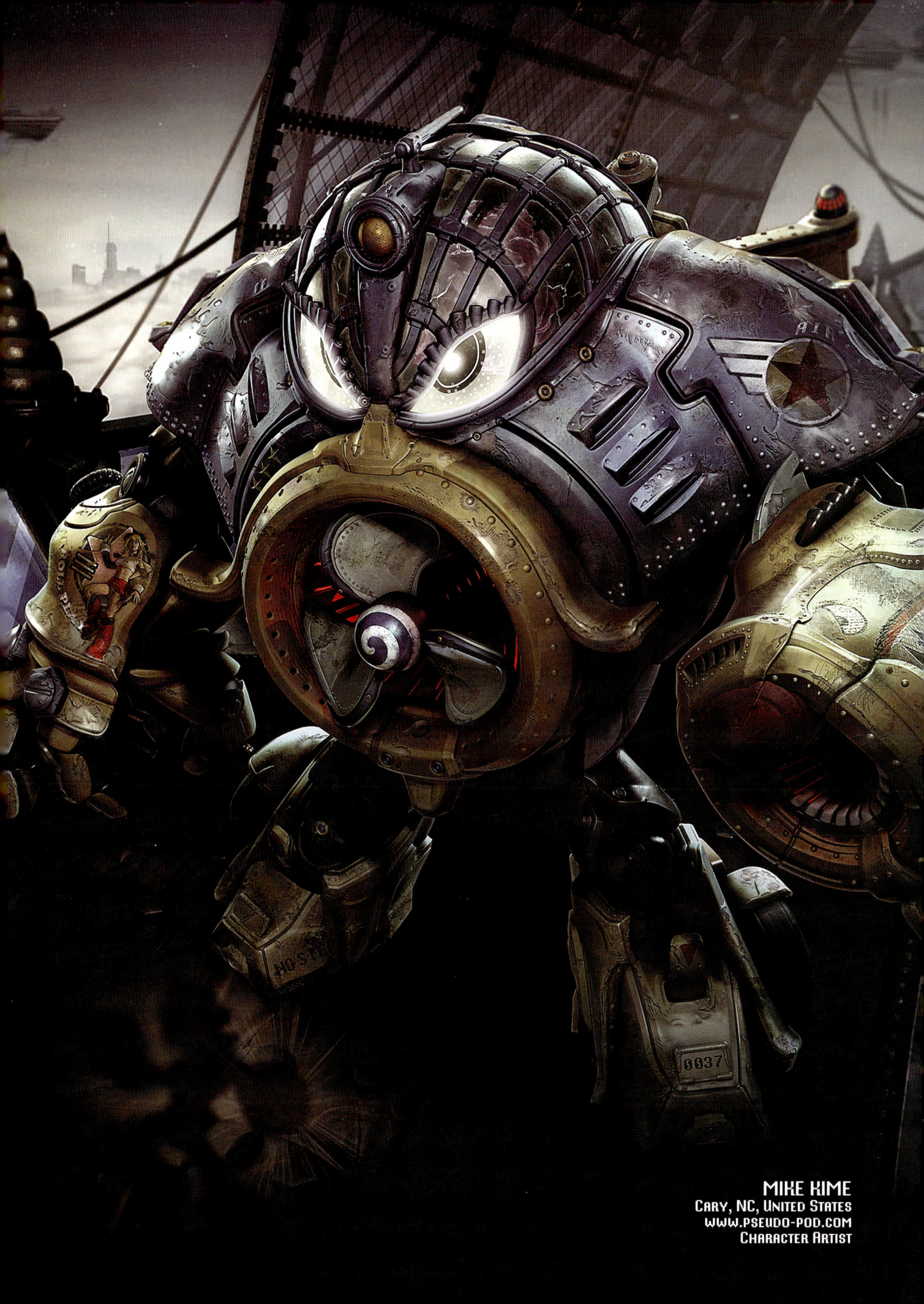

MIKE KIME
Cary, NC, United States
www.pseudo-pod.com
Character Artist

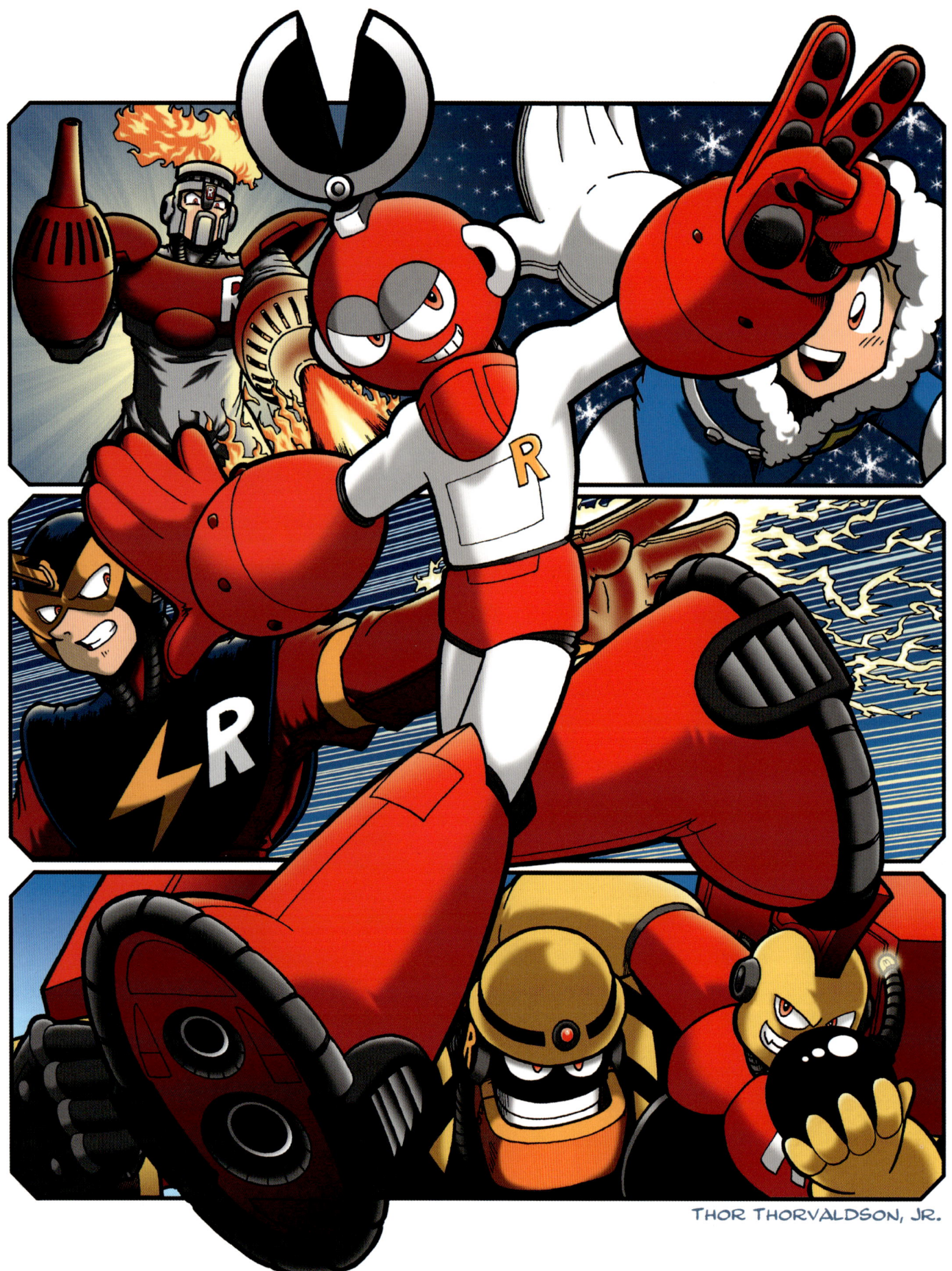

THOR THORVALDSON JR.
Columbia, SC, United States
thormeister.deviantart.com
Artist/Writer
(Tales of Marga - Radio Comix / Gold Digger: Pink Slip - Antarctic Press
/ Ninja High School Yearbooks - Antarctic Press)

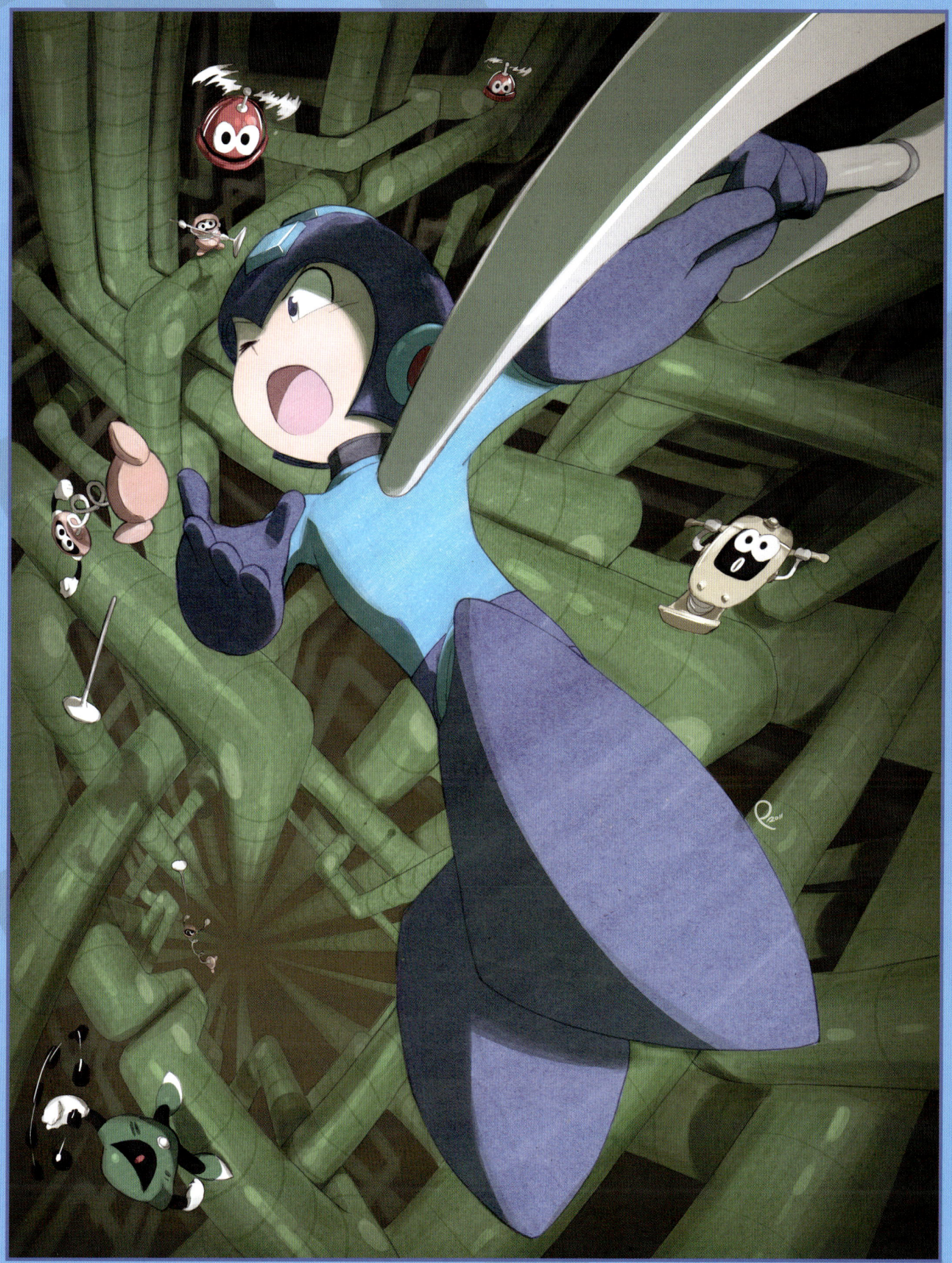

JOHN DY
Manila, Philippines
pharan.deviantart.com
Illustrator

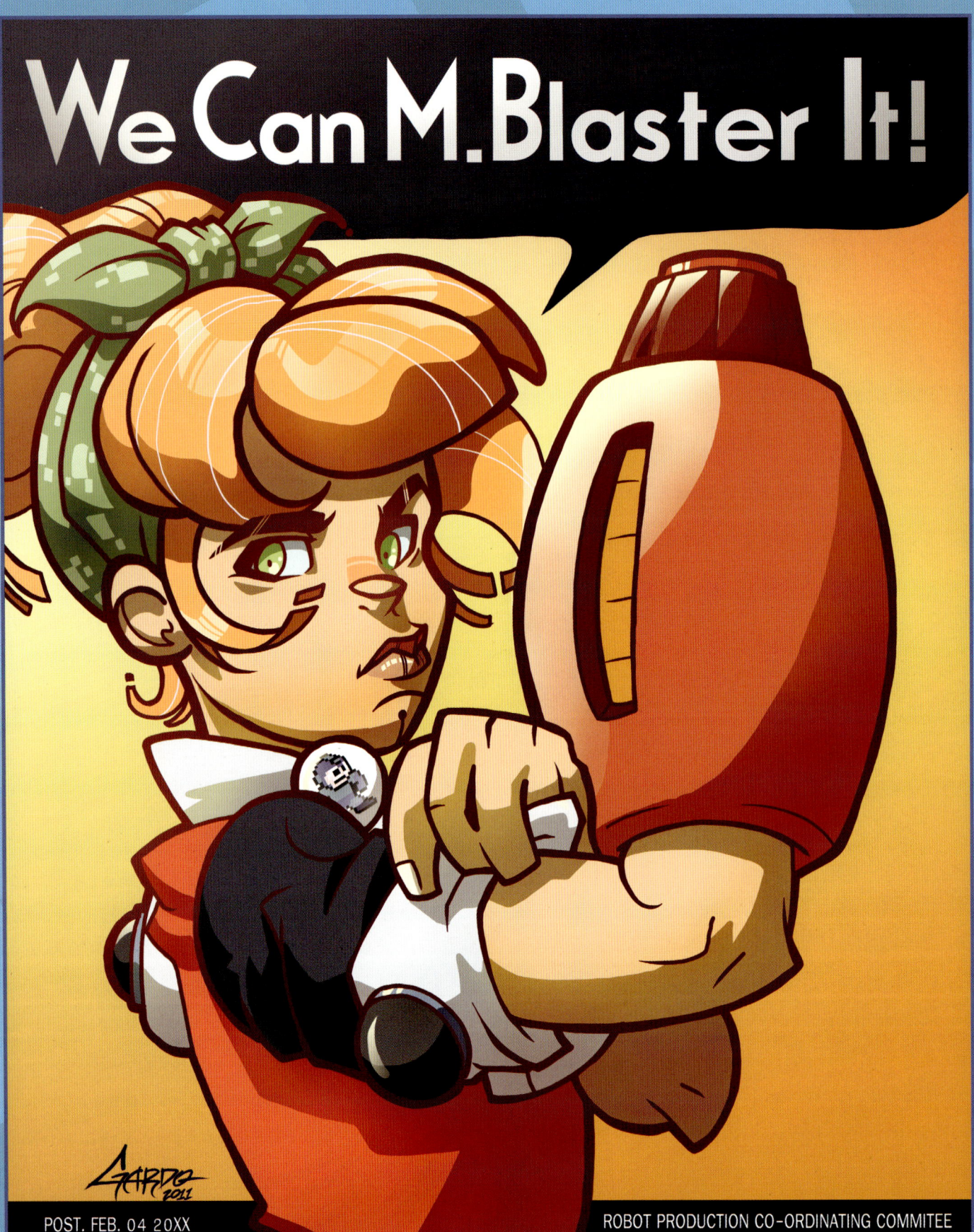

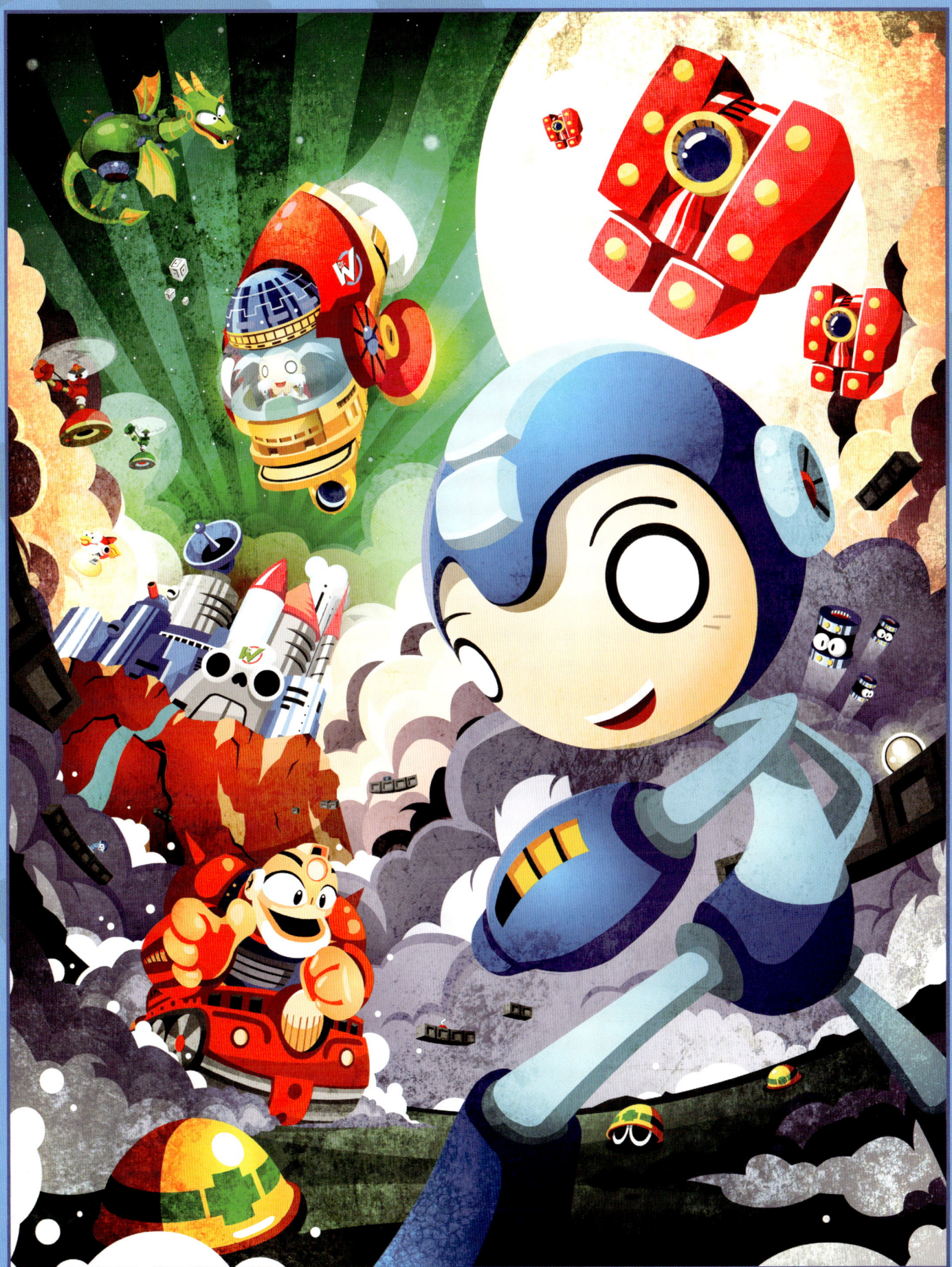

JAMES FRANZEN
OLYMPIA, WA, UNITED STATES
WWW.RADIOGOSHA.COM
GRAPHIC DESIGNER

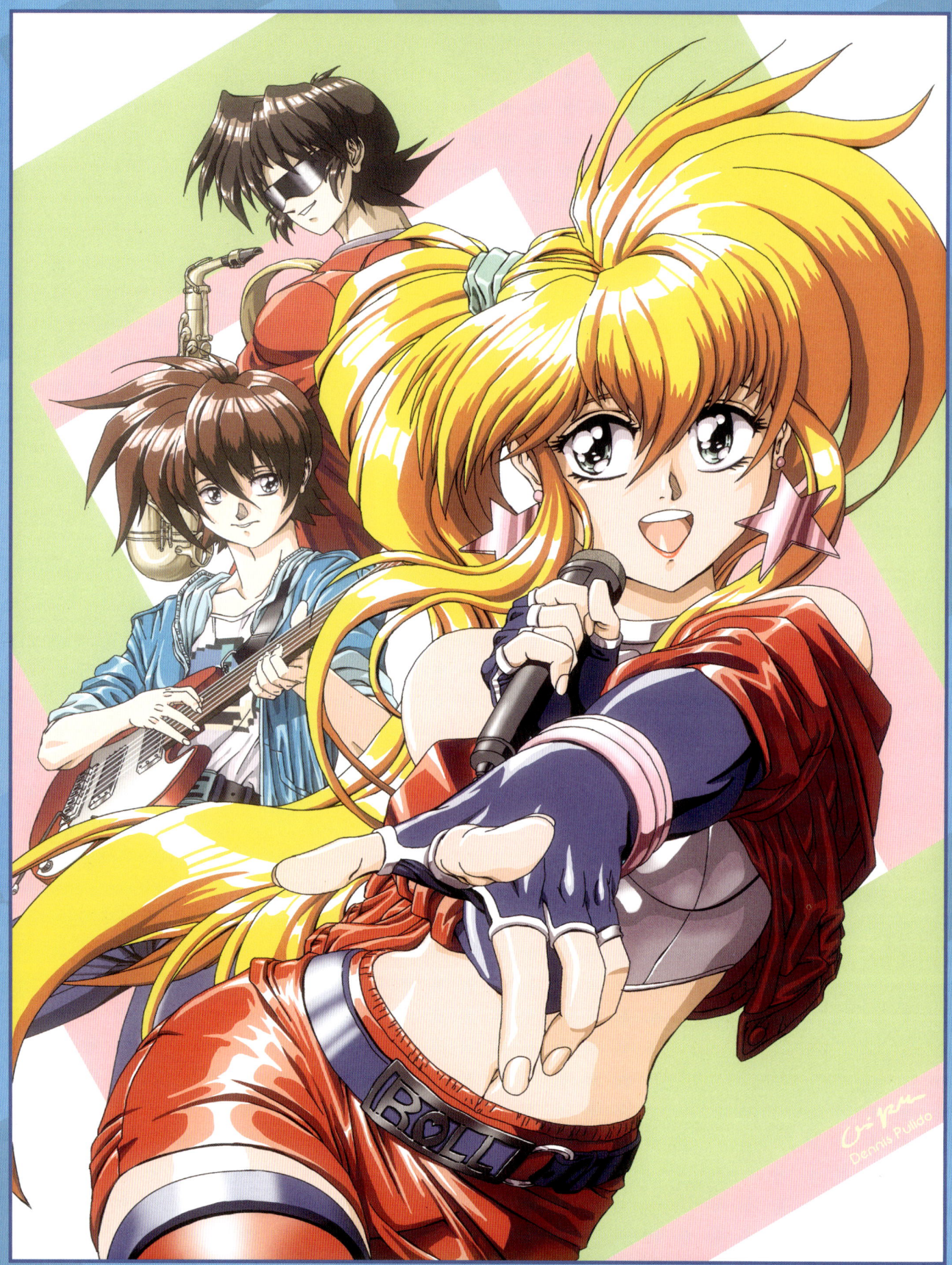

DENNIS PULIDO
Cerritos, CA, United States
haven9270.deviantart.com
Illustrator
(The Art Institute of California Orange County)

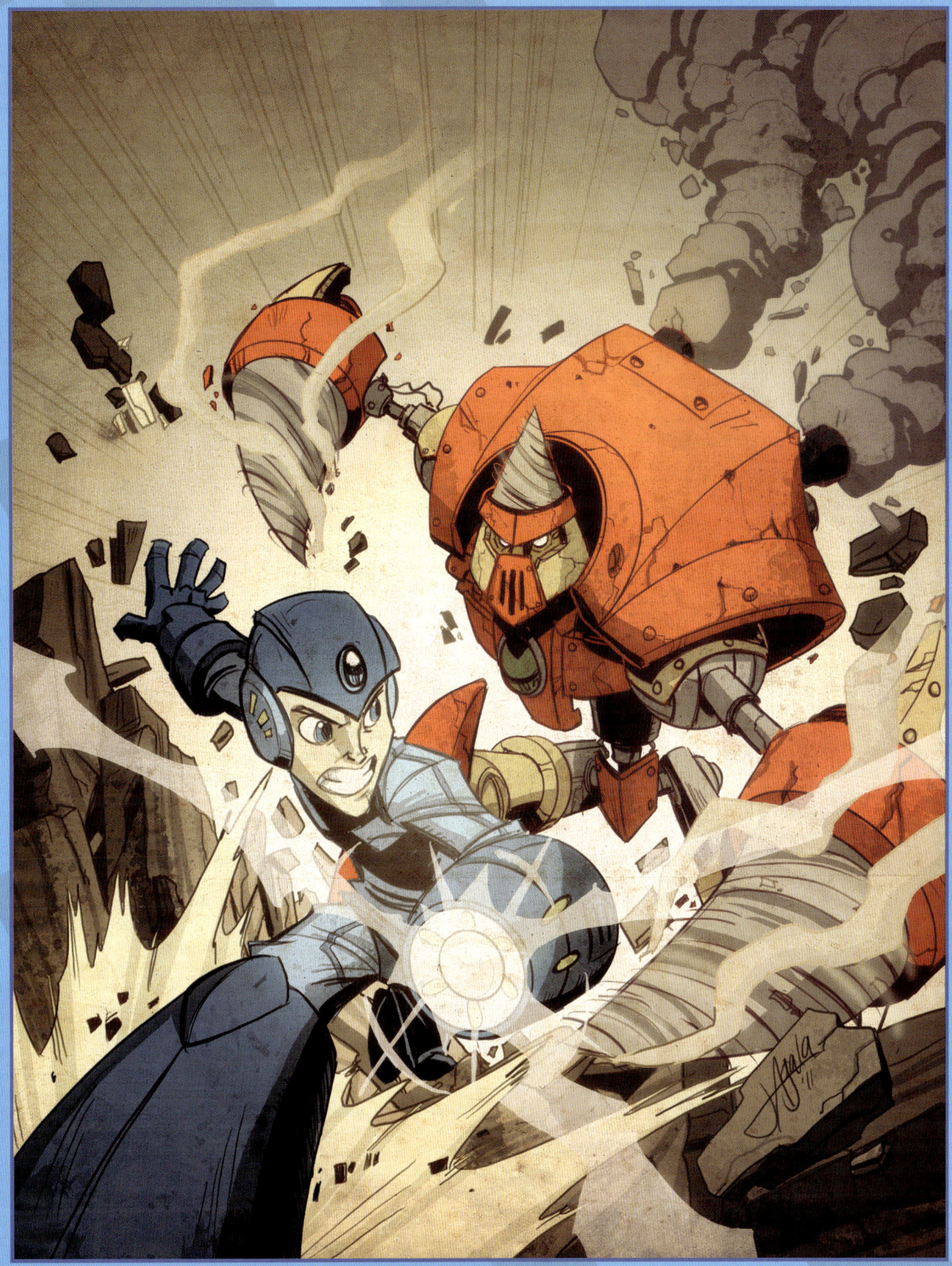

JEFF AGALA
Vancouver, BC, Canada
jeffagala.blogspot.com / jeffagala.deviantart.com
Creative Director - Klei Entertainment
(Creator of Shank (video game) / Director of Atomic Betty)

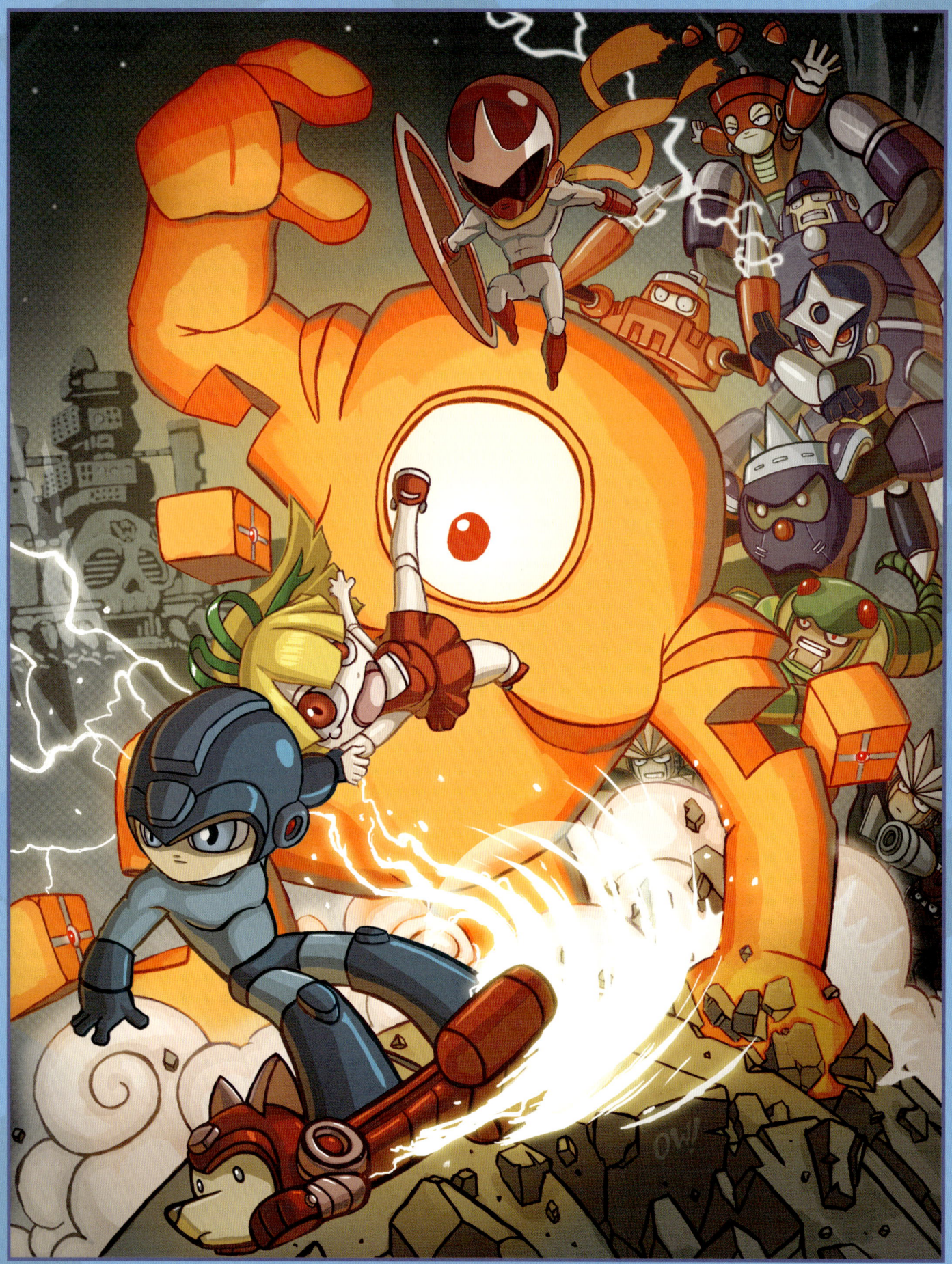

OBRAY WILLIAMS
Katy, TX, United States
elbrazo.deviantart.com
Video Game Generalist
(Mercenaries 2, Rockband 1 & 2, Bonk: Brink of Extinction)

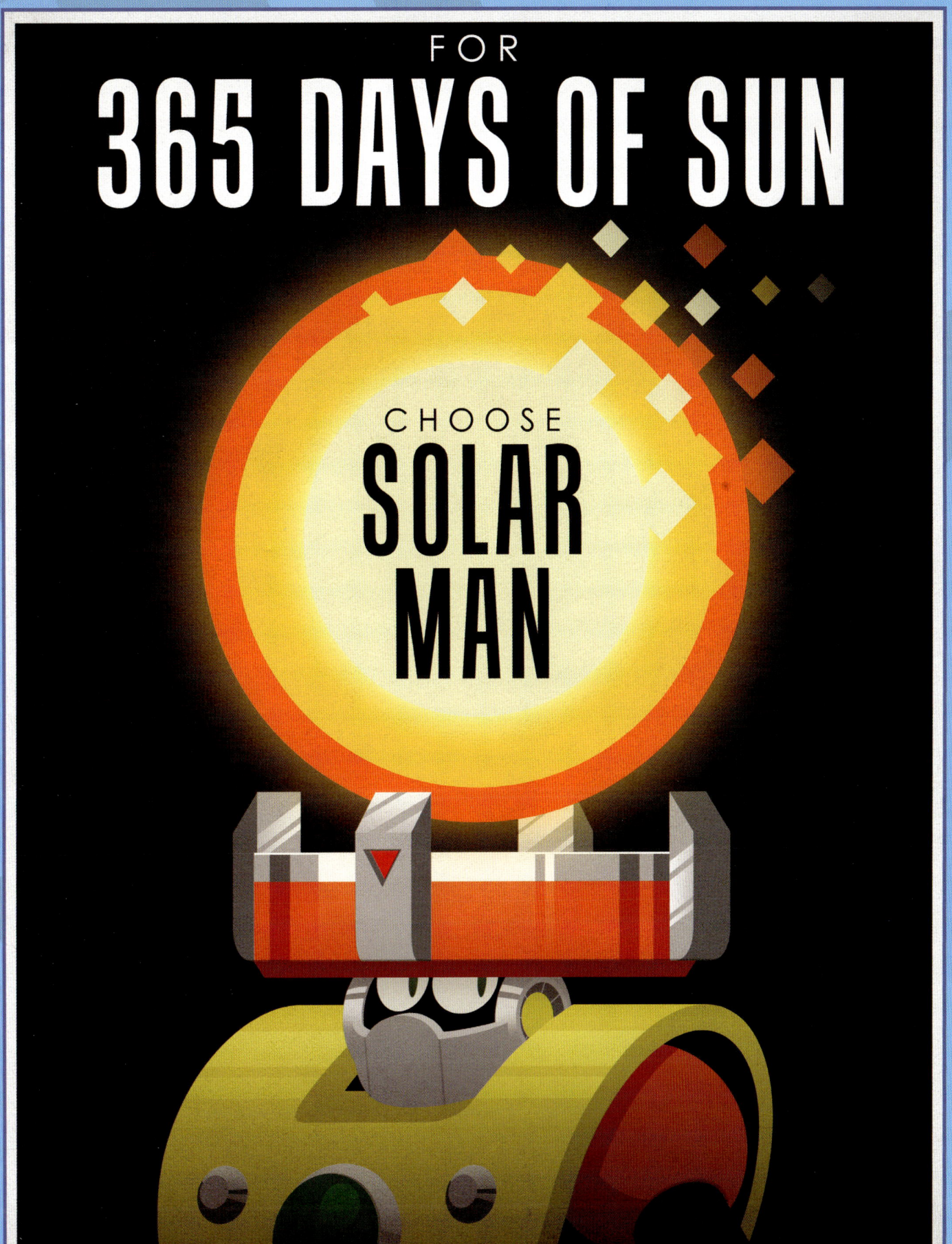

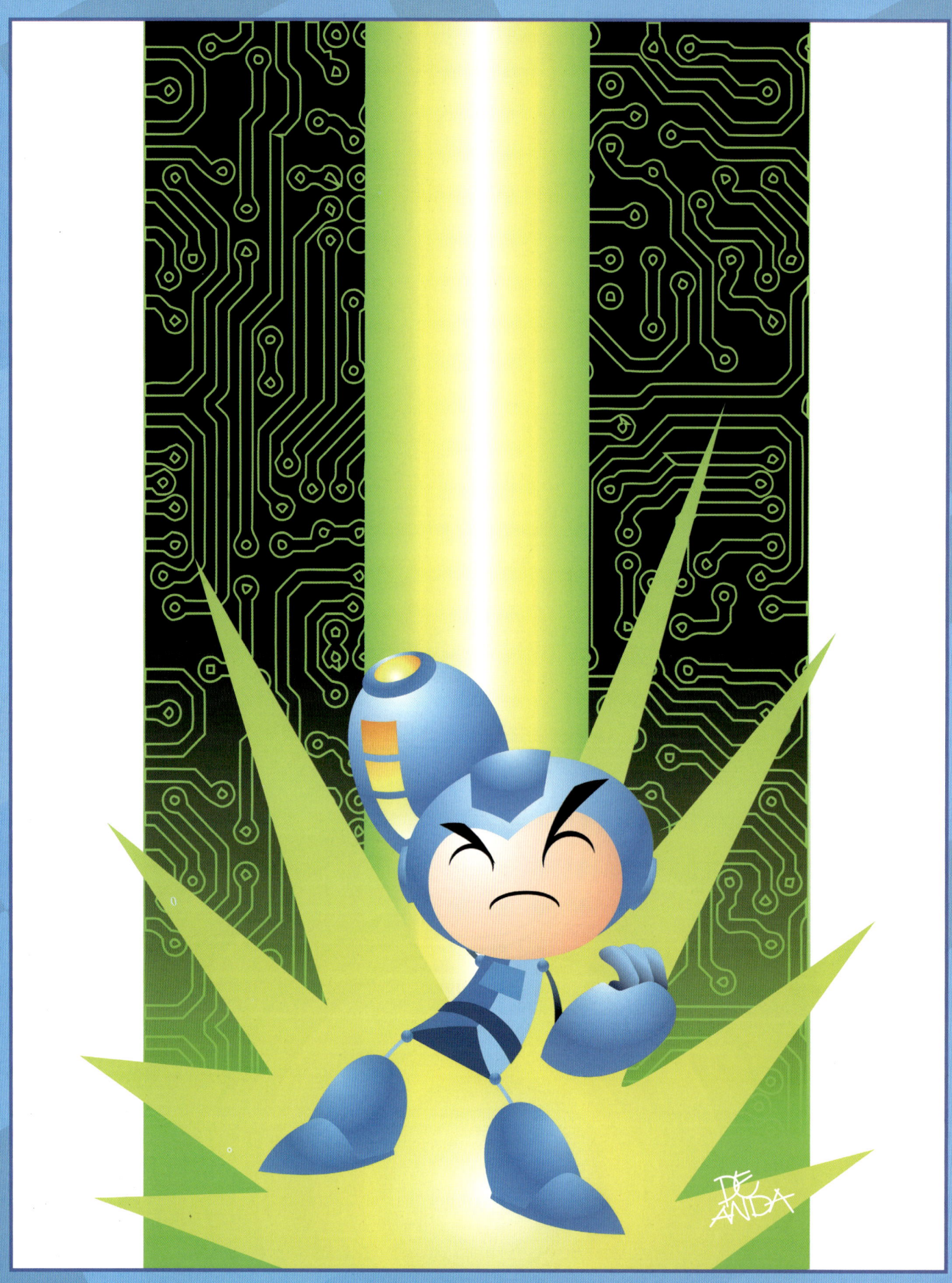

CARLOS DE ANDA LÓPEZ
Aguascalientes, Mexico
charlydeanda.blogspot.com / chachaman.deviantart.com
Graphic Designer
(Creator of Arcana Obscura comic /
IAJU Graphic Design Award Winner 2005 / Esthel Girls)

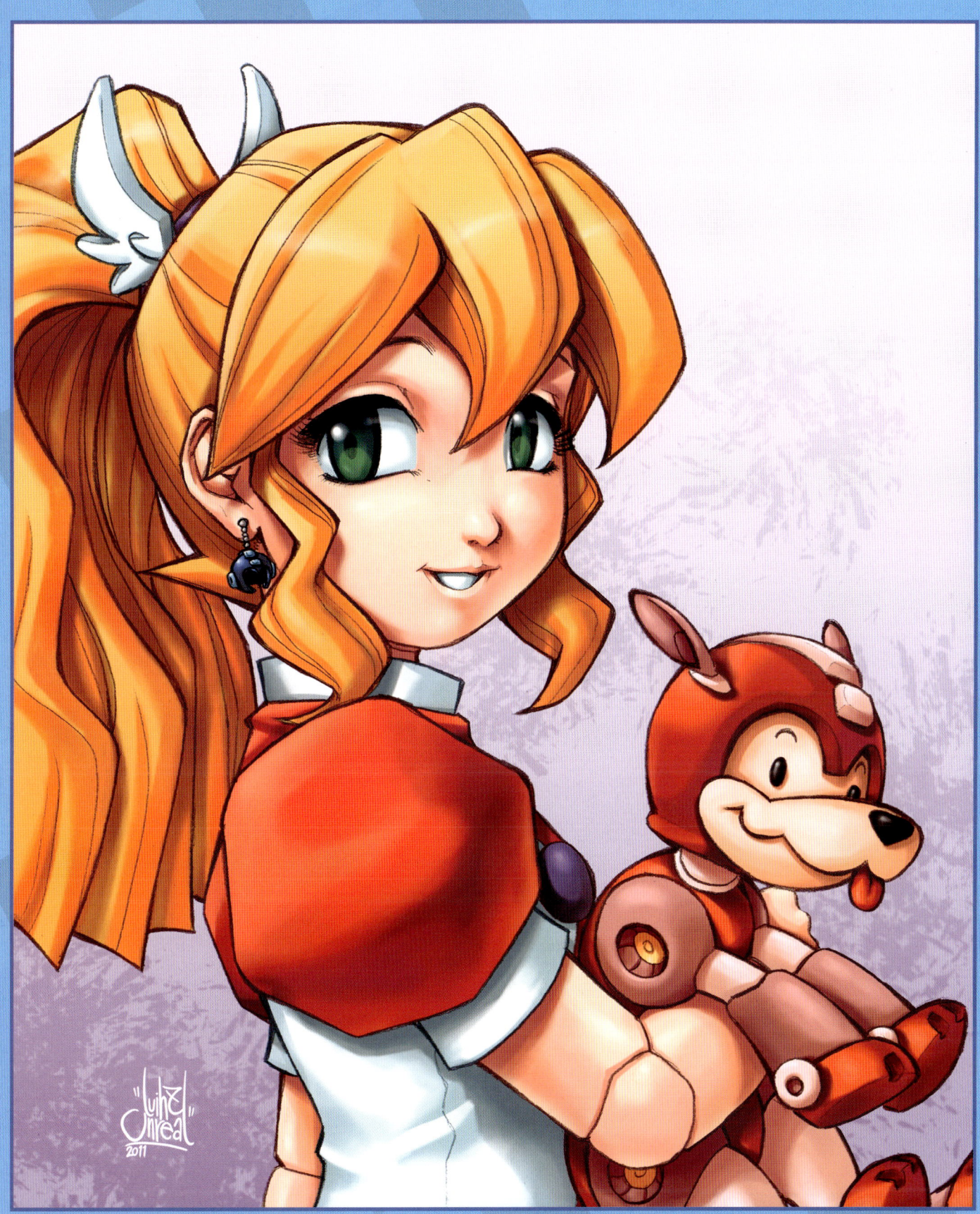

LUIZ CARLOS
São Paulo, Brazil
luihzumreal.deviantart.com
Illustrator

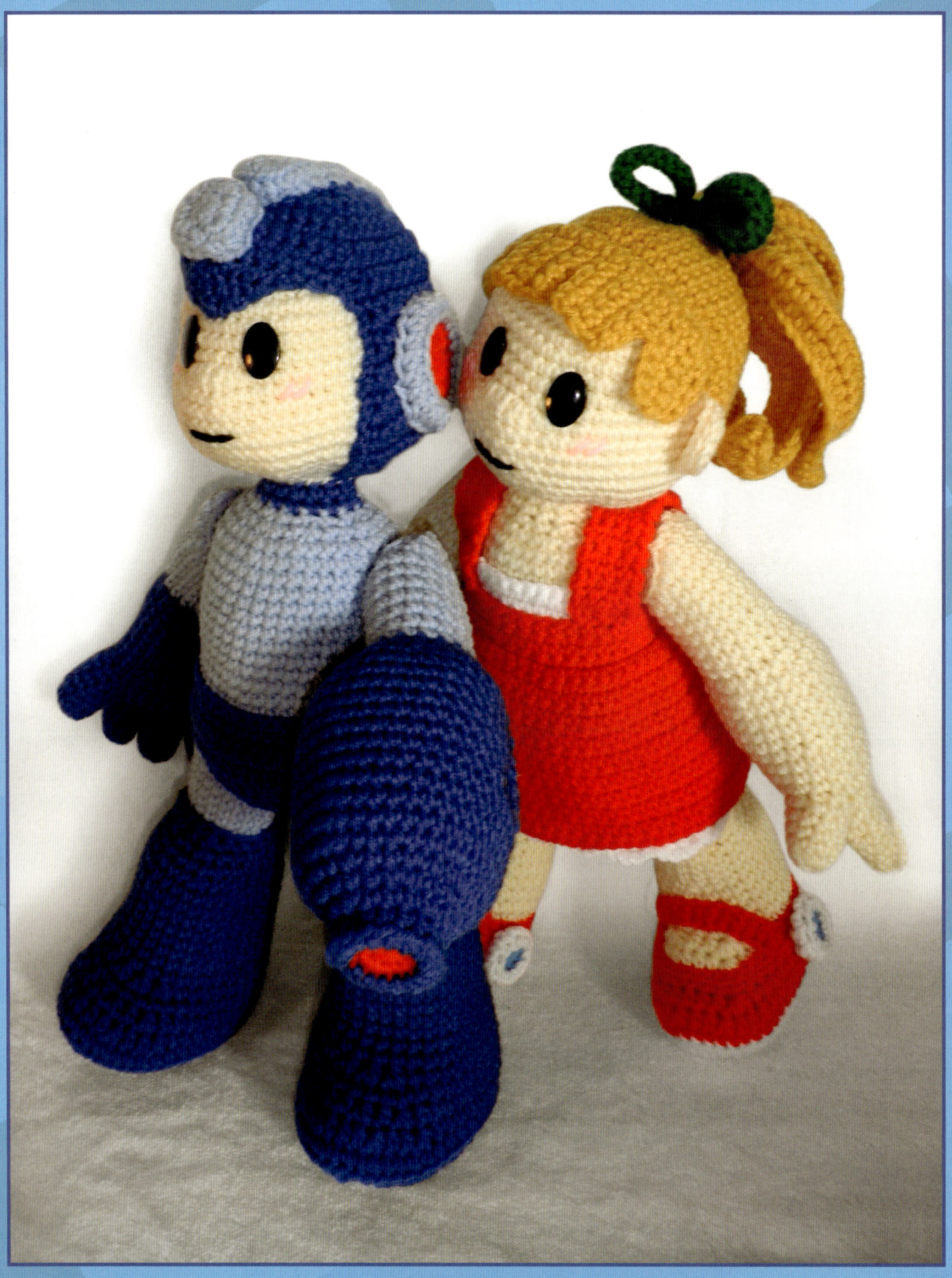

ELIZABETH REMSEN
Oswego, IL, United States
www.anothercastlecrochet.com / bunniebard.deviantart.com
Crochet Artist

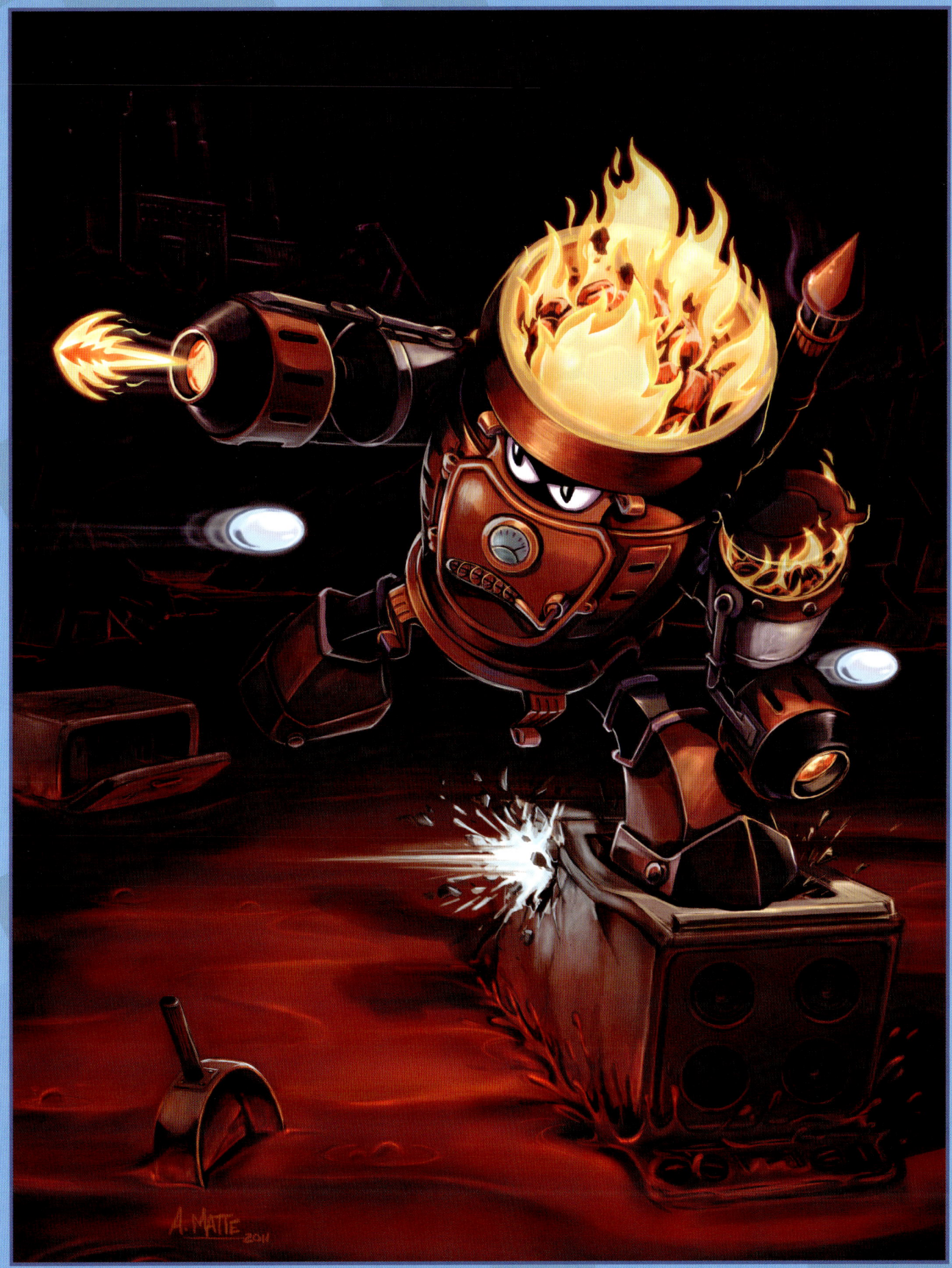

ALAIN MATTE
St-Nicolas, QC, Canada
alainmatteportfolio.blogspot.com
Illustrator

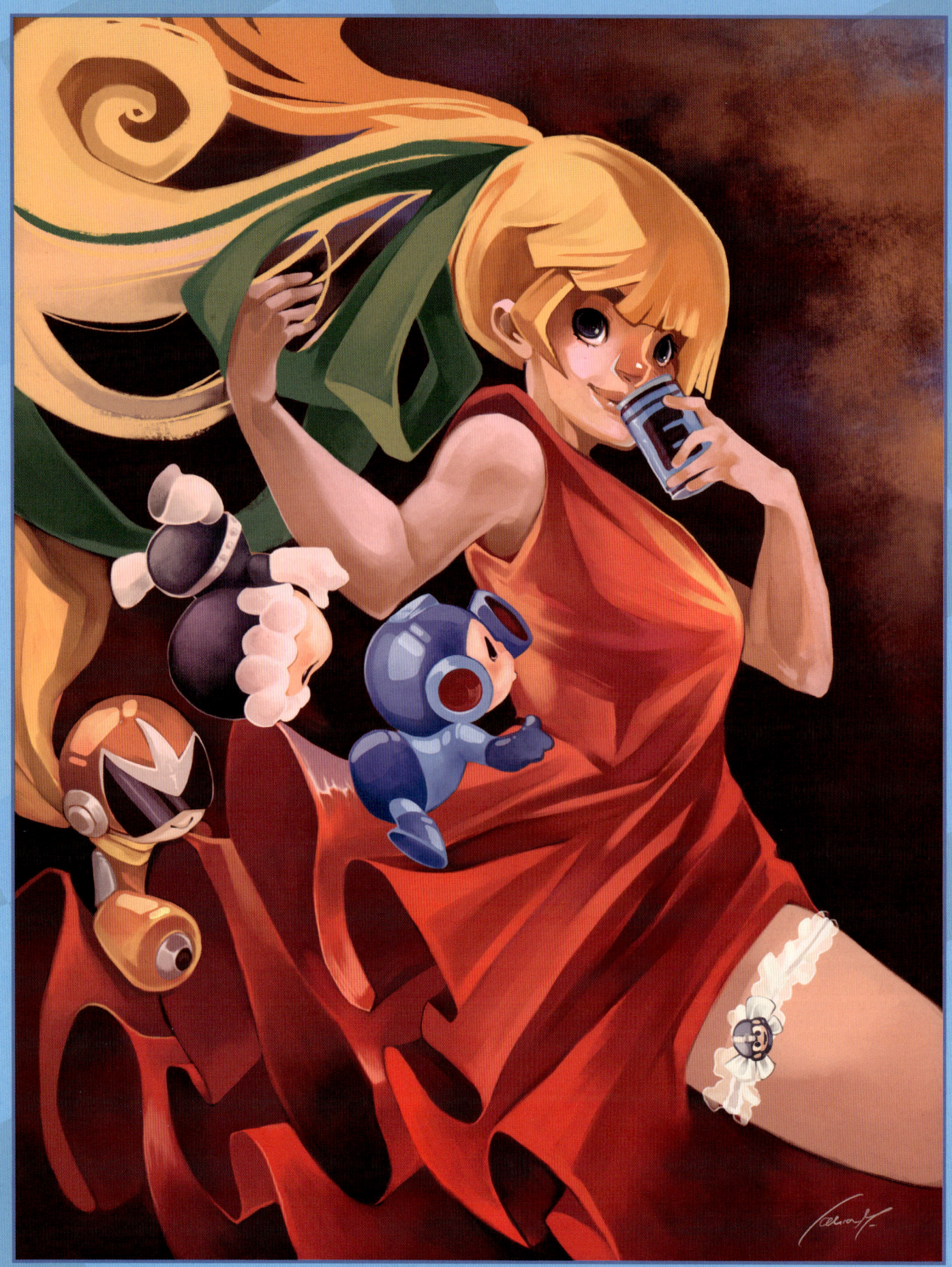

LAURA MÜLLER (LAUMILINE)
Waldesruh, Germany
www.laumiline.com / laumann.deviantart.com
Illustrator

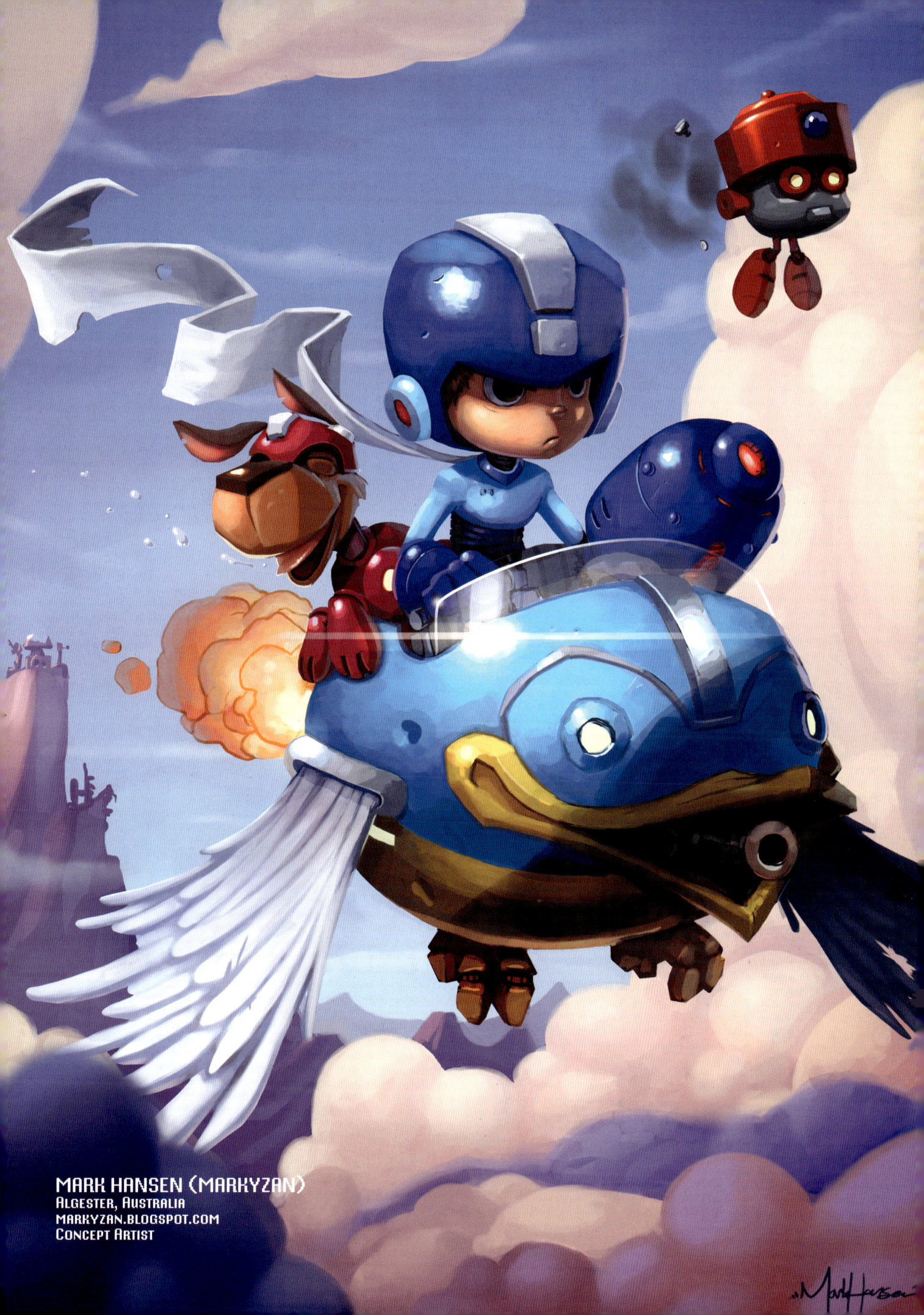

MARK HANSEN (MARKYZAN)
Algester, Australia
markyzan.blogspot.com
Concept Artist

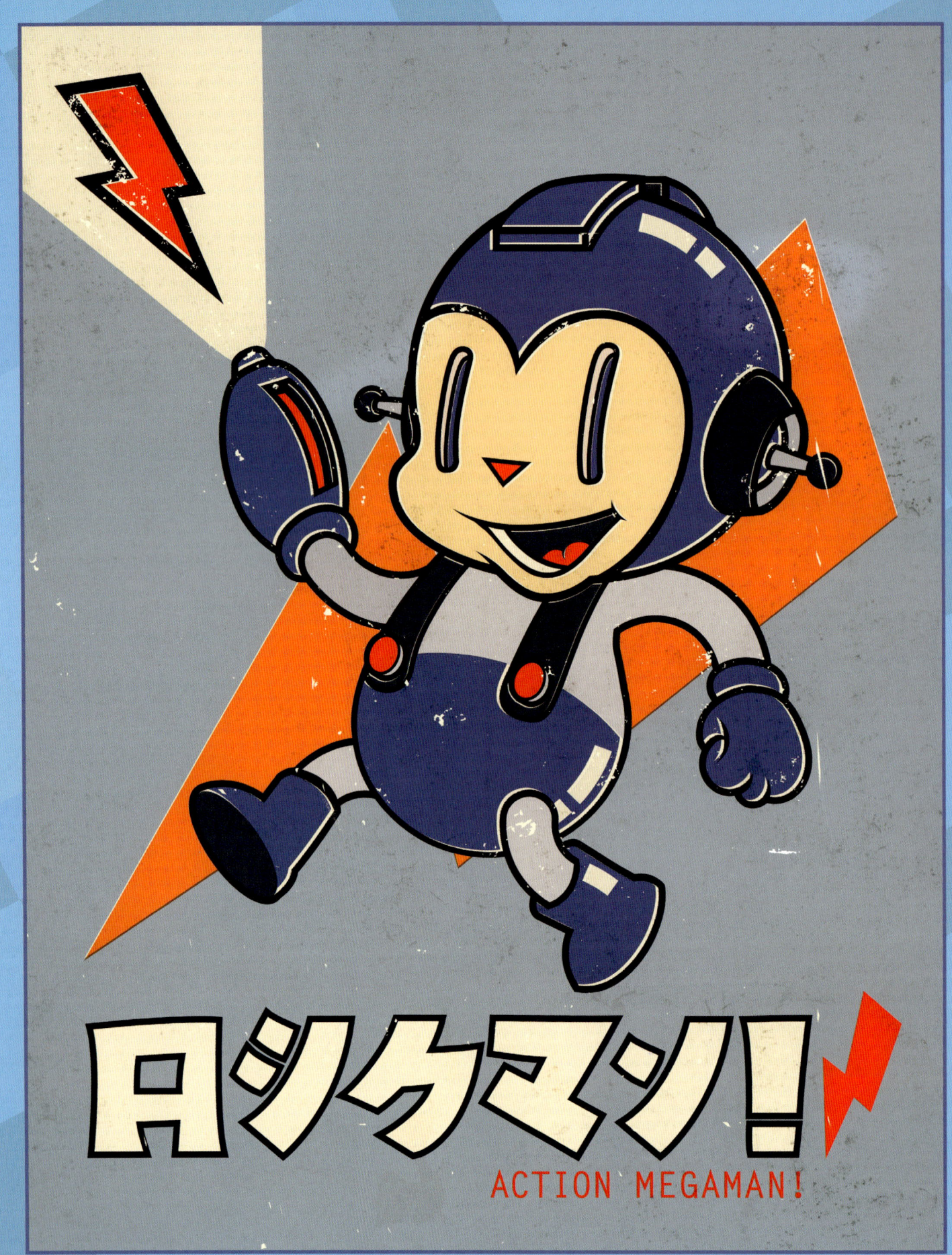

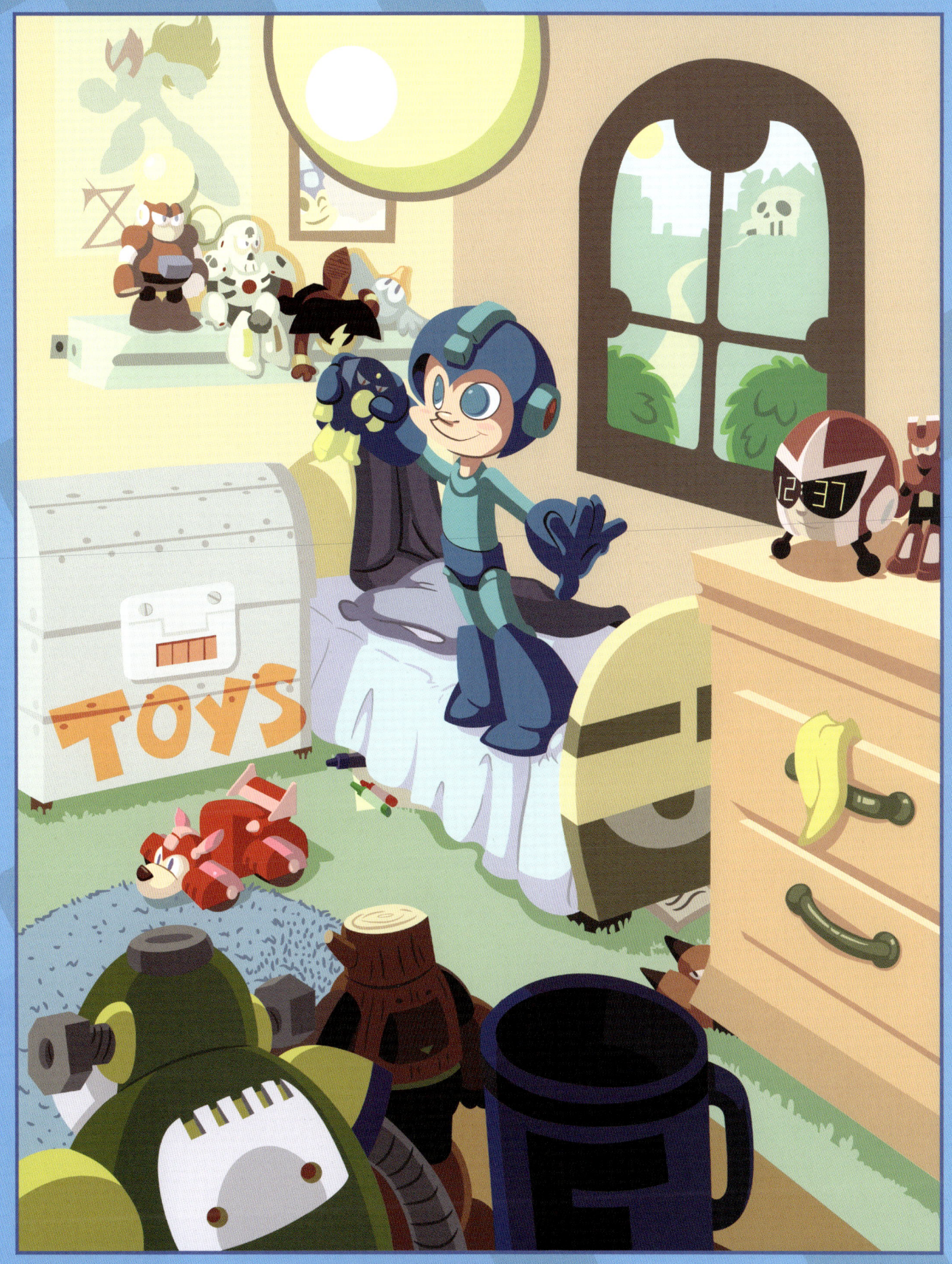

KEVIN CAMERON (HEROGEAR)
LONG BEACH, CA, UNITED STATES
herogear.deviantart.com
ILLUSTRATOR
(Clothing Icon/Badge Design - Disney / Darkstalkers Tribute /
"Pedal's & Prints" @ Crewest Gallery)

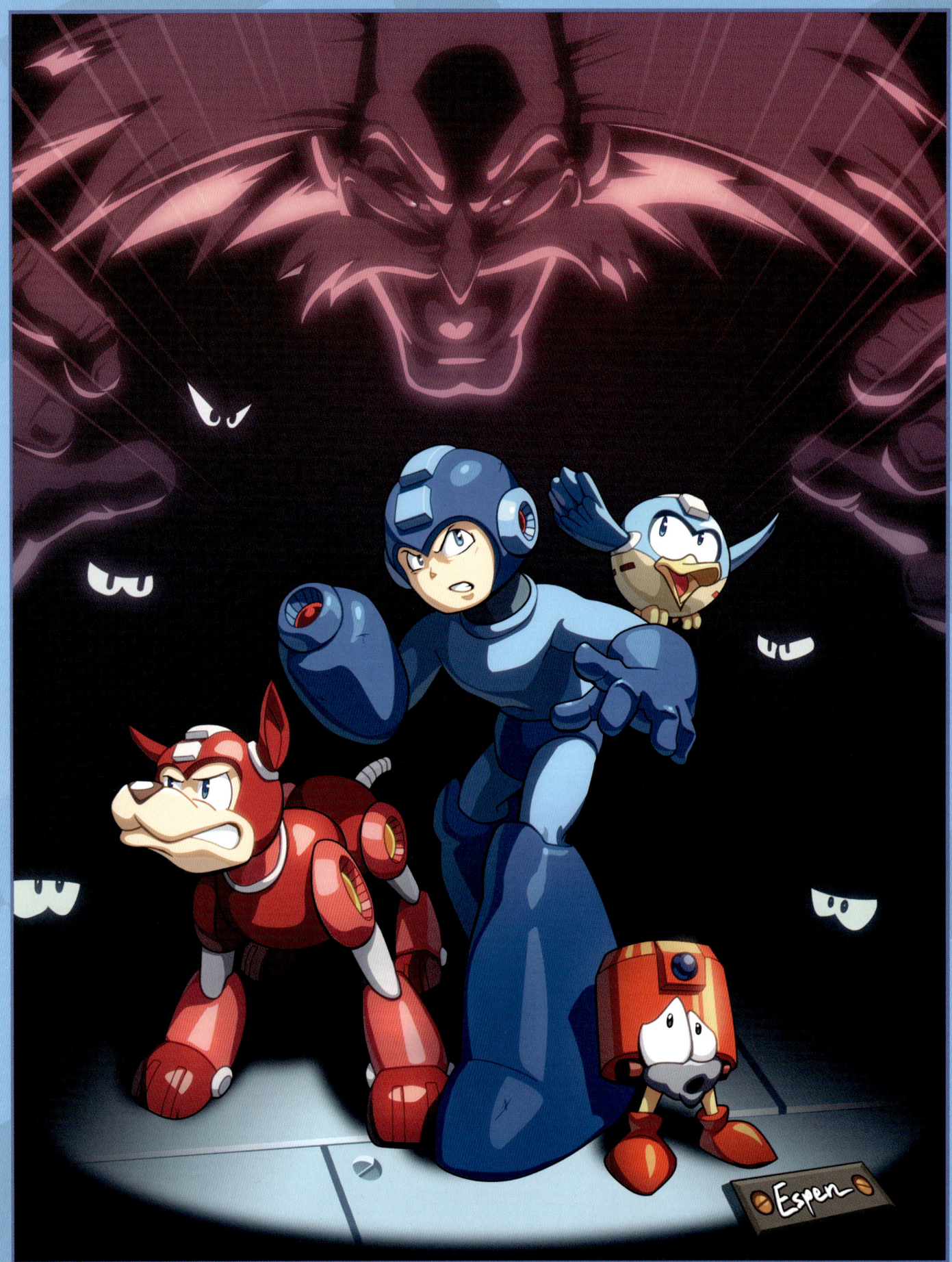

ESPEN GRUNDETJERN
Norway
espeng.deviantart.com
Colourist
(Street Fighter, Darkstalkers, Transformers)

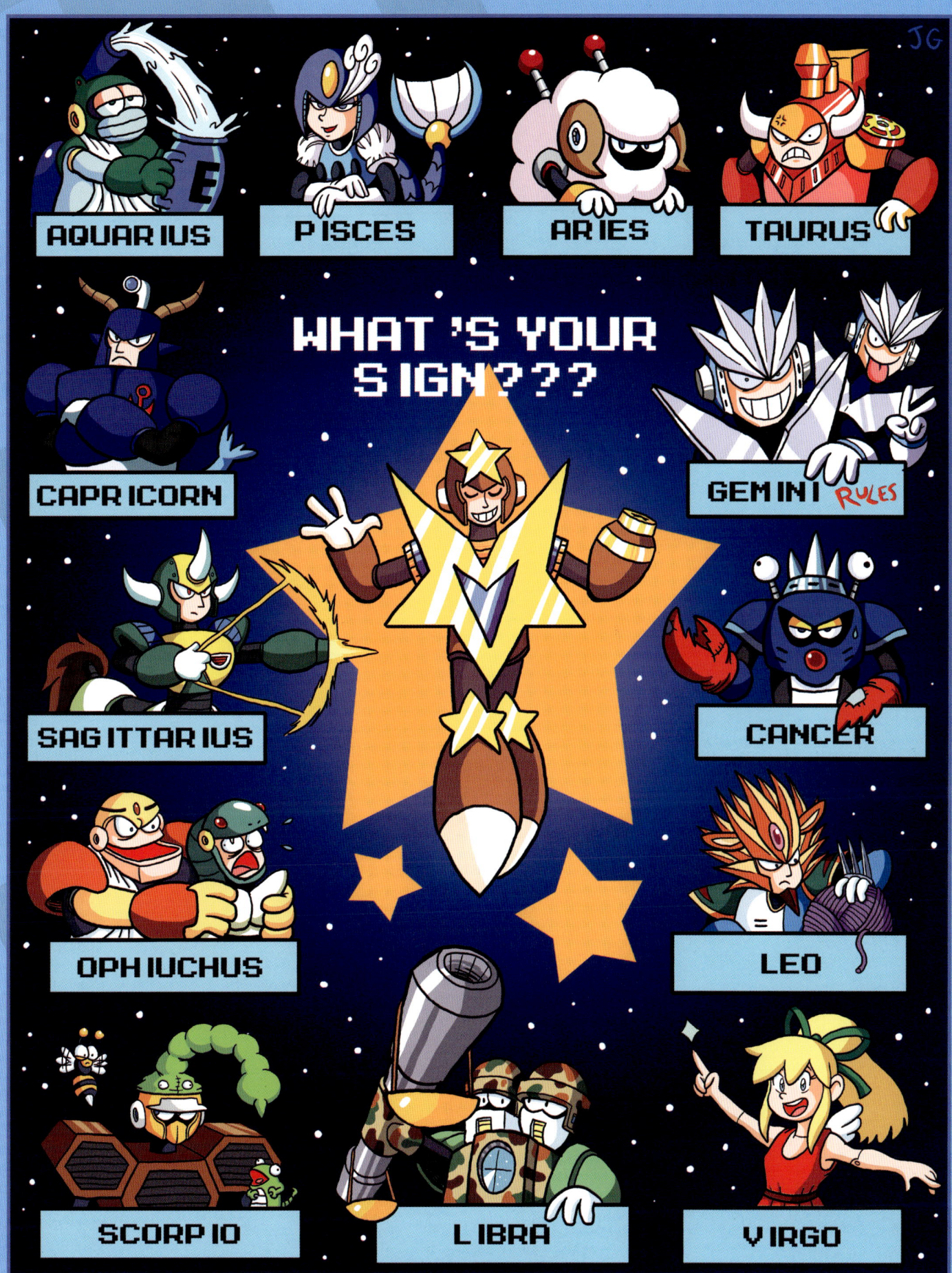

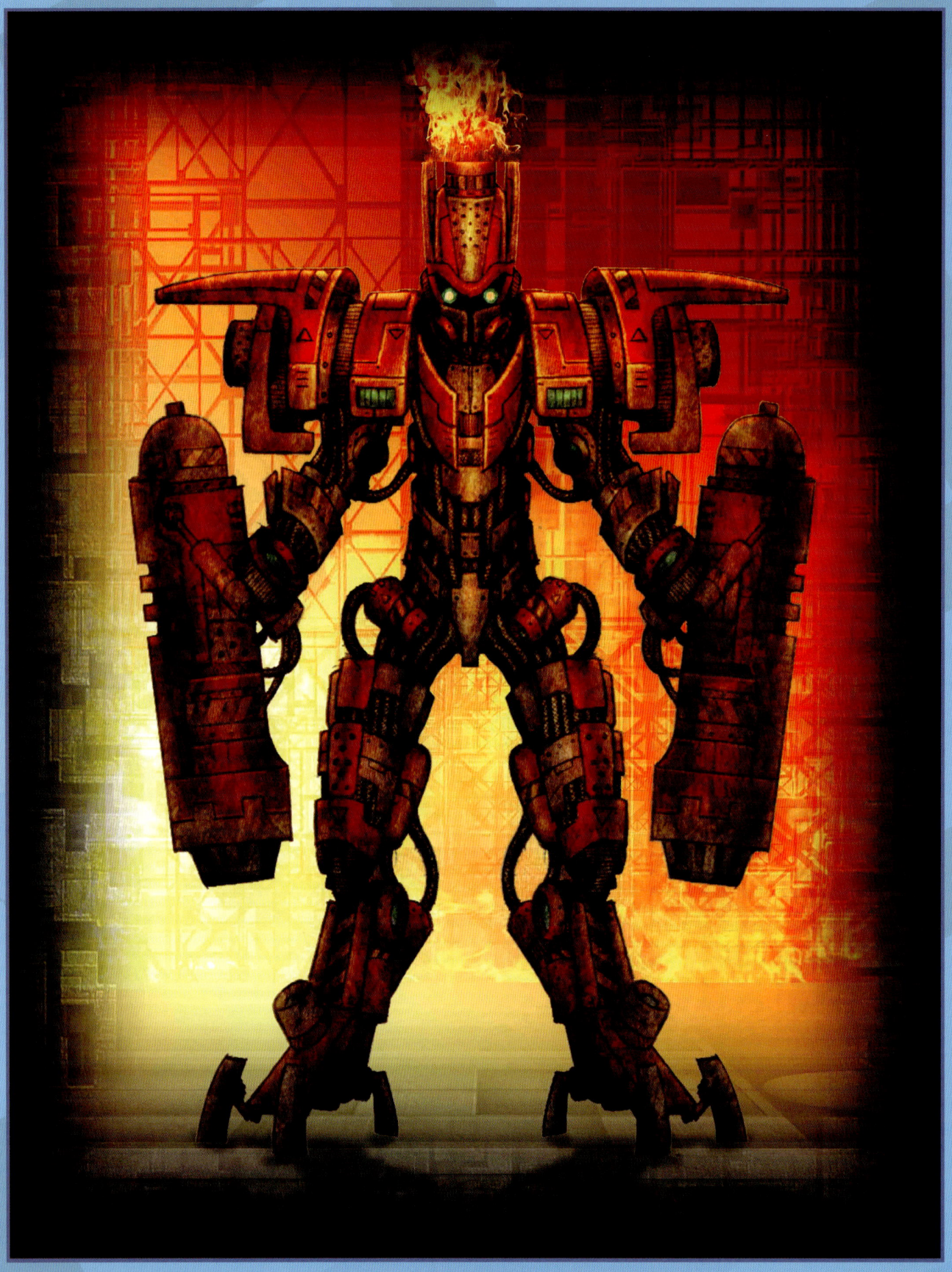

ALEX RUDE
San Francisco, CA, United States
Illustrator

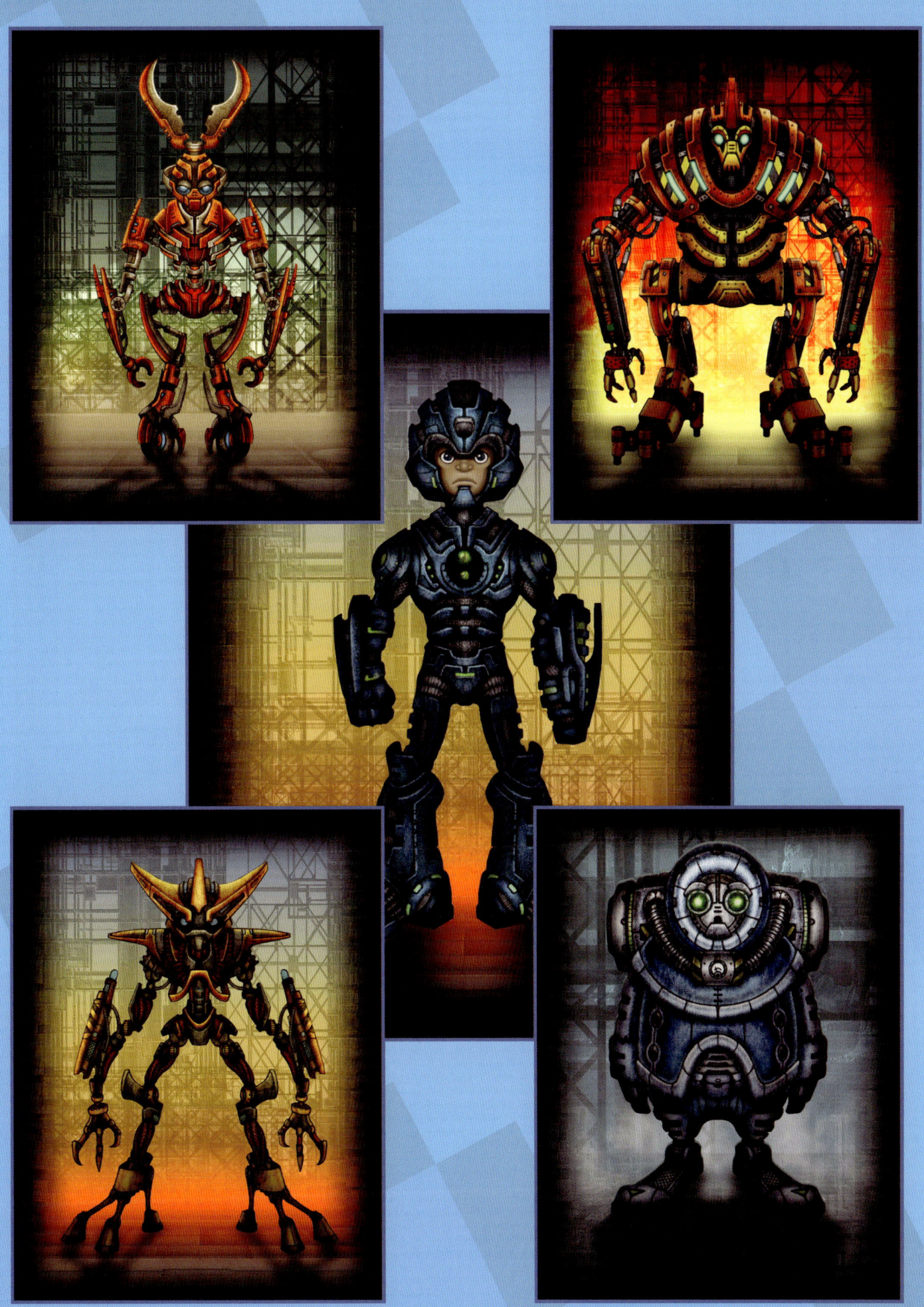

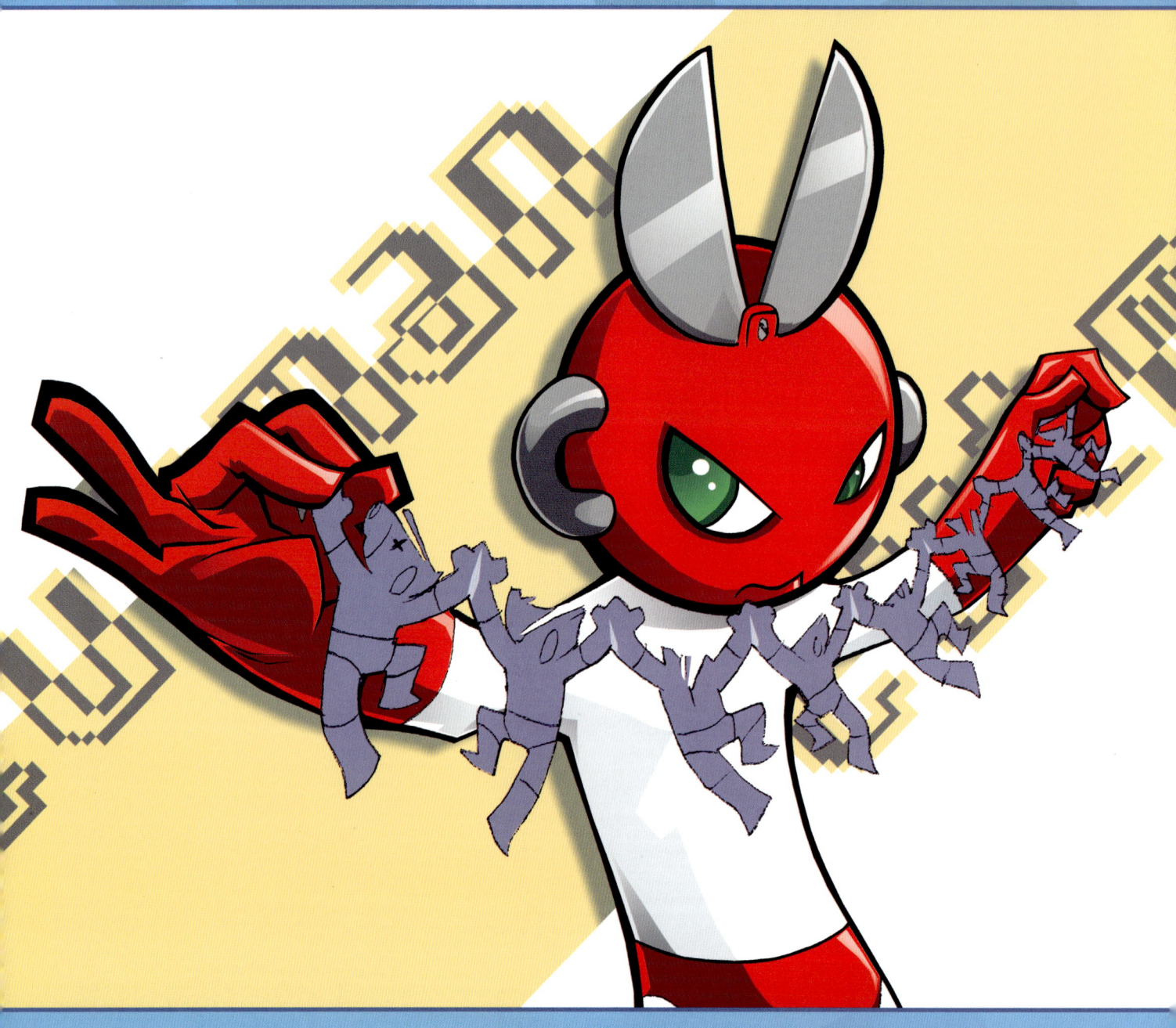

BRIAN WIMBERLY
Beltsville, MD, United States
www.sanctuary-school.com
Comic Illustrator
(Sanctuary School)

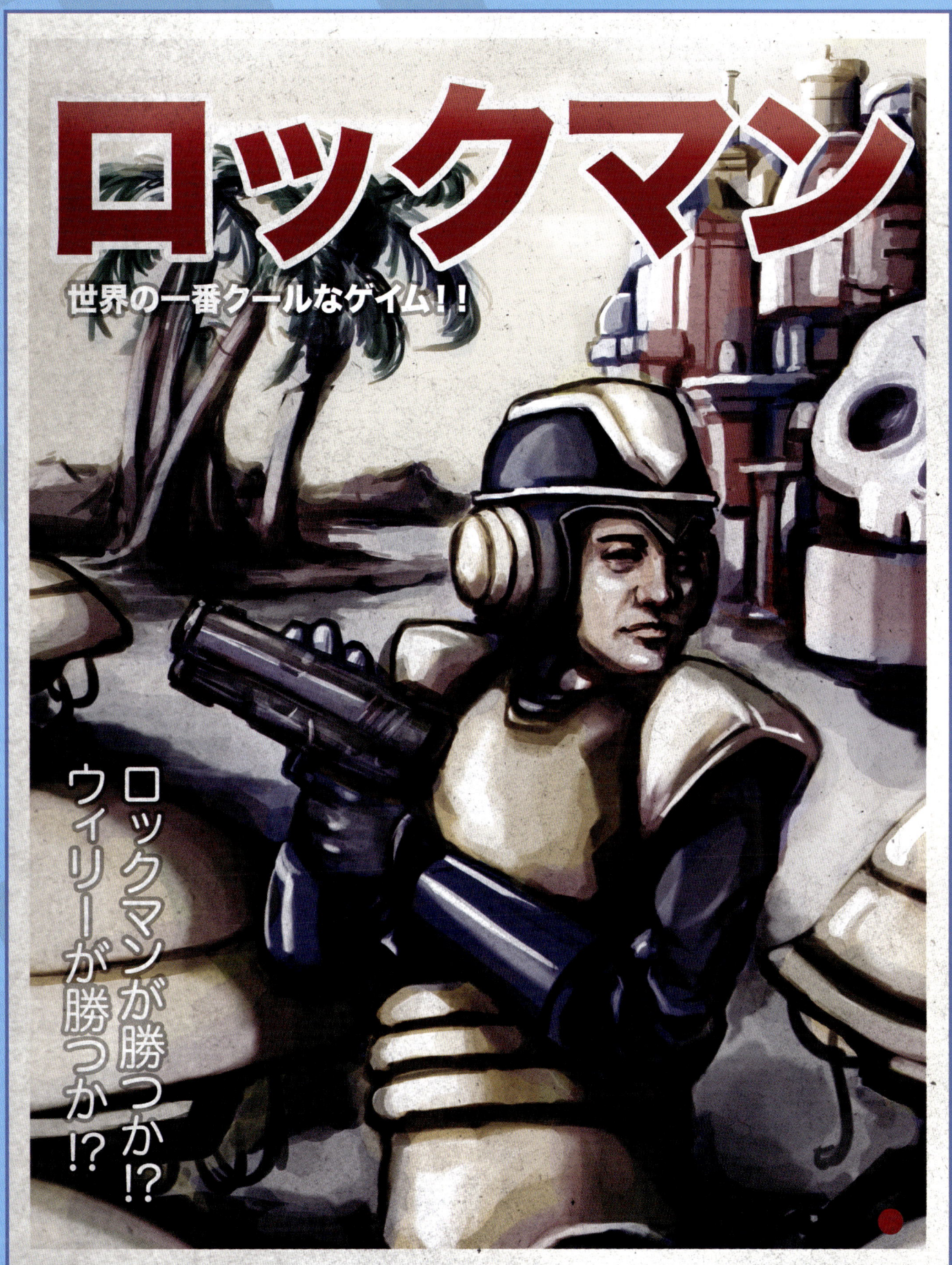

MIKE YEH
Cupertino, CA, United States
www.super-minus.com
Illustrator

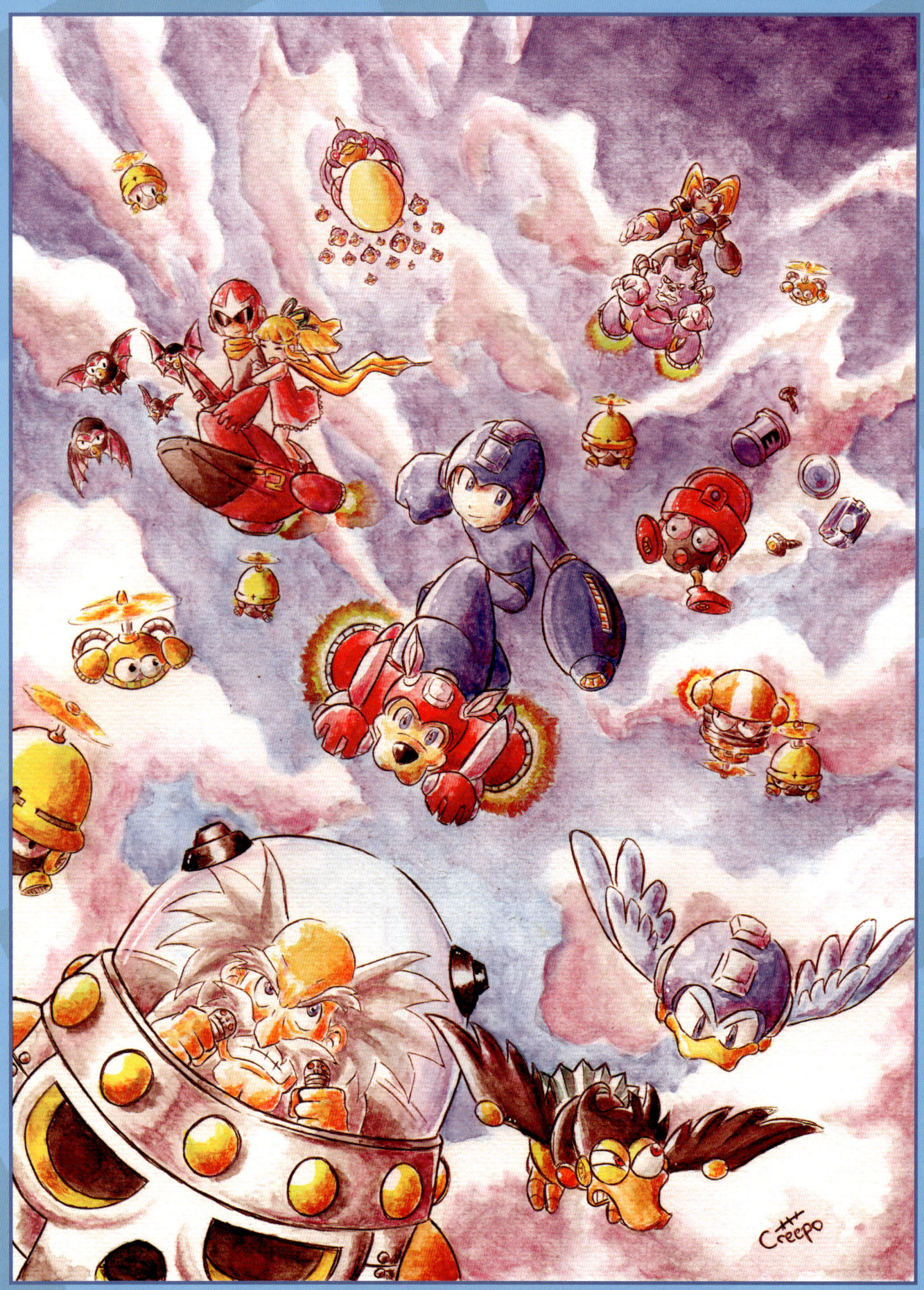

FELIPE LIRA (JUST-A-CREEP)
Valparaiso, Chile
just-a-creep.deviantart.com
Psychologist

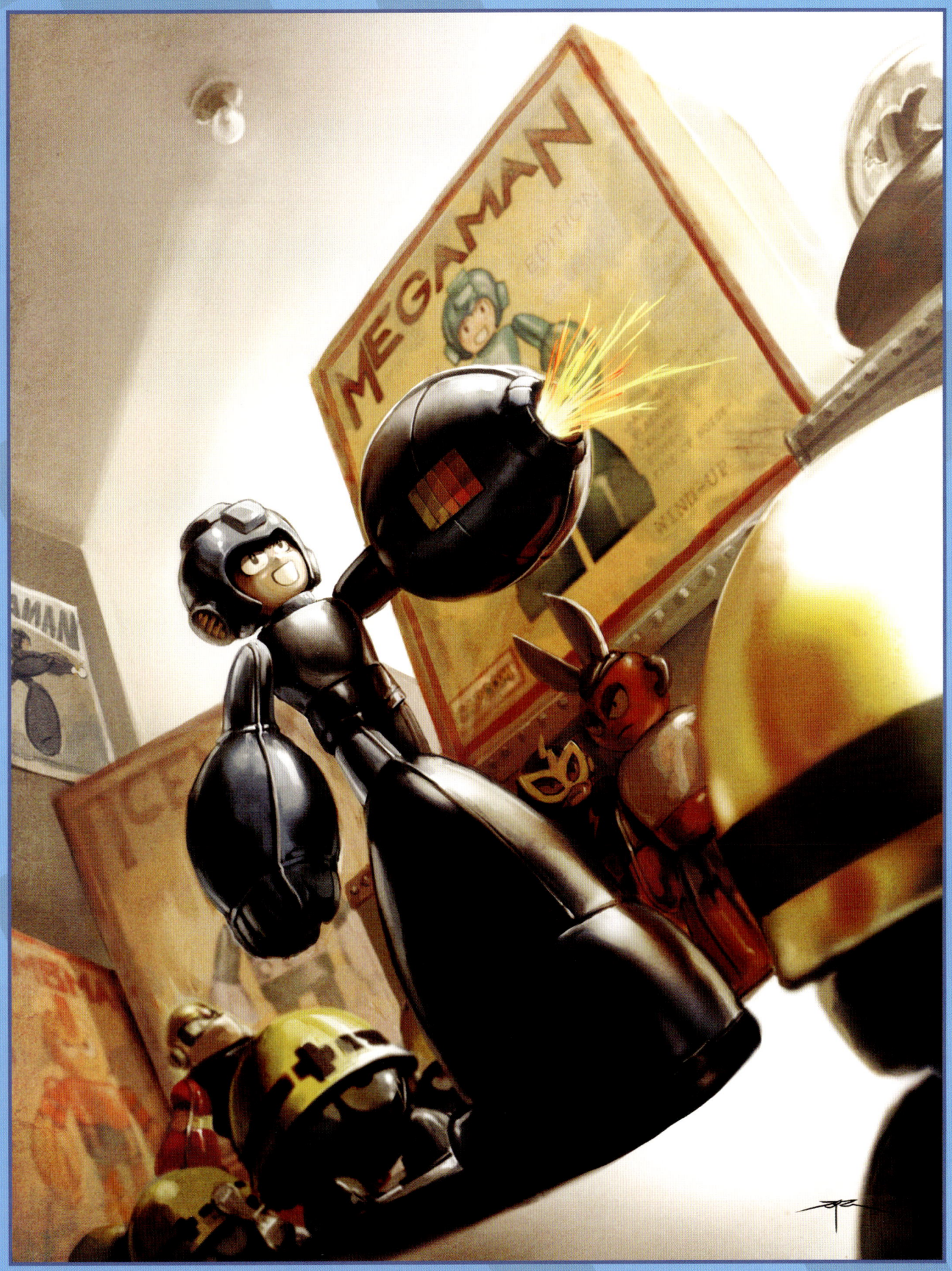

ALEJANDRO MORENO GONZALEZ (MAGNOZZ)
Ibagué, Colombia
mgnz.deviantart.com
Illustrator

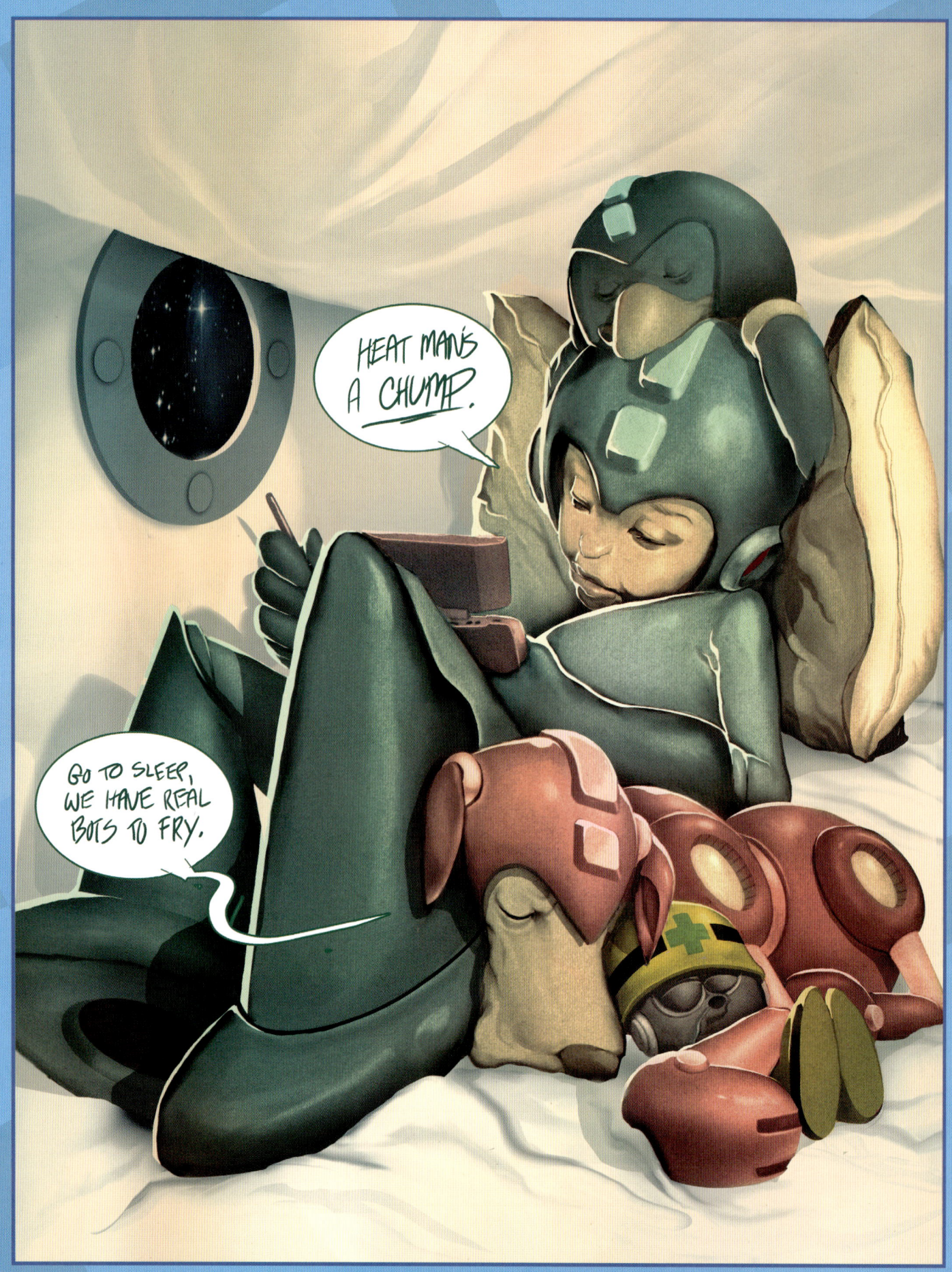

MIKE DEL MUNDO (DEADLY DEL MUNDO)
Unionville, Canada
www.deadlydelmundo.com / deadlydelmundo.deviantart.com
Illustrator
(1MONTH2LIVE Covers / IRON MAN by Design Covers / Thor Goes Hollywood Covers)

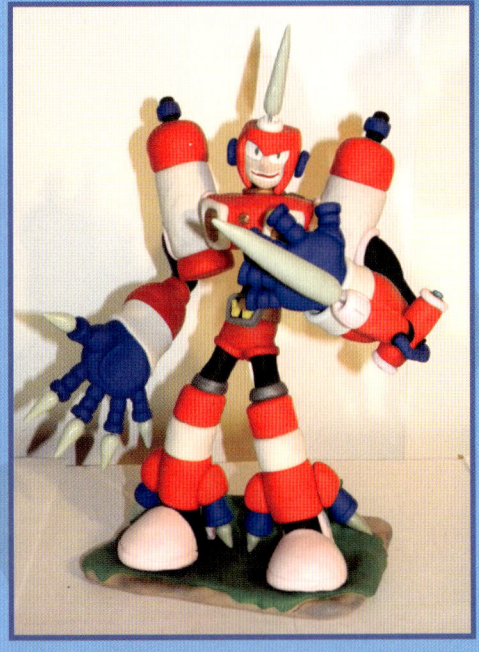
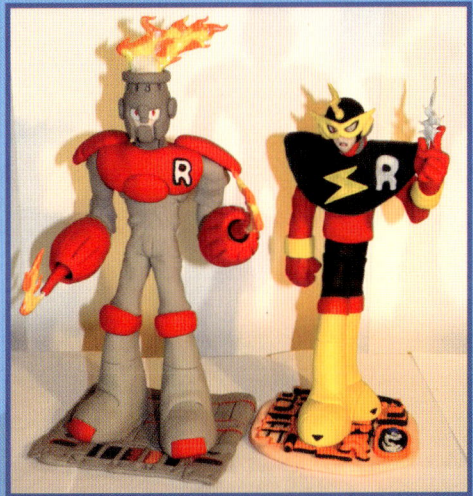
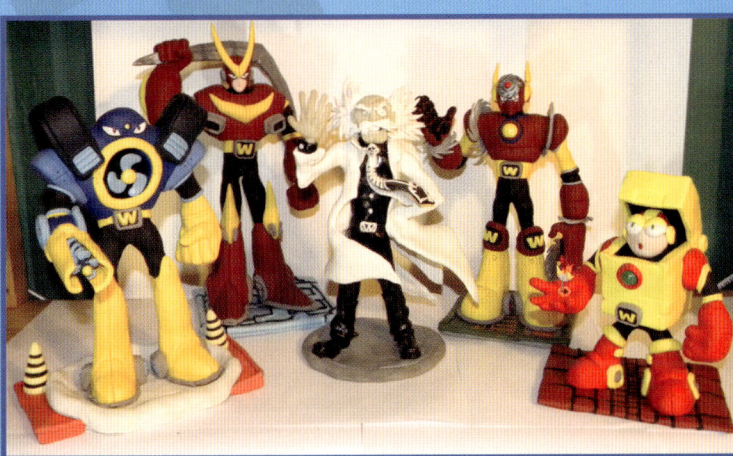
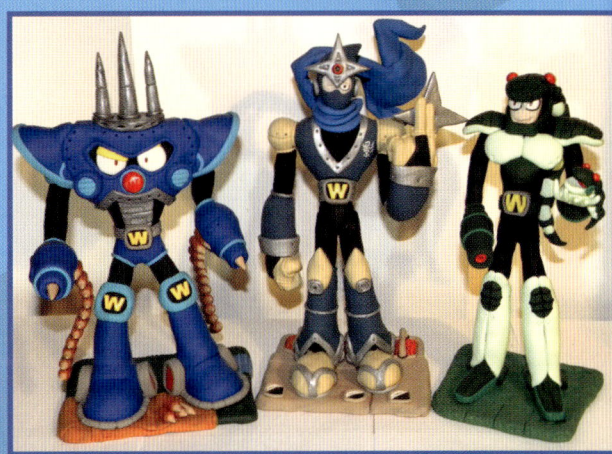

CALEB COOK
Nyack, NY, United States
Student
(Artwork Published in Japanese "One Piece" Volumes)

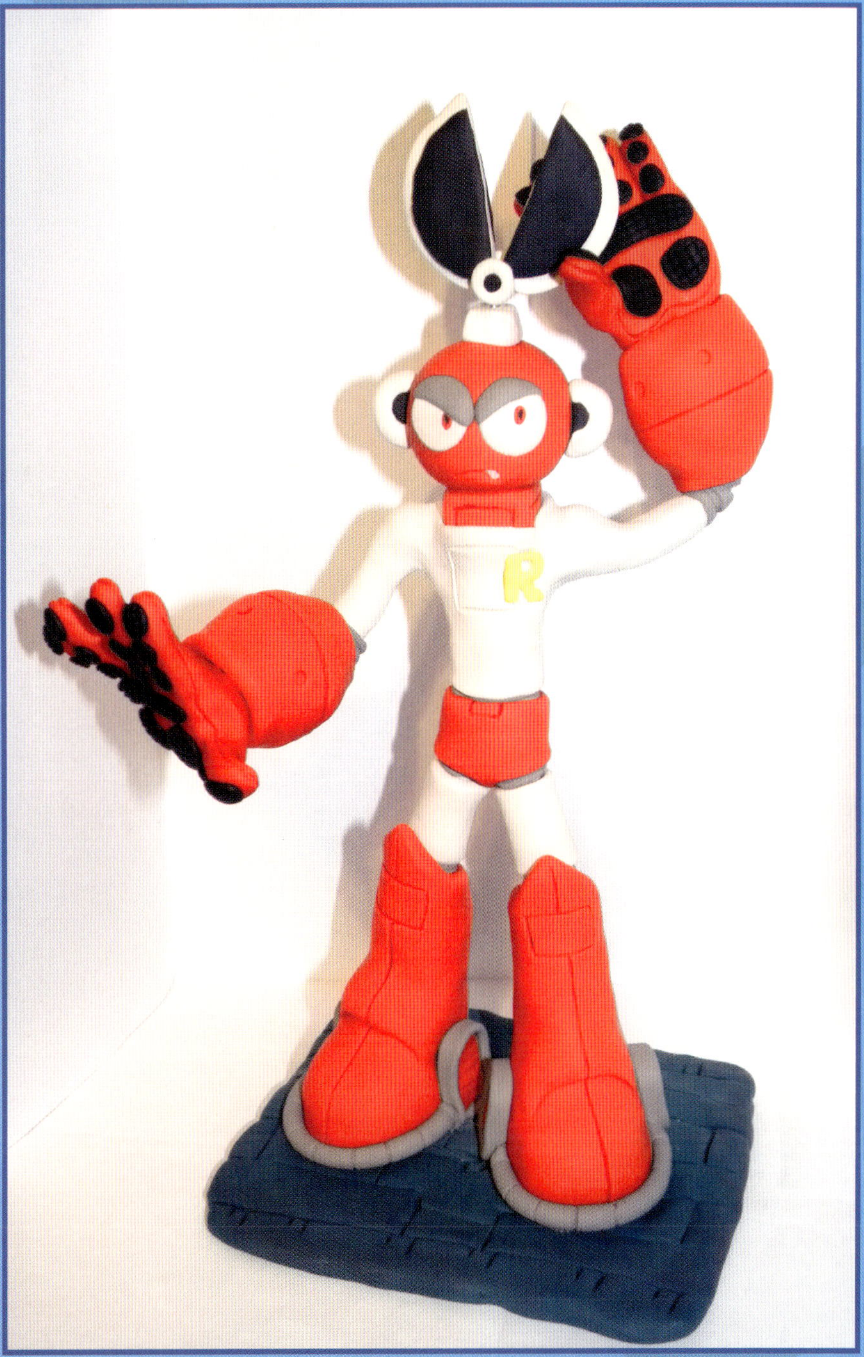

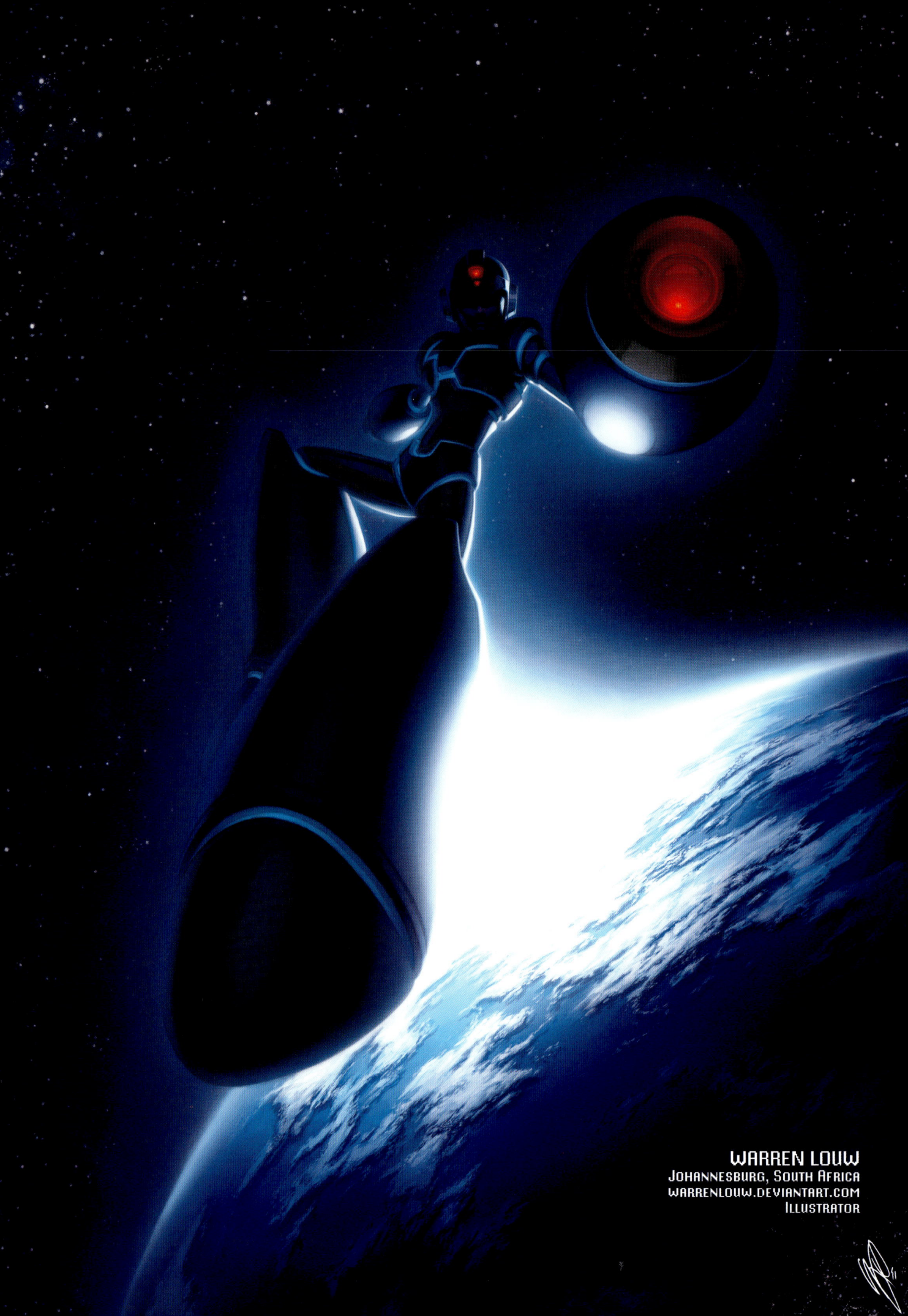

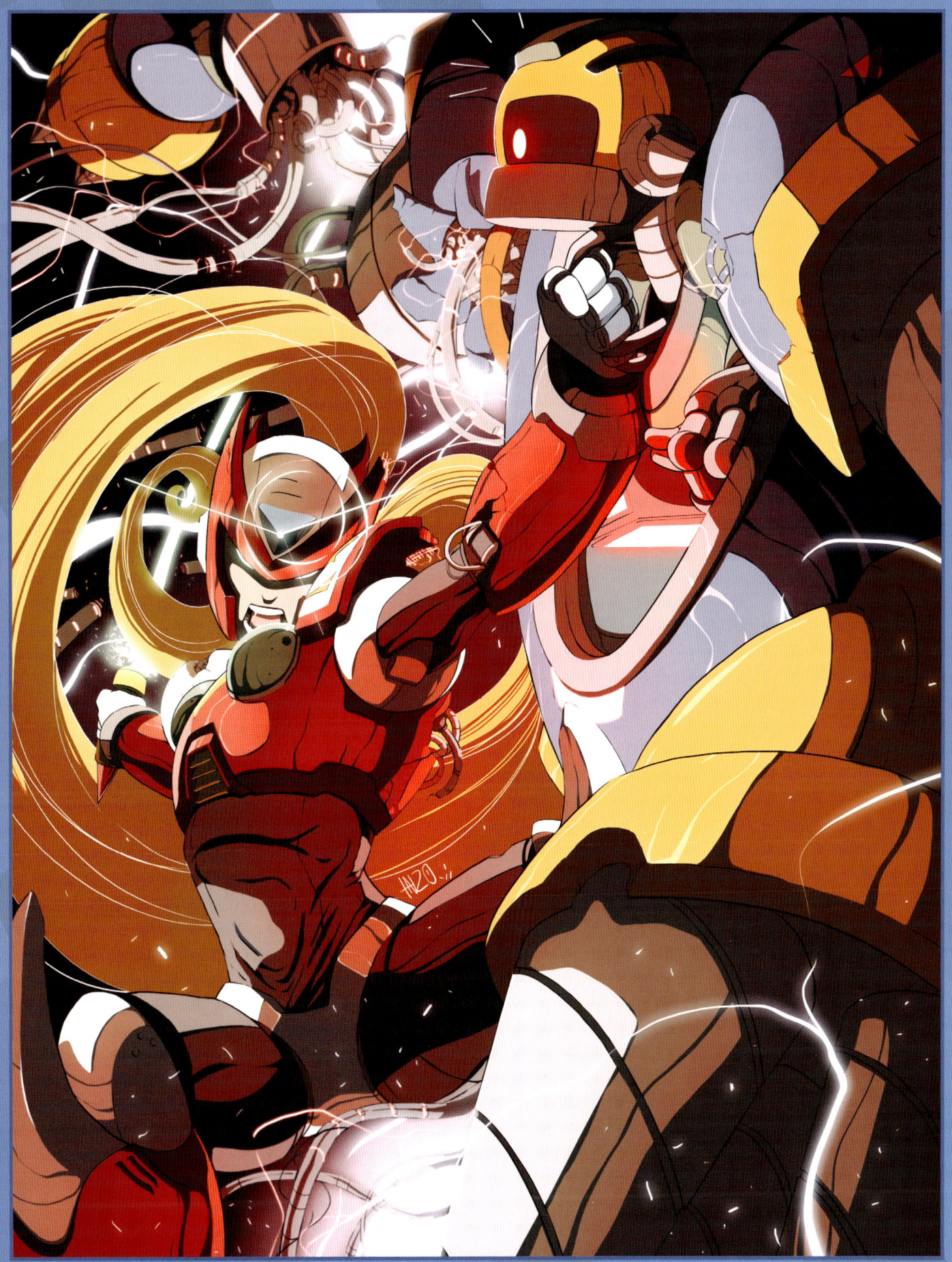

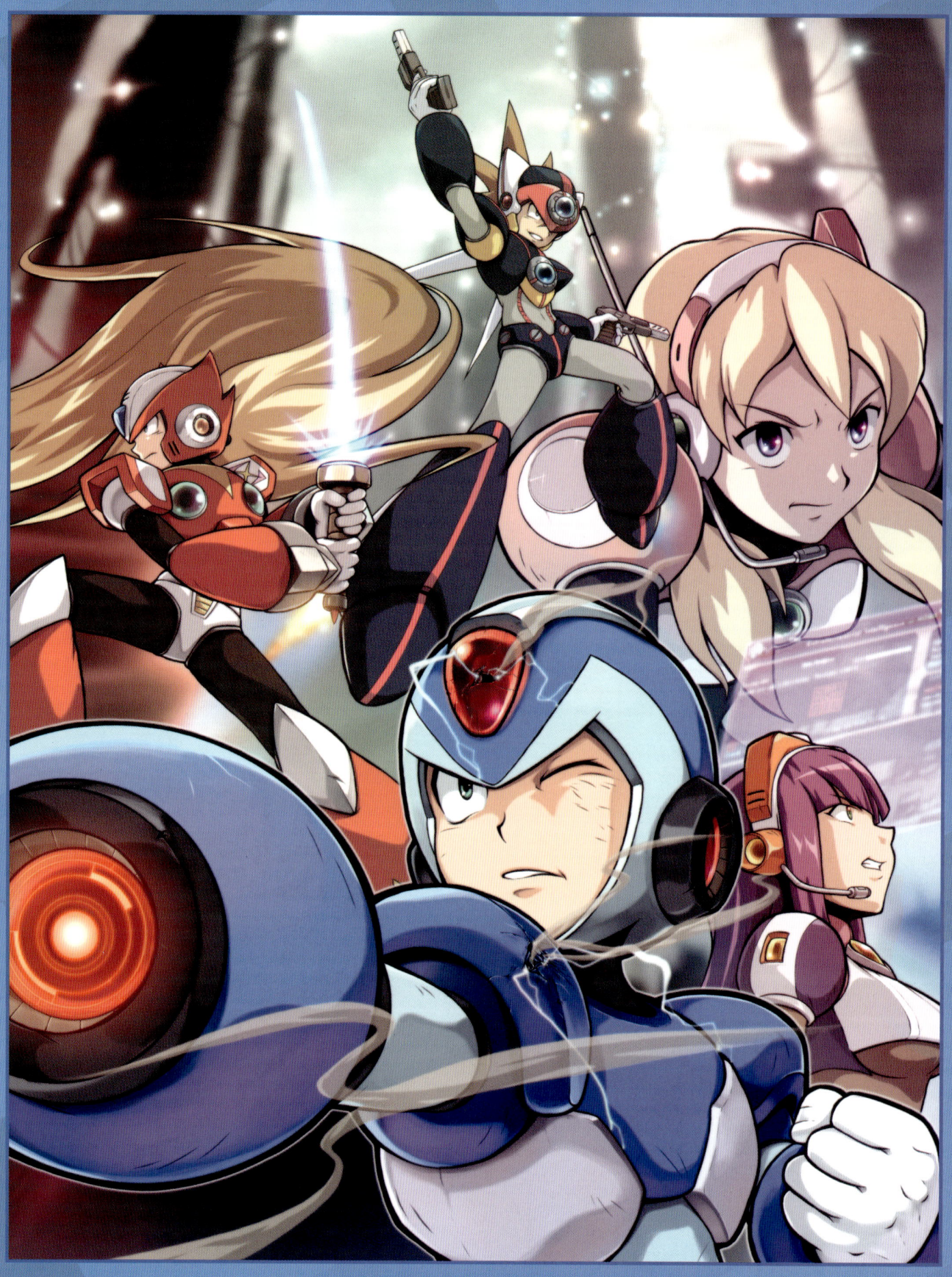

GARY YEUNG
Canada
Illustrator
(Mega Man X Collection / Rockstar Games)

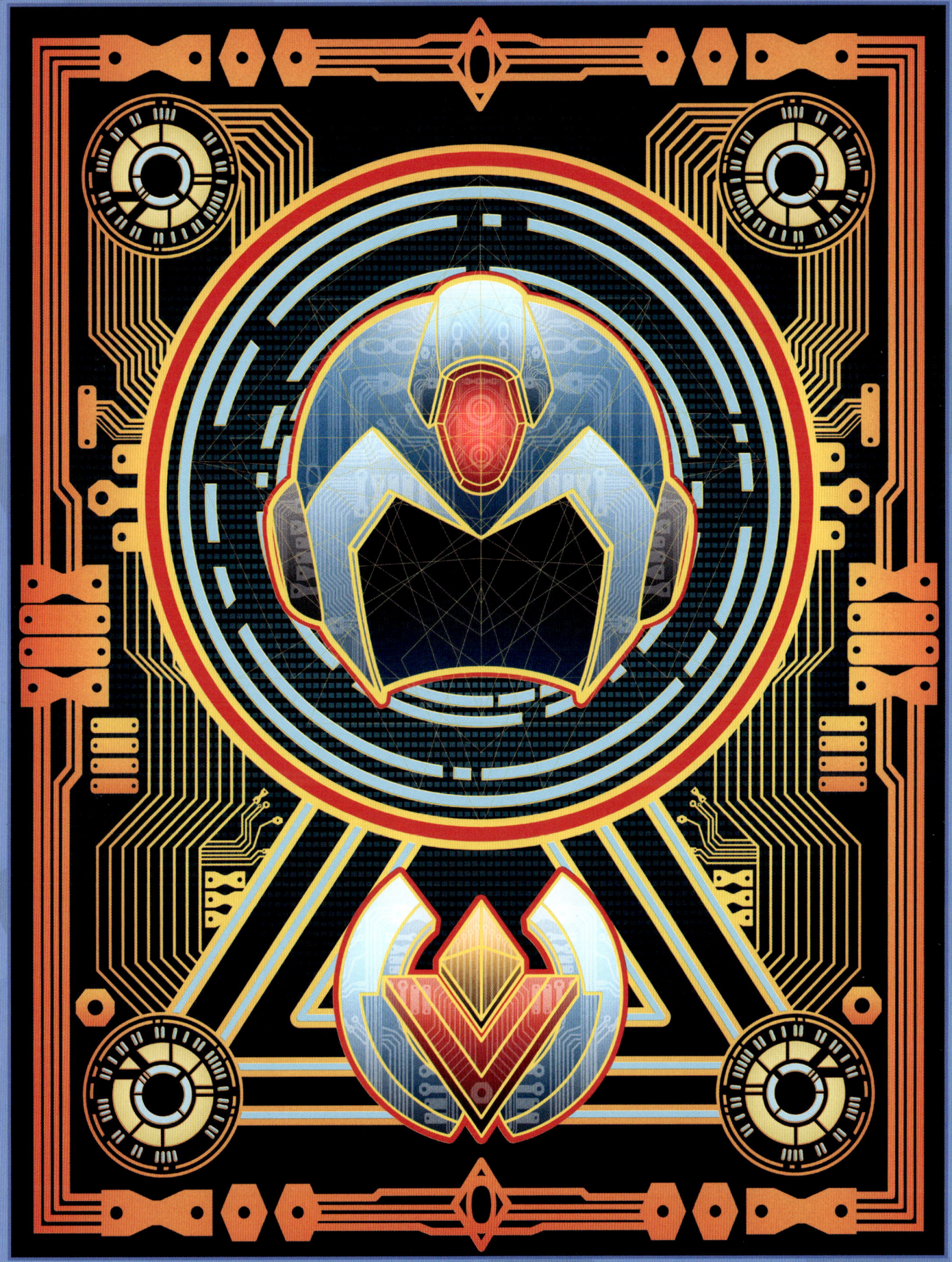

BENJAMIN LAM
Wolverhampton, United Kingdom
lxq.deviantart.com
Illustrator

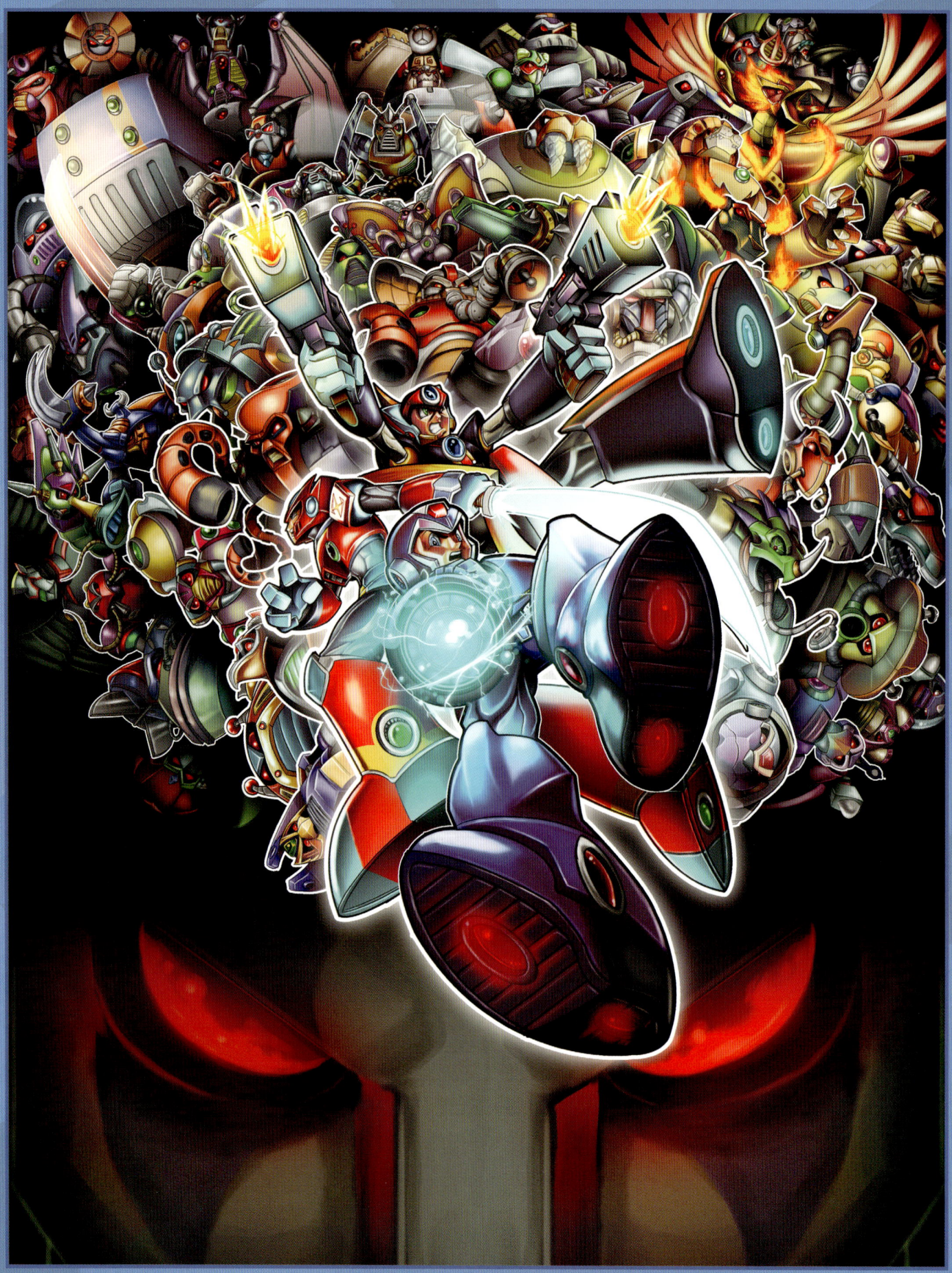

DANIEL VÉLEZ
Medellín, Antioquia, Colombia
daniel-velez.deviantart.com
Animator / Illustrator
(Street Figther Tribute / Doki - Discovery Kids / Bombillo Amarillo)

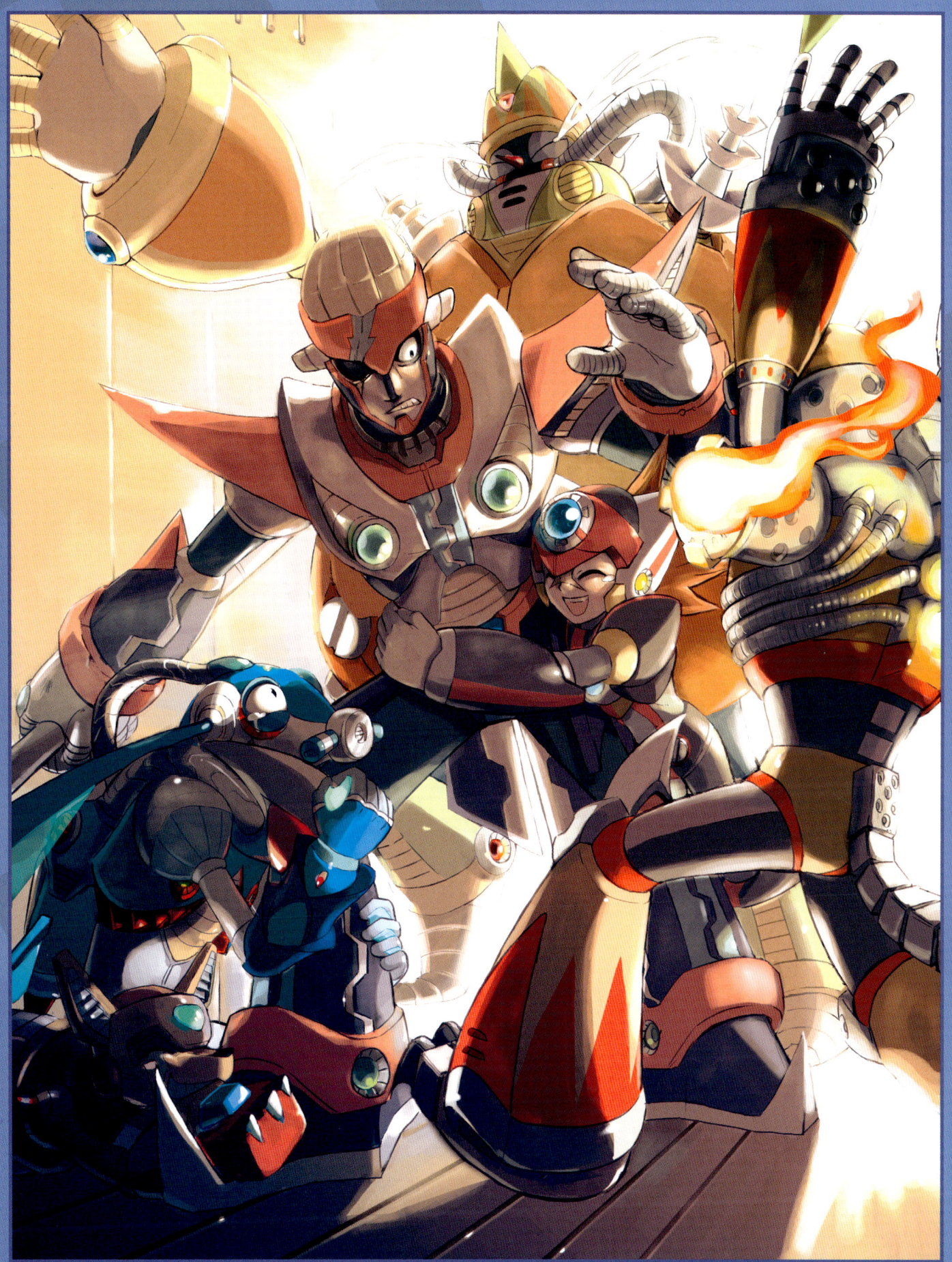

MAYA PETERSEN (RNN)
GAITHERSBURG, MD, UNITED STATES
ILLUSTRATOR

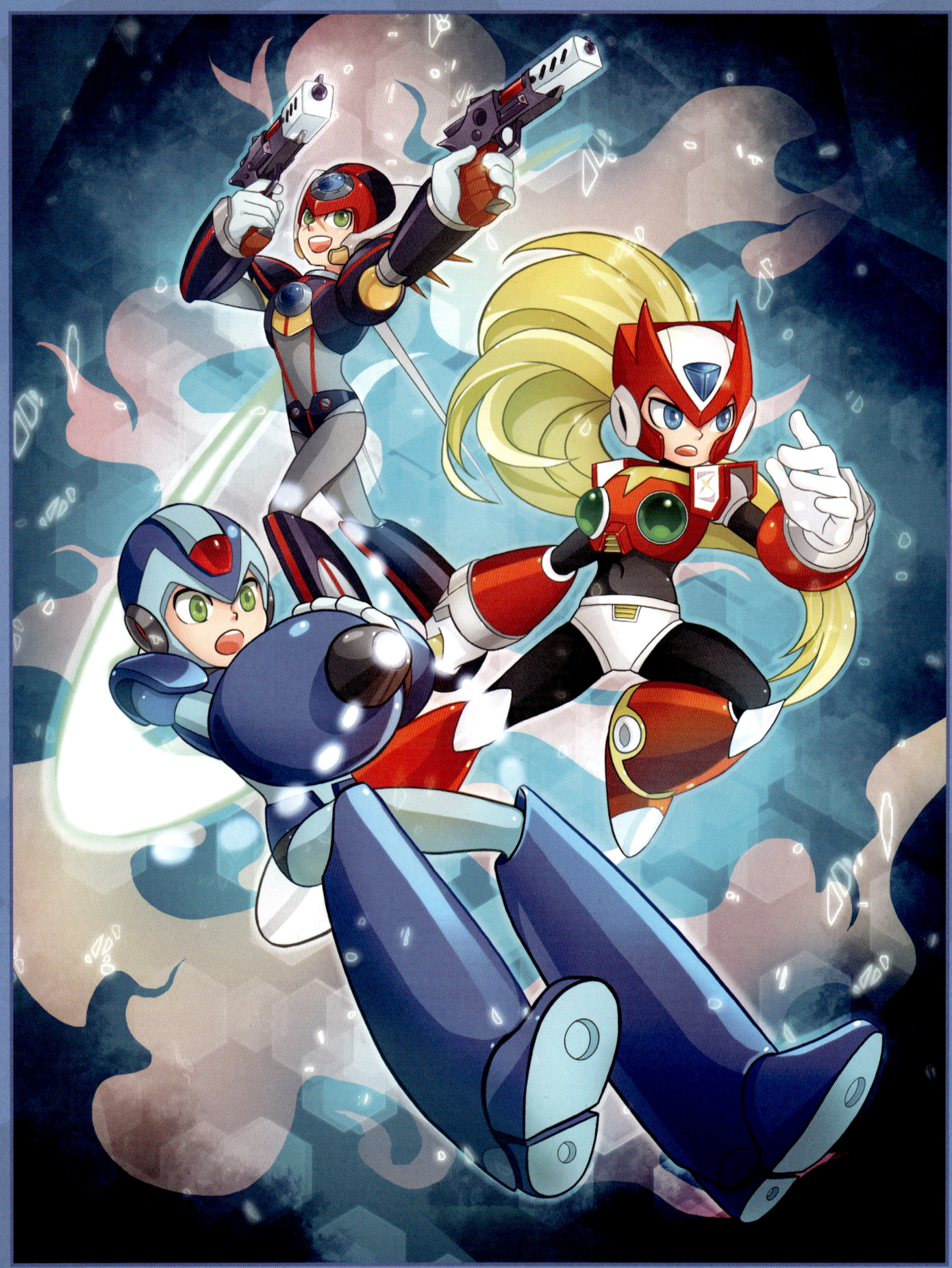

ESTHER CHOW (KUZU)
Batu Pahat, Malaysia
Illustrator

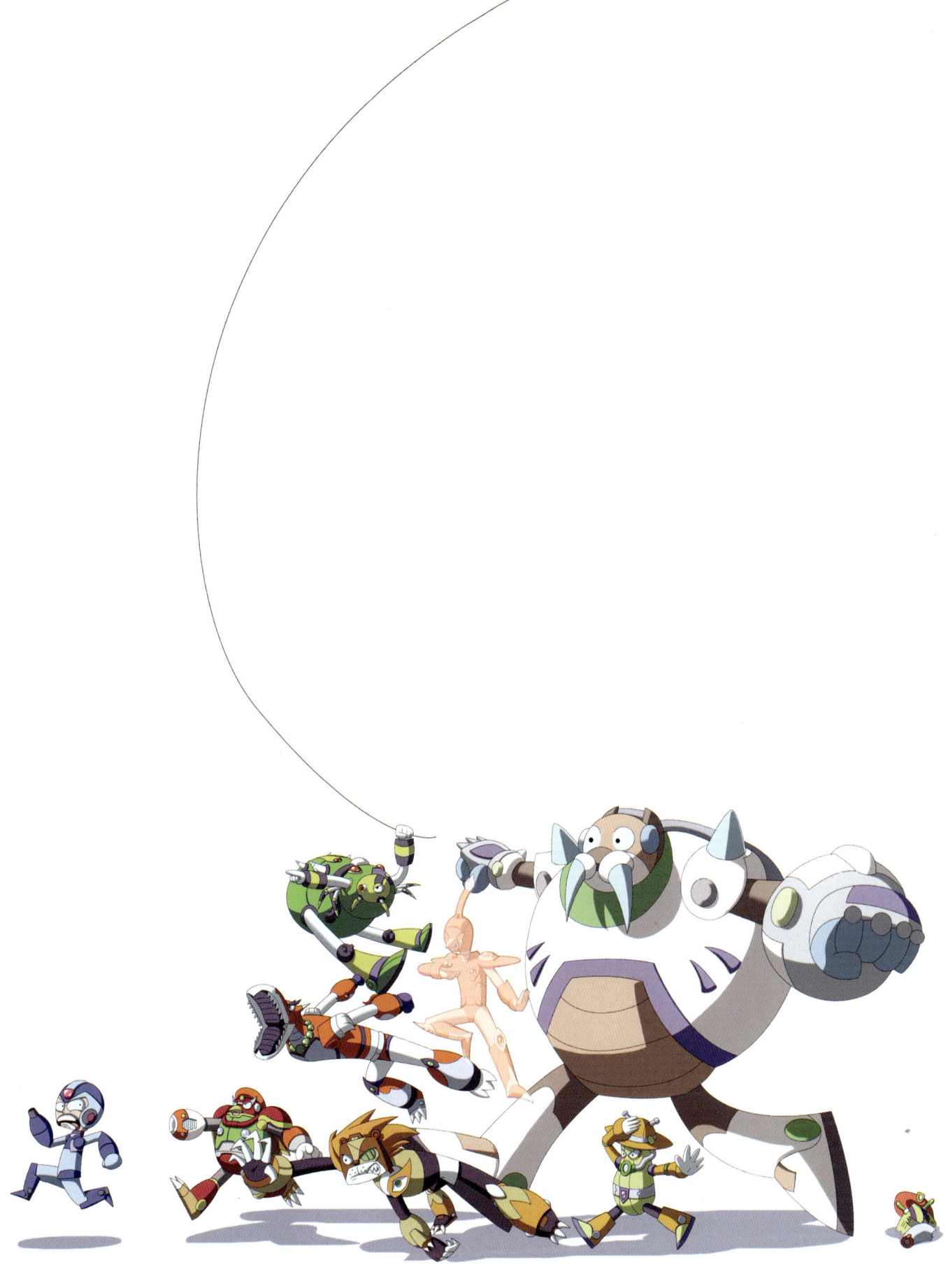

EMMANUELL Z (E-M2)
Monterrey, Mexico
e-m2.deviantart.com
Animator / Illutrator

LAURA RIVERA
Monterrey, Mexico
paper-rabbit.deviantart.com
Illutrator/Animator

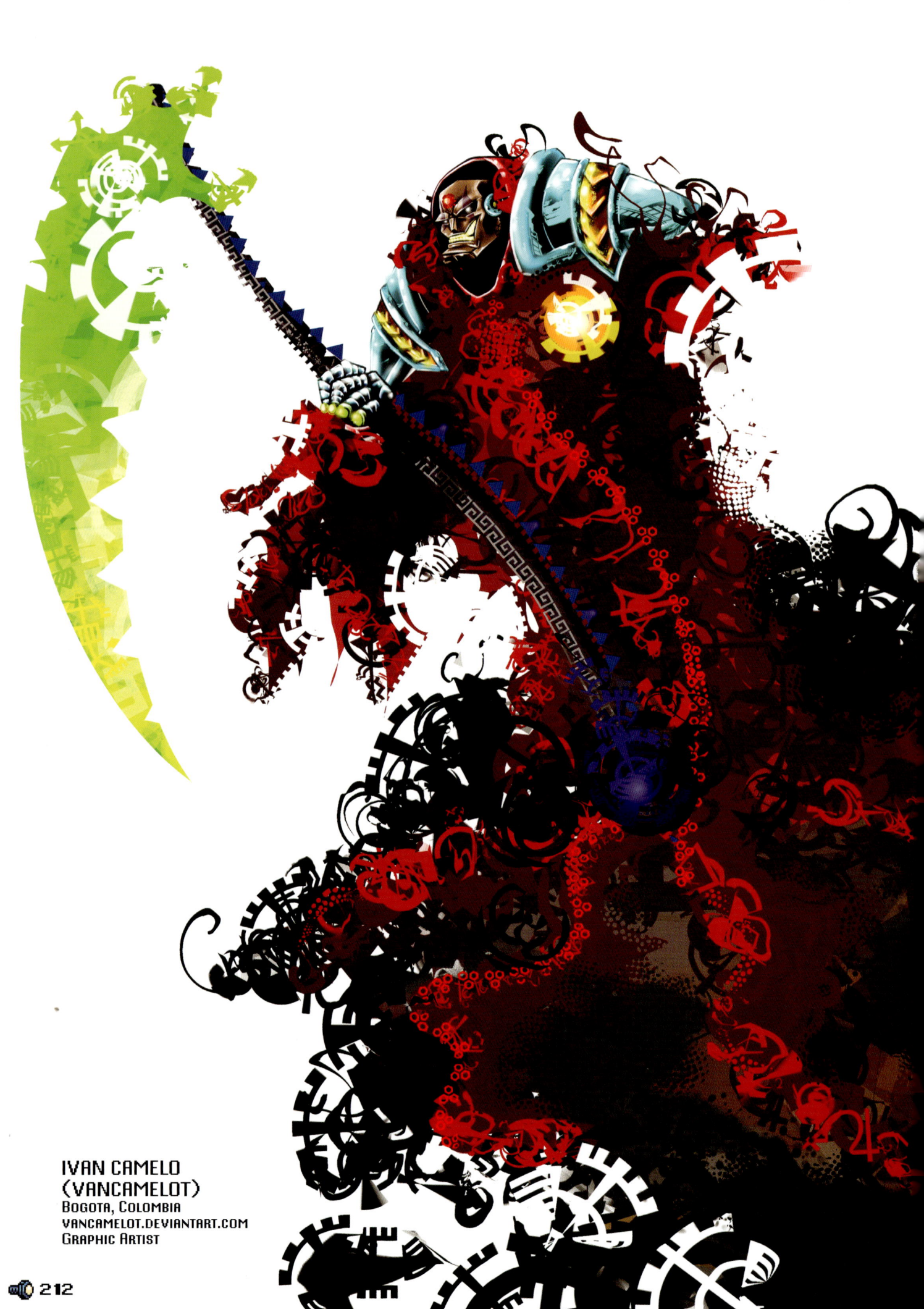

Ivan Camelo (Vancamelot)
Bogota, Colombia
vancamelot.deviantart.com
Graphic Artist

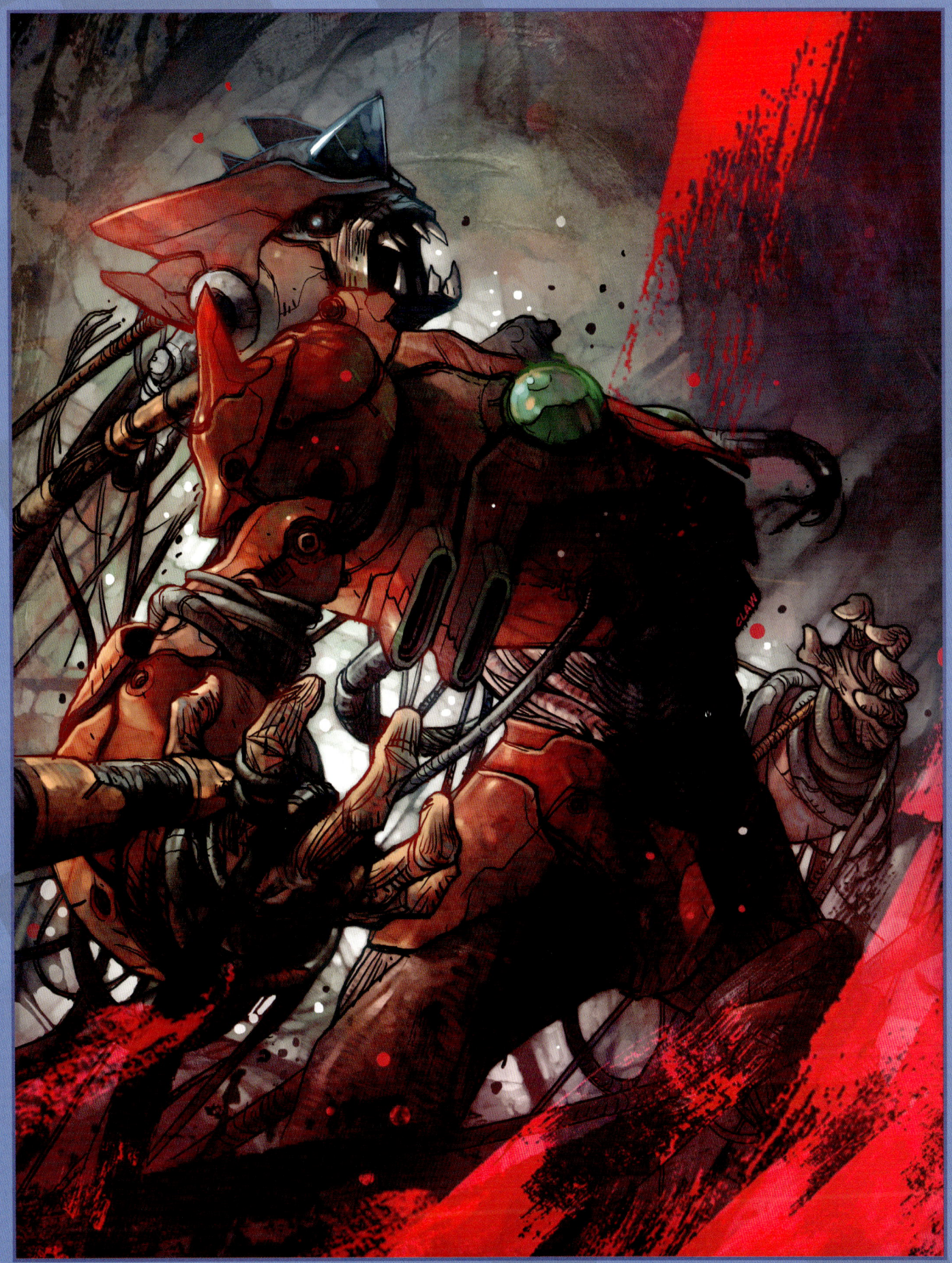

CHANG LIP WEI
BUKIT MERTAJAM, MALAYSIA
claw0208.deviantart.com
Lecturer / Tutor
(The One Academy)

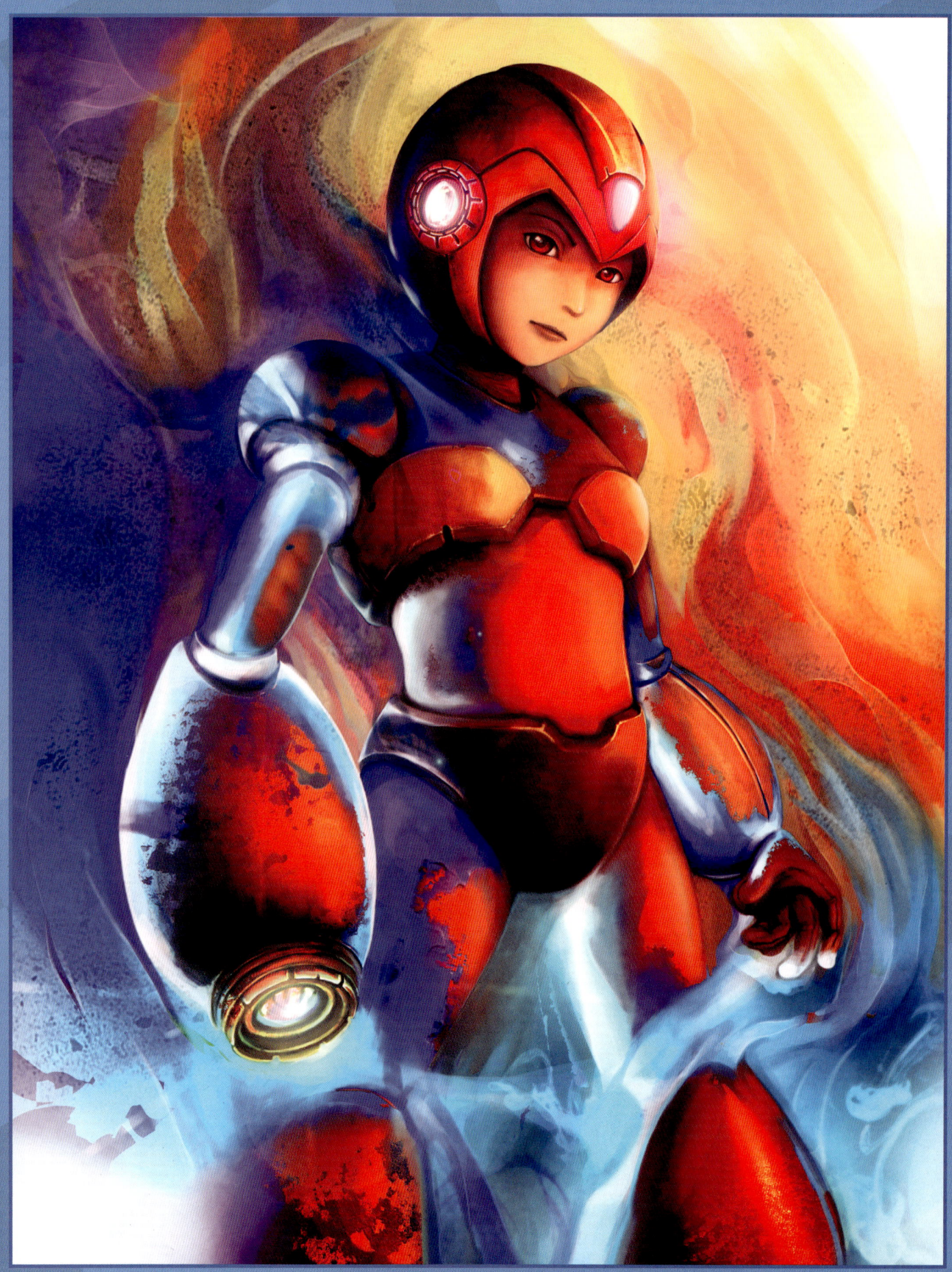

ARTHUR WONGKOKWAI
Kuala Lumpur, Malaysia
arthurwkw.deviantart.com
CG Artist
(Passion Republic)

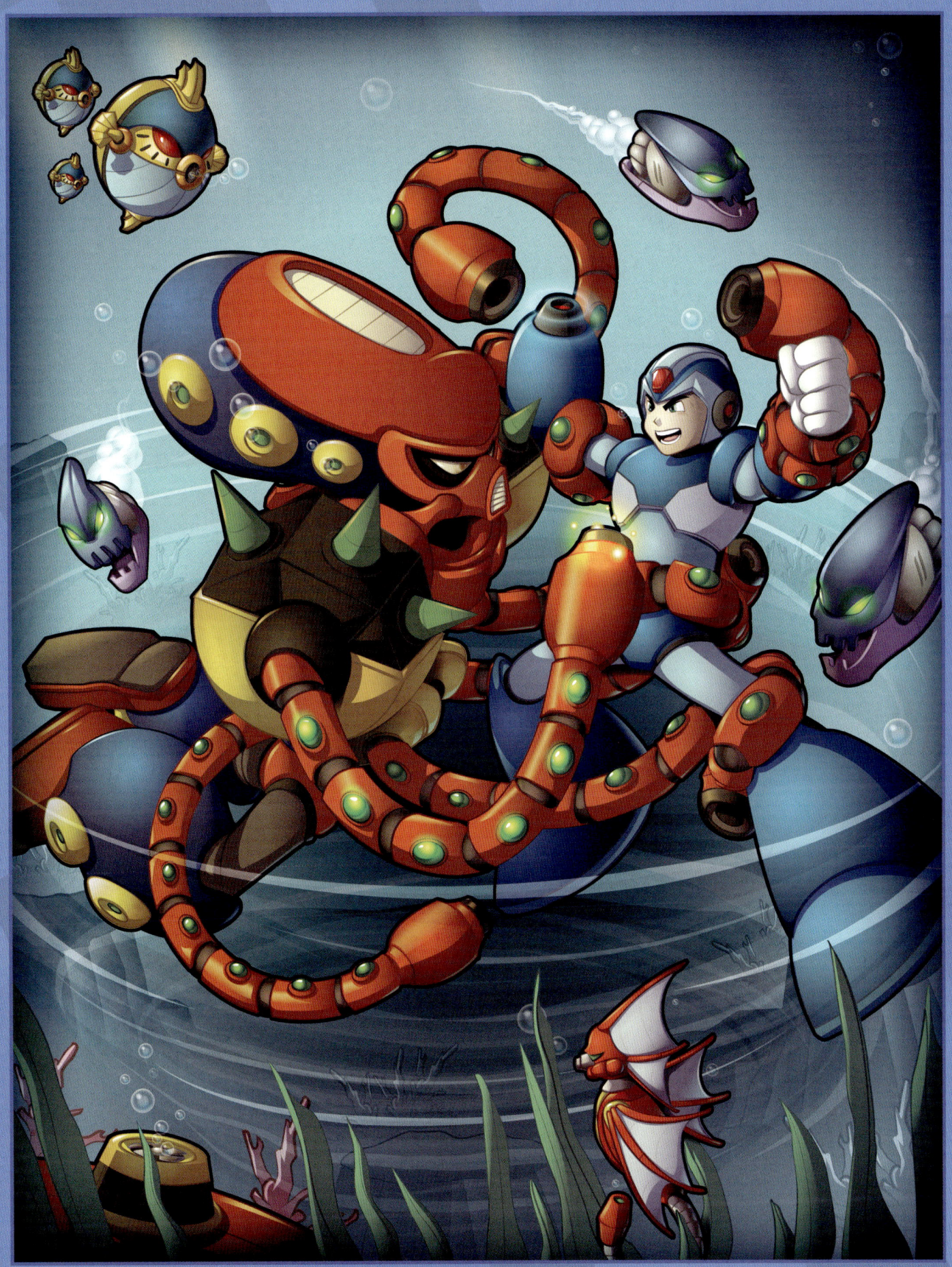

BILLY GARRETSEN (PERFECT DORK)
Cedar Park, TX, United States
www.perfectdorkstudios.com
Game Artist

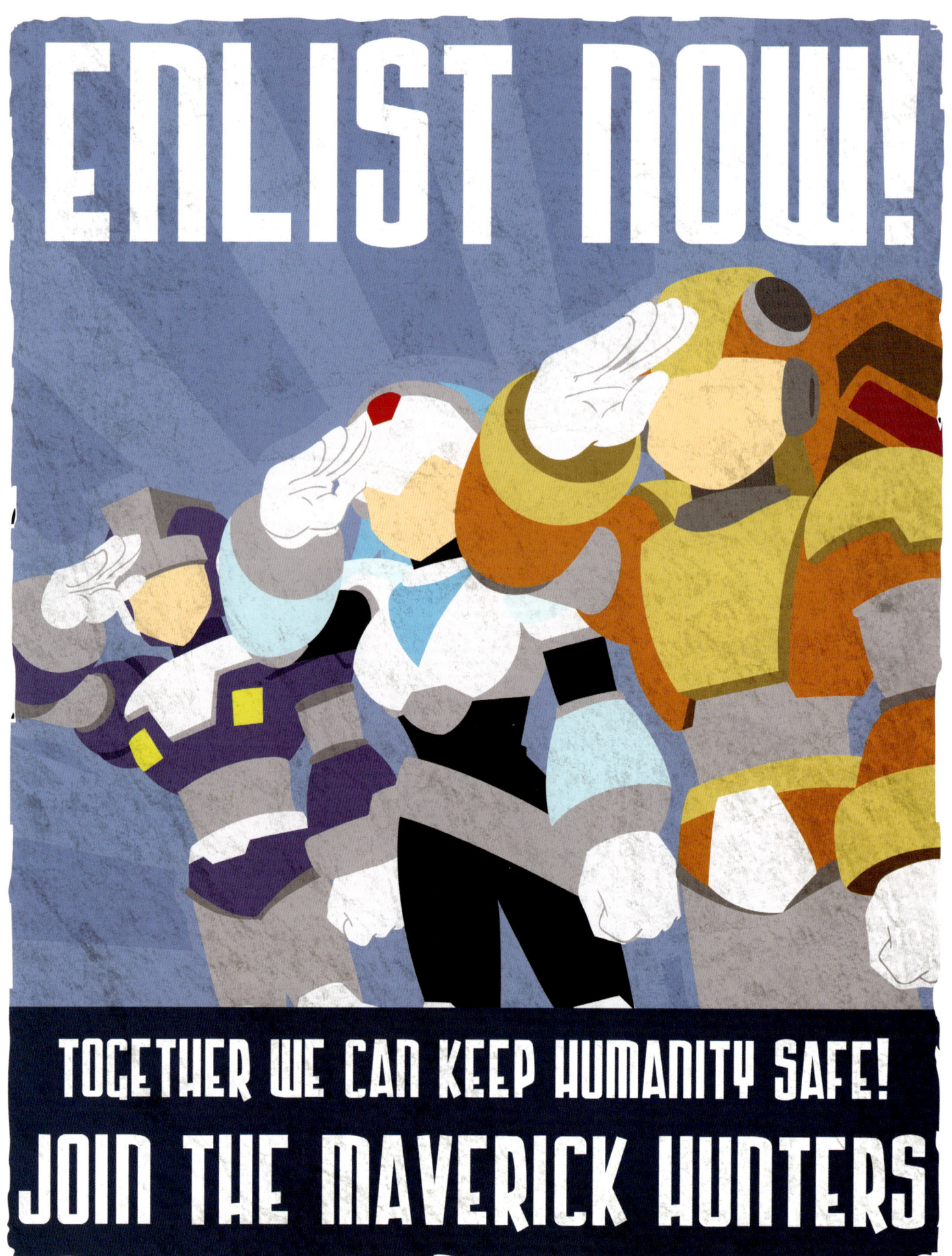

Greg Sepelak
Morrisville, NC, United States
msipher.deviantart.com
Artist / Writer
(Artist, "Shatterd Expectations", BotCon 2008 / Character bio artist)

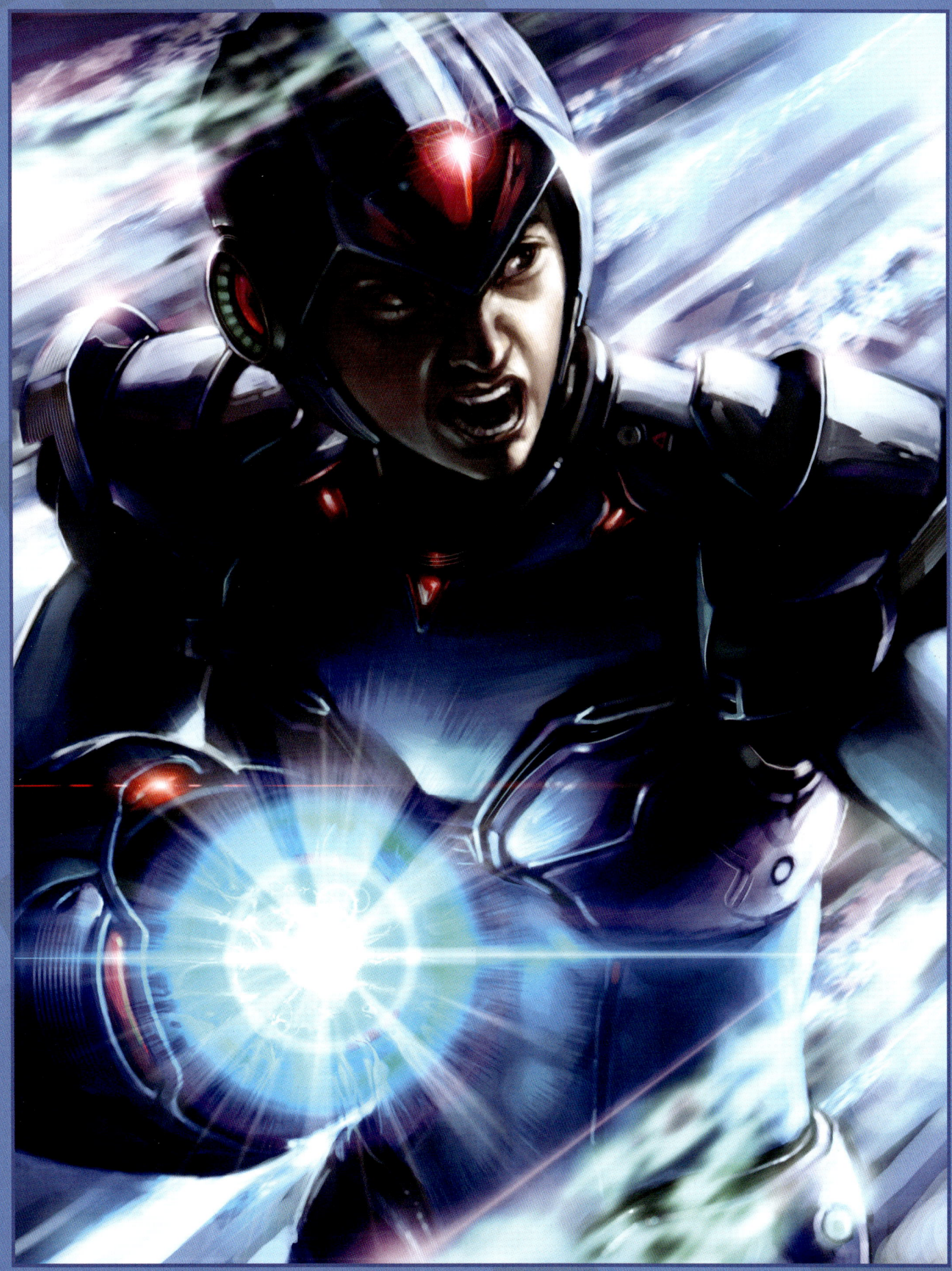

CHUN KIAT WONG
Kuantan, Malaysia
junj.deviantart.com
Illustrator
(The One Academy)

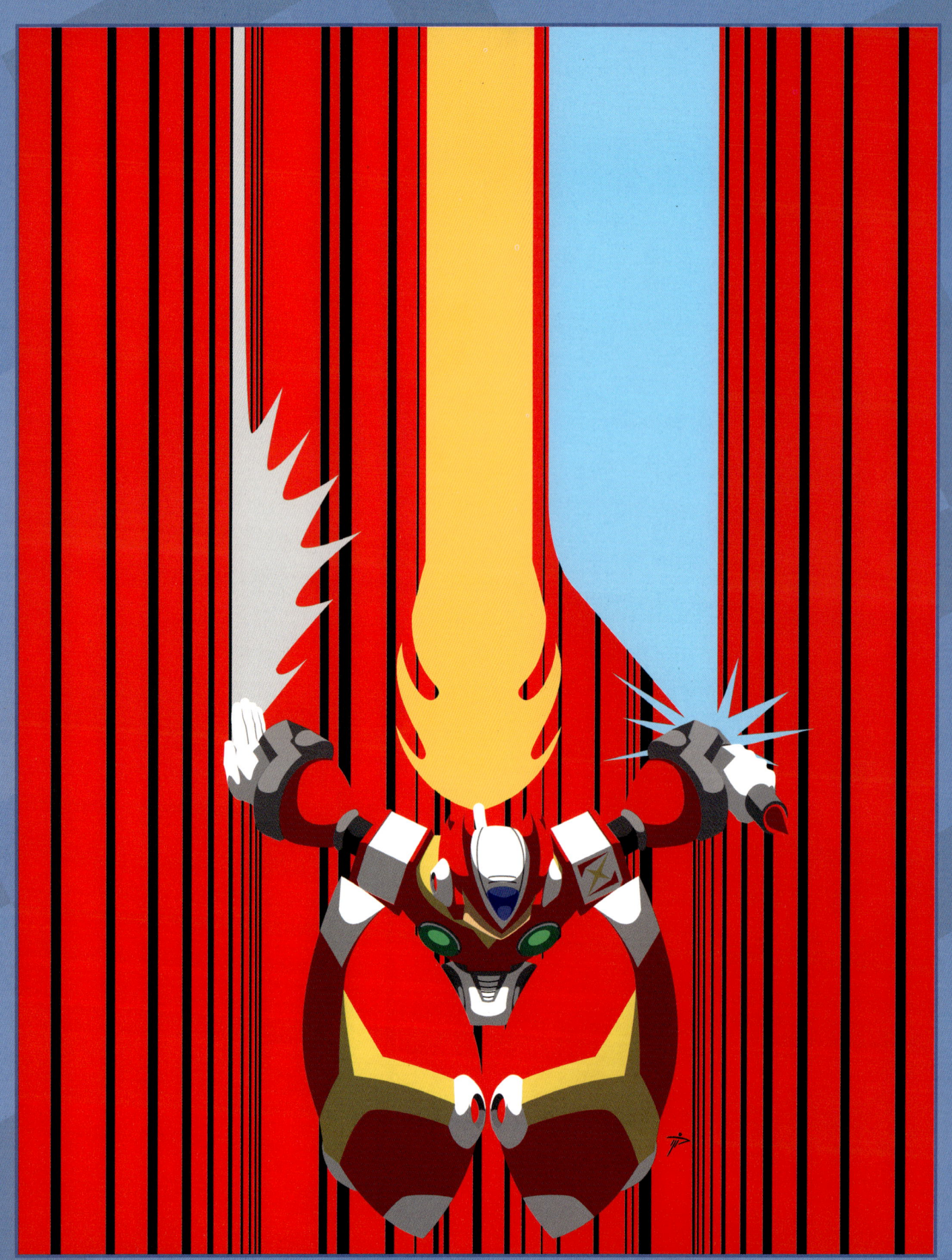

DENNIS PATZELT
Neukirchen-Vluyn, Germany
artofdpi.deviantart.com
Illustrator

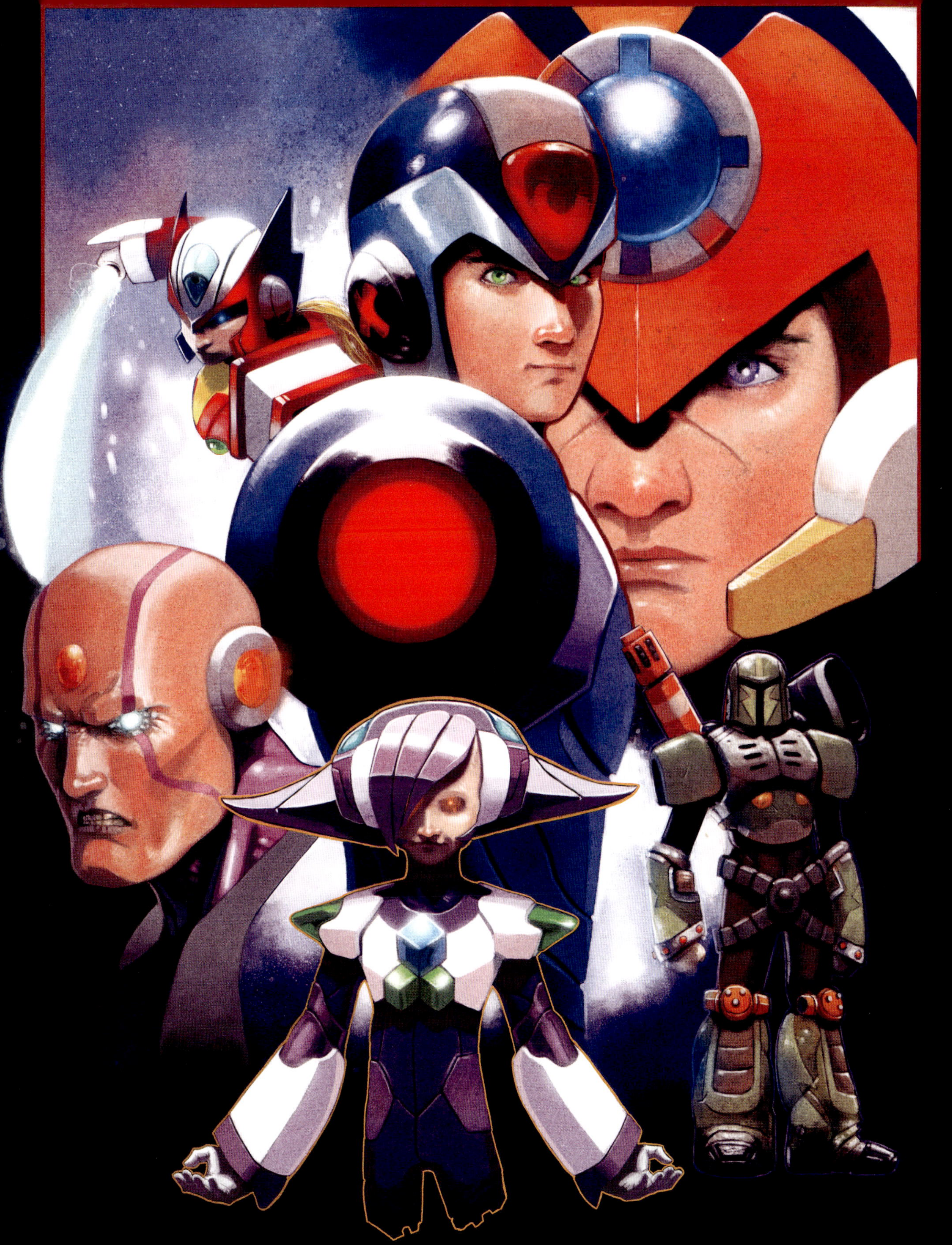

FRANCISCO MENDEZ
Tuxtla Gutierrez, Mexico
packo-mx.deviantart.com
Digital Artist

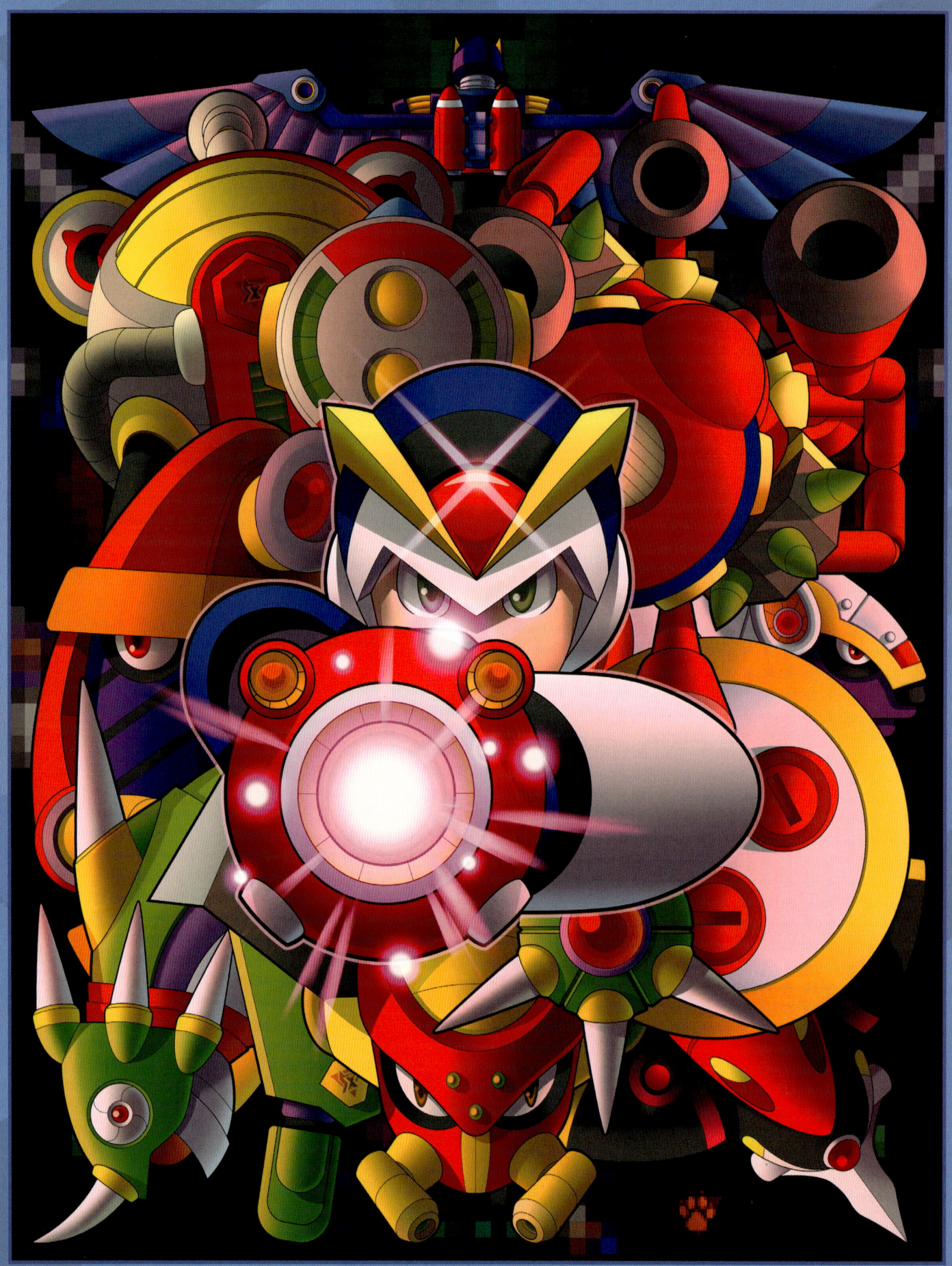

LUIS ROBERTO RAMÍREZ CRUZ (LOBO GRIS)
México City, Mexico
lobo-gris.deviantart.com
Illustrator / Comic artist

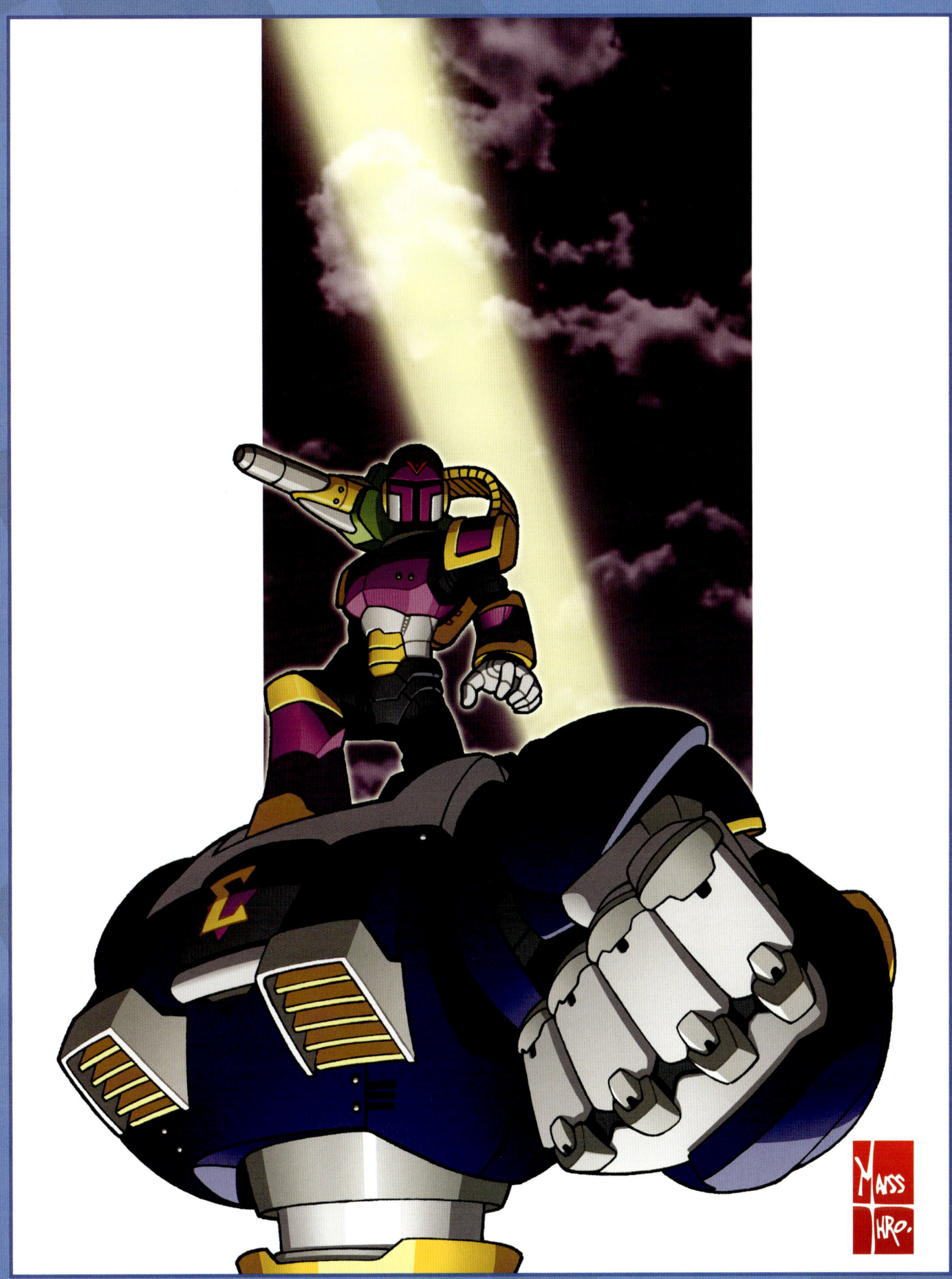

EDUARDO PÉREZ
Maracaibo, Venezuela
maiss-thro.deviantart.com
Illustrator / Grahic Designer

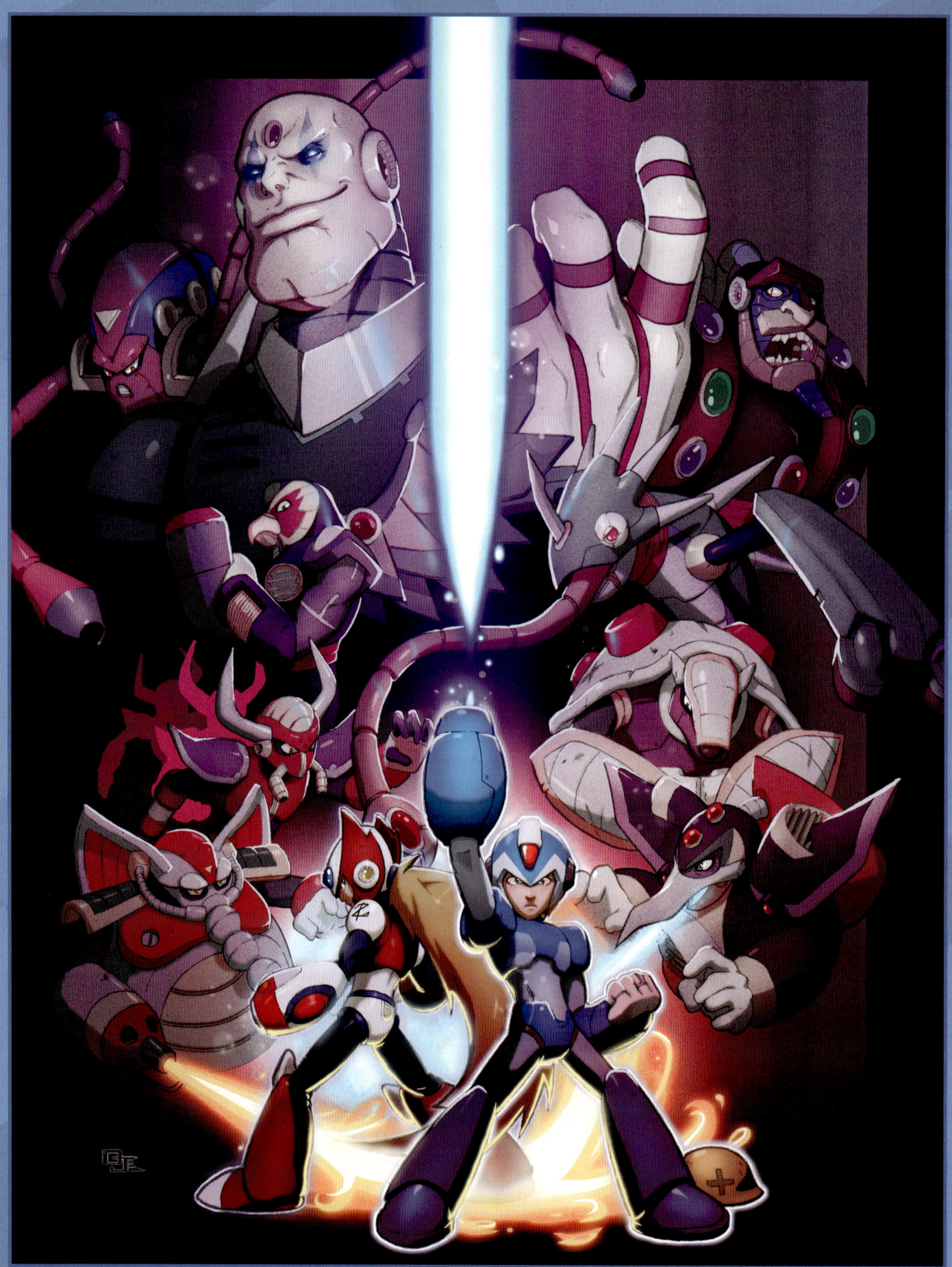

DJ Welch (Dark Kenjie)
San Francisco, CA, United States
darkkenjie.deviantart.com
Concept Artist/ Storyboard Artist
(Academy of Art University)

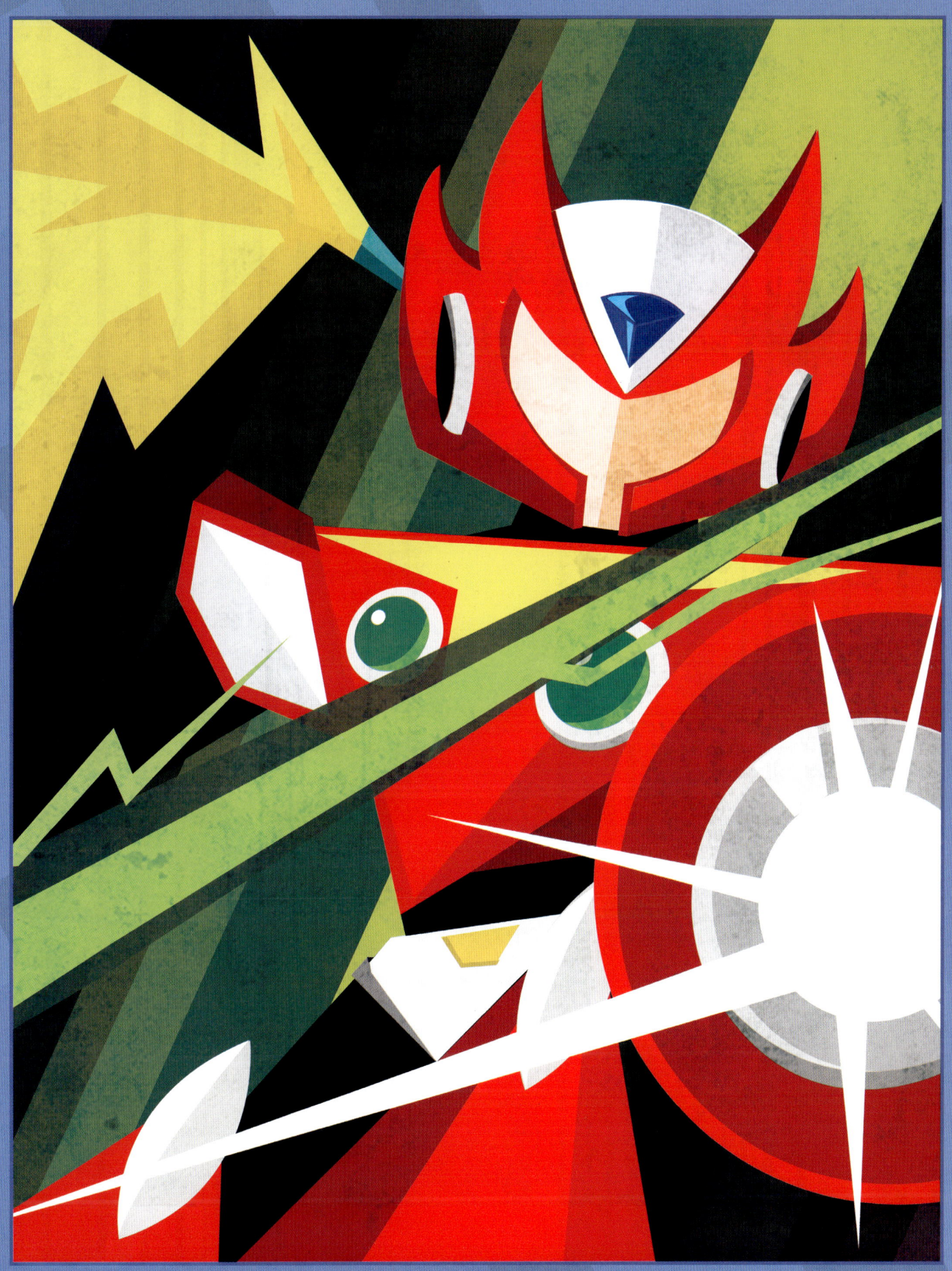

MICHEL MALAGUETA
Barueri, Brazil
michelmalagueta.deviantart.com
Illustrator

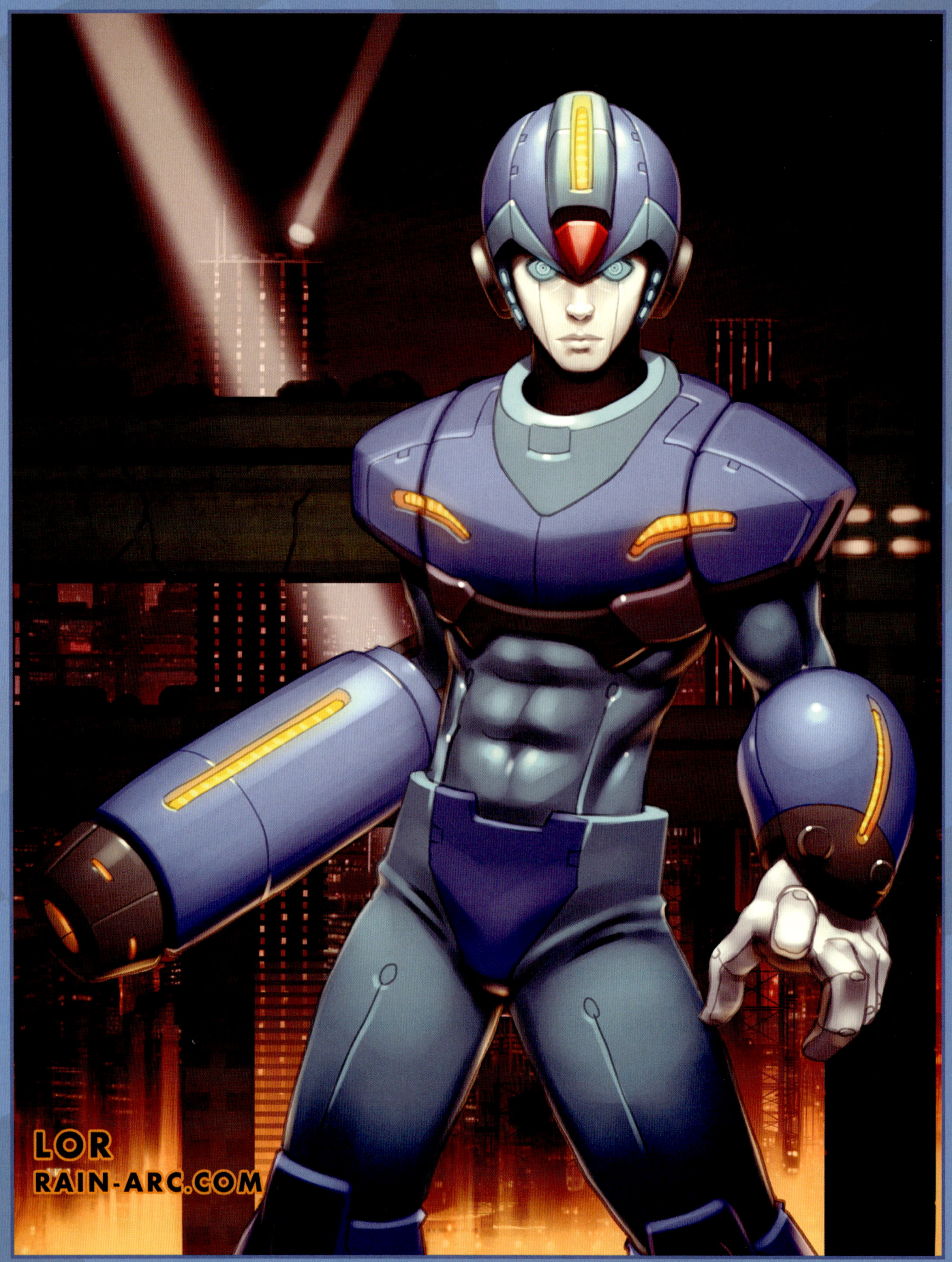

STEPHEN RAFFILL
Madison, WI, United States
www.rain-arc.com
Artist

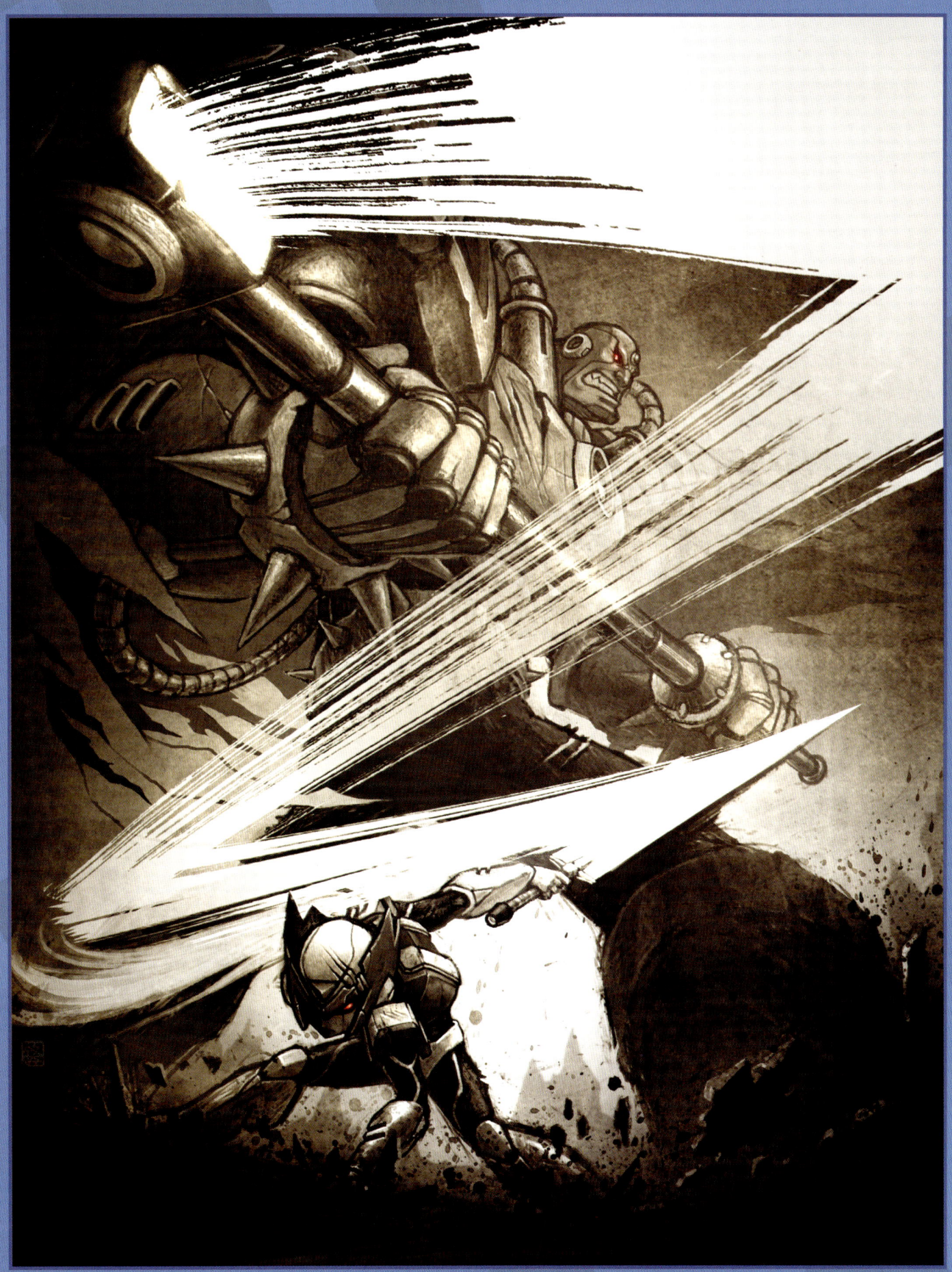

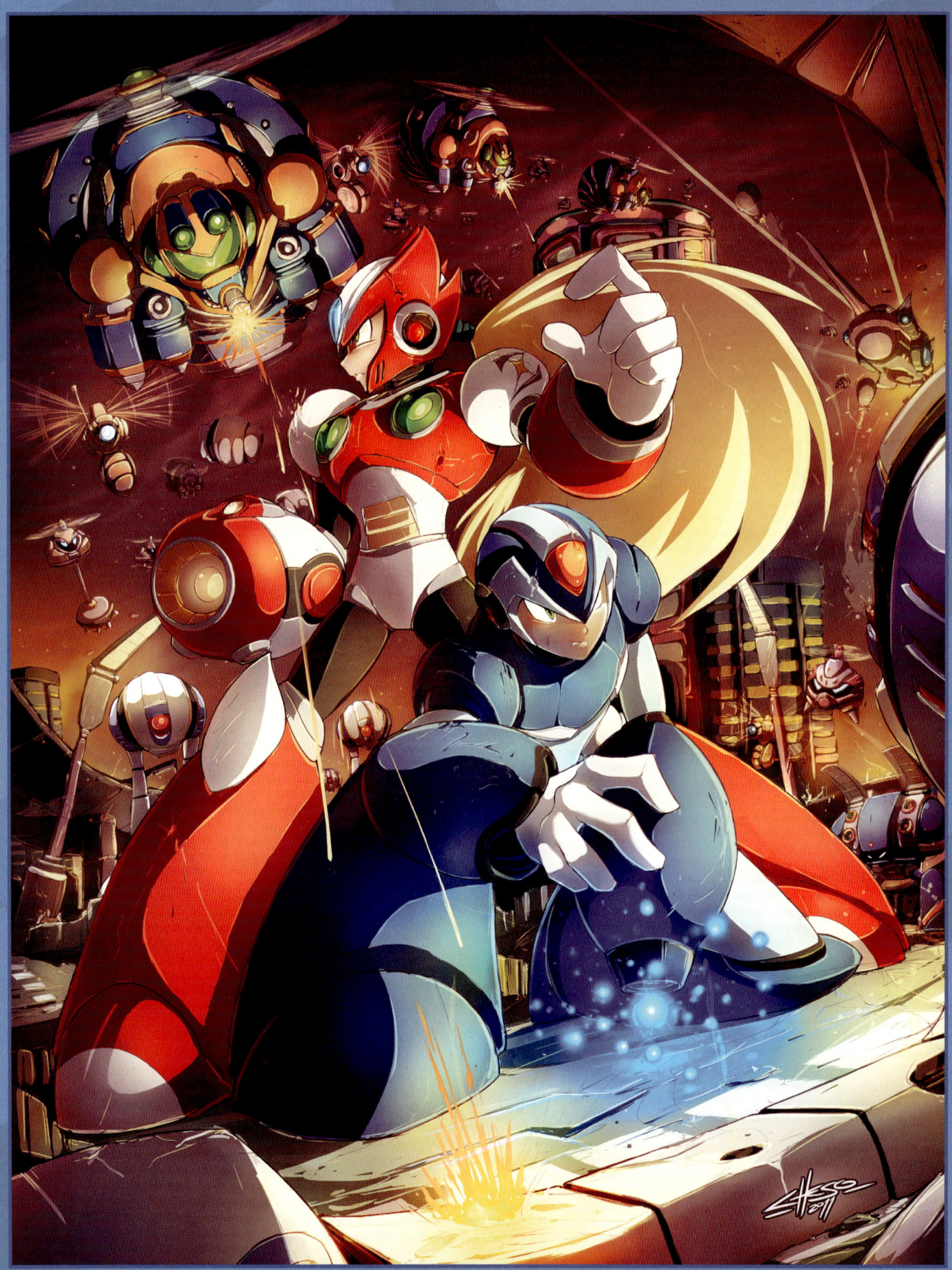

JESUS BAUTISTA (JESONITE)
Chihuahua, Mexico
jesonite.deviantart.com
Illustrator and Graphic Designer
(Okamibox Studios / Running Wild! - Artist and Writter)

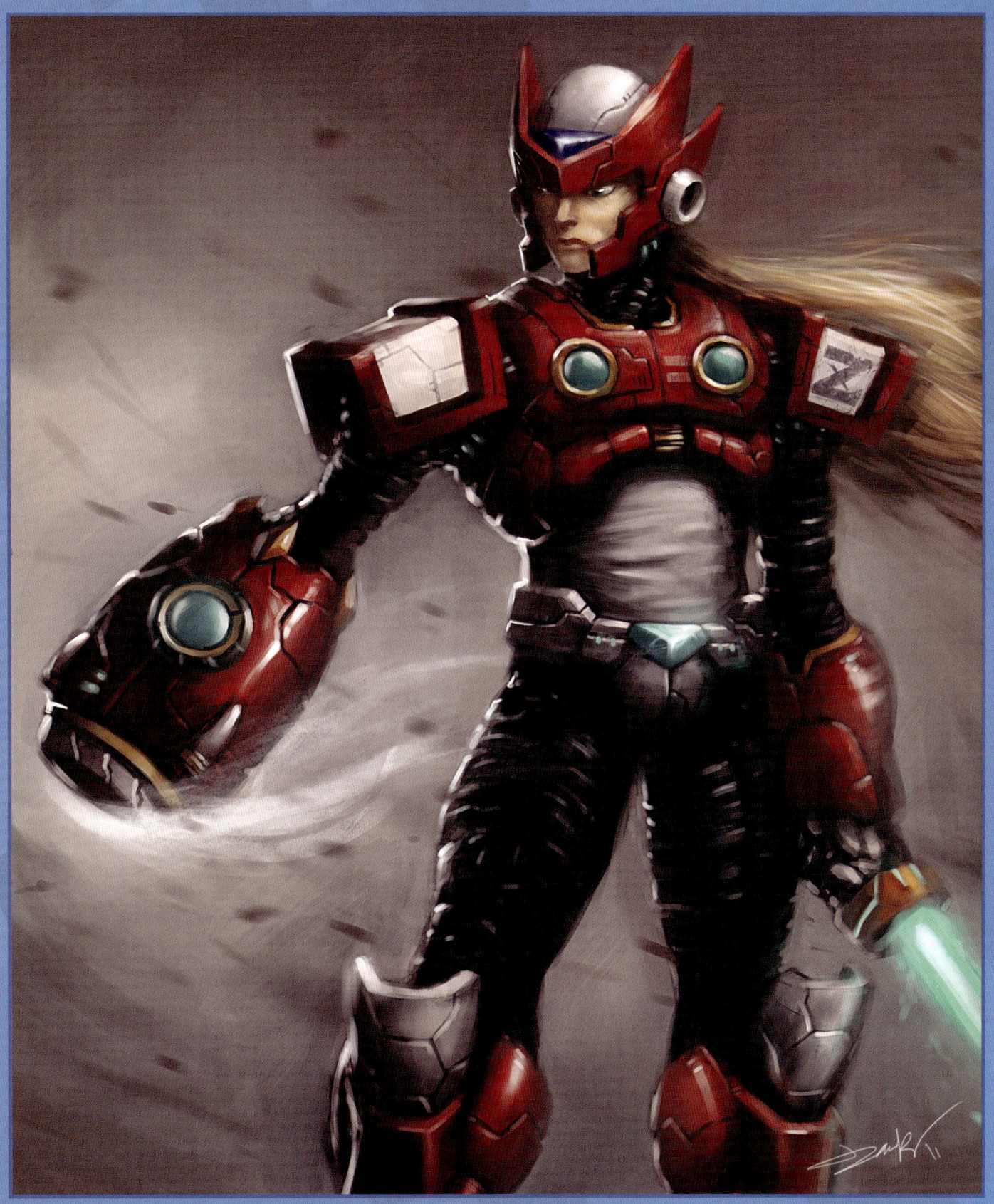

DANIEL KHO
Subang Jaya, Malaysia
daniorrr.deviantart.com
Student
(The One Academy)

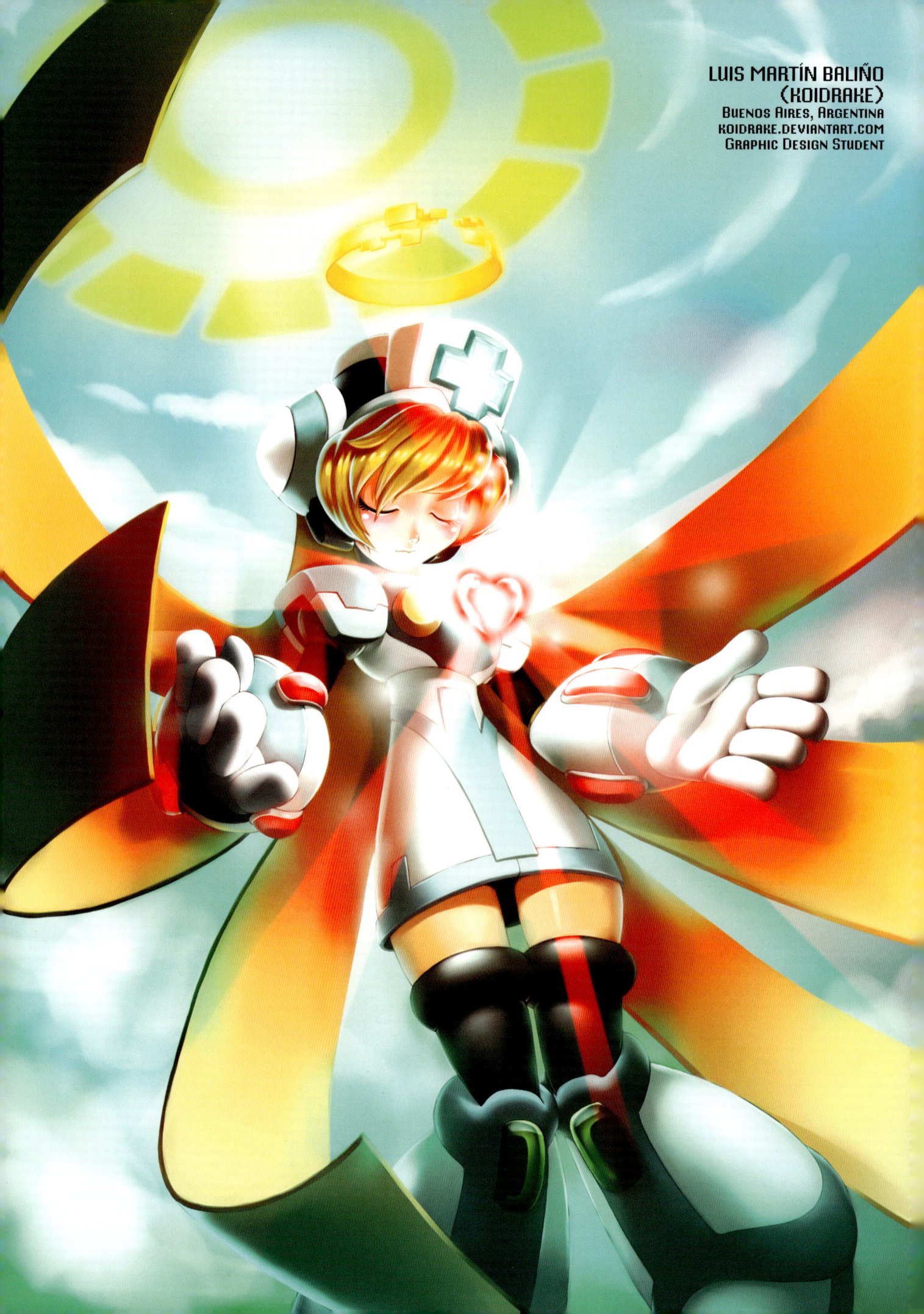

LUIS MARTÍN BALIÑO
(KOIDRAKE)
Buenos Aires, Argentina
koidrake.deviantart.com
Graphic Design Student

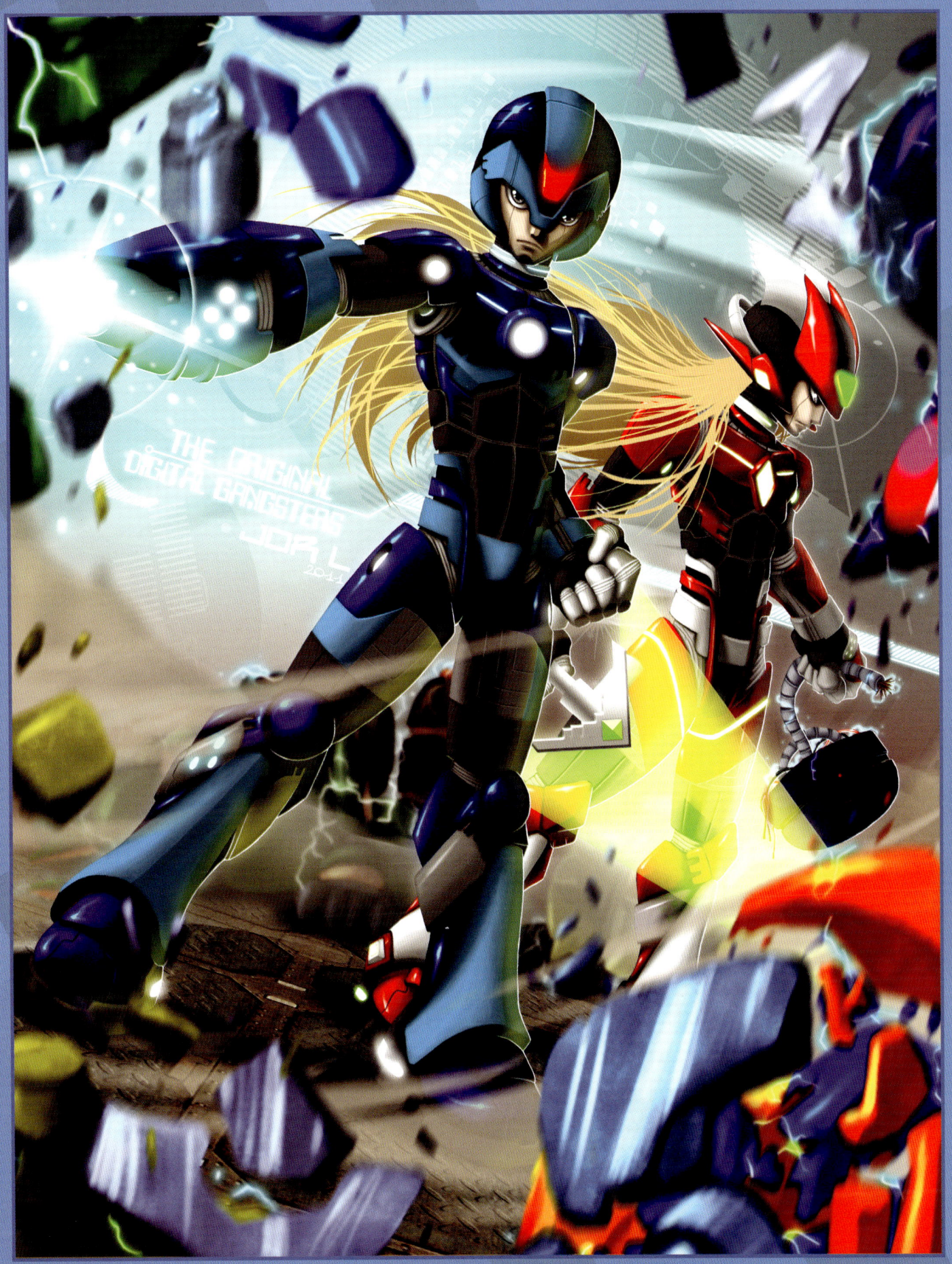

JORGE LUIS MALDONADO MOROCHO (JOR L)
Machala, Ecuador
jorgesuke.deviantart.com
Designer / Illustrator

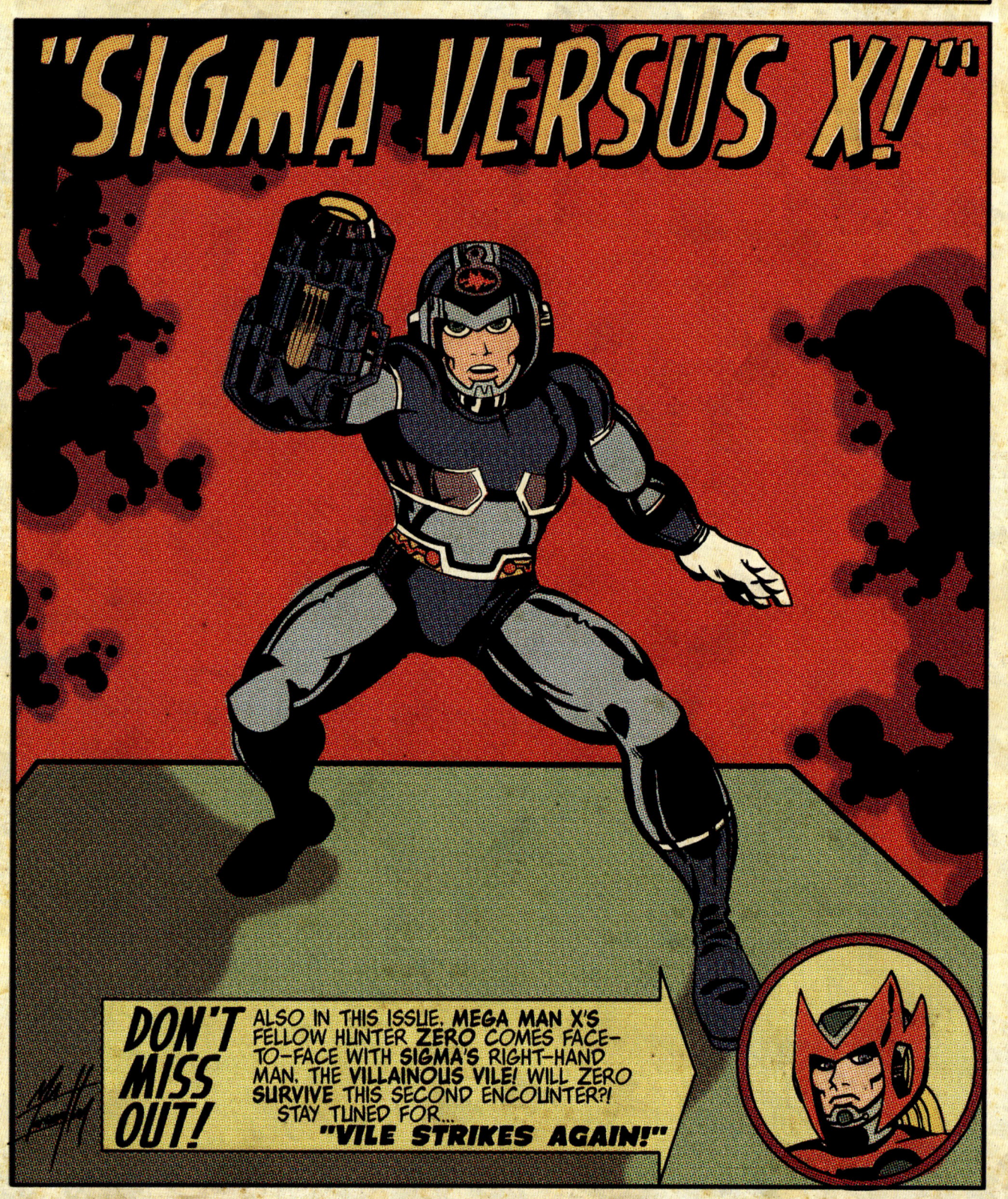

Matthew Ingraham
Kitchener, ON, Canada
cyber-kun.deviantart.com
Illustrator

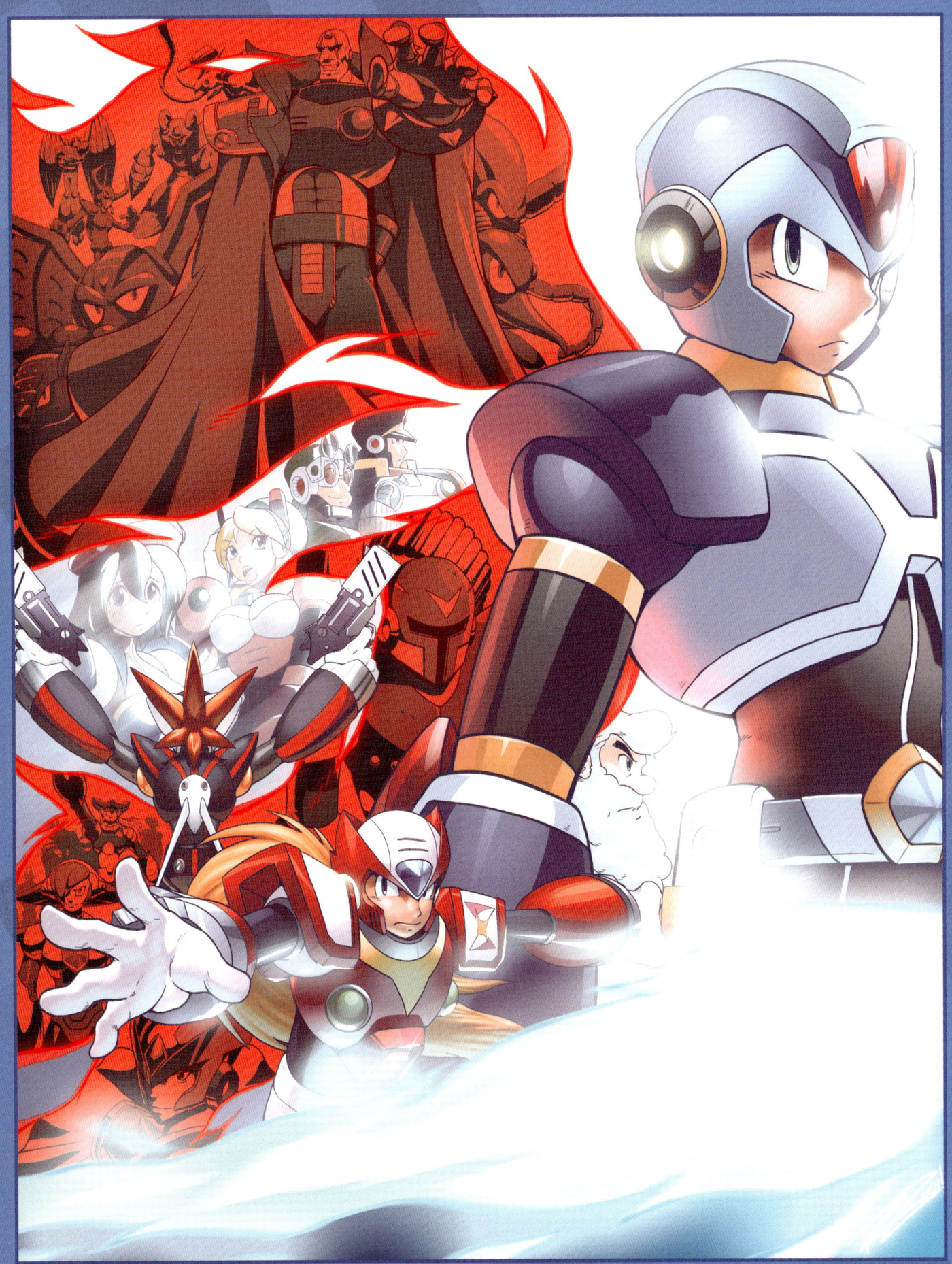

ROBERT PORTER (ROBAATO)
Romeoville, IL, United States
robaato.deviantart.com
Illustrator
(Rat Rage (Creator))

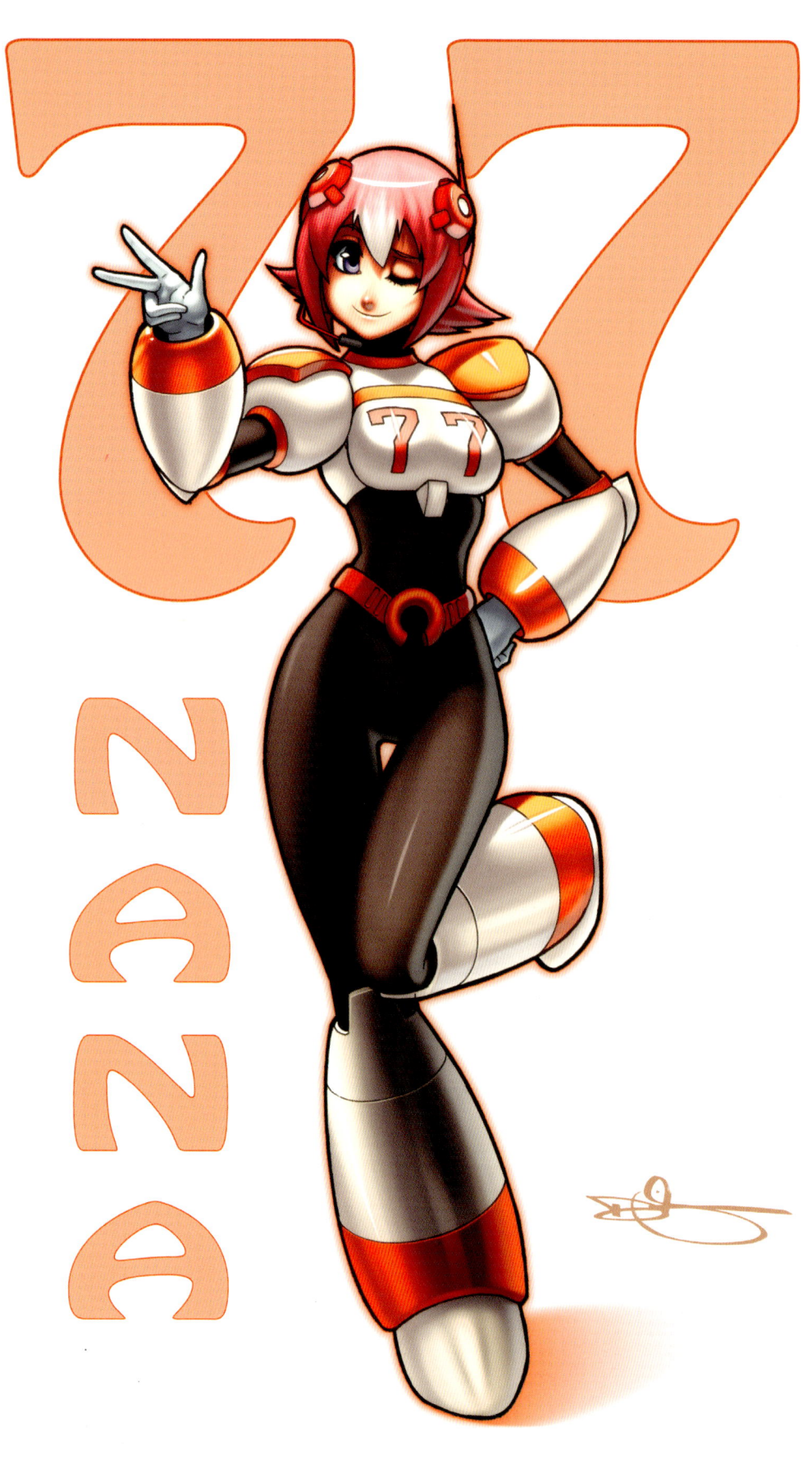

OMAR DOGAN
Mississauga, ON, Canada
omar-dogan.deviantart.com
Illustrator (Street Fighter Legends, 5th Capsule)

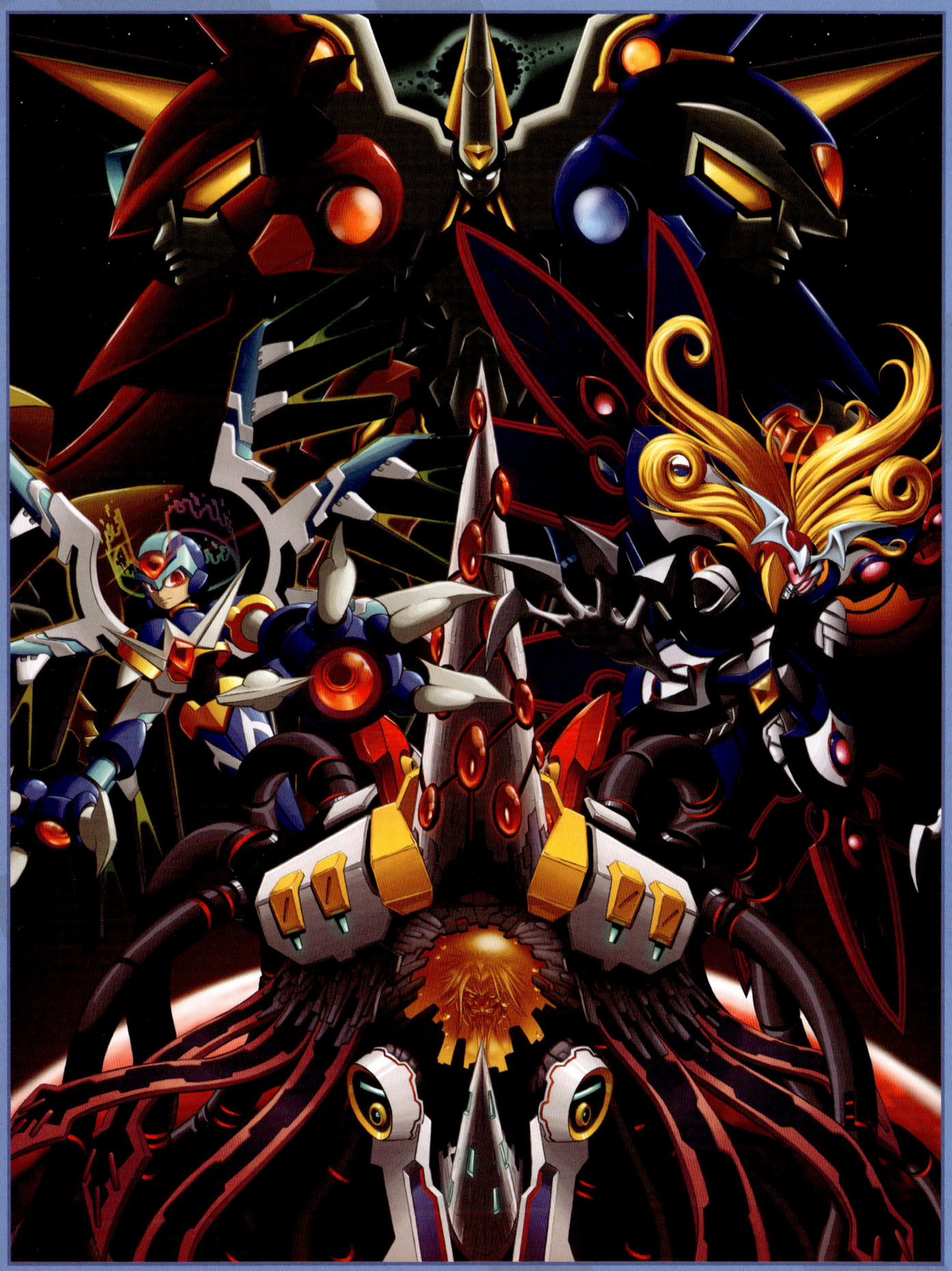

ROBERT JOHNSTON
Plymouth, MN, United States
Comic Artist
(Minneapolis College of Art and Design)

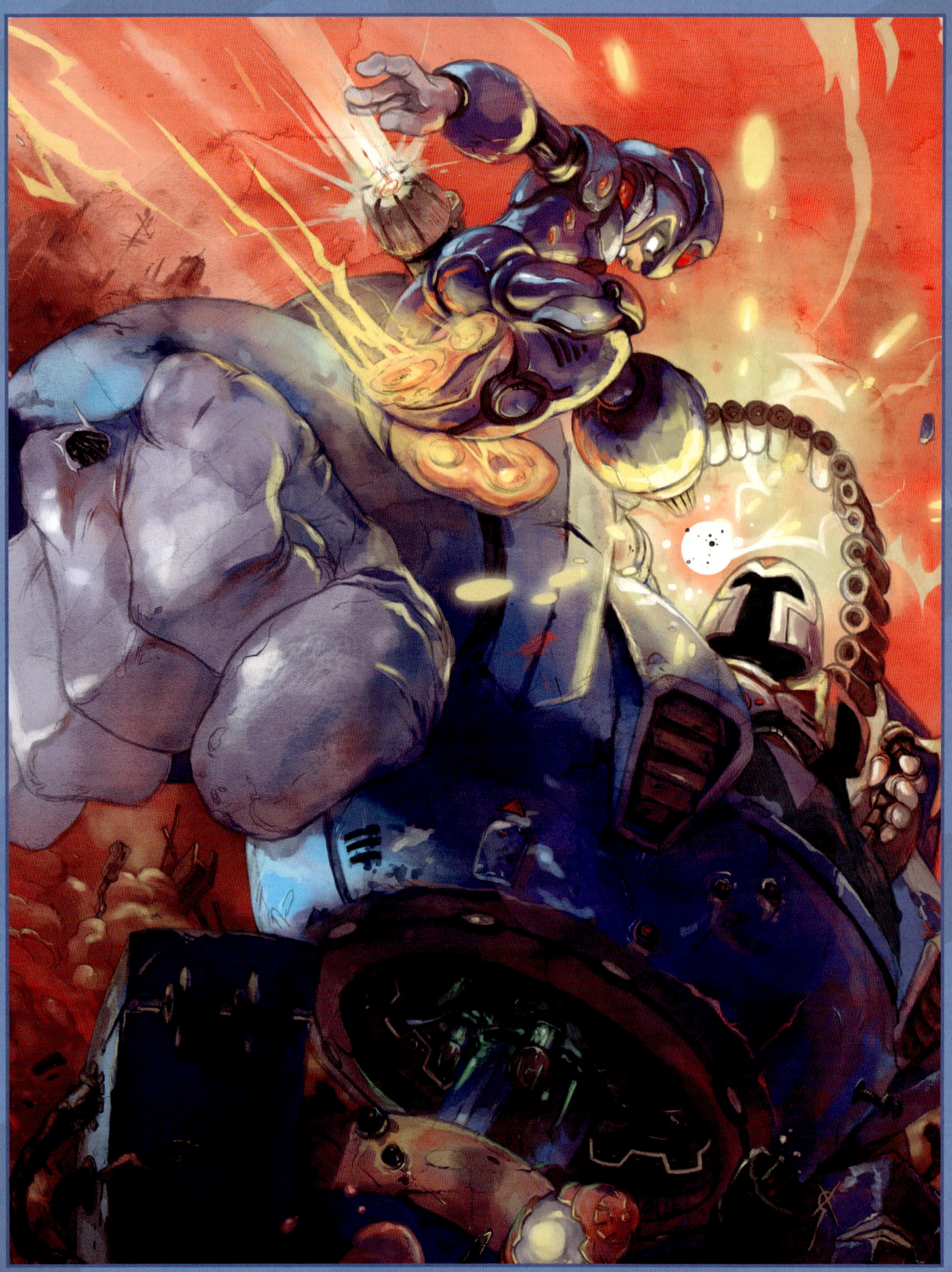

XAVIER GARCIA
Brooklyn, NY, United States
www.ragingspaniard.com
Game Artist at OMGPOP
(Inside Cover: Street Fighter IV / Concept Artist: MySims
/ Graduate at the Joe Kubert School)

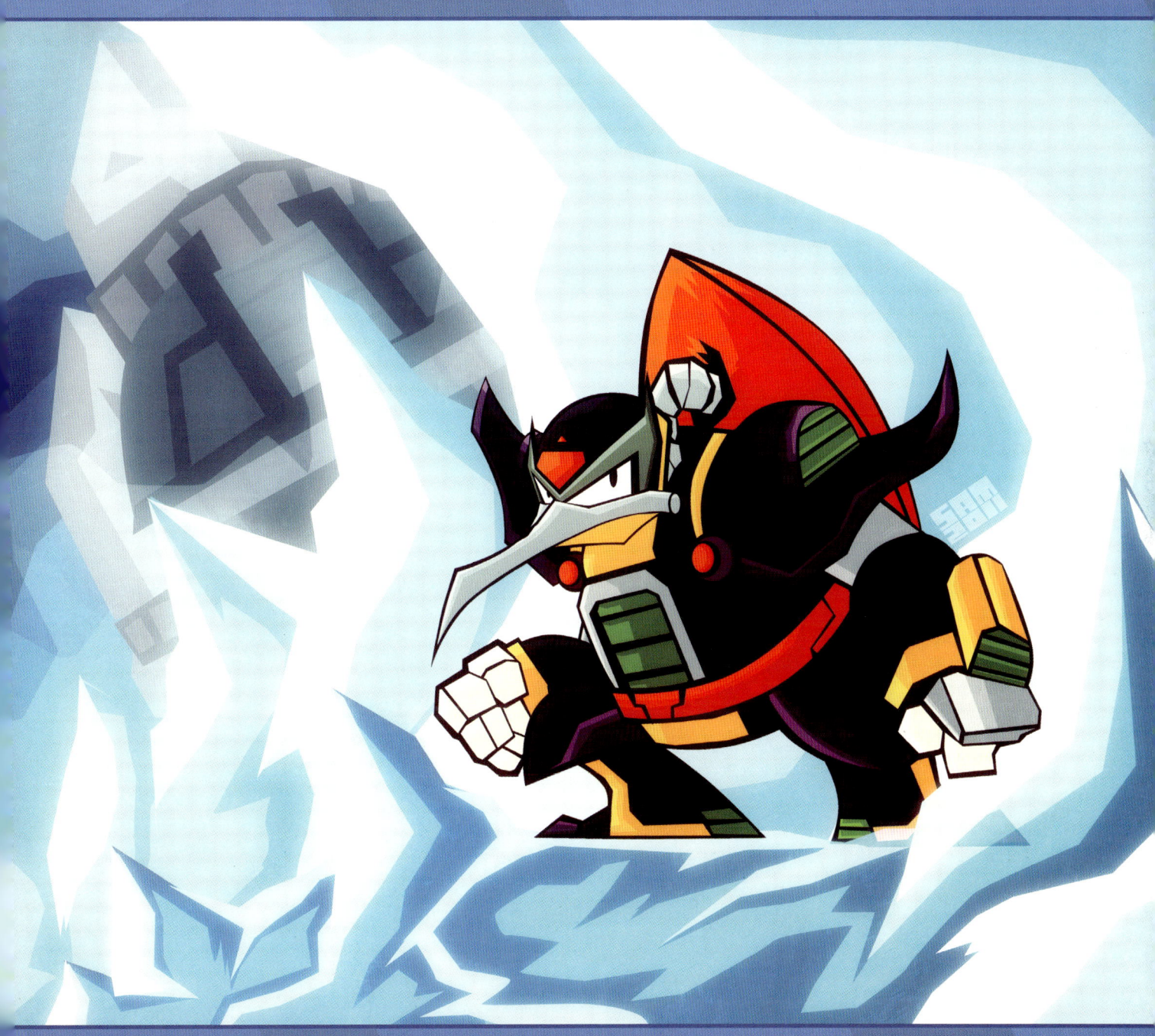

SAM FILSTRUP
Concord, CA, United States
tigerhawk01.deviantart.com
Art Student
(Academy of Art University)

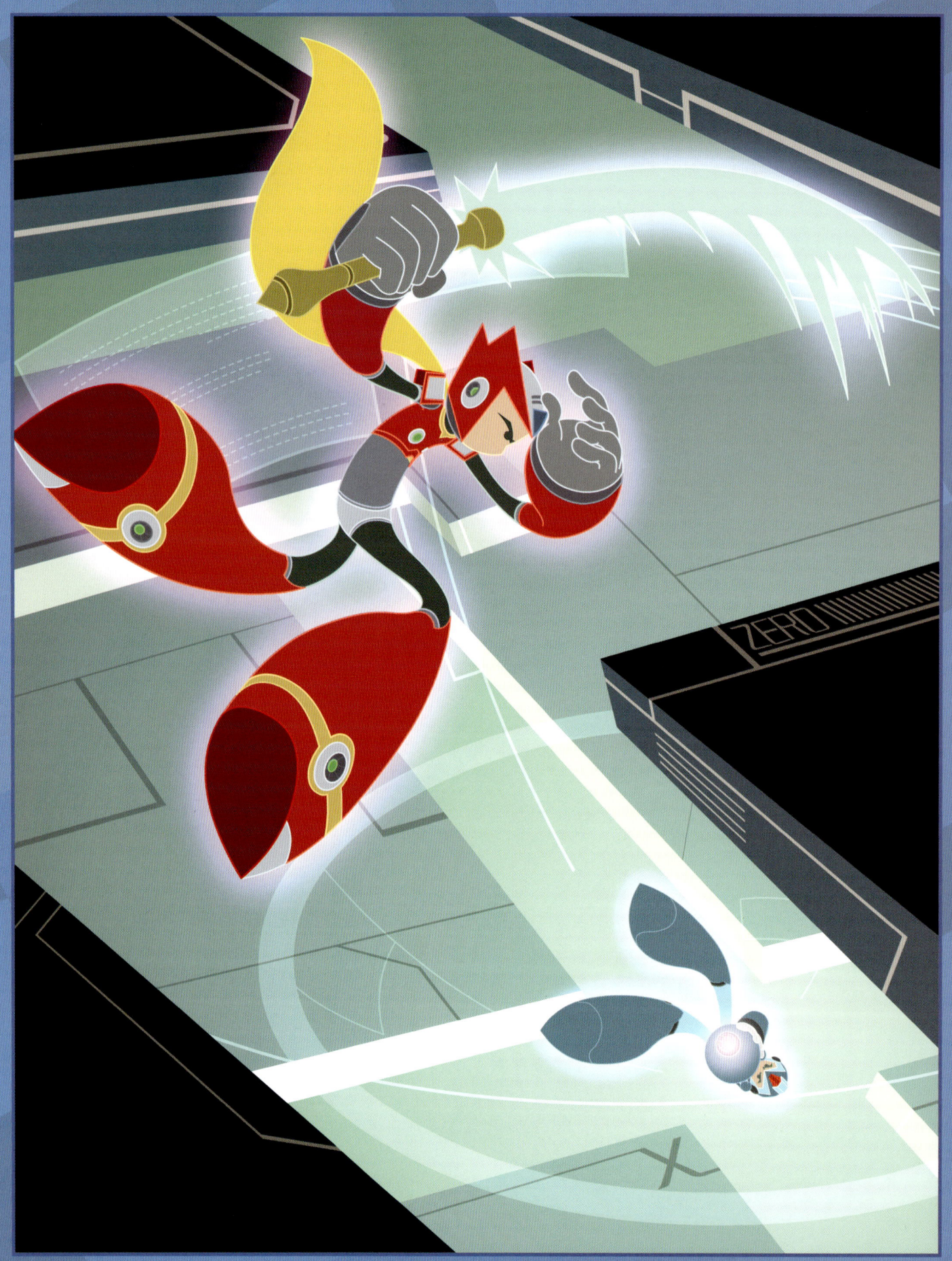

CHING FEI KANG
Seremban, Malaysia
zeander.deviantart.com
Illustrator

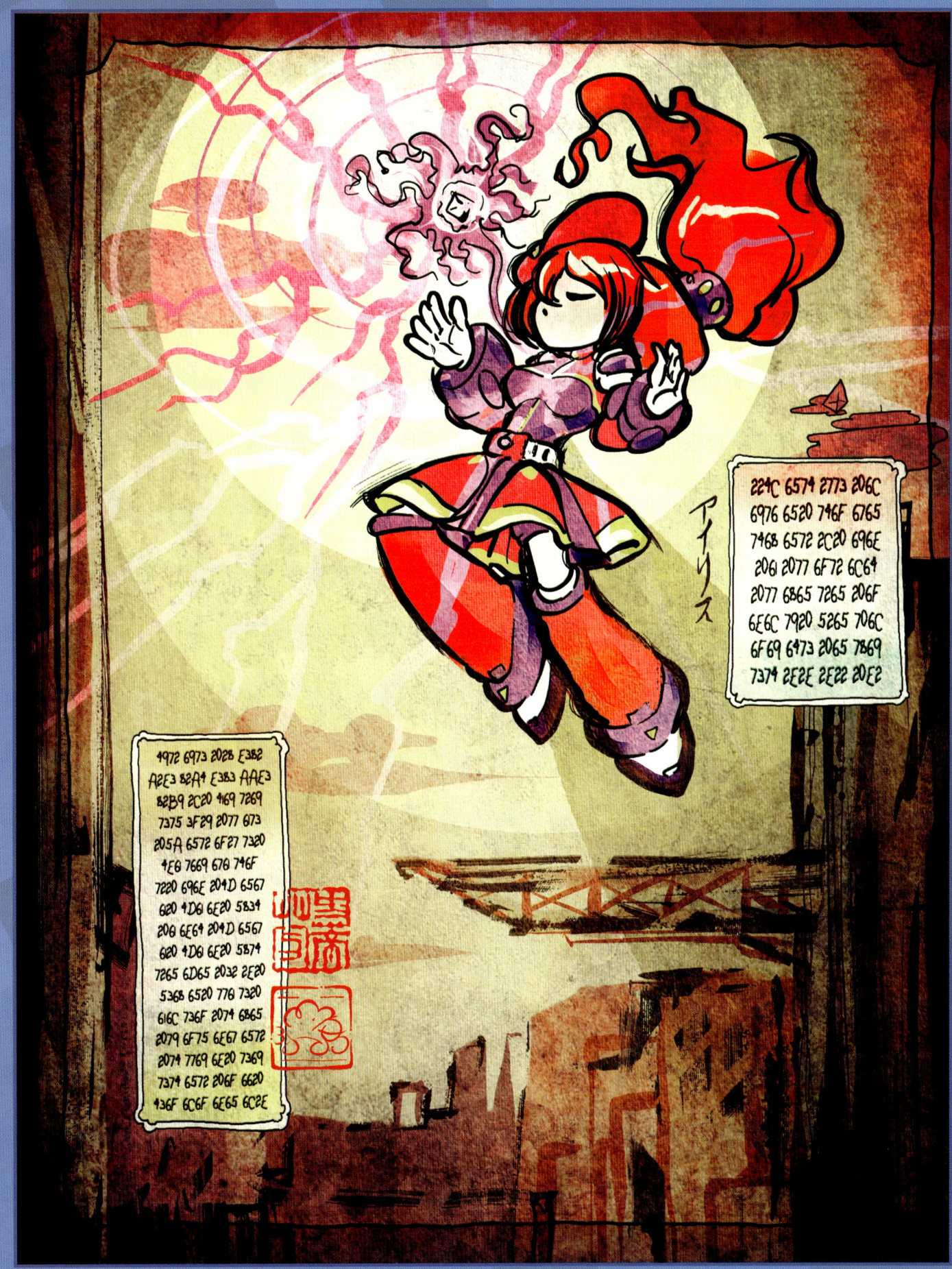

STEFANO COLLAVINI (NEFASTO)
Nantes, France
yeppoh.stage-select.com
Artist
("So Blonde" Adventure Game /
"Manga Without Border" Japanime / Pivaut Art School)

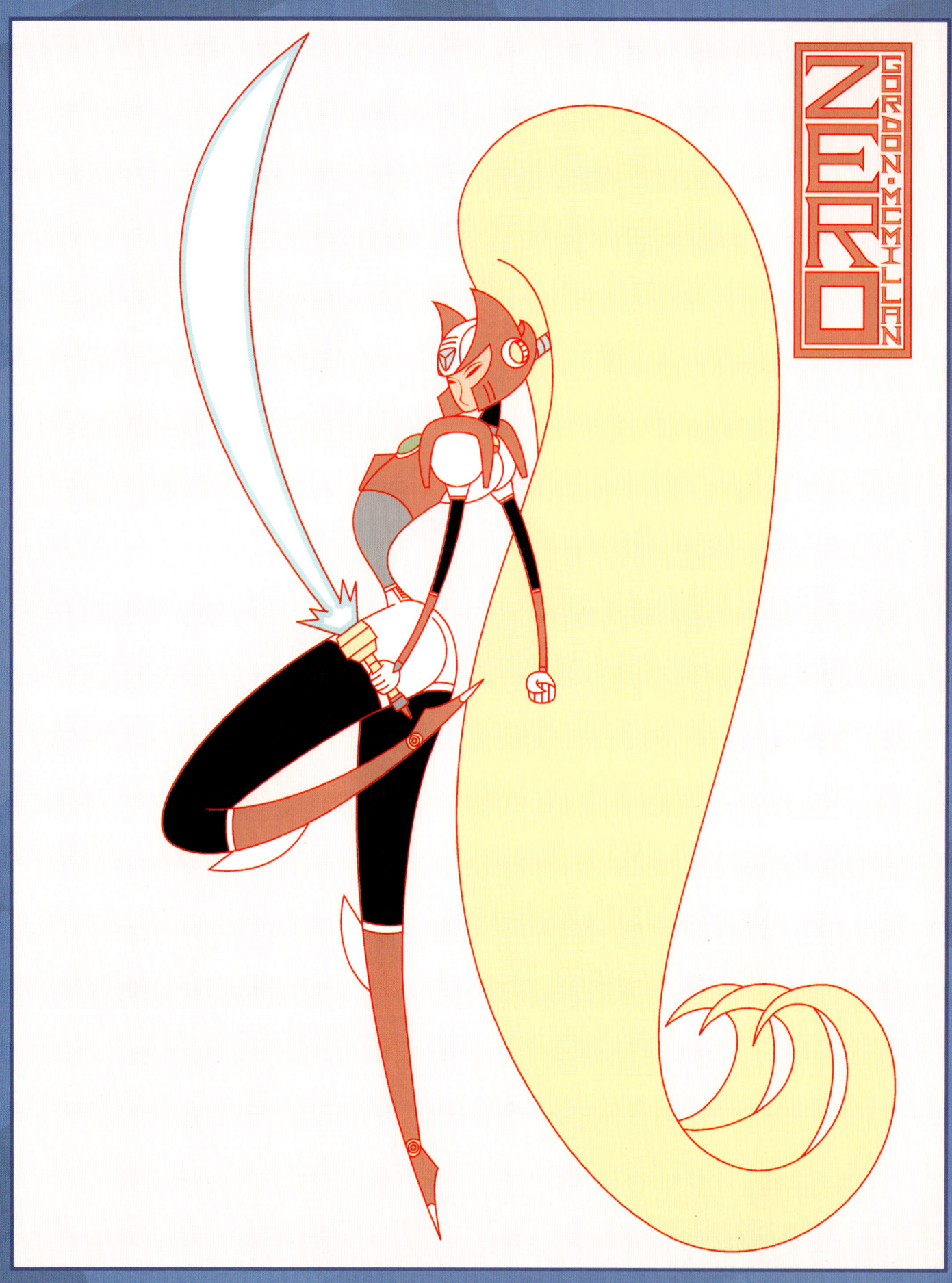

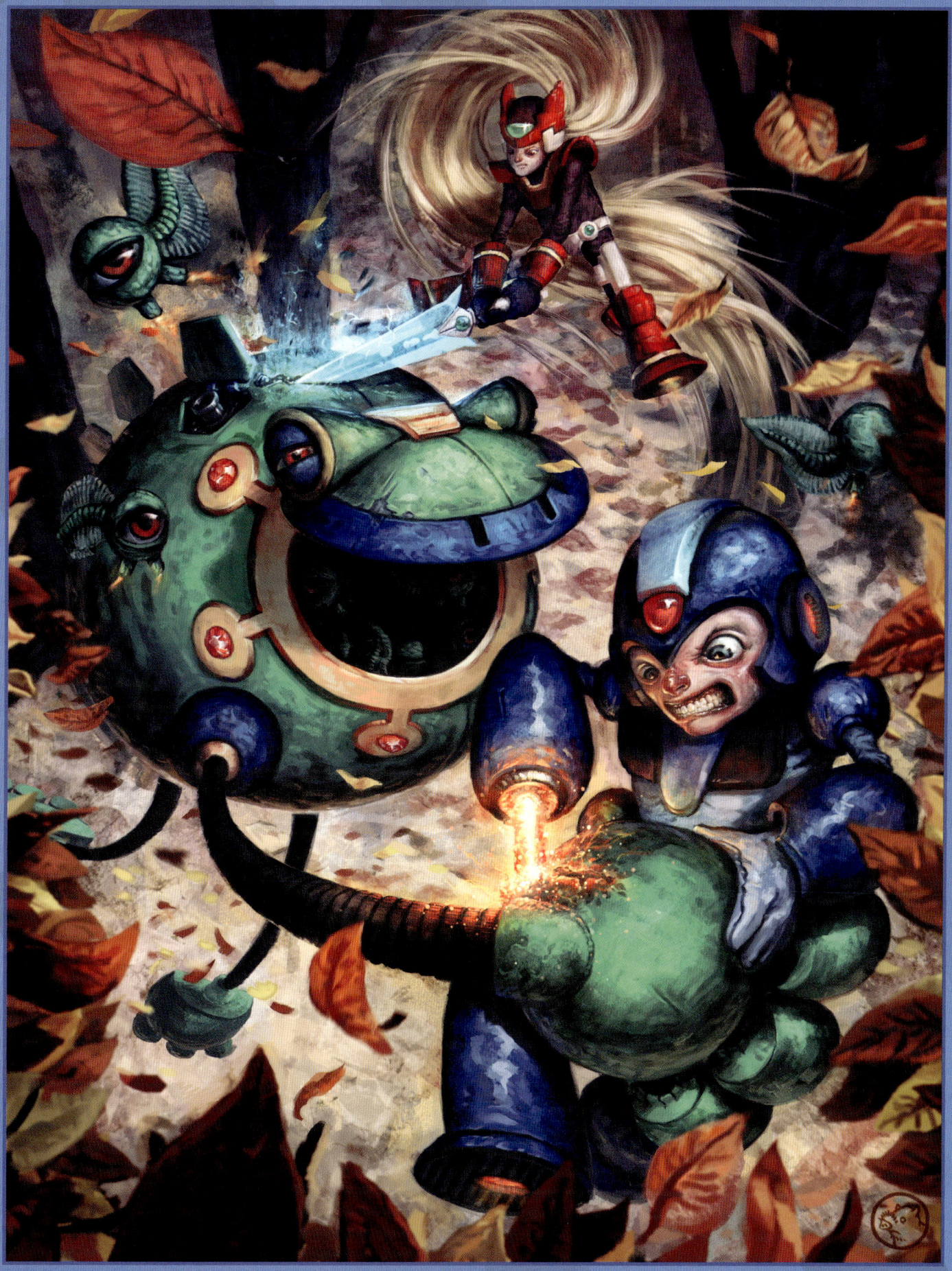

MATHIAS BARTH (BARTHSCHWEIN)
Hamburg, Germany
barthschwein.deviantart.com
Illustrator

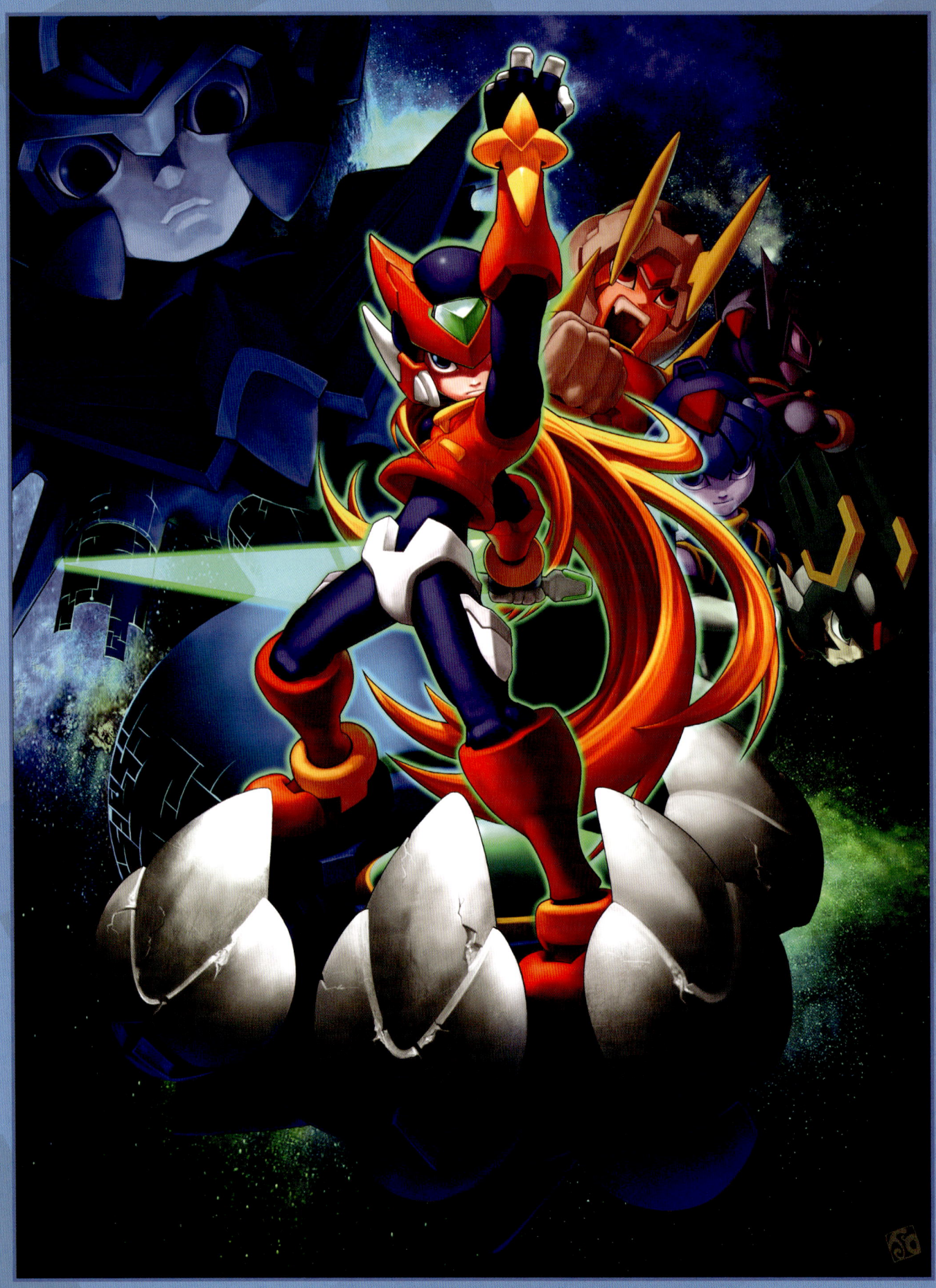

LE DUY (JO)
Ho Chi Minh, Viet Nam
Concept Artist

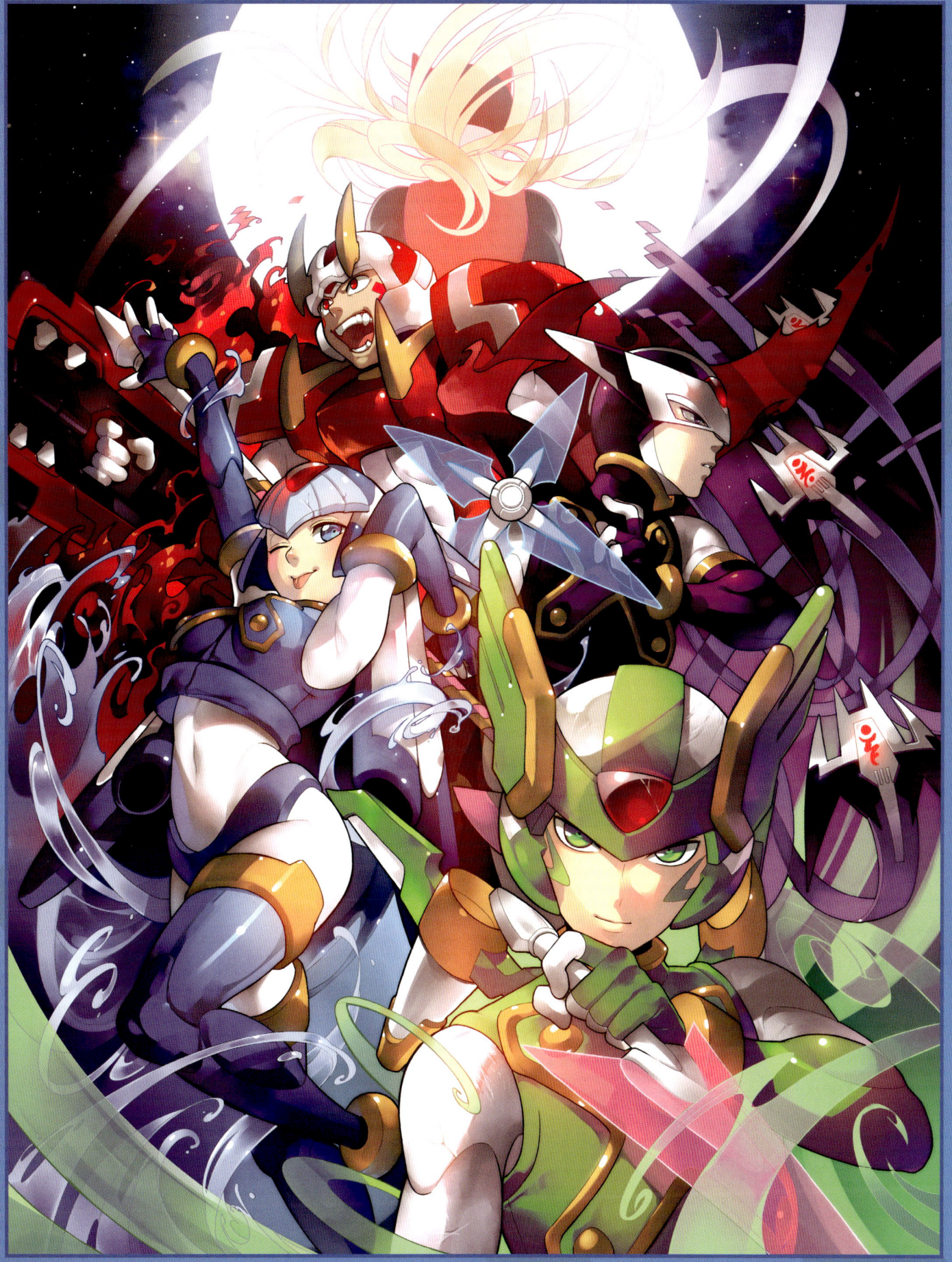

EIN LEE
Nantou City, China
www.einlee.net
Illustrator
(Illustrator of French storybook Princesse Pivoine /
Character designer & colorist at Sodapop Miniatures/application artworks for Omegasoft)

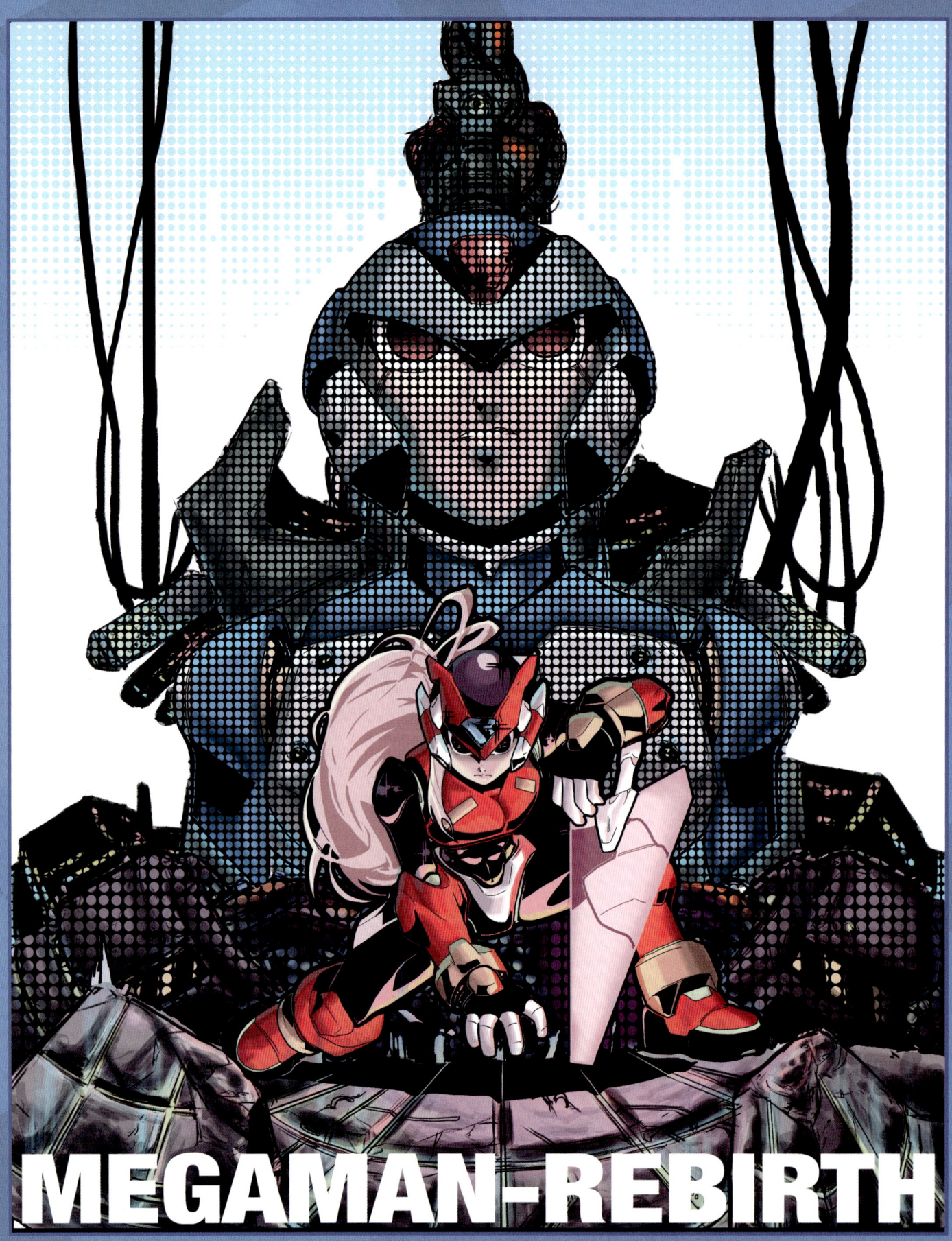

MEGAMAN-REBIRTH

MALCOLM WOPE (MALCOLM.XY)
Cape Town, South Africa
malcolmxy.blogspot.com / beatboxsamurai.deviantart.com
Illustrator
(Quest-Crew / Rocket-boi t-shirts)

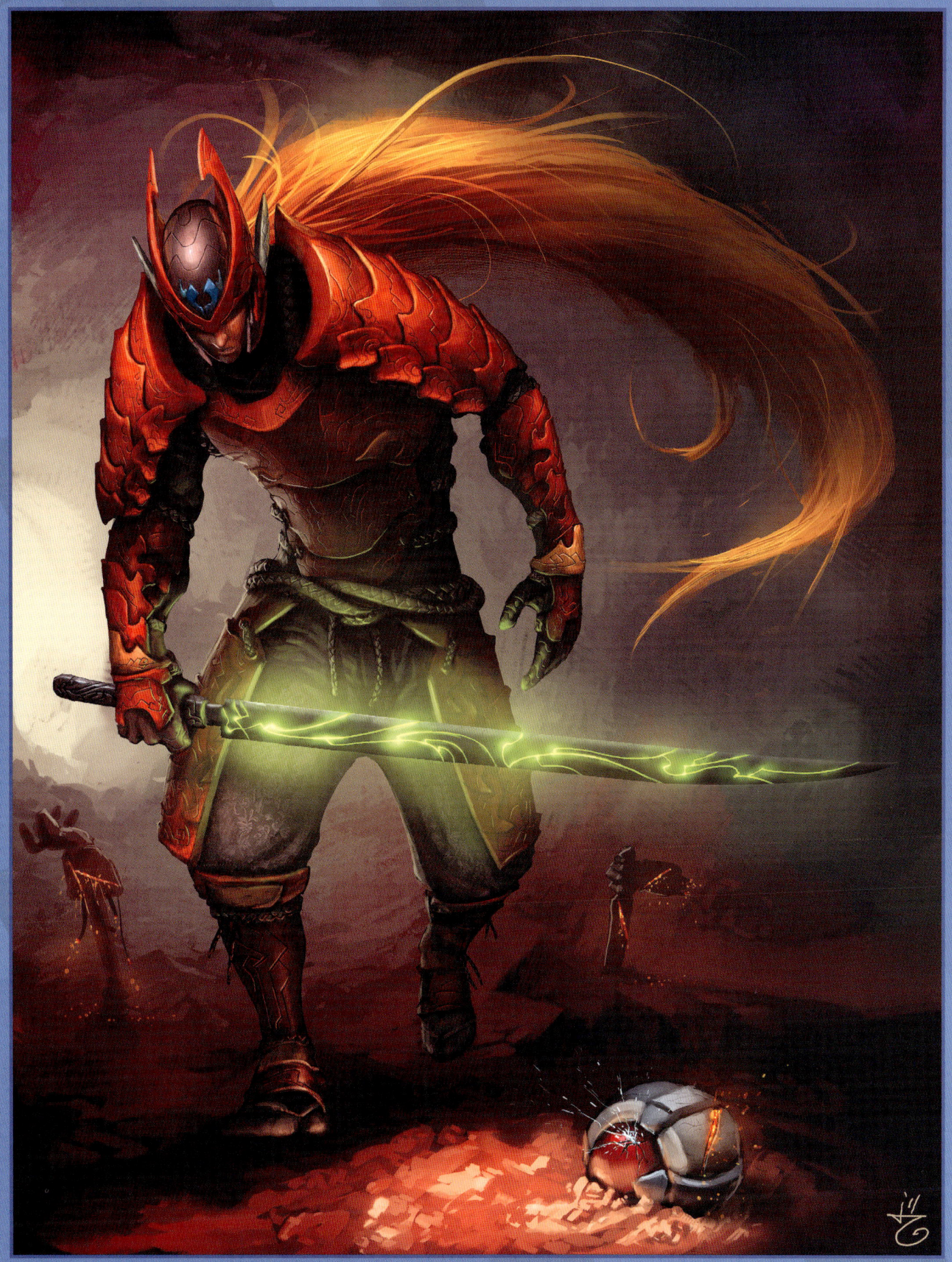

ZULKARNAEN HASAN BASRI
Solo, Indonesia
ijul.deviantart.com
2D Artist

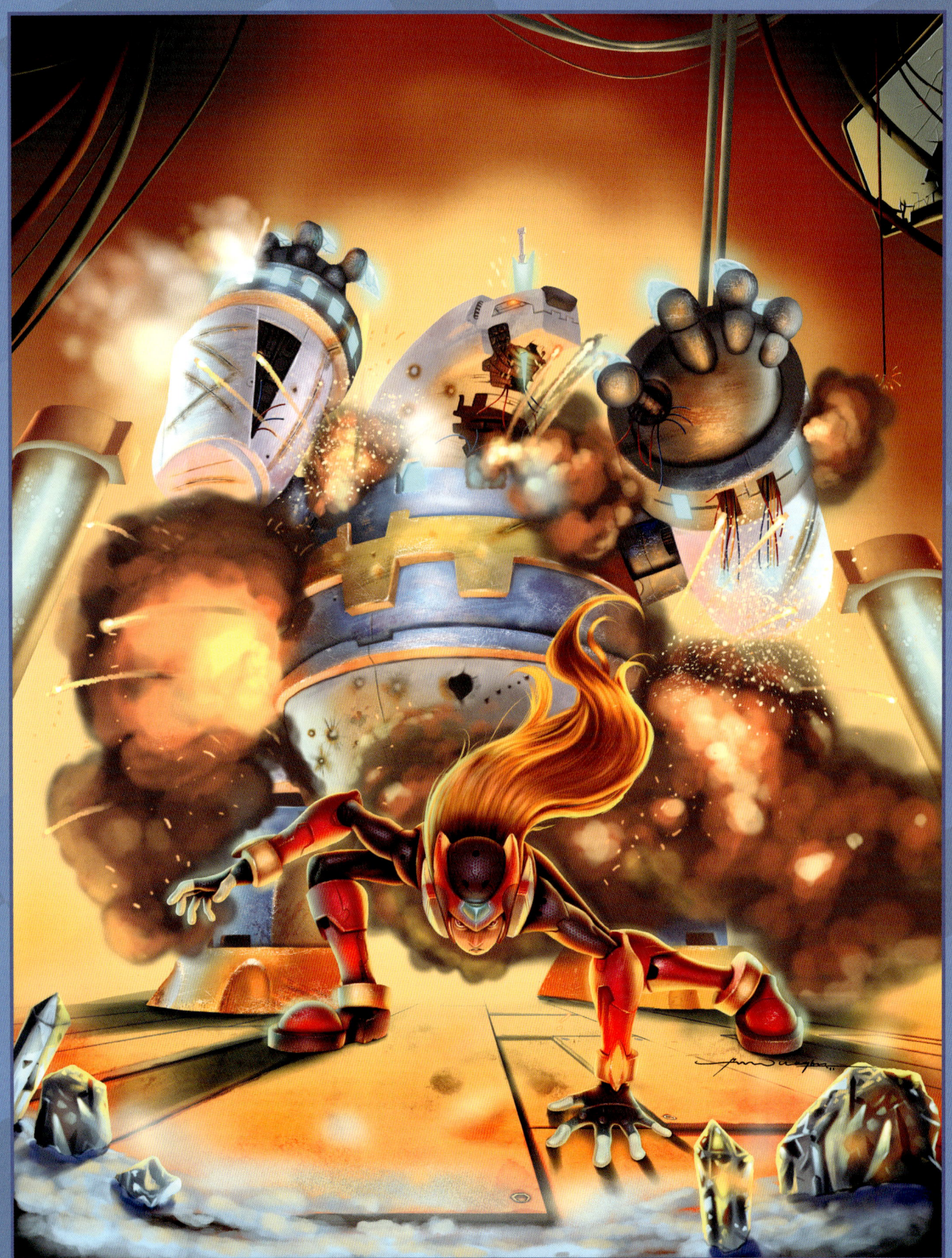

IFEANYI PAPPY ONWUAGBU (POPSAART)
Johannesburg, South Africa
popsaart.blogspot.com / popsaart.deviantart.com
Illustrator / 3D Artist

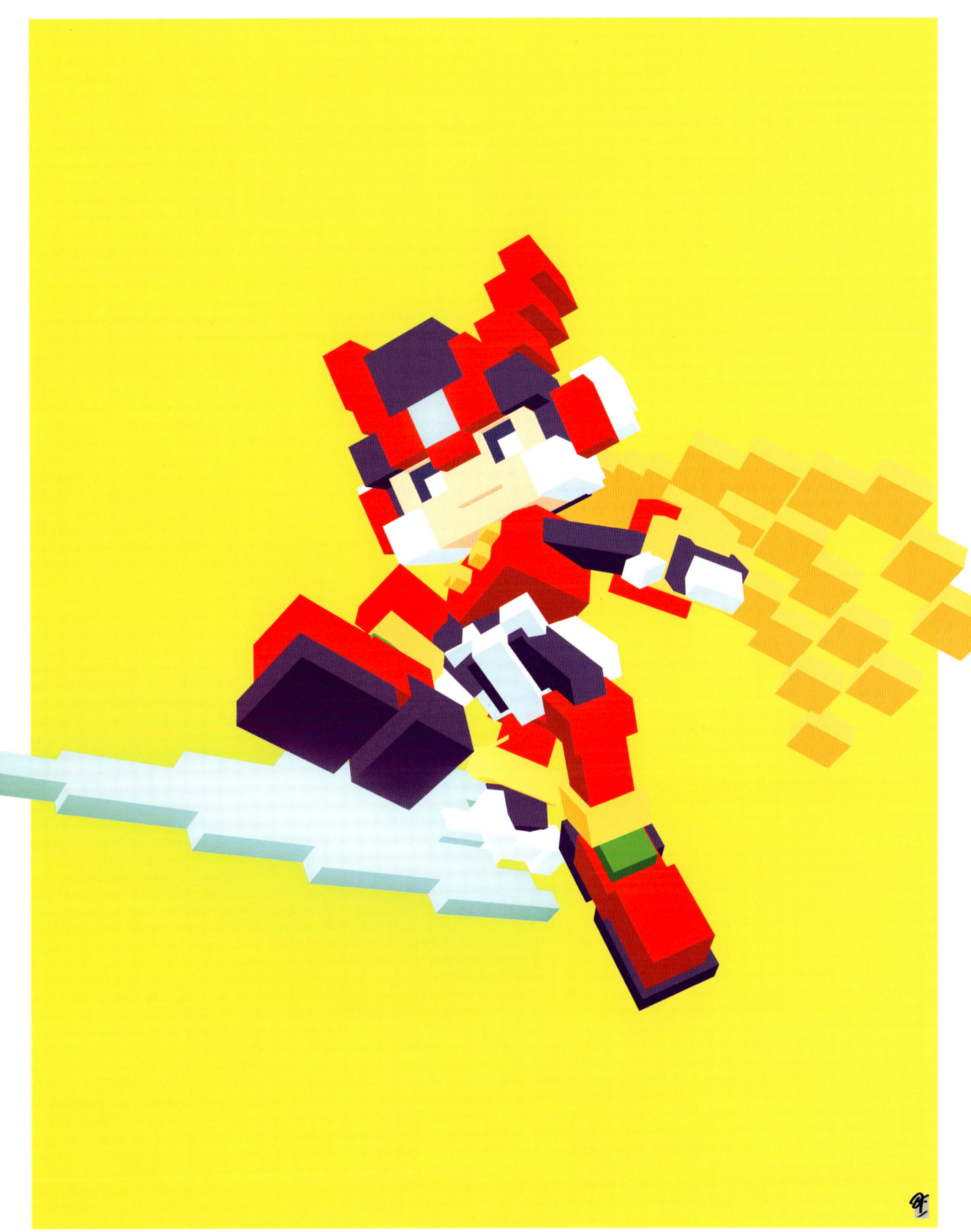

OSCAR TRIANA
Bogotá, Colombia
oscartriana.deviantart.com
Graphic Designer / Animator
(Star Wars in a Notebook)

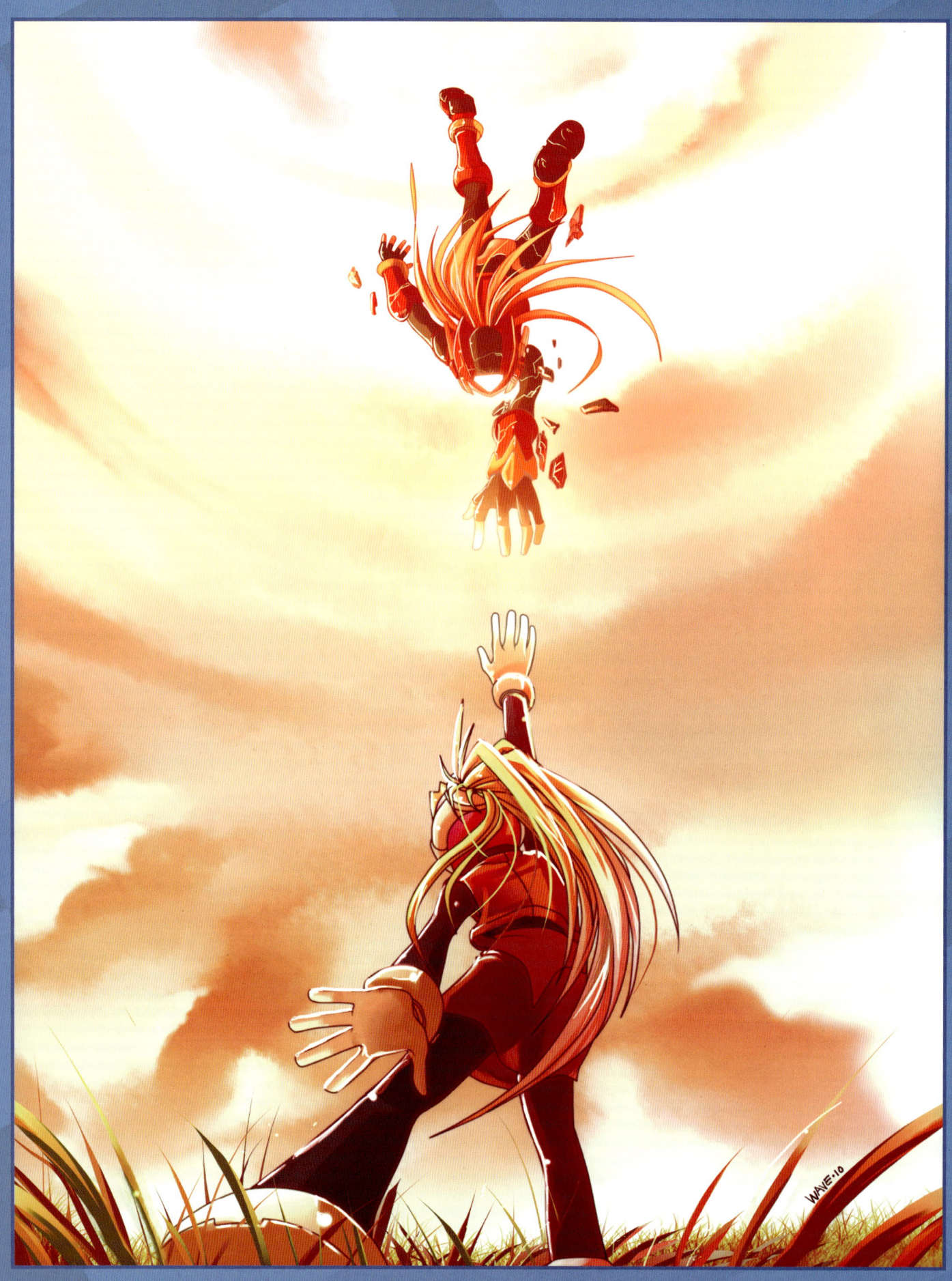

IRENE LEE (WAVE)
Woodhaven, NY, United States
suzuran.deviantart.com
Comic Digital Compositor
(Marvel Comics)

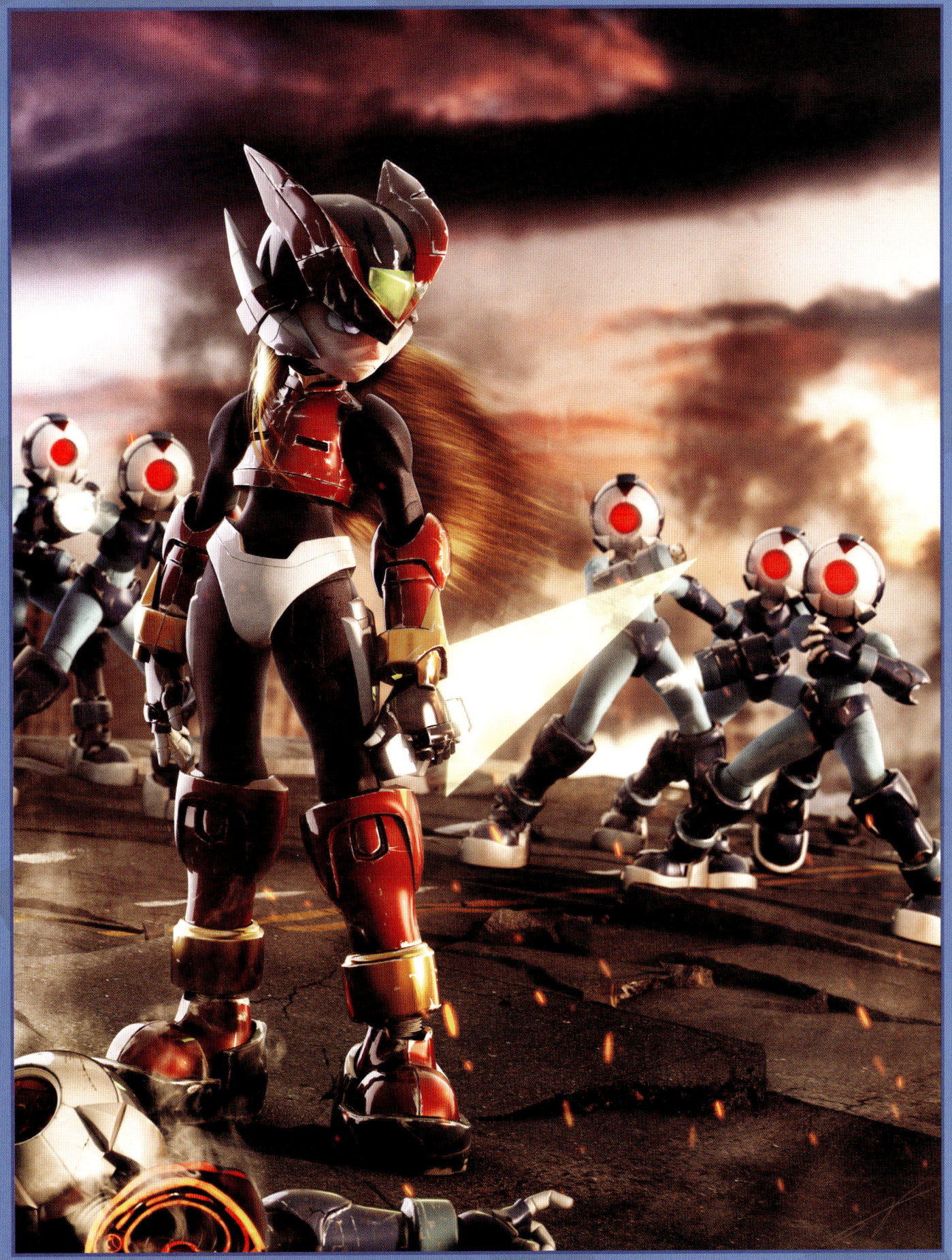

VICTOR HUGO QUEIROZ (VITORUGO)
Sao Paulo, Brazil
torugo.wordpress.com
3D Artist

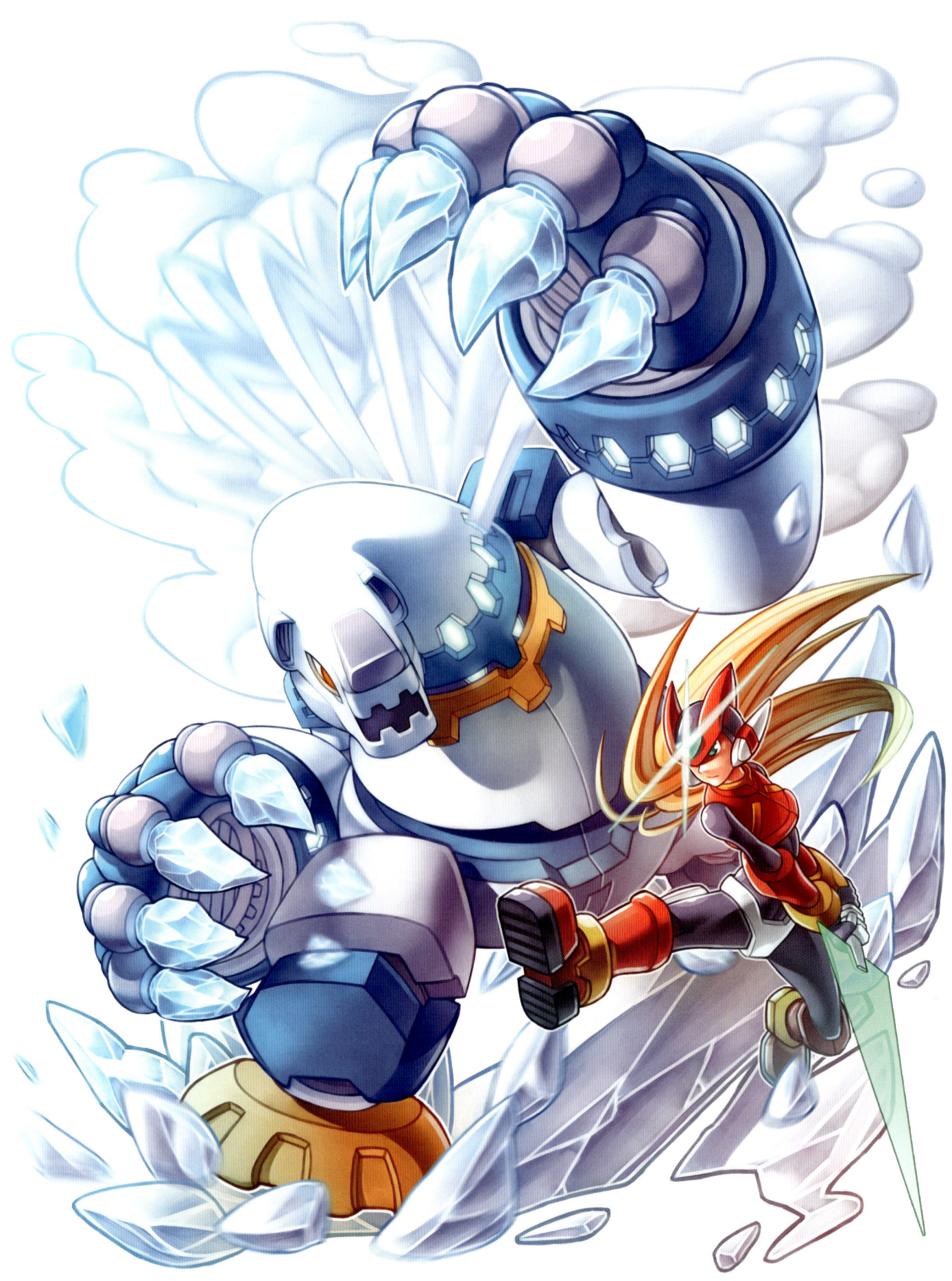

JUSTIN VU
Milpitas, CA, United States
silverava.deviantart.com
Illustrator

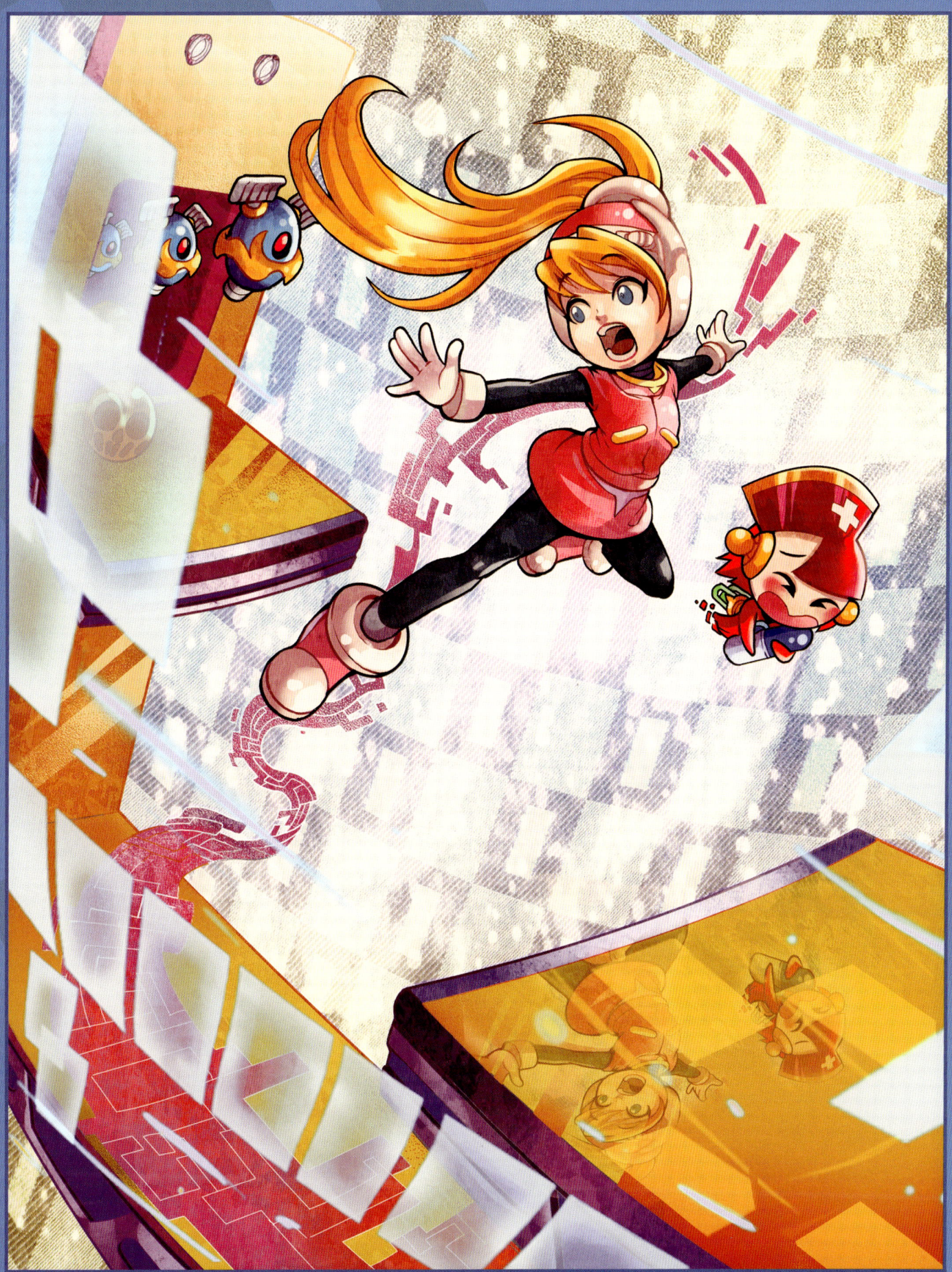

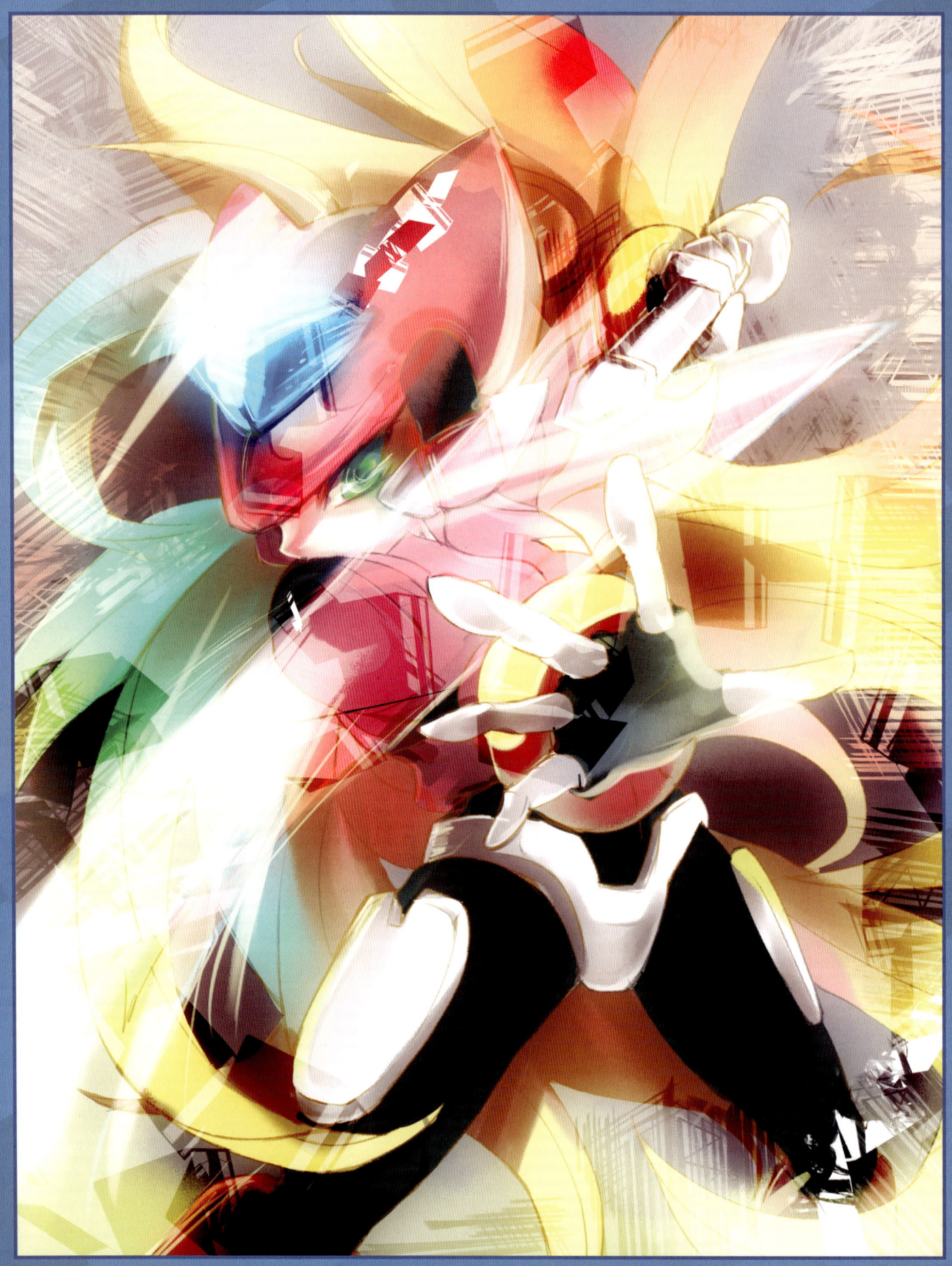

MIYUKIKO
Frenchs Forest, Australia
www.fatalholic.net
Illustrator
(University of New South Wales)

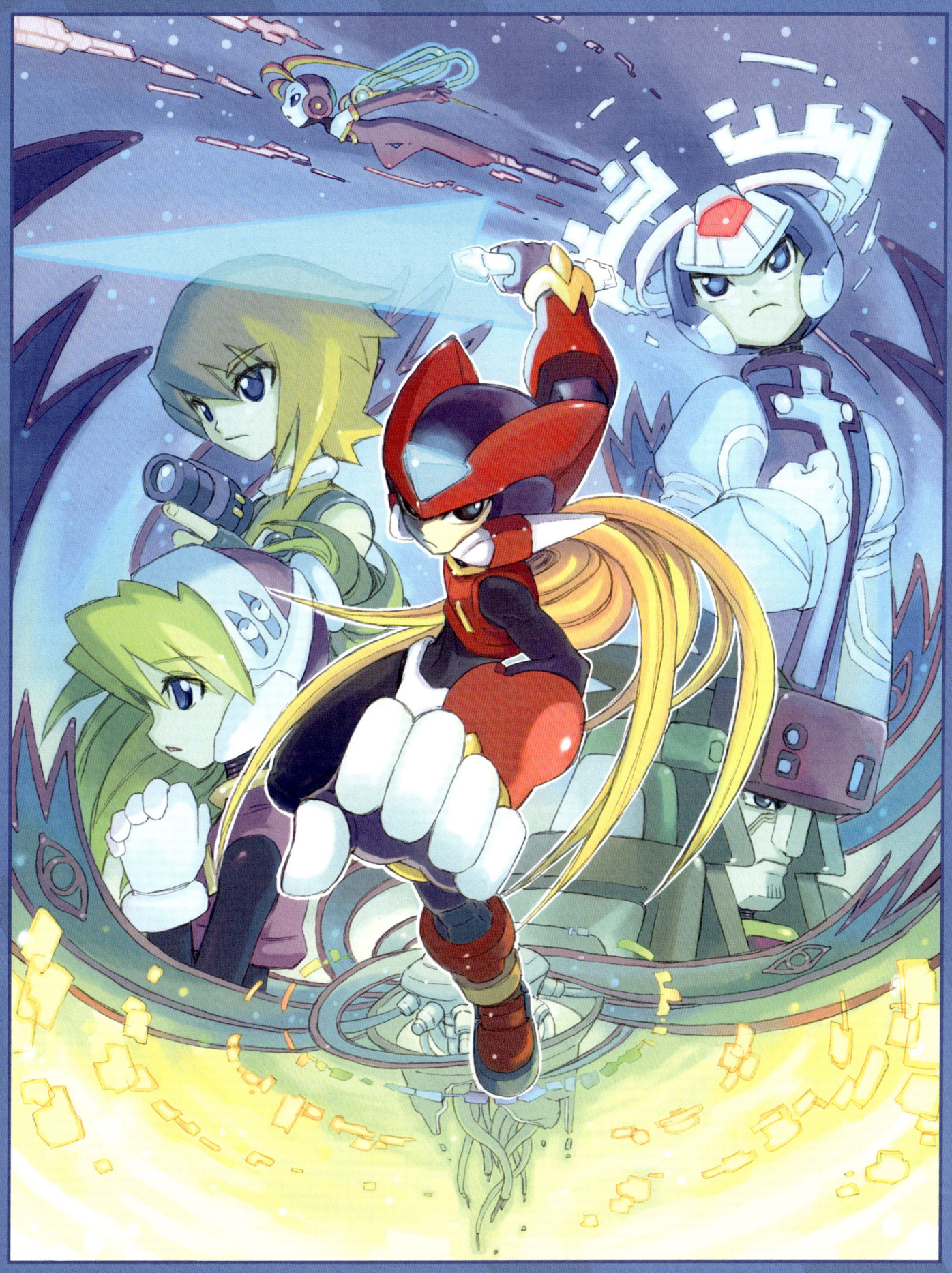

MASUMI SUGIYAMA (NASU)
Kawasaki City, Japan
Illustrator

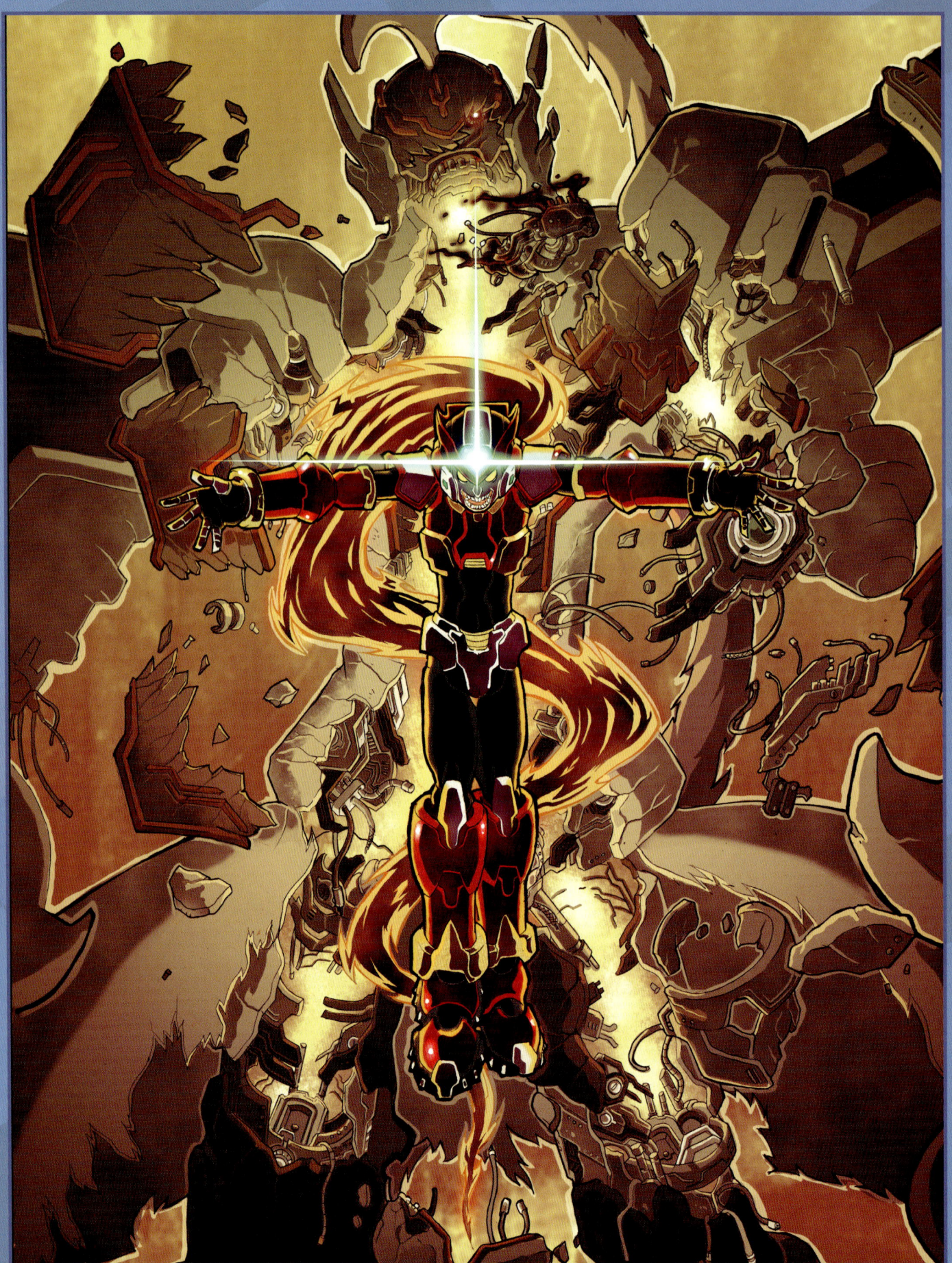

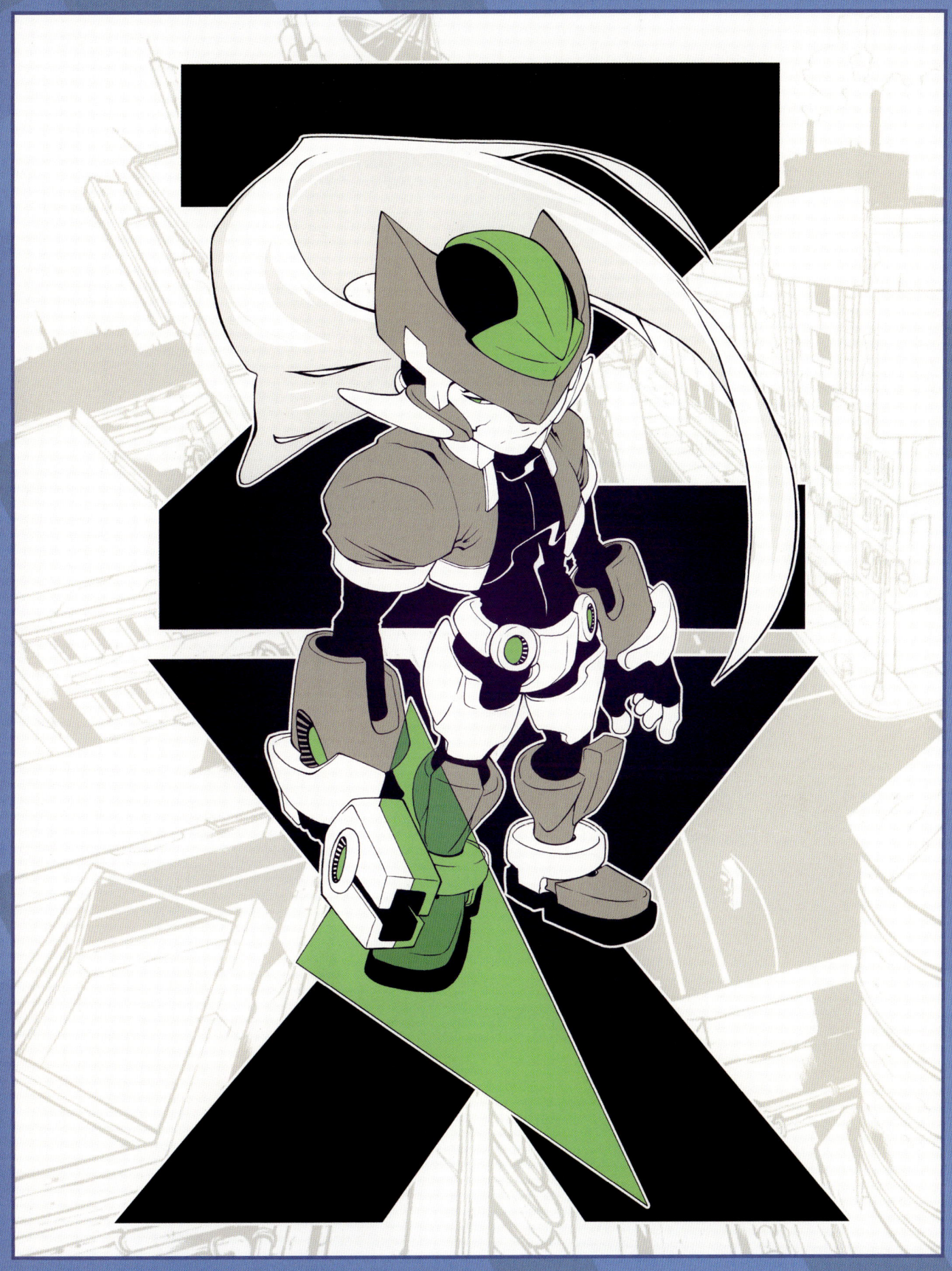

EDWIN HUANG
New York, NY, United States
www.edwinhuang.com / ongakujunkie.deviantart.com
Illustrator
(Skullkickers)

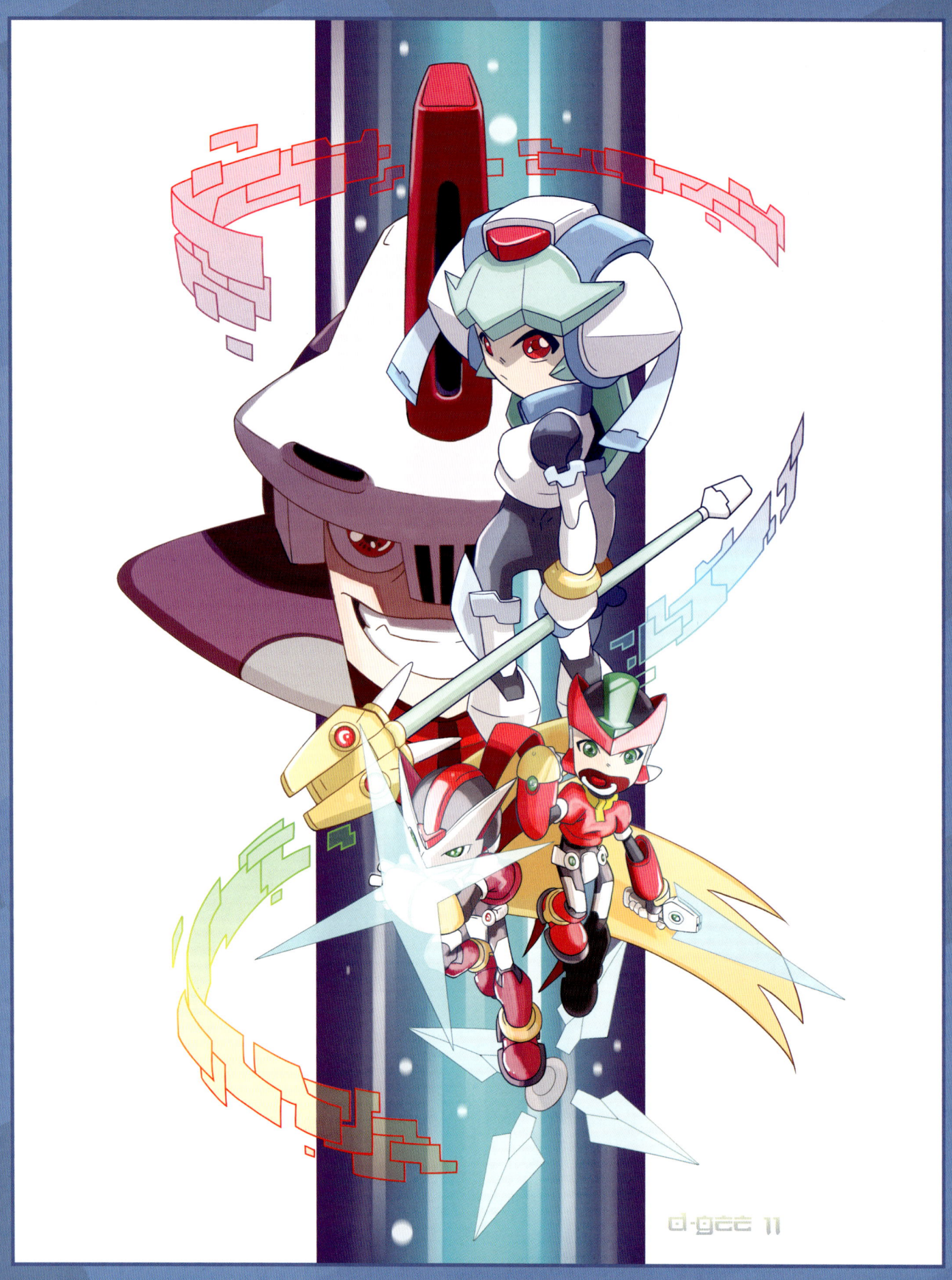

DAX GORDINE
Brampton, ON, Canada
d-gee.deviantart.com
Animator
(Silicon Knights)

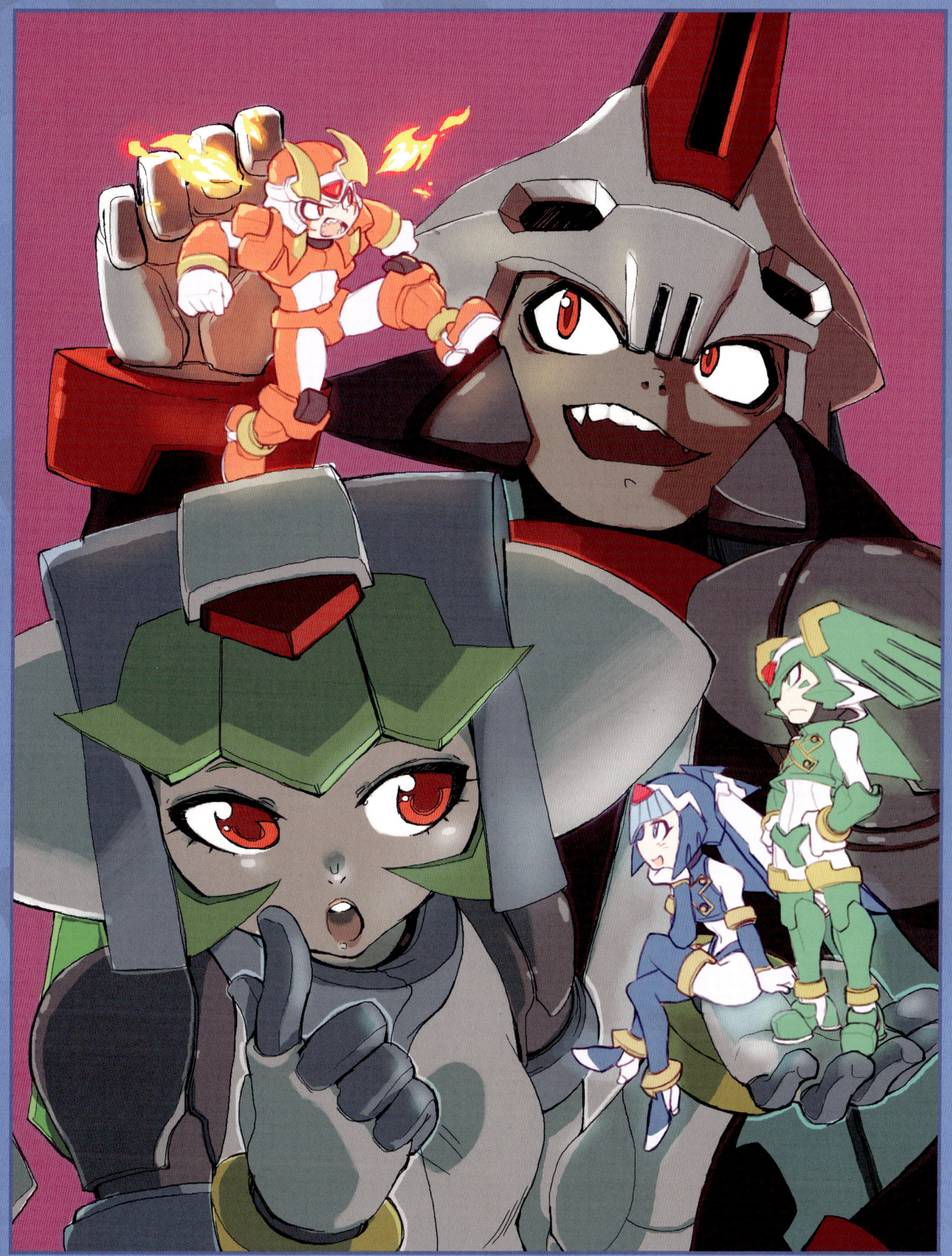

JASON ROBINSON
Beltsville, MD, United States
crybringer.blogspot.com / crybringer.deviantart.com
Artist
(The Demon Mages)

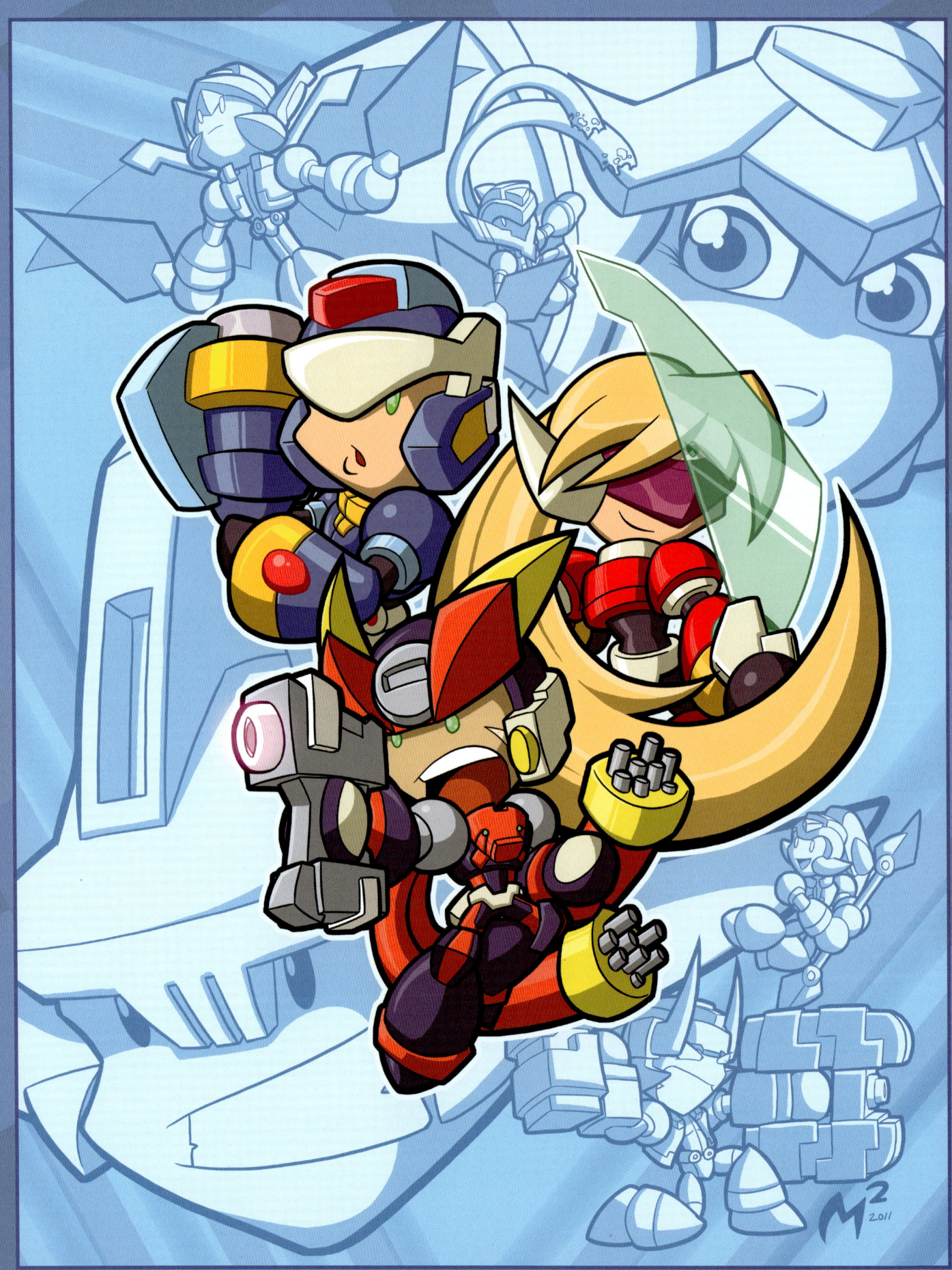

MATT MOYLAN
Toronto, ON, Canada
WWW.LILFORMERS.COM / MATTMOYLAN.DEVIANTART.COM
UDON Managing Editor / Cartoonist
(Lil Formers)

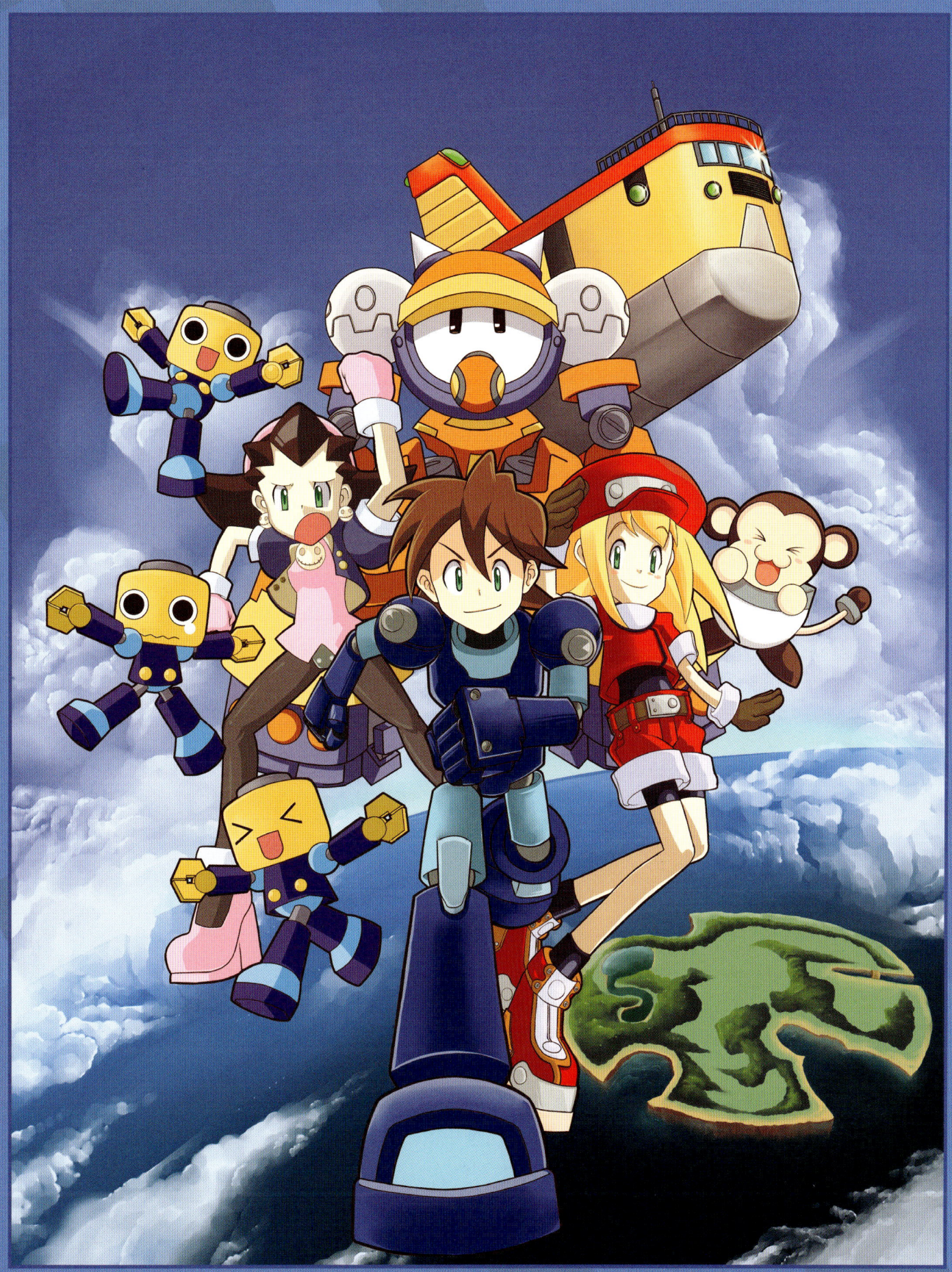

JOHN LEYTON
Santiago, Chile
zanahoriaman.deviantart.com
Ilustrator

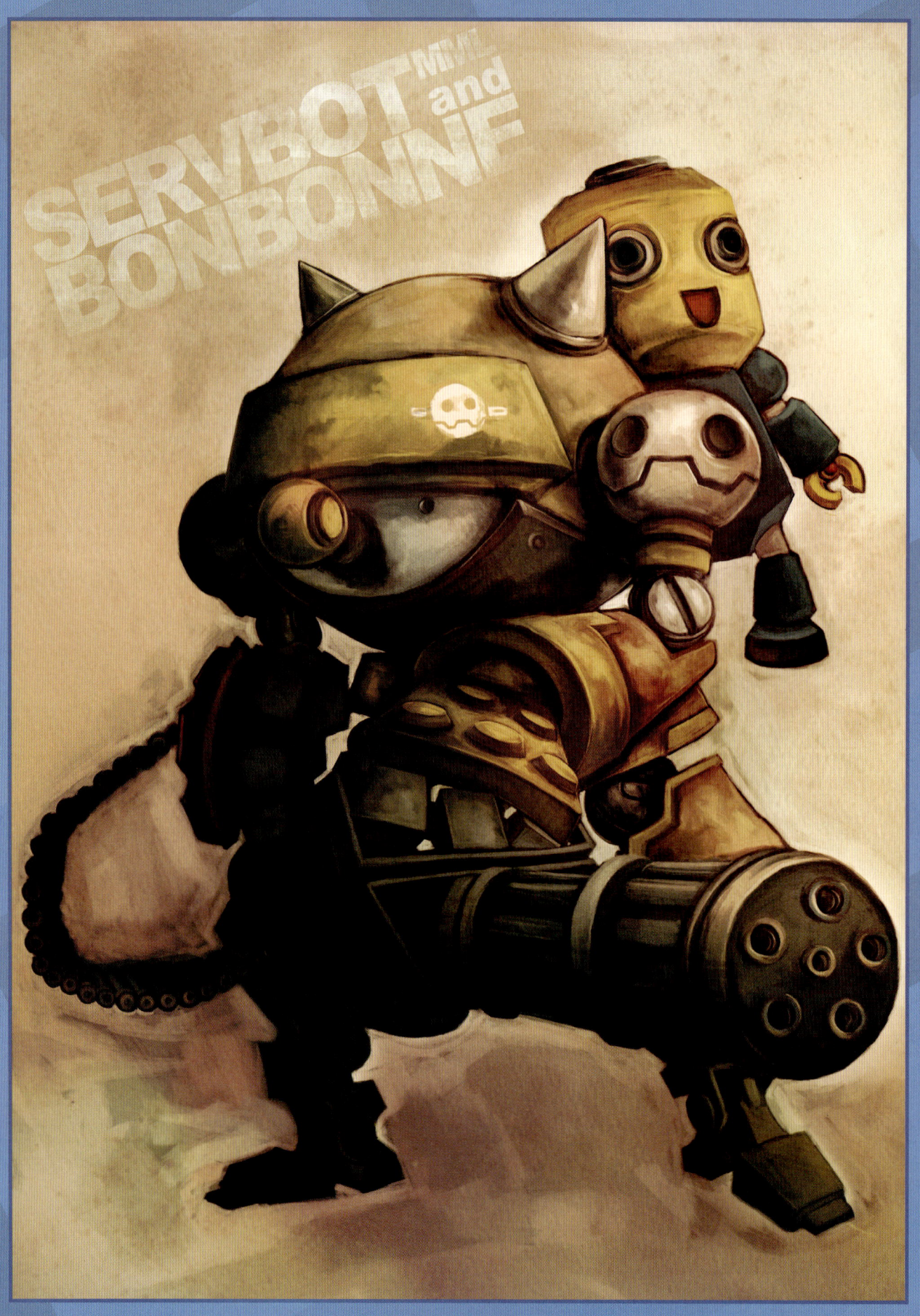

KOK YIP SUN
Puchong, Malaysia
nichiyobi.deviantart.com
CG Artist

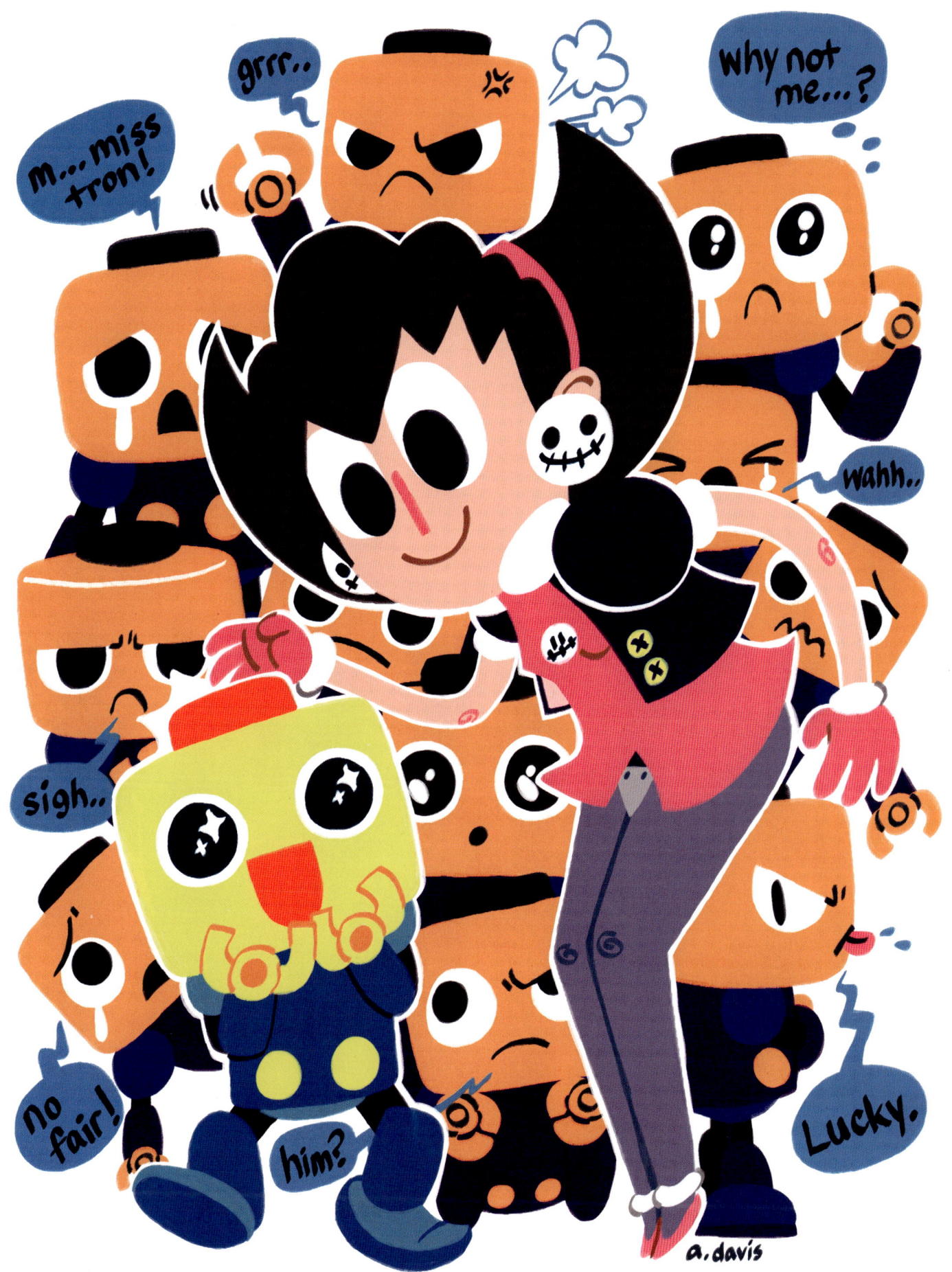

ASHLEY DAVIS
Plano, TX, United States
www.oddlookingbird.com / heartpuncher.deviantart.com
Illustrator
(Once Upon a Pixel)

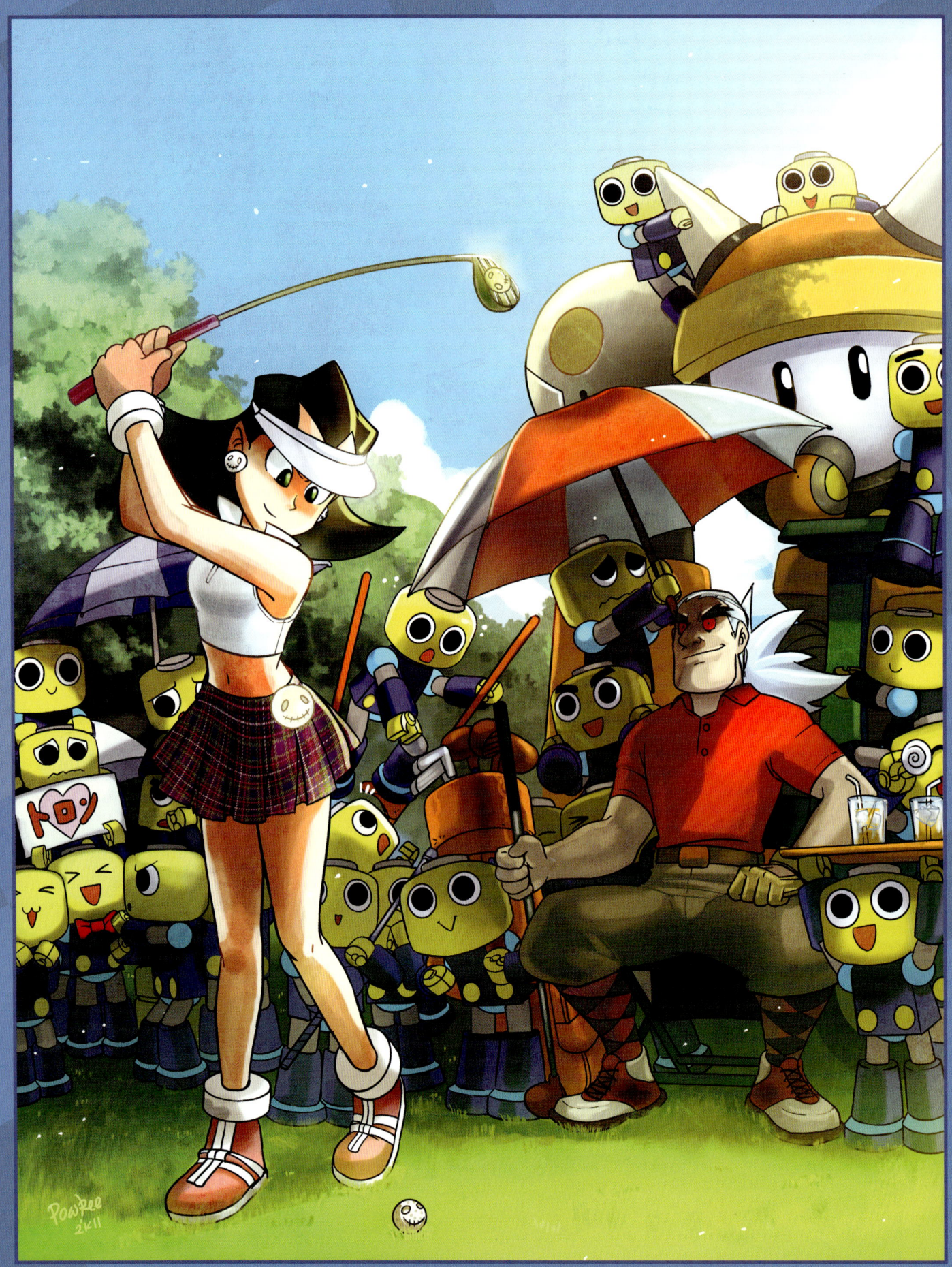

PURI ANDINI (POWREE)
Bandung, Indonesia
froggiechan.deviantart.com
Artist
(Menara Games)

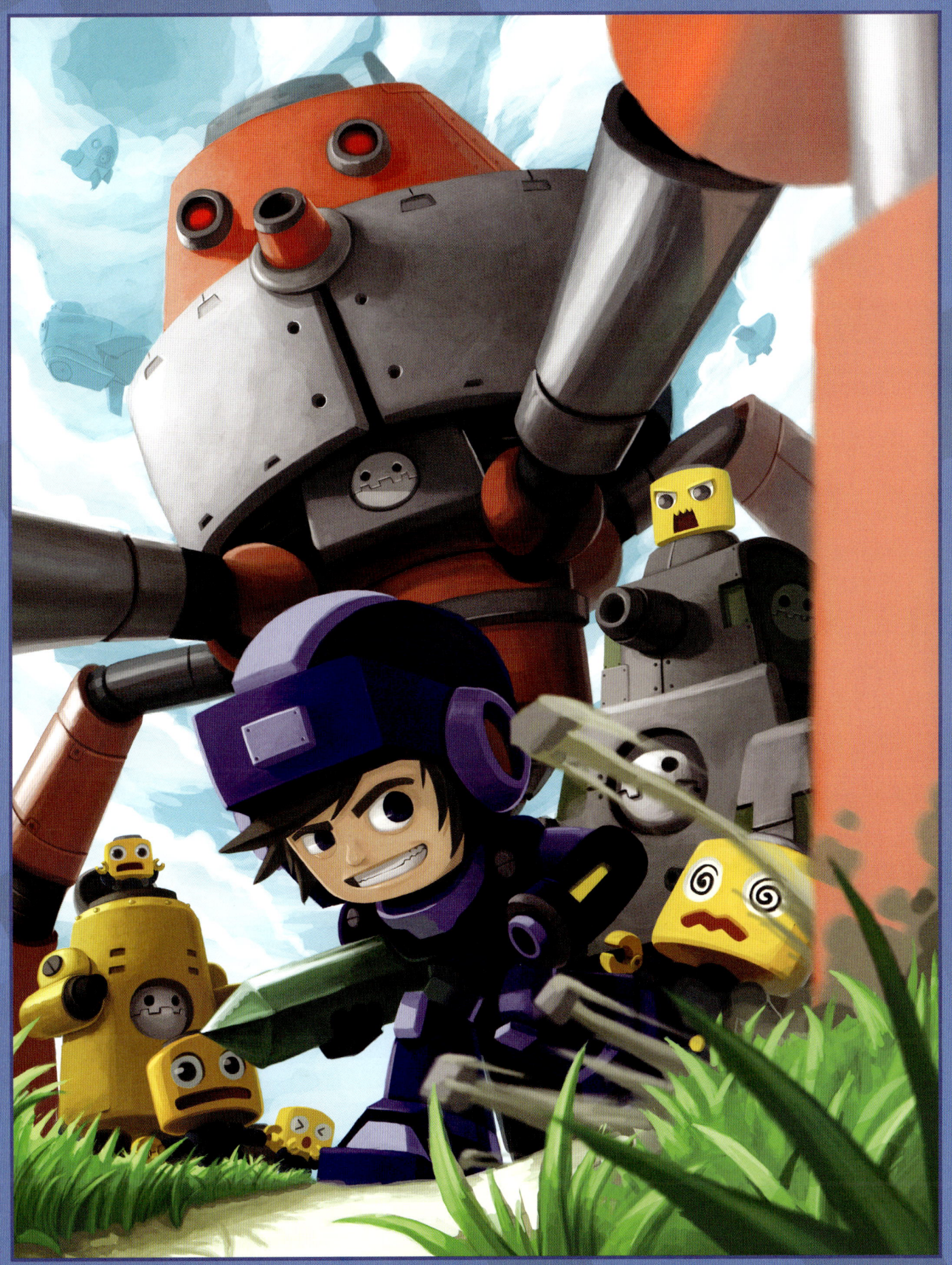

JORGE EDUARDO RUIZ
Arecibo, Puerto Rico
www.jorgeruizanimation.com
Student

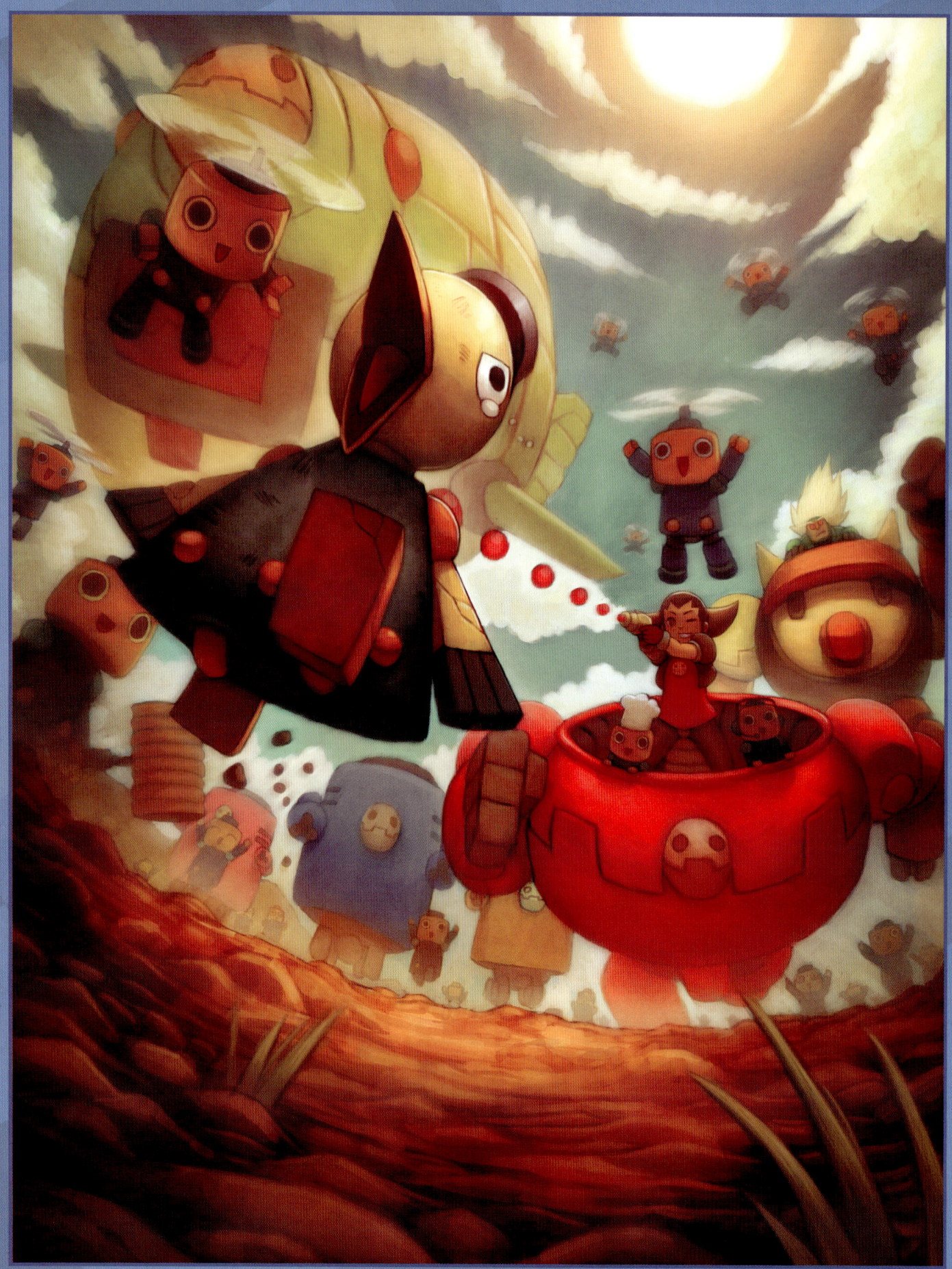

RYAN SHIU (RY-SPIRIT)
Carlingford, Australia
ry-spirit.deviantart.com
Illustrator

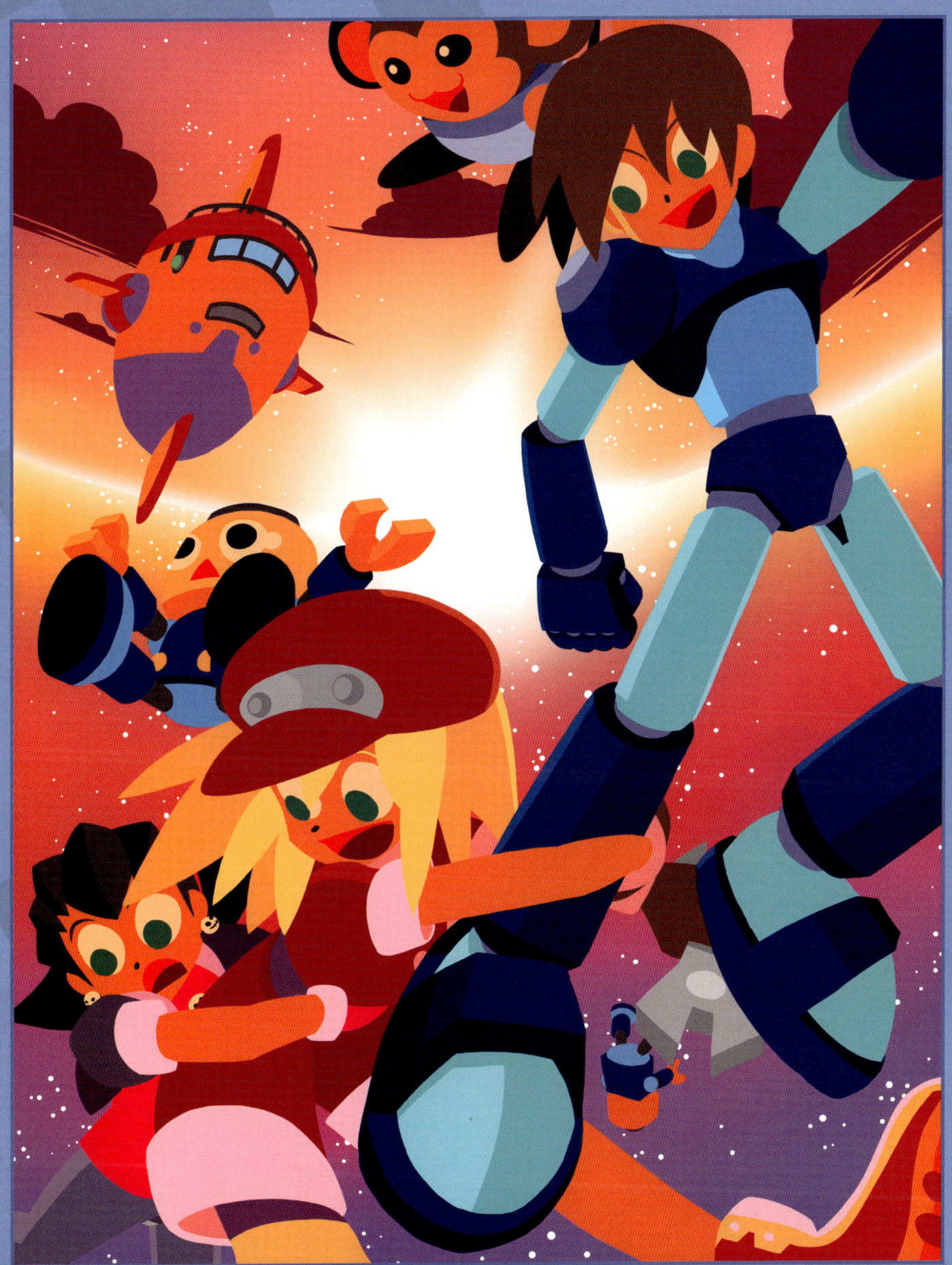

SAPPHIRE WONG YING CHEE
Petaling Jaya, Malaysia
sapphire1010.deviantart.com
Concept Artist
The One Academy

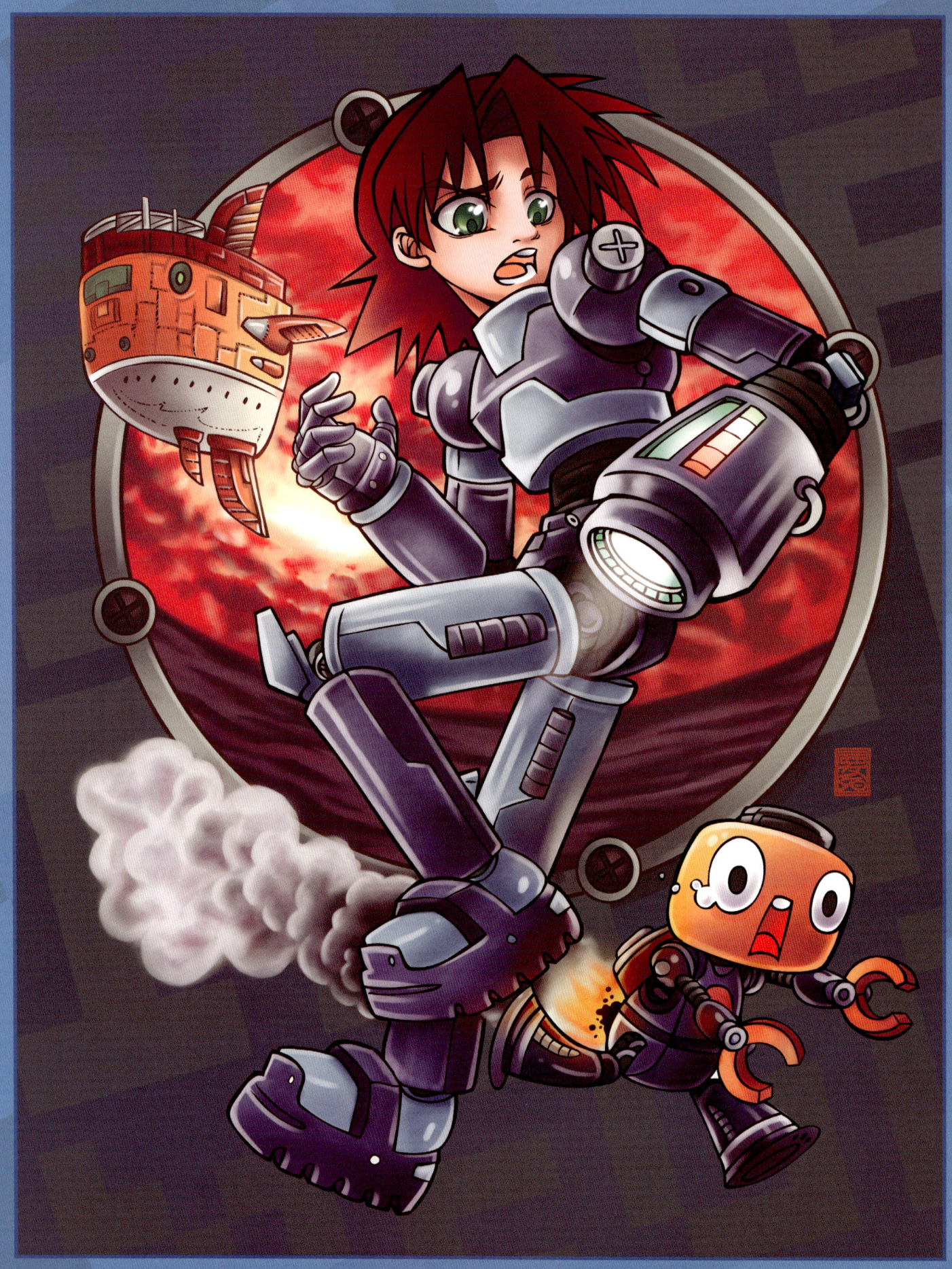

CAIO YO
Sao Paulo, Brazil
yo-tan.deviantart.com
Illustrator

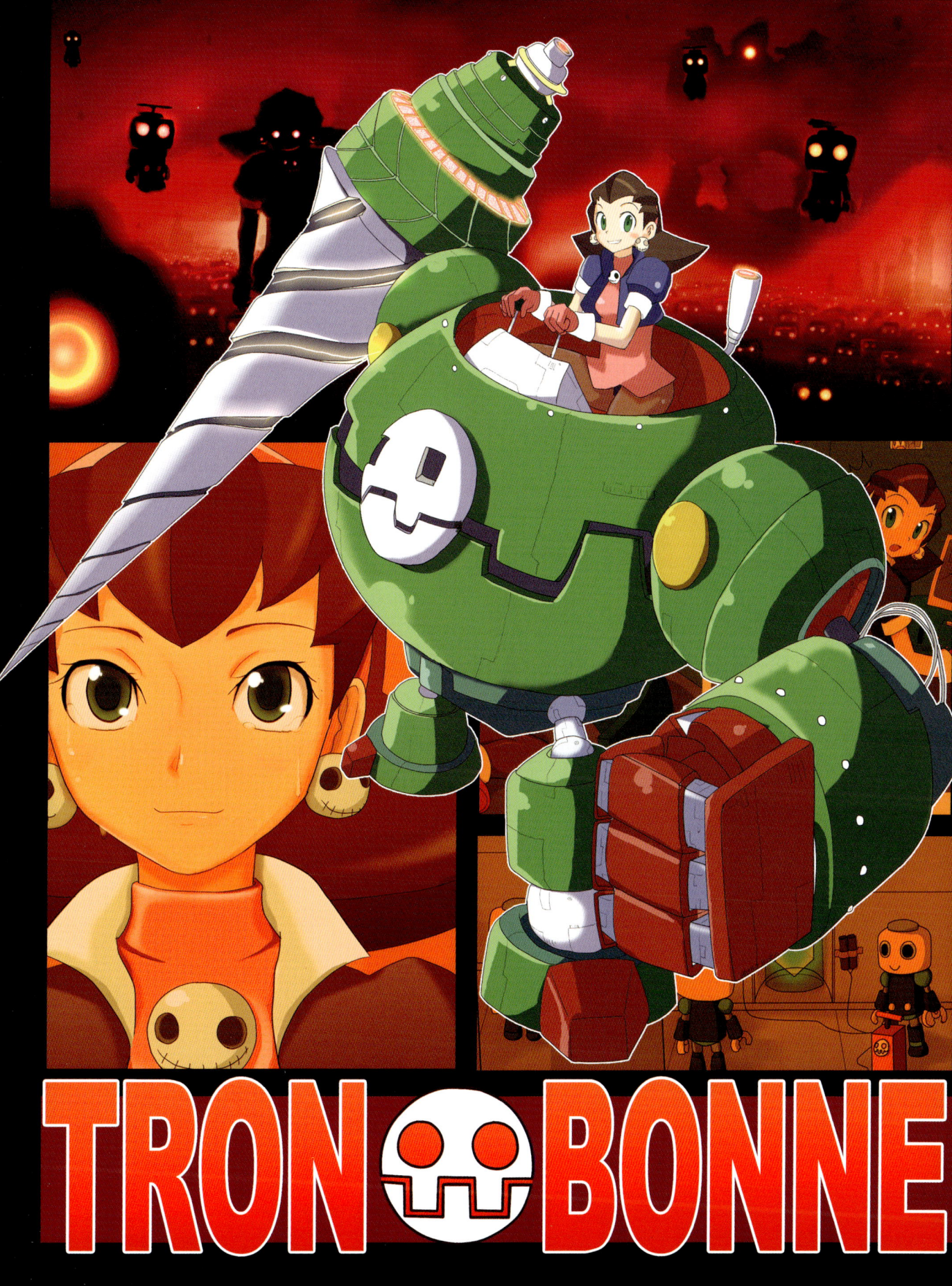

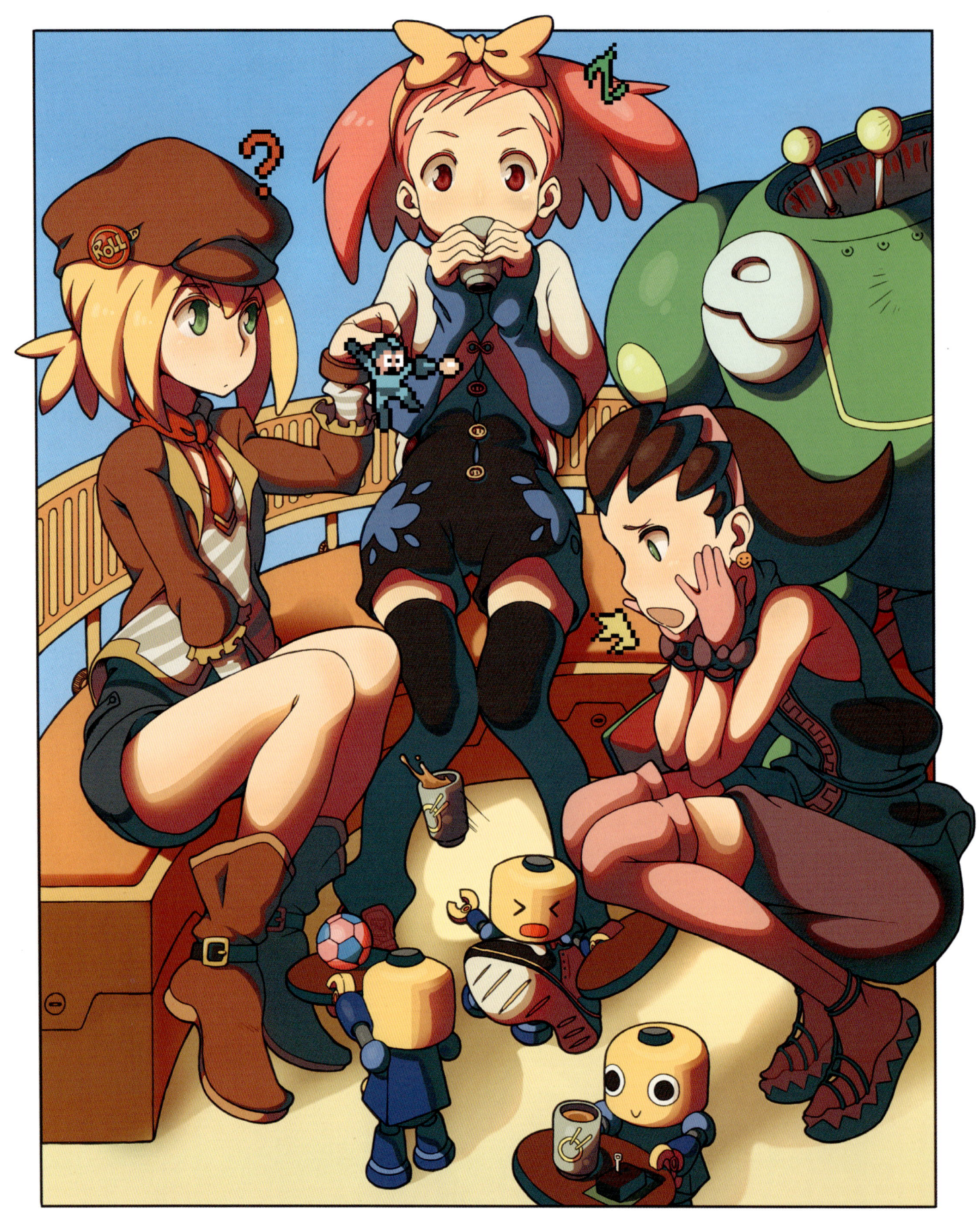

VINHNYU
Sainte Savine, France
vinhnyu.deviantart.com
Electric Engineer

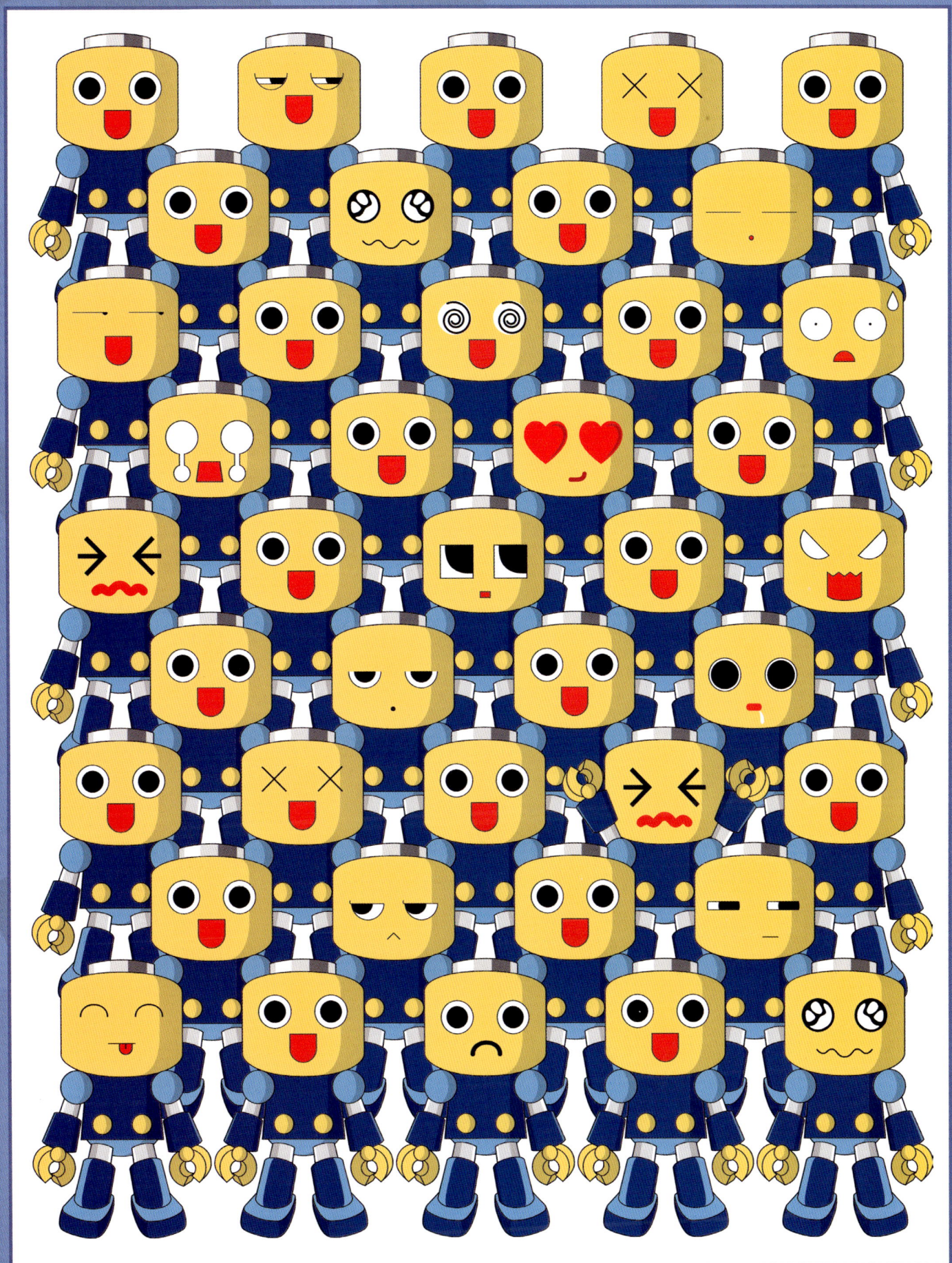

CARLOS BALDO
Tijuana, Mexico
Graphic Designer

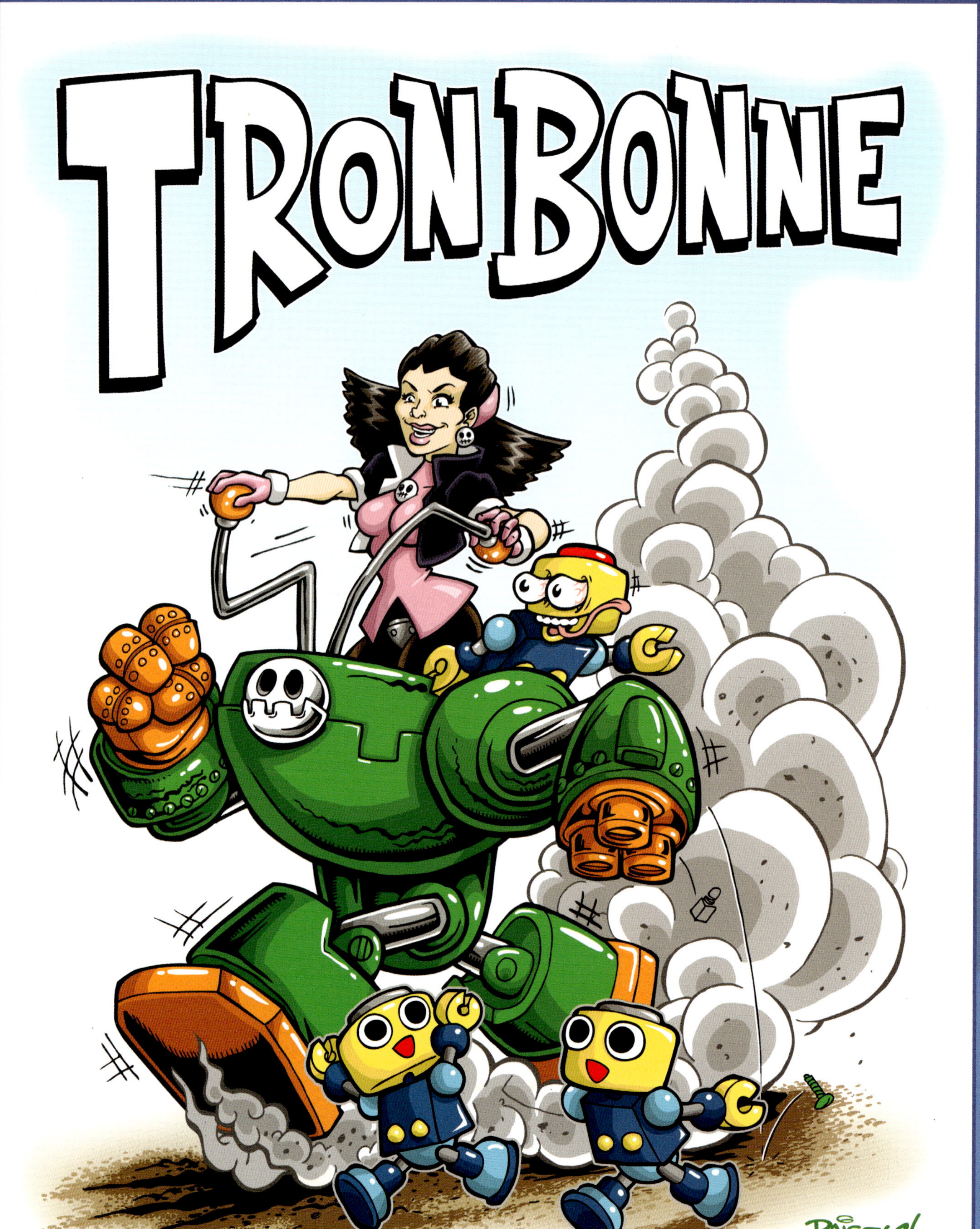

PAIGE PUMPHREY (PAIGEY!)
Brooklyn, NY, United States
theartofpaigey.blogspot.com / paigey.deviantart.com
Artist
(Joe Kubert School Alumni / Charm City Roller girls posters
/ Charter East Coast member of Girls Drawin Girls)

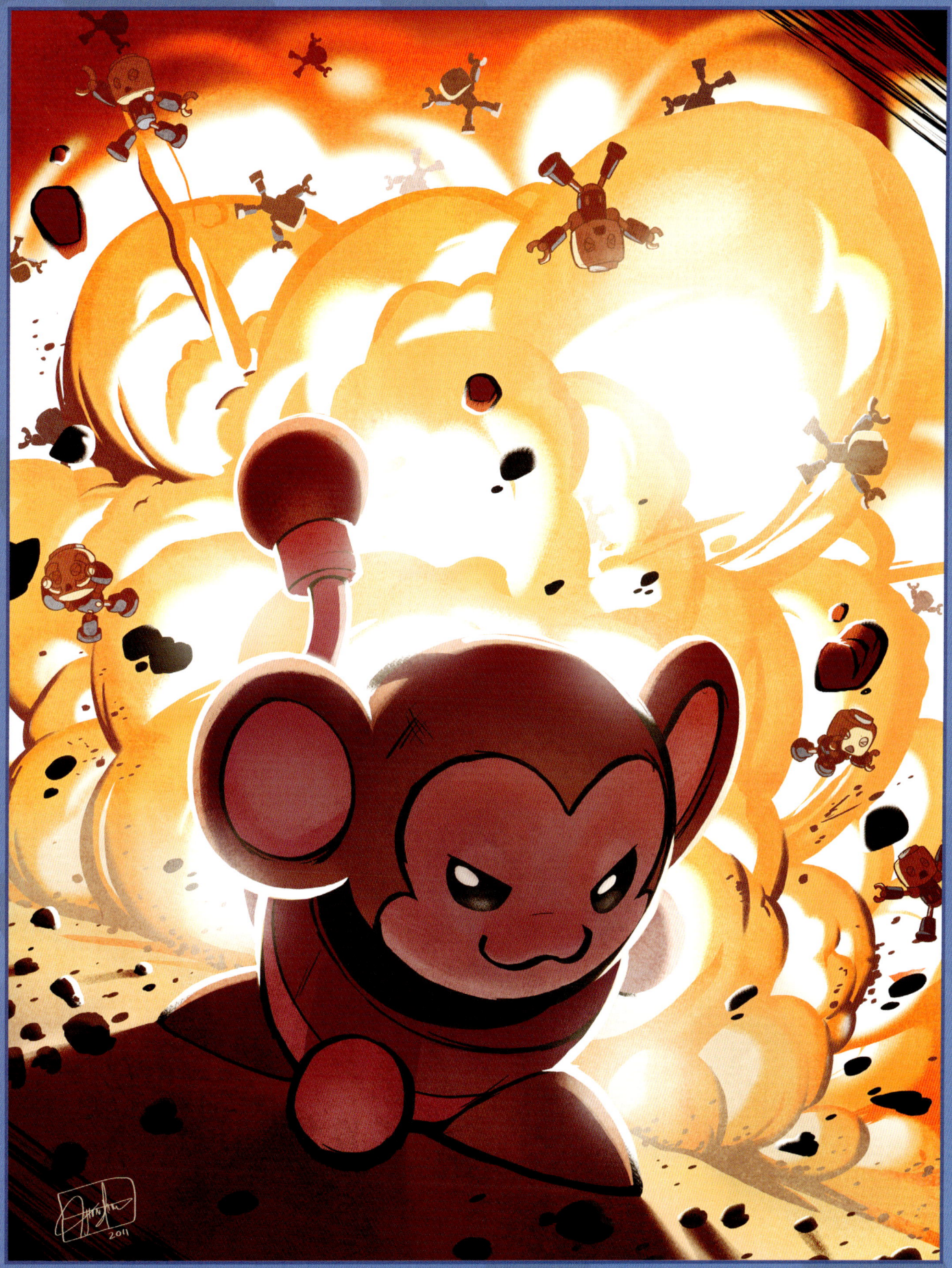

TYSON HESSE
Charlotte, NC, United States
www.boxerhockey.com / mechanical-penguin.deviantart.com
Webcomic Artist
(Boxer Hockey / Savannah College of Art and Design)

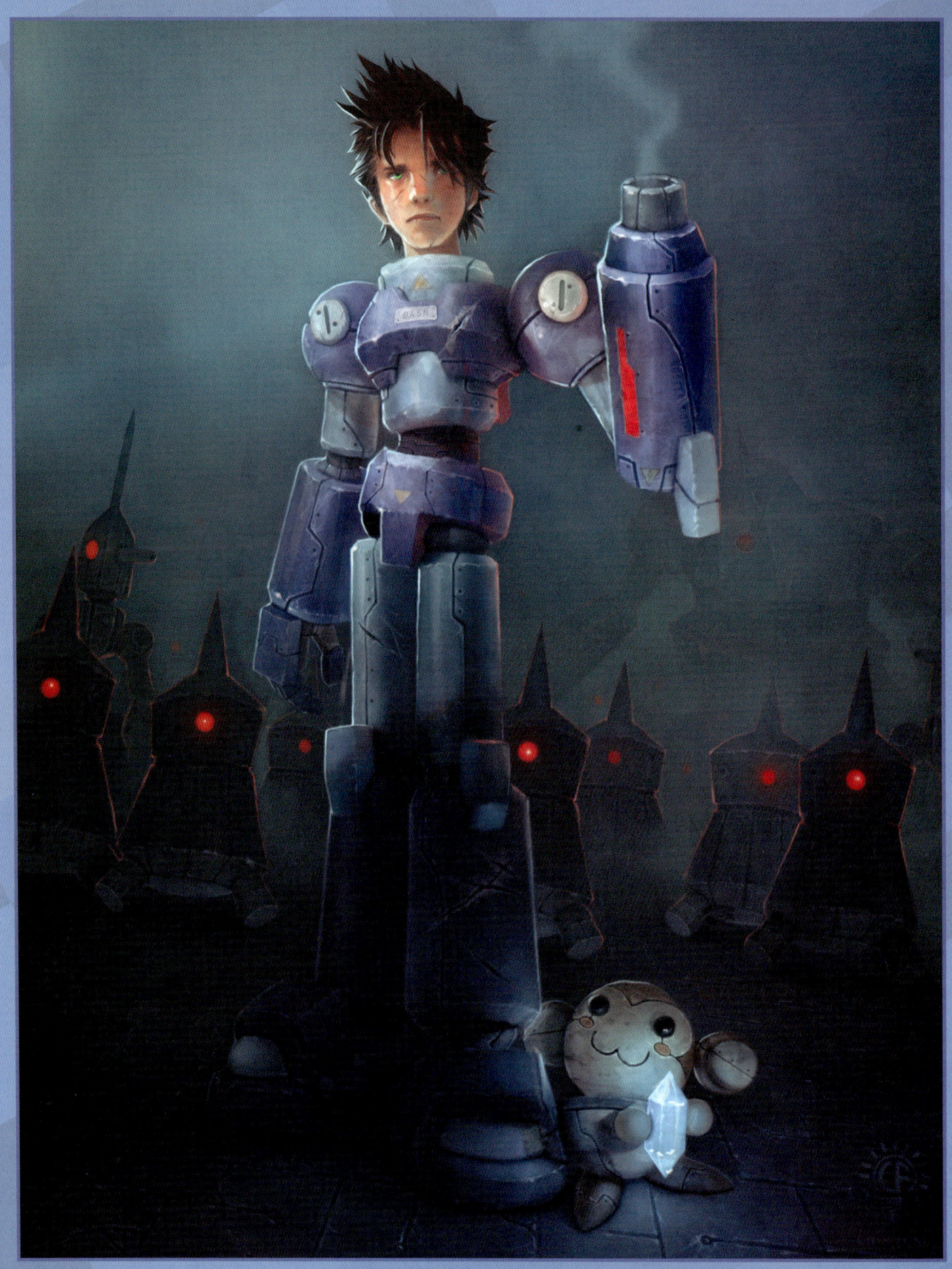

CHIN FONG
Cherry Hill, NJ, United States
chinfongart.blogspot.com / phongshader.deviantart.com
Student

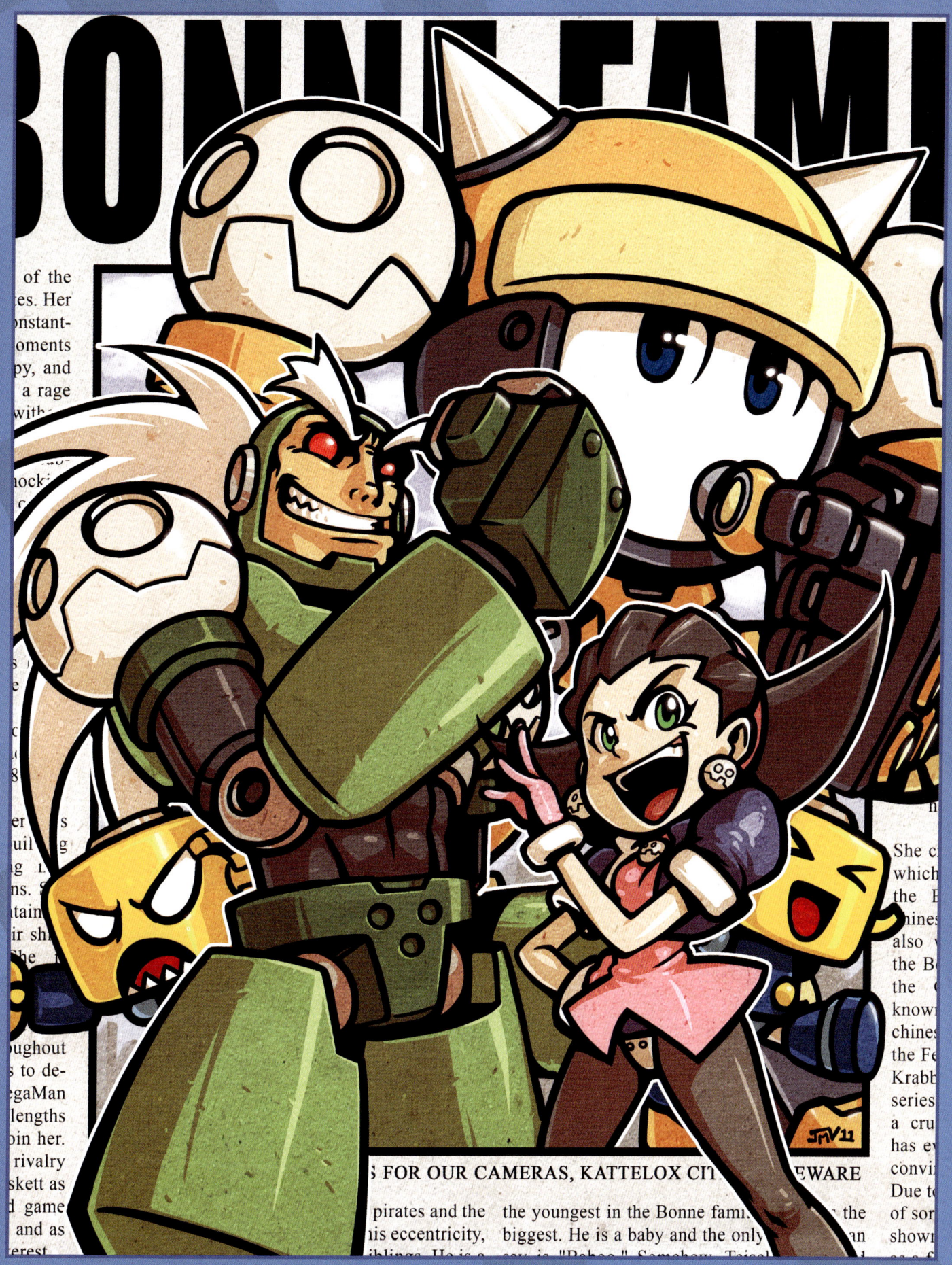

JORGE M. VELEZ
Smyrna, GA, United States
kaigetsudo.blogspot.com / kaigetsudo.deviantart.com
Illustrator
(Atlantic College)

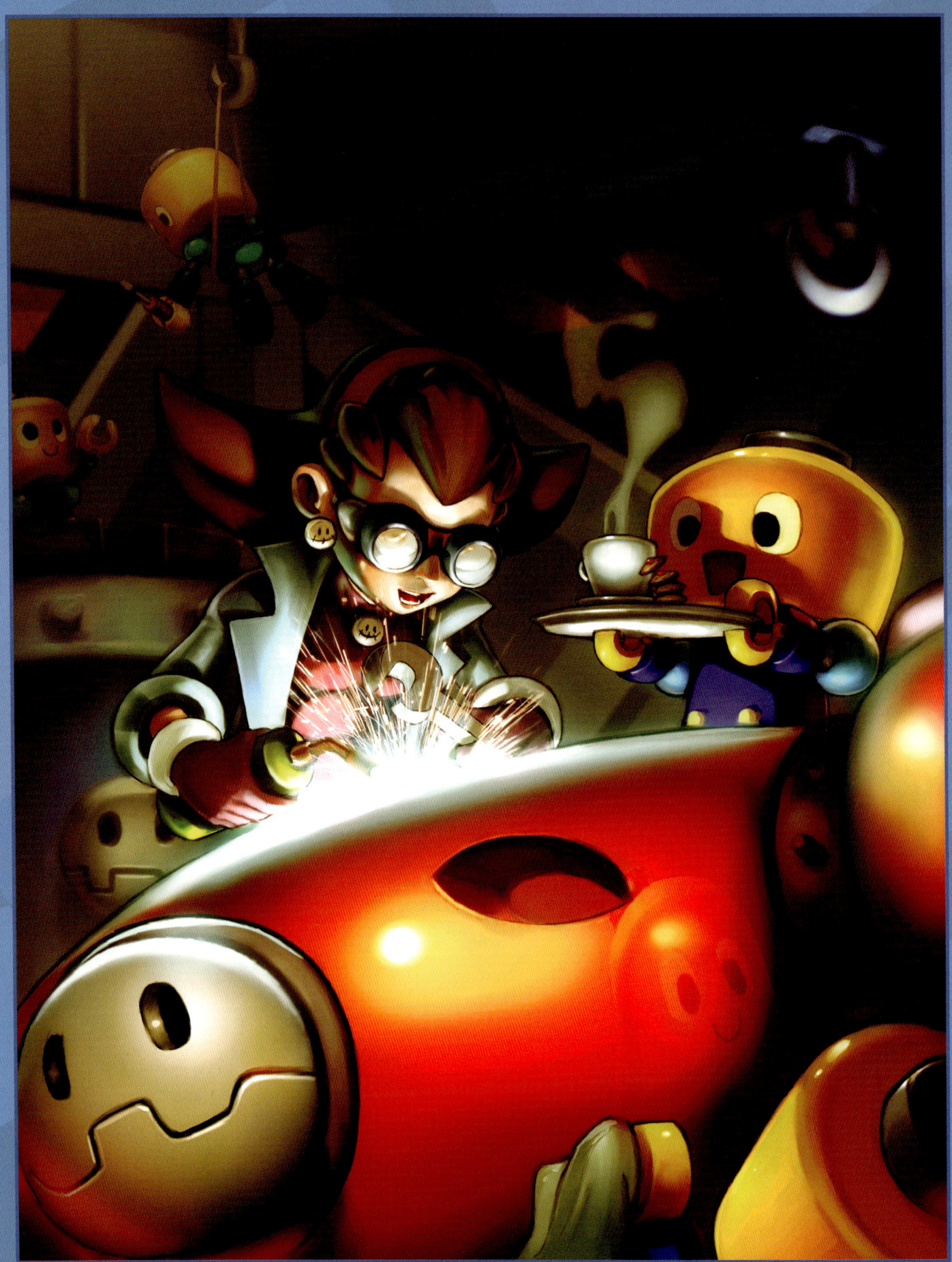

BEN ELLEBRACHT
Ferguson, MO, United States
fightingfail.blogspot.com / fightingfailure.deviantart.com
Illustrator

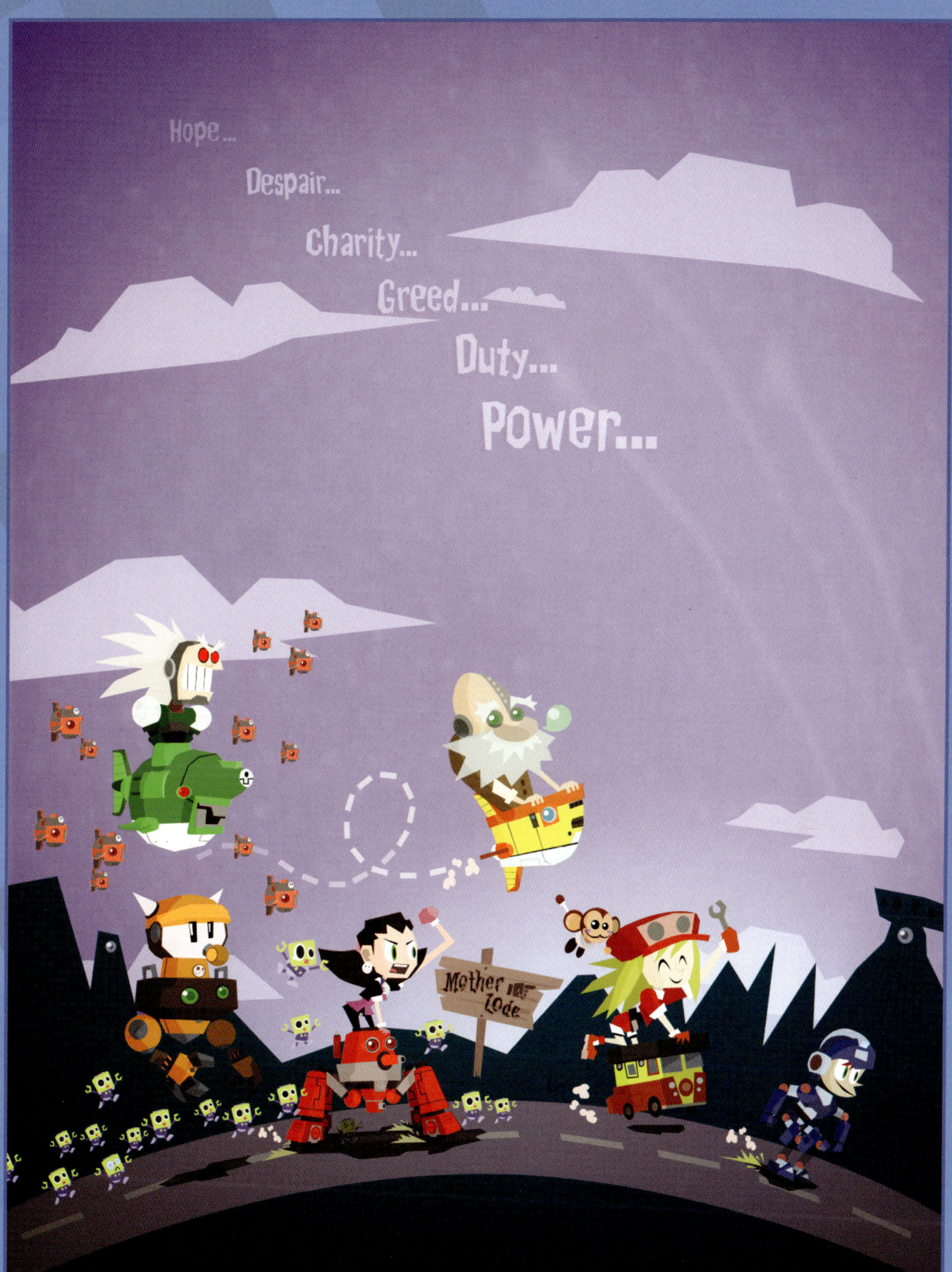

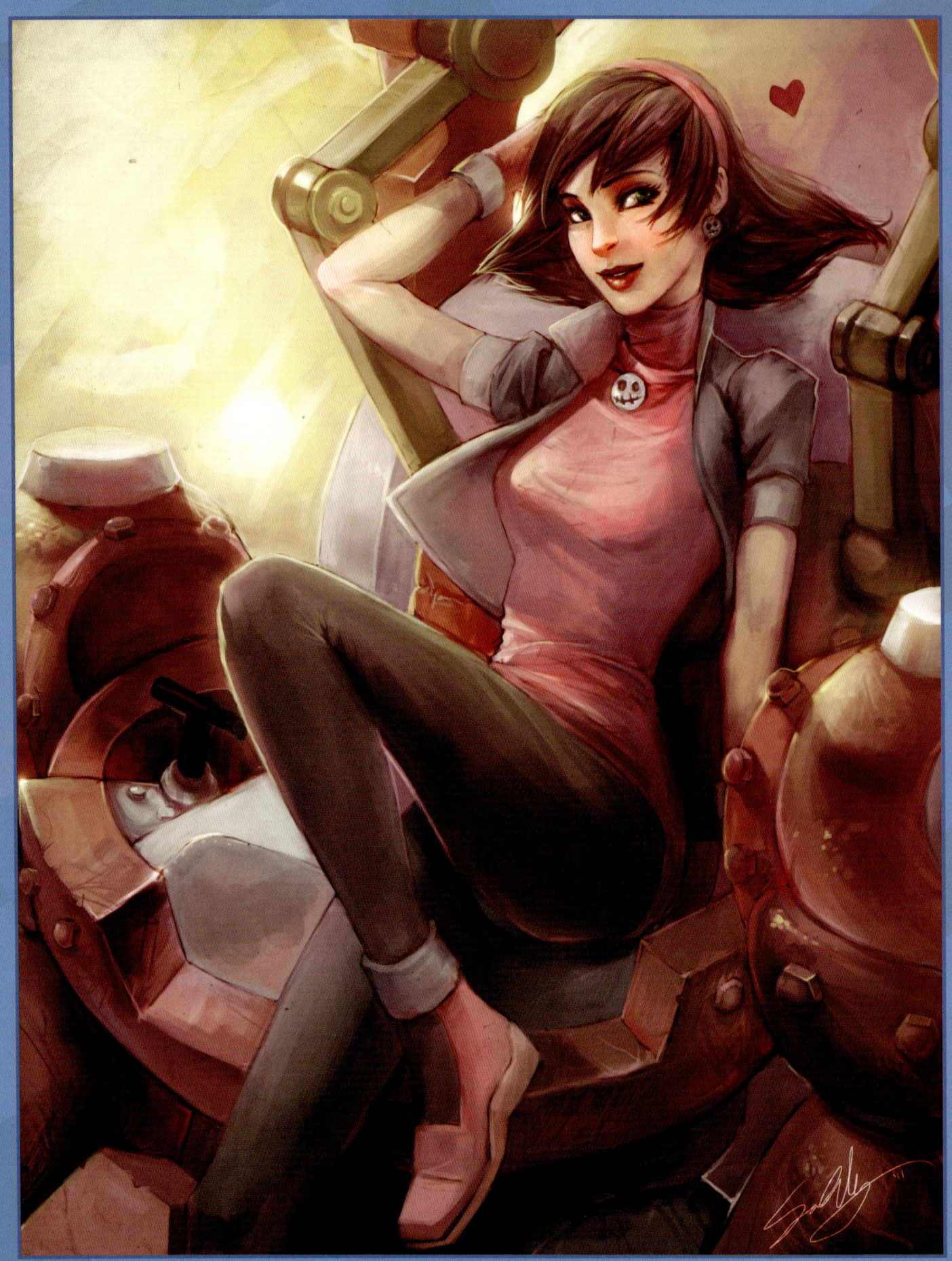

SARAH ELLERTON
Newtown, Australia
www.arts-angel.com / artsangel.deviantart.com
Comic Artist
(The Phoenix Requiem)

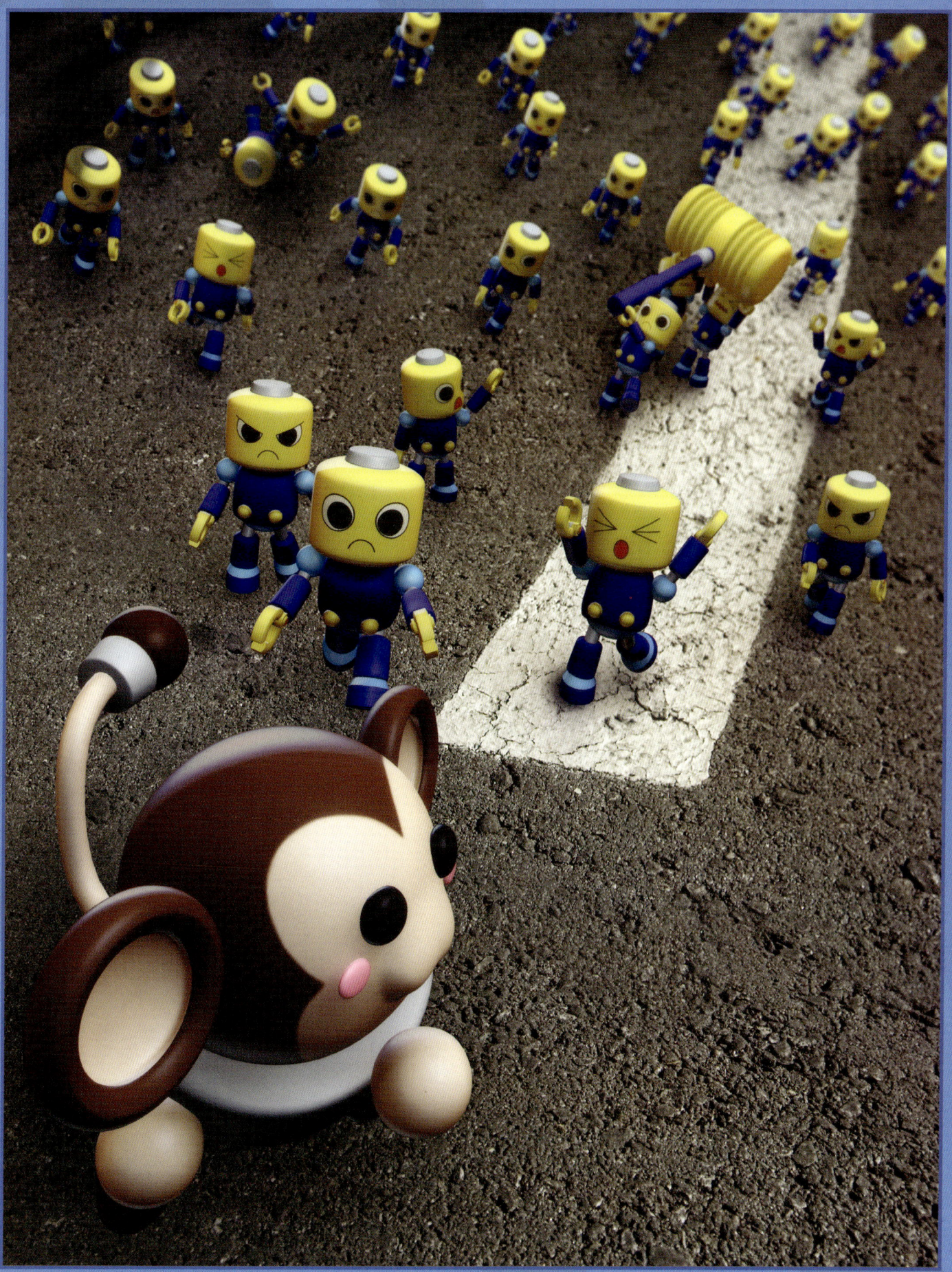

CHRIS WHITAKER
San Jose, CA, United States
funkybunnies.deviantart.com
Game Artist

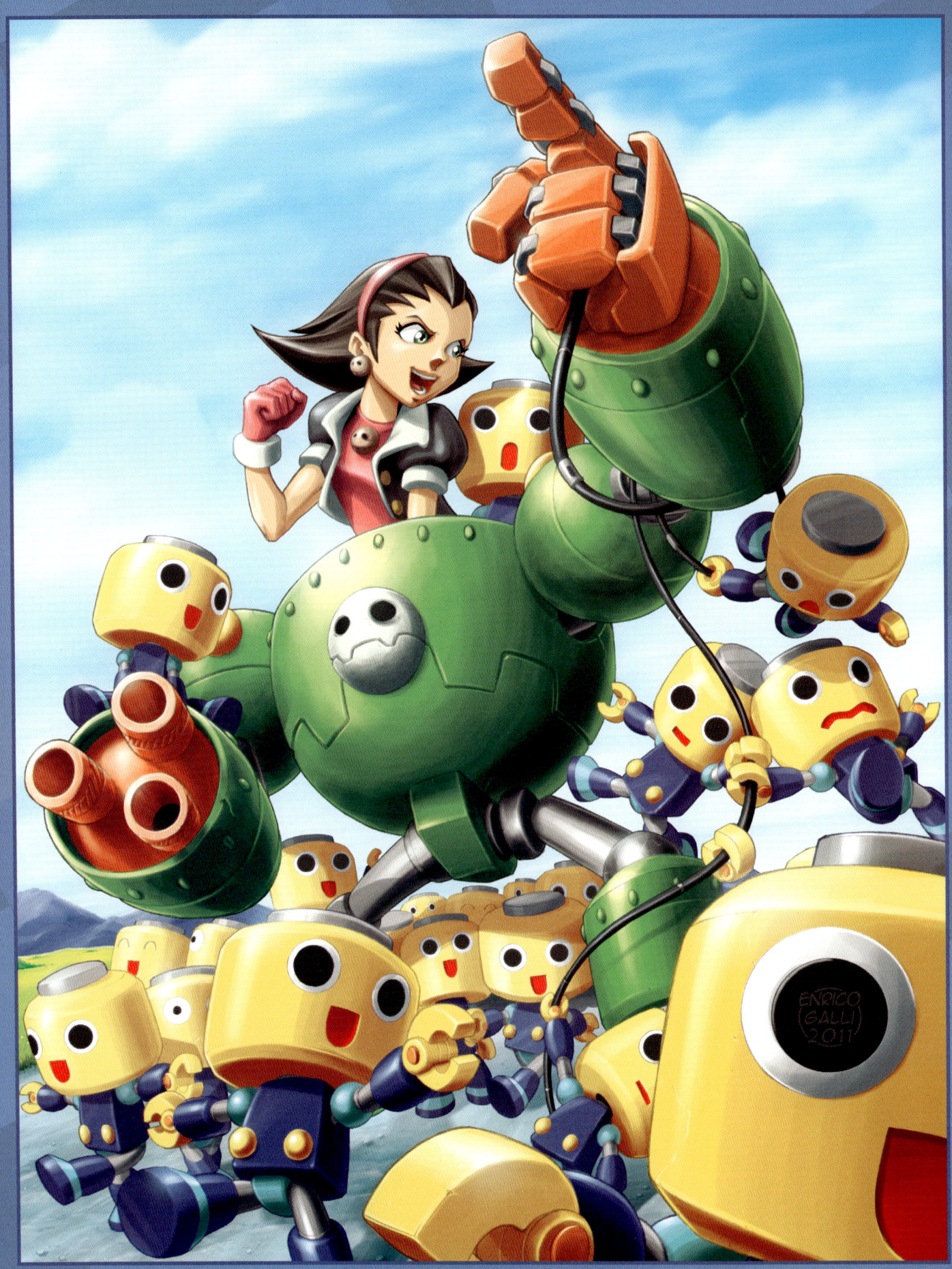

ENRICO GALLI
Rome, Italy
enricogalli.deviantart.com
Illustrator / Cartoonist / Colorist

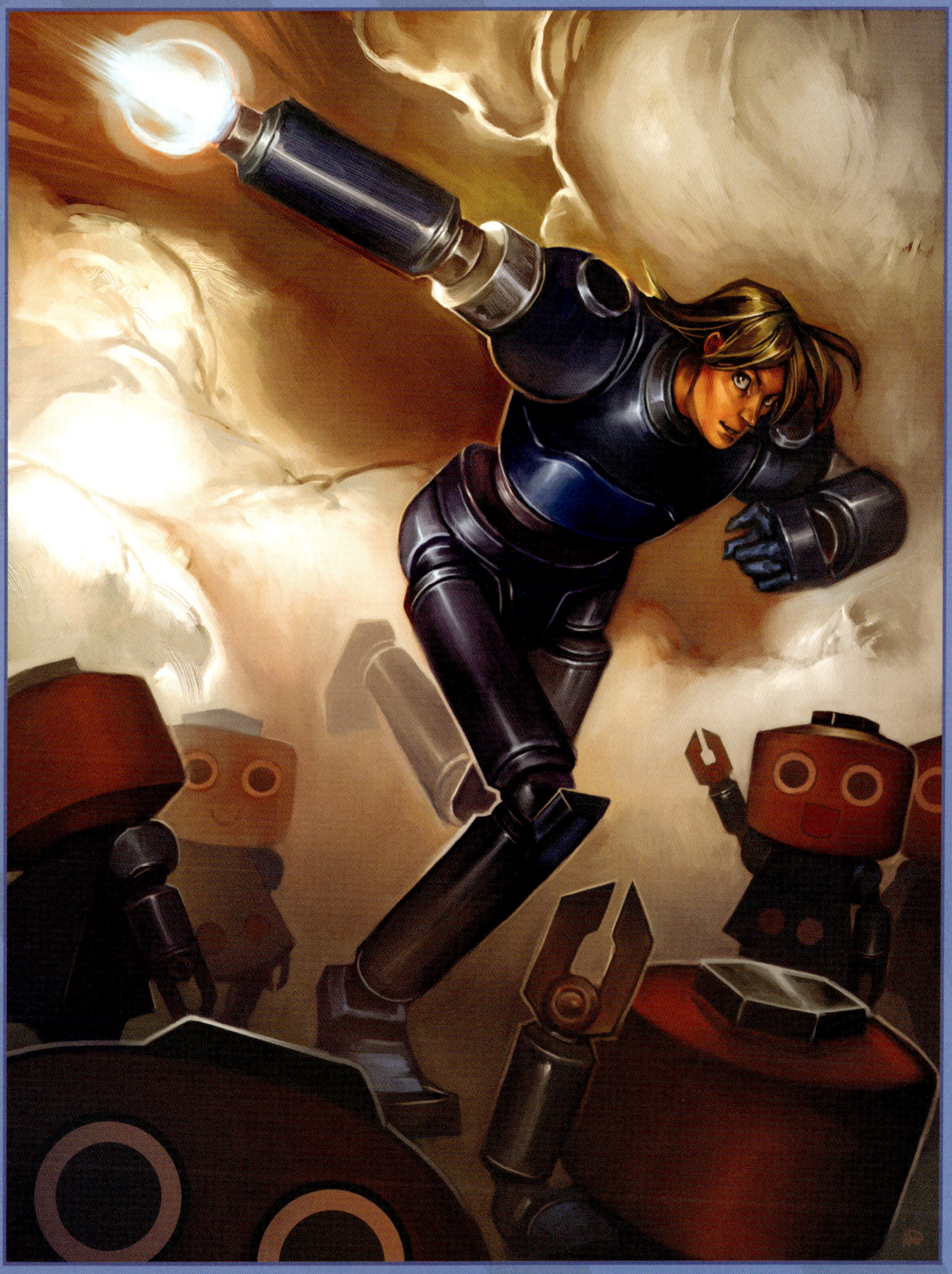

JEFFREY LAI
Wellington, New Zealand
jeffrey-lai.blogspot.com / jeffreylai.deviantart.com
Illustrator

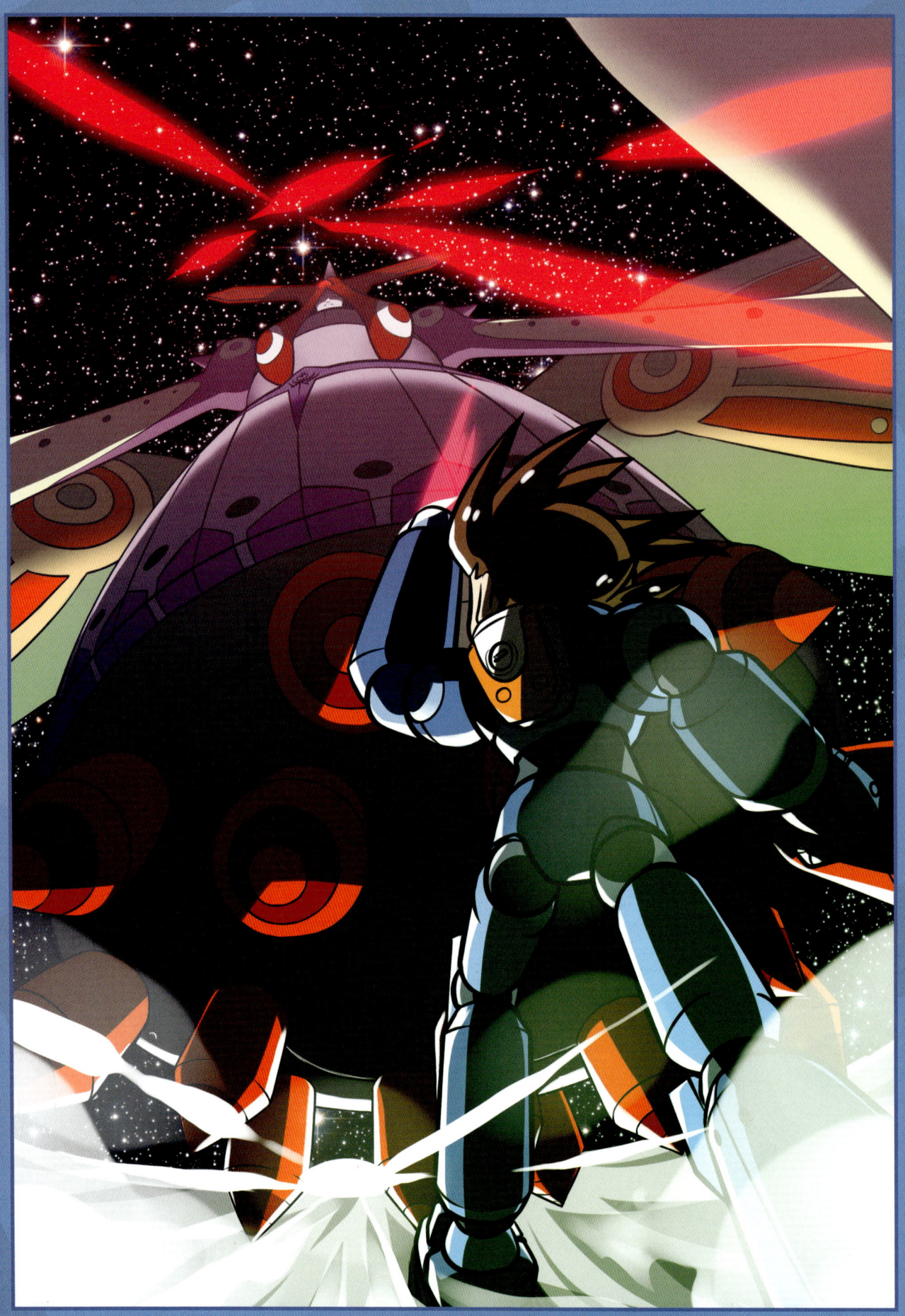

LAE DONALD (DONALD)
SUN YAT-SEN UNIVERSITY CAMPUS CITY, CHINA
ILLUSTRATOR

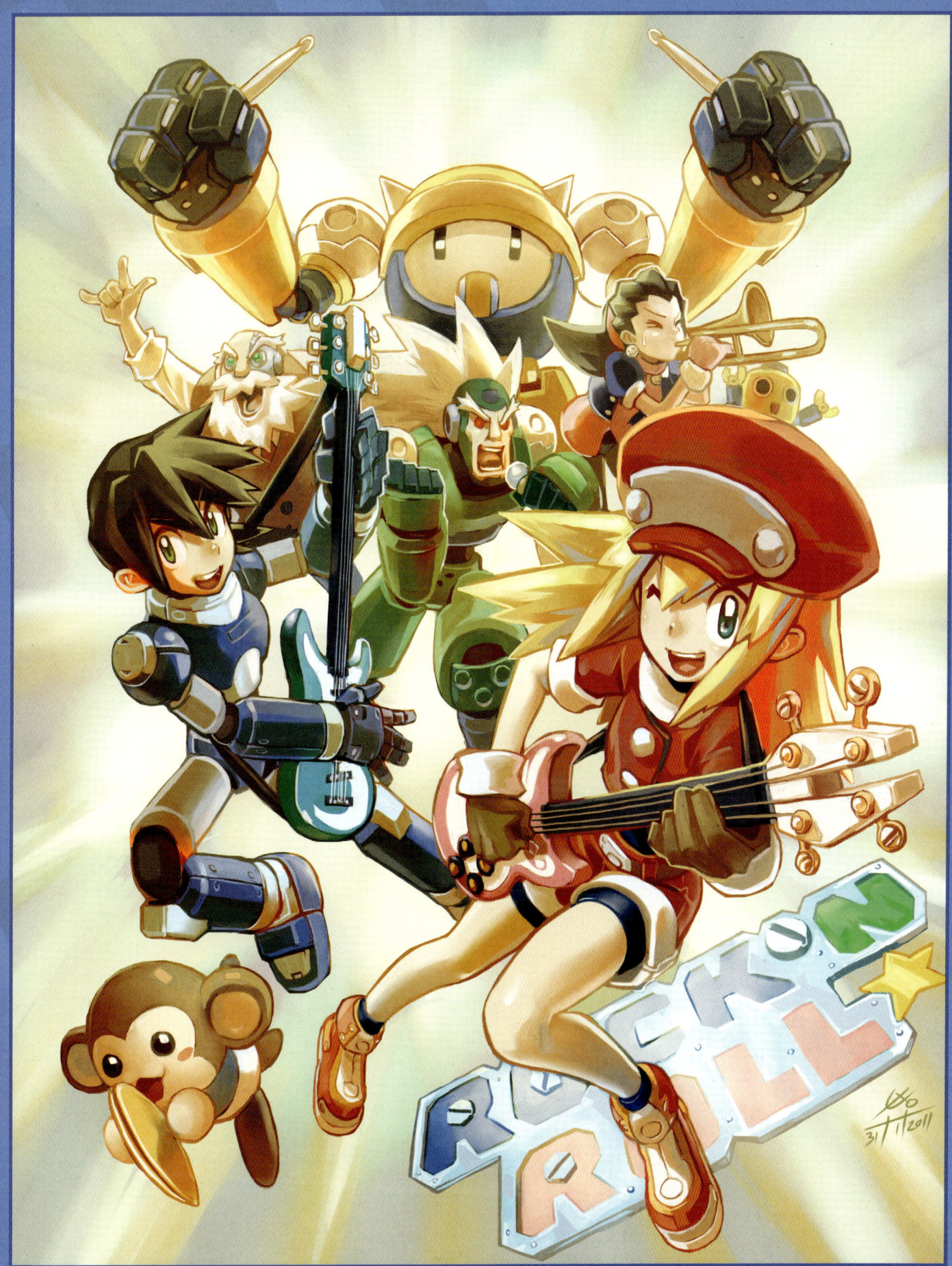

PORAMED CHONRATTANAKUN
Daokanong Thonburi, Thailand
kyokimaru.deviantart.com
Artist

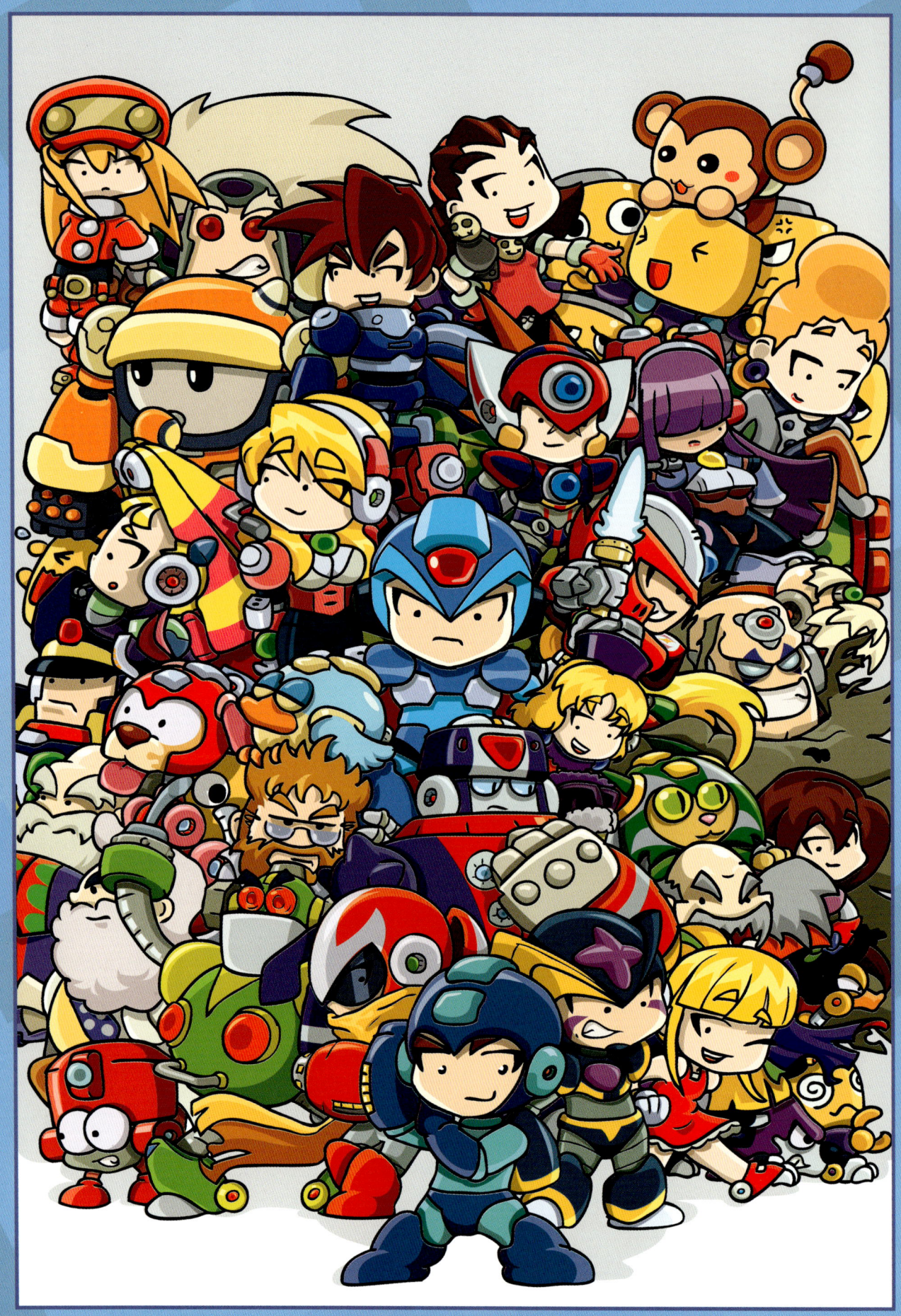

VICTOR BOGGIANO
Lima, Peru
galleryllustrata.blogspot.com
Illustrator

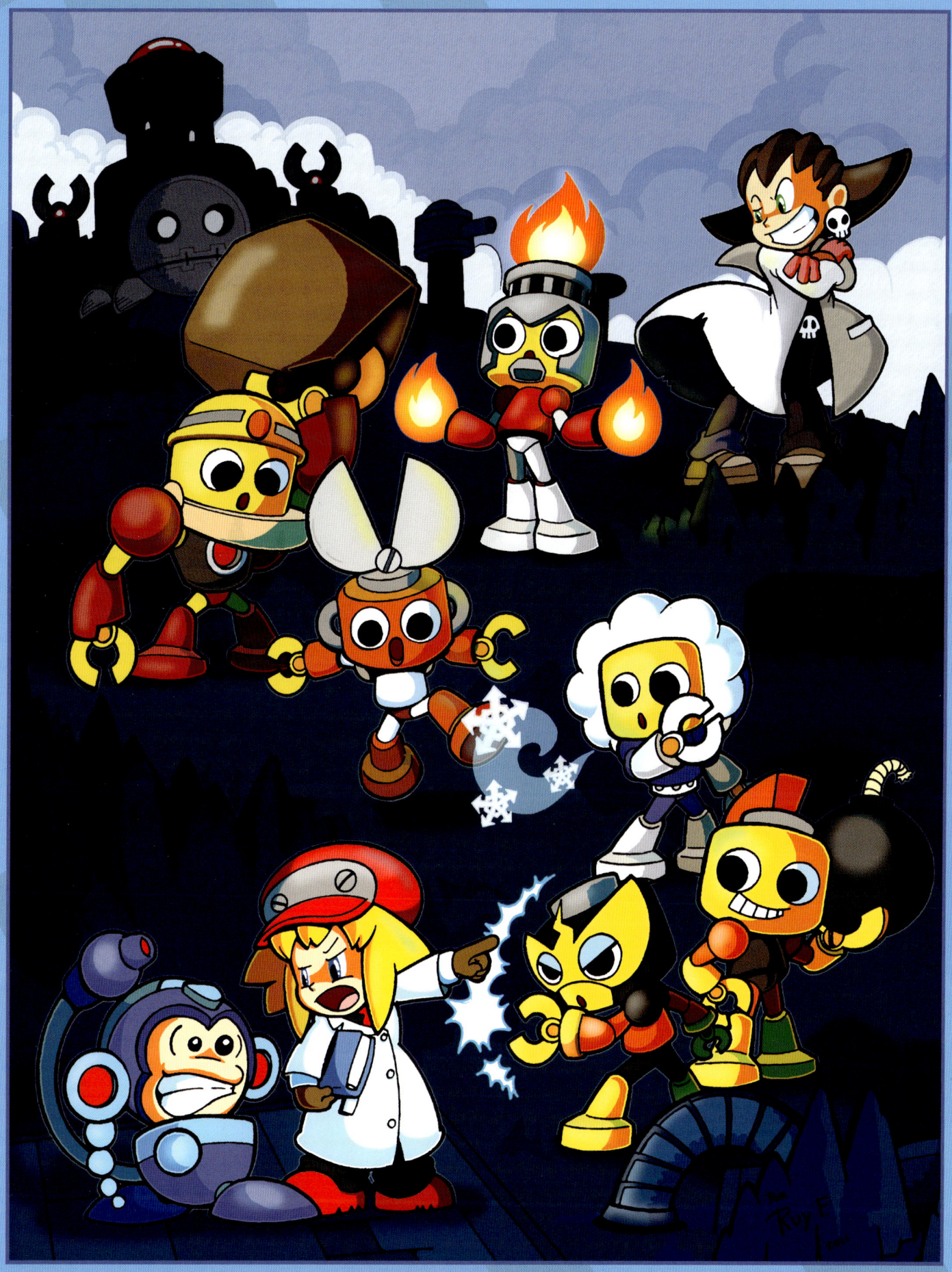

RUY FERNANDO (FLINT)
Guadalajara, Mexico
flintofmother3.deviantart.com
Art Director
(Nikte (animated feature) animator / Juan Escopeta (animated feature) animator
/ Sam Brennan's tale (animated short) art director)

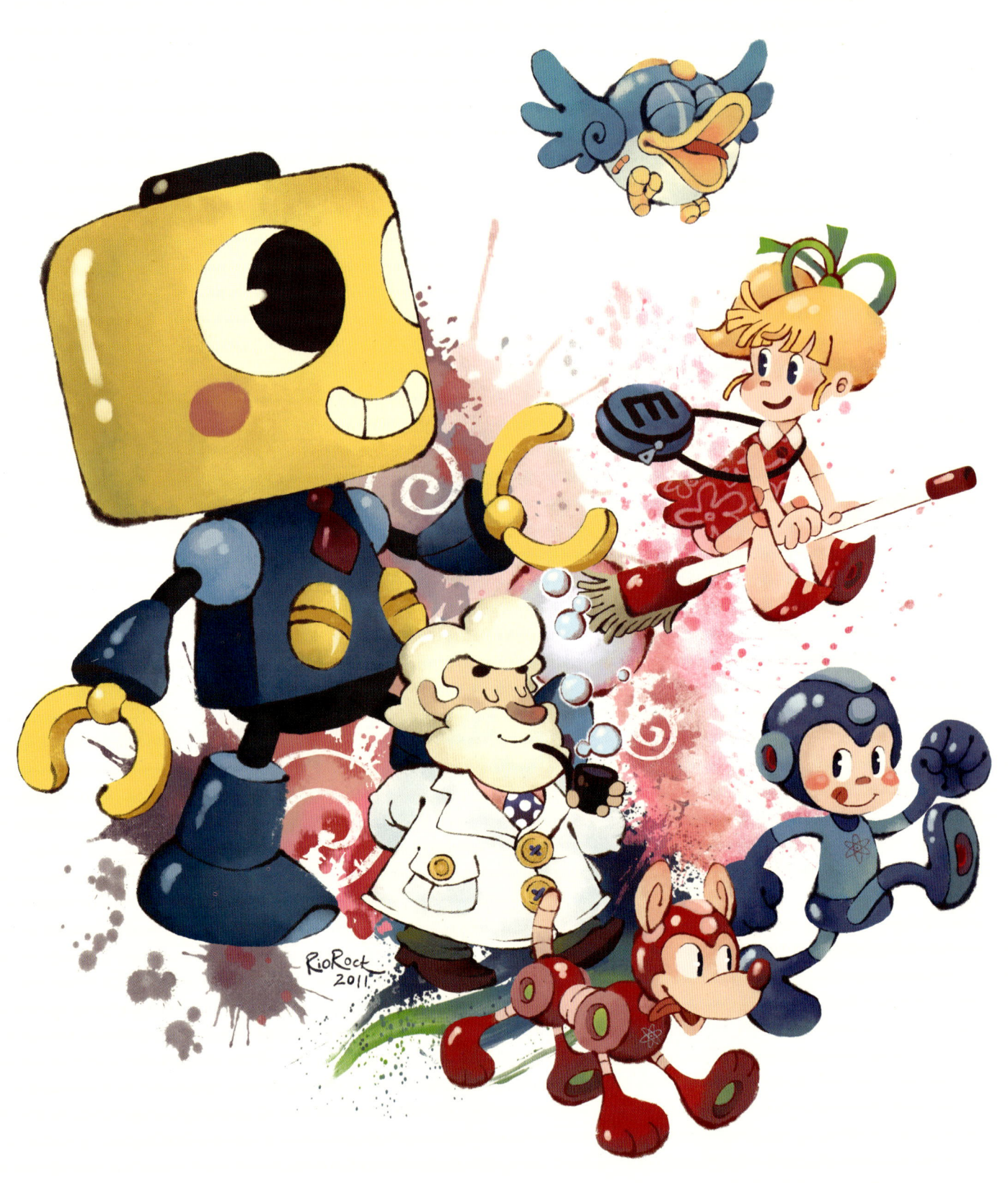

RIO ROCK
Heilbad Heiligenstadt, Germany
riorock.deviantart.com
Comic Artist

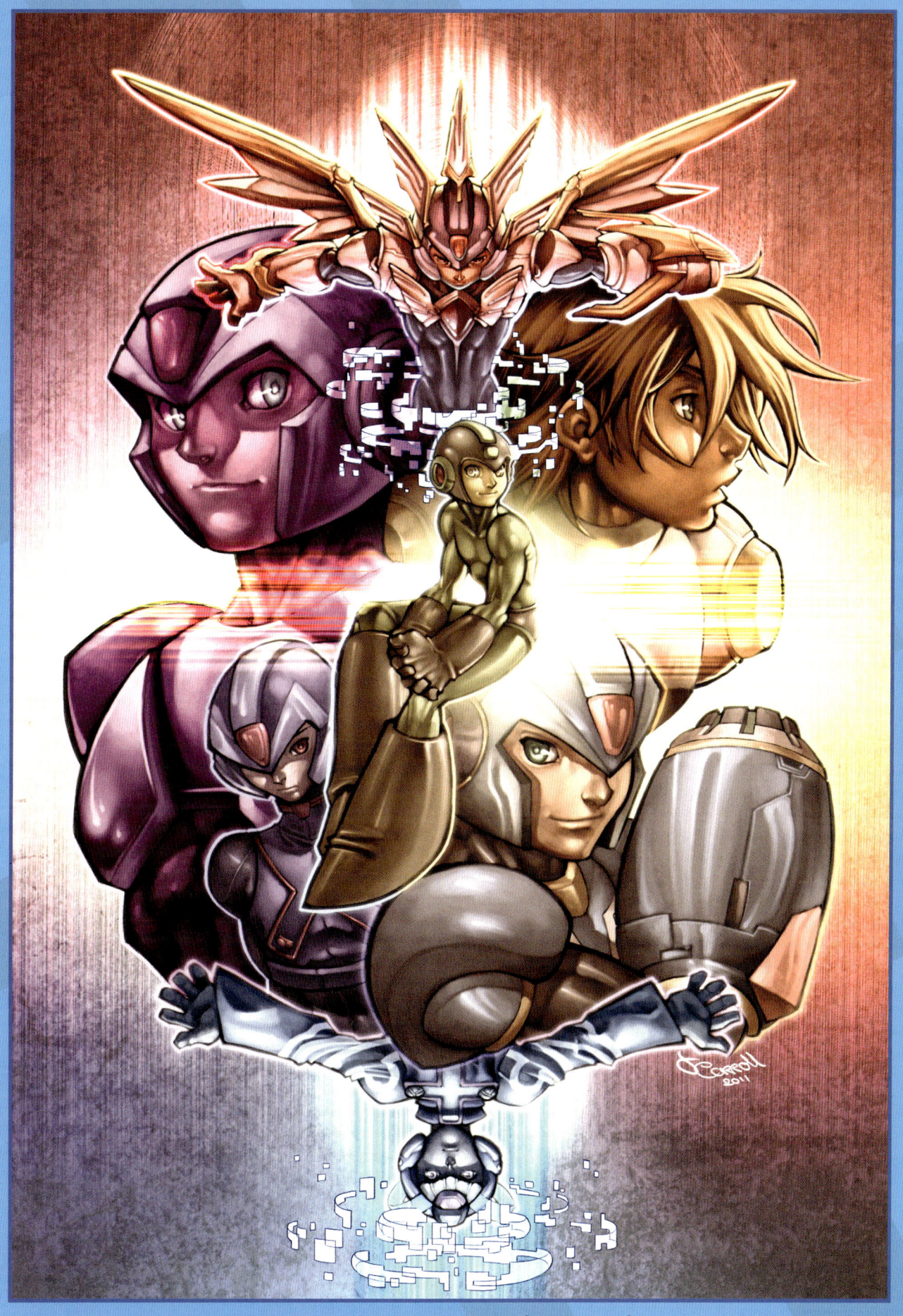

JEAN-BAPTISTE NANTEAU (JCARROLL)
RENNES, FRANCE
ILLUSTRATOR

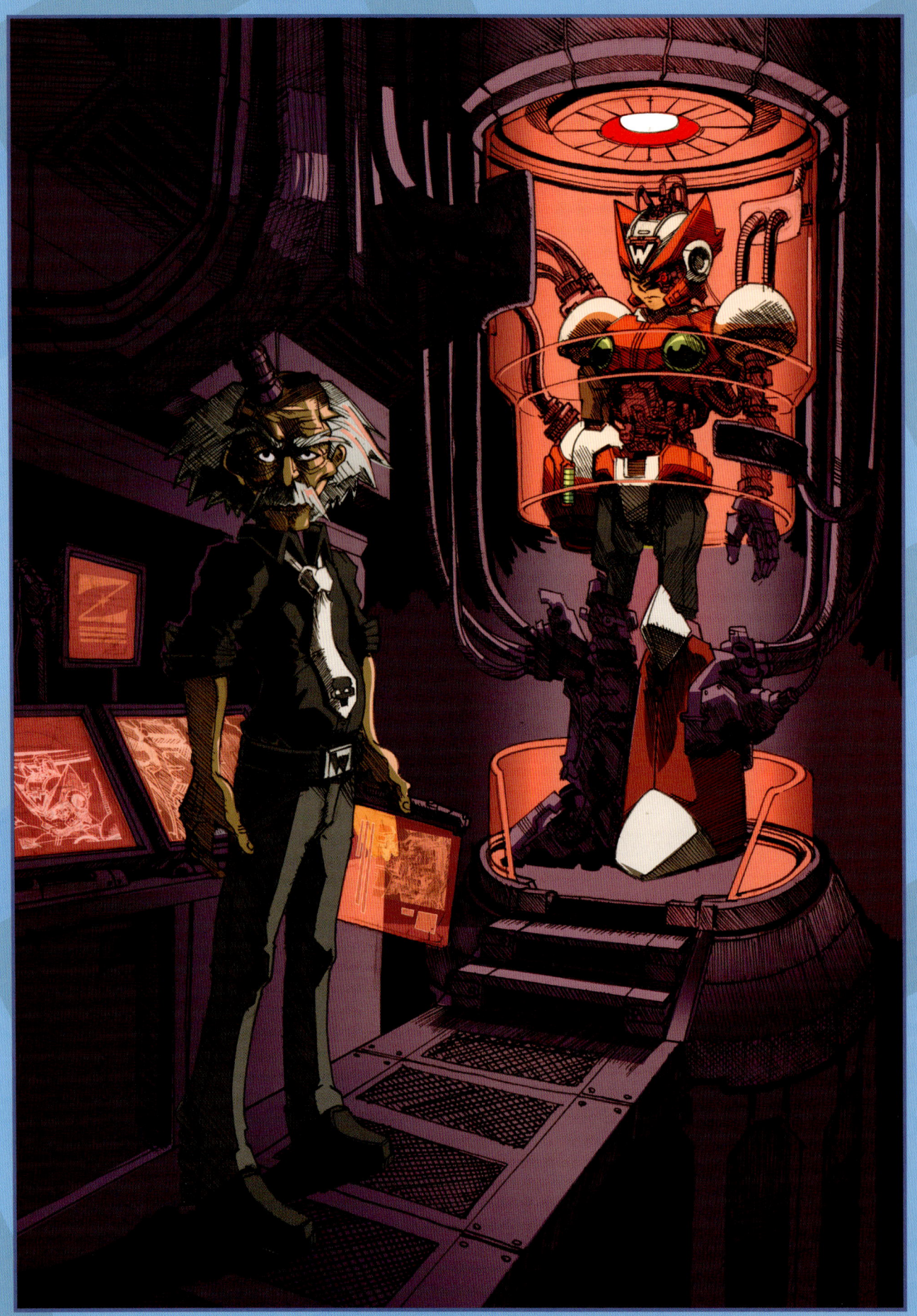

COLLIN OTTO
Commerce, MI, United States
www.collinotto.com
Illustrator

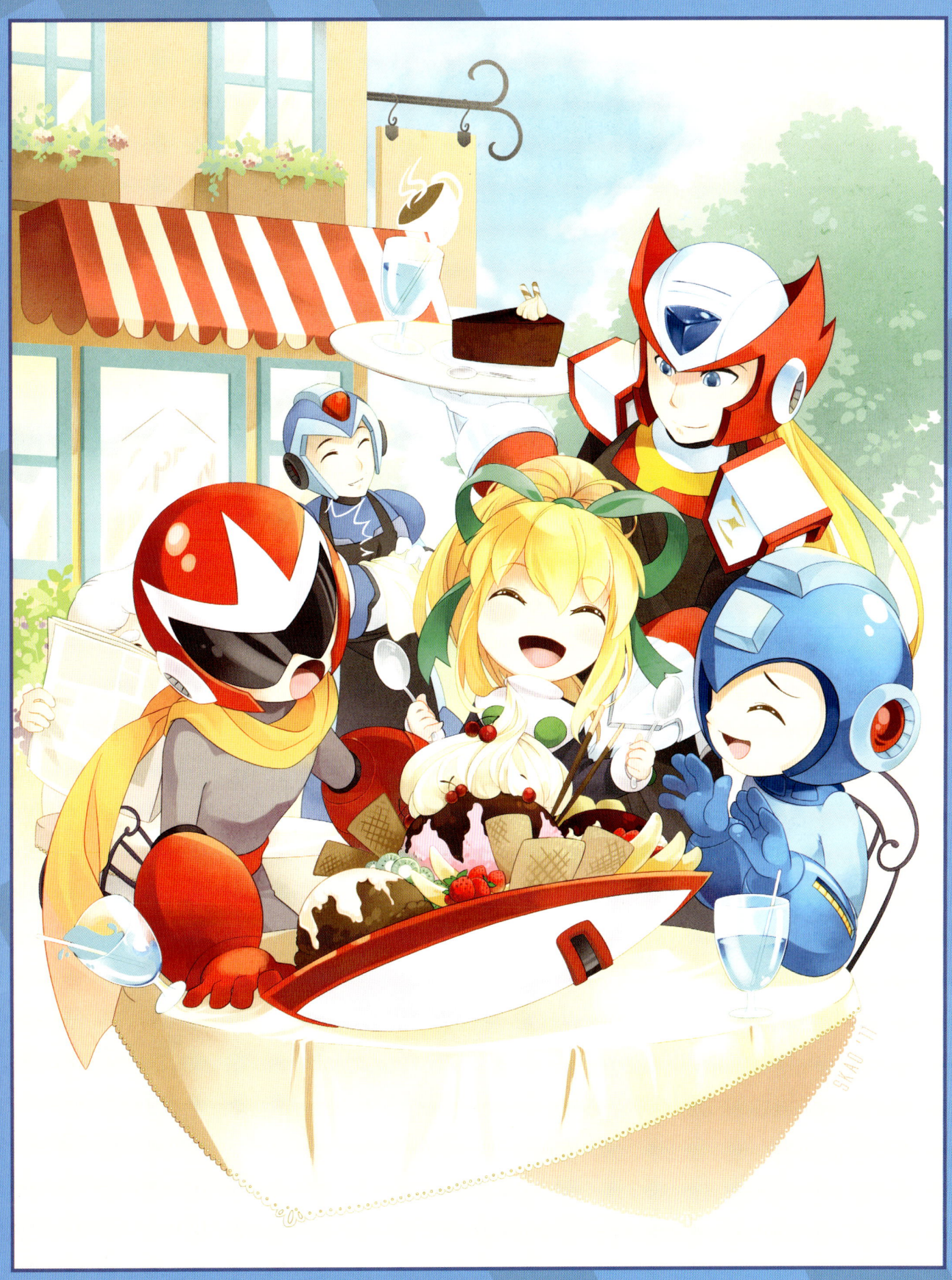

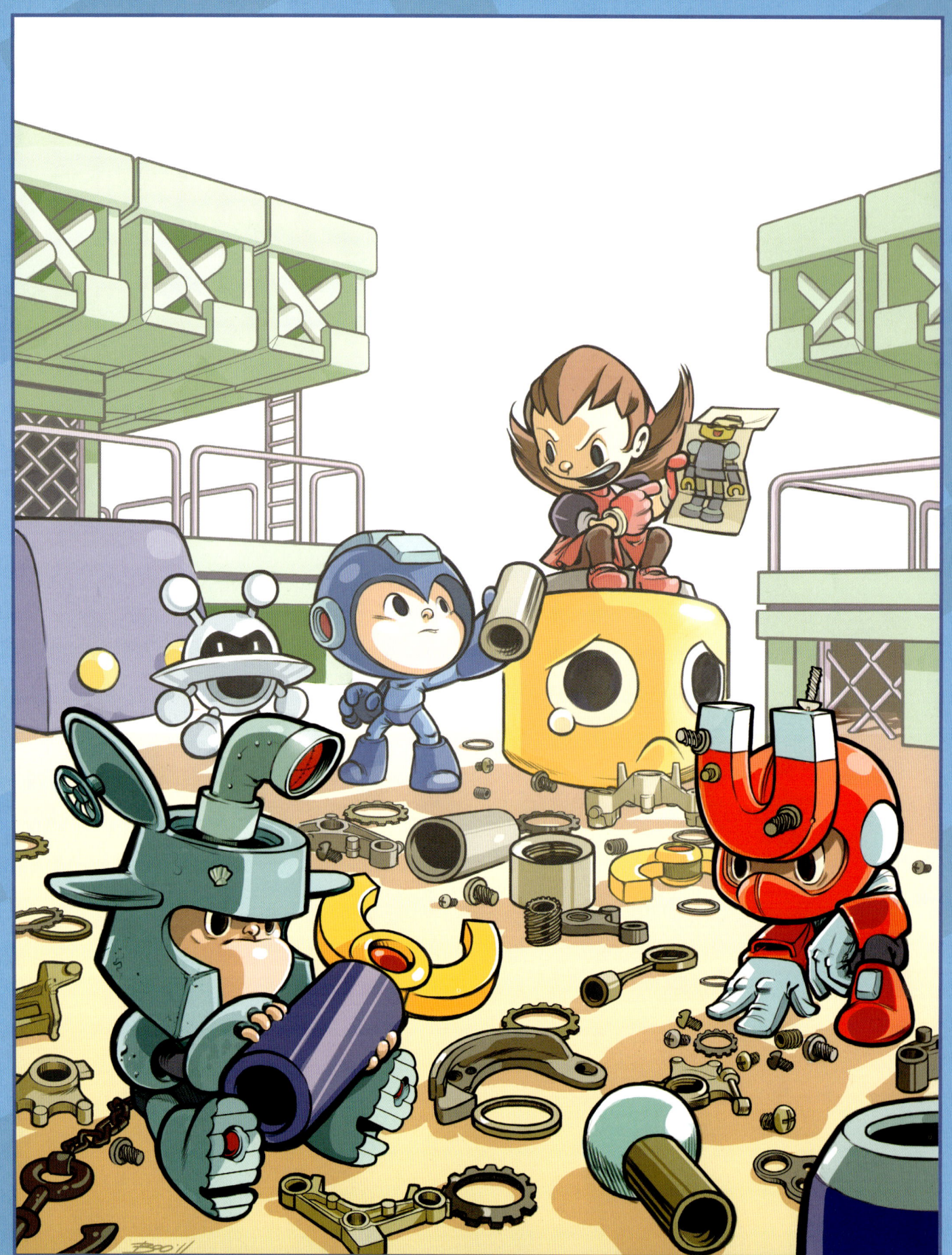

DANIEL BOULANGER
Quebec City, QC, Canada
wallambamboo.blogspot.com
Illustrator

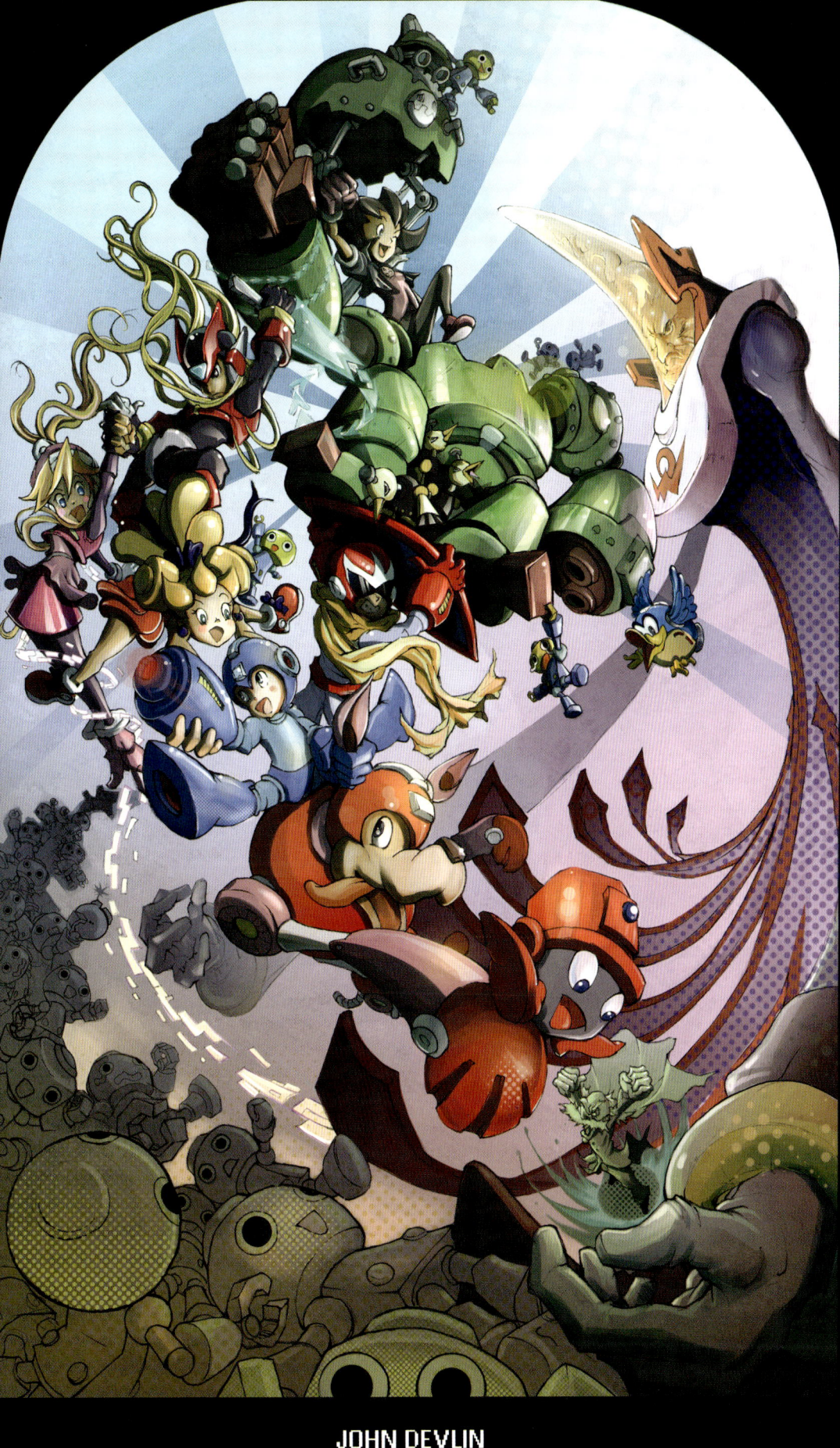

JOHN DEVLIN
Dublin, Ireland
revenant-wings.deviantart.com
Illustrator

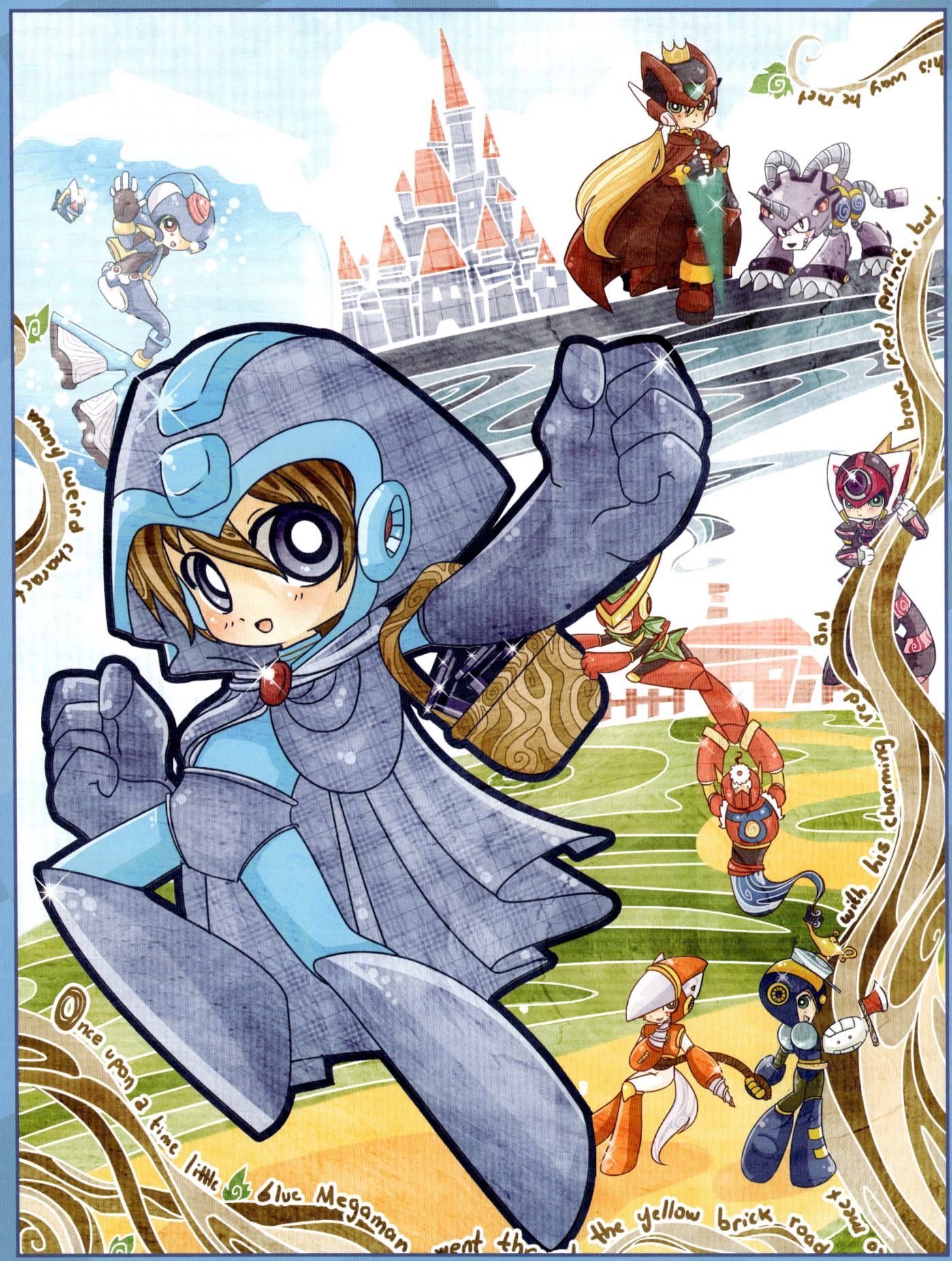

ALEJANDRA ZÚÑIGA MIRANDA
CHIHUAHUA, MEXICO
SILICEB.DEVIANTART.COM
Graphic Designer
(STUDIO XIII)

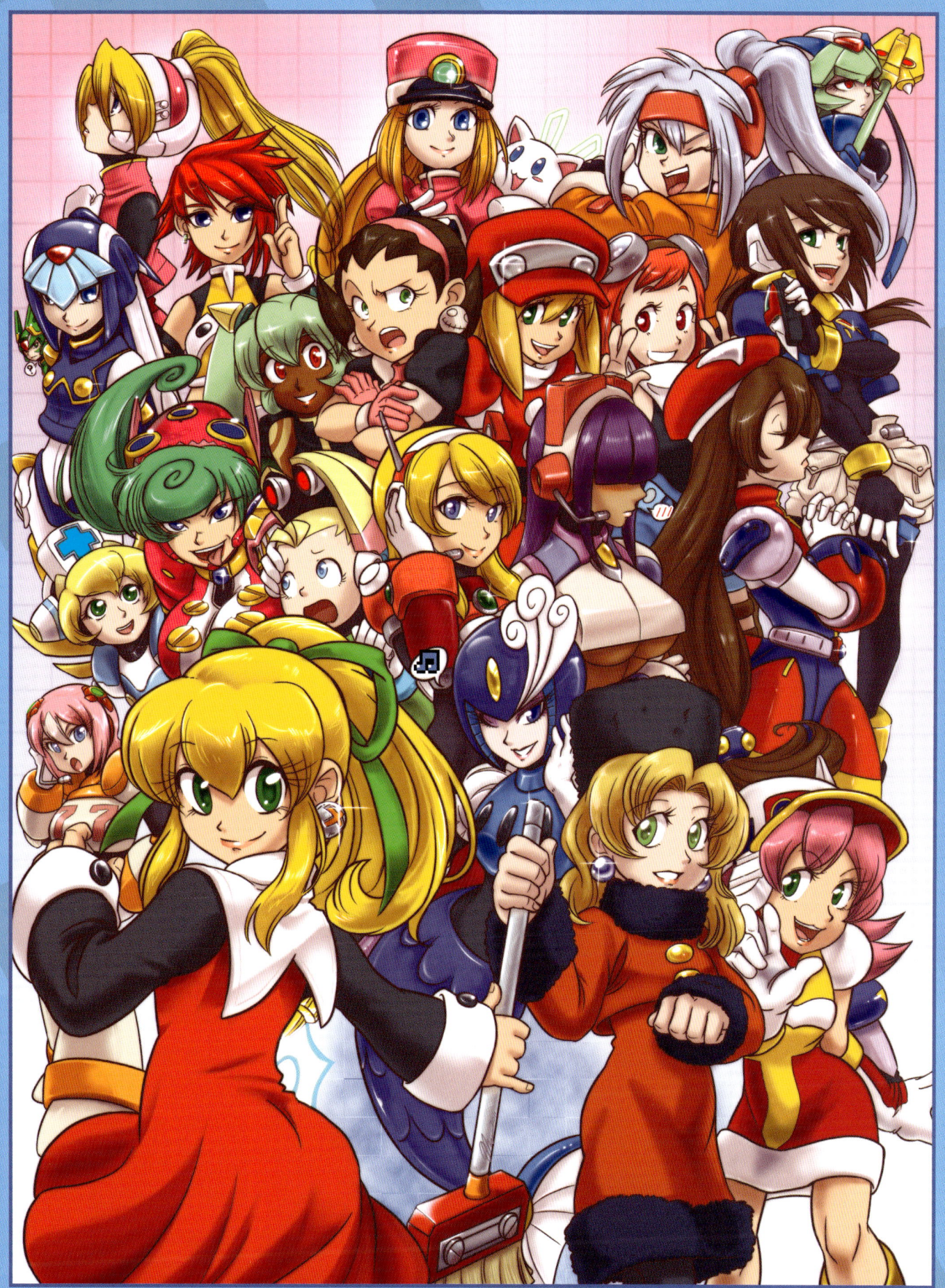

AUDREY KARE
Coquitlam, BC Canada
audioerf.deviantart.com
Illustrator

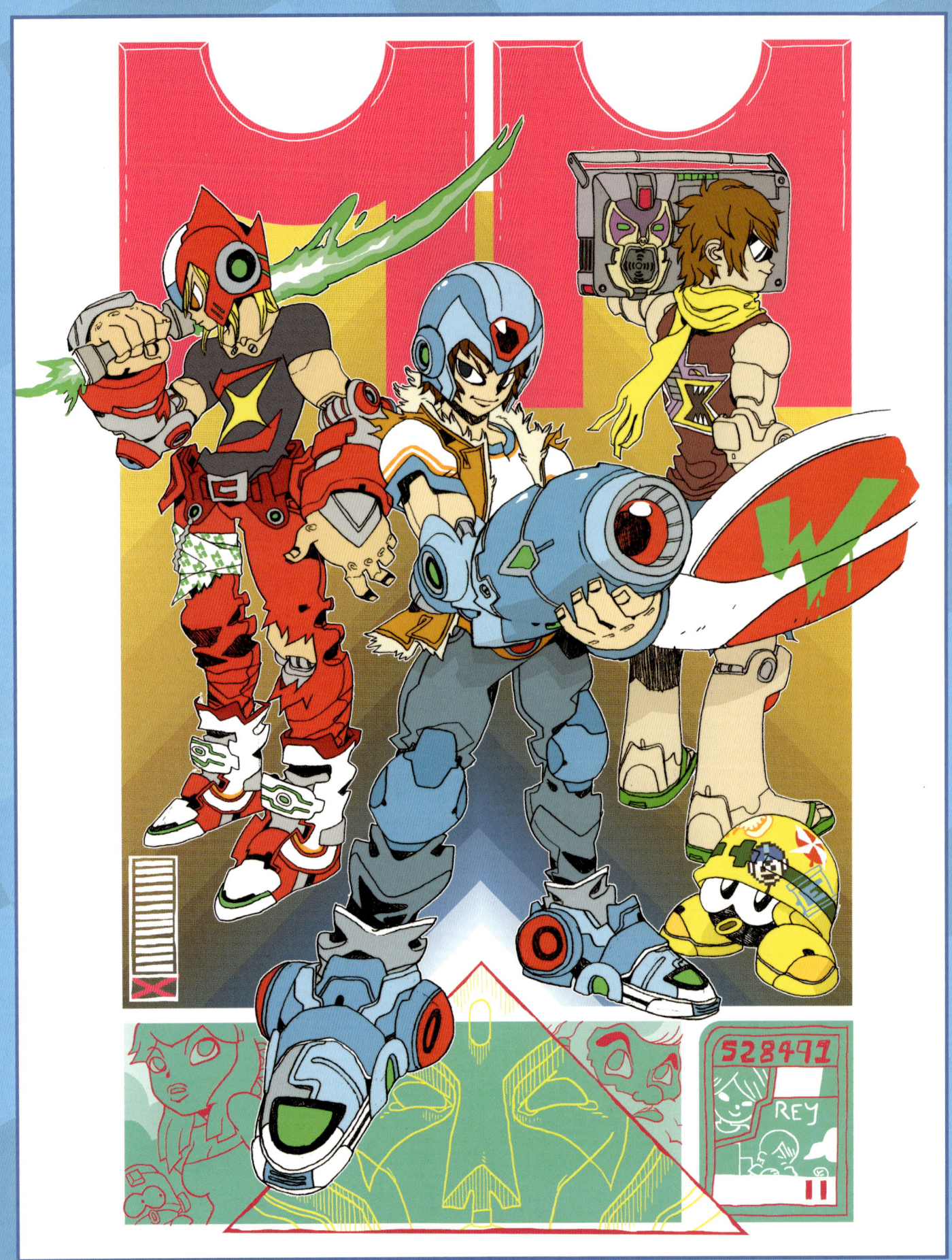

COREY LEWIS
Seattle, WA, United States
www.reyyy.com
Comic Artist
(Sharknife / Peng! / Seedless)

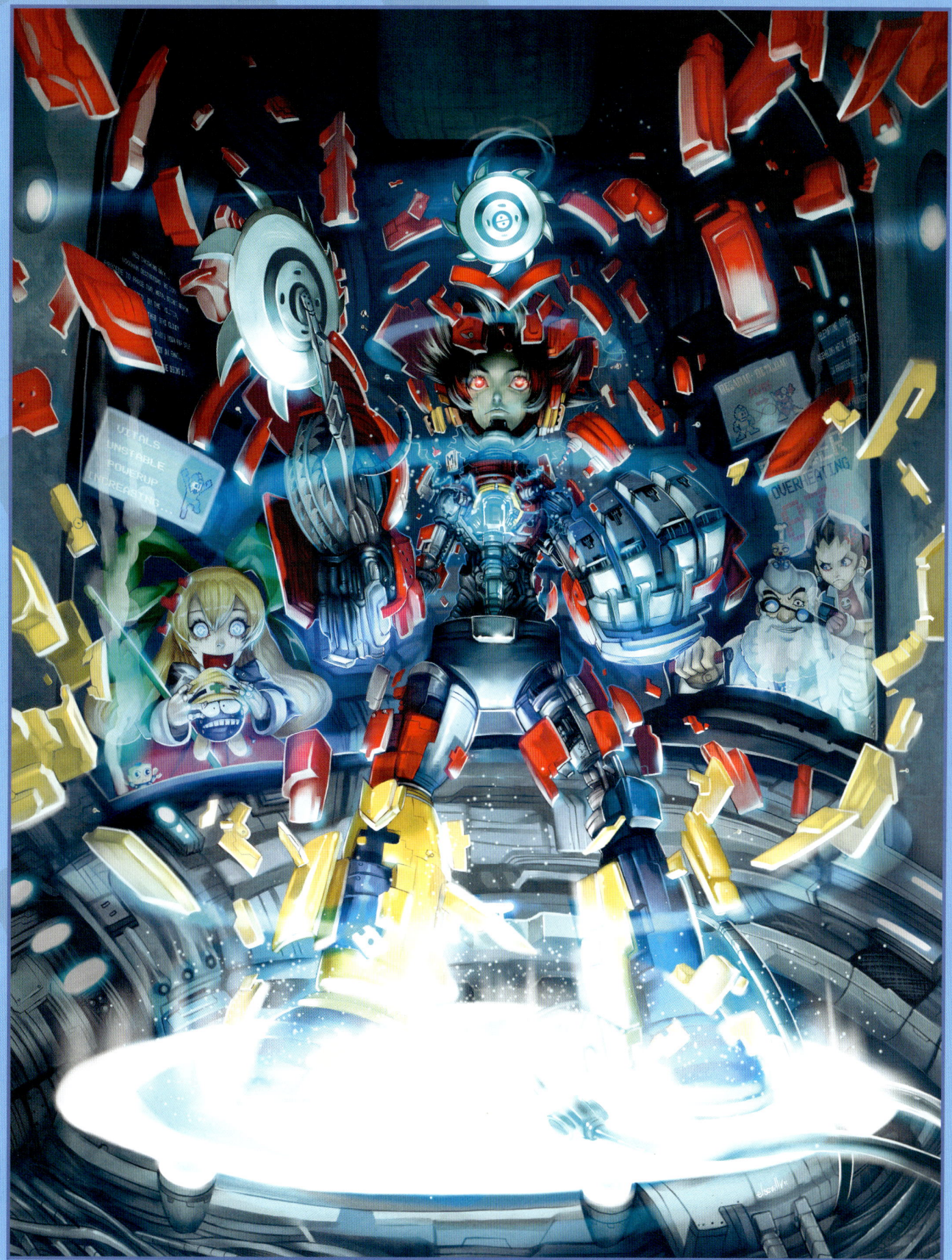

HECTOR SELVILLA LUJAN (ELSEVILLA)
Chihuahua, Mexico
elsevilla.deviantart.com
Illustrator

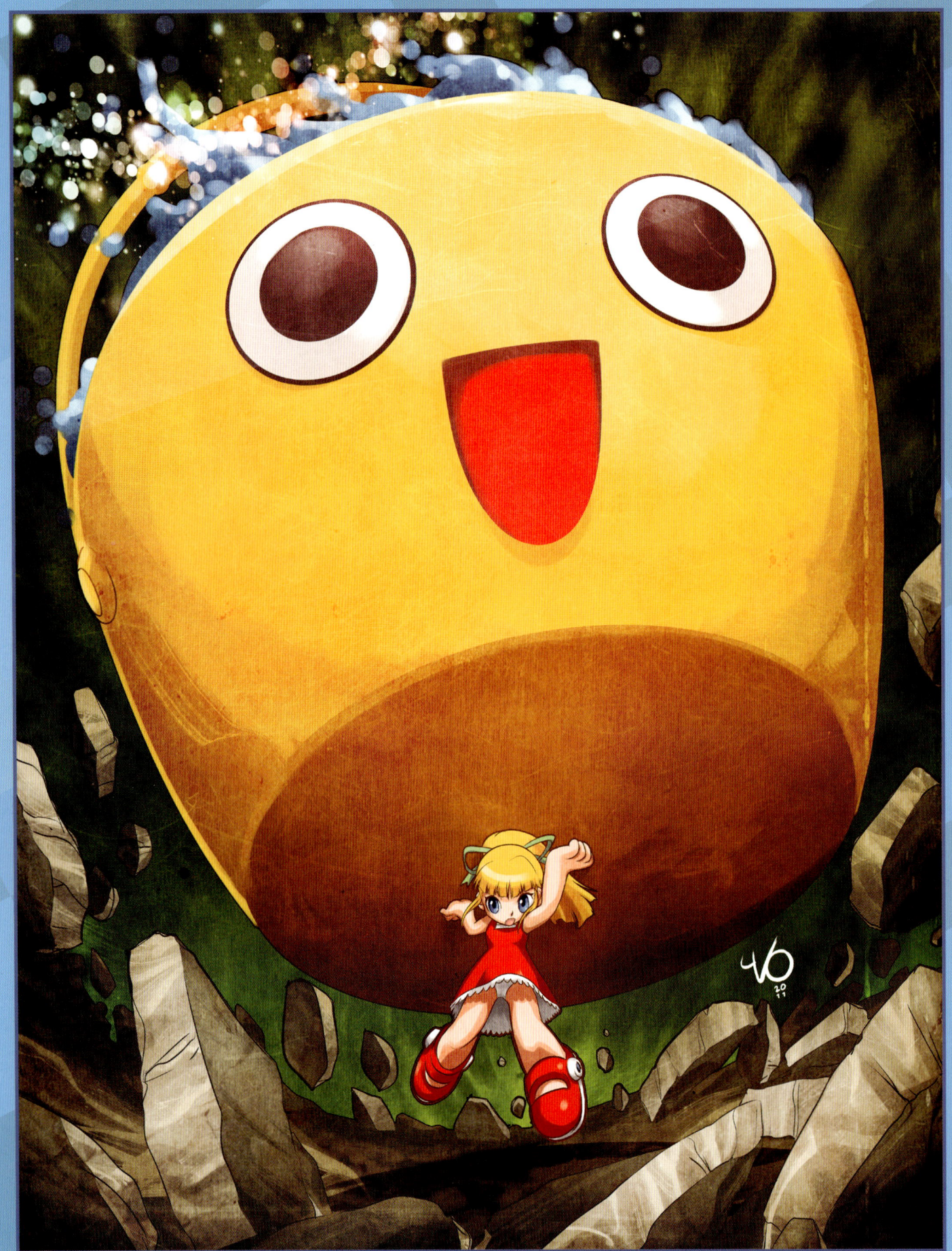

LONG VO
Long Beach, CA, United States
www.vostalgic.com
Illustrator
(Inception: The Cobol Job, Super Street Fighter II Turbo HD Remix)

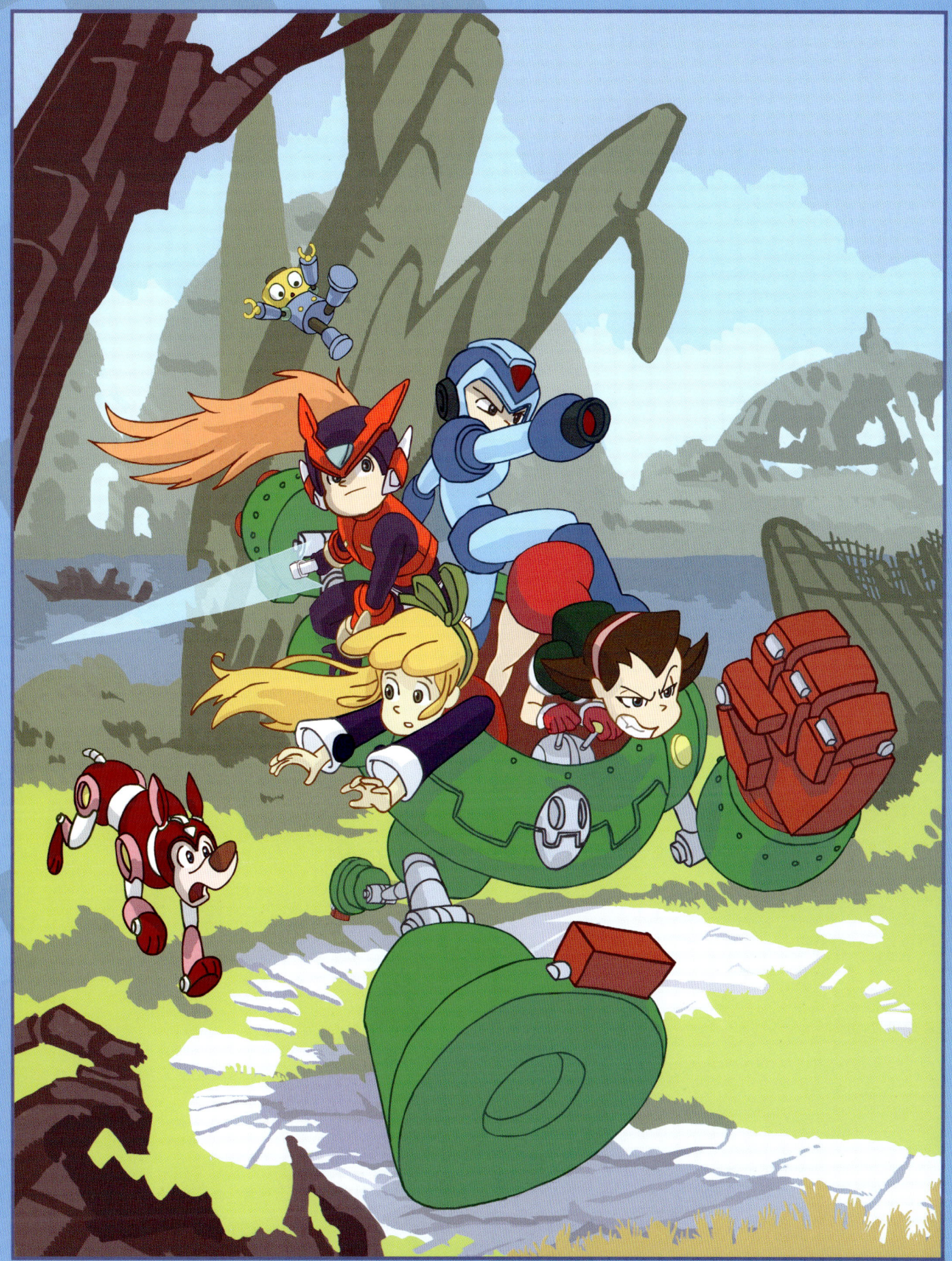

PHILIP RODRIGUES
Toronto, ON, Canada
invisible2blog.blogspot.com
Flash Animator

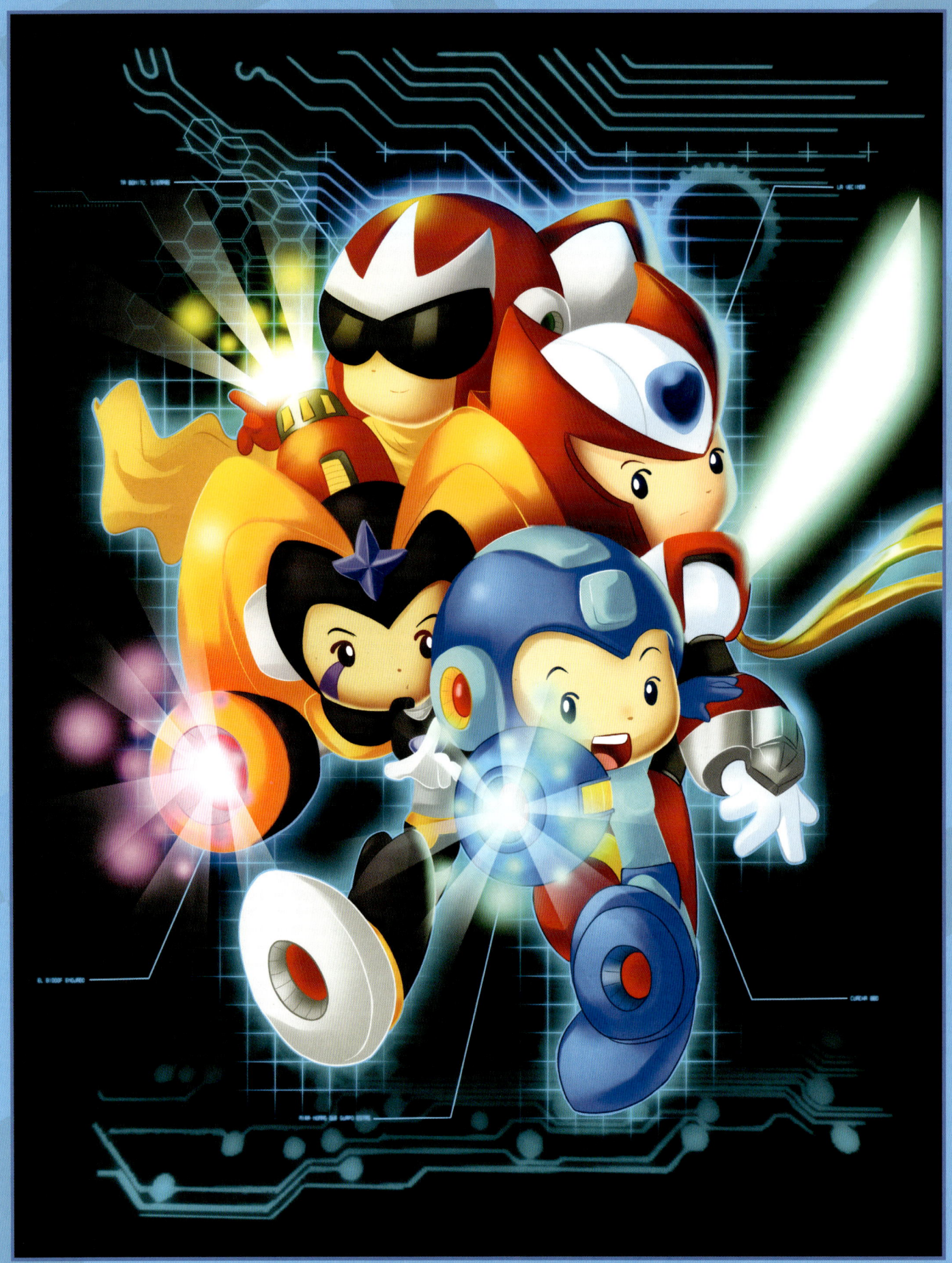

JONATHAN CASTILLO
Chihuahua, Mexico
www.potatows.com
Illustrator

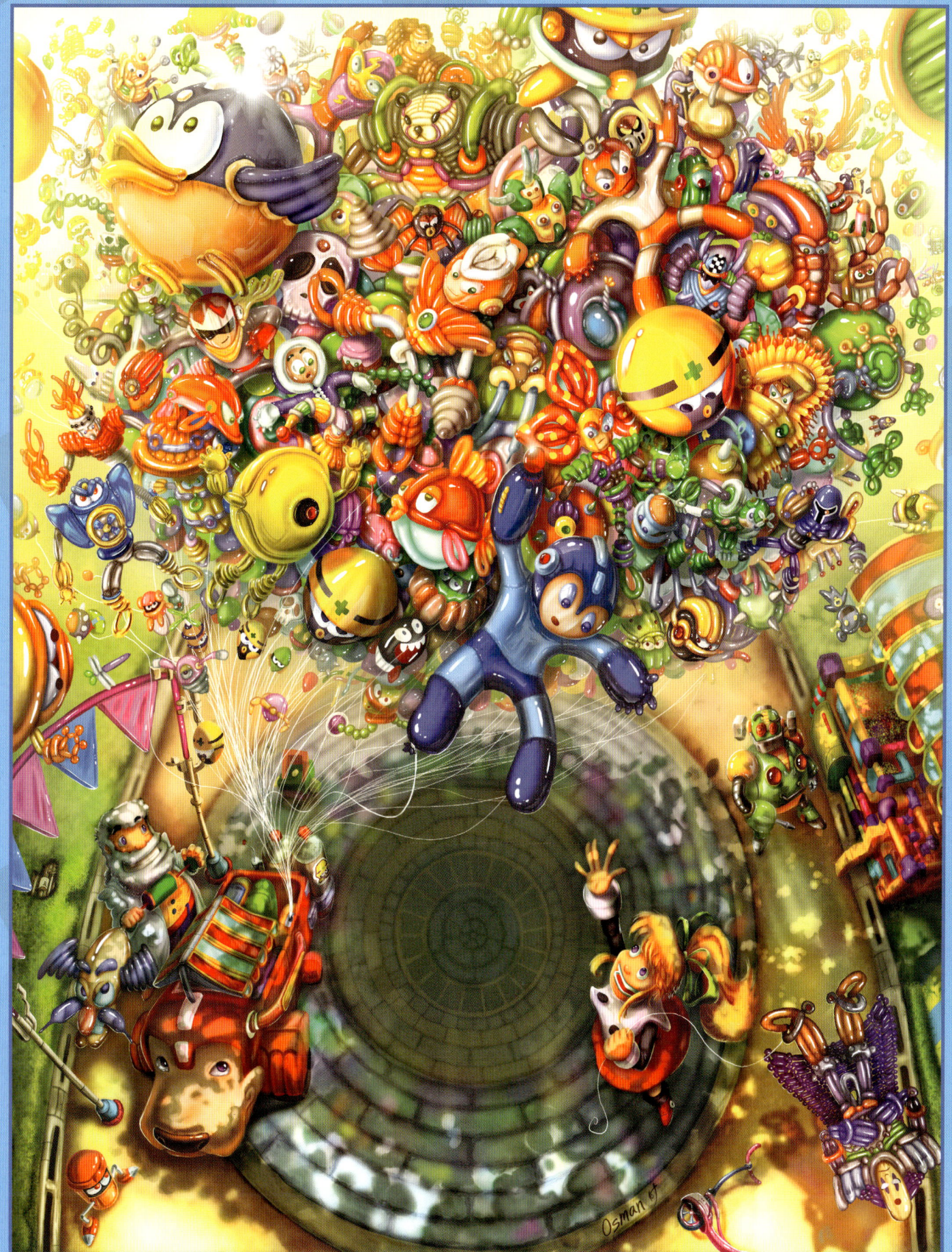

OSMAN HERNÁNDEZ
San Salvador, El Salvador
www.osmanhernandez.com / keops7.deviantart.com
Graphic Designer

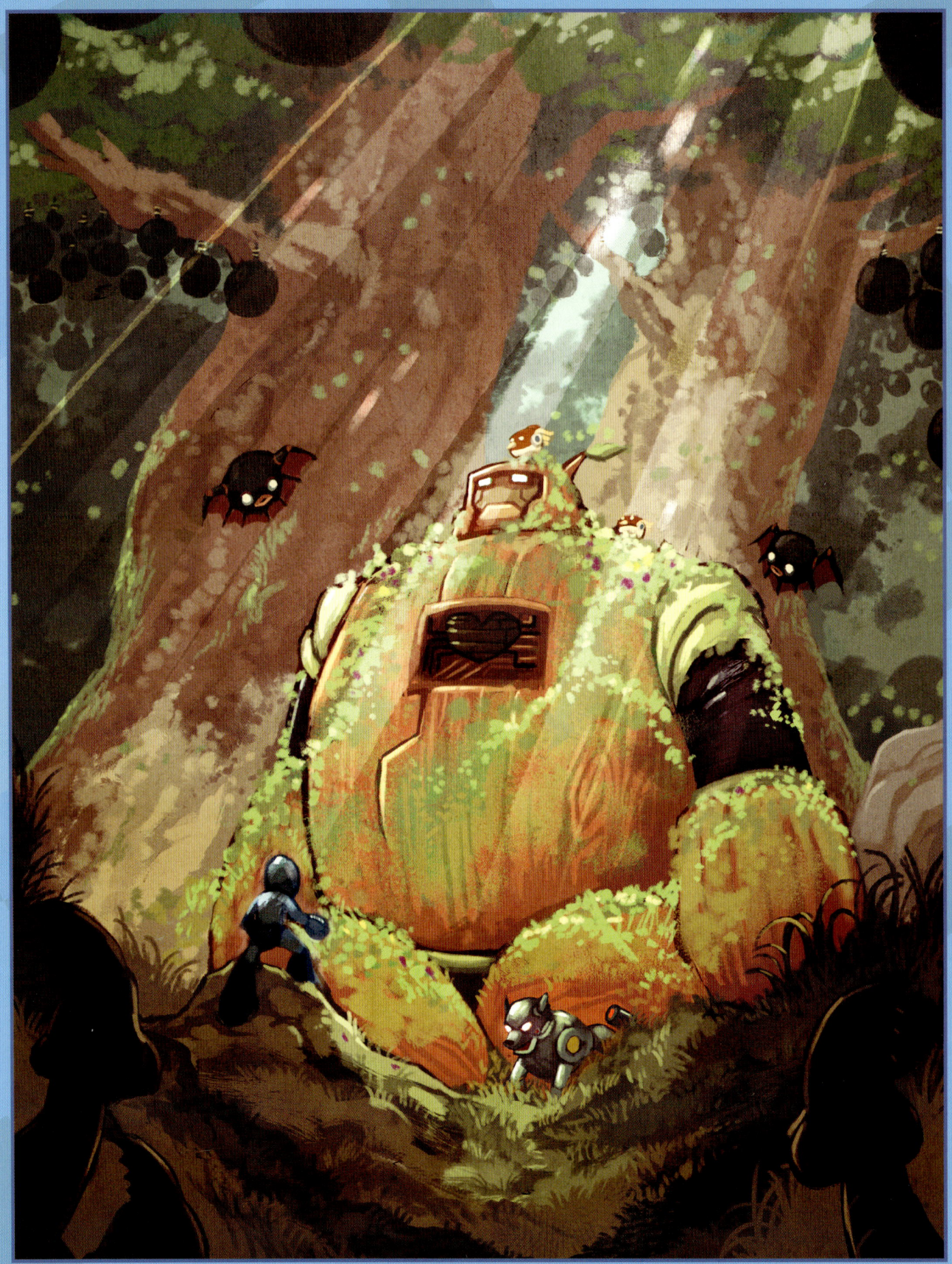

DAVID ALEGRE
San Francisco, CA, United States
Graphic Designer / Illustrator

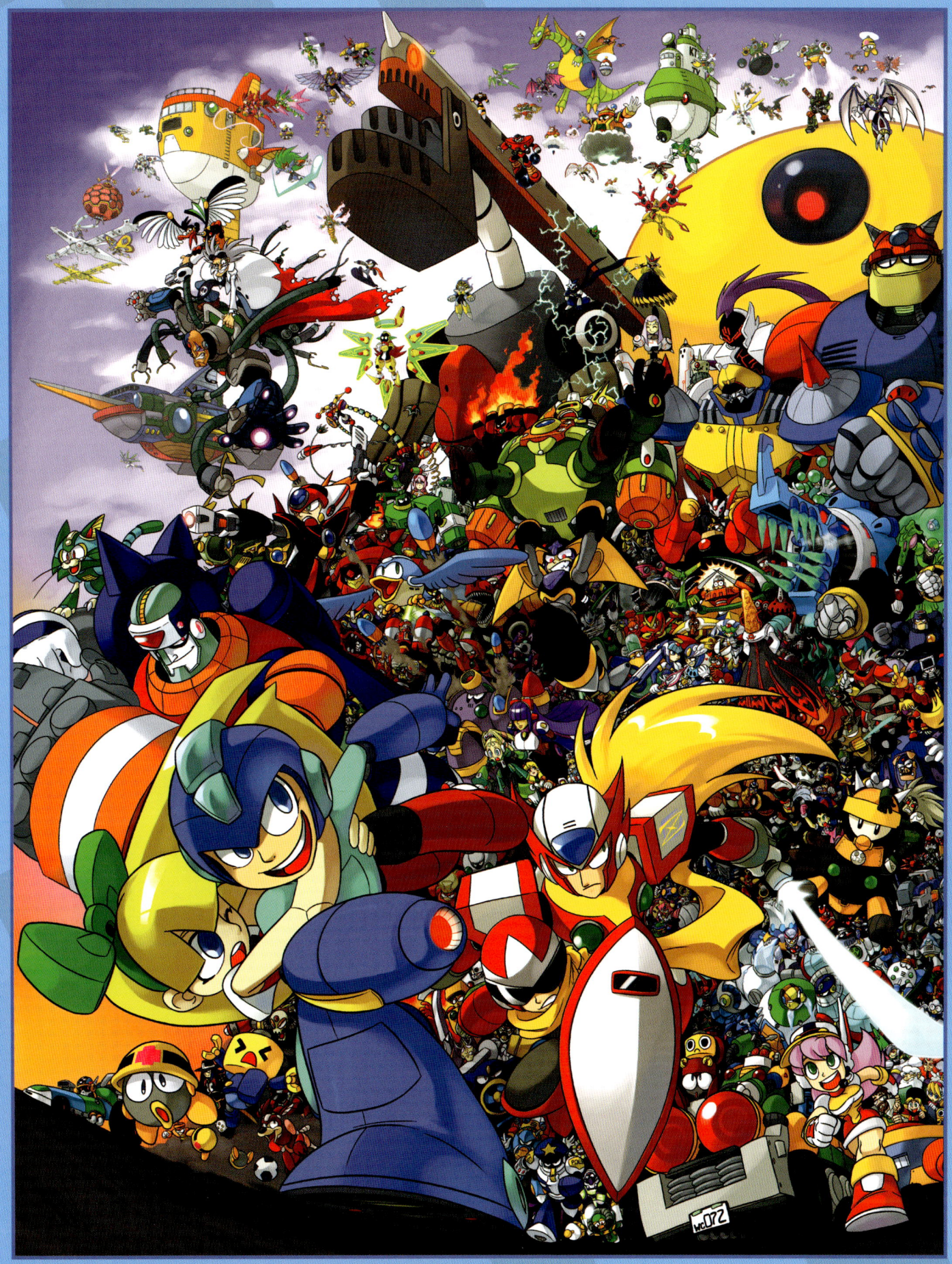

ANDREW DICKMAN
Burbank, CA, United States
andrewdickman.deviantart.com / www.starfieldcreations.com
Storyboard Artist
(Ivan the Unbearable - Creator / Dinosaur Train - Storyboards / ThatGuyWithTheGlasses.com - Title Card Artist)

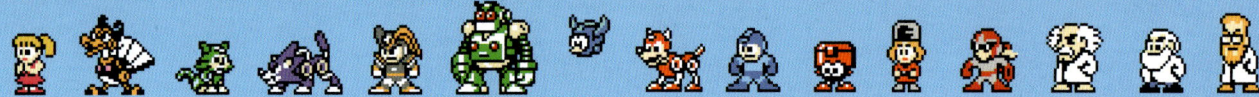

AFTERWORD

Thank you for joining us again for another great Capcom Tribute volume! Personally, I've been looking forward to giving the blue bomber the Tribute treatment ever since we had our very first art competition.

As you've seen in this book, the iconic design of Mega Man allows him to be recognizable in almost any art style, giving Mega Man Tribute arguably the most diverse works of any of our Tribute books so far. Of course, having a supporting cast of hundreds of bosses, enemies, and secondary characters helps keeps things interesting as well!

Choosing the final line-up for the book was also tougher than ever. We received over 2500 entries, surpassing the totals of both Street Fighter Tribute and Darkstalkers Tribute. Not bad for a little blue 24-pixel tall robot!

A big thank you goes out to not only the final artists chosen, but also everyone else who entered the competition. I hope you'll all be back to try again for our next Tribute project.

MATT MOYLAN
Managing Editor
UDON Entertainment

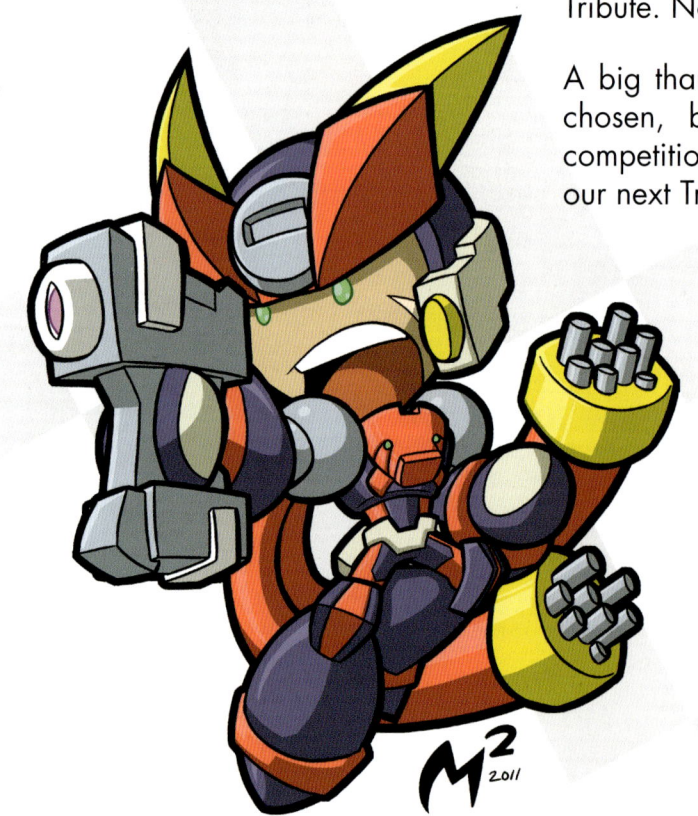

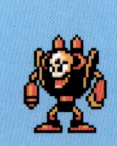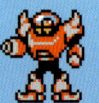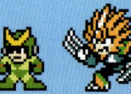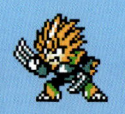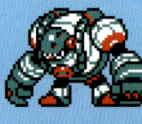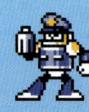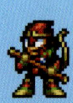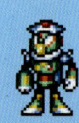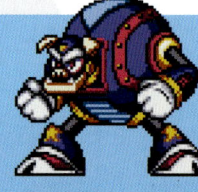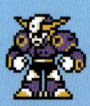

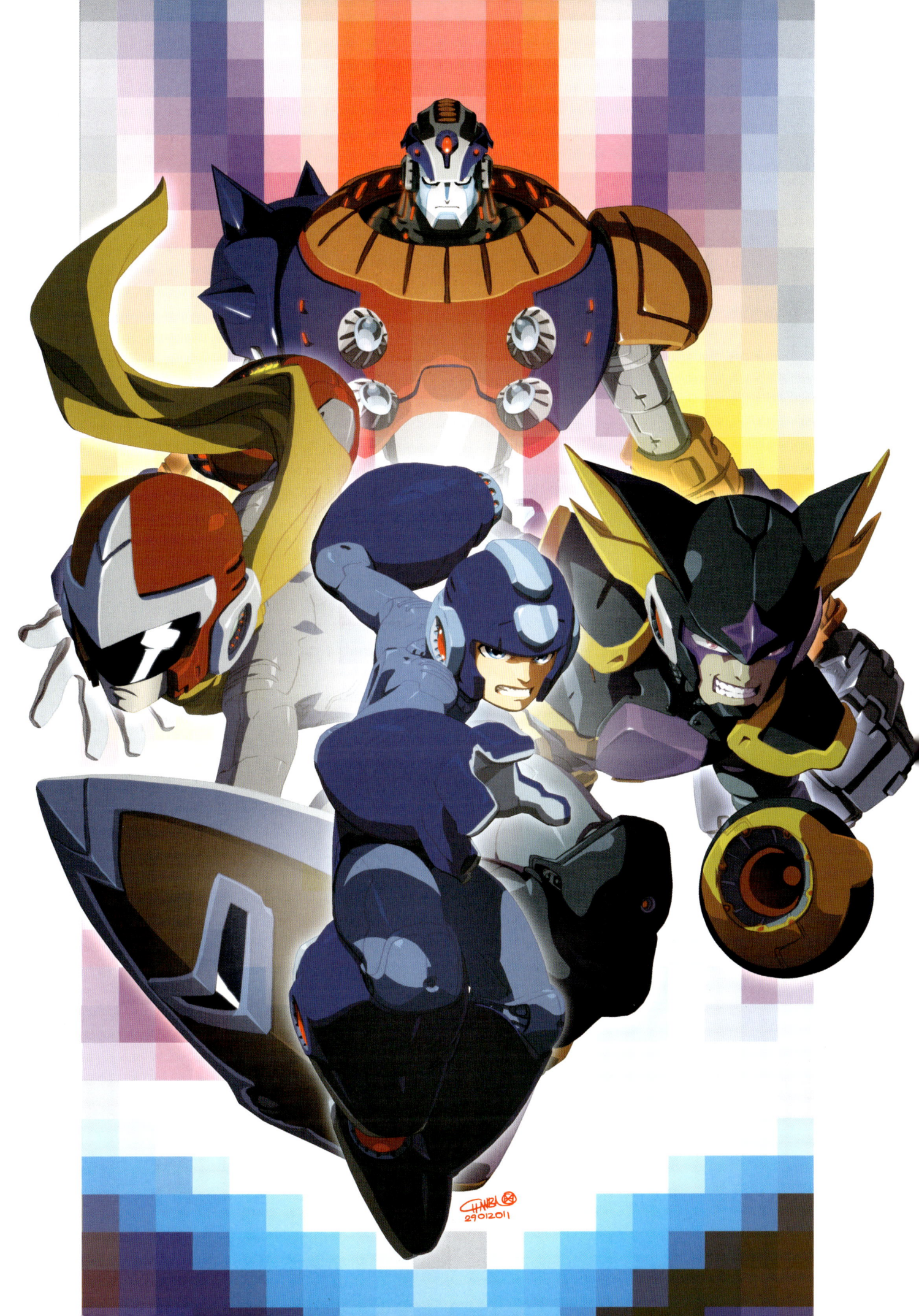

A

Adam Ford 45
Adam Hines 24
Adriana De La Torre (Akimaro) 151
Alain Matte 189
Alberto Rios 158
Alejandra Zúñiga Miranda 288
Alejandro Moreno Gonzalez (Magnozz) 201
Alexander Diochon 142
Alex Milne 39
Alex rude 196
Alise Gluškova (AlexaSharlOt) 173
Alvaro Amaya (avalon) 52
Amr El-Wakeel (Frobman) 162
Ancor Gil Hernández 159
Andrea Jen 141
Andres S. Blanco 25
Andrew Dickman 297
Andrew Wilson (Fourthwish) 165
Andry Rajoelina (Shango) 30
Andy Genen (-ND!-) 32
Andy Kluth 153
Angel Barba Barrera 54
Anthony Brennan 78
Arianna Pushkin (Aipe) 50
Arthur WongKokWai 214
Arttu Ilomäki 136
Ashley Davis 259
Audrey Kare 289

B

Ben Camberos 175
Ben Dale 145
Ben Ellebracht 272
Benjamin Lam 207
Beto Garza (Helbetico) 115
Billy Garretsen (Perfect Dork) 215
Bob Cassella 80
Bob Rissetto 117
Bob Strang 60
Brett Nienburg 118
Brian Luong 167
Brian Wimberly 198
Bryan Newton 273

C

Caio Yo 264
Caleb Cook 203
Cameron Ahmadi 63
Camila Fortuna 166
Camilo Suarez 163
Carey Chan (P-RO) 150
Carlos Baldo 267
Carlos de Anda López 186
Cathy Campbell 300
Cesar Augusto Sanchez Sandoval 144
Chang Lip Wei 213
Charles Hamwey 125
Chin Fong 270
Ching Fei Kang 236
Chito Arellano (Kwestone) 174
Chris Ayer (Air-City) 38
Chris House (Rikyo) 33
Christian Ramirez (creepstian) 16
Christopher Reavey (Glitcher) 46
Chris Whitaker 275
Chun Kiat Wong 217
Claire Schumacher 156
Collin Otto 284
Corey Lewis 290
Cristian Melián 119
Cristina Díaz 7

D

Damian Buzugbe 132
Daniel Boulanger 286
Daniel Hooker 62
Daniel Kho 227
Daniel Rosini Dimas Machado 40
Daniel Vélez 208
Dan Schoening (Dapper Dan) 160
Darren Rawlings (Rawls) 152
David Alegre 296
David Espinoza 106
Dax Gordine 254
DeAnna Belle (LadyRuby) 53
Dennis Patzelt 218
Dennis Pulido 182
Diego Pachón (Doppel) 122
Diego Zúñiga (Novanim) 252
DJ Welch (Dark Kenjie) 222
Drew Green 51
Drew Tetz 116

E

Edgardo Najarro 180
Eduardo Pérez 221
Edward Chow (Edatron) 23
Edwin Huang 253
Ein Lee 241
Elizabeth Remsen 188
Emilio Pilliu (Exemi) 57
Emmanuell Fuentes (E-m2) 211
Enrico Galli 276
Eric Phan 174
Eric Vedder 11
Espen Grundetjern 194
Esther Chow (Kuzu) 210

F

Felipe Lira (Just-a-creep) 200
Fernando Cano 98
Francisco Mendez 219
Francisco Perez (pac23) 140
Frank Simmonds 48
Freddy Carrasco 47

G

Gabo 158
Gabriel Luque 171
Garrett Hanna 21
Gary Yeung 206
Gene Goldstein 29
Georgina Chacón 65
Gerardo Alba 43
Gijs Hermans 155
Gonzalo Ordóñez Arias 15, 35
Gordon McMillan 238
Greg Sepelak 216
Greig Rapson 14
Gustavo Cosio 111

H

Hainanu Saulque 72
Hans Steinbach (Hanzo) 205
Hector Selvilla Lujan (Elsevilla) 291
Hino 43
Hitoshi Ariga 36
Holly Segarra 94
Hugh Freeman 148

I

Ifeanyi Pappy Onwuagbu (Popsaart) 244
Ilias Patlis 20
Irene Lee (Wave) 246
Ivan Camelo (Vancamelot) 212

J

Jaime Herrera Rivera 27
Jake Kalbhenn 172
James Franzen 181
Jason Blakely (Jabone) 78
Jason Hazelroth 127
Jason Robinson 255
Jean-Baptiste Nanteau (JCarroll) 283
Jeff Agala 183
Jeffrey Cruz (Chamba) 13
Jeffrey Lai 277
Jeff Stokely 26
Jerome Patrick Jacinto 12
Jesus Bautista (Jesonite) 226

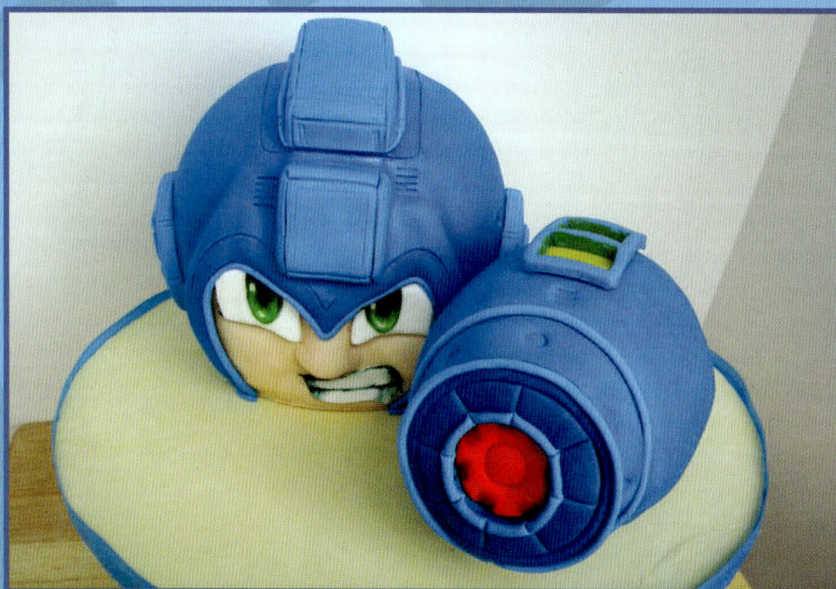

CATHY CAMPBELL
Ottawa, ON, Canada
www.cakewhisperer.ca
Cake Designer

INDEX

Jhosephine Tanuwidjaya 10
Jim Zubkavich 168
Jin-ha Kwon 41
Jin Han 18
Joe Bluhm 42
Joel Mackenzie 34
Joe Martin (Joerocks1981) 139
Joe Ng 35
John Devlin 287
John Dy 179
John Leyton 257
John Michael Carreon (koi) 44
Jonathan Castillo 294
Jonathan González Gómez 161
Jonathan Griffiths 195
Jon Murakami 146
Jon Sommariva (Red J) 6
Jorge Eduardo Ruiz 261
Jorge Luis Maldonado Morocho 229
Jorge M. Velez 271
Jose Carlos Salvio Pereira Jr. 143
José Luís Jiménez Díaz 163
Josh Mirman 154
Joshua Perez (Dyemooch) 37
Joshua Shepherd 157
Juan Molinet 192
Juan Pablo Riebeling (Joven Paul) 58
Justin Orr 110
Justin Vu 248

K

Karith Densmore 61
Keith Morris 31
Ken Wong 55
Ken Wright 81
Kevin Cameron (Herogear) 193
Khairul Ammar Jamal 49
Kinson Yung (Pyauki) 176
Kok Yip Sun 258
Koté Carvajal 252
Kwok-Hei Mak (Kei) 56

L

Lae Donald (donald) 278
Larry Gilbert 147
Laura Müller (Laumiline) 190
Laura Rivera 210
Le Duy (Jo) 240
Leonardo Martinez Manfredo Morales 73
Liang Feng Wang 225
Long Vo 292
Luis Martín Baliño (KoiDrake) 228
Luis Roberto Ramírez Cruz 220
Luis Santiago 164
Luiz Carlos 187

M

Makoto Koji 137
Malcolm Wope (Malcolm.xy) 242
Manuel Molohua (Samolo) 100
Marcus Penna 113
Mark Fionda 149
Mark Hansen (Markyzan) 191
Mark Pellegrini 83
Masumi Sugiyama (Nasu) 251
Mathias Barth (Barthschwein) 239
Mathieu Beaulieu 71
Matthew Armstrong 135
Matthew Ingraham 230
Matt Moylan 256
Maximiliano Martinez 73
Maximo V. Lorenzo 93
Maya Petersen (RNN) 209

May Wa Leng 22
Michel Malagueta 223
Miguel Delicado 59
Mike del Mundo 202
Mike Henry 72
Mike Hiscott 64
Mike Kime 177
Mike Yeh 199
Miles Donovan 126
Miyukiko 250
M. S. Corley 185

N

Nagayoshi Ryosuke 265
Nate Bear 105
Nicholas Maradin 67
Nicole Dubois (Neolucky) 101
Nina Matsumoto 28

O

Obray Williams 184
Oliver Lee Arce 111
Omar Dogan 232
Omar Lozano 98
Oscar Celestini 74
Oscar Triana 245
Osman Hernández 295

P

Pablo Praino 68
Paige Pumphrey (Paigey!) 268
Papang Pangketepang 169
Patrick Ballesteros 170
Pedro Reyes (Bug!) 131
Philip Rodrigues 293
Piximix 138
Poramed Chonrattanakun 279
Puri Andini (powree) 260

R

Raul Velasquez (Zeo) 69
Ricardo Ruiz-Dana (Rick R-D) 76
Richard Bouden 120
Rio Rock 282
R. L. May III 133
Robert Case 99
Robert Johnston 233
Robert Kim 103
Robert Porter (Robaato) 231
Robin Keijzer 97
Roborock (Albert Covarrubias) 75
Robot Soda 85
Rocco Commisso 104
Rory Keller 95
Rosa Ramirez (Rosa Fresina) 114
Ruben De Vela 19
Ruben Lara (Pingolito) 112
Ruy Fernando (Flint) 281
Ryan Hall 66
Ryan Odagawa 102
Ryan Shiu (Ry-Spirit) 262

S

Saeijin Oh 128
Salvador Ramirez Madriz 70
Sam Filstrup 235
Samuel Thomas 9
Sandro Hojo 82
Sanford Greene 89
Santiago Calleriza 91
Sapphire Wong Ying Chee 263
Sarah Ellerton 274

Sawpea Keo 96
Sean Galloway (Cheeks) 121
Sergio Lantadilla (Peero) 8
Sergio Olivares (Sercho!) 84
Shane Law 134
Spikytiger 123
Stefano Collavini (Nefasto) 237
Stéphane Boutin (JGSB) 92
Stephanie Kao 285
Stephen Raffill 224
Steven Tran 130

T

Ted Kim 109
Teerawat Palanitisena 88
Thor Thorvaldson Jr. 178
Timothy Lim 83
Tonny Jiménez 90
Tony Christou (Pthallo) 124
Tozani 43
Tracy Tubera 77
Tyson Hesse 269

V

Victor Boggiano 280
Victor Hugo Queiroz (Vitorugo) 247
vinhnyu 266

W

Walter Gatus (Waltdog) 87
Warren Louw 204
Wes Louie 86

XYZ

Xavier Garcia 234
Yadza Lafalika (cessa) 107
Yasmin Sheikh 79
Yenny Laud (Y2laud) 249
Yoshi Vu 106
Zack Giallongo 108
Zulkarnaen Hasan Basri 243

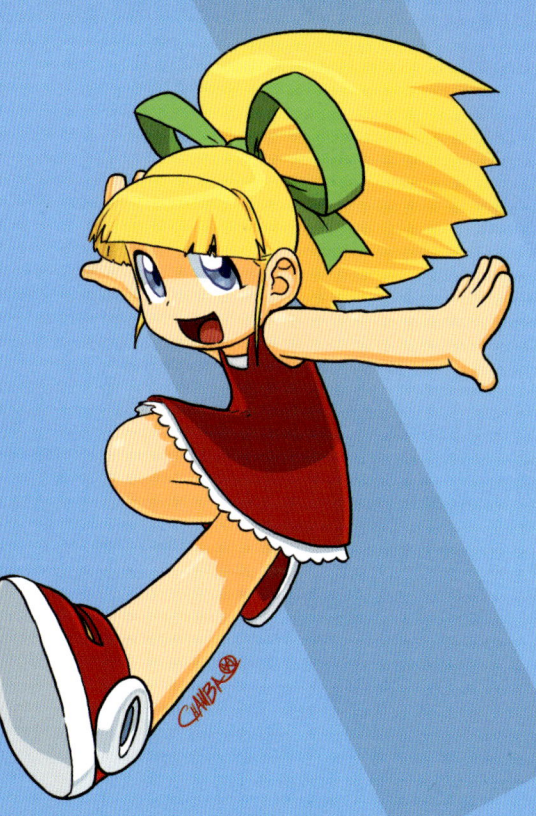

COMPLETE YOUR COLLECTION:

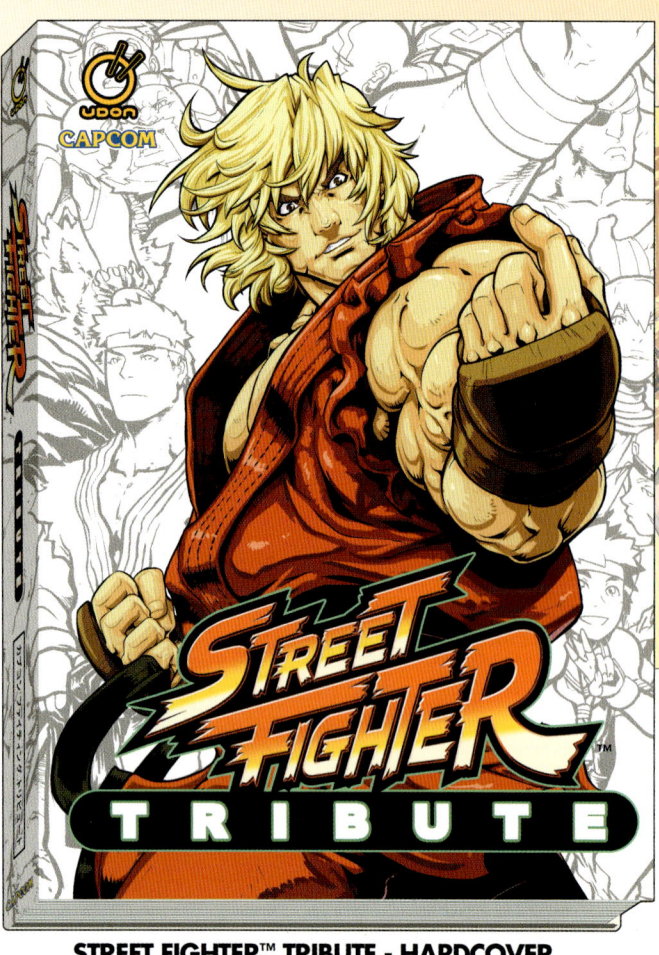

STREET FIGHTER™ TRIBUTE - HARDCOVER
296pgs, Full Color, Hardcover
ISBN: 978-1-927925-53-9

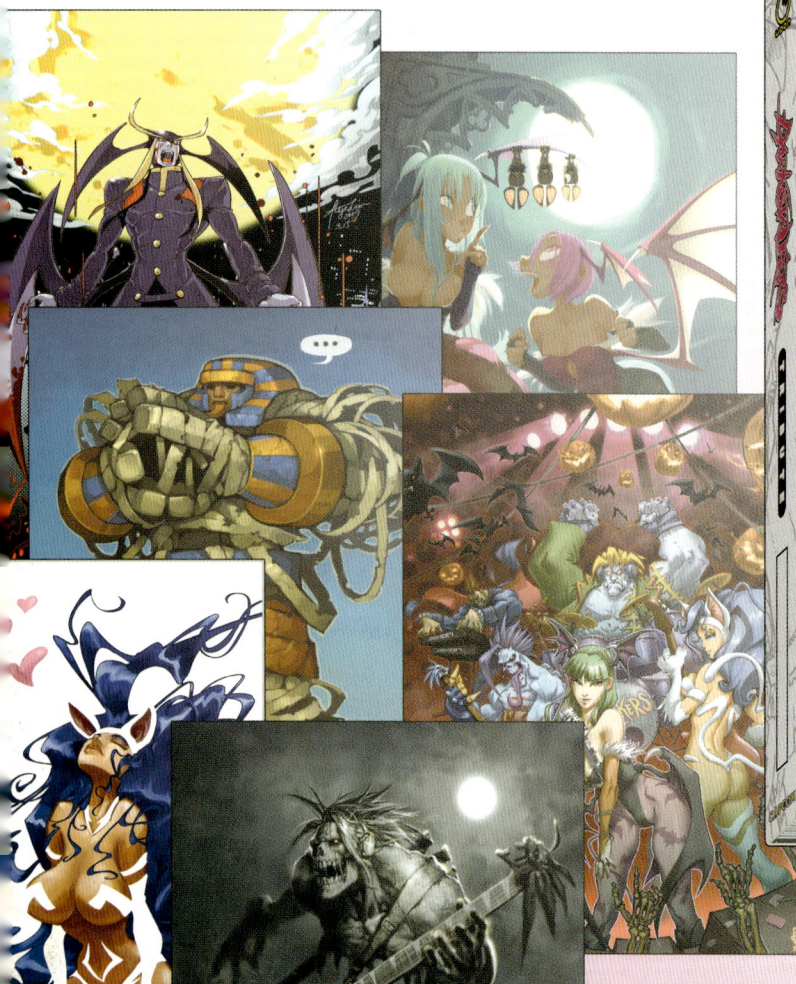

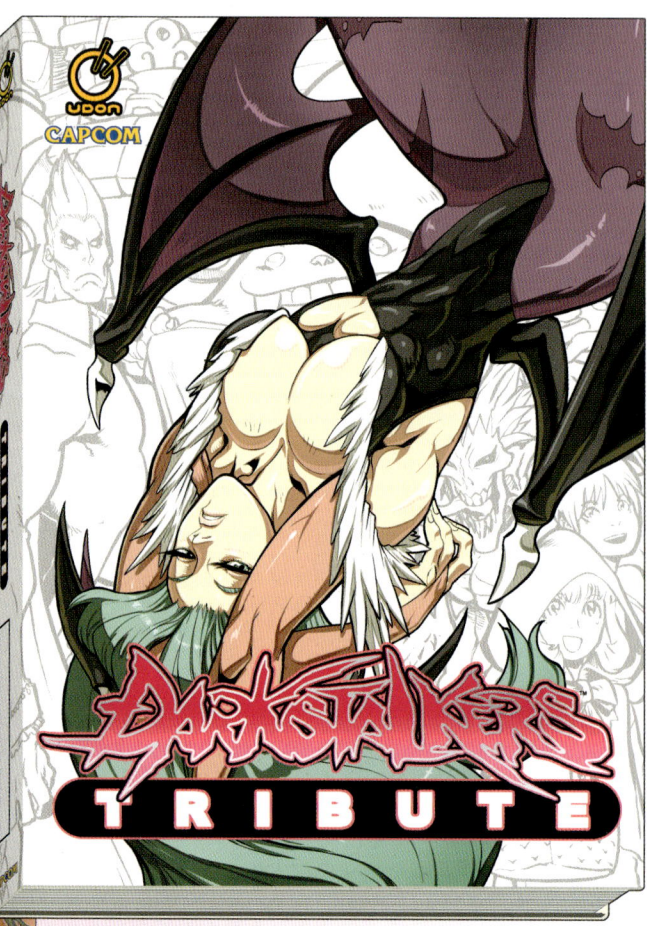

DARKSTALKERS™ TRIBUTE - HARDCOVER
296pgs, Full Color, Hardcover
ISBN: 978-1-927925-59-1

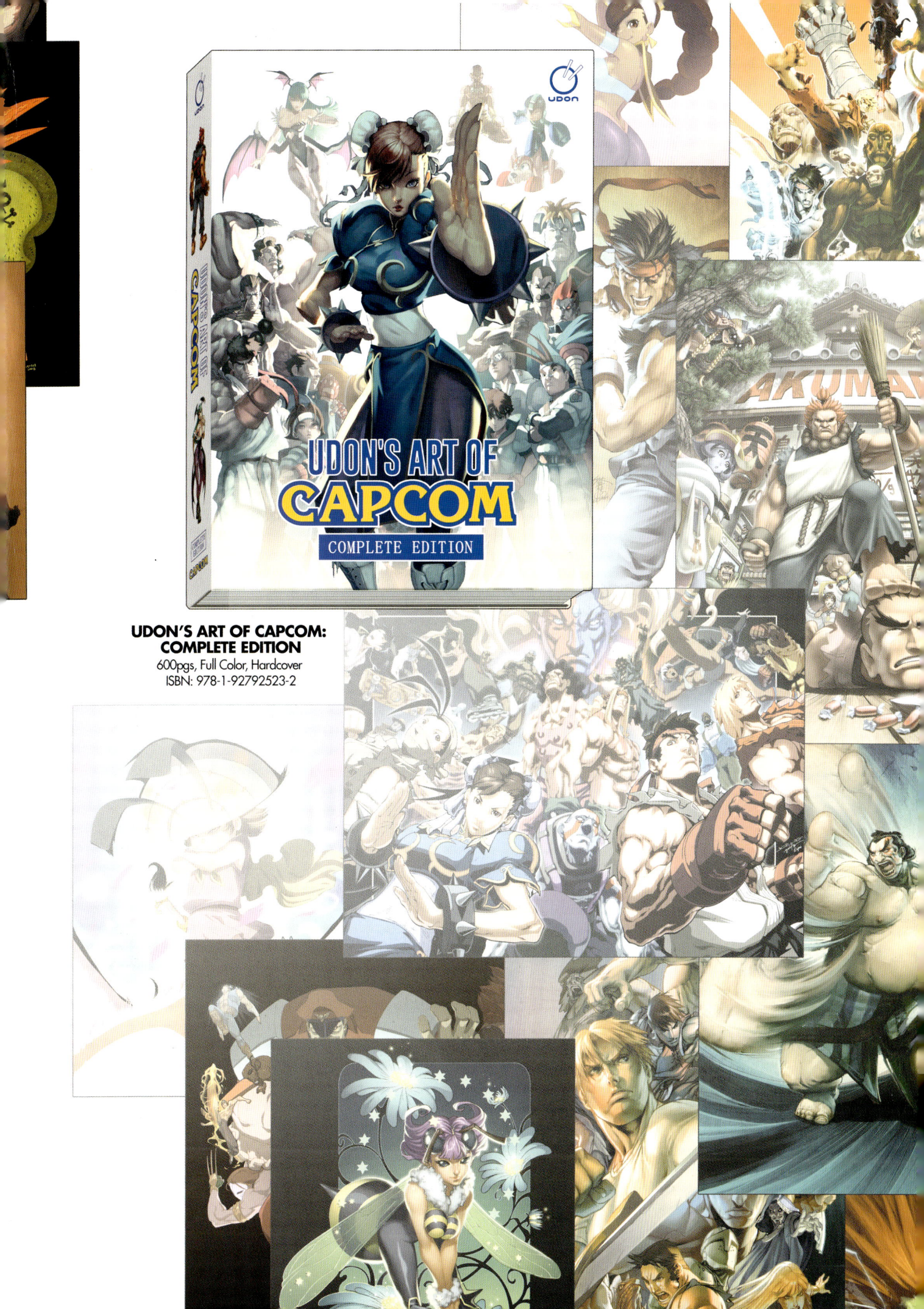

UDON'S ART OF CAPCOM: COMPLETE EDITION
600pgs, Full Color, Hardcover
ISBN: 978-1-92792523-2

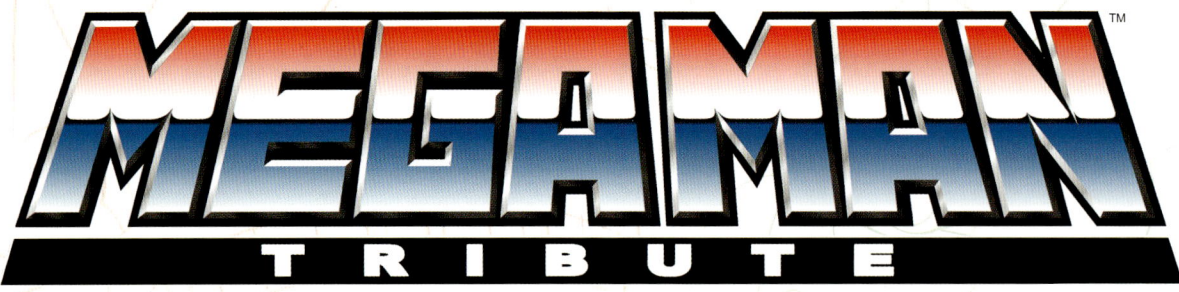

MEGA MAN TRIBUTE

PROJECT EDITOR
MATT MOYLAN

COVER ARTISTS
HITOSHI ARIGA
(FRONT COVER MAIN CHARACTER)
JEFFREY "CHAMBA" CRUZ
(WRAPAROUND BACKGROUND)

PG 1 & PG 300 ART
JEFFREY "CHAMBA" CRUZ

CREDIT PAGE ART
SEAN "CHEEKS" GALLOWAY

UDON STAFF
CHIEF OF OPERATIONS: ERIK KO
DIRECTOR OF PUBLISHING: MATT MOYLAN
SENIOR EDITOR: ASH PAULSEN
SENIOR PRODUCER: LONG VO
VP OF SALES: JOHN SHABLESKI
PRODUCTION MANAGER: JANICE LEUNG
MARKETING MANAGER: JENNY MYUNG
JAPANESE LIAISON: STEVEN CUMMINGS

CAPCOM U.S.A., INC.
FRANCIS MAO
TAKI ENOMOTO
NORIKO NATSUNAGA
HIROMI IWASAKI
SUSAN SUAREZ

www.UDONentertainment.com

© CAPCOM CO., LTD. ALL RIGHTS RESERVED.
Licensed for use by UDON Entertainment Corp.

Published by UDON Entertainment Corp.
118 Tower Hill Road, C1, PO Box 20008
Richmond Hill, Ontario, L4K 0K0 CANADA

All artwork in this book was created specifically for UDON Entertainment's "Mega Man Tribute" art competition, and for use in this book.

Any similarities to persons living or dead are purely coincidental. No portion of this publication may be used or reproduced by any means (digital or print) without written permission from UDON Entertainment except for review purposes.

Second Edition, First Printing: November 2015
ISBN-13: 978-1-927925-67-6
ISBN-10: 1-927925-67-3

Printed in China

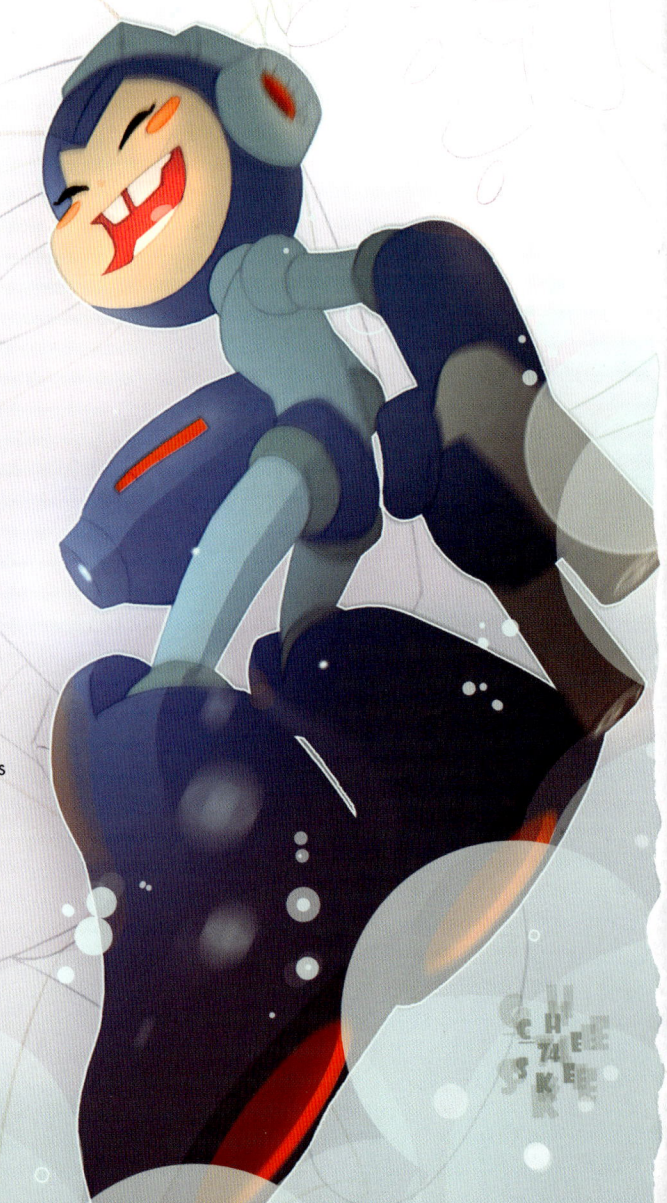

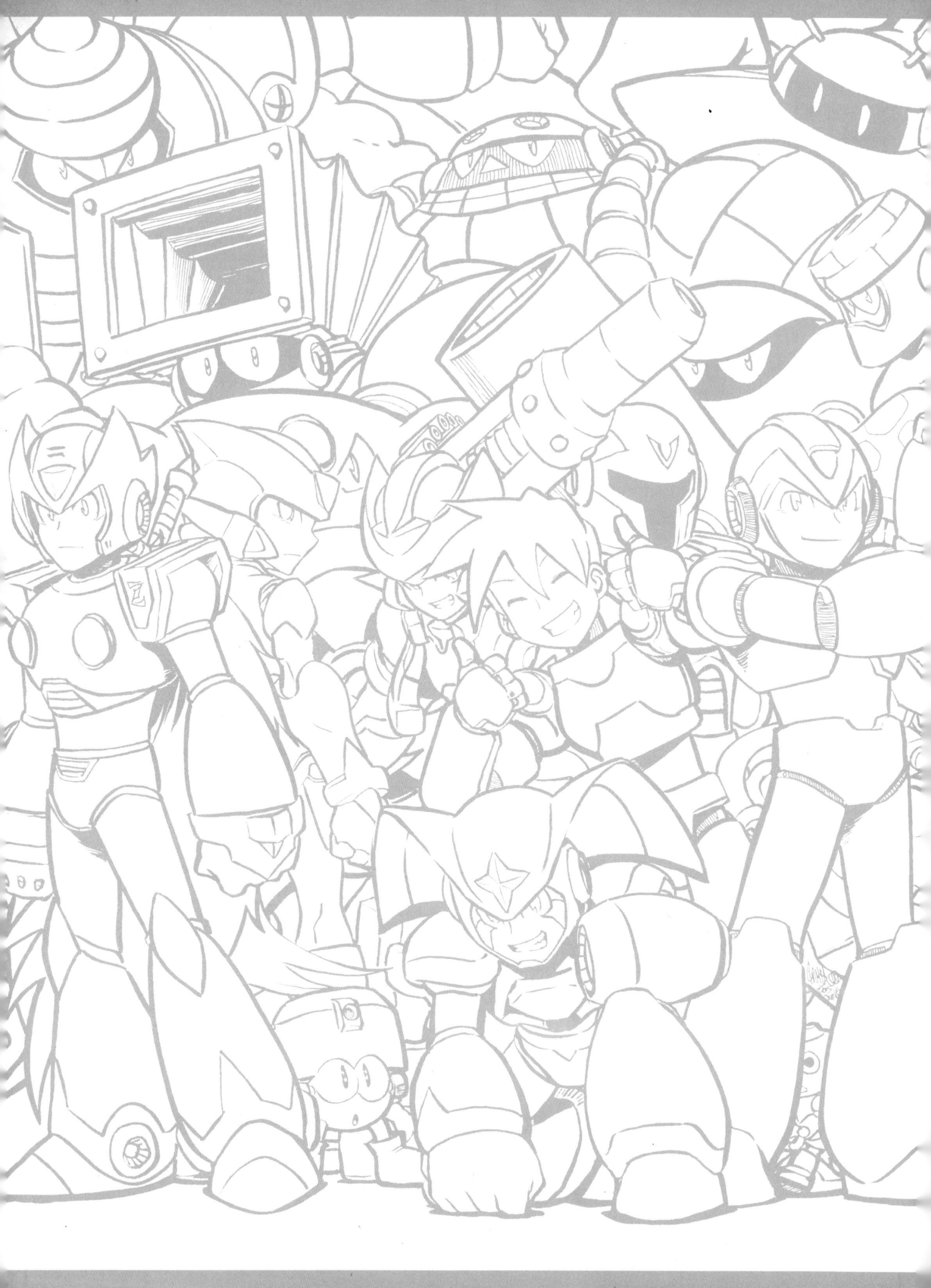